ALSO BY ADAM LEVIN

The Instructions

Hot Pink

BUBBLEGUM

A Novel

Adam Levin

DOUBLEDAY
New York

This is a work of fiction. Names, characters, places, and incidents either are the product of the author's imagination or are used fictitiously. Any resemblance to actual persons, living or dead, events, or locales is entirely coincidental.

www.doubleday.com

DOUBLEDAY and the portrayal of an anchor with a dolphin are registered trademarks of Penguin Random House LLC.

The writing of this book was supported in part by an award from the National Endowment for the Arts.

Jacket illustrations: bubble © boykung / Shutterstock;
gears © Besjunior / Shutterstock
Jacket design by Michael J. Windsor
Book design by Michael Collica

Library of Congress Cataloging-in-Publication Data
Names: Levin, Adam, author.
Title: Bubblegum : a novel / Adam Levin.
Description: First edition. | New York : Doubleday, [2020]
Identifiers: LCCN 2019001907 | ISBN 9780385544962 (hardcover) |
ISBN 9780385544979 (ebook)
Classification: LCC PS3612.E92365 B83 2020 | DDC 813/.6—dc23
LC record available at https://lccn.loc.gov/2019001907

MANUFACTURED IN THE UNITED STATES OF AMERICA

1 3 5 7 9 10 8 6 4 2

First Edition

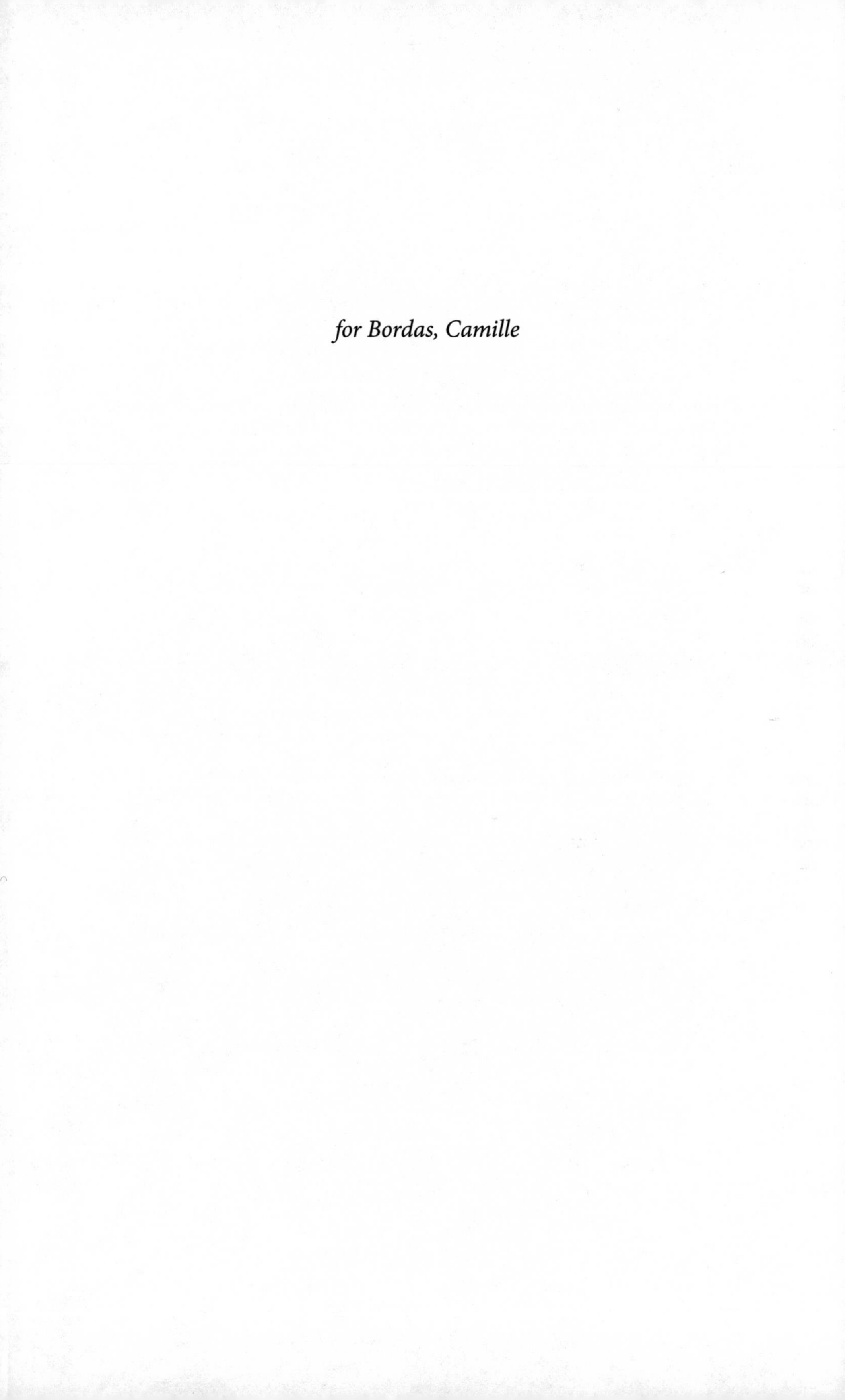

for Bordas, Camille

As flies to wanton boys are we to the gods
They kill us for their sport

—Shakespeare, *King Lear*

Self-determination does not follow from complexity. Difficulty in calculating the orbit of the fly does not prove capriciousness, though it may make it impossible to prove anything else. The problems imposed by the complexity of a subject matter must be dealt with as they arise. Apparently hopeless cases often become manageable in time.

—Skinner, *Science and Human Behavior*

The panther was all right.

—Kafka, "A Hunger Artist"

CONTENTS

I
INVITATION
1

II
THE HOPE OF RUSTING SWINGSETS
177

III
PORTFOLIO
309

IV
COMPOUND
477

V
GATES
631

I

INVITATION

JONBOAT SAY

GROWING UP, I'D HEARD, "Shut your piehole, cakeface," a couple or three times a week from my father. The piehole thats shutting he'd demand was rarely mine, though. It usually belonged to someone well outside shouting range—as frequently a radio or television newsman as a bested foe in a dinner table anecdote of everyday interpersonal victory—and never to my mother. She'd never been a cakeface. Not to my father or me at least. Nor had she ever used the saying herself, and, after she was gone, I wondered what, if anything, that might have meant. Except for when she'd hear it from my father's mother, who'd put a bite behind the *piehole* that somehow made it sharper than whatever slur the *cakeface* was being used to euphemize, the saying seemed always to incite her to smile, yet I may have been too young to distinguish true amusement from motherly indulgence. I may have been too young to tell a smile from a smirk.

Come to think of it, I can't recall my mother ever smirking.

But all of this to say that while Jonny "Jonboat" Pellmore-Jason, by eventually having made it his catchphrase, popularized "Shut your piehole, cakeface," it had been ours first. My family's. We Magnets'. He learned it from me.

There used to be a couple of tetherball courts in the middle of the playground next door to our house, and one day, around the start of seventh grade, Blackie Buxman and I were facing off on one of them, playing best-of-nine for a soda and chips, when Jonboat, who'd moved to town a week earlier, declared his intention to challenge the winner. Buxman wouldn't rob liquor stores for years yet. He was, at that time, our school's starting pitcher and basketball center. I lacked strength and was average of stature. My competitive streak was the width of a noodle. Having grown up so close to the playground, however, I dominated foursquare and tetherball the both. Blackie must have forgotten, or maybe never known. When I beat him five-zip, he evinced disbelief. He said, "No way," then spoke to me rudely. "Go assfuck a swingset, you psycho," he said.

That cut me a little, but I came back fast. I said, "Fetch me my cold Cherry Coke and Pringles. In the meantime, though, shut your piehole, cakeface."

Jonboat laughed.

The crowd around the court took a couple steps back, alarmed and confused. I possessed at that time a fair-size, however provisional measure of blacksheepish cool, and so was someone who'd have normally been able to get away with wising off to Buxman in response to a slight—it would have looked like we were riffing—but Jonboat's laughter bent the social calculus. No one quite understood where he fit yet. Girls seemed to like him. He was certainly big. His father was Jon "Jon-Jon" Jason, and his granddad Hubert "All Hell" Pellmore. Nevertheless, Jonboat was the new kid; the new, rich, blond kid. He didn't have friends, or we were, all of us, his friends—none of us were sure. For all we knew, Jonboat was *too* blond and rich—was that a thing? It seemed like it could be and it seemed like it couldn't. Did he have the right to laugh at Blackie's expense, though? And if he had the right to laugh at Blackie's expense, did I have the right to get credit for his laughter? Did Blackie Buxman have to save face?

Blackie thought he did. So it was Jonboat or me. Someone had to hurt. I was the easy choice, and Blackie liked it easy, simple as that. He stepped in my direction. Jonboat shoved him sideways. Blackie reached for Jonboat, and Jonboat smashed his nose.

"You'll pay," Blackie said.

"Shut your piehole-cakeface, gaylord," said Jonboat.

Blackie loped home without buying me snacks. Jonboat roundly defeated me at tetherball—five to three—and took me out for pizza. We were friendly for a while, though not really friends til a few months later when he beat me up at school.

•

• •

After spending a semester using "piehole" as a modifier and pushing back the comma so the saying could abide the direct address "gaylord," Jonboat—who'd by then taken Blackie's starting spot at center, gotten to third with a sitcom ingénue at a party at the White House over winter break, and become, hands down, the goldenest goldenboy in Wheelatine Township, perhaps in all the greater Chicagolandarea—realized, I think, that even as "Shut your piehole-cakeface, gaylord" had entered the everyday parlance of our school, it was ineradicably branded Jonboat, and thus he felt free to change it up. I'd heard versions ranging from G- to X-rated. "Stuff your greasehole-fryface, burgerking." "Hide your oofhole-bruiseface, punchingbag." "Plug your stinkhole-assface, widehind." "Wipe your meathole-lipsface, cumdump." Etcetera. All versions got laughs, though none beat the original—at least not to my taste—and, ultimately, I think I felt flattered to have had my family's best saying appropriated by someone as handsome and affable as Jonboat. It helped, too, that he acknowledged my role in the process. When, just before Easter, he came up with the idea to add "Jonboat Say" to the front of the catchphrase and put it on T-shirts, he consulted me directly, and accepted nearly all the advice I gave. All of it except for one small piece, which eventually, though indirectly, caused the brief spasm of trouble between us.

We both agreed the T-shirts should be all-cotton and Superman red. We agreed that the image Jonboat had drawn—a balding and openmouthed fatman's head (colossal uvula, flappy underchin fold) beside a disembodied hand and a motion-line array expressing an imminent, four-fingered slap—should be printed on the chest below "Jonboat Say" and above the catchphrase. We agreed that the lettering should look like it had the texture of spray paint, that the image should be black on a square white background, and that "gaylord" shouldn't appear on the shirt, as "gaylord" would make it unwearable at school. I, however, was of the opinion that, absent "gaylord," the comma should be restored to its original position between "piehole" and "cakeface," whereas Jonboat claimed restoring it would ruin the shirt. He said that, first of all, with a comma before "cakeface," the shirt would have to be considered "officially punctuated," which would require a period be placed *after* "cakeface," not to mention a colon, if not another comma, after "Jonboat Say," and quotation marks around the catchphrase itself, i.e.,

JONBOAT SAY:
[almost-slapped fatman image]
"SHUT YOUR PIEHOLE, CAKEFACE."

This, believed Jonboat, was more punctuation than a T-shirt could abide.

Secondly, he explained that, as his use of the saying had long since demonstrated, he thought it sounded better without the comma; that commanding a person to shut his piehole-cakeface was stronger than just commanding some cakeface to shut his piehole. With that I disagreed, though not too heartily, and I kept my opinion to myself. But I did suggest that a hyphen be placed between "piehole" and "cakeface" in order to really bring across the compoundedness of the two already-compound words. Jonboat wasn't sure. He thought a hyphen might suggest "official punctuation," giving rise to the problem that ditching the comma had already solved. Then again, it might not. A hyphen might be more like a spelling thing—more like an apostrophe. We briefly tossed around the idea of making "piehole(-)cakeface" a single word, i.e. "pieholecakeface," but it looked like Italian spelled by a Slav, and we figured that even if readers of the shirt could recognize "pieholecakeface" as English, they were bound to be confused about where the stresses fell. And so we were back to do- or don't-hyphenate.

Jonboat suggested we sleep on it.

•

•   •

I awoke the next morning erect and depressed. I was twelve years old, wanted someone to touch me, and knew no one would. In the months since Jonboat had bloodied Blackie's nose, some things had changed. First and foremost, my mother had died, a loss so fundamental that it didn't, much of the time, seem possible. I knew I would never see her again and, when I thought about that, I'd pull neck muscles crying, yet after having mourned just five or six weeks, I no longer thought about it—at least not so directly. Which may as easily have meant that I'd "entered a self-preserving state of denial" as that I'd "arrived at acceptance of the loss." The therapists differed; I didn't care. I didn't know what any of it meant, and to try to sort it out seemed self-destructive, masochistic at best. The loss was too massive, the thought of it too painful, to analyze the style in which I chose—or was compelled—to feel it.

Plus there was my skin—newly oily and porous. And I'd developed dandruff, slight myopia, and whiskers over my upper lip too sparse and feline to call a mustache. The UV-sensitive, autotinting lenses of my overlarge glasses (black wire frames, vaguely aviator-shaped) never fully clarified; even in basements, milk was beige. My father no longer cared to fight about my haircut, and although it had remained the same for the most part—long in the back, short on the top, shorter yet on the sides—horizontal stripes above each of my ears were now clippered down to stubble so my temples looked vented. Eight of these stripes. Four per temple. I'm pretty sure I smelled. Something did. And the stoic, ringbound–Kid Dynamite approach to basic ambulation I'd been trying to affect since seeing Tyson KO Biggs—ground-focused glares and smooth rollings of the neck punctuated by sudden, prey-tracking head-tilts—came off less gladiatorial than Crispin Gloveresque (I learned this through observing how Blackie Buxman spoofed me when we passed in the hallways: all unswinging arms, tightened lips, and startled twitching), and I wanted to quit it, and I tried my best, yet I couldn't seem to teach myself to walk how I used to; my muscles refused to shake their training. The fire in my eyes, perhaps wild once, sputtered. In mirrors, I suffered, appeared to be crooked. To my peers, my blacksheepishness had ceased to seem elective. Where before I'd been an outsider, now I was an outcast. Even authority figures—even the smiley ones—emptied their expressions when I entered their shops, their classrooms, their offices.

I don't know why all of this struck me that morning, or if it really did, but that's how I recall it—being in my bed thinking it. "Outcast, retard, psycho, creep." My erection uselessly sweating in my briefs. Worse than uselessly. It was getting in the way. My bladder was full.

I headed for the bathroom, where I leaned and angled, aiming not to tag the seat or the lid. I tagged the lid a little, tagged the seat a lot. There was sprayback on the tile, the side of the tub. I sopped the mess with tissue and returned to my room to wait for the pinch in my loins to subside.

There I heard my cure rustling around in its PillowNest. The flushing toilet must have awakened it. I removed the nest's lid, and found the cure sitting up beside its rear ejection. "Morning, Blank," I said. It played at deafness. I repeated my greeting, and it lay on its belly, closed its eyes. "Blank," I said to it. "Blank, Blank, Blank." But Blank wouldn't stir.

Blank was short for *Kablankey,* the name I'd given it, at my mother's suggestion, for the sound of its sneeze. It had responded to *Kablankey* since the age of four days, but within a couple months—right around the time I'd vented my temples—I'd determined that *Kablankey* was overly cutesy. Yet because my mother had liked the name, I couldn't abandon *Kablankey* entirely; to do that would have somehow dishonored her memory. So I'd been calling it *Blank* for maybe four or five weeks, and although it had started responding to *Blank,* which indicated that it knew it was *Blank,* the responses seemed to follow too much hesitation, and for the past few mornings, the cure had faked sleep til I'd called it by its full name. The faking, in itself, didn't bother me at all; I found it as adorable as anyone would. I just didn't want to have to say *Kablankey* anymore. Especially that morning. I wasn't in the mood.

"Blank," I said.

Its eyes remained closed.

I removed the rear ejection from the nest with a tissue, brought it to the bathroom, flushed it down the toilet.

When I returned to the bedroom, Blank was still faking sleep.

"Blank," I said.

Nothing.

I refused to lose a battle of wills with a Curio. I had a closet-door-mounted toy basketball hoop and, after finding the inflatable ball that went with it, I started taking shots by the foot of the bed. Inside a minute, Blank climbed from the nest, leapt from the nightstand onto my pillow, and, as I continued pretending to ignore it, shinnied down the comforter and stood at my feet.

"Blank?" I said.

Blank showed me its palm.

I cupped a hand by my ankle and the cure climbed in. It slumped for a moment, still catching the breath it lost getting to the floor, then lay along my forearm, an ear to my pulse, and embraced my wrist like a watchband. I cooed affirmations, scratched it on the neck. It pushed a closed eye against my wrist skin and squeezed. This was nice for a minute, but soon I was antsy, and I got the idea to play a game of chase: I would set Kablankey back down on the floor, roll the basketball at it, then watch it bound adorably away in fear.

Of course the trouble with this game was Blank over-trusted me. Or maybe it wasn't a matter of trust—it might have been more a matter of stupidity. It seemed, however, like trust to me, or possibly even something like faith, for I'd seen Blank flee things I *hadn't* set in motion. One time a cricket, down in the basement. Another time the sound of Jon-Jon's chow chow killing a squirrel beneath the elm across the street. That morning with the ball, though, Blank watched me setting up. It saw me providing the force behind the roll. And yet, until the ball—an object roughly twice its width and half its weight—was entirely upon it, it just stood there, waiting, the same expression on its face as when I'd give it a candy.

The ball ran it over and kept on rolling as Blank smacked its head against the rim of a nickel that was standing on end, half-submerged, amidst the rough fibers of the wall-to-wall carpeting. At first it didn't seem too hurt. It sprung up as quickly as it had been knocked down and even seemed poised to do the shuffley little dance thing it so often did when it would sense I was worried or angry about something. But then the ball, having bounced off the baseboard and traveled the path on which I'd set it in reverse, ran Blank down again, this time face-first. I swept the ball out of action—set it firmly on the bed—and when I turned back to look, Blank, though wobbly, was upright once more, shifting its weight from foot to tail, its elbows pointing outward like wings, and its hands autistically flapping the air by the sides of its pinkening, rugburned muzzle.

This was already the single cutest thing I'd ever witnessed, yet before I even thought to reach down and offer comfort, one of Blank's welling eyes squeezed out a plump tear, cutening it further. The tear spilled onto the rugburn and puddled, and the pinkened muzzle reddened, visibly swelled. I would not have been surprised to hear a low sizzling or see rising steam, and, for a moment, Blank must have experienced some relief, for its hands ceased to flap, and its posture relaxed. After that moment had passed, however, any cooling effect the tear's wetness may have had was, it seemed, dramatically reversed by that same tear's salinity.

Blank's hands resumed flapping, and its eyes began to gush. The rugburn became increasingly inflamed, and, through trembling lips, which were pursed as if to whistle, my cure began singing its sublime, plaintive painsong.

Something like thirst, or even lust, overcame me. I tried to understand. What more did I want? Shinier tears? Shakier quivering? Richer vibrato? Spazzier hands? I wanted all of those things, but not only those things. I wanted the painsong to sing from my lungs. I wanted Blank's tears to stream down my face. I wanted its shakes to convulse my own muscles. I wanted to engulf it, to make it a part of me. I wanted to fuse. And I wanted, at last—and for the first time—to crush my cure in my fist and ingest it. Preferably whole. In a long, single swallow.

Though I know how mundane that must seem today, this was still the first half of 1988, and little involving cures was mundane yet. A couple kids, true, had made the nightly news for having gone into overload, but they'd *made the nightly news*—that seemed to mean that what they'd done was weird. Ghastly, even. It had, at least, seemed that way to me. I'd raised Blank from a marble, and I'd never made it clone, had never fed it formulae (formulae hadn't been heard of yet; Curios, for that matter, were still branded *Botimals; cure overload* didn't even have a name). I had never pinched it, much less punctured it, nor blocked its airways, nor shown it a cat. I'd never pulled any of its limbs from their sockets, nor thrown it down stairs, nor thrown it at a wall. I'd never thrown it.

What I wanted to do made me feel like a monster, yet I didn't move away. I wasn't reaching for Blank—I knew I wouldn't follow through—but I let myself remain there, in that state of total wanting, until the phone rang, and Blank stopped singing.

I lunged across my bed, picked up before the second ring—my father was asleep, still.

"No hyphen," said Jonboat. "It just—"

"Hold on," I said. I set the phone down, took the thimble of water from the slot in the PillowNest, and brought it to Blank, which was still on the floor, flapping its hands, looking up at me for guidance. I tapped my mouth with my index finger, then dipped the same finger into the thimble. The cure understood. It dunked its face in, up to the eyes, and as it started to rub the tiny knot on its skull, which had risen on the spot that had smacked the nickel's rim, I said, "Blank, I'm sorry. I didn't mean to hurt you." It kept rubbing the spot, kept its face in the thimble. I said, "I'll never hurt you on purpose again, okay? Kablankey?"

It stopped the rubbing and showed me its palm.

It resumed the rubbing, and I picked up the phone.

"So I was saying no hyphen," Jonboat said. "It just isn't needed."

"You're right," I told him. "The hyphen's implied."

"You don't sound like you mean it. You sound all negative."

"I mean it," I said.

"I hope so," said Jonboat. "Cause that hyphen's an ostrich. Not an ostrich, an aubergine. An ocelot, I mean. Around the shirt's neck. Dragging us down. Cursing our voyage. I really believe that. Using it's—what? Inappropriate, right? Not exactly inappropriate, but not quite . . . I don't know."

"It's pissing through a boner," I said.

"It's what? It's pissing through a *boner*? You come up with that yourself?"

"Just now," I said. "Yeah."

"Nice one!" said Jonboat. "And thanks for the help. Word to the muth, homey. Smellya on the later. Pissing through a boner! You rule, Belt. You rule."

The compliment rattled me free of my despair, made me like myself a little. I'd even say it buoyed me for a couple of weeks. And when next I looked at Blank, I only wanted to be kind. When its rugburn healed, I would teach it to somersault.

•

•   •

At a stand beside the bleachers at the baseball season-opener, Jonboat's driver, Burroughs, was selling the shirts. My father bought two—one for each of us—though only after announcing to Burroughs, and those in line behind us, that I'd "played no small role in designing these garments," that the catchphrase was, in fact, Magnet-family trademarked, and he was looking forward with great anticipation to toting up our royalties with Jon-Jon Jason over postgame tallboys—"On me!"—at Blimey's Tavern. He was joking about the royalties. He was, it seemed, proud. He even seemed happy. Laughing it up for the first time in months. Throughout the game, he kept pointing at his chest (he was wearing the shirt), patting my arm, saying, "Nice work, son."

Jonboat pitched a no-hitter, stole home twice, hit one RBI, and was given the game ball.

On the drive home, my dad tuned to 88.1, community radio, to hear the local sports show. An interviewer said, "We're live in the dugout with Jonny 'Jonboat' Pellmore-Jason and his Washington Mustangs, who Jonboat just led to a ten-to-nada, no-hitter victory over the mighty Twin Groves Eagles.

Now, Jonboat, I'm serious here: What gives? In fall you're a triple-doubling center one day, and the next you're a golden-armed-quarterback-slash-blitz-a-quarter-nose-tackle. That's confusing enough. Now it's spring and you're telling me you've pitched a no-hitter and gotten on base at your every at bat? How do you do it? Is there anything can stop you?"

"I don't know," Jonboat said. "I really don't know. I guess I try to keep my head down and do the necessary work. This is sports. It's for real. It matters to people. I think others could do the same things I do. Other teams could do the same things we do. The physical machinery, it's there to be honed. To be made useful. I really believe that. I mean, you saw the Eagles. It's not like they're shrimpy. They've got legs, arms, and eyes. Brains in their heads. They've got the same equipment we Mustangs have. It's just they're not willing to put in the work. They're—I don't know. I guess . . . How can I put it? They're pissing through a boner."

"Come again, Jonboat?" the interviewer said. "I didn't quite get that."

"Well, you know what I mean. They're pissing through a boner. They're pissing through a boner, and that's not why they have one."

" 'They're pissing through a boner, and that's not why they have one!' Aphoristic wisdom from our own Jonny 'Jonboat,' scion of the Pellmores and Jasons the both. Kids these days. So tell me, Jonboat. Rumor has it Papa Jon-Jon's about to buy—"

I shut off the radio.

"Hey," said my father.

"He stole that from me. Pissing through a boner. I invented that. It's mine."

"Relax," said my father. "Stop with the crying. Stop kicking the glovebox."

"Stop kicking the glovebox? He stole my *line*. I made it up myself. I was sad when I thought of it. It meant something specific, and he changed the meaning so that now it's too broad, and then he added a clause to explain it all to dummies. 'And that's not why they have one!' No kidding, huh? Boners aren't meant for pissing through, dude? I had no idea. I really didn't. Thanks for the clarification, Jonboat. He ruined it completely. First he stole it, then he destroyed it."

"Billy, listen—" said my father.

"That's not my fucking *name*."

•

•   •

The next day at school, I rushed up on Jonboat, flailing my arms and squealing away about theft and betrayal. He threw me at a locker, the rebound from which bounced me venting-first at a Pellmore-Jason palm-strike that knocked me out cold.

When I regained consciousness a couple seconds later, he was kneeling beside me, holding my glasses, straightening out the arm he'd bent. "Sorry," he said, and slipped them back on my face. "That was all just reflex."

"*Pissing through a boner*," I said. "You stole it."

"I'm sorry you feel that way, Belt. I didn't know," he said. "I thought you were giving it to me, like with piehole-cakeface. Did I get that wrong? I guess I got it wrong. Listen. Let me buy you some stuff after school. Maybe some clothes. Your clothes are really wanting, man. That's why no pussy. We'll go to the mall, alright? Then get pussy."

"You want," I said, "to take me to the mall?"

"Of course I want to take you to the mall," said Jonboat. "I don't see any reason we can't still be pals. We just had our physical confrontation, right? That's an important developmental stage in the friendships of boys. That's what they say. At least that's what my dad says. He's beaten up *all* his friends at one point or another. And Jon-Jon Jason—you know as well as I do—Jon-Jon Jason's got a lot of friends."

"Alright," I said.

"Friends then. Good. And listen here: *pissing through a boner*. I'm not gonna use it ever again, unless you want me to."

"You can use it," I said. "You already used it. But just, look, leave off *and that's not why they have one*. It's really redundant. It kills all the subtlety."

"Deal," Jonboat said. "Let's get you to the nurse, now. We'll tell her you tripped and banged your face on a locker. After school, I'll ditch practice and meet you in the back of my Phantom, by the bike rack."

I agreed to the plan. But then it turned out I might have had a concussion, and the nurse called my father, who took me to the hospital, where the doctor confirmed I might have had a concussion.

I missed the mall.

I told my father the locker tale. He told me I needed to watch where I was going.

•

• •

Jonboat brought me clothes at lunch the next day. One bag from Guess? and one from Z. Cavaricci. Also a hairbrush with an air-powered gel compartment built into the handle. The clothes didn't fit and, even when wet, my hair was too wavy to pull a brush through, but the thought was what counted. I didn't complain. I pasted up bangs and tucked in the shirts, cinched the waists of the pants with silver-tipped belts and pegged the cuffs thick on my shins like a pirate.

Jonboat said I looked great and introduced me to girls, a couple of whom took my calls when I phoned the first couple times. It wasn't as though we had become bosom buddies, but throughout all the rest of junior high, and then high school, I always had the sense he was protecting me a little—that had it not been for the occasional light he shone upon me in public (the hellos in the hallways, the cafeteria line-cuts), I'd have been just as bullied as any other greasy and motherless weirdo. The conversations we had, however brief and infrequent, didn't feel like charity the way my conversations with other kids did. I could get him to laugh, to slap me on the back, to admiringly echo things I'd just said. Correctly or not, I thought of Jonboat as a friend.

After graduation, he went to Annapolis. I wrote him three times in as many months, but received no response. Yet there were no hard feelings. At least not on my end. For a while I felt forgotten, but I never felt ditched. Well, not never, but not often. He was different from the rest of us. He always would be. He'd bow-hunted grizzlies since the age of thirteen. Flown jets at sixteen and dined at Camp David. At Kensington Palace. He would marry at the Hermitage. Buy and sell airlines. Push legislation. Make and break currencies. Underwrite charities. Explore *outer space*. As he had turned down Oxford and Yale senior year, he'd eventually (at least according to rumor) turn down vital ambassadorships—to Russia, to China, Israel, and France. Everyone wanted a piece of the guy, and I knew it back then as all the world knows it now. Within weeks of sending that third, unanswered letter, I'd come to accept that the piece I wanted was worth far more than I could offer in return, that he didn't have time for me, was just too busy, and I took satisfaction—took *pride,* in fact—in swearing him off.

Not swearing him off, but determining, rather, to do the decent thing and leave him alone.

When the press began to turn on him during his divorce, I'd fail to change the channel—in the end I'm only human—but I wasn't ever happy to see him attacked. I always hoped Jonboat would be alright.

TWO HUNDRED-SOME QUILLS

THEN A BIRTHDAY AGO, while drinking from a tumbler of water in the kitchen, I saw the front page of that Sunday's *Daily Herald* wrapping the present my father had left for me next to the sink. A Post-it note crookedly stuck to the banner read, "38YO! Well that's just nutso. A Happy and a Healthy to YOU, Young Master! Sorry not to be here to say that in person. —from Clyde the Dad." Under the note was the following headline:

RETURN OF THE PRODIGAL PRODIGY CONFIRMED

PELLMORE-JASONS LIVING IN WHEELATINE

"THEY'VE BEEN HERE SINCE APRIL," MEMBER OF GROUNDS-KEEPING STAFF TELLS *THE HERALD*

This was stale, sound news disguised as hot gossip, *confirmed* the headline's operative word. Everyone in town knew Jonboat was back. His compound was lit, had been lit since spring, his armored fastback '65 Mustang (aka "The Boatmobile") photographed approaching the ramparts at Pellmore Place, hulking men in immaculate livery spotted on corners speaking into their collars, and at least one Wheelatine-area merchant (Main Street Sloga Nero's, according to the pricetag ($20.98) stapled to the hem) was carrying bootlegged JONBOAT SAY shirts with the catchphrase replaced by I'M BACK IN 'TINE GAYLORD—this last fact one I was, admittedly, only just discovering there in the kitchen amidst the ripped newsprint. I looked at the label. The shirt was a medium. At least Clyde had gotten the size right, I thought.

The phone started ringing.

Owing only to its timing (the possibility would never have otherwise occurred to me), I wondered if maybe Jonboat was calling, which wondering then triggered a number of thoughts to overcome me at once, all gooed up and twisty as an orgy of tree snails. Unpacked and organized, their images grammarized, they would have, these thoughts, gone something like this:

- Maybe, since returning to Wheelatine, Jonboat's been wanting to get back in contact but, given all of the time that's passed, has waited til today because opening the dialogue with a "Happy Birthday" would, by virtue of explaining why he's calling *now,* lower the pressure he's probably feeling to explain some other whys, e.g. why he never called before, why he never wrote you back, and perhaps why he might owe you some kind of apology.
- That you'd even imagine he'd feel such pressure means you're not as much at peace with the end of your friendship (or whatever it was) as you like to tell yourself, and that the pride you've taken in not having reached out to him for all these years was a dishonest kind, a loser's pride akin to the sort would-be suicides who fail to pull the trigger from fear of what's next exhibit with pronouncements on the sanctity of life and nobility of suffering when in fact they're only cowards.
- Though not necessarily. You might just be too good at empathy. You're a fiction writer, after all. Your tendency to imagine how others might feel given who *they* are and what *they've* experienced, might have, by now, become knee-jerk, unwitting. It might even have been that way before you wrote fiction. Like after that time on the bus, in fourth grade, when Blackie Buxman pantsed you and punched you in the asshole, and then later that night, while you were trying to fall asleep, you imagined a chubbier, toddling Blackie getting pantsed and punched in the asshole by his dad (who you'd never met, but who, in your mind's eye, resembled Bill Sikes from Hollywood's take on the musical *Oliver!*), and you went downstairs in tears to your parents, tears for toddling Blackie, and explained how you felt, and your mom said, "Oh, baby," and squeezed your shoulders, and your father told your mom that she shouldn't do that, that it encouraged weakness. "What he's doing . . ." he said to her. "What you're doing," he said to you. "It's like suffering from Stockholm syndrome in Auschwitz."
- If only you were as gay for Jonboat as you seem right now! That would probably mean you could be gay for other men, i.e. that you could be gay, in which case you might have better luck in love, since gay men are notoriously curious and open-minded, and might find your quirks not only acceptable, but even attractive.
- How can your father think this T-shirt is an okay gift? It's hostile, isn't it? Not just because it's plainly cheap and joke-gifty, nor even because

he must know it's the only birthday gift you'll get, but because of that day in the car, after the game, when he was all full of pride about the family catchphrase appearing on the T-shirt, and you were upset about "pissing through a boner," and he told you relax and stop kicking the glovebox. Ever since, things have been tense between you, especially around the subject of Jonboat. Do you even really care if it's Jonboat calling? Maybe you don't. Did you ever really have a friendship with Jonboat? Maybe you didn't. And maybe you only think about Jonboat in order to avoid thinking about your dad.

- Unless maybe it's the reverse. Or maybe neither. After all, you're thinking about the both of them right now, aren't you?
- You're such a whiner. You're such a weenie. You're such an introspective ham. What seems to be insensitivity on your father's part is just as likely oversensitivity on yours. He's a good guy, your father. His life has not exactly been easy, and yet he's put up with you, his useless, freeloading failure of a son, so grow a sense of humor. You could just as easily understand the shirt as a kind of malformed olive branch, a message to the effect of, "Hey, Belt, we're different you and I, but you're my son, and the way I've learned to deal with this terrifying world that took your mother away is to approach emotionally complicated matters with levity—a type of levity that, at times, resembles cruelty, sure, but for that reason is more effective, engenders bigger laughs. I'd like you to learn to do the same, and am only trying to teach by example. I'm your father after all. Can't we get past that time in the car? Can't we get over our bullshit, already? Can't you just laugh about the shirt with me a little?"
- Your father doesn't remember that time in the car. He's never made a big deal out of birthdays, yet he felt a little bad for leaving town on your birthday, felt bad enough to want to buy you a gift, and the shirt's the gift he chose because he thinks it's funny in the first degree.

This mess of thoughts, despite its intensity, receded just as quickly as it had emerged once I caught sight of the clock on the stove. It read 9:43, which meant the caller was Grandmother. She'd call me every birthday, with birthday wishes, just after 9:40, the minute of my birth. "Happy birth-hour," she'd say.

I didn't want to hear her.

Our telephone's handset was sleek and ultralight, though. Earlier that morning, if not before then, my father had left it keypad-side-up on the topmost couldn't get lost, couldn't even manage that; the town wasn't big enough, the chemist wasn't dumb enough. The chemist was glum. But then one night, as he was plodding past an alley, he overheard an orphan saying to a dog, "Don't you think this gum should have a lot more chew in it? I bet if it chewed more I could blow it up into a ball-type shape, see. Like stretch it with my tongue, then breathe it out round. Make like a bubble. Call the stuff bubbleychew. How do you like that? Ah, you don't understand. You're just a stray animal I once fed a scrap to, and me I'm crazy and stupid the both. Doomed and crazy with my stupid ideas, just like Sister Alameda says. Doomed. *Blow it in a ball shape and call the stuff*—what was it? yeah—*call it bubbleychew*. Sounds like a faggot's name. A queer baking cookies. A homo in an apron with sprinkles on top. Honest to Christmas, what's wrong with me, muttso?"

Regardless of the source of the chemist's inspiration, though, his recipe, I supposed, revolutionized gum. It was far less a failure at retaining sweetness than it was a success at sustaining chewability and, epiphenomenally, enabling bubbling. It forced the tide to rise. All the other brands of bubblegum still around today—your Hubba Bubbas, Bazookas, Bubbliciousi, and Bubble Yums—developed in its wake. Dubble Bubble stood for progress. And the sun was high, too, and the pantry was stocked. So was the fridge. I had 150 Quills.

Then again I had only 150 Quills, an empty wallet, no credit to speak of, and this was 2013—shouldn't Dubble Bubble, in the intervening decades, have figured out a way to make the sweetness longer-lasting? If so, did that mean Dubble Bubble stood for regress? Maybe it did.

And yet a case could be made for original formulas—the benefits of sticking to them. Cases could no doubt be made for nostalgia (I wasn't as against it as the thinkers said I should be). One could argue Dubble Bubble had come to stand for regress, but that regress in a world that had gone to the dogs was a form of progress, or, at worst, digression. Had the world gone to the dogs, though? Who was I to judge? I wasn't even creditworthy. Or maybe I was and nobody knew it. They sent me those offers, but I never signed up. I was sure of this much: it was past 12 p.m., which meant the mailman had come, and I wanted to believe Dubble Bubble stood for something. Digression, progress, regress—something.

I walked to the mailbox, dragging at my Quill, determined to blow a bubble full of smoke. Though not too determined. A couple failed attempts, and I forgot all about it. The mailbox held a *Newsweek* and three or four catalogs, atop which lay an envelope from Social Security. Inside was a check for $1,100 made out to my father. My SSDI check.

The change that came over me wasn't dramatic. I still wasn't sure Dubble Bubble stood for anything. I still wasn't sure what I wanted it to stand for. I realized, however, that I'd ignored the possibility it might stand for stasis, and

I found myself hoping it didn't stand for stasis. I'd have rather it stood for nothing than stasis.

•
•   •

At the bank I lined up behind one or two customers, depending on whether you counted the one who was already being helped at the counter. I hadn't been to the bank since my mother was living, yet the teller looked familiar. Her eyes did at least. They were gray, though, which threw me. The gray-eyed seemed always to be on the verge of offering a hug to whomever they were looking at, or stretching their limbs out in hopes of getting belly-rubbed. Since strangers aren't like that, at least not usually, you think, "Not a stranger's," when you see some gray eyes. You think it automatically. On top of that, her body was round as a pie. She had to be at least twice the recommended weight. Wouldn't I have remembered a person with that build if she had those eyes? I tried thinking back to high school, then junior high school—the teller looked my age, give or take a couple years—and came up with nothing. Then again, "heavy with lovely eyes" was such a rampantly trampled cliché—what prom-going beauty ever lacked a best friend who matched that description?—that maybe the teller, back in our school days, wouldn't have even stood out enough to register, let alone be remembered twenty years later. And to complicate matters even further, it was possible adulthood had compromised her shape. She might once have been thin, or not so unthin.

The man she was helping headed for the exit, briefly decongesting my line of sight and allowing me a glimpse at her nameplate on the counter. It read LOTTA HOGG, white letters on woodgrain. Dementia plus ninety-nine blows to the head couldn't force you to forget a girl named Lotta Hogg. So the matter was settled. It was just the gray eyes.

Another teller appeared at the next station over while Lotta helped the customer who'd been in line in front of me. This new teller hadn't put his nameplate on the counter, so I didn't think his station was officially open and, assuming he needed more time to set up, I remained between the queue poles, which seemed to annoy him. "Um, sir?" he said. "I'm open *here,* sir."

He wore a pinstriped vest and decisive mustache. From the vest's top button fell a golden chain that disappeared inside the watchpocket, forming half a smile. My father, had he been there, would have probably asked the teller if Halloween had come early. Or, if he were in a not-good mood, he might have called the teller *chief* and offered mock solace like, "I know it must be hard to stay so true to yourself, but one day, believe me, the whole neuters-impersonating-railroad-barons look will have a big-time comeback, most people won't want to pound your teeth down your throat, and you will, mark my words, have consensual sex, chief." I wasn't like my father, though. I wasn't good at dominance. Approaching the teller, I said, "You've got a pocketwatch! I love those things."

"Oh, this," the teller said. He tugged the golden chain, and a pale infant cure attached by a collar the circumference of a dime crawled out from the watchpocket, blinking and sniffling. It was medium-tailed, two-legged, and its velvet was black—it seemed as standard as they came—but when the teller cupped his chain-tugging hand at his ribs, the cure didn't climb in.

I said, "I've never seen that."

"A cure on a watch chain?"

"That too," I said. "It's not going to your hand, though."

"Oh that," said the teller. "I gave it Independence."

"How?" I said.

"By 'How?'" said the teller, "I suppose what you mean is, 'How did you, a mild-mannered young bank teller, manage to get hold of the most exciting and buzzed-about line of Graham&Swords PlayChanger PerFormulae for Curios since 2008's SloMo, or perhaps even 1993's BullyKing, when said line of PerFormulae won't be made available to mainstream consumers for another like month?' Am I right? Is that what you mean?"

"Independence is a formula?"

"Where have *you* been?" he said. "Yes. It's a formula. A *PerFormula,* holmes. No off-brand syrups para *mon* cure. It's PlayChanger line. Licensed and patented. Countdown engaged for worldwide launch. T-minus roughly five weeks or whatever. And my answer to the question you should have been asking about how I got ahold of it ahead of the launch is: Well I guess how it happened is I was spotted backstage at a DJ Crystal Worms show a little while back. I think it must have been probably three or four or maybe even five months back because Crys-Dubs wasn't exactly Crys-Dubs yet. Like his style of new sleazebeat was still, at the time when I was at that show, which wasn't even sold out, a revolution on the scale of Wang Kar Pourquoi's first fortes into fuzzdub or, if it's fair to go outside genre to compare revolutions, even Murderer-ers' invention of the whole demonkraut sound back in like Murderer-ers' trademark-infringement days when they were still called Murderers Jr. Anyways, there I was, backstage for Crys-Dubs, just doing my thang. My thang that night was handing out flyers to VIPs to promote this sponsored afterparty at Killer Queen Marmalade's for . . . I can't remember, actually, what the afterparty was for. I mean, I've VIP-flyered for so many sponsored afterparties by now, it would really blow your mind. Like I just can't keep track. I'm pretty sure that the sponsor was Que Padre Mezcal, though.

Whatever. It's not really urbane to what I'm trying to say because point being is that right when I was VIP-flyering Crys-Dubs himself (he said he couldn't make it, even though he wished he could, and you could tell he really meant it, too, he was really disappointed), I got spotted by a Graham&Swords outreach marketing liaison who was standing right next to him. She admired how I did my thang, she said, and she thought I might—and it's embarrassing to say, but I'm only quoting here—she thought I might be able to 'help sexen up the profile of the Graham&Swords PlayChanger brand,' and she asked me if I'd like to be a beta tester/demonstrator, which is something I obviously said, 'Oh sure why not,' to."

The cure seemed sleepy. Clinging to the teller's vest by its footclaws, it rubbed its eyes with the heels of its palms, arched its back, and yawned repeatedly. To get a closer look, I'd leaned forward a little, onto the counter, and in so doing must have jarred my CureSleeve, for I felt an insistent, three-part knocking on the meat of my forearm—Blank's signal that it had woken up. I knocked twice lightly on the top of the sleeve—my signal to Blank that it couldn't come out.

"And the answer," said the teller, gaining verbal momentum, "to the follow-up question you're about to ask is: Nope. I can't hook you up with the liaison so you can become a beta tester/demonstrator. If I hooked everyone up with the liaison who asked me to hook them up with the liaison then I wouldn't have time to do anything but hook people up with the liaison, and that's not my job. That's not why they hired me. There's something I can do for you that you might appreciate, though. I'm not like officially allowed to do this, however that's not to say I'm officially unallowed to do this, but it could be considered a little bit of a risk to my employment situation—not here, the boss is cool here, but with Graham&Swords, I'm saying—and that's why I'd have to ask you to offer payment for the service—the service *and* the product—but I do happen to have a couple extra ampules of Independence on me, and although I wouldn't be willing to let you actually handle one of these extra ampules—they've got serial numbers on them that could lead right back to me—I would, for some cashious-type consideration, if you get what I'm saying, be willing to meet you out in the parking lot, and like *empty* one of these ampules into your CureSleeve's dropper-bottle. If you're into it, I mean."

"Aw, no thanks," I said.

"Really? That's—I guess that's kind of not what . . . Well how about can you open your sleeve up for me? Because I'd love to get a look at your little robot."

"I better not," I said.

"Oh damn, is it a hobunk? I wasn't even thinking about that. I'll put this one away, and then—"

"It's not a hobunk," I said. "It's just asleep."

"It's what?"

"It's asleep."

"Well *it* doesn't care!"

"Still, though," I said.

"Come on," said the teller. "Wake the punk up."

"It really needs its sleep," I said.

"Okay then, I guess, but, well, main reason I asked to see it to begin with, though, is cause I'm wondering: Is it full-grown?"

"Yes," I said.

"Good. That's good. That's all I wanted to know. Because if you're worried it'll run away if you dose it with Independence: don't. I mean, I don't know what rumors you have or haven't heard, but I don't think it'll happen. I think it's seriously unlikely. Like Tiddleywinks here is, as you can see, just a couple weeks old, so the effect of the Independence is particularly strong, stronger than it would be on an older cure. I've dosed a couple full-growns and they still went to my hand is what I'm saying—they just weren't all like *enthusiastic* about it, you know? I had to coax them a little. And they didn't autodact, or even get grievey when I left them untouched for a couple of days. Anyway, say I'm wrong and yours does run—well, *wick*ed, right? It'll be the first cure on record to ever run away—not that it would be 'on record,' of course, because that would mean you'd told someone I let you have some pre-launch Independence if you wanted to even begin to be believed, and that would get me in trouble, but *you'd* know, right? that yours was the first, I mean? Not to mention that I can throw in a collar, too. I've got extras. They're thinking every ampule of Independence is gonna come with a leash and some kind of collar—Graham&Swords hasn't decided what kind of collar yet, which is one of the reasons they haven't launched Independence yet, or at least that's the rumor—but the liaison gave me all these different collars to try. I've got adjustable one-size-fits-alls, and then I've got specifically sized ones, too. I still haven't given any feedback to the liaison about which I prefer—which, note to self, eh?—but only because I haven't developed a solid preference yet, and that means you're in luck because it means I'd hook you up with whichever one of those collars you wanted. I can't give you a bangin gold watchchain or anything, but you can maybe go up the street to the new toy shop they opened there next to the video store, and buy yourself a yo-yo, use the string as a leash, or even just allow me to present the free gift of a rubberband I'll get from this very supply cabinet to my left if you'd like. I'll gladly secure it to the collar for you, free of charge and so on. Enticed, now? All in, I'm talking, what? Two hundred dollars."

"I don't feed my cure formula."

"Right. Who would? But like I said before, this is *PerFormula*. Graham&

Swords-branded, Graham&Swords-tested, and totally Graham&Swords-official. Or at least it will be in just a few more months. And listen, I can go as low as one seventy-five, maybe even one fifty, and plus I didn't even tell you the best part yet because I'm definitely forbidden to mention it, but listen, okay? The marrow of a cure that's been Independenced? Let's just say it acquires certain heretofore-unseen and wicked-rad *properties* if you know what I mean. That's *way* off-the-record, though, feel me? You do. I can tell. I can. You feel me."

By this point, the teller was leaning in to whisper, and Tiddleywinks had jumped from his vest to the counter, where it lay on its side, clawing at the collar and jerking its head around. It hummed through pursed lips in two- and three-note bursts, too young still to piece a whole painsong together.

"I don't think it likes wearing that collar," I said.

"Word," said the teller. "Cute as hell, right? Hey, though, watch this." The teller remained bent forward at the waist, but he took a step back, which yanked the cure off the counter, into open air, where it dangled by the neck, kicking its legs around. "Adorable." said the teller. "So *freakin* adorable!"

"Chad-Kyle," Lotta Hogg said. Her customer had left.

"Oh right," said the teller. "Unprofessional. Sorry. Thanks for the feedback. And thanks for calling me Chad-Kyle." Turning from Lotta and winking at me, he straightened his posture. The cure collided hands-first with his belt, clung and breathed heavy, eyes squeezed shut. "People tend to call me C.K.," the teller told me, jamming the cure back into the watchpocket. "That's partly because I used to introduce myself as C.K. It's also partly because lots of people know me through my VIP-flyering work, and, in the lower-right corner of every flyer I print to promote the events I VIP-flyer for, there's a little stamp that says, 'C.K. Productions International.' But mostly it's because people don't, for some reason, like to say Chad-Kyle, which is why I started introducing myself as C.K. to begin with, and also why I branded my little VIP-flyering-slash-VIP-flyer-design-and-consulting side venture 'C.K. Productions International' instead of branding it 'Chad-Kyle Productions International.' Vicious cycle. Circle? I don't know. It's vicious either way, right? *Vicious*. I don't personally see anything wrong with Chad-Kyle. It's actually a pretty great name, I think. But now I'm just babbling, and this isn't about me. And I'm sorry if I pressed you about the Independence—it gets me all enthused, and I want to share that with people. If you change your mind, you know where to find me. Just keep it lo-pro, alright? Okay. I know you got my back. Now how can I help meet your banking needs?"

I showed him the check.

"Would you swipe your ATM card for me, please?"

"I don't have one," I said.

"Oh, that's okay. Do you have another form of ID?"

I showed him my state ID.

"Now *that* is a name," he said. Then he stroked keys, paused, stroked more keys.

"You probably won't find me in there," I said. "I don't have an account. I've just got this check."

"Ah-ha," said Chad-Kyle. "You'd like to *open an account* with this check."

"If that's what I need to do," I said.

"Well that's . . ."

"I'm sorry," I said. "I'm totally new at this. I don't really know how it works."

"No no no. I'm a teller. This is a bank. We like new accounts. So, let's see here—well, thing is, it looks like this check isn't made out to you, unless maybe you changed your name since you got that ID?"

"Right," I said. "I mean I haven't changed my name. The check's made out to my father. But it's meant for me."

"For you."

"It's my SSDI check. I'm the beneficiary. My father's my guardian, though, so it's made out to him. He's out of town, is the thing, and he forgot to leave me any money. He won't be back for a week, so I thought probably I could maybe come here and get the money myself since this is his bank."

"I see," said Chad-Kyle. "I see now, but—you know, this isn't . . . I'm not sure exactly how to handle this kind of thing," he said. "I think I better go up the chain a little here."

The manager came. The manager was nice. He quietly explained why they couldn't cash the check for me—why no one could. I'd be lying if I said I didn't feel pretty low. To have become an adult without having learned how to bank—which it turned out wasn't very complicated at all—was embarrassing. On top of that, Chad-Kyle, while the manager explained things, kept biting his lip and trying to throw at Lotta, who was too busy closing down her station to notice, these wide-eyed looks that seemed to say, "This poor idiot here who has to rely on his father to bank—makes the heart just bleed and bleed. Too bad we can't help him." So I wasn't merely ignorant, unworthy of credit, and in need of more Quills—I was also pitiful. And this is how pitiful: when the manager finished talking, I asked where the bathroom was, and Chad-Kyle, apologetically, informed me that the bathroom was employees-only, and the manager overrode it. Said he'd make an exception. He gave me the four-digit code for the door.

I didn't use the toilet. I only blew my nose. After blowing my nose, though, I saw how they could think that I had used the toilet and not washed my hands, given how little time the whole process took. So I decided to stay there another minute or two. Except then I thought, "No. Let them think what they will. Your hands are clean," and I resolved to leave, yet my resolve was not as strong as I liked to imagine, so I washed my hands and didn't dry them, but rather walked past the counter conspicuously wiping them off on my shirt.

I could have wiped them on my shirt without having first washed them and still produced the effect I was after, except that didn't occur to me til I was back in the lobby, halfway to the exit. It was probably all for nothing anyway. No one seemed to be paying attention. No one waved at me. No one said goodbye.

• • •

Lotta Hogg was out front, leaning on the building and eating a blondie.

"Belt Magnet," she said. "I *thought* it was you."

"You did?" I said.

"Yes!" she said. "But I didn't believe it til Chad-Kyle made a comment about how unique a name you had, which must seem like a really dumb way to say it to a wordsmith like you because of how a thing's 'unique' or 'not unique,' but I guess that's just—I don't know—how people talk. 'So unique!' 'Very unique!' It's colloquial! Anyway, I asked him what it was, your name, just to be sure. And sure enough, right? So I guess this must be totally weird for you. You don't have the faintest idea who I am."

"I should, though, shouldn't I? I'm sorry," I said. "You looked familiar to me the instant I saw you, but then I thought it was just your gray eyes."

"It probably was. People tend to remember them. Big girl with gray eyes. You catch a glance and move on because of the big part, but you never *fully* move on—because of the gray part. Or maybe *you* move on, but these suckers stay with you. These peepers *linger*. You'd probably be surprised by how often I hear that. Then again, maybe you wouldn't be surprised at all! This isn't a blondie, by the way. Not really. I mean it's a blondie, but it's made with fake sugar. It's not very good, or I'd offer you some. How have you *been*?"

"Same as always," I said.

"And how's that, Belt Magnet?"

I said, "You never told me where we knew each other from."

"Well that's because we don't know each other, and I'm really nervous because I realize I sound like a complete weirdo who's talking way too fast!" said Lotta. She swallowed some blondie, rolled up her eyes, loudly inhaled the summer air through her nose. "Okay," she said. "Okay. Okay. Confession time. It's confession time because the thing is, me and my girlfriends? We had a total deadly hot crush on you back when, but you were a couple grades ahead of us, and then, by the time it would have been alright to do something about it, well—you know."

"I don't," I said, though I thought I probably did.

"Well you kind of went from trouble to troubled is how I think my grandma would say it."

"Who's your grandma?" I said.

"Who *was* she's more like it. She passed on, oh my, it must have been twenty years ago. We're getting so old, Belt. I'm thirty-five years old next month. You must be thirty-seven, thirty-eight now, right? But Grandma, may her kind, granny soul be at rest, was a big fan of Elvis is what I meant, and what she'd always say about Elvis was how, at the start, with 'Hound Dog' and 'Heartbreak Hotel' and so on—at the start he was trouble, but then, by the time he was wearing those capes, he was . . . troubled."

"So you liked me end of summer, 1987."

"I guess it *was* 1987. Wow, that's so long ago. But not just liked, though, Belt. Deadly hot crushed on. And not just end of summer. A little into fall, too. We saw your performance at the Feather place and, I swear, you were—you were beautiful. Our hero. We all got our first periods the following morning. Oh, that's a gross thing to say, isn't it? I'm sorry. That was gross. I'm gross. It's true, though. Mostly. Not all of us got them, but three of us did. Me and Kelly and Jenn. Ashley, however, it should probably be noted, is now a lesbian, so I don't think her crush was real anyway. We were, like, nine years old, though. I mean it was definitely a phenomenon. Or maybe we were ten. Still, though. You turned us into women. God, I don't say things like this. I don't talk this way. I'm really not a bubblehead. I'm so, I'm just . . . I mean, I'd heard you were in an institution, and then I heard you wrote a novel, which I read—*awesome* by the way—and I sent a letter to you through your publisher, but I never heard back from you, which made me pretty angry—I took a lot of time on that letter!—but then I heard that you were in an institution *again* and so I forgave you for not writing back, and but now you're here. At my *job*. And what's even weirder than that is that so was Jonboat. Just yesterday. I knew he was back, but *still*, you know? It's different to see him in the flesh than on some front page. It's like hearing your voice after having read your book. At least that's what I imagine it's like. I mean, I wasn't actually here when he came in, but Chad-Kyle was, and he compared it to a time when he saw some singer from some band thats name I can't remember right now—I never heard their music but I definitely heard *of* them—Chad-Kyle saw this singer eating eggs at the IHOP like a regular person, and he said that seeing Jonboat come in here to bank was exactly just like that, except times two, or squared or whatever. Squared? Whichever's bigger. Which is I guess always squared. Not always. Almost always. If the number's greater than two, or . . . wait. Yes. Squared's always bigger than doubled if the number's greater than two *or less than zero*—and what a shitty movie, by the way, ha! yeah, I know, I know, it was also a book too—but like . . . No. Yeah. I'm totally right. If the number you're squaring is greater than two or less than zero, then squaring it always makes it bigger than doubling it. Because of a negative times a negative is always a positive. So squared. That must have been what Chad-Kyle said. That when Jonboat came in, it was like the time he saw the singer at the IHOP eating pancakes, but *squared* because Fondajane was right beside him, holding his hand, getting kissed on the cheek by him. The both of them at once! Just banking away. Except unlike me, and unlike you, Chad-Kyle hadn't even ever once seen Jonboat in the flesh before, not even as a kid, so maybe it was more intense for him to see Jonboat in the bank than it is for me to hear your voice after reading your book. But also, Chad-Kyle, I don't think, ever had a crush on Jonboat, because of how he's straight, and he definitely didn't have a deadly hot crush on Jonboat like I used to have on you so many years ago now, so maybe the intensity he was feeling was equal after all. To mine. Unless he used to have a deadly hot crush on Fondajane. Which, duh duh duh, is almost definitely the case. I mean, *more* than the case because he probably still *does,* right?"

"Maybe?" I said.

"I mean, every guy's had a crush on Fondajane, haven't they?"

"Well, a lot of guys, sure, but—"

"You?"

"Me?" I said. "No."

"Come *on*. Admit it. You find her attractive."

"Not really," I said.

"Not into rich blondes with PhDs and ideal bodies?"

I made a couple laugh sounds.

"Wait—are you a bigot? That's it, huh? You're a bigot."

"I'm—"

"Totally kidding. I know you're broad-minded and intellectual. *Anyway,* I can't even remember the point I was trying to make. Jonboat . . . you . . . Yeah. That was it, I guess. Jonboat, then you. That's what I was getting at—no maybe it's not what I was getting at. But still, it bears saying: it's like everyone's coming back to Wheelatine all the sudden, you know?"

"I never left," I said.

"Well except for when you were in those institutions, though."

"I was never in an institution," I said.

"You can tell me," she said. "You don't have to, obviously, but I'm not judging. I was actually in an institution for a little bit, myself. It's hard being bigger, you know, as a younger person."

"I really wasn't ever in an institution," I said.

"Then why didn't you write me back? You had something *better* to do, Belt? Belt Magnet? Beltenhauer? Magnetron? Beltinya Magnetovich?"

I said, "I never got your letter. Believe me, I'd remember. I've never gotten a letter about my book from anyone."

"Well I'll tell you a secret. The reason you never got my letter is because I never wrote one. I was pulling your chain. And now I feel guilty about that because you just went from looking all like, 'This heavy girl is totally weird but she's making me feel really validated,' to more like, 'Why is the world against me? Even this chunkster with the pretty eyes who seemed so nice and awkward has to mess with my head.' Also, I'm not exactly sober, and this blondie isn't even a little bit sugar-free. It's actually a really good blondie, but it's got some spidge baked into it—some new, special blend of Chad-Kyle's which, well, you heard how *he* was going on in there—and it's coming on *fast*—ha, like duh, like you couldn't tell, ha. Ha! Anyway, I didn't actually understand your book. I tried, but I couldn't. The writing was *awesome,* though. From what I read. And I mean that. But, wow, Jesus, Belt—maybe it's the blondie, but you really do look pretty crestfallen now. You look really messed up and sad and that's the exact and total opposite of everything I wanted when I decided to come out here which was because I couldn't help overhear what went on inside with that check for your dad, and how it sounded like you could really use some cash flow, and then once you went to use the toilet and Chad-Kyle confirmed that you were the you who it turned out you were, and still *are,* duh duh duh, I decided I wanted to help you out. I still want to do that! I want to give you some money. That's the main reason I came out here, I'm saying. The main reason I stayed out here, actually. Because I just got off work and I could have got in my car and gone home, but instead I stayed here, to wait for you til you finished using the toilet so I could give you some money. How much do you need? I've got this much." Lotta pulled from her pocket a short stack of twenties, fanned them out.

"Oh no. I couldn't," I said. "That seems—"

"It seems decent and good is what it seems. I've got a full-time job. I get paid twice a month. This money in my hand, it's from my savings account, and interest rates are nothing, now, Belt, did you know that? Not really nothing, but next to nothing. You know what that means? It means if you don't take this money, it'll sit there, doing next to nothing, and what a waste, you know? What a waste of having money. When I could use it to help. Plus it's not like you're not gonna pay me back, right? Because your dad's coming home in a week, isn't he? That's what I heard you say to Chad-Kyle. So: good. So your dad'll come home, cash that check, give you the cash, and you'll pay me back. Simple as that. I know you know where to find me, so you'll come here and find me and pay me back."

"You're very kind," I said, "but the thing is, Lotta, I can't take your money. I have food and shelter. I have all I *need*. The only reason I was even trying to cash the check was to buy some cigarettes, which isn't—"

"But it *is*. Cigarettes are important. I mean, they're terrible and everything, but my parents are smokers, and I know how smokers get when they can't smoke their cigarettes. And plus you're this artist. How can you make art without your cigarettes? You need to make your art!" In place, it seemed, of a fist's gesticulation, or maybe a vigorous putting-down of foot, Lotta thrust into her mouth what remained of the blondie.

"You may be right, at that," I said, "but I have some cigarettes. Quite a few, actually, by normal standards. If I had any willpower, I could make them last the week, so I'll just—"

"Why *should* you?" she said, still chewing a little. "That is my question. 'Why *should* you, Belt?' You don't have to, I'm saying. You've suffered enough. *I've* suffered enough. I mean . . ." Here she did stomp her foot. "If you don't take this money, Belt . . ." she said. "If you won't accept my help. If you won't . . . I'll just. Oh. Oh God." Lotta crumpled the fanned stack of twenties in one hand and showed me the index finger of the other. She turned away from me, bent at the waist, and heaved three times.

Nothing came out.

Moneyed hand over diaphragm, she turned back around. A bulge beneath the silky arm of her blouse traveled rapidly upward onto her shoulder. The snout of a cure with a touch of overbite protruded from her collar, nuzzling her clavicle. It moaned with an interrogative lilt for three or four measures while Lotta caught her breath and wiped her eyes and a bulge on her opposite arm went shoulderward. The second cure didn't poke its snout out at all, but it harmonized its moaning with that of the first, which Blank must have heard, for it stirred in its sleeve, cleared its throat, and joined in.

"Hey!" Lotta said, and swallowed hard. "Hey," she said, "let's see your little guy. It wants to have a singalong."

I said, "I wish. It's a hobunk, though—it could tear your friends to pieces." I knocked one-two-three-*one* on the roof of the sleeve—i.e. "Quiet down!"—and Blank obeyed.

Lotta opened her mouth, as if to protest, but instead she bent over and dry-heaved again.

I led her by the elbow past the corner of the building, into the parking lot.

We sat side by side on a Cadillac's trunk. As her breathing slowed down, her cures flattened out and descended her back, where they clung, I'd imagine, to the straps of her bra. Lotta spit drily, wiped at her mouth, set her hand on my knee.

"You always seemed nice," she said. "Even at your peak. We always said that about you. No one ever said different." She hiccupped, blinked heavily, coughed, and hiccupped. "I'm sorry about your life," she said.

She got off the trunk and bent at the waist—to heave more, I thought, but no. No heaving. Then as quickly as she'd bent, she was walking away, getting into a Beetle a couple spaces north. I thought she must have been embarrassed. To be sick is embarrassing. To have had too much.

She started the Beetle and pulled it up beside me, lowered the window. "You know where I work," she said. "Pay me back whenever."

"What?" I said. "Listen. Are you sure you should be driving?"

She pointed at my shins, but not at my shins, and as I looked to my shins, she drove away.

There were twenty-five twenties in the Cadillac's tailpipe.

ABOUT THE AUTHOR

Why did Lotta Hogg think I'd been in institutions, though? What did she mean, she was sorry about my life? What happened the night I purportedly incited her first menstruation? What was this book that she'd mentioned I'd written? And why did I twice refuse to show off Kablankey? These questions, and others, need answering, reader. I understand that. And I know that if I fail to provide the answers soon, you'll think me withholding or, worse, a bumbler. I worry you might even be starting to think those things already—and maybe you'd be right to—but before you pass judgment, please allow me to mount a brief defense, after which I'll address all those questions one by one.

To begin with, I have been diagnosed since childhood with "psychotic disorder not otherwise specified." The "symptoms" of my "illness" come and go, and although it's true (as it is for sufferers of any chronic illness, particularly chronic mental illness, and *especially* chronic mental illness with psychotic features) that my "illness" does to some degree affect how I think and behave even during periods in which I suffer none of its "symptoms," I'm nonetheless pretty much like anyone else. Or as the self-empowerment salesmen would have me phrase it: I'm not a disease, but a human being. If I'd prefaced this memoir with anything resembling, "My name is Belt Magnet, and sometimes I'm psychotic—at least that's what they say," then, even had the rest of the text remained the same, you would have spent the previous pages reading not about a recently young American writer and onetime semi-intimate of Jonny "Jonboat" Pellmore-Jason on a quest for cigarette money in 2013, but rather about a disturbed man. You wouldn't have been able to help but to do so.

Please understand that's not a hostile accusation. I'd do just the same. Show me, for instance, a blank-faced man atop some bleachers who's watching a bunch of kids play baseball, and I figure he's on fatherly Little League duty, tired and bored. If before, while, or immediately after showing me that man, though, you tell me he was sexually molested as a child, I'm no longer thinking he's tired and bored. I'm thinking maybe he has suspicions about one of the coaches, and he's keeping a close eye out to protect his son. Or maybe he doesn't have a son, and he's picking a victim from among the players. Or he's picking a victim and does have a son, or fighting the urge to pick a victim. Or maybe while knowing what others watching might imagine him thinking if they were to learn he'd been molested as a child, he's bittersweetly appreciating that, despite what he suffered, he has no desire to harm any of the boys who are out on that field, or any children anywhere else for that matter. Whatever it is that I think he's thinking, though, I assume it concerns his having been molested, regardless of the fact that he's been alive for decades, and spent 99.99+ percent of those decades' moments not getting molested.

But show me this blank-faced guy in the bleachers, then show me him taking his son out for ice cream, struggling at a job interview, fighting with his wife, visiting an oncologist, dancing with his wife, then drinking with a friend he's known since childhood who keeps telling him everything will be okay, and only *then* tell me he was molested as a boy—I won't, when I recall his sitting blank-faced in the bleachers, assume he'd been thinking about child molestation; or, at least I won't assume he was mostly, let alone *only,* thinking about child molestation. Nor do I imagine that you would either.

In light of all that, and considering that I wasn't suffering any "symptoms" of my "illness" during any of the scenes I've so far described—not to mention that I've never been entirely convinced my "symptoms" even indicate an "illness" (as I'm pretty sure you've gathered by way of all the scare quotes, which, from this point forward, I'll happily dispense with)—I thought it would actually be *more* straightforward to begin this memoir—again: a book about me, not my illness—without pushing my diagnosis in your face. Obviously, I still feel that way. And as you'll see momentarily, I'd pretty much have to push my diagnosis in your face to sufficiently answer any of the aforementioned questions. But it was not my intention to *trick* you, reader, into thinking of me as a human being, and I can only hope you'll accept my assurances that no further surprises of this nature lie in store for you.

•

•   •

How does your psychotic disorder not otherwise specified manifest?

Sometimes I converse with inanimate beings. Sometimes a sense of alienation ensues, other times a sense of profound connection and gratitude. The sense of alienation doesn't count as a symptom. The sense of connection and gratitude sometimes does (depending on whether the attending psychiatrist perceives my reaction to it as joy or mania). The conversing, however, counts as two symptoms: the hearing of the inans and the responding to them.

Though I do respond to inans by conventional means (i.e. speaking or, far less often, writing), I don't, when I talk about "hearing inans," mean to suggest that my ears are involved. The inans communicate straight to my brain. I've known that pretty much from the beginning. At eleven years old, my age when the inans began to address me, I conducted a test with an Olive Garden booth and confirmed its results with multiple inans on any number of occasions thereafter. The booth had said, ||My upholstery's cracked. Steam from the pasta condenses inside me,|| and I plugged both ears with the tips of my fingers. ||My stuffing is swelling and it's straining my seams. Help me,|| it continued, clear as a syllogism.

And so thusly ergo: straight to my brain.

What's been harder to figure—impossible, really—is whether or not the inans speak English, or any other human language. It seems no less likely an organic mechanism etched in my gray matter translates inan language(s) automatically. I'll probably never know. Inans are slippery, epistemologically. I've tried to corner a few, but it hasn't ever worked. I once asked an heirloom woolen afghan from Austria (knitted by an aunt of Grandfather Magnet) whether it preferred to speak German or English. ||What's English?|| said the afghan. "That's weird," I said. ||What?|| "You didn't ask about German, which suggests you know what German is, but you don't know what English is, and yet you used English, or seemed to use English, to ask me what English is." ||So?|| said the afghan. "Do you know what German is?" ||Of course,|| said the afghan. ||Who doesn't?|| it said. "Do you speak it?" I said. ||Do I what? Yes, of course.|| "Will you show me?" I said. ||The edges of my holes are fraying,|| said the afghan. ||It's like an itch and a pinch all at once plus a burning.|| "Can you say that again in German, though?" I said. ||How do you know I didn't?|| said the afghan. "I heard it in English." ||Maybe that's your *own* problem.|| "Did you say it in German or not?" I said. ||You disappoint me,|| said the afghan. "Please?" I said. "Say something in German." ||I'm not your damn pet,|| the afghan said. And that was the last I ever heard from it.

To reiterate, I do recognize the possibility that I hallucinate—I'm entirely aware of that possibility. I'm a rigorous thinker, and I pay attention. I've noticed, for instance, how the inans have a greater tendency to speak to me when I'm feeling desperate (desperately happy, desperately sad, desperately afraid: any kind of desperate)—though they don't speak to me *every* time I'm feeling desperate, nor *only* when I'm feeling desperate—and since desperation is a flavor of stress, and stress a well-known trigger of psychotic reactions,

I understand how this tendency might seem to indicate that I'm having a psychotic episode when I hear the inans. Yet I think it would be foolish, and I know it would (at least from my point of view) be counterintuitive, to dismiss the possibility that those times during which I'm feeling desperate are times when I'm more sensitive to the world around me and might thereby be capable of superperception.

When I've asked the inans themselves to account for why they speak to me (i.e., not just why they speak to *me*, but why they do so only some of the time, and why most of them never speak to me at all), they tell me it's because I'm available to be spoken to and they feel like having a conversation. The reasons they might or might not feel like conversing are as varied and capricious as any given human being's, but the conditions under which I'm available to be spoken to are, at least to them, clear and constant: we're in physical contact and our gates are open.

All beings, according to the inans, have gates, and every being's gate can be closed or open. If two beings with open gates come into contact, one can initiate communication with the other. If, conversely, a being with an open gate comes into contact with a being whose gate is closed, then no matter how badly the open-gated being might want to communicate with the closed-gated being, communication cannot be initiated.

I don't know what a gate is, let alone how to determine (assuming I'm not, in the moment, already conversing with an inan) whether my gate—or any other being's—is closed or open, and asking an inan to describe what a gate is hasn't ever gotten me very far at all. Sometimes it's like asking a layman what makes art art, or maybe porn porn; other times like pulling a definition of life from a labful of virologists. It's either "Come on, man! You know it when you see it," or "Instead of what it is, let me tell you what it isn't." The reasoning gets circular almost immediately. What's certain, though, is this: to be a being—as distinct from an insentient object—is to have a gate. At least no inan with which I've spoken has ever claimed otherwise. A minority of inans do, however, believe there's no such thing as an insentient object, i.e. that every thing is a being; that those things in the world which appear to us (i.e. to inans and myself) to be insentient objects (nonartifactual inanimates like rocks, for example, but also "constituent" artifacts like the strips of adhesive along the edges of rolling papers, the space bars on keyboards, or those rough, golden threads that stitch the inseams of blue jeans) are actually beings with imperceptible gates.

•

•   •

What, according to Lotta Hogg, provoked the onset of puberty in herself and her friends?

Toward the end of summer break of 1987, before an estimated 350 Washington Junior High Schoolers, I, Belt Magnet, days away from turning twelve years old, spent nearly two hours—fervently at first, and then more methodically—swinging an aluminum baseball bat and, briefly, a five-pound firefighter's ax in the service of deforming past salvageability a rusting, neglected backyard swingset belonging to a man named Conrad Feather. It was the ninth of what the press would soon be calling "the swingset murders," all eleven of which were committed by me.

Apart from my role in it, I barely remember the event at all. I was told half the kids there got kissed that night; that the cheerleading squad, atop the elevated porch beside the swingset, performed a mock striptease that became a real striptease; that alcohol was present and Mini Thins and Whip-it!s (spidge wasn't in play—no one even had a cure yet); that the spirits of belonging and anonymity—those biggest of all the big crowd-moving spirits—uncommonly united to pervade the gathering in a way that even those blessed with older siblings who'd let them tag along a couple weeks earlier to see Metallica headline the Aragon claimed to have never before experienced; that somehow nothing terrible happened; that there weren't any fights; that there wasn't any bullying; that no one got petted against her will; that of the 350ish suburban children present, all between the ages of ten and fourteen, not a single one of them was bored.

One seventh-grade boy later told the *Daily Herald*, "It felt how they tell you that church is supposed to feel."

Another one said, "The last second of the last minute of the last day of school and plus you've got a ride to Six Flags and a girlfriend—that's how it was the whole entire murder. I got Frenched twice, by two different girls, and one of my friends got Frenched four times, by three different girls, and he went up two shirts, and down one *pants*. Plus did I mention that the first girl who Frenched me *started out* Frenching me? I never even heard of that being a thing. My friend who Frenched four of them said it happened sometimes, that when they're really horny they just skip the batter's circle, take you straight to tongue city. The official thing it's called is a 'no-pitch walk,' he said. I think that's funny, but it's also dumb though. Baseball has nothing to do with girls. Our school's starting shortstop only got Frenched once—I asked him straight out, and that's what he told me, and he did it like bragging, like, 'You bet I got Frenched!' and I'm thinking, 'Ha! You, the shortstop, only got Frenched once—I didn't even make the team.' Anyway, it was such a good night, really inspiring. I'm saving up for a guitar now, just because of it. I want to turn these poems I've been writing into songs."

"We saw boobies," a fifth-grader told the reporter, "but it wasn't like a magazine. The boobies were *nice*. They looked like breasts. Or maybe like chests. I don't know the right word. Not boobies though, I'm saying. Not titties, either. Young women's nice what-do-you-call-thems, bare bosoms. You didn't want to squeeze them really hard or shake them, just stare like, 'Thank you, don't let me forget this,' and maybe put your ear against one and listen."

"[The accused] was so cute," remarked a girl (identified only, to my great frustration, as a "member of the popular set at WJH") to the reporter from the *Chicago Tribune*'s Sunday supplement, where appeared, two weeks after my second run-in with the cops, the fifth and final major newspaper feature to focus on the murders. "He was always kind of quiet at school," she went on. "And maybe weird. So I never paid attention to how cute he was, but then he was up there, doing this crazy thing that I still don't understand why everyone liked it so much, even me, except he really like *meant* it, whatever he meant. And I agreed with what he meant. I really believed in it and couldn't stop watching. I stared at him *a lot*. And like I was saying: cue-oo-*oot*. I don't know how I missed it all these years. It really makes you think. Not that I would date him, though. My mother would kill me. My friends would *totally* kill me. But if he told me he loved me, though, I think I'd run away to the city with him maybe."

What I do remember is that the swingset wasn't nearly as rusted as I'd initially believed, and that the moment I realized that—about twenty minutes into exerting myself to no gainful effect (I was usually halfway-to-two-thirds done by minute twenty)—I had the rare experience of being able to choose my emotional response. I could be angry at myself and—never one for self-harm—take it out on the roiling, shouting child-wall surrounding me by walking in a circle clubbing smiles down gullets. Or I could let myself be sad for the swingset, for my failure to help it, and leave, defeated.

I didn't at all want to see those kids suffer. They'd done nothing wrong. They were trying to have fun. Plus hurting them wouldn't help the swingset, anyway. Nor had I ever been much of a sadist. So maybe I didn't choose anything at all. Maybe it only seemed like a choice. Sadness it was and would be either way. I lowered the bat.

As the sadness took me over, though, my muscles relaxed, and my vision clarified. Like I had with all the swingsets I'd previously murdered, I'd started by swinging at the legs of Feather's, and now I could see how this had been a mistake. The legs, for some reason I couldn't make sense of (they were in tall grass, which, sure, must have offered protection from the sun, but also meant greater exposure to moisture, and thus—at least I'd have thought—deeper rust), were far less corroded than the overhead crossbar. They wouldn't even dent, let alone bend. All I'd managed with the bat was to shake up the frame, chip off some paint flakes, rattle the swing chains. It would have been better to have attacked the crossbar from the very beginning. It might, I thought, *be* better, to attack the crossbar. It could, I thought. It *will* be better.

But even jumping, I could barely reach the crossbar with the bat. I had to tip the swingset onto its side. I knelt in the grass and searched with my hands til I found the taut chains that fixed the legs to the anchors—two chains per leg—which anchors went who-knew-how-deep into the ground. I pulled at one chain to no avail, then another, then a third, with the same result. At this point someone passed me the ax. I didn't know who, much less where they'd gotten it. An unsleeved arm reaching down from in between a couple of the child-wall's frontmost torsos—that's all I was able to see of the ax-bearer.

I got on my feet and started to swing.

Each chain took more effort to snap than the last. The sun had gone red and was rapidly setting. Sweat blurred my vision. To repeatedly hit one strike-point became as much a matter of luck as aim, and I was getting weak, plus I might have drunk alcohol—kids were handing me cups, and much of what I swallowed didn't taste quite right (at the time, I thought I'd gotten paint in my teeth). After freeing the two back legs from their chains, though, I saw, with relief, I didn't need to free the front two. I dropped the ax, put a shoulder to a leg, pushed forward and upward, and knocked the thing down. The applause hurt my ears. Kids shouted my name. I began to attack the crossbar with the bat.

Why I picked up the bat again instead of the ax had nothing to do with helping the swingset. Unlike the eight I'd already murdered, each of which had nagged and cajoled me to destroy it, Feather's swingset hadn't uttered a single word to me. I'd been led to it by a group of seven boys who'd watched me murder the Blond family swingset—murder #8—through the glass back door of the Blond family's house a week or so earlier. I hadn't known they were watching til the murder was through; I'd thought the house was empty. Then they all came outside, and the Blonds' youngest son, eighth-grader Ron Blond, high-fived me and said he'd always hated the swingset. "It made me depressed, and made me want to puke," he said, "but now it just looks like a sculpture or something. Like maybe like it's kneeling. Or was kneeling when it died. Yeah, more like that. Like it fell asleep kneeling and died or something. I'd have kicked your fucken ass when I saw what you were doing, except then I didn't because I changed my mind since first of all you had that bat with you and I could fuck you up later when you didn't have the bat I thought, and second of all it made me want to puke anyway, and now thirdly I don't want to kick your ass because the swingset looks as useless as it is and always has been for years, I'm saying, except it isn't depressing is what I'm saying because it looks like it knows it. Or knew it. That it's useless. It doesn't look forgotten, like I'm supposed to feel guilty. We could throw it away and not feel bad. We could just leave it sitting there and not feel bad. It doesn't matter either way now. We won't feel bad. And I don't want to puke. So I won't kick your ass. That is what I'm saying."

"Ron Blond digging deep deep deep," said Rory Riley, who was one of those giant-eyed, cute-mean, small kids in overpriced clothing who gets to be a bully because pretty girls convince stronger kids to look out for him. "Whatever, though, whatever. Main thing is it was choice and you should do it again."

All of them agreed I should do it again, and they wanted to know when I would do it again. I said I couldn't say for sure; I'd have to find the right swingset. I left off explaining what that might entail, partly because I wasn't sure what it entailed (although the eight swingsets I'd already murdered had each, as mentioned, asked me to help them, I'd begun by then to wonder if, given that my gate was sometimes, perhaps even often, closed, it wouldn't be kinder on my part to go ahead and murder swingsets that appeared neglected even if they didn't ask me to help them, i.e. kinder to assume they wanted my help and would have asked for my help and yet, because my gate was closed, were unable to ask for it), but mostly because I knew I'd sound crazy.

The boys said they'd scout around Wheelatine for prospects.

One of the boys, eighth-grader Chuck Schmidt, lived in "Old Wheelatine," Feather's part of town, which was mostly composed of disused corn- and soybean fields owned by old Germans holding out for bigger bids from property developers. Schmidt's mom, the day after I'd murdered Blond's swingset, saw Feather have a stroke in the checkout lane at Dominick's, and she rushed to Feather's place to drive his wife to the hospital. Mrs. Feather died in the car of a heart attack. That same afternoon, Schmidt biked to my house with Rory Riley in tow and told me all about it. "Their only kid got killed in the Nam," Schmidt said, "and Feather's stuck at Sheridan for at least a few weeks. He can't even walk. The swingset's right there, all rusted and ugly and sixties-looking, in a yard surrounded by farmland. We're the nearest neighbors and we're half a mile away."

"Let's go," I said.

"Better to wait til Thursday," Schmidt said. "My parents'll be downtown for a Sox game, and plus we should spread the news around, too."

"Leave that last part to me," Rory Riley said, winking. "I spread news well."

"No doubt," Schmidt said. "You are choice at spreading news."

I never learned what the news was. Nobody told me. It may have been, "This Thursday, Belt will wreck a swingset," but it may have been, "Belt will wreck a swingset *with a bat* this Thursday." *With a bat* is how I'd always done it, after all. It was how the seven boys had seen me do it at Blond's. And til that arm reached out to hand me the ax, I'd never even considered not using a bat. I'd felt it was okay to use the ax on the chains only because the anchors had been getting in the way of the murder, but to use the ax on the swingset's frame—to use the ax to do the actual murdering—might, I felt, be somehow cheaty, and would definitely render the murder less elegant.

All of which is to say that as soon as the anchors ceased to be a hindrance, I picked up the bat instead of the ax from a desire to maintain the integrity of the performance, as well as from a desire to give the audience what it might have come for.

There were writers who insisted in their *Herald* op-eds that the swingsets functioned as symbolic metaphors of juvenescence; that the children of Wheelatine had all gathered round to see them ruined, or "ritually murdered," in order to "celebrate" or "mourn" "the end of childhood" or "the birth of empowerment" while "sating violent impulses through vicarious means." And I don't know—maybe. But to me, those explanations seemed overblown, if for no other reason than that I'd never heard them spoken by any kid who was there. I think it was probably all a lot simpler. I think the aesthetic pleasures of watching a boy destroy a swingset were vastly underrated by our town's editorialists. I think those kids found the act to be beautiful—not its "meaning" (at least not *so much* its "meaning"), but what the act looked like, sounded like, felt like. A sky full of fireworks is no less thrilling on the seventh of August than the fourth of July. Not to me at least. And what I'm getting at is that while the "meaning" of a group of children standing around to watch a boy murder a swingset with a bat might not be much, if any, different from the "meaning" of a group of children standing around to watch a boy murder a swingset with an ax, the *experience* of seeing the boy use a bat differs markedly from that of seeing the boy use an ax. A bat requires greater effort from the boy, causing him to sweat more, color darker, groan; the impacts produce sounds of thumping and pinging and gonging and bonking rather than chopping and thwacking and slicing; the crowd has more time to get tighter, closer—to get more crowded—and thus more intimate; the swingset, rather than snapping, contorts.

A few swings into my attack on the crossbar, I seemed to disappear. I guess it was a fugue state. Fugue isn't one of the symptoms of my illness; I hadn't entered a fugue state before that night, nor have I entered a fugue state since. I'd imagine it was physical—rather than psychological—exertion that put me there; that all the energy I'd have normally spent on possessing a coherent sense of myself and my surroundings was being siphoned off to power my muscles. I didn't feel as though I'd gone somewhere else—I just wasn't *there*. At least not for the most part. I do remember that at some point a voice was whispering, ||Finish.|| I remember not knowing if the voice belonged to the swingset or the bat. And I remember deducing that, because I heard it only in those moments when the bat was touching the crossbar, it was likely the swingset's.

I don't recall standing the nearly finished-off swingset back on its legs, but I was told I did so. And I was told that after delivering the blow that finally M'd the swingset's frame (I jumped from the roof of Feather's toolshed, swinging both-handed, executioner-style), I collapsed in the arms of those who broke my fall, and was dragged to McDonald's, hanging from their shoulders. And that's the next thing I remember of that night: wanting a Shamrock Shake at McDonald's, finding out I couldn't have one, that the timing wasn't right—it was summer, mid-August, Shamrock Shakes were sold only in March—and how, in the end, I settled for vanilla.

•
• •

Are you prescribed medication to treat your illness?

Yes. Every six months or so, I visit Dr. Eileen Bobbert at Sheridan State Hospital, and we spend fifteen minutes together, during which she checks my vitals, asks whether I've experienced any new symptoms of my illness or troubling side effects of my medication, tells me a couple of pun-driven jokes, then writes me a refill prescription for an antipsychotic pill called Risperdal. At least that's how it's been the past fifteenish years. Prior to that, the doctor's name was Emil Calgary, the jokes, though often pun-driven, were more scatological, and the prescriptions he wrote were for a pill called Haldol.

I've tried each medication. The Haldol I tried in junior high, but it kept me in a viscous, cotton-mouthed stupor, and terrorized my stomach. To say it left me feeling desperate could hardly be more of an understatement. When I wasn't near-suicidal with boredom (nothing would relieve it—I couldn't even focus enough to watch television, let alone read), I was clutching my guts to quell stabbing pains, or moving as quickly as I could toward a toilet. The inans seemed to speak to me a bit less often than they had before I'd started the Haldol, so from a certain point of view it probably looked like the drug was "starting to work," but I was sleeping fourteen hours a day, my grades had gone to hell, and I just couldn't find anything to like about being alive.

After nine or ten weeks, I quit the stuff with my mother's blessing, which she said was conditional on my promise to do my best to never again destroy any property that didn't belong to me regardless of how strongly I believed it wanted help. Even if I'd refused to make that promise, I doubt she'd have withheld the blessing, though. She'd been hesitant to let me take meds to begin with. Having read about the side effects, she'd feared that in addition to what ended up happening—transient zombiehood via chemical lobotomy—I'd wreck my liver. Or maybe it was my kidneys. At the same time, she was holding out hope that my symptoms would—as such symptoms sometimes (though rarely) did—disappear on their own once I'd gone through puberty. She died with that hope a couple months later.

Dr. Calgary retired when I was twenty-four years old, at which point I was assigned to Dr. Bobbert, who suggested I "quit" Haldol and try out Risperdal. Whereas Calgary, who'd worked at the hospital for decades by the time I was his patient, had always seemed resigned to merely doing no harm, Bobbert, who was youngish and infectiously hopeful, got me thinking: Maybe. Maybe the Risperdal would be different from the Haldol. Maybe it would allow me to work a steady job so I could make enough money to move out of the house. Maybe it would empower me to be my own legal guardian. Maybe it would even unweird me to the point that I could meet a woman to fall in love with. Maybe I still had a shot at being normal.

At first, my father supported my decision. He even got me hired at the Wheelatine Palace, a second-run movie theater owned by Mal Vaughn, a guy with whom he drank and sometimes played poker. The job itself—tearing tickets and pointing, righting tilted displays, sweeping spilled popcorn—was dull and easy, but owing to the Risperdal, which kept me as stuporous and desperate as had the Haldol (it wasn't, however, as hard on my stomach), I struggled. I struggled not to slouch, not to sit, not to sleep. Nor did the host of old, neglected inans that occupied the theater incentivize wakefulness. Between the cracked marble tiles atop which I stood, the water-damaged podium against which I leaned, and the rope of rotting velveteen that hung between the podium and wall between shows, I heard a lot of complaints—complaints I couldn't respond to without raising eyebrows, much less resolve without getting fired, if not arrested, and breaking my promise to my mother in the meantime. Nonetheless, I wanted badly to succeed, and I stuck with the Risperdal, telling myself that once it had a chance to build up in my system, it would quiet the inans, leave me less drained, and make the job feel as manageable as I knew it really was.

I'd been employed six weeks when my father, who'd spoken to a lawyer at the tavern, informed me that, if I continued to work, my disability status would change. The Social Security benefits he received biweekly on my behalf would either—depending on murky legal technicalities that even the lawyer didn't quite have a handle on—be reduced by the amount that I earned at the theater, or be canceled entirely. In other words, unless I could make more working at the theater than what the government had been giving me, my financial situation would at best remain the same, and at worst become meaner. To earn at the theater what I already received from SSDI would require nearly double the salary and twice the hours Mal Vaughn had allowed me, which, even if he were able to offer them, I could hardly stand the thought of having to show up for. And all those extra hours would be to *break even.* My father said he was proud of me for giving work a try, and if I wanted to continue he wouldn't stand in the way, but that he wasn't a sucker, and he hadn't raised a sucker, and if he were me he'd probably quit.

The meds, which by then had surely built up in my system, weren't treating me any better than they previously had, and in the meantime I'd learned—just a few days before my father talked to the lawyer—that a small-circulation literary journal had accepted a couple short stories I'd sent them. It would be my first publication—my first *and* second publication—and it wouldn't pay much, just an honorarium of $80, yet I couldn't help but dream it might lead to bigger things. On top of that, I hadn't, since starting the Risperdal, written one stitch of decent fiction. I didn't have the energy. I'd sleep at my desk. So I rolled with my father's suggestion—I quit. Both things at once: the job and the drug.

After that, I did with the Risperdal the same as I'd previously done with the Haldol: every six months I'd fill the prescription, flush it down the toilet, and tell the doc I'd taken it with no major side effects or change in my condition. Though we had our problems, my father and I, he never objected to my refusal of meds. Whether that was more because he wanted to honor the final wishes of my mother, who he hadn't stopped missing, or because he figured the physical side effects of the meds would eventually render me a bigger pain in his neck than I was already is hard to say, but both considerations were likely in play. As for Dr. Bobbert, I have difficulty believing she believed I took the Risperdal; by our second appointment, she was already busy with too many patients, worn down and baggy-eyed, no longer hopeful, and since I didn't live in a state institution, and there was little-to-no threat that I'd need to anytime soon (as I'd told Lotta Hogg, I'd never lived in one before), I imagine it was no less convenient for her than it was for me to just pretend.

* * *

Having said all that, there are those who would argue that I've spent the majority of my life using nonprescription meds; that that's what nicotine is for me. Even I might make that argument. I've read that allowing schizophrenics to smoke can lower the frequency of their psychotic episodes by up to 60 percent, and I bet there are psychiatrists who'd attest to there being a fairly high probability that the frequency with which I conversed with inans was lower than it would have been, had I not been a smoker. Whether or not they'd be correct, I have no real idea. The studies I've seen, which look at people who are already smokers (prescribing nicotine to mentally ill subjects for the sake of research could never get past any ethics committee), fail to make clear whether it's nicotine itself or the habit of using nicotine that lowers the incidence of psychotic episodes. That is, it might be the case that nicotine directly inhibits the kind of brain activity that causes psychotic episodes, but it might also be the case that the kind of brain activity that causes psychotic episodes is disinhibited (or even encouraged) by the stress a nicotine addict experiences upon deprivation of nicotine. Or both might be the case.

I can say with certainty that smoking decreased the sense of alienation that sometimes arose from the conversations I had with inans. (It decreased the sense of alienation that sometimes arose independent of my conversations with inans as well.) Although that sense of alienation did not, as previously noted, count as a symptom of my psychotic disorder not otherwise specified, it was the only aspect of my illness I'm 100 percent certain I'd have chosen to be 100 percent rid of. Had I the choice.

•

• •

Did Lotta and Chad-Kyle really speak to you in the way you've reported, or have you taken liberties in reconstructing what they said?

Something about me, something inadvertent and perhaps uncontrollable, some quality, maybe, of my face or my posture—the spacing of my eyes, say, or the hang of my arms—encourages others to monologize at me, especially those who I've only just met. I've never been able to figure it out. For a while, during my early twenties, I'd ask this or that monologist some version of the question, "What about me is causing you to go on at length?" but doing so only provoked their defenses: they'd clam up, deny, or tell me I was rude. I understood their defensiveness—I'm not an autistic—but at the same time considered it reasonable to hope that one or another of them, since they seemed more than comfortable monologizing at me, would be comfortable enough to acknowledge they were comfortable monologizing at me, and would be open, in turn, to discussing what about me made them so comfortable.

Reasonable or not, my hope was never realized, and, eventually, it died. The monologues stopped while I was taking the Risperdal, and owing to the sizable number of people with whom I interacted at the Wheelatine Palace—a far greater number on any given day than I'd been used to interacting with over any given season since high school had ended—their absence (i.e. the monologues' absence) was especially conspicuous. I began to miss the monologues, to miss them rather keenly, and I learned, as I missed them, to appreciate them more: not only were they excellent sources of material (of voices, dilemmas, and patterns of thought from which to develop my fictional characters), but they made me less lonely.

I came to figure (correctly, I believe) that the Risperdal had somehow taken from me that inadvertent certain something that got people talking, and in turn I expected I would get it back as soon as the drug was out of my system. Not knowing what it is, I'm unable to say when I got it back, but the next time someone monologized at me—in the checkout line at Pang's, a bleary-eyed woman with a basket full of yo-yos, squirt guns, and bubblegum enumerated for me the lengths to which her ex had gone to turn her son against her—was four months after I'd quit the Risperdal, and although I was grateful for the dry spell's having broken, and grateful to the bleary-eyed woman for breaking it, it wasn't only gratitude that kept me from asking her what it was about me that caused her to monologize, but fear of the answer.

I feared that her answer would be correct.

The same way a child mispronouncing a word can be cute, whereas a child mispronouncing a word *to be* cute annoys, a lisping woman can be very sexy, whereas a woman who lisps *to be* sexy repels, and I feared that my inadvertent certain something, like the child's cuteness or the woman's sexiness, might be one of those qualities self-consciousness could ruin, or (put another way) one of those behaviors, like the child's mispronouncing or the woman's lisping, that, in order to produce its desired effect, must not seem deliberate, i.e. *had* to seem, and perhaps had to *be,* inadvertent. In short, I feared that, were I to find out what exactly my inadvertent certain something was, I would lose the power, as it were, to encourage others to monologize.

I still have that fear, and no plans to find out how well founded it is. Well—maybe on my deathbed if the opportunity arises. It's not that I've lost interest in knowing the nature of my inadvertent certain something, just that I have a far greater interest, as both a writer of fiction and a borderline shut-in, in continuing to hear people like Lotta—even people like Chad-Kyle—monologize.

I think that covers the first part of the question, but in case it doesn't: yes. Chad-Kyle and Lotta spoke to me in the way I've reported.

As for the second part of the question: also a yes, but more qualified a yes. I have taken liberties in reconstructing what Chad-Kyle and Lotta said. I've taken liberties, and will continue to take liberties, in reconstructing what anyone in this memoir says, including myself.

I possess, I believe, a very strong memory, one specifically (however inadvertently) trained by having journaled daily for most of my boyhood. What's more, that daily journaling, which often focused on my conversations with inans, particularly strengthened my ability to recollect the speech of others: not only what they say, but how they say it. Yet my brain is by no means a tape recorder. Not everything I report hearing or saying in this book is transcribed verbatim.

For example, I've written that Lotta said,

> That must have been what Chad-Kyle said. That when Jonboat came in, it was like the time he saw the singer at the IHOP eating pancakes, but *squared* because Fondajane was right beside him, holding his hand, getting kissed on the cheek by him.

But she might have said,

> That must have been what Chad-Kyle said. That when Jonboat came into the bank, it was just like the time he saw the singer at the Denny's eating waffles, but *squared* because his wife was right next to him, squeezing his hand, getting shoulder-hugged by him.

Or,

> What Chad-Kyle said must have been that it was like the time he saw the singer at the Golden Nugget eating fries but *squared* because of how, when Jonboat came in, he was with Fondajane, and they were all over each other, husbandy-wifey, touching and kissing.

I've reported Lotta saying what she said the first way rather than reporting it the second or third way not because the first way seems to me to more accurately depict what Lotta said or who Lotta is than do the second or third way, but because all three seem to me to be highly and equally accurate depictions and, to my ear at least, the first way *sounds* better (it's more in keeping with the rhythm of the paragraph from which I've excerpted it, and it comes across more clearly with regard to pronouns) than the second or third way. And I suppose that I could indicate, throughout the memoir, every instance in which what I'm quoting is other than verbatim, and then, much as how I have above, offer, perhaps in a footnote or endnote, alternate versions of what the speaker in question might have said, but that would, in addition to repeatedly breaking the spell of the narrative, become far more tiresome far more quickly than even this tiresome paragraph has.

In sum: Since I don't have audio recordings of any of the dialogues or monologues spoken with or to or at or by me during the period this memoir covers, and because I wish to include some of the dialogues and monologues in the memoir—to disinclude them, let alone describe them (e.g. "Chad-Kyle, in the course of blathering on about all the hip bands he was one of the first people to ever see, eventually explained how he got ahold of Independence.") would portray them (and the whole fabric of my reality) less accurately than do my reconstructions of them—I *must* take liberties in reconstructing the dialogues and monologues. That said, I reconstruct them as truthfully as possible, without any slant of which I'm aware, without any hidden or sneaky agenda, as all conscientious memoirists reconstruct what the people in their memoirs say to them.

If you're reluctant to trust in my conscientiousness, I do understand. I rarely trust in that of other memoirists myself. It's one of the reasons I so rarely read memoirs. With just a couple exceptions, the only way that I've gotten through the ones that I have read is by pretending they were novels. I even enjoyed a few of those. So were I to somehow learn that you were reading this as a novel, I'd say, "Go ahead." I'd probably do the same, were I in your shoes.

•

•   •

Why wouldn't you show Blank to Chad-Kyle or Lotta?

Maybe you've already determined that my refusal to unsleeve Blank upon request stemmed from an ignorance of basic social norms that was somehow symptomatic of my psychotic disorder. That's not the case. And I know that the following statement, coming as it does from a thirty-eight-year-old uncelebrated novelist who lives with his father, receives SSDI, and converses with inans, is going to sound even more unbelievable than it otherwise might, but the Blank I refused to show to Chad-Kyle and Lotta was the same Blank at which I rolled the mini basketball the morning I coined the phrase "pissing through a boner." I.e. Blank was not a clone of an earlier Blank. I.e. Blank was one of the oldest cures in the world.

It may, in fact, have been *the* oldest. There's no way to know for certain, of course—there could have been others like me, keeping quiet—but even if that monk from the *Inhuman Self Denial* documentary hadn't succumbed to temptation (I, like millions of others, and perhaps you, too, reader, saw the tabloid headlines that claimed he hadn't (i.e. succumbed); that after he'd sworn a vow of humility which prevented him from taking any part in a sequel, his documentarians had spread the false rumor of his overload in order to drum up publicity for *Inhuman Self Denial*'s home video release), little Basho would've been only eighteen years old, whereas Blank was twenty-five. Nobody knew.

Whenever I was asked, I'd lie about its age. By the time it was nine, though, lies weren't enough. Kablankey had continued, like the TV spots promise, to become more adorable with each passing day, and people who'd catch sight of it, even just a glance, could sense there was something different—better—about it, and their eyes would go thieflike and murderous quick. As such, I'd taught Blank to return to its sleeve (I still wore an original, windowpocket-less model) when people came near, or, if it couldn't get there in time, to hide its face. Like the majority of other single-legged tripeds, its four-fingered hands were disproportionately large (large enough for juggling uncracked walnuts and jumbo gumballs), so although its head was slightly bigger than average, it could, while pressing its palms to either cheek, interlace its digits atop its skull, leaving just the very end of its muzzle exposed.

But no defense is foolproof. Occasionally, someone would sneak up on us, get a good look, and press me to account for Blank's excess of cuteness. More often than not, I'd just respond with incredulity, sometimes going so far as to accuse the interloper of making fun of my cure, which might not, I would say (in a wounded/hostile voice), be all that much to look at, but was loyal to me, and warm, and decent, and, *at ten weeks old,* an age of such extreme impressionability, shouldn't be made to suffer the ridicule of strangers. In most cases, the interloper, as subject as most of us to the power of suggestion, would back off apologetically, doubting what his own eyes had seen—i.e. the unparalleled cuteness of my cure (Blank would have, by this point, gone back inside its sleeve)—and would explain that, well, no, no ridicule was intended whatsoever; that my cure, at least from the brief glance the interloper'd caught of it, seemed really very cute, and would I please reveal to him what, if anything, it was that I had done to mature it so adorably. Pretending at begrudgement, I'd make something up about allowing it to drink only filtered water, feeding it boutiquey herbal supplements, and making sure it slept on a regular schedule. The interloper would often write down what I told him (or at least pretend to), then walk away, vaguely embarrassed for the both of us. When, however, that tactic didn't work—when the interloper's eyes retained their criminal set even after I'd performed my incredulous routine—I would say strange things and behave erratically. I dropped to the ground once, and did twenty push-ups while muttering about church bells and the Mexican president. Another time, I pretended to converse with a spider. Twice I'd mumbled, "It hurts! It smells!" and scratched inside my pants and reached forward. The rare few times the madman act failed, I ran away, shouting "Fire!" and "Rape!" I'm a pretty good sprinter, despite all the Quills, and not a bad climber. I shout as well as anyone. The getaways were clean.

More subtlety, however, was required with my father. He knew I was fundamentally harmless, averse to confrontation, and STD-free. Furthermore, he could often tell when I was lying. On top of that, the threat he represented was different from that represented by others: I did of course fear that if he caught too long a look at Blank he'd best me physically and overload on it, but what I feared far more was that if he learned Blank's age he'd best me with guilt, perhaps even litigiously, and compel me to sell Blank. I was, after all, his financial dependent, and although we weren't by any means poor, we weren't *set,* let alone rich, plus he *was* my guardian, and thus upon Blank he might have had a legal claim, regardless of whether I thought he had a moral one. So what I'd do whenever he caught sight of Kablankey—he'd sneak up on us every couple of years or so (though not usually, if ever, on purpose, I don't think)—and express surprise at its adorability, was tell him the kind of clumsy, overworded lie that seemed to shed light on its own motivation for being told when in fact the "motivation" itself was a lie in which was nested a second "motivation" that was also a lie. Specifically: after claiming that Blank was a recent clone (my father had little interest in overloading on those that were two years or younger, so I'd divide Blank's actual age by two, add one, and claim that number was the "clone's" generation's), I'd say that "like I['d] told [him] last time," I'd really wanted us to overload on Blank together, father and son, to strengthen our bond, but that the moment in which the sweet compulsion overwhelmed me, he wasn't around, owing to which—i.e. owing to my failure to wait for my father to get home from work/the brothel/the tavern to join me in the pleasure of overloading on Blank—I already felt weak and guilty enough, so would he please stop making me feel even worse, and let me, for Christ's sake, forgive myself at last. This rant would incite my father to accuse me of being selfish, and a lousy liar. He'd assert that I hadn't thought twice about sharing in the destruction of my umpteenth-generation-cloned cure, that I'd planned from the beginning to overload on it alone, and that my whole transparent song and dance insulted his intelligence. I'd insist that his assertions were false, but would, as with the telling of the initial lie, do so in as stammering and clumsy a manner as I could manage. A day or so of the cold shoulder would follow, and I *would* feel guilty for having made him feel insulted, but the guilt was worth it: he never suspected Kablankey's true age.

•

• •

How were you able to overcome the urge to kill Blank, yourself?

I won't say it was easy, but it certainly got easier as time went on. Or maybe not *easier,* given Blank's perpetually increasing adorability, but more automatic, more habitual. Like the monk did with Basho, I developed a regimen, early on, of staring at Blank for extended periods, getting right up next to the point of overload, staying at that point for as long as I could tolerate it, then turning away til the feelings diminished. Afraid the sound of its painsong could defeat my resolve, I also went to great lengths to protect Blank from injury, rarely allowing it out of my sight unless it was inside its PillowNest or sleeve.

Why I wouldn't want to kill Blank is at once much simpler and infinitely more complicated to explain. In case it hasn't already come across by my use of the word *kill* to describe the action in question, I'll state it more plainly: I didn't think it was right to dact a cure. (It's probably more accurate to say that I didn't *feel* it was right to dact a cure.) Despite all that we've always been told about them, they seemed to me to be sentient creatures—higher-order animals. A cure denied water did not, to me, look *dry,* but thirsty. A cure denied pellets looked hungry, not empty. An expired cure, pleasant smells aside, did not appear to me to be *deactivated,* but dead. You might guess these sensibilities owed to my psychotic disorder, and it's possible that, to some extent, they did (that's the infinitely complicated, unknowable part), but I believe they must have owed at least as much to the peculiar situation in which I'd been introduced to Blank.

You see, I hadn't been just any early adopter; I'd been one of the earliest. Maybe the sixth. Maybe the seventh. Certainly one of the first seventeen. A couple months after the last of the swingset murders, I participated, however briefly, in the now-(in)famous Graham&Swords Friends Study at the University of Chicago. When Dr. Manx, the study's lead researcher, assigned me the marble that Blank would emerge from, he said it was an egg from which an animal would hatch, a "new kind of animal" that would require my affection in order to survive, and I believed him. Why wouldn't I believe him? Granted, he told me the animal was called a *Bot*imal, but look: he told me the animal was called a Bot*imal.* And, yes, he was indeed explicit (as was the owner's manual) about its being "a robot made of flesh and bone," but, given the context—I was getting a pet! a new kind of pet!—the information seemed parenthetical to me, parenthetical enough to pretty much forget about until some eleven or twelve weeks later when, amidst the eruption of press and publicity preceding the nationwide product rollout, I couldn't help but hear others, in public and private forums the both, referring to Botimals as "flesh-and-bone robots." Few of these others had ever met a Botimal, let alone owned one, but all of them, it seemed, had reached a happy consensus about what it meant for a Botimal to be a Botimal. My response to this consensus—or so I would imagine—resembled the response a loyal daughter must have upon hearing others brand her father a war criminal. At first, the daughter thinks it can't be true at all, but then, as evidence seems to mount, and everyone around her insists that it's true, she either tells herself that even though her father may have done what he's said to have done, he was somehow fundamentally different from others who do those same things—i.e. maybe the father *had* committed war crimes, but nevertheless he was not *a war criminal*—or she begins to question the very meaning of war criminality, developing arguments against the notion that there could even be such a thing as a war crime. And maybe she's right. Probably not, but maybe, just maybe. And maybe's enough to keep on believing—she loves him, he raised her, she loves him, she loves him. In either case, I, correct or confused, have never been able to believe any cure, let alone Blank, was a robot.

I didn't fancy myself a protector of cures, though, and I never stopped anyone from killing their own. I never judged anyone for killing their own—not a lot, anyway. My convictions, I guess, weren't all that strong. Few of my convictions ever really were. Had I been a vegan, I would not have been the kind to bomb factory farms, nor even the kind to write letters to Congress to protest the practices of factory farms. I'd have probably drunk a soda at McDonald's now and then.

Blank was *my* pet, though. My friend. My sibling. I didn't *want* to kill it, even when I did.

For those squint-prone, harder-hearted readers among you, that doesn't likely suffice to explain why I'd never endeavored to profit off Blank. Since losing my companionship would, obviously, kill it with grief, you can see how I wasn't willing to sell it, but considering the offer George Lucas had made to purchase little Basho in 2007 (or, for that matter, those offers made earlier by Oprah Winfrey and Prince Al Saud), just renting Blank out a couple days at a time probably could have earned me at least a few hundred thousand dollars—Blank was, after all, years older and more adorable than Basho—so why not do that? Why not rent it out? Well, I thought about it, sure, about trying to contact Industrial Light & Magic and offer them some kind of very short lease at a very high rate, but the risk of Blank's death—if not by the hand (or mouth) of an overloading Lucas once he'd gotten his footage, then by the hand (or mouth) of any one of the hundreds of people who worked for him—was way too high. Ditto the Saudi prince and Oprah.

As for licensing its image, appearing on talk shows, or even just hocking some photos to the tabloids, the amount of money I'd have had to spend on security afterward—security I'd doubt I could ever fully trust—would have rapidly outpaced my earnings, leaving me just as penniless as ever, with a cure that everyone now wanted (and wanted to kill), and no one but my scrawny, shrinking self (and maybe—*maybe*—my father) to protect it.

But so couldn't you, say you entrepreneurial squinters, *couldn't you—after earning your boatload of money on licensing its image, appearing on talk shows, or hocking photos to tabloids—couldn't you put out a press release that falsely announced Kablankey's death? Don't you think that would keep the barbarians from storming your gate?*

To which I respond: No. I don't think so at all. Look what's happened in the wake of the announcement of little Basho's death. Hardly a month has gone by in which there hasn't been some story in the papers about a crazy fan or group of crazy fans who, suffering from the wholly unsubstantiated belief that Basho's death was falsely reported, have attempted to break into the monastery in which Basho used to live; a monastery that, unlike my father's house, is not only situated in a remote part of the country, but is filled with a one-hundred-plus-strong brotherhood of armed monks.

Having said all that—and all you squinty hardhearts will like this part—I did snap my own photos and shoot my own videos to document Blank's increasing cuteness, as well as every new song and gag it learned, figuring that one day, if I were to outlive it, I would sell these still and moving images for a comforting sum: if not for hundreds of thousands, then for a reasonable fraction of hundreds of thousands.

A sentimental psychotic I may be, but never have I been a sentimental fool. At least almost never.

•

• •

What is the book that Lotta Hogg mentioned?

It's a coming-of-age/detective novel called *No Please Don't,* and was published in paperback (deckle-edged, French-flapped) in 2006 by Darger Editions, a not-for-profit press "dedicated to providing a platform for outsider voices from the greater Chicago area." To the surprise of many—including Darger, which printed only two thousand copies—the book received notice (positive, for the most part) in a number of mainstream venues, *Rolling Stone* and the *New York Times* among them, and the Dutch translation rights to the novel were bought (for nine hundred euros) by Sobchak, an independent publishing house in Amsterdam, which I was told would put it out as *Geen Kont Voor De Trieste* in 2007, but then it took three years to sell out its print run (its American print run; I don't know what happened with the translation—I never held it in my hands, nor heard from Sobchak once they sent me my advance), after which it wasn't reprinted (Darger went under). It concerns a character named Gil MacCabby who has lost his most beloved plastic action figure, an intergalactic smuggler called Bam Naka. In Part 1 of the novel, ten-year-old Gil, deeply upset by the action figure's loss, spends a number of weeks searching his parents' house for it, and, in the midst of his search, a family tragedy strikes, leading Gil to discover some paradoxical truths about himself and his life. Part 2 of the novel sees Gil, fifteen years later, once again searching the house for Bam Naka, which has now become a valuable collector's item (whether Gil failed, at age ten, to find the action figure, or perhaps found it only to lose it a second time is very deliberately left unclear), and, in the course of the search, he reexamines the truths that he discovered at the end of Part 1, and comes to see how they aren't so much paradoxical as they are just plain ambiguous. If that sounds uninteresting, it's probably because I've left out some key information (e.g. the discovered-and-then-reexamined truths, the specifics of the tragedy that strikes the MacCabbys) for fear of spoiling their impact on anyone who might be enticed by this summary to read the novel. My hope is that the memoir you're currently reading will be successful enough to persuade whoever publishes it to bring *No Please Don't* back into print. I'm proud of that book.

The one difficulty I have enjoying its (admittedly minor) success is that reviewers had a tendency to spend a lot of words discussing the way my life granted the narrative extra (unfair?) power. I don't blame the reviewers, for Darger had printed a full-page author biography at the front of the book in addition to the more conventional capsule biography below my photo on the cover's back flap. Not to say I blame Darger, either. Their stated mission, after all, was to provide a platform for "outsiders," so it only made sense that they'd have wanted anything that could testify to that mission's fulfillment to be as prominently displayed as possible. However, the message they were going for (something along the lines of "Our authors may be mentally ill, but that doesn't mean they can't write great novels!") unfortunately came across, at least in my case, as "Seeing as the author of this book is mentally ill, we invite you to admire the ways in which this thing he calls a good novel actually resembles, at times, a good novel."

Then again, maybe I'm being paranoid and needy, or I'm just less talented at receiving compliments than I should be. Possibly just less talented in general. Still, I couldn't help but notice how often the reviewers quoted from the bio, especially from the paragraph that stated, "In the wake of a pair of arrests, at age twelve, for trespassing and destruction of property, Magnet took part in the Graham&Swords/University of Chicago Friends Study, the seminal research (and development) project that aimed—purportedly—to examine the therapeutic effects of companion animals on children diagnosed with psychotic disorders. He was one of a handful of the study's subjects to be given what, at that time, was still called a Botimal; he was one of the first people in the world to own a Curio."

I do recognize that, apart from my proximity to the Pellmore-Jasons, my having been in that study is, to the general reader, likely the most interesting aspect of my life, and, as you'll see, I will describe it—in *this* book—soon enough, but *No Please Don't* has no more to do with cures or studies than it does with swingsets, childhood psychosis, or encounters with North American royalty. It's not about me at all, but a boy—and later a man—called Gil in search of a lost and beloved action figure. If you ever get to read it, I hope you'll remember that.

•

• •

Have you published anything since No Please Don't?

In fact, I haven't. Mostly for lack of trying, but also—a little bit—for success at failing. Since publishing *No Please Don't*, I've completed seven short stories, two novellas, and a novel, and all of them, I think, are likable, but none of them can stand beside *NPD*, which I hope is great (only time can tell greatness, but I have a feeling; *NPD* is the one work of fiction I've written that I'm able to imagine—even seven years after its publication, now—that I'd fall in love with were someone other than me to have written it), and because the paltry advance (if any at all) I'd receive for these merely likable works wouldn't be enough to get me out of my father's house, and because to publish fiction that's anything less than potentially great could as easily thwart as benefit *NPD*'s chances of being reprinted, I never bothered submitting them to publishers or magazines.

So that covers my lack of trying.

As for my failure, I did once try to publish a short work of nonfiction that I think is quite good. My journals aside, it's the only work of nonfiction I've written other than the one you're currently reading, and I wrote it, quite reluctantly at first, only because my editor at Darger, in the months leading up to *No Please Don't*'s publication, went out of his way to interest a friend of his at *Harper's*—a junior editor—in me. For those of you readers who don't closely follow the publishing industry, one of the things a fiction writer is supposed to do when that fiction writer has a book of fiction coming out is try, in the weeks preceding his book of fiction's publication, to publish as much nonfiction in periodicals as he possibly can in the hopes his nonfiction will entice those who read it to read his forthcoming fiction. If successful at all, writers usually end up publishing one or two newspaper book reviews, but occasionally they publish personal essays that relate in some way to the subject of their forthcoming fiction, and *that*, my editor at Darger told me, was the sort of nonfiction *Harper's* wanted from me; they wanted, he said, an essay on my childhood. They wanted that, I reasoned all on my own, because a full half of *NPD* takes place during its protagonist Gil MacCabby's childhood.

As I said, I was at first reluctant to accept the assignment—I just wasn't that interested in writing nonfiction—but soon I came to realize that if I didn't do everything I could to increase the likelihood that my novel would be read, I'd hate myself later.

I settled on a subject rather quickly: a memorable night I once spent as a boy at the house of an aged, middle-tier Chicagoland gangster. To my surprise, I quite enjoyed writing it.

Three weeks and it was finished. I went to Kinko's and faxed it over to my editor at Darger. A couple hours later, he called me at home and said he loved the essay, but didn't think it was what his friend at *Harper's* wanted. His friend wanted, he said, an essay about my time in the Friends Study. He'd thought I'd understood that. I asked him how he thought I could have understood that, since the Friends Study had nothing to do with *No Please Don't*; plus how did his friend even know about my time in the Friends Study? His friend knew, he said, because he'd pitched him on my bio. I'd assumed he'd shown him my novel, I said. His friend didn't have any time to read novels, he said, and his friend, truth be told, he said, didn't seem to like novels. What he'd liked was my bio, so . . .

My editor sent my essay in anyway. Why not at least give it a try? was the reasoning. It was good, after all, and therefore his friend might—should—want to publish it regardless of what it was about.

A few weeks later, his friend rejected it nicely, said that he'd enjoyed it, but had trouble believing in the boy-me I depicted—too reflective too young, not childlike enough—plus it didn't fit the issue for this or that reason. I was welcome, the friend said, to try again with a piece about my time in the Friends Study, but I'd need to have it finished by the end of the week if I wanted a shot at getting it into the issue that would come out the month of *No Please Don't*'s publication. It was already Wednesday afternoon at that point, and, having gotten my hopes up about being in *Harper's*, I was now too deflated to conceive, much less deliver, a whole new piece in under forty-eight hours. There just wasn't any way.

When I explained this situation to my father, he clapped me on the shoulder and said I should ask my editor at Darger to collect me my kill fee, so that's what I did. My editor at Darger said I wasn't owed a kill fee; kill fees were for writers who'd been contracted to write articles the contracting magazine eventually rejected, whereas I was but a writer who'd been granted a friendly invitation to submit.

"Well, shit," my dad said, when I reported to him my editor's response. "I guess it's best to just roll with the punch, then. Focus on the book. You're publishing a book! Better yet: fuck *that*. Unfocus on all of it. Come on out with me. Brothel. My treat. Let's go."

I thanked him and declined to go to the brothel, taking, instead, his first piece of advice: to focus on the book. I thought: "I'm a novelist. Whether or not I publish a personal essay has nothing meaningful to do with that."

And I started, then and there, to work on a brand-new novel—the one I decided, eventually, wasn't good enough to publish—and, for the most part, I forgot about the essay.

It wasn't til I started doing "research" for this memoir (mostly rereading journals and newspaper clippings, staring at old photos, watching old movies) that I again read the essay, at which point I determined it possessed no small amount of relevance to this memoir—not just because I've spent some thousandish words describing it in the course of answering the question "Have you published anything since *No Please Don't*?" but because it'll help me answer the question that follows it, here in the "About the Author" chapter—and so, I've decided to include it below.

The Magnets, the Birds, and the Balls
(June 2006)

When I was six, or maybe seven years old, my parents, for their seventh or eighth anniversary, spent a Friday night at a downtown hotel, and left me in the care of my father's mother, my Grandmother Magnet. As my father told it, Grandma Magnet had agreed a full month in advance to stay the Friday night at our house in Wheelatine, but then, on the Saturday prior to their getaway (though my parents wouldn't learn of this til after their return), she and her mahjong pals had thrown aside their tiles in favor of an outing to Arlington Racecourse, where Grandma'd met Salvatore "Sally the Balls" DiBoccerini, with whom she was instantly stricken by the thunderbolt, and from whom she had, purportedly (there wasn't any ring, and the ostensible engagement was called off inside a fortnight), accepted a hasty proposal of marriage.

Had I heard of Sally the Balls? she asked me, beaming, as we drove to the Balls's house in her LeSabre. I had no idea we were going to his house—after seeing my parents off, we'd packed me a bag for a "surprise, secret overnight" at what I'd nonsensically hoped would be Disney World—nor had I heard of Sally the Balls, but, given her tone, it seemed like I should have heard of Sally the Balls, so I told her I might have heard of Sally the Balls. She told me that she didn't know what I'd heard, but she'd heard of some things that other people had said, and I asked her what things other people had said, and she said those things were not worth repeating, and she wanted me to know, in case those were also the things that I'd heard, that those things were false, and that there wasn't any good reason at all to think Sally the Balls was anything less than a wonderful man. It was true, she told me, that when the Balls was younger, he'd had some friends who had gotten him in trouble, and that was why, ever since 1970, he hadn't set foot inside Chicago city limits, and it was one of the reasons he didn't like to leave Cicero if he didn't have to, which was why we, ourselves, were going to Cicero—but the past was the past, was the past not the past? And I asked her how the past could *not* be the past and I asked her if Cicero was close to Disney World. She said that I'd hit the nail on the head regarding the past, said the past could by no means fail to be the past, and as far as Cicero went, it was the best of all suburbs, I was going to love Cicero, Disney World compared to Cicero was nothing. And I asked her if the reason they called the Balls *the Balls* was because the Balls was good at lots of different sports, and she said maybe that was it, though she couldn't say for sure, and if she had to guess, he was probably good at sports, or at least used to be: he was getting old for sports, now, was nearly seventy. And I suggested that maybe he was the owner of a sports team, like probably not the Cubs or the Bears or the Bulls because all those teams were inside Chicago where he wouldn't set foot because of when he was young, but maybe there was also a Cicero team that I hadn't ever heard of? And she said that, no, the Balls didn't own teams but probably he'd be good at owning teams if he owned them; what he did own was a club, at least in part; he co-owned a club at which pretty girls danced, and he was good at co-owning it, did well for himself, made lots of money, and so did the dancers, and some people looked down on that, but where did they get off? I didn't know where they got off, and I told her as much. I said I liked pretty girls, and liked to see them dance, and she said that was because I was a red-blooded boy, just like my father'd been, just like the Balls had been, and each of them had grown up, as would I grow up, to be a red-blooded man, which was the best kind of man. I asked her what other kinds of blooded people there were, and she gave it some thought, then told me that people were all kinds of blooded, and the worst kind of all the kinds of blooded were the blue because of how they looked down their long, thin noses at boys like me and men like my father and men like the Balls, and the worst part about them was how some of the uncommon things they did were made out to be interesting, and sometimes even good, but when the red-blooded did those same kinds of uncommon things, they were made out to be strange, and sometimes even bad, like for instance the Balls had some uncommon ways, and if the Balls were blue-blooded then the word the blue-blooded would use to describe him would be "eccentric," but since the Balls's blood was red, the blue-blooded called him less generous words. I asked what kind of words. She said she wouldn't repeat them. I asked her again. She told me shut my piehole about the kinds of words. She told me take a hint, she was getting annoyed. I hadn't wanted to annoy her, I had only been curious, she needed to see that all I was was just curious, so to show curiosity I asked what kind of uncommon ways the Balls had that would be eccentric if he were blue-blooded, and she said she'd already told me a couple—didn't like to leave Cicero, had some troublesome friends, owned part of a club where pretty girls danced—but the main one, she said, was that he loved exotic birds, and he kept some as pets, and he called them his *fids,* which was short for "feathered kids," and when he did leave Cicero, he missed his fids the way some parents miss their children, which was, she thought, very sweet of the Balls, something that suggested he possessed soulful depths, wouldn't I say? I told her I would. Her annoyance abated.

When we entered his bungalow—Grandma Magnet had the key—the Balls was in an easy chair that faced the bay window. "Slowly now," he told us, in a high, soft voice. "Don't want to startle our beautiful man here."

Our beautiful man here was a slate-gray parrot the size of a rabbit. It was perching on the shaft of a shovel on the rug, halfway between the Balls and the window. Its head was the size of a healthy tangerine, its eyes a pale yellow—skeptically, if not accusatorially, set—and its hooked black beak looked like something a ninja might strap to a thumb on his way to a regicide.

"Belt," said my grandma. "Come on, it's okay."

We approached the Balls on tiptoe. The bird puffed its feathers, made itself big.

"Easy, buddy," said the Balls, rising from his chair. He wore a Hawaiian shirt tucked into chinos, laid an arm on my shoulders, and I didn't really mind. He smelled like a barbershop, of talcum and aftershave, clean and strong, and appeared as though he'd just been to one, too. His cheeks and white widow's peak shone as if shellacked. There were no errant nose- or eyebrow- or ear-hairs. I won't say he seemed young—I was six or seven, and the Balls was an adult—but apart from the watery quality of his gaze, his senior citizenship was not in evidence.

"So you're Belt," he said, "and I'm the Balls, or Uncle Sally, whichever one of those you're more comfortable with. My friends call me both, and you're my new friend, so I want you to feel at home here, alright? So that's the first thing: you call me whichever. The second thing, now, is that you gotta meet Mouth, the real prince of this palace, so I want you to wave your hand like this, just once, like this, up then down, right? You do that and you say to the beautiful man: 'Hello.' Same time as the wave. 'Hello' and the wave. Got it? Simultaneous. The wave and 'Hello.' Go on now. Do it."

I did as instructed, and, in a voice far less screechy and far more androidal than I'd ever have imagined, Mouth said, "I'm the Pottymouth shitforbrains fucken the prince. Pottymouth. Mouth. Prince Mouth cock shitforbrains."

I laughed at the swears, as did Grandma Magnet, who giggled her way into the arms of the Balls, and Mouth's even tone gave way to loud squawking: "Shut the fuck up Mouth! Eat shitforbrainscock! Shut your! Shut your!"

The Balls gave my grandma a squeeze on the flank, and, nudging her aside, told us, "Mouthy gets jealous." Mouth ceased its squawking. The Balls said, "Come here, now."

With a tilt of its head, Mouth stepped from the shovel onto the loafer-shod foot of the Balls, then climbed, beak and claw, up his clothes to his shoulder.

The Balls made some kissing noise.

"Kisses," said Mouth. "Kisses fucken. Kisses."

We followed them down to the wood-paneled basement. Its main room, which the Balls referred to as "the parlor," featured a pair of pinball machines—a Playboy and a Star Wars—warmly glowing in opposite corners, and in the center of the room a billiards table, oxblood felted with hand-carved legs resembling an elephant's. Between two doors on the parlor's left wall stood a Mountain Dew– and Pepsi-stocked miniature fridge as well as a shelf holding two kinds of chips, three kinds of cookies, jars of chunky salsa and oily cheese, and bags upon bags of brand-name candy. One of the doors opened up on a bedroom with a television in it and a folding table stacked with paper napkins and plates, and the other to a bathroom redolent of lemons. Along the parlor's right wall was the doorless entrance to a room half its width and matching in length. At one end of this room, Mouth's wrought-iron cage, about the size of two phone booths set side by side, stood next to a much smaller, hairpin-legged cage, in which six small birds with marbled pink and gray feathers perched wing-to-wing on a branch, blinking slowly.

Strangely or not, I was far more interested in the opposite end of the room, where sat a leather-padded benchpress near a rack of gleaming dumbbells, but because I worried that revealing this interest might cause the Balls to lock the weights away—my parents, for reasons that, to me, were less important than possessing large biceps, explicitly forbade me from using my dad's weights—I kept my back to the workout area, grinned widely at the sextet inside the small cage, and greeted them using the same hello-wave with which I'd greeted Mouth. In response to my greeting, the leftmost bird emitted a trisyllabic, sirenlike *fweep*, and then, as if passing the message along, each bird to its right fweeped identically in turn.

The Balls said these birds were called Rosy Bourkes, and they weren't as clever as African Grays, which was the kind of bird Mouth was, but boy were they sweet and a feast for the eyes, eh? I asked the Balls their names and he named the seven dwarves, and I said there were only six birds in the cage. "Yeah, I guess you're right," he said. "But they don't know the difference. All they know is *foo-WEE-ip*. That's their only word. Everything else to them is just a noise anyway. Ha!"

The Balls then explained the basement had a few rules that he wanted me to follow. I could eat and drink whatever was down there—he'd laid all the food and soda in specifically for me—but I was not allowed to set any food or drinks on the billiards table. The second rule was not to free any of the birds from their cages. I could stand around and talk to them as much as I liked, but Mouth, even though he looked as though he wanted a hug, didn't ever want a hug; he did not want to be touched in any way, shape, or form by anyone but the Balls, and if anyone else ever tried to touch him, Mouth would use his frightening beak, which was strong enough and sharp enough to sever a finger, and as for what it could do to different parts of a face, like the eyes, the lips, the ears, or the tongue, the Balls didn't even want to start to suggest to have me begin to consider imagining. As for the Bourkes, they couldn't really do a person any damage, but they were far too innocent to be set free; they might stick their heads through the bars of Mouth's cage, and that would be the end of them. Last but not least, I shouldn't feed the birds anything that wasn't in the cabinet under the small cage. I could feed them as much bird food as I wanted, but anything else could poison and kill them. The Bourkes, he told me, might or might not eat if I offered them some food—they had a lot of food in their cage and might not be interested—but Mouth would absolutely eat anything that I offered because Mouth's food bowl, as I could see, was empty, since keeping Mouth hungry was part of his training.

I didn't understand the part about the training, and I didn't really care to, but I could tell that the Balls, who I'd decided I liked, would be disappointed if I didn't express a lot of curiosity, so I pressed him for details on how Mouth was trained.

The Balls said that was the question of a smart individual and chucked me on the chin. He said Mouth wouldn't learn if its belly were full; that the way you got Mouth to say new words and phrases was to stand in front of Mouth's cage while Mouth was hungry and hold out a morsel—a hazelnut or tiny nugget of granola—so Mouth could see, and repeat a word, over and over. When Mouth said something back that sounded like the word you were repeating, you gave Mouth the morsel. Then you repeated the process again, maybe once or twice more, but after that you had to be very careful not to keep feeding Mouth for saying the same almost-word—you had to wait til Mouth formed the word even better. And so on and so forth: you fed it in degrees until it got the word perfectly. After that, you moved on, if you wanted, to a second word. Mouth, for its part, understood how this worked, the Balls said, and was, for a bird, a very quick learner. The main thing was just you had to keep it hungry, even if it did the adorable bowing thing that it sometimes did which made you want to feed it all the morsels in the world.

"It's hard to resist it when it begs," Grandma Magnet said, "but believe you me, Belt, it's completely worth it. I taught it 'Shut your piehole' in under an hour. I taught it 'cakeface,' too, but, for some reason it wouldn't put them together."

I wowed and grinned for Grandma Magnet's benefit, and to Mouth, I said, "Cakeface?"

"Cake. *Fay,*" said Mouth, and I wowed and grinned more for the Balls's benefit.

"See, if it would've said it right," the Balls informed me, "I'd've given it a morsel, but it didn't say it right, so it don't get a morsel. You want to strive for perfection, both here, and in all other things in this life that we live on this beautiful earth, which can try us at times, but also reward us with all sorts of types of rewards that produce satisfaction like the love of a beautiful woman, young Belt. And even in our very October, which may have seemed like December til the sun and the balm came and now all the sudden it looks like August, at times even like June, depending on the point of view and such."

"Aint that the truth, Sally," said my Grandmother Magnet.

The Balls gave her a wink, put Mouth in its cage, and showed me where the towels were, and how the remote for the television worked. "Last thing," the Balls said, "is if the birds start screaming and it's bothering you, you just turn out the lights, and they'll pipe down fast." He was having some pals over to meet his new gal, he said; they'd be right upstairs if I needed anything. Meantime, they'd leave me to my own private party. Grandma Magnet kissed my cheek and said she'd come down later to see how I was doing.

She didn't come down til the following morning. Judging by the crooner music, laughter-bursts, and footfalls I heard through the ceiling, she and the Balls and his pals had a blast. For a while, I did, too.

The inside door of the bathroom was mirrored, and I brought a couple dumbbells in there and pumped, looking up every couple minutes or so to witness the enlargement of my biceps and forearms, which happened, at first, even faster than I had dared to imagine. When, after three sets of ten, the enlargement plateaued, I strained slowly through a final set, then went to the bench, pressed twenty, then thirty, then thirty-five pounds before I felt a shift at the base of my abdomen, and feared what would happen if the thing that shifted tore—I didn't know from hernias, but thought a sudden pain could make me drop the bar, which could land on my throat—and decided to lay off working out for the night.

Mouth, in the meantime, had been reciting near continuously; running through, it seemed, every last word and phrase it had ever been taught. There was a lot of swearing, and, much of the time, I couldn't help but imagine, what was said wasn't voiced in quite the same way that Mouth was taught to say it. "Good birdy!" it would scream, as if to ward off attack, and then, in the android voice, "Fucknuts" and "Jagoff," and, later in the evening, still androidally calm, but with more of an interrogative lilt: "Don't?" and "Water?" and "Bite the salam?" Once its humor wore thin, the nonsense of all this verbal behavior—or, rather, what at first struck me as the nonsense of it—confirmed my core belief regarding pets, a belief I had readily adopted from my father: that they were little more than high-maintenance furniture, they were decorative home appliances that smelled and made a mess, and guys who claimed to "love" them were shallow, or lonely, or shallow and lonely—tasteless dummies, friendless losers. At least for the most part. After all, there was the Balls, who seemed kind of tough. The contradiction didn't really bother me, though. I was only a kid. I solved it readily: I told myself the Balls had tasteless dummies for parents, or friendless losers for parents, and that these tasteless, friendless loser-dummies raised him with birds, and so, despite everything good and right with the Balls, he got saddled with this bird-loving thing too early to shake it. Then again, he may have had a loser-dummy, bird-loving older brother, or a non-loser-dummy, bird-loving baby sister (it wasn't loserly or dumb, I didn't think, when girls said they loved animals) who died when the Balls was still just a child, and when he looked at a bird he thought of his beloved, departed sibling who, in the case of a sister was truly a sweetheart, and in that of a brother was as much a loser-dummy as any other bird-lover, though his death had come before the Balls was old enough to understand that.

Mouth's cage, true enough, didn't really have a smell, but it was certainly a mess, the bars and the floor of it caked with brittle feces that itself was caked with bits of down and pinfeather wax, nutshell particles, who knew what else. Ditto the Bourkes' cage. Had I not thought that doing so would hurt the Balls's feelings, what I would have told him when he'd finished explaining the rules to me was that setting any of these animals free was the last thing I'd want to do in the basement, even if none of them were capable of violence—I was too afraid of getting shat upon by them, and too afraid to step in shit, too afraid to inhale a beak- or claw-loosed flake of crust a wing aflap might set afloat.

So when I finished lifting weights, I turned off the light. The birds, as promised, went quiet at once. While watching TV, I guzzled Mountain Dews, ate half a bag of Ruffles with a full jar of cheesefood, any number of Smarties, and a snack-size Twix. For dessert, I had some Orange Milanos and Thin Mints, then fell into a half-sleep in the middle of Carson. Shortly thereafter, I was startled awake by spasms in my legs that must have owed to the Mountain Dew's caffeine. I stretched my thighs and occasionally rubbed them til, by Letterman's end, my arms started stiffening. I got out of bed, thirsty, tried the tap in the bathroom, which tasted like minerals and seemed a little thick—"Neosporinish" is how I phrased it to myself—and glugged another Dew to clean my palate. I played a game of pinball on the Playboy machine, found my reflexes dull, and the game not-relaxing, the sound effects grating when they weren't startling. I gave up on pinball, took a stick off the wall rack, shot twice and missed, and gave up on pool.

I lay down again to sleep, and sleep wouldn't come.

I sat up in bed, started getting emotional. An eyelid kept twitching, my mouth was dry, I was hungry yet full, and the thought of the available food made me nauseous. My arms kept getting stiffer, my back a little too, and when I went to the mirror on the bathroom door, my biceps, I discovered, had shrunken back to normal. My face looked like cheese.

It was 2 a.m.: a time of day I'd never encountered awake. The thrilling aloneness that Grandma Magnet and the Balls had permitted me had turned inside out, into desperate loneliness. The sound of the thoughts in my head was whiny. The imagery with which I tried to comfort myself—my mom bringing me a mug of hot broth in my sickbed, singing my name; my father and I playing Whac-A-Mole and Skee-Ball, side by side, at Showbiz Pizza Place, high-fiving twice every ten tickets won—was stock and Vaseline-lensed and made me feel wimpy. Here I was in this suburban basement Pleasure Island, and instead of gamboling between all the fun-machines, laughing like a donkey, and feeling like a man, I was sitting on a shaggy, teal bathroom throw rug, frowning and missing my mommy and daddy.

I hurled myself to my feet and out of the bathroom, paced around the parlor, eyes aching, pits damp, heartburn welling, learning self-hate, not liking it at all. Maybe the problem with self-hate, I thought, in my instinctive six- (or seven-) year-old way (and rather insightfully, I must say, looking back now) was less the hate than it was the self. That is: instead of pacing around trying not to hate myself, maybe it would be better to try not to think about myself; to try not to think about how I thought; to try to think about something, or someone, else.

Or maybe I'm remembering my intelligence too fondly. Maybe I was just so bored and incapable of sleep that I was willing to try anything I hadn't yet tried.

In either case, I returned to the birdcage/weight room, thinking I'd try to train Mouth to say a word or two—"Grandma," I was thinking, "Grandma Magnet" if possible—the idea being (at least as I recall it) that doing so would please the Balls, and my grandma in turn. When I turned on the light, though, Mouth, who'd been sleeping, did a yogic-type stretch: stood on one leg extending the opposite wing, and then did the same with the other wing and leg. This was such a nice and surprising thing to see—such a graceful, calming thing—I wanted to reward it. I held a chunk of granola up, about an inch outside the bars, and Mouth came forward slowly, deliberately, and, just as slowly and deliberately, pushed its beak between the bars, clamped down on the chunk without touching my fingers, and gently tugged til I released the chunk. This was also quite nice—it seemed almost polite—and what was nicer yet was how the bird then climbed a couple bars to a perch, removed the chunk from its beak with a foot, and, standing on the other foot, ate the chunk, bite by bite, as if—single-legged surefootedness notwithstanding—he were just some kid enjoying an apple. A sloppy kid, yes—the granola chips sprayed in every direction—but a kid nonetheless. Not a piece of furniture.

As I watched him eat, I blinked, and Mouth blinked back. Or so it seemed. I blinked a second time, longer—one-one-thousand, two—and Mouth blinked a second time, also longer. I didn't blink again til he'd finished the chunk, and he didn't blink until after I'd blinked, and when my third blink garnered that third blink from him, I knew he was definitely mimicking me, and this thrilled me for reasons I didn't quite understand.

Suddenly, I yawned. And then Mouth either yawned or just opened its beak and showed me its muscly, dry black tongue.

I yawned again—faked it. Mouth yawned again or faked it.

And here was the thing. Here was what thrilled me: its beak and my mouth just didn't look the same. One was black and sharp and obtruding, the other pink and meaty and round. For Mouth to determine that its beak was like my mouth—which is what it must have had to determine before mimicking the movements of my mouth with its beak—was a pretty big leap. It was a much larger leap than I'd have ever credited an animal capable of making. Even looking at my eyes and determining they were like his eyes—which I saw he'd had to do to mimic my blinking—even that struck me, on reflection, as a fairly big deal, for remember, I had, til about five minutes before, thought of animals strictly as machines that stunk and made messes. Suddenly I had to think of them as capable of reasoning.

"Shitcockfucker?" Mouth said. He didn't know what that meant—hell, I didn't really know what that meant—but if he'd had any idea at all what it meant, there's no way he would have said it so tenderly. So why did Mouth say it? Because the Balls, at some point, had taught Mouth that saying it—or saying some slightly different version of it—would get Mouth some food. And why had the Balls done that? Why'd he taught Mouth that? He'd done it because when a bird said words, it entertained the Balls.

It had entertained me a little bit too, but not any longer; now it depressed me. In a blink—or three blinks and a couple of yawns—I'd decided it was wrong to train Mouth to swear. Correction: it was wrong to train Mouth to form any words at all. It robbed him of his dignity. It made of him a fool. The most foolish kind of fool I was able to imagine—the kind who doesn't know he's being laughed at, if even he can hear the laughter to begin with, if he's even aware of what laughter is at all.

And maybe you're someone who says of such fools, "What they don't know can't hurt them," and maybe you're correct, and maybe I'm a sap. If you're incorrect, though, what does that make you? I don't know the word. I didn't know it then.

Please know I'm not attempting to moralize here, for I feared I was a sap, down there in the basement, amidst my revelations; feared becoming a guy who my father would laugh at. And had I not more strongly feared remaining whatever that other, unknown word is, or if I hadn't ceased to find Mouth's speech-acts entertaining, I have no idea how—if at all—I would have responded when Mouth again said, "Shitcockfucker?" and it seemed to mean "Please, sir, may I have some more?" and perhaps seemed so only because I assumed I myself would have begged for food if all I'd eaten in hours were a chunk of granola.

I found a tiny door on the side of his cage. Inside it was a ledge. On the ledge was a bowl. I opened the door, took the bowl from the ledge, filled it with nuts and granola, and replaced it. Mouth ate it all up over twenty-some minutes. He broke away once or twice to drink water from the bowl on the next ledge over, but otherwise chomped continuously, punctuating swallows with tail feather shakings and tilts of the head, glancing at me in what I took to be a state of hope fighting disbelief, though it could have been anything at all, or nothing.

After that, I turned the lights out, went to bed, and finally slept.

In the morning, my upper body was so sore and stiff, I was having trouble walking. I couldn't hide the pain, and couldn't seem to summon a lie to explain it, so I fessed up to having used the Balls's weights. The Balls, who in daylight seemed a little different—blubberier of lip, yellower of eye-white, wheezier of lung, and less flirty with my grandma—gave me the impression it was no big deal, my having used his weights, and I said I wished someone would tell that to my parents, and he chuckled and said that he bet my grandma would tell them, then gave me a Cotylenol he'd been prescribed for a broken hip the year before.

I didn't have the chance to say goodbye to Mouth; the drug's effects didn't start til we were halfway home, and I was in too much pain to move more than I had to. Around the time the opiate started kicking in, my grandmother offered to do me the favor, just this once, of helping me keep a secret from my parents. She wouldn't mention the weights, she said, if I didn't want her to. I said I didn't want her to. She said that since I looked so sleepy and slack, we should say that I hadn't felt well since late last night. I agreed to the plan; it was, at least, half-true.

When we got to the house, though, my parents were waiting in the kitchen for us, and when they asked where we'd been—they'd missed us, they said, and had come back a little early to take us to brunch—I, high on opiates, joyfully shouted, "At Sally the Balls's!" and my dad said, "Sally the Balls's, huh? Ha! Where'd you hear of that scumbag? I haven't heard that name in—"

"He's nice," I said. "He's one of the red-blooded."

"Fuck's wrong with your voice? And your eyes? What the fuck? Ma, what's going on here? He sleep last night? He looks . . . drunk."

"He's not feeling well," she said. "He should go to his room and get some rest."

I sat on the floor. My mom helped me up, walked me to the couch, and turned on *The Smurfs*. In the kitchen, my dad said, "So Sally the Balls—how'd the kid hear of *him*?" to which Grandma Magnet responded at a volume too low for me to make out her words. Not two minutes later, I heard the word *Cicero* pronounced a few times in a few different tones, all of which were loud, but didn't interest me so much as did Brainy Smurf's imminent abasement. As usual, Brainy was, in this episode, aggravating everyone else in the tribe, especially Handy Smurf, who was trying to fix some broken instrument I couldn't keep track of while Brainy stood by, nagging him about the superior ways he might fix the thing if he were the one in charge of fixing it. I hated that Brainy—that fun-killing, know-it-all, bespectacled stiff. I looked forward to when the others Smurfs would have enough. I hoped they'd beat him with the hammer this time—it had been too long—but worried they might only exile him again.

I fell asleep before finding out.

When I woke, my parents grounded me over the weights—my Grandmother Magnet had ratted in the end, maybe to ease their worries that

I might be really ill, or maybe out of resentment for my unknowingly blowing some intricate plan she'd developed for more softly breaking the news of her love for the Balls—but while I was grounded, my dad taught me how to use his own weights safely, and I worked out religiously for three days straight.

•

• •

A couple answers back, when you mentioned you recorded "every new song and gag [Blank] learned," what exactly did you mean by "gag"?

Given the revelatory moment I had (or felt I had) with Mouth, and the views I've already expressed about Curios, I trust that it isn't too hard to imagine how the idea of training Blank—or any Curio (or, for that matter, any animal)—to perform tricks intended only to entertain humans might strike me as distasteful, even repellent. In the vast majority of cases it does. In those cases where it doesn't, the motivation "to entertain humans" belongs to the trainee at least as much as to the trainer; it is in those rare cases that the tricks engendered by the training are what I call "gags."

Blank's tricks are gags because Blank performs them *in order* to entertain me, or, at the very least (i.e. for those who won't allow that Curios possess a theory of mind), it performs its gags in order to hear the sounds and/or see the movements I tend to make when I'm feeling entertained.

But how can I claim to know what Blank's motivation is when Blank performs a trick? To answer that, I'll have to first explain how I know what Blank's motivation *isn't.* Toward that end, here's an excerpt from Chapter 1 ("Early Training") of Abed Patel's (truly stellar) 1991 *New York Times* best-seller, *How to Shape Your Cure:*

> Suppose you find it entertaining when your two-legged Curio stands on one leg, and thus you'd prefer that it do so more often. Here is the most efficient way to make that happen:
>
> 1) Don't touch your Curio for a number of hours.
> 2) Once your Curio begins to exhibit early-stage grieving behavior, coax it into a standing position on a flat surface without touching it. If you cannot coax your Curio into standing on a flat surface without touching it, get someone else to set your Curio standing upon the flat surface.

3) Use a pen or pencil to bend one of the Curio's legs back at the knee and, very briefly, with the hand not holding the pen, scratch it on the head. Set the pen down.
4) Repeat step 3.
5) Repeat step 3 again.
6) Bend back the leg with the pen again, but rather than scratching the Curio's head while you're bending the leg, set the pen down. If the Curio continues to keep its leg bent after you have set the pen down, scratch it on the head. If it doesn't keep its leg bent, don't scratch its head: bend its leg back with the pen again, set the pen down, and repeat this step until it keeps its leg bent without aid of the pen, at which point you should scratch it on the head.
7) Repeat step 6 until the Curio has kept its leg bent without aid of the pen three times in a row.
8) Hold the pen near the Curio's leg, but do not touch the leg with the pen. If the Curio bends its leg back on its own, let it climb into your hand. Then set it down. If the Curio does not bend its leg back on its own, repeat step 7.
9) Repeat step 8 until the Curio, three times in a row, has bent its leg when the pen is held near its leg.
10) Hide the pen.
11) Wait two minutes. If in those two minutes, the Curio bends its leg, let it climb into your hand. If the Curio does not bend its leg within two minutes, repeat steps 9 and 10.
12) Set the Curio down. Repeat step 11 until the Curio, three times in a row, has bent its leg within two minutes of being set down, but after the third time you've let it climb into your hand, don't set it down; let it stay on your person for at least an hour. The next time the Curio seeks your body heat, it will stand on one leg to get some.

Although Patel's readers are vastly fewer and farther between than they were in the nineties (I'd assume a rather large proportion of you younger readers haven't even heard his name), I doubt many people reading this memoir would fail to recognize in the excerpt quoted above a method fundamentally similar to (though, perhaps, a tad more systematic than) that which they use to train their own Curios. In turn, I trust most wouldn't hesitate to agree that one's Curio, in the course of being so trained, is motivated to participate successfully in its training (i.e. to learn whatever trick it's being taught) by its need/desire for direct exposure to its owner's body heat (I prefer the terms "affection" and "human warmth" to "body heat," but I see no need, beyond mentioning my preference, to stir that pot here); that just as Mouth, when deprived of food, did what he had to do to get food, so does a Curio, when deprived of its owner's body heat, do what it must to gain exposure to that body heat.

I suppose that the reason we're so easily able to accept the aforementioned motivations while often having such difficulty accepting the existence of other motivations is that we know that birds require food to survive, and that Curios require their owner's body heat to survive (or "to prolong activation" if I must). (Of course, Curios also require food to survive but, incidentally or not, the reason one trains one's Curio via body heat reinforcement rather than food reinforcement is threefold: 1) The Curio doesn't require food as frequently as it requires the administration of body heat from its owner, thus the Curio takes longer to sense its need for food than it takes to sense its need for its owner's body heat; 2) the minuscule amount of food that satisfies a Curio's hunger—a single pellet a day—is difficult to break down into morsels systematically proportioned enough to reinforce with effectively; 3) Curios experience their need for human affection more acutely than they experience their need for food: as shown by Steiger et al (1993)*, a Curio deprived of food for as many as forty-eight hours will, if also deprived of its owner's body heat for as few as four hours, climb onto its owner before picking up a foodpellet even if the distance at which the cure stands from the foodpellet is significantly shorter than the distance at which the cure stands from its owner; even, in fact, if the foodpellet is situated *directly in between* the cure and its owner (i.e. the cure will actually leap over the pellet on its way to its owner).) I don't mean to belabor the obvious here, but to some—to most—what I'm getting at is all too often not obvious enough: because we can all comfortably agree that a Curio deprived of its owner's body heat is motivated to do (or attempt to do) whatever it must do to come into contact with its owner's body, it shouldn't be so uncomfortable a leap to suppose that whatever is done by a Curio that's already in contact with its owner's body is motivated by *something other* than that Curio's need/desire for its owner's body heat.

A Curio blinks, sure, to moisten its eyes, breathes to oxygenate its blood, but assuming the Curio's been properly fed, why might it dance upon its owner's shoulder, or do a headstand on its owner's anklebone? Why might it, as the case may be, keep rubbing at its eye while astride its owner's knee?

* N. Steiger, V. Klaus, H. Hyde, and R. Clydefellow, "The Strength of the Imprint," *Applied Behavioral Science* 28 no. 2 (1993): 10–29.

One needn't be familiar with Patel's bestseller, nor words like *conditioning, operant,* and *stimulus* to approach these questions empirically.

I certainly hadn't known those words, let alone even heard of *How to Shape Your Cure* (it hadn't yet been published), when Blank, at the age of five months, sat astride my knee and repeatedly rubbed at its eye with its finger as I read "The Hat Act" by Robert Coover, yet I didn't for a moment suspect Blank was rubbing its eye in order to get me to give it some body heat. At first, of course, I assumed it had something in its eye it was trying to remove. Within only just a couple of minutes, however, I realized that any time I ceased laughing at "The Hat Act," Blank would drop its hand from its eye for a moment, then bring it back up and start rubbing again.

What I deduced (or induced) by the time I'd finished reading "The Hat Act" was that Blank believed it was inciting me to laugh by rubbing its eye, and that it lowered its hand so as to then rub its eye anew each time I stopped laughing because it wanted to get me to laugh some more. What must have happened, I figured, was that Blank had happened to be rubbing its eye for an entirely different, though typical reason—likely to get something out of its eye, as I'd originally suspected—right at the moment when I first laughed at "The Hat Act," and then, after it had noticed my laughter, had determined that, given its timing, the eye-rubbing was what had caused that laughter. And so then Blank must have rubbed its eye again while, coincidentally, "The Hat Act" must have made me laugh once again. That could have happened any number of times: "The Hat Act" is a terribly funny story at which I laughed frequently—at which I still laugh frequently whenever I go back to it—and, assuming my laughter was what Blank sought, I may have accidentally reinforced the eye-rubbing (though I thought of it as having accidentally "rewarded" the eye-rubbing) thirty or even forty times in the fifteen-or-so minutes the story took me to read.

Once finished with "The Hat Act," I set it aside and watched Blank rub its eye, but didn't laugh. It rubbed at the other eye. Still I didn't laugh. It rubbed then at both eyes frantically, which did make me laugh—the idea that it was struggling to make me laugh was, I thought, very funny—and Blank stopped rubbing, and I stopped laughing, and then it rubbed at both eyes frantically again. After laughing some more, I started to worry about Blank's ocular well-being (it was rubbing very hard), and I embraced this worry so as to keep from laughing.

For a minute or so, Blank rubbed even more frantically than it previously had. Then it seemed to tire out for a moment and, in this new, tired state, it made a peculiar, slightly painful-looking face: it showed its gritted teeth between the flared lips of its muzzle and rolled up its eyes as if to gaze upon its own brow. I laughed at that and stopped, and again Blank frantically rubbed at its eyes, and again I declined to laugh (though I found the repetition of the eye-rubbing funny), and I reached out and gently took its hands from its face, and it showed me gritted teeth and rolled-up eyes. At that I made laugh sounds—I was forcing it, yes, but I thought that if I could get Blank to see that this far less self-destructive face-making behavior would make me laugh on its own, it might cease the eye-rubbing.

After a few more cycles of eye-rubbing/no-laugh/face-making/forced-laugh, that's exactly what happened: Blank dropped the eye-rubbing in favor of making the painful-looking face. (Within a few hours, I stopped laughing at the painful-looking face as frequently, and Blank stopped making the painful-looking face as frequently, but for years afterward, apropos of nothing—or so it would seem—Blank would make the painful-looking face two or three times a day, and I would laugh, I'd guess, about once per every five painful-looking faces made.) So those were the first of the gags I taught Blank to perform—the eye-rubbing accidentally, the painful-looking face more deliberately. After that, I taught it countless other gags, a few of them accidentally, a few of them deliberately, most of them somewhere right in the middle.

How it usually worked was that Blank would see me laugh at something and then attempt to perform or approximate whatever thing it was that it thought I'd laughed at (e.g. if someone on TV groaned after receiving a blow to the testicles, Blank might strike—or mime the striking of—its own testicle-free "crotch" (being single-legged, and thereby crotchless, Blank would strike/mime striking the "perineal" zone between the back of its upper thigh and its exit) and then groan). Sometimes what it thought I'd laughed at would be so far off from that at which I'd actually laughed that it was funny in itself (e.g. I might laugh at the groaning of someone who'd just been nutstruck, but Blank would think I'd laughed at the sight of an overweight bystander to the nutstrike and would stick out its stomach and inflate its cheeks). Sometimes what Blank thought I'd laughed at *was* what I'd laughed at even though *I* didn't realize that it was what I'd laughed at til after Blank's performance or approximation of it (e.g. the throat-clearing/coughing thing Woody Allen often did to signal he was about to deliver a quip, rather than the quip itself; or Julia Louis-Dreyfus's posture, rather than the words she spoke while she was adopting that posture). More often than not, though, Blank and I shared a basic understanding of what I'd laughed at, and gag training was a matter of exposing Blank to a greater variety of that thing, thus enhancing its understanding of that thing's potentials and subtleties.

Given cures' incapacity to converse in human language, I realize it might strike some readers as controversial, or even objectionable, to speak of a cure "sharing a basic understanding" with a person, let alone "understanding subtleties" (or, for some—for many—"understanding" anything at all), yet I have no better word to describe what I mean, so it's probably best I just give an example of the ways in which Blank manifested these various kinds of understanding:

Just this past summer (i.e. summer 2013), I went through one of my many Marx Bros. phases—a Groucho-focused one. We had, at the house, the twenty-one-volume *Collected Bros.* (an office Secret Santa gift my mother had received some thirty years earlier), which, in addition to all the films the Brothers Marx made, featured tapes of rare outtakes, highlights from *You Bet Your Life,* and a couple documentaries, as well as talk show appearances and newsreel footage. So I was spending a couple hours a day, sometimes more, watching the Brothers, and laughing quite a lot. A couple days into the week-plus Marxathon, Blank, which had been viewing the tapes with me, began making tentative, up-stressed laugh sounds—"tchi-*tchi*?"—when Groucho flexed his eyebrows, then turning to me, presumably to visually confirm that I was laughing at Groucho's flexing eyebrows, too. I was. I had been. After maybe two or three post-eyebrow-flex tchi-*tchi*?'s that successfully predicted my own laughter (which does not, incidentally, sound like "tchi-tchi"), Blank, when Groucho flexed his eyebrows, began to tchi-tchi less tentatively (no stress of any sort on the second tchi), and ceased turning to me for (ostensible) visual confirmation.

All of this was relatively typical. From previous Marx Bros. viewings, for example, Blank had learned, via the same process, to tchi-tchi when Harpo horn-humped something or someone or gookied, when Margaret Dumont grasped her chest and raised her voice, when Chico, looking away from whomever he was talking to, pouted his lips.

Less typical was Blank's determination not only to laugh at what I laughed at (again, Groucho's eyebrow-flexing), but to perform Groucho-style eyebrow-flexing itself. This determination was made plainly evident when, after a couple more appropriately timed tchi-tchi's, Blank jumped from my knee to the floor in front of me, and flexed its brow in the Groucho style.

I laughed when it did so. Of course I did. It eyebrow-flexed again and I laughed even harder. The third time was only half as funny as the first, and the fourth time wasn't really funny at all, so after that I didn't laugh when Blank flexed its brow, and within another few minutes, it stopped.

Over the next few days, though, for whatever reason (likely because we continued watching *The Collected Bros.,* and I continued laughing when Groucho flexed his eyebrows), Blank brought the eyebrow-flexing back any number of times, thus making known its desire to add the move to its repertoire and, presumably (and I think it's very reasonable to presume), to master the move, i.e. to get me to laugh whenever it deployed the move. As you can probably guess, I shared Blank's desire, and so I set out to more deliberately train it. The trouble, of course, was that mastery of this specific move was less about developing a physical ability (i.e. *how* to flex—which Blank had down pat) than it was about developing a sense of timing (i.e. *when* to flex—of which Blank seemed ignorant) and proper context (or, as the case may be, improper context): two concepts (i.e. timing and context) that were no easy thing to bring across *with* human language. And *without* human language, well . . .

Language-free object lessons (unless laughter counts as language) seemed the only option. So I trained Blank with language-free object lessons, by which I mean Blank and I watched every on-screen appearance of Groucho Marx in the fifty-some hours of *The Collected Bros.* Twice.

Though I can't say this resulted in Blank's mastery of the Groucho-style eyebrow-flex, it most definitely led to improvement. Likely because Groucho rarely eyebrow-flexed without having first delivered—or been a party to (the party of) the delivery of—a zinger, Blank learned to eyebrow-flex after having first performed another gag from its repertoire (e.g. a pratfall, a hammed-up sneeze, a solo waltz paired with humming). Additionally, Blank picked up the habit of tapping a phantom cigar in the air when, in the wake of a particularly well-deployed eyebrow-flex, my laughter was especially hearty.

What kept Blank from mastery was its tendency to eyebrow-flex anytime anyone on television or the radio had just finished saying anything. "Tune in tonight." Eyebrow-flex. "I miss that girl." Eyebrow-flex. "Mom says I can do my homework later." Eyebrow-flex. "Next up, a two-for-Tuesday from everyone's favorite quartet of Liverpudlians." Eyebrow-flex. In other words, upon hearing a stop, Blank would act as though whatever preceded the stop were a zinger worthy of facial punctuation. Sometimes that which preceded the stop coincidentally was a zinger, and then I might laugh. Sometimes it was so far from a zinger, I'd laugh. It wasn't often either, though. Not often enough.

And that's what we were working on—or what I hoped we were working on—around the time of my thirty-eighth birthday: distinguishing utterances that were either appropriate or highly inappropriate to eyebrow-flex in the wake of from those that were neither. I wasn't going to attempt to teach Blank English (I'm not *that* kind of crazy), but I believed that there might exist some universal set of specific human vocal dynamics (e.g. certain kinds of volume- or pitch-shifting) that were only ever manifest when someone cracked a joke and/or said something deadly serious, and the hope was that Blank, with enough exposure to these ostensible dynamics, would develop an ear for them, and thereby learn to make the aforementioned distinctions. Toward that end, I went through all fifty-plus hours of *The Collected Bros.* (I'd ordered the DVD box set by then), logged all the moments when Groucho eyebrow-flexed in response to something said by someone else, and made what turned out to be a seventeen-minute compilation of those moments (i.e. of each statement followed by the flex it incited). We watched the compilation as often as I could stand to—laughing every three to ten seconds, even when it's forced (perhaps especially when it's forced), is exhausting—which was once every two or three days or so, which meant that by the time I'd met Lotta Hogg, we'd seen the compilation only four or five times, and so even though our viewings had failed to noticeably improve Blank's sense of the kinds of statements that did and didn't merit eyebrow-flexing, I was still quite hopeful that future viewings might.

•

• •

Why did you lie to Lotta Hogg about having a crush on Fondajane?

Strictly speaking, I didn't lie about that. To *have a crush* on someone—at least by my lights—one has to sense one has a shot at becoming involved with that someone, and I, never even having met Fondajane, didn't have that sense. That said, I did have eyes. And I lived in this world. I possessed a libido. Inside my trousers, everything was jake. Saying I didn't find Fondajane *attractive*—that was a lie. I found her, in fact, *inspiringly* attractive, and had, for a while, thought about her quite a lot. Not just about her looks (though I was, I'll admit, one of the million or so readers who shelled out $60 for the special deluxe edition of her first memoir, *My Procedures,* in which the pre- and post-op nudes were full-color), nor even just about her role in recent history, but about what it must have been like to *be* her.

The third novel I wrote (two novels prior to *No Please Don't*) was narrated by a very loosely disguised (i.e. only in name) Fondajane I called Josephine Singer: a staggeringly gorgeous intersex sex-worker-slash-wunderkind of critical theory for whom a billionaire astronaut leaves his wife, and who, by the time she's married to that astronaut, becomes world-renowned as an author, human rights activist, public intellectual, and sex symbol credited with all-but-single-handedly 1) bringing about the full legalization of prostitution in America, 2) bringing about the legalization of gay marriage in America, and 3) launching us into the post-gender epoch.

One big problem I had with the novel was that I never got Josephine to convincingly grapple with questions I imagined were central and unique—or nearly unique—to Fondajane: Was she truly a force behind social change, or merely an emblem of social change? Both a force and an emblem? One and then the other? If one and then the other, then which one first?

Instead of embodying these questions, or even addressing them directly, Josephine writes a lyric essay—included in the novel—about Harriet Beecher Stowe, who, according to Josephine, was always conflicted about 1) whether she (i.e. Beecher Stowe) really had, as per Abraham Lincoln's famous quote, started the Civil War by publishing *Uncle Tom's Cabin*, and 2) whether starting the Civil War was something she *wanted* to think she'd done by publishing *Uncle Tom's Cabin*. My idea was that the reader—in the course of thinking about how Josephine thought about Harriet Beecher Stowe—would realize how Josephine must have thought about herself (i.e. in terms of emblem vs. force, etc.), and thereby understand, on a deeper level than Josephine could communicate deliberately, what it must be like to be Josephine.

An even bigger problem I had with the novel was that it wasn't—as I'm guessing you must have by now imagined—much fun to read. That's why I never tried to publish it.

But as for why I told Lotta that I didn't find Fondajane attractive, I suppose I thought it was the nice thing to say. One time, at Denny's, I eavesdropped on some women in the booth beside mine, and three of them agreed that they didn't like six-pack abs on men. Six-pack-less man that I am—on my hungriest mornings, if I really suck in, shadowy outlines of my upper couple "cans" momentarily show inside the arc of my rib cage—I was cheered. Because I assume that response was typically human, and because it would be hard to find two more physically dissimilar women than Fondajane and Lotta, and because Lotta seemed so nervous, and seemed so kind, I thought it would please her to "learn" that at least one man failed to find Fondajane attractive.

•

• •

Why did Lotta Hogg think you'd been in institutions?

I never asked, and so it's impossible to really say for sure, but since graduating high school, I hadn't left the house much in daylight except to buy cigarettes or—a couple times a year—go to Sheridan Hospital. I did have brief and infrequent—as brief and infrequent as I could make them—conversations with my grandmother, and even less frequent conversations with Pang and my former editor at Darger, but with the exception of my father, there was no one I spoke to on an even remotely regular basis, let alone anyone in my and Lotta's cohort. So given that she knew I'd been diagnosed with mental illness as a boy (everyone in town who knew of me knew), and given that I hadn't, since graduating high school, spoken to anyone who she and I should have presumably had in common, it would make sense that if some person—or *some people*—in our town were to (somewhat understandably) assume I'd been institutionalized and then say so to Lotta, she wouldn't have all too much trouble believing them.

•

• •

Why was Lotta Hogg sorry about your life?

Again, I never asked and so couldn't say for sure, but I imagine she said she was sorry about my life because she knew I'd been diagnosed with a psychotic disorder, and she was, as noted, under the illusion that I'd lived in institutions. Furthermore, she mentioned that I'd always been nice, even at my "peak" (presumably the twenty to thirty days following the murder of Feather's swingset, during which I enjoyed a measure of popularity at school), indicating her belief that I was past my peak. Also maybe she remembered that I lost my mother young, which, to me at least, would have been the best reason for someone to be sorry about my life, though I can see how, given everything else, that probably wouldn't have been what she was thinking of.

ALL-ENCOMPASSING AND TYRANNICAL

I LEFT THE BANK parking lot, performing calculations. Supposing I were to smoke my maximum eighty Quills a day every day until my father's return—six to six-and-a-half days away, depending on traffic—I would smoke between 480 and 520 Quills. I still had 150 (149 not including the one I'd just lit), which meant that, assuming bad traffic, I'd need to buy 370. Three hundred eighty, really, since they came in packs of twenty—so nineteen packs of Quills. With the cost of Quills at ten dollars a pack, I'd require $190 at most, then. I had a fin in my wallet, so, of the $500 Lotta had left me, I'd need only $185.

Lotta may have supposed I had a fin in my wallet, or even a ten, or a twenty. And because I'd told her I had enough smokes to last a normal person a week, she must have supposed I had at least a couple packs. But even supposing that she supposed I had nothing—no smokes, no dough—and that I needed, therefore, 520 Quills, i.e. twenty-six packs, that would mean I needed just $260, which would mean that her $500 would leave me a $240 surplus, i.e. her $500 would have been nearly twice what I could have possibly needed.

And I didn't see how she could know, or even guess, how much I smoked. I had read about people who smoked as much as me (I had read about three of them—Keith Richards of the rock-and-roll band the Rolling Stones; Adam Levin, author of the novel *The Instructions;* and that guy who wrote the *Easy Way to Stop Smoking* book, Allen Carr), but I had never *met* anyone who smoked as much as me. Not that I'd met all that many people, but still. Of the people I had met, few of them smoked even a third as much as me, and so it seemed extremely unlikely that Lotta would suppose I smoked more than forty cigarettes a day, which would mean she'd left me, at minimum, nearly *four* times the money it was reasonable for her to imagine I'd need.

So there were no two ways about it: the loan wasn't just generous, but conspicuously generous. What Lotta's conspicuous generosity meant, however—

that was hard to say. It could have been, to begin with, *inadvertently* conspicuous: she may have been too spidged to perform the kinds of calculations I was performing and, knowing that, had determined it was better to err on the side of giving me a little too much, but, intoxicated as she was, had vastly overestimated the amount I smoked, or the amount smokes cost, and ended up giving me a lot too much; or perhaps she was too high to even see how much she'd given me (e.g. maybe she thought, in her intoxicated state, that the twenty-five twenty-dollar bills she'd left me were twenty-five five- or ten-dollar bills, or five or ten twenty-dollar bills (having never used spidge, I had no real sense of how being spidged might affect one's perceptions, or ability to count)). In either case, it would have been okay, I decided, for me to do as she so kindly wished: to purchase Quills with the money she'd lent me, then pay the money back when my father returned.

But what if her conspicuous generosity was *intentionally* conspicuous? What if the sizable loan wasn't merely an act of kindness, but a subtle, or not-so-subtle, communication? What if she was trying to tell me something? What if she was trying to tell me she loved me? Was that not a possibility?

Granted, no one had ever fallen in love with me. I was under no illusions about my prospects, nor had I been—not even once—since childhood. But that was the thing. I had for so long been so entirely free of any suspicion that I might be someone's object of romantic interest that the novelty, itself, of having the thought—the thought that a person was possibly in love with me—appeared to lend the thought credence. Maybe Lotta'd displayed some kind of love behavior that, owing to my inexperience, I couldn't put my finger on despite having sensed it. Or maybe it was just the fact of the loan. People announced their love for one another in all kinds of different, sometimes subtle ways that didn't entail using the phrase(s) "I('m in) love (with) you." It happened all the time. In books, at least. In certain movies, too. Was it crazy to think that an overly generous short-term loan could serve as a proclamation of love?

One thing I was sure of was I didn't love Lotta. And if she loved me, and I accepted her loan—if, in fact, I didn't return it, unused, ASAP—it might lead her on, suggesting to her that I did in fact love her, or would love her soon, for what kind of person would accept a loan being offered out of love when he could not himself imagine reciprocating that love? A duplicitous sleaze. A blackhearted dirtbag. Just the kind of person who nice, smitten girls always seemed to have the most trouble getting over. Not the kind of person I wanted to be. Not, at least, to the ostensibly smitten, nice girl in question.

Then again, if Lotta loved me and I didn't use the loan, it might suggest to her that I wasn't merely not in love with her, but that the thought of her loving me repulsed me so much that I'd rather suffer the hovering anxiety and physical discomfort of nicotine withdrawal than accept a simple act of kindness from her. That could cause her more pain than would being led on.

Unless maybe the opposite.

Maybe my refusal to accept her loan could cause her to think I *was* in love with her, to think I was afraid that she'd question my feelings if I accepted the loan; to think I was afraid she'd wonder whether I truly loved her or just needed money. I.e. she might think that I refused the loan for fear of letting money defile our love's purity. Because that would have been romantic, I thought. Of me. To refuse a loan on those grounds. And then romantic of her to think it romantic. It would have been romantic of the both of us, I thought.

I knew a stalemate of hypotheticals when I saw one. So, much as I wanted to stop by White Hen, buy a couple cartons, and let Pang know that at least one person—a veritable stranger, no less—believed me credit*worthy,* I didn't. I couldn't. Not yet at least. Not without an unclear conscience. Plus what was my rush? Why keep pressing? There wasn't any rush. It was better not to press. I had 147 Quills and, even if I wanted to, couldn't return the money til morning (morning at earliest—for all I knew, Lotta had the next day off). I'd head back home, watch the eyebrow-flexing compilation with Blank, do a little reading, have a bite to eat, and maybe get some writing done. By these means, I would cease to press, and then I would sleep on it. It was always best to sleep on it.

•

•   •

I did cease to press, but didn't need to sleep on anything. Having slipped the eyebrow-flexing compilation into the living room player, I was just sitting down to unsleeve Kablankey when my father, bruised greenly below the right eye, appeared in the doorway. He had come back home an hour earlier, he said. He'd been sitting out on the dock that morning, reminiscing, he said, with his old friend Rick, and Rick's son, Jim, about the time we'd all gone fishing with some other father-son pairs on a rented pontoon boat thirtyish years ago, the time when Jim, who was mildly mentally retarded, had reeled in a crappie too small to keep, and Rick had told Jim that he had to throw it back, but Jim didn't want to take the hook from its mouth, and Rick had said he had to or the fish would die, and Jim began keening and said he couldn't touch it, he was too scared to touch it, and Rick told Jim that he had to man up ("Man up, son," he'd said. "Remove that hook and throw that fucking fish back, or I'll do it myself, and throw you in after it!"), and Jim, still wailing, and gushing snot and tears, had planted a foot on the flopping fish's back and, before anyone could understand what was happening, wrapped the line around a fist and pulled with all his strength, ripping out the hook along with half the fish's face, then punted what remained on the deck into the lake. My father said he'd been out on the dock in Michiana, reminiscing about that time with Rick and Jim, and that Rick had remarked on how gravely the Jim-manning-up ruckus must have upset me, given that I hadn't gone fishing since, and went on to suggest that I'd overreacted (I had, in fact, vomited), saying that, sure, it had been bad, but it hadn't been *that* bad, and my dad said, well, yes, it had been pretty bad, that fish got no mercy, was allowed no dignity, he'd nearly puked too, and Rick said no way, no way my father'd nearly puked, Clyde Magnet wasn't a puker, Rick said, which my father took to imply that I, his son, *was* a puker, and he expressed his resentment of the implication, which, Rick, rather than apologizing for, tried to make light of by insisting repeatedly that I was, yes, a puker, a master puker, a hall-of-fame world championship puker. " 'The Duke of Puke,' they call your boy," Rick said to my father, and my father, in his turn, though he knew Rick was trying to mend fences via ribbing him, nonetheless took "Duke of Puke" pretty badly, he just didn't like it, and who was Rick to talk about someone else's son anyway, he wondered aloud, and Rick asked what he meant, and my father, who'd meant, "Your son is retarded," or "I'm not the one with the retarded son," already felt, if not bad, at least a little conflicted about having meant that, and he tried to make up for it by saying to Rick, "I just mean that Jim's the one who lost control of himself and stomped a perfectly viable, inedible fish to death while tearing off its face, and then kicked it in the lake," but Rick, no dummy, knew that wasn't what he'd meant and, cutting closer to the chase, he told my father that Jim, despite having been born with many challenges, had overcome a lot, had only gotten stronger and, for that, Rick was proud, which my father, no doubt unmistakenly, understood to imply that Rick held the opinion that I, the author of *No Please Don't,* had not done anything to make a father proud, which meaning incited him to once again express resentment, and before Rick had a chance to say anything to repair the offense he'd caused my father, Jim piped up. "I'm not the pussy son!" he said. "It's your son who is! He is the puker! He puked on the deck! He puked and puked!" to which my father responded by slapping Rick with the back of his hand, to which Rick responded by punching my father just under the eye, which my father countered by socking Rick in the belly and then in the mouth and again in the belly, left-right-left, and he was just hauling back to strike a blow to Rick's nose when Jim—"Strong as an ox, that doofus!"—stood up (they'd been, all three of them, sitting side by side on the edge of the dock while the fathers provoked and punched each other) and lifted my father above his head, and bodyslammed him into the lake.

My father sobered instantly and floated on his back, watching the dock he'd been thrown from and thinking, "Who's crying now? (Jim!) Who's puking now? (Rick and Jim both!)," and it was then, he said, that he realized he'd forgotten to stuff the bust of Hagler, and he'd better get home. So he left Michiana, stopped by the tavern, and came straight home.

He handed me some twenties, said, "Sorry about that."

"Thanks," I said.

"I can't decide if I should go back or not," he said. "To Michiana. If I don't go back, that's it for me and Rick, I think. What do I care, though, right? Who the fuck is Rick? More importantly, how was your birthday? What'd you think of that shirt? Did you like the wrapping? I saw the shirt in the window of Sloga Nero's a couple weeks back and I thought it was funny, but I didn't know if you would think it was funny, so I didn't buy it. But then, on Sunday, when I saw the front page of the *Herald,* I thought, 'That Jonboat's everywhere! If I wrap that shirt in this front page, then the kid'll get a chuckle, at *least* a chuckle,' right?"

I said, "Thanks for the shirt."

"I guess I'll choose to understand that to mean, 'Yes, Dad, I liked the shirt. Gave me a chuckle.' By the way, you know—that whole story I just told you? Not exactly true. We got in a fight, and the oaf did bodyslam me into the lake, and that's when I remembered I forgot to leave you money, but the fight was about who should pay for bait, which, I mean, since that isn't really worth getting in a physical confrontation with a friend about, might mean that all the other stuff I told you was kind of underneath it—been brewing for twenty-however-many years, probably—but none of that stuff about the fish's face or the puking got *said,* not outright at least. I guess last night, just after I got there, Rick had asked me something about 'Why doesn't your son ever come out fishing with us, Clyde?' and it just built up inside me, that question, like, 'Is this guy really asking me this question? Who is this fucking guy to ask me this question?' Anyway, it was mostly about bait, so don't feel guilty about me getting in a fight to defend your honor or anything. I *am* glad you liked the shirt so much, though, and while we're on the topic of it having been your birthday, I'm wondering about that tumbler of water in the middle of the kitchen table."

Then he asked if it was I who'd left the water on the kitchen table, and, if so, then why had I left the water on the kitchen table, but before I could answer either question, he'd already begun to sarcastically offer a number of reasons why someone who had just celebrated his thirty-eighth birthday might feel entitled to leave water on a table instead of feeling obligated to spill it in a sink and wash its container or, at the very least, rinse its container. He didn't say *container* but he didn't only say *tumbler*. He named a large assortment of containers—glass, cup, mug, tankard, stein, grail, chalice, etc.—as if he felt that uttering an exhaustive list of names for containers from which one might drink was necessary to bringing his point across with clarity.

When at last he finished speaking, I told him I wasn't yet finished with the water.

"So finish it," he said.

•

• •

I headed toward the kitchen. My father followed. With my father behind me, especially in a hallway, I always felt as though I were about to flinch, and I knew that if I flinched or even seemed to him to be on the verge of flinching, he'd enjoy my flinching or the promise my being on the verge of it conveyed, and he'd attempt to make me flinch again and again, and so I'd do my best, when my father was behind me, to appear to be casual, even devil-may-care. That evening, in the hallway that led to the kitchen, I extended my arms to run my fingers along the walls.

The walls were warm and their paint was blistered. I pressed down hard and the blisters flattened, though not crunchingly or poppingly as I might've expected. It was more like the blisters reluctantly withdrew, like the nosy extras' heads that stick out of windows overlooking courtyards when lovers' quarrels end in old romantic comedies set in Manhattan.

Because, I guess, the reaction of the blisters was unexpected, I tried to think of the unexpected word for what I was doing to the wall, the unexpected word for the act of touching. It seemed important to recall the word.

Taction. I got it. Almost instantly. In a hallway with my father behind me, no less. I was sharpening, sharpened, extra-alert—the one advantage to being made to feel jumpy.

And no sooner had I gotten hold of *taction* than I noticed a short, fuzzy coil of carpet fiber at rest just beyond the slim metal bar that marked the line where the carpeting stopped and the tile began—right there at the threshold of hallway and kitchen. I wanted to tact the coil with a toe, but the movement of my feet as I approached the coil created a vacuum, causing the coil to be sucked between my ankles into the space behind me. I doubted that my father, whose legs bowed widely, made any kind of contact at all with the coil, but I didn't turn around to confirm this doubt, for fear that my turning might look like a flinch.

However, just a pace from the metal bar—which, owing to a superstition thats origins I can't recall, I had, for years, taken care to step over, never on—I saw something else: I saw that one of the screws intended to hold the bar to the floor had come up in its hole. I didn't think to crouch to better fasten the screw, but I realized that in order to maintain the casual, unflinching character of my stride, I would need to step directly onto the bar.

I silently apologized to whom- or whatever one apologizes upon failing to behave in accord with superstition, and did what I had to do to seem casual. The weight of my body caused the bar to flex, which propelled the loose screw from its last bit of threading. The screw became airborne and entered the hallway. Yet I didn't get to hear what I imagine must have been the small thump it made when it landed on the carpet; I didn't even think to attempt to hear it. I was far too distracted. Even through the sock, the bar was cold on my sole, and the shock of the coldness caused me to shudder.

My father mistook the shudder for a flinch, and said, "Any second thoughts there, Young Master Billy?"

Though Belt was the name my mother and he had chosen to give me, my father no longer liked that name, hadn't liked it in decades, and would call me Billy—Young Master Billy if I had just flinched, had seemed to flinch, or had seemed to him to be on the verge of flinching.

"I asked if you were having second thoughts," he said.

"Maybe," I told him.

"*Maybe*'s a shrug. A shrug and a dodge. *Maybe*'s the sound second thoughts make, son, the pumping of blood in their lily-livered hearts. May-BE, may-BE, may-BE, may-BE . . ."

Dusk was gaining and the house was mostly dark. The little bit of sunlight that did achieve the kitchen through the sliding glass door was orange and split into rails by the blinds. Each rail widened and dimmed as it traveled away from the door, and the effect on the kitchen was Japanese, especially on the table. Thirteen sun-rails achieved the table and they made the table look *extremely* Japanese, like the backdrop of a Japanese stage romance, or a paper fan between the fingers of a Japanese actress.

The tumbler I'd forgotten there was half in shadow and the lip at its base bent the edge of a sun-rail. The water in the tumbler's lit half appeared stale, depleted of fundaments. A blanket of tiny white bubbles on the surface—three and four bubbles deep—was hardly jarred at all by a bubble that rapidly climbed from the bottom to collide with its underside.

"Drink up," my father said, and brought down his fist, rattling the table, sending more bubbles climbing. He'd never told me exactly what his job as "impeller" at the plant entailed—I think he (rightfully) assumed I wasn't that interested—but I imagined he pushed heavy things via handcart, or broke those things down, or carted them somewhere to be broken down, maybe with heat. In summer he was often shirtless, barefoot. He strode high-leggedly around the house like a young mountaineer in a fable of derring-do, or a gunslinger high on good paregoric, and although the house shook with his every footfall, his walking occasionally sounded hopeful, an end to something dangerous, the clanging of the change in his pocket silver lining.

He crossed his arms and leaned back on the fridge, worried the hair on his shoulders with his fingers.

I set the cup against my mouth and tilted it.

Ever since I can remember, I've taken a certain misguided delight in the tilting of partly filled vessels. Even as an adult—and it's embarrassing to admit this—but even as an adult, even to this day, in the moment before I ruin it with thought, I believe with all my heart that the vessel I'm tilting is doing more than bounding the demonstration of a larger absolute; I believe the vessel is, itself, the absolute. The way the surface of the contained substance appears to be getting pulled from under by the vessel, even though it's just gravity doing the usual.

I sipped the water slowly. It clotted my saliva. Dried out my teeth. It clung to the walls of my throat like dust.

"That's drinking?" my father said. "That's not drinking." He clambered around me to get to the sink, opened the tap, and gulped at the stream. "That's drinking!" he said. He swallowed awhile, then nodded mock-smugly, caught some water in his eyes. "This is drinking," he said.

I didn't want to make laugh sounds.

"Okay, Dad," I said.

He kept drinking and telling me, "This is drinking."

"Okay," I said. "I understand."

He closed the tap. He left the kitchen. Walking down the hallway, he stepped on the screw. He said, "What could this screw be doing in our hallway?" Crouching where he'd stood, he pinched the screw between fingers, then held the screw high and addressed himself to it. "Maybe," he said, "you thought there was a shortage of loose screws in our carpeting. Maybe you believed there was some kind of shortage of aggravation in the world. Or maybe you're just a funnyguy, and you think it's funny. You think he thinks it's funny, Billy? Do you? Well, tell him. Tell him how we do with loose screws around here. Tell him what we do with funnyguys, Billy. Hey there, Billy, I'm talking to you. Young Master Billy. Hey there. So forget it. I'll tell him myself. We screw 'em back down. We screw 'em back down where they belong, see," he said. "See?" he said. "See? You see?"

He kept saying "See," until I made laugh sounds. Then he tossed the screw down the basement stairwell and went up the street to the Arcades Brothel.

•
• •

I can see how you, if you were a more considerate version of me, might have cared about the screw your dad had tossed down the basement stairwell. You might have felt that the screw, despite being just a tiny component of the threshold bar from which it had sprung (from which you had sprung it, however accidentally), was worth more consideration. It might have occurred to you, right on the spot, that although the bar was fastened by two other screws, the tossed one's absence was straining those two—left, as they were, to do work meant for three—and would eventually strain them beyond their abilities, allowing the bar to curl up on one side and thereby malfunction years (perhaps decades) earlier than it would were it still screwed down in all its holes. You might have even been cognizant of how the tossed screw, were you to leave it stranded in the basement, would likely be kicked into a corner or crevice by some oblivious shuffler's insensate foot (maybe even your own) and, owing to the basement's being sealed and sturdy, remain preserved and undiscovered until such a time when a natural calamity or act of war or property developer razed your home and exposed the screw to corrosive heat and cold and moisture, if not birds or rodents or possibly insects with screw-size gaps in their nests in need of plugging. I'm very well able to imagine how you, as a more considerate version of me, might have retrieved the screw from the basement and screwed it back into the threshold bar in order to save both screw and bar from any or all of the fates described above.

So I *can* understand why you might expect that I would have cared about the screw and the bar, and yet I didn't. Care, that is. I cared about neither the screw nor the bar. Had either one of them ever spoken to me, I might have cared, and maybe even cared enough, depending on my mood, to spend energy helping them, but probably not. Even when I'm moved by the plight of an inan—which happens less and less often the older I get—I'm rarely moved enough to do anything about it. Nor do I judge myself harshly for that. No more harshly, at least, than I judge myself for spending money and effort on books instead of spending that money and effort to help put an end to genocide in Africa, famine in India, global warming, animal cruelty, child abuse, or any other of the world's presumably stoppable, certainly diminishable, absolutely unnecessary causes of suffering, including the hunger of the homeless man begging next to the bus stop in front of Barnes & Noble. I hope you don't judge me too harshly either.

If you do judge me harshly, though, perhaps you'll find it pleasing to learn that I was bored. I was terribly bored, and perhaps you believe I deserved to be bored. And perhaps you'll determine—despite my protests to the contrary—that I was bored *because* I failed to care about the screw and the threshold bar. As much as I would disagree with that determination, I have no better an account to offer. I've never once known why I was bored when I was bored. My boredoms always seemed to strike me out of nowhere; they lacked salient causes, which made them hard to cure. My first impulse when bored was to play with Blank, yet since my boredoms, by nature, felt like personal failures—failures, that is, to be not-bored—and since feelings of failure could rapidly lead to feelings of frustration, and feelings of frustration increased muscular tension, which could in turn foster brash and/or clumsy applications of strength (e.g. the slamming of doors, the over-pulling of drawers, the over-scratching of mosquito bites, the snapping of pencil points), I feared that if I, while bored, were to play with Blank, I would do so too aggressively, and possibly harm it, so I'd keep Blank sleeved whenever I was bored.

So I kept Blank sleeved, and went down to retrieve the screw from the basement, not to save the screw from eons of uselessness, nor to grant the threshold bar greater longevity, but only because it seemed the most Curio-safe and readily available approach to killing some time til the boredom wore off, or, at least, til I could get to sleep.

I hadn't been down there for at least a decade—not since our first washer-dryer combo died and the new one was installed in the first-floor bathroom. As far as I could tell, nothing had changed; even the busted laundry machine remained. The carpeting was rough, the walls wood-paneled, the window wells grimy and leaf-obstructed. Cartons of clothing that used to be my mother's were stacked along one wall, a couple old computers and some dated small appliances were lined against the baseboard along another, and sharing the wall with the washer-dryer combo was a fireproof cabinet for medical records, insurance policies, property titles, and other such documents. My father's workbench—a leather tool belt, a drill case, and a pair of plastic goggles all resting on a plank-and-sawhorse table—abutted the wall that was opposite the stairwell and, above it, in a frame, hung one of the original JONBOAT SAY shirts.

He'd gotten it a few weeks after purchasing the first two, saying he thought it could become a collector's item. Although eventually a couple local shops would start carrying them, the only place to get a JONBOAT SAY shirt at the time was a Mustangs game, and he had invited me to go to another one, and then get some ice cream. I refused the invitation. So my father went to the game without me, and inside five minutes of his departure from the house, I found myself wishing I hadn't refused. True, he didn't know Jonboat had apologized (via bags of eighties mall couture) for having given me a possible concussion via beating, but then he also didn't know that I'd been beaten at all—I'd told him I'd fallen. And maybe another dad, upon having learned that Jonboat had stolen "pissing through a boner," would have shown more loyalty to his son—maybe another dad would have been outraged on his son's behalf and thrown away the JONBOAT SAY shirts he'd already bought—but then again, I thought, maybe not. Maybe I was just being oversensitive. Maybe I was just expecting too much. Maybe's the sound second thoughts make, son. Plus I knew for certain that if my father *had known* I'd been beaten up by Jonboat, he wouldn't have stood for it, bagsful of Guess? and Cavaricci or no. He'd have gone to the compound, knocked on the gate, and . . . then what? Knocked on Jon-Jon's face? Well, that seemed a little much—but he would have done *something*. There would have been some kind of confrontation. Some kind of demonstration of his fatherly devotion. And yet, I'd refused to go to a game with him. To go, with my father, to a baseball game, then afterward get some ice cream—I'd refused.

I rode to the ballfield to apologize and join him. I locked my bike to a leg of the bleachers. He was sitting up top, elbows on knees, looking out at the diamond, blank-faced, alone. His wife was gone and his son was insane. It wasn't his fault, neither one nor the other.

It wasn't mine either, though.

I unlocked my bike. I rode back home.

The basement was dim, lit by one bulb. I'd have to get on my knees to find the screw. As I was bending to do so, the framed JONBOAT SAY shirt's fatman seemed to wink.

I leaned over the workbench to get a closer look, and the winking stopped. Probably it had just been a weird reflection. Maybe a silverfish standing on the glass. Nonetheless, it unsettled me a little.

I took the frame off the wall, brought it under the lightbulb, tilted it some, and . . . there—the winking. No cause for discomfort, much less alarm. Just a shadow effect at play on the glass. I could get the fatman to appear to wink if I held the frame at a particular angle while partially eclipsing the bulb with my chin.

I hung the frame.

No sooner had I back-stepped to confirm it was centered than it dropped to the workbench.

The bang of the initial impact wasn't loud, but it was paired with a crunch, and instantly followed by silvery tinkling as the frame, glass-first, fell upon the rusty handle of the drill case. Shards blasted everywhere.

The hook the frame's picture wire had formerly rested in no longer occupied its hole in the wall; it was lying on the workbench by a pile of shattered glass. Maybe it had never been properly inserted. Or maybe I'd let the wire down too hard. Was there even a difference? There probably wasn't. It certainly wouldn't make a difference to my father. He'd believe I'd damaged the frame on purpose.

I knew it would be best to just take it on the chin, but I also knew I wouldn't; I'd try to dodge the blow. Though I'd never expressed my resentment toward my father for having displayed the T-shirt in our house, he had once accused me of harboring such resentment—right after he'd hung the framed shirt above the mantel, just over Hagler, and I'd said it looked tacky—and I'd denied the accusation (*convincingly,* I'd felt at the time; he had, after all, moved the shirt to the basement), but now he would, if (when) he discovered the damage, believe he knew something he *had* once known—something that was, anyway, no longer true—and he'd lord the "knowledge" over me til one of us died.

•

•   •

Apart from the glass, the fallen frame was intact, the T-shirt still mounted without a wrinkle. I drilled a new hole just over the old one, secured the hook, and successfully carried out the evening's second hanging. I swept up the shards with an old *Daily Herald,* and discovered in the shovel I was using as a dustpan the screw I'd been seeking. At least there was that.

As I pocketed the screw, though, my fingers grazed something rough and unexpected—Lotta's money. I'd forgotten all about it.

A mistake I'd made earlier came cruelly to light.

The mistake was this: from the very outset, I'd dismissed the possibility that Lotta had given me the money out of pity. I'd dismissed it because she'd told me she knew I would pay her back, which had seemed to indicate the money was a loan. And pity did not give rise to loans. Pity gave rise to charitable donations. There in the basement, though, sweeping up glass, I recalled what I'd always been taught about charity: that the highest form of charity is anonymous donation. It's the highest form of charity for two big reasons. First of all, the giver's anonymity makes it impossible for the recipient to pay the giver back, allowing the recipient to receive the donation without feeling indebted to a particular person. Secondly, though—and more to the point—the giver's anonymity prevents the recipient from experiencing the shame of being seen accepting charity (or, at the very least, it prevents the recipient from experiencing the shame of being seen *by the giver* accepting charity). Owing to the circumstances under which I received the $500 (our immediate proximity, and my relatively immediate need), Lotta couldn't have made an effective, anonymous donation to me even if she'd wanted to and, there in the basement, sweeping glass, what occurred to me was that she might very well have wanted to. She might very well have wanted to grant me an anonymous donation, and on seeing that she couldn't, did the next best thing: she spoke of what she privately understood to be a donation (i.e. money she counted on never seeing again) as if it were a loan. Calling it a loan couldn't spare me the feeling of being indebted to a particular person (her), but it *could* at least spare me the shame of being seen accepting charity (and it had! at least up until I started thinking these thoughts). And I supposed she supposed that if ever I did try to pay her back, she could act as if she'd expected repayment all along—as if the donation, all along, had been a loan—and by those means, I'd never register her pity; I'd lose no face. Either way, she'd have saved me from that initial shame. What a sweetheart she was!

And what a conceited schmuck I'd been. Mistaking some nice girl's pity for love. She'd even said, "I'm sorry about your life." And yet somehow I'd managed to imagine that sentiment had been independent of the rest of the encounter. Something was wrong with me. What was wrong with me? How could I possibly be such a fool when all that I ever seemed to do was *think*?

Having finished cleaning the mess in the basement, I went to the bar at the kitchen/hallway threshold and screwed the screw down into its hole. I tightened the other two a couple of turns, and boredom was upon me even worse than before.

It was still too early to go to sleep, so I fixed an egg sandwich, from which I took a bite, but I wasn't hungry. I tossed out the sandwich, poured some juice in a glass and took a couple sips, but I wasn't thirsty. I emptied the glass of juice in the sink and rinsed it with soap. I looked at my books, and looked at my magazines, and turned the TV on, and then the radio. None of it engaged me. Could I sit at my desk and write? I could, but should not. All I'd be able to write about was boredom, and there was nothing new available to write about boredom—at least nothing new that was also true.

I lit up a Quill and lay on the couch and I thought about boredom, how boring it was, how unsympathetic (or maybe oversympathetic? what other feeling, when discussed at length, so dependably inflicted itself on the listener?), how all-encompassing and tyrannical it was. It's boring, reader, for me to write this passage. It's boring for you to read this passage. As I'm telling you the truth about a time I was bored, the truth can't be new, can't help but be boring. And of course the same goes for thinking about boredom, and I knew it then as I know it now, yet I lay there on the couch, and thought about boredom. My boredom. Others'. Boredom in general. Was it the state of desirelessness it seemed to be? Or was it more like a state of pure desire, the sole object of which was its own negation? Was there any difference? What was desire? Wasn't desire that which motivated action? But if desire was that which motivated action, then how could boredom—if boredom was "a state of pure desire, the sole object of which was its own negation"—fail to motivate action? the action, that is, of attempting to negate itself? Or maybe it couldn't fail? Maybe it never failed? Could I think of a time that boredom had failed to motivate an attempt to negate itself? I couldn't. But then why was it so boring to hear about boredom? So boring to read and write and think about boredom? Motivated action—action motivated by human desire—wasn't that the stuff of which ripping yarns were made? Maybe the problem was that, by definition, the only action boredom could motivate was indirect action? random action? action for which a meaningful outcome (i.e. one beyond the actor's overcoming or failing to overcome his boredom) could not be anticipated by the listener/reader/thinker, and therefore couldn't entice the listener/reader/thinker to invest in it?

These questions were nothing new and they bored me.

I got off the couch and extinguished my Quill, then headed to the playground next door to our house.

ON THE CHIN

AT THE EDGE OF the SafeSurf playground turf, I broke into a sprint. I hurdled the seesaw and the motorcycle bouncetoy, then ran up the broad metal slide and sat. Within ten rapid breaths, the fresh air and raised heart rate transformed my boredom into despair. I wished a rabid rabbit would bite me, or a death cult abduct me, that a horn would burst forth from the center of my forehead. I was out of print and no one was in love with me. I was lonesome and lonely and unimportant. Alone and pointless and principally a nuisance. A scratch on a windshield covered in smudges.

The slide spoke up.

||I'm achy,|| it said. ||My bolts are throbbing. I worry I'm beginning to oxidize.||

Sloping sharply off the deck of a pipe-and-log jungle gym shaped like a Vietnam War–era gunboat, the slide was a plank of silvery steel, five feet wide and entirely flat. Because it wasn't walled or even ridged at the lips, anxious local parents fearing premature fall-offs forbade their small children to ride it. My mother and father had been two such parents and once I'd turned eight and they'd lifted the ban I rode the thing daily til that winter's first storm, never failing to feel like I was living on the edge—the slide was fast, even faster than it looked—and I had, amidst attacks of nostalgia most gummy, ridden it a few times a year ever since. Nonetheless, we hadn't once conversed.

I craned my neck to inspect its surface, and could see no corrosion or discoloration. A tract of shallow dings I'd never noticed before, though, was bending the moonlight halfway down. I covered my mouth and mumbled the news.

||So *what* you never noticed my tract of shallow dings before? You stare at me a lot?||

"Not a lot," I said. "But I come here enough, to the playground I mean, and I think I'd've noticed if—"

||Well I'd think so, too. Aren't you the boy who helped all those swingsets?||

This was the inans' favorite question to ask me. Sometimes they'd ask out of authentic curiosity, sometimes from suspicion, and other times—like this one, if tone was any indication—for rhetorical reasons.

"I haven't been a boy for a really long time," I said.

||Do you have to mumble into your hand? It's annoying.||

"You never know who's watching."

||Why not just silently *think* at me, though?||

This was their second-favorite question to ask me.

"My words," I said, "don't come through clear enough unless I'm talking them or writing them down. If you'd rather I wrote them, I've got a pen in my pocket. I can scribble on my palm."

||No, no,|| the slide said. ||That'll take too long. But your voice is unpleasant. You've got a lousy voice. Your lousy voice bothers me way deep down. Can't you just *try* to think silently at me?||

I knew it was useless, but I gave it a go in the hopes that doing so might placate the slide. I thought, ||I'm sitting on a slide, feeling lonesome and dumb, and my rear is kind of sore, and the air is still,|| because those were the most immediate truths available, and therefore, I reasoned, they might have a shot at getting conveyed without too much of the usual interference.

Once I was finished, though, the slide started laughing.

||You weren't lying,|| it said. ||That was really—wow.||

"That bad?" I said.

||It's almost as if you're retarded or something. First there was this field of, like, screechy, pulsing, kind of blindingly fluorescent gray thats hue cooled down until the whole thing resolved into this scene from a traveling circus or carnival. A shiny black panther inside a small cage was pacing and roaring, and people were crowding at the front of the cage, lots and lots of people, a hundred maybe, standing nine- and ten-deep, watching it move, listening to it roar, whistling and cheering and clapping and so on. They couldn't look away. Then the panther, it reared up on its hind legs and roared so loudly that the image started shaking, and the crowd got even more enthusiastic, and the roar got even louder and that blinding gray field closed in from the edges, blotting everything out, muting the roar, and when the gray cooled down again and resolved, there was no more panther, no more cage, no more crowd, but this tall, thick glass with some spitty-looking stuff in the bottom like third of it. The glass was tipping sideways, and something was off: the spitty-looking stuff didn't move like it should, it didn't move like a liquid, moved more like a slime, a really thick slime, or a molten metal, kind of rippling a little and maybe kind of trembling but mostly holding its shape, keeping its form while the glass went horizontal around it. Just when the glass

was about to get completely horizontal, *it* started to tremble and ripple, the glass I mean, and these little spidery crack lines started appearing, but before they were deep enough to really break the glass apart, a glint near one of the cracklines expanded suddenly, almost explosively, and everything went bright gray again.||

"You didn't catch a single word?"

||There was one wordy moment, right at the beginning, during the panther part. Some voice in the crowd said, |Ma, what's it mean?| and then another voice responded, |It's saying, ||I'm freeeeee! I'm freeee! I'm free-ee-ee!|| Isn't that beautiful?| The words barely got through, though. Like whispers and hums fighting radio static. Scratching and buzzing. How do you live in that head? It's a mess.||

"Enough with the digs. I'm about to walk away from you."

||No surprise there. That's just how you are now. That's what's become of you. You could've been a hero, too. It's sad.||

I leapt from the slide and could no longer hear it, which fact (i.e. my no longer hearing it) serves, incidentally, to highlight one of the major reasons that I tend to doubt my conversations with inans are symptomatic of a psychotic disorder. Were the conversations hallucinatory, the rules governing them wouldn't hold, I don't think. The slide, or any other inan for that matter, would be able to speak to me from any distance, regardless of whether we were touching each other. I'd have less control.

•

•   •

As my soles met the SafeSurf, the SafeSurf spoke up. ||Hey, Blight!|| it said. ||What's wrong? What's the problem?||

"It's *Belt,*" I said. "And there isn't any problem."

||Your sneakers betray you,|| the SafeSurf said. ||Not on purpose, of course. I mean, it's not like they said anything. They never would. Go ahead and ask me why. Don't you want to ask me why?||

"I'm tired," I said.

||You're not just tired, you're also upset. I can tell by the action in the soles of your sneakers, who would never, incidentally, say anything to me. And if you want to know why, but maybe don't feel like asking, well, I'll tell you why: it's because they resent me. All sneakers do. Sneakers feel threatened in my presence—diminished a bit, half-obsolesced. Hi-tops being an exception, of course—they support your ankles laterally, which is to say that they support your ankles in a manner that's totally beyond my means. Not that I've

had many conversations with hi-tops. They tend to snub me, out of clan-like solidarity with their bitchy, mewling lo-top cousins.||

The thing about the SafeSurf was it had always been kind to me and, as little as I felt like talking about sneakers or feelings, I could tell it needed company—its telephone-pollster-like cadence was a giveaway. Acting like a friend would only cost me time, a currency on which I was not short. So, "You don't keep feet warm, though," I said, "or dry. Plus you're outside of fashion. No one can wear you, let alone be made more exciting by wearing you."

||You're preaching to the choir,|| the SafeSurf said. ||I think sneakers are useful. But all those skills you just named—sheltering feet, attracting like-minded friends, and being outward, however dubious, expressions of one's wearer's individuality—these are skills that any old shoe might possess, and sneakers understand those skills as their birthright. It's the grip and pressure-absorption capacities inherent in their rubber soles that make them *sneakers,* though. Their group identity is rooted in their ability to prevent slippage and diminish, if not entirely forgo, damage to joints and tendons—abilities I can't deny I possess.||

"Do lo-tops resent hi-tops, then?" I said. "Don't hi-tops do all those things and more? I mean, they've got the same soles, *and,* like you said, they support the ankles."

||I think lo-tops probably tell themselves that hi-tops, sure, provide ankle support, but the cost of that provision is they're heavier, bulkier, more confining. Who knows, though, right? Like I said, these aren't beings I've ever been too intimate with. The best I can do to understand what they're thinking is observe how they behave and what it gets them, and assume that getting what it gets them is what motivates their behavior, and then after all that, imagine what it would be like to have the same motivations. In the end, however, I'm just not footwear, let alone a sneaker. I'm not even apparel. I'm the floor of a playground. A large, flat swath of molded polymer. I've never, as it were—and ehem and oof—I've never walked in their shoes, nor will I, nor can I. At this depth of analysis, I'm kind of just making stuff up, I guess.||

"I guess," I said. "But I think I know what you mean. I think your method's sound. Plus at least you're trying."

||And I'm glad to hear you think that, but we started out talking about you and *your* sneakers, and how, when their soles met my surface, I sensed a flex in the area below the balls of your feet, which indicated there was rigidity in your toes, i.e. that your toes were *clenched.* If clenched toes isn't the surest sign that Belt Magnificat's feeling upset, well then I guess that, even after all these years, I don't know you any better than a schoolboy's Jordans.||

"Magnet," I said.

||Magnet?||

"Not Magnificat."

||Right! Blight *Magnet*. I mean *Belt* Magnet. Forgive me. I'm sorry. I knew *Magnificat* sounded off. But just talk to me, Belt. What's eating you up?||

"Nothing," I said, still not wanting to talk about it. "Everything," I said, not wanting to be rude. "I don't know," I said. "It's just one of those days. Like, the slide, okay? Out of nowhere, the slide just started bugging me—insulting me sideways, being really hostile."

||The *slide*? So what! Don't listen to *that* chump. That slide's a sourpuss. Everyone knows that. The information's famous.||

"Well, I had no idea," I said. "I just met it."

||Yeah right, |just met it.| You've been coming here for years.||

"You're the only one in the playground who ever talks to me," I said. "I mean, the rocket talked once, but I offended it somehow."

||I have a hard time believing that,|| the SafeSurf said. ||What about the tank? The tank never talks to you? That thing can't shut up. Nyar nyar nyar. Jabber jabber jabber. It's been greeting into my gate for days. It's greeting this very moment, as we speak. I have to *actively* ignore the tank, like twenty-four/seven, and you're telling me you never had a single talk with it?||

"You're not really making me feel any better."

||Come on,|| said the SafeSurf. ||All's I'm saying is communication's a two-way street, right? Maybe the slide's hurt that you never opened your gate to it before—maybe it doesn't believe you can't. The tank too, for that matter, though I guess that's a boon. But the slide's the point. It's always been a whiner and a sadsack and a jerk. At least ever since *I* got laid down here it has been. Like, I guess I replaced some pebbles, right? And so you know what it calls me? It calls me |Notpebbles.| Even after all these years. |Notpebbles.|||

"It was woodchips you replaced."

||Woodchips?|| said the SafeSurf.

"Wait," I said. I thought I'd heard a human sound. A couple of footfalls. An exhalation. "You hear that?" I said.

||I don't hear anything.||

"Over by the alley," I said. "Behind the fence."

||You know I can't hear things that don't touch—||

"Right, sure. Hold on."

I listened, and failed to hear any more human sounds, but still I felt self-conscious, standing there and mumbling into my hand, so I sat down to mumble into my hand.

||What were you saying about woodchips?|| said the SafeSurf.

"It wasn't pebbles you replaced. It was woodchips," I said. "There were pebbles til maybe 1989, but some study came out that said woodchips were safer."

||That seems pretty obvious.||

"Not as obvious as you'd think. The study actually found that woodchips led to more falls than pebbles because kids tripped more often on woodchips when running, but the thing was the falls on woodchips weren't as injurious. And that was the more important factor to consider—the injuriousness of the falls, not the rate of falling. Woodchips only lasted here a couple of years, though, because the miracle of affordable SafeSurf had arrived, and SafeSurf, as I'm sure you know, decreased both injuriousness and rates of falling in one fell swoop. It's a really great technology."

||You're a regular encyclopedia, aren't you? And a sweetheart, too.||

"Tell that to the slide," I said.

||Bet your sweet bippy, I'll tell it to the slide. I'm sure it knows it anyway. Thing's just a stresscase. A bitter sourpuss. No one knows why. I'm confident it likes you, though. All of us do. How couldn't we, you know? You're the only person who really gets us. Well, at least the only dude. There's also the girl.||

"I hate you," I said, and stood up. I left.

Sort of.

I walked ten steps to the long, gravelly strip that bordered the playground, and sat.

•

• •

I'd heard about *the girl* since I was fourteen years old—a local girl who, like me, could talk to inans. For nearly ten years, I believed what I'd heard, but I'd never met her, try though I did. The task of finding her was doomed from the outset. Most inans don't understand the concept of proper names, and the few that do, all of which, themselves, go by brand names (e.g. Zippo lighters, Jacuzzi bathtubs, Air Jordan sneakers, and, of course, SafeSurf playground turf), have very little motivation to learn proper names, let alone to commit proper names to memory, for the vast majority of their conversations—if not all of their conversations—are with unbranded inans that, when the need to refer to a specific being arises, use behavior- and function-oriented phrases like *the rusty-edged teaspoon that once cut a lip* or *the sewer cap children like to rattle by stomping on*. So when it came to the local girl who could talk to inans, they called her *the girl who talks to inans* or, on occasion, *the person who talks to inans who has never been the boy who helped the swingsets.*

Nor could any of them describe her to me. Apart from the fact that humans all look alike to inans, none of the inans who'd told me about the girl had ever actually encountered her themselves—they'd heard of her only through other inans—so even if the inans who *had* met the girl had for some reason noted her height or the color of her hair or any other potentially identifying physical attribute, by the time the news had traveled telephone-game-like through all the gates it would have needed to travel in order to get to me, the odds that the information I'd receive would be anything like accurate were miserably low.

Nonetheless I spent my every spare moment seeking out and trying not to stare at lone females who were writing something down or speaking into their hands. Over the course of five years, I even approached a few—seven in total—and made a creep of myself at each encounter, only then to learn, from the very stretch of SafeSurf from which I'd just fled, that the girl who talked to inans was able to do so via thinking silently, which meant I'd not only wasted those first five years using incorrect search criteria, but that said criteria might have actually *blinded me* to the girl. She might have been sitting at the counter of the Denny's right next to the diarist I'd fixated on who jotted away in her small red book while continually fondling and intermittently gazing at a blue paper packet of synthetic sugar until I scared her off with my anxious demeanor (I was young and lonely) or crazy-sounding questions (I was young and tactless) or probably both. Or she might have been eating an ice cream on a bench across from the fountain at the Plaza Beige strip mall when the young divorcée who'd sat the ledge of the fountain while angrily muttering in the direction of her handbag threatened to tase me and drown me in the fountain if I came any closer or said another word "about or to" my wallet (I was faking the conversation—my wallet's never spoken to me—in the stupid hopes that doing so would invite an approach by the divorcée herself).

Whoever the girl who talked to inans was, I'd have looked right past her without a second thought, bent as I'd been on finding mumblers and scribblers.

I'd continued to search, though, continued without knowing what it was I should search for. What might a girl who conversed with inans via silent, unwritten thought look like? What might make such a girl stand out? Would she have a quality of contented stillness to her? Would being able to silently communicate with inans be the pleasure I imagined it would? Or would the girl, despite her gift, doubt her own perceptions like I so often did, and feel apart from all the people she encountered? And how would she respond to that? Certainly not with contentment. But how would her lack of contentment manifest? Would she appear to be agitated? Withdrawn? Maybe she'd construct a big, welcoming personality to compensate for how unwelcome she, herself, always felt? I had no idea. I assumed she'd be attractive, though. And this wasn't merely wishful thinking, I don't think. I assumed she'd be attractive because I assumed that I, personally, couldn't fail to be attracted to someone who was like me in the way she was like me. I didn't believe in justice or God—I never really had—but I didn't believe in irony the way so many people do, either. That is: I didn't believe that everything was ironic. I didn't believe that the girl with whom I should, at least according to reason, fall in storybook love, had to be someone with whom I was romantically incompatible. I knew it *could* be that way, but I didn't think it *had to* be that way. And I really hoped it wouldn't. I really thought we could be happy, together in our hallucinations or superperceptions—whichever. So when the SafeSurf informed me, ten years after I'd first heard of the girl, and five years after it had told me she could talk with inans via silent thinking—when the SafeSurf informed me that she'd ended her life with a stomach full of pills in a clawfooted bathtub . . . I just wasn't expecting that.

And when, on the night after my thirty-eighth birthday (i.e. over twenty years after I'd first heard of the girl, i.e. over ten years after I'd given up all hope and come to delicate terms with what looked to be my permanent state of loneliness), the SafeSurf spoke of her as if she were alive—as if it, itself, hadn't been the one to inform me of her death—I felt not only betrayed and manipulated, but deeply insulted. How could it forget that it had told me she was dead? or think I was dumb enough to have forgotten it had told me that? or daft enough to believe that she had come back alive? Even if our conversations were hallucinatory, how could it? *Especially* if our conversations were hallucinatory . . . Because that would mean I did it to myself. To tell myself via extremely convincing hallucination that a girl who might be able to love me actually existed, and then that she died, and then that she was somehow alive again—the level of self-contempt it would take for me to do that was impossible to justify. I wasn't a bad person really, I didn't think. I was unkind to my grandmother on the telephone sometimes, and I resented my father for the way he occasionally lorded over me, but on the grand scale these were minor offenses. Small potatoes. Someone was hurting me and I didn't deserve it, even if I was that very someone. Unless maybe I deserved it *because* I was that someone. Because I unjustly persecuted myself. Oh God, I felt crazy and ludicrous and worthless.

I unsleeved Blank and set it on my knee.

•

•   •

I unsleeved Blank and set it on my knee. It blinked heavily, twice, scratched its chin with its tail, and whistled an interrogative melody.

I lit up a Quill.

It whistled again—same tune, higher-pitched.

I shrugged, smoked.

Blank leapt from my knee to the gravelly strip, started humming the cancan, then bobbing to the cancan, then dancing the cancan upside down on its hands and brassing the hums up with tuba-like lipfarts.

Just as I began to feel cheered by the performance—as much by its intent to entertain away my misery as by its content (which was old-school Blank; it hadn't done the cancan since it first learned to Hora a couple or maybe three years earlier)—I heard footsteps approaching from across the playground. Not wanting to appear like I had anything to hide, I turned my face forward, in the footsteps' direction, and very casually extended my arm—as if I were merely stretching out my triceps—to allow Blank quicker access to its sleeve.

Blank's hearing had always been keener than mine, so I can only assume that, given its ears' proximity to the gravel, the scraping noise of the cancanned pebbles must have drowned out the sounds of everything else, for Blank didn't race back to its sleeve as it should have, nor did it cover its face.

By the time it stopped dancing, the boys were before us.

Four of them. Fourteen-year-olds. Maybe fifteen-. They wore cardigan vests over turtleneck T-shirts, and each had a sailor cap, Dixie cup–style, with a name in felt block letters stitched to its brim: *LYLE, BRYCE, CHAZ, CHAZ JR*. A fifth kept his distance. He was over by the slide, half the playground away.

Of the four before us, two—the Chazes—actually rubbed at their eyes with their wrists.

"No way," Chaz said.

"No way," said Chaz Jr.

"What?" Bryce said.

Lyle pointed to Blank.

Bryce said, "Oh my dang donkey! Is that item real, mud?"

Lyle and Bryce both knelt on the SafeSurf to get a closer look. Centered on their throats, at the folds of their turtlenecks, *yachts* was embroidered in golden thread. Silhouettes of sailboats embossing the swooshes of their Nike CureSleeves were also done in gold, and earthwormy stains shone dully like smears of petroleum jelly near the Velcro closures. Similar stains marred the legs of Lyle's shorts. He saw me seeing them.

"Sloppy," he said. "I know. I do. Judge not, though, kind mud. Our domestic, Pilar, took ill on laundry day."

"What is it this time?" Bryce said, winking. "Croup? The grippe? I hope it's not pertussis, or, God forbid, dropsy. Your Pilar's always down with something, what what. You need to tell your mother to find a new girl."

"Pilar," said Lyle, "is irreplaceable. Vigorously loyal, kind, and—"

"Buxom? Vigorously buxom and oral you were saying? Buxom and foxy and docile and oral?"

“I surely wouldn’t,” said Lyle, “regret a sudden change of subject, dear Bryce. For example, golly me, this mud’s cure over here.”

“Indeed, we might table the Pilar conversation for another, better time. The mud’s cure *does* merit further discussion.”

By this point, Blank had turned its back to the boys and was creeping sideways on the tips of its fingers, slow as a loris, in the direction of my arm.

“It is so tootin cute—the way it’s hiding?” Lyle said. “As though it thinks it’s clever? As though it thinks it can elude us? As though it believes that treading lightly enough will grant it the power of invisibility? Word it up on the real now, how adorable is that! Holy jams I want to smash it. Holy jams holy jimmy.”

“Holy jimmy to the jimjames jammety jimjam, that stripe down its back—that stripe looks *painted,*” Bryce said to Lyle. “Is it painted,” Bryce asked me, “or did it grow that way, mud? Don’t you guff me on this.”

“Painted?” I said.

“You needn’t feel you have reason to say it that way—in that voice. As though I’m a cretin. It’s an honest question.”

“Know this one thing if no other,” said Lyle. “Bryce is neither cretin nor weisenheiming rogue. The fellow shoots straight with whomever he addresses, be they mud, chap, lady, chippy, harlot, or tot. I believe you should apologize. Word is bond, now, what.”

“No need,” Bryce said. “It’s all entirely good. Were there any hard feelings, why, they’d soften in an instant, yo. May I hold it, though, please? Your cure, mud, what.”

“It wouldn’t like that,” I said. “It’s shy. It fears strangers.” Blank was in arm’s reach, both mine and Lyle’s. I swooped it up. Not wanting to secure it inside its sleeve—the sleeve was on the outs, the zipper catchy—which would grant the boys more time to ogle it, I stuck it in my shirt. It clung to the fabric just under the collar and emitted happy beeps in three sets of two.

“Nonsense,” said Bryce. “No cure fears strangers. And would you listen to that voice it has! I’m completely in its thrall. You really shouldn’t hide it, mud. Hiding it is rude. You should really let us hold it, mud. That is what I’m saying, and we all of us agree. Hear hear, Chaz Jr.?”

“Hear hear,” said Chaz Jr. “And Chaz agrees, too.”

“I do agree, too. That’s the truth,” said Chaz. “Not to mention Lyle, who agrees, too, also.”

“And I would wager my trousers Triple-J agrees as well. Triple-J!” Lyle shouted to the boy near the slide. “Come on over here, chap! We need your help. You need to vouch for your opinion.”

“What opinion?” Triple-J said.

“Your opinion that this fellow should let us hold his cure.”

"I'm occupied, Lyle-san," Triple-J said. His voice sounded like someone's. I couldn't place whose. I didn't know any kids.

"Are you beginning without us, Triple-J?" said Lyle. "Don't begin without us!"

"I'm starting," Triple-J said. He backed up away from the slide a few yards and sidearmed something from his pocket at it. Probably a rock. The sound of the impact was a flat, raspy click.

I remembered the tract of shallow dings I'd noticed earlier.

"He started without us! Wait a minute, Triple-J. We'll be there in a minute. Come on, lads, let's go."

"Hold up," said Chaz. "I think first we should ask this kind citizen here to quote us a price for that bugger in his shirt."

"That's clever. I like it. You heard the gent, mud. How much'll you sell it for? I've got fifty clams in this very billfold. Will fifty cut the mustard?"

Triple-J whipped something else at the slide. Another raspy click.

"What are you doing to the slide?" I said.

Triple-J ignored the question, or failed to hear it.

" 'The slide,' " Chaz said. " 'The slide,' the man says."

"Don't insult the man, Chaz, for the man will speak nonsense. That is the lesson he means us to take. And take it we shall. That adorable bugger's worth eighty beans, easy, sure as I'm standing here."

"One hundred at that, Chaz Jr.," Bryce said.

"One hundred's high, Bryce. That's four new, factory-sealed, LuckTest EmergeRigs—six, by golly, on three-for-two Tuesdays over at A(cute)rements. High odds from six marbles we'd emerge one just as cute."

"Be reasonable, Chaz. You know that's not true. You saw how it was sneaking—it had to *learn* that. It isn't a baby. It's at least what, two, even three years old, hey."

"Bryce is right," said Lyle. "The price is wrong. And when I think about it sneaking, I just want to—dear! I just want to pin it to a wall with my thumb is what I want. I want to pin it to a wall by the throat and mash . . . mash its rootin-tootin face in slowly with a twig til it . . ."

"Pops?"

"Til it pops! Yes, indeed. Til it pops and gushes forth. Now hear me out, mud. Lucre we've got. On loot we're not short. Fifty a chap is two hundred, I say, two-fifty assuming Triple-J pitches in, and we'll call it a deal, yes, hey, what, word?"

Triple-J's arm blurred. No raspy click. "Bullseye," he said.

I said, "What's your friend doing?"

"He's starting *without* us. Word up now, I say, let's settle our business."

"My cure's not for sale."

"Everything's for sale." "All our fathers say so." "Indubitably."

"I don't know your fathers."

"Very few do." "If any at all." "And especially not you." "Our fathers are beyond you." "They're beyond even us." "Light-years beyond us." "Not quite as many light-years as they are beyond you, though." "Let us cease speaking of our fathers at once." "Yes, enough about our fathers." "Name us your price."

"Really, guys," I said. I stood up to go home, and to get, on my way, a closer look at whatever Triple-J was doing. The four formed a semicircle, blocking my path. I took a step to the right, to get around them, and Chaz kicked my thigh. It was not a strong kick.

He said, "Consider that a warning. Forewarned is fore—"

I pushed him harder than I meant to. He fell on Chaz Jr. and they both hit the SafeSurf. Bryce put his fists up, and I knew he couldn't hurt me—he could hardly have reached my chin if he'd uppercut—but my cure was vulnerable, there in my shirt, and the pleasure I took in striking Bryce's forehead with the heel of my palm was greater than I would have liked to admit. His neck bent back, and his hat popped off. Beneath the hat he was yellowly mohawked. He did not look okay. Twice he whimpered, "No," and his eyes started streaming. He lunged forward anyway. I caught him by the throat and threw him back at the fence, which bounced him to his ass on the gravelly strip. He sat there and wept. Lyle ran away. I looked at what I'd done, knew I needed to fix it. I moved first to Chaz Jr.—after all, he'd done the least—but before I had the chance to extend my hand, something crunched against my temple, stung my left eye shut.

I heard hurried footfalls. My left cheek was cool. I touched it—wet. Blood. Mine. Where was Triple-J? I turned toward the slide. He was crouching before me.

Crouching? Why?

He sweep-kicked my ankles.

I fell on the SafeSurf, cradling my cure, and he jumped on my kidneys—just once—and leapt aside.

"We done?" he said.

The pain was too much for a mere pair of organs. It throbbed all the way to the ends of my extremities.

"Yes," I gasped. "Done."

"You sure?" he said.

"Yes."

"Go home," he told his friends, "and don't forget your stupid hats, you stupid bunch of fucking idiots."

* * *

As the remaining three Yachts donned their caps and limped off, Triple-J lit a smoke and perched atop the motorcycle bouncetoy's sidecar, pressing a whale song out of its spring. "I don't feel good," he told me, "about you being hurt." Then the middle of his chest started blinking bright orange and giving off beeps. He tapped the brightest part with the heel of his palm: one, one-two, one-two, one-two. The beeping continued. "Pain in the fucking *dick*," he mumbled, and, lipping his smoke, fished a vitreous pendant up out of his collar. He tapped at the thing with his index finger: one, one-two, one-two, one-two. It ceased to beep, blinked green, went dark.

"What is that?" I said.

"Take it easy," he said, and stuck it back in his shirt.

The position I was in—half-sitting/half-lying, leaning back on an elbow—was suddenly embarrassing. I pulled in my legs, raised myself higher.

"So look," said Triple-J. "Listen, alright? All that stuff that just happened? Completely regrettable. Bums me out hard. I want to say it's not me. I want to say it's all them. But it's a little bit me cause those guys are my friends and I let them be my friends. They think we're a gang and I don't stop them thinking that. They think we're called the Yachts and they think I'm their leader. They read some stupid novel. New kid at school bands the losers together. Starts an uprising. I don't want an uprising. Maybe—I don't know—a *revolution*, but only if it's fun. And I've told them that, but still, they keep on following me. They really look up to me. They try to impress me. They're just so *nice* to me. And life is so easy. Mine is, I'm saying. I mean, I'm really lucky. I'm seriously privileged. I can't disappoint them. I have no right to let anyone down. So I wear the silly hat and cut the arms off my turtlenecks. I try when I'm around them to talk how they imagined I would talk before they met me. Like a polo-playing dicksneeze who listens to hip-hop and goes on safari. I talk about the sky above the Kenyan savannah, thoroughbreds for birthday gifts, backgammon strategy, girls named Cebrin with sisters named Colombe. I reminisce about Manhattan, which I don't even miss, not even a little—there's so much space here, so many ballfields and places to park—and I throw some Slick Rick on when they come to my houses. Why am I telling you this? There's something about you. Something familiar and maybe not bad."

"Thank you," I said.

"Yeah, well, still. You shouldn't have hit them. That's what I should tell you. They're a bunch of fucking idiots, but they're smaller than you and they're serious pussies and they're good in their hearts. Or maybe they're not that good in their hearts. It remains to be seen. But the main thing is this: main thing's they're with *me*. You shouldn't have hit them and that's where I stand.

Don't do it again. And I'll tell them not to narc you. I'll say we're evo-stevo, and they'll listen, believe me. But mum's gotta be the word on your end, too. Not that you'd want people to know a kid laid you out, even this kid. Or I don't know. Maybe. Maybe you would. Maybe you're the kind who'd think the big headline would mean real fame. I'll tell you, though, it won't. Before word one about me made it into print, your life would be ruined. You know who my father is. You know he's no pussy. So you no say, I no say, entiendes, amigo?"

"Entiendo," I said. "We say nada nunca a nadie." To my surprise, I felt extremely amiable. Partly, I think, because my attacker seemed to be revealing himself as an overall decent human being who'd thought he was righting a wrong when he'd hurt me, which meant that he didn't have anything against me—against who I *truly* was. Partly because some really vigorous endorphins were bathing my nerve ends, overcompensating me with warmth and calm for the pain induced by the blow to my kidneys. Partly because, although I hardly knew Spanish (I'd had just a couple years of it in high school), Triple-J's punning had not been lost on me. Also partly because I'm basically a coward; I'd rather be finished taking a beating than have to continue to be in a fight. Mostly, however, my amiability owed to the fact that I *did* know who Triple-J's father was. His father's, I'd realized—when Triple-J'd said "dicksneeze"—was the voice of which his croaky own reminded me.

"Nunca a nadie, for sure-o," Triple-J said. "You're funny, jefe."

"And you're Jonboat's son, right? You're Jonny Pellmore-Jason, Jr. Your father beat me up once, too, you know?"

"Oh?"

"It's true. When we were kids. And after that we were friends. At least kind of, I mean."

"My father," said Triple-J, "is friendless. He's never had friends. And listen: you're smiling. You're smiling in the way that some people call beaming, and it's making me uncomfortable. Don't beam at strangers. Jesus you're weird. I better get going. You're really creeping me out."

He straightened his cap, chucked his smoke at the fence, and walked off in the direction of his father's houses, taking with him, it seemed, the last of my endorphins.

I drew a deep breath, which hurt, and lay down.

•

• •

I was, somewhat literarily, yards from where I'd lain when my father first taught me all he knew about suffering. We'd been playing tetherball. Game upon game. Despite our height differential—I was five years old—I was holding my own. My father was impressed. I'd score and he'd shake his head in admiration, call me "killer" and whistle, promise all kinds of ice cream. The sun, that afternoon, was murder, the air like sap, and, more and more frequently, he'd bend to catch his breath—hands on knees, shoulder involvement—but he didn't want to quit. Best-of-three had become best-of-five, then of-seven, -eleven . . . -twenty-one.

I didn't want to quit either. Not only was I getting better at tetherball, and pleasing my dad, but, during the breaks we took between games, I kept seeing this chipmunk dart across the blacktop (this was two or three years before the pebbles were installed), back and forth between the rocket and the gunboat. It may have been the first chipmunk I'd ever encountered, it was certainly the first one I'd ever been drawn to, and I found myself wondering what it was doing there. The nearest tree in which it could have viably nested would have been in the copse by the man-made pond. (Our housing development was younger than me; the trees along the playground's perimeter were saplings, staked to the sod with hazard-orange-streamered tethers, same as those planted on the trapezoids of grass between the bottoms of the driveways of all the local homes.) The copse by the pond was three blocks away—an epic journey, I'd thought, in chipmunk terms, especially considering the bulldozer-flattened Wheelatine landscape's general paucity of protective cover. The chipmunk probably had a burrow in a neighboring lawn—potentially our lawn—but that prospect didn't occur to me at the time; I thought burrows were for rabbits, and trees for squirrels (I didn't think of the chipmunk as a *chipmunk* but a *squirrel*).

I supposed that in the course of chasing a female it had fallen in love with, or fleeing a predator that had murdered its family, the chipmunk had left the copse and gotten lost. But that didn't explain why it remained on the playground. Why wasn't it trying to find its way home?

To me it seemed the chipmunk might have wanted to play. I thought it might have sensed that I wasn't any danger; I thought it might have felt that, this far from its nest, it needed a friend, and I could be that friend. Plus it appeared, in a way, to already be playing with us, or maybe rather attempting to play with us; it showed itself only when one of us was readying to serve, whereas during the volleys it stayed beneath the rocket. True, when it hid, it may have chosen to do so for fear of those volleys' startling sounds—I *did* accept that possibility—but because it repeatedly darted back and forth across the same small stretch when the sounds let up (seven separate times over someteen minutes before I quit counting) rather than running away from the playground (a nestless, foodless, and mate-free area), I came to see the rationale behind its timing (darting only during the breaks in the match) may just as well have been to invite me to chase it when I was least distracted (and thus most likely to receive the invitation), and I even registered the possibility (though, even at the time, this did seem far-fetched) that the chipmunk kept itself out of my sight while the ball was in play so as not to distract me from scoring on my father.

I wanted very badly to hold that chipmunk. More specifically, I wanted to catch it, cup a hand around its head to show it I was safe, then stick it in my pocket, feed it dried apricots, and set it free just a few minutes later, only to discover it the following day, and every day thereafter, happily awaiting my return to the playground.

The tetherball pole was as far from the gunboat as it was from the rocket, and the rocket and gunboat as far from one another as they were from the pole. I, behind the pole, was feeling fast; not chipmunk-fast, but maybe half that fast. If I were actually as fast as I felt, I imagined, the time it would take me to race to either the gunboat or the rocket would be twice the time it would take the chipmunk to race between them. To put that another, more functional way: in the time it would take the chipmunk to go from the rocket to the gunboat and back to the rocket, I could get to the rocket. So the plan I hatched was to head for the rocket as soon as the chipmunk left the rocket, for that would see me arriving at the rocket just as the chipmunk returned to the rocket. Granted, the chipmunk would have a head start—I wouldn't go for the rocket til I saw the chipmunk take off toward the gunboat—but then it would also have to turn around when it got to the gunboat, and, given that all I'd have to do to get to the rocket was traverse a vector, the time the chipmunk's turnaround would take to execute should have, according to my calculations, sufficiently neutralized that head start's advantage.

I can't say with confidence that my thoughts were as organized as they appear above. I wrote a similar scene in *No Please Don't*—one of just two or three vaguely autobiographical moments in the novel—and in the course of doing so, I may have permanently confused my fiction with my memory (though not on the bigger points; I'm well aware, for example, that for ten-year-old Gil MacCabby, who's newly mourning the loss of his beloved Bam Naka, the whole chipmunk episode metaphorically resonates quite a bit more tidily than the real one did for five-year-old Belt; I won't spoil the novel by revealing more than that). I can, however, say with confidence that I did not know geometry or fractions at the age of five, and thus using words here like *vector* and *calculated* and *twice the time* is potentially misleading. But even if my mathy reasons weren't as concise at five years old as I've reported them being at thirty-eight years old, I certainly hatched the plan I've described; if there's any real difference between the way I thought and the way in which I've conveyed the way I thought, it's no larger than the difference between calling a man "tall" and calling a man "over six feet tall." And for whatever it's worth, the memory of the time I'm describing—the time my father taught me what suffering was—is really quite vivid to me, despite the potentially fictional nature of some of it. In fact, it happens to be the earliest coherent memory I have of my father, all those preceding it being flashes and noise from which any narratives I'm able to produce require far too much induction to trust.

My plan, it turned out, was less than sound. A few strides from the rocket, I realized that I was going to make it. That is, I realized that I would get to the rocket just as the chipmunk got to the rocket (maybe I was actually as quick as I'd thought; maybe the chipmunk, seeing me coming, slowed its pace because, as I'd imagined, it wanted me to catch it—I'll never know), but I realized, also, that I would overshoot the mark. I was going too fast.

So I dropped to my knees and slid to a stop. Right on target. As I'd slid, I'd rotated—not on purpose, and just a little, maybe forty-five degrees—in the direction of the chipmunk, and the chipmunk had leapt. The timing was lucky. For me at least. The chipmunk bounced headfirst off my neck, landed on my lap. I cupped its haunches and lifted it up in front of my face. We exchanged stunned looks, both our mouths open. Its arms were outstretched, its little fingers twiddling.

"I got it!" I shouted out to my father, and the chipmunk wriggled, gained purchase with its feet against the muscles of my thumbs, shat down my shirt-front, sprung over my shoulder, and gave me a scratch on the ear as it passed.

I wouldn't find the scratch til later that night. I had far nastier wounds to contend with. Over the course of my rotating slide, the blacktop had rubbed half the flesh off my shins. Suddenly I felt it. The rapid-fire stinging. Thousands of stings. I fell to my side, looked back toward the pole, saw the chipmunk licking at a curled scrap of skin in one of the gore trails, and started to cry.

The chipmunk bolted. My father rushed over, saying my name. Not shouting my name, just saying my name. "Belt," he said. "Belt. Belt, you've gotta breathe."

And he knelt beside me and said I had to breathe, and he held my hand and said I had to pay attention, to breathe in when he squeezed, breathe out when he released, and I did as he said, but soon the pain increased, and I told him so, I said, "You're making it worse."

"No such thing," he said. "It's you getting worse. Trying to dodge a blow you've gotta take on the chin."

"You're a horrible father," I said. "I hate you."

"You don't hate your father, you listen to your father, so listen to your father. There's your pain, and there's your suffering. There isn't all that much you can do about your pain, but your suffering—that's all yours to control. This stupid shit you just did—it isn't going to kill you. It isn't even going to lay you out for that long. In a week you won't hardly remember it happened. You're just surprised, and so you're afraid, and that's why you're suffering. The pain surprised you. The pain from what you did. You're afraid of the pain so you're turning away from it. That makes it worse. Face it down."

"It hurts."

"So what? It's supposed to hurt. Let it hurt. It's a message from your body. Listen to your body. Do nothing but listen, and your suffering will stop."

"There aren't any sounds. You're crazy. You're mean."

"Listen to the *feeling*."

"There aren't any sounds!"

"I know. But . . . Look, forget the word 'listen.' Just pay attention. Pay attention to the pain."

"I am! I can't help it!"

"You're arguing with me. You're not paying attention. Stop arguing with me and pay attention. Stop trying not to feel it, and it won't hurt so bad. Stop trying to distract yourself. Feel it *more,* feel nothing *except* it, and son, I promise, you will stop being scared and you will no longer suffer."

I did as he said. I shut my eyes, and paid attention to the stings, the thousands of stings, then closer attention, til I fell into a trance in which I came to see that *I* was the stings, that these thousands of stings, rather than assaulting me, *were* me, or at least part of me. And the negative valence of the stings receded. They weren't good, but they weren't so bad. The stings, which were me, like me, just were. Even calling them stings came to seem incorrect. They were more like not-quite-comfortable pressures; I was more like not-quite-comfortable pressures. I stopped calling us anything.

When I snapped to—a minute, or three, or maybe five later—my father was there, right where he'd been, holding my hand, squeezing and releasing it in time with my breathing.

"Okay?" he said.

"Yeah."

"That's cause you're badass."

He picked me up off the blacktop, and sat me on his shoulder, then carried me all the way back to the house. I was way too old to be carried like that, but I didn't argue. I didn't say a thing. I was focused on the pain, on being the pain.

At home, he installed me on the couch in the living room. He Bactined my legs and wrapped them in gauze, then turned the TV on and ordered a pizza. The Bactine incited a new kind of sting that I successfully entered the trance to fight (or rather to not-fight), and, over the course of the next couple weeks, as the scabs formed and dried and slowly fell away, I found the trance also worked to take the edge off itches.

I haven't since come across an acute sensation that I couldn't, given the opportunity to concentrate, reveal to be a not-quite-comfortable pressure. The more acute the sensation, the heavier (and also—maybe paradoxically—the easier to enter) would be the trance.

The one I entered the night I met Triple-J wasn't the heaviest in which I'd ever been (I'd landed splay-legged on a balance beam once; lost a ring finger's nail to a Little Leaguer's fastball; broken a molar on the pit of an olive), but it was still pretty heavy. Heavy enough, in any case, that I fell asleep right there beneath the stars.

•
• •

The nap must have been brief, for Blank hadn't moved. It would have gone to its sleeve had it realized I was sleeping, but it was still in my shirt. Huddled there, shivering. I think that's what woke me—this hot vibration against my ribs.

||You alright?|| said the SafeSurf.

I didn't respond. I wanted to ignore it; to freeze it out. And I was hearing something else. With my ears, I mean. Something awful and saccharine from over by the slide. Rather, I was trying to hear it; no sooner had I noticed the sound than it stopped, or got carried off by the low-power breeze.

||I'm really sorry,|| said the SafeSurf, ||that you got your ass kicked. Even though you told me you hated me before.||

Blank wouldn't quit shivering. I scratched the back of its head through the cotton, dragged a knuckle along its curved spine. Neither gesture seemed to calm it in the least. We had to get home. I'd give it half a lollipop stick to chew on, light up a Quill. It liked to pretend we were smoking together.

I lurched to my feet, wobbled, and sat. It wasn't my kidneys—their pain had dulled down into something like cramp—just a big headrush from rising too fast. Blank came out of the bottom of my shirt, stood on my thigh, looked up at my face. I smiled to let it know I was fine. Still shivering, it nodded, climbed back in my shirt.

||I feel so damn helpless right now,|| said the SafeSurf. ||I feel like I failed you. Like I could have protected you. I know that's crazy, but still. I feel

ashamed. Do you really have to ignore me on top of it? You know I can't move.||

Again I heard the faint, awful sound from by the slide. I held my breath, the better to listen, but the rubbing of a passing car's tires undermined me.

||You *know* I can't move,|| the SafeSurf whined. ||What could I have done? Tell me. What?||

"Nothing," I thought.

||I know,|| said the SafeSurf, ||nothing at all,|| pronouncing the words as if in agreement with my unspoken thought; as if my thought had passed through its gate unadorned by noise. Maybe it had. But if it had, so what? It was just two syllables, a one-word response, and, given the context, a highly predictable response at that. No. I didn't believe the SafeSurf had heard me think ||Nothing.|| And I was made freshly angry by what seemed to be yet another attempt on its part—or, worse, my own—to mess with my head. We both knew, after all, how I wished for the ability to silently communicate my thoughts to inans.

"Absolutely nothing," I said. "Agreed. You're completely worthless."

||Oh man. That's harsh. |Completely worthless.| Jeez. That's harsh. But at least we're talking, right? I appreciate that. Look, is there something I could do? Like to make you feel better?||

"Could you go back twenty years and untell me about the girl who talked to inans who probably never even existed? Or maybe you could go back ten years after that and untell me that she died? Or even just, you know, go back twenty minutes and untell me that she was still alive after all?"

||I never said that girl was still alive,|| said the SafeSurf. ||Why would I say that? It's not just untrue—it's . . . it's crazy. She's gone. And I'm sorry if I got you thinking about her. I was talking about the other one.||

"The other one, right. What other one?" I said.

||The other girl,|| said the SafeSurf.

"Yeah, sure. What's her name?"

||I wish I could tell you.||

"You're lying," I said. "I got angry at you for messing with me, and now you're lying. You're saying you didn't mess with me, but you're messing with me *more*."

||Belt, man, please. I'm not messing with you. I never even met that first girl once. I didn't find out she was dead til at least a month after she swallowed those pills, and, tell you the truth, I don't even know if she really swallowed any pills. She didn't live that close, at least I assume she didn't, and the number of gates the news had to pass through to get to me from the bathtub she died in's uncountable. You know information transforms a little with each

transmission, even if every inan whose gate it passes through is honest and well-intentioned, which—who knows, right? We only know who we're touching, and maybe we don't even really know them. Like right now, I feel like you don't even know me, which makes me feel like I don't even know you. But this other one, though. This other girl, I mean. The one I mentioned earlier tonight—I *met* her. And she seemed really sweet. I just didn't catch her name. I didn't think to ask. I should have. Now I feel even worse. I should have gotten her name for you. I suck at that. I'm sorry, man.||

I wanted very badly to believe the SafeSurf—not only because I wanted to believe there was a girl in the world who might be able to understand and love me, but because, apart from having just been thrashed by the adolescent son of the only male friend I'd (at least thought I'd) ever had, I'd proceeded, in the course of attempting to befriend that son, to accidentally scare him off, thereby proving to myself for the millionth time that I was even more repellent a bumbling pariah than I'd formerly imagined, which, in turn, pretty powerfully suggested that, with the exception of Blank, inans were the closest things to friends I'd ever have—and, owing to that, I doubted the SafeSurf. Its telling the truth would have been just good enough to be untrue.

"What did she look like then?" I said.

||Well, she looked like a female person,|| said the SafeSurf. ||There were mammary glands above a waist that tapered, earth-tone hair that fell past her shoulders, and she didn't have an Adam's apple. Is that any help?||

"Not really."

||How about this: I *think*, but I can't say for sure—I might just be filling in blanks here—I *think* she had different kinds of teeth than yours. Like more white-like. Not so yellow.||

"Great."

||Belt, I'm sorry. You all look pretty much the same to me—to all of us. I couldn't describe you to her any better. If she asked me right *now,* with you standing right *here,* I couldn't do much better. |Person,| I'd say. |No mammary glands. Visible ears. Mumbles in his hand.|||

"You recognized me the moment I landed on you."

||Sure I did. Your gate was open, which meant you were either her or yourself, or some human being I've never met or even heard about who can open his or her gate. Your waist didn't taper and your chest didn't bulge, so I knew you weren't her, so I thought you might be you, and it turned out you were. Which made me happy. It *makes* me happy. It's been too long, Belt.||

"I come here almost every day," I said.

||Well then my feelings are a little bit hurt because I'm here every second of every day, and you've had your gate closed to me since when? When's the last

time we talked? Months ago, Belt. And here I thought I was different. I guess I might as well be the tank as far as you're concerned.||

"Hey, that's not fair."

||I know, I know. You can't control your gate. I'm not really offended. I know you don't think I might as well be the tank. But I guess what I'm getting at is that you told me you hated me a few minutes ago, and, given how rarely we end up being able to talk to each other, I just want to hear you say you don't hate me before this conversation ends, cause otherwise it might be another however-many months of me wondering if maybe you really do hate me. And I'm not just being selfish here, either. If I know you at all, and I think I do, the kind of satisfaction I'm asking for will save you a lot of worried feelings as well. A lot of potentially guilty feelings. I mean, I don't think you want to risk spending the next however-many months of us not being able to have a conversation regretting the lack of kindness you showed me, and maybe even feeling a little bit tortured by the thought that the reason we're not speaking over the course of those however-many months isn't, after all, because your gate is closed to me, but rather because you alienated me so much here tonight that mine is closed to you.||

"I don't hate you," I said, though maybe I did, but the SafeSurf was right: there wasn't any profit in letting it continue believing I did. And I was just so tired. I'd just had my ass kicked. And Blank was still shivering. I had to get home. Plus what was that sound from over by the slide? It had come back a couple or three minutes earlier, and it seemed to have gotten a little bit louder.

Slowly—to forgo another headrush—I rose.

"You hear that terrible *sound*?" I said. "From over by the slide?"

||I can't hear sounds that—||

"Right. I forgot." I went to the slide. The conversation was over. Maybe my gate had closed. Maybe the SafeSurf's. I didn't have the presence of mind to wonder; I was far too disturbed by what I saw before me.

In the center of the slide, colorlessly bleeding from a swollen-shut eye and a rip in its torso, a tiny, short-tailed, double-legged cure was fastened to the area of shallow dings by Band-Aids at its throat, its ankles, and its wrists. Its snout was bruised where it wasn't caved in, its whiskers uneven and singed at the ends. It was missing the claws on nearly half its digits; in their places were wet-looking scabs and dirt. And yet even as the muscles of its wrenched legs and arms twitched and bucked against its restraints, the heaving of its chest was slow and full, granting the poor, mangled cure possession of no small measure of animal grace.

I pulled off the Band-Aid that held it at the neck. It kissed the side of my finger, repeatedly, gasped a couple times, then returned to its painsong, which wasn't so awful or saccharine after all; not, at least, when you could see where it came from.

I couldn't help but see. I couldn't look away.

And it was looking right back. Its roving, open eye was the green of tart apples.

The painsong got better. Sadder, more vulnerable.

Though young, very young, barely out of its infancy, it was too old not to have already imprinted. If I saved its life—supposing that was possible—but didn't get it back to Triple-J (who I assumed was its owner), it would grieve itself to death inside a week. Yet I could only imagine that if I returned it, saved, to Triple-J, he'd torture it again.

Two of the rocks he'd thrown lay at my feet, and I found myself reaching down for the sharper one.

The cure stopped singing and shut its open eye. It pressed the swollen side of its face against the slide.

The raised tendon in its neck, jumping with strain underneath the taut skin, was too much to abide, too sublime, too much.

I wanted to soothe the cure, wanted to embrace it, to hold it closely, to grasp it firmly, to smother and destroy it once and for all.

I dropped the rock.

If it had to die anyway, why shouldn't I allow myself to overload with it? Why should I slit its fine throat with a rock if what I wanted to do was crush it in my fist? or break it in my mouth and swallow it down? or, maybe better, swallow it whole? or . . .

Dead was dead was dead was dead.

But maybe dying wasn't always just dying? There was, after all, the question of pain—how much pain one died in. But who could say whether bleeding out from the throat would hurt any less than being crushed in a fist? It could go either way. Except then, also, there was the question of terror (arguably just a subcategory of pain): even if bleeding out would hurt less than being crushed, it would take a bit longer. No doubt about that. And during the interval between the cut and the expiration, the cure, presumably, would be aware that its death was imminent; such an awareness could, I imagined, terrify the cure. I could see how that could be. And yet, I also saw how it might be a kind of blessing for the cure to possess an extra few seconds (even maybe an extra few minutes) of life in the shadow of rapidly encroaching death, some extra bit of time in which to make peace with mortality, to have final thoughts, to review, to re*live*—as the dying do in so many works of fiction—the most meaningful moments of its all-too-brief life. Which would mean that slitting its throat—

Blank.

So entranced had I been, so verging on overload, that I'd failed to even notice Blank had climbed to my shoulder until it jumped off, onto the slide. It crouched beside the tortured cure, placed a hand on its bleeding forehead, and, softly, started to harmonize with it. That just wouldn't do. I could not allow Blank to see me overload. I don't mean I'd have been ashamed to have it see me—though maybe I would have—but rather that if it saw me kill another Curio, it might become afraid of me. We might grow apart.

And, corollarily, I saw that I might also become afraid of me, for I could lose the ostensible advantage of my ignorance. Those times Kablankey had caught me off guard with an adorable new acrobatic or gag, one thing I always told myself was that overloading couldn't possibly be as exultant an experience as everyone claimed. But what if I were to find out that it was? Before my father, for my twenty-seventh birthday, bought me an evening at the brothel up the street, where a gentle-voiced, Gender Studies grad, Grete, held me in her arms and ended my virginity, I was able to believe that sex without love was overrated, maybe even unpleasant. Since then, although I'd never again had sex or returned to the brothel (I feared slippery slopes—feared that to have more loveless sex, commodified or no, would somehow decrease, or even annihilate, my chances of ever finding true love), my desire to have sex with someone I loved only grew more desperate, for, given how great it had been *without* love, I could only assume . . . And Blank—Blank was very likely the most adorable cure in the world, so if overloading on the tortured cure were, in the end, to live up to the hype, the thought of overloading on Blank, in the analogy I'm trying to draw here, would (maybe, at least) come to seem, just as the thought of sex with someone I loved had come to seem in the wake of Grete, even more appealing. And it would become harder than ever—perhaps even impossible—to refrain.

At the same time, if I overloaded on the tortured cure, doing so might prove to be disappointing after all. Maybe I wouldn't like it that much. And maybe, if it did prove disappointing, it would actually strengthen my ability to resist future temptations to overload on Blank.

There was only one way to find out.

Yet I didn't.

One big advantage—or disadvantage, depending on your angle—to having second thoughts is the way they lead you to have third and fourth ones. Fifth and sixtieth and seven hundredth ones. They pile on, and draw attention to themselves, away from their objects, distance the immediate, slow things down.

I wasn't even looking at the cure anymore. My eyes were on my hands, on the Quill in the one held up to my lips, and the Bic in the other held under the Quill, and I ignited the Quill, and the Bic made a sound, that sound

Bics make, which admen, for ages, have claimed to be *flick*, but is, as anyone who's lit a Bic knows, duosyllabic—there's the scrape of the sparkwheel (that's where the stress falls), followed by the clack of the fuel fork's release—and that sound, dear reader, sounds a lot like *CHAD-kyle*. To me it does at least. Or did that one time, that night on the playground.

And to think of Chad-Kyle was to think of Tiddleywinks—that cure at the end of his golden fob, that cure that didn't care to rush to his hand—and the PerFormula he'd fed it, the one he'd tried to sell me—Freedom! Not Freedom, but rather Independence.

The following morning, when I would go to the bank to return Lotta's money, I could buy some Independence PerFormula from Chad-Kyle, dose the tortured cure with it, and if the Independence worked like he'd said, the cure could live free of Triple-J's specific warmth (or that of whomever it had in fact imprinted on) for who-knows-how-long—indefinitely, maybe, assuming the supply of Independence were steady—but long enough in any case that putting the poor thing out of its misery right then and there had ceased to be a moral imperative.

I had to try to save it.

Kablankey had already removed the Band-Aid that bound the ankles. I removed the other two, cupped my hand, and the cure slid gently down into my palm, struggled up onto its hands and knees, then backward-crawled, slowly, a couple of inches. It straightened its legs out against my forearm, and, hugging my wrist, pressed a cheek to my pulse.

TOE

ONE SATURDAY MORNING NEAR the start of eighth grade, my father roused me early to try a Cajun breakfast joint he'd heard about the previous night at the tavern. The joint had just opened, and his friends had all been there. They raved about the sausage, but bitched about the crowds. Mal Vaughn said he'd had to queue for an hour before his family of three got a table. Clyde's tolerance for lines was little better than a rabbit's, as low as his love for strong sausage was deep, and the joint was a twenty-minute drive northeast, in Deerbrook Park, off Sanders Way, so I wasn't given time to wake Blank, or even wash.

I gargled Scope while I emptied my bladder, misted my pits with scent til they dripped. My feet I socked and shod in the Bronco.

We were served our hyped meat well ahead of the rush, along with poached eggs, cheesed hash browns, and toast. The food was, if anything, a little overcooked, and my dad, although he was disappointed—"That sausage," he'd said, once we'd left, "was *mild*—what in the fuck is wrong with my friends?"—did not get sick, so the corruption I swallowed had probably been borne by an unclean finger someone dipped in my plate, rather than by any of the intended ingredients.

It would take a few hours for the poisoning to peak, but the earliest symptoms came on pretty quick. Since the joint was near Khron's, our favorite German deli, we stopped to buy black bread, cold cuts, and beer. As the stubble-wattled counterman sliced our smoked beef, he chattered away, trading familiar cracks with my father, jocular insults and puns about meat, and I came to understand he hated his life. That glint in his eyes wasn't mischief: it stung him. With every pull of the sawblade, he fought the compulsion to mutilate himself, maybe even end it all. Short of that, all he wanted was to lie on his side, by a low-wattage lamp, and cry, and cry. What I couldn't tell was whether the jabbering hilarity he faked for Clyde's benefit was helping fend his pain off, or making it worse, but the question seemed important. It seemed more important than just about anything. I had no idea I'd eaten poison, and although my psychic insights did feel real, no less real than the voices of inans, their invasive quality—the novelty of it, of knowing things without knowing how I knew them—led me to suspect they weren't real, that I was going crazy, or a new kind of crazy. I turned from the counterman, looked at my father, and saw much the same thing—a desperate man barely holding it together. That twisted upper lip of his: it wasn't just toughguy wiseass stuff. It wasn't, as I'd always previously assumed, only there to keep you out; it was there to keep whatever was behind it intact. And what was behind it? I didn't want to know. I didn't want to wonder. It seemed important not to. It seemed more important than just about anything.

I went outside, took a breath of autumn air, shivered a little, and lit up a Quill. Within a couple drags, I was back to normal. Or maybe not really. Had I gone back to normal, I'd have worried about what the episode meant, and I wasn't worried, just full-body tired. Sluggish. Syrupy. I wanted to sleep.

But I couldn't sleep yet. We had to go to the mall. As long as we were near it, and I needed new shoes, and my father new jeans (his iron-on patches, like my thinning rubber soles, were coming unglued), we might as well, my father said, stop at Deerbrook Park Mall. He jerked his chin at the Quill in my hand—he'd never, to my knowledge, seen me smoking before—and said he thought smoking was a bad idea, "for all the reasons they tell you at school, and plus it's expensive, and the prices only rise," and left it at that. He didn't raise his voice, or invoke my mother, and it wasn't, I don't think, for any lack of love or parenting instinct that he ceased to press. I think he figured, correctly, that there was nothing he could say to get me not to smoke, if for no other reason than that the seven-month-going-on-forever-long absence of the woman we'd both loved most in the world was a fact from which smoking could reliably help one get briefly distracted. It was something we shared, this distraction strategy, and perhaps without his having known til just then. And on top of that, of course, this dead woman we loved, this wife and mother, had been a rather heavy smoker herself, and we remembered her as such, at least in large part. To picture her in motion was mostly a matter of recalling the way she handled her Quills, the way she'd turn her body to block the wind rather than cupping the flame when she lit them, the way she switched her grip from index-middle to index-thumb when the burn met the feather stamped over the filter, the way her exhalations got louder when she drove, and the way she coned the cherries against the curves of ashtrays while listening intently to whatever often petty, too occasionally kind, and always lamentably mortal information we thought we should convey to her about what we had done or what we would do or what we might want from her or who we might be.

She had liked, a lot, to smoke, my mother, and it wasn't what had killed her. It was something that had helped her to enjoy not being dead. If I'm reluctant to insist that by way of smoking cigarettes we communed with her spirit, it's only because none of us—least of all her—believed in spirits.

So I appreciated my father's decision not to press. I admired it, even. We had an understanding, something in common. I was sluggish? Felt syrupy? I'd seen a chatty counterman verging on suicide? Well, whatever. If my father wanted to take me to the mall, I would let my father take me to the mall, and he would—and did—let me smoke in the truck on the way to the mall.

It was the tongues of some Jordans displayed on a dais in the Foot Locker window that announced the next symptom: the reflective white around the Jumpman logos appeared to be swelling, squeezing the Jumpman. I squinted, attempting to make the swelling stop, but all the squinting did was cause venous lines of purple iridescence to bulge from the tongue, somehow ringing my fillings, which wasn't, this ringing, strictly speaking, unpleasant. It tickled a little. I remember thinking the following words: "The depths of this silver." And then I was clammy.

I don't know if that happened before or after I regrettably asked for the Agassi Air Techs with the marbled pink panels and tiny black swishes—shoes that my father, until I outgrew them, refused to replace (less, I would think, because he was a skinflint than because he so relished coming up with new names for them; my Swishies, my Fagassis, my Likey Cutey Boots, my Fagassi Swish Techs, my Fagassi Fairy Techs, my Likey Fagassis, my Fagassi Air Pinks, my Pinky Swish Boots, countless other derivations)—nor do I recall my dad buying his Wranglers.

The next thing I remember is listing in bed, so dizzy and depleted that flipping the pillow cooler-side-up took planning, drained strength, and indicated thusly that to cuddle Kablankey against my bare chest—which, apart from not feeling the way I was feeling, which is to say *poisoned,* was the only thing I actively wanted to do—to cuddle Kablankey would be impossible. Just the thought of raising my arm to reach for the PillowNest brought on vertigo.

I passed out for hours. When I woke, the sky in the window was navy, I was gushing with sweat, abundant with need, and I ruined my boxers as I ran the eleven steps to the bathroom to sit on the toilet and puke in the tub.

I hadn't thrown up in a number of years—not since Jim tore the face off that fish—and I'd never once shat myself outside diapers. The trauma was manifold, disgust upon pain upon fear upon shame, and it lasted for hours, wrecking multiple garments and pieces of linen, freeing my GI tract of every last graspable particle and hope. Once it was over, I slept through til Sunday, a little past noon. With an acid-ravaged throat, and limp, trembling muscles, I managed to brush my teeth and shower—my father must have cleaned the bathroom while I'd slept—and then, still in towels, had another night's sleep before Sunday night had even started to fall.

I dreamed of a Jumpman squeezed by a tongue til its dunking arm snapped in very slow motion. I woke sitting up, opened the PillowNest, and found Blank grieving, lying there prone, head under elbows, hiccupping wildly. We'd been out of contact for nearly two days. I knew, of course, what the hiccupping meant, and I thought another cure could be a nice thing to have, but Blank's suffering, however admittedly adorable, looked so harrowing, and Blank so defeated—chunks of velvet had fallen from the stripe on its back, its neck appeared scaly, and, though I sang-sung its name in ever-sweeter tones, it wouldn't stand up, or even show me its face—I could not, in good conscience, let it keep grieving, much less for all the hours that cloning would require. I picked it up and cupped it against my bare chest and, within a few minutes, the hiccupping stopped. Blank hummed a couple bars from its pain-song's opening, then, twice, told me, "Anks," which is how it said, "Thanks," which was one of the only words it knew—a word I hadn't deliberately taught it—and by which it meant "Please," having learned to associate the sound of "Thanks" with the making of requests, rather than with the fulfillment of them.

"Anks," Blank said, and I took that to mean, "Please feed and water and continue to hang with me," and so I filled its thimble, gave it a pellet, and we stayed up late playing Box with the Shoelace, Rock Paper Scissors, and Make This Face. Its skin reacquired its smoothness by morning, and by the end of the week the stripe on its back was no longer patchy.

The only other time I ever saw Blank grieve was ten or so years later when I accidentally OD'd on Risperdal. *OD'd* sounds dramatic. It wasn't dramatic. About a month into my soon-to-be-failed attempt to become a normal citizen, I thought that, maybe, if I doubled my dosage, the inans in the lobby of the Wheelatine Palace would quiet down for good and I'd learn to love work, like work, or not dread work. I swallowed the pills right after dinner, went to bed early, slept twenty hours, drank a glass of water, went back to bed, and didn't rise again til well past midnight. The symptoms Blank displayed when next I opened its PillowNest were the same as the last time: major hiccups, patchy stripe, scaly neck, stricken mien. I wouldn't swear they manifested less severely this second time (though that would stand to reason, given that this overdose episode had kept us out of contact for only about two-thirds the number of hours the previous, i.e. the food-poisoning, one had), but I seem to recall the hiccups being fewer and farther between, and Blank's healthy pallor's recovery more rapid. I do admit my memory here is a little bit iffy—I was, after all, still fairly stewing in antipsychotics—and so I suppose it's possible that Kablankey's claws had also been afflicted by the grief, but, if so, they couldn't have really been *too* afflicted. They certainly weren't bleeding. I'd remember that for sure.

I've described here the times I witnessed Blank grieve not in order to *excuse* the mistakes I made with Triple-J's cure once I got it back home, but rather to simply account for those mistakes and, perhaps, mitigate my culpability a little. It isn't just that my experience with grieving cures was less extensive than most American toddlers', nor just that I hadn't read the manual since childhood, but that Blank's style of grief—the style of grief I was, naturally, most alert to—had never entailed any (memorable) damage to its claws. I know now, of course, that the state in which I found the claws of Triple-J's cure, claws I'd assumed to have been smashed and pried by a Yacht (if not more than one Yacht) in the course of inflicting a medieval torture . . . I know my first thought on seeing the devastation of the poor thing's claws should have been that it was grieving and would soon attempt to clone. I know that likely would have been your first thought, whoever you are, and I assure you that had it been my first thought—or my tenth or my hundredth—I would have approached my ministrations differently.

Namely, I wouldn't have taped the cure's ribs, three of which I had discovered broken, while I cleaned and dressed its more obvious wounds. It's not as if rib-taping had always been something I longed to do. I was, truth be known, hesitant to do it. Though I believed, and still believe, I understood the basic principle—to minimize how much they shift around—I didn't really know *how* to tape ribs, and, on top of that, the cure, when it saw the Band-Aids I'd originally intended to use for the taping, backed away so fast it fell in the sink, stubbing its tail, afraid, I would guess, that I was planning to bind it to a slide and stone it.

I improvised with gauze and self-stick postage. Once I was finished, it breathed more evenly, stopped clutching at its chest, and didn't seem, when it inhaled, to wince as hard as it previously had. Still, I was nervous I may have taped it incorrectly, and I monitored it closely for signs thereof while Blank taught it Dance This Dance and Peekaboo. Its condition didn't seem to worsen, and after an hour or so of observation, I heard my father coming through our front door. Not wanting to have a sentimental conversation—my father, whenever he returned from the brothel, would, if he happened to find me awake, try to get heart-to-hearty—I turned off the lights, and set the cures in the PillowNest. They spooned in a corner and closed their eyes. I shut the lid, and went to bed, myself.

Next morning, as I'm sure you've long since deduced, I discovered the younger cure had died in the night. It was lying on its back, some inches from Blank, its eyes half-shut and its mouth wide-open. The reproductive pearl on which it had strangled—the ovumseed my tape job had left it unable to gather the necessary wind to eject—winked from the base of its lolling tongue, gleaming and smooth as a brand-new milktooth.

Blank had never been near a dead cure before that. It hadn't been near many living ones, either. Triple-J's had been the first with which it shared a PillowNest. Under the impression the corpse was just sleeping, Blank initially tried to rouse it with a catcall, then a light cuddle, and then a more vigorous, shoulder-rubbing cuddle. This was not a happy moment. Something needed doing. What I did—I don't quite know why—was offer Blank a pellet. I guess I was trying to pretend all was well, just another normal morning, time to get fed. And maybe I should have separated them. Maybe I should have removed the dead cure the very moment the fact of its death became known to me. Or removed Blank.

Then again, maybe not, because what happened next was truly weird, perhaps unique—I surely hadn't heard of it happening before—and, in some ways, also kind of beautiful. What happened was that Blank, which had taken the pellet out of my palm, attempted to feed it to Triple-J's cure, and, in the process of doing so—while pressing the pellet to the corpse's bottom lip—spotted the pearl, dropped the pellet, reached two fingers inside the corpse's mouth, and, slowly, gently, extracted the pearl. And I haven't even gotten to the kind of beautiful part yet.

The kind of beautiful part, which was, to be certain, also very weird, was that Blank—a cure that, remember, hadn't been grieving, hadn't grieved at all in nearly ten years, and had never once grieved for long enough to mouth-eject—treated the dead cure's pearl as its own. It hiccupped until it spat pinkly on the surface, then rubbed the spit in, blew the spit dry, hiccupped, spit, rubbed, blew . . . the whole second-phase reproductive banana. A couple hours later, having finished the shell, Blank removed the thimble of water from the ovumslit, replaced it with the ovum, and went back to sleep. I had already—while Blank was busy, and perhaps making history—hidden the dead cure's body in the sock drawer, found the old manual under my bed, in the same locked box that held all my photos and videos of Blank, and read the section on cloning, and the FAQs. The possibility of a cure producing the shell of another cure's ovum wasn't even mentioned. The only pertinent advice the manual offered was:

> If you'd like the ovum to hatch, all you need to do is follow the steps described above, in the section entitled HATCHING YOUR BOTIMAL®.
>
> If you don't care to hatch another BOTIMAL®, simply cuddle your BOTIMAL® so it can't see what you're doing, and dispose of

> the ovum the way you would a rear ejection. Whether or not your BOTIMAL® will remember the ovum—if it even knew it WAS an ovum—we can't say for sure. What's certain, however, is that your BOTIMAL® won't miss the ovum. It will continue to behave as it always has, like a *flesh-and-bone robot that thinks it's your friend®*.

Even if a cure could hatch from such an uncommonly (perhaps uniquely) generated ovum, I knew I didn't want another. What if it died? The sadness and frustration I'd felt when I'd discovered the dead one that morning had, it's true, been relatively light and quickly overcome by this new sense of wonder Blank's behavior had inspired, but it was just the kind of thing that could happen only once—the wonder, not the frustration and sadness (which, had I known the dead cure longer, would have, I imagined, been all the more powerful)—and plus it had already started to fade. Already I was feeling a little annoyed that I'd have to dig a hole in which to bury the corpse. Or maybe it's more accurate to say I was annoyed because of how I *didn't*, in fact, have to dig a hole—I'd seen countless cures in gutters and trash cans, all of us have—but would dig a hole anyway, from a sense of obligation that no one else shared, sentimental psychotic that I am.

I cuddled Kablankey inside my shirt and removed the ovum, and, partly from the fear that the manual was wrong—that Blank *would* miss the ovum, and so wouldn't, thereafter, continue to behave as it always had—though mostly because the ovum was a rarity (if not a uniquity), I didn't flush it. I stuck it in the box beside the old manual.

Blank, when I returned it to the nest, didn't behave as if anything were off, let alone missing, but it did seem tired, so I whispered it to sleep, and, considering the calories it must have expended on making the shell, I set an extra pellet beside its thimble before I closed the lid and pulled the corpse from the drawer.

•

• •

I chose a spade from the wall of our backyard shed, and dug in the shade of our weeping willow. When, a couple feet down, the spade struck a root, I removed the dead cure, which I'd shrouded in a sock, from the pocket of my cargos, and interred it supine, head to the east. All of this took just fifteen minutes. A gesture to induce a sense of closure seemed needed. I wasn't about to start talking to the corpse, though, let alone the sky, plus I wasn't really sure how I felt about closure, wasn't too sure closure even existed. I lit up a Quill, and missed my mother, and thought about closure. "Closure," I thought. "To have it, to feel it. Closure, closure . . ." At best it was one of those words, like *mind,* thats meaning squirmed with increasing vigor at each of your attempts to pin it down. Each of my attempts to pin it down, at least. No shortage of people seemed to know it when they saw it—like *art,* or *porn*. Like *self,* or *life*. Maybe my problem with closure was me. My weirdo mind. But if closure *were* more than a bankrupt concept gurus in neckties advanced to sell books, no gesture, I concluded, should have a better shot at inducing one's sense of it than filling a grave.

I packed the dirt tight, returned the spade to the shed. When I came back out, my father was there, on the patio steps, holding a steaming mug and squinting.

"Are you sick?" I said.

"Do I look sick?" he said.

"You aren't at work. You're drinking something hot."

"Just woke up. Plus it's Saturday," he said.

"I forgot," I said.

"Yeah, speaking of *forgot,* I hope you're better at remembering which hook you took that spade from than you are at remembering to lock the shed door."

I had locked the shed door. "It's locked," I said.

"Sure," said my father. "I can see it's locked *now,* but it wasn't while you did whatever you were doing with my spade over there for however long you did it."

"No one would've broken in while I was standing in sight of it."

"I didn't say they would. I'm talking about habits. The more often you fail to lock the shed when you leave it, the more likely you are to forget to lock the shed."

"Maybe," I said.

"Trust me," he said.

"I trust you," I said.

"Don't get all autistic. I'm fucking with you, Billy. Lighten up. Take it easy. What were you doing out back here, anyway? With the spade, I mean."

"Digging. Backfilling."

"Yeah, no shit, but that's not what I meant."

"Lighten up. Take it easy."

"So, alright. Touché. You want to hang out?"

"Hang out?"

"Like brunch or something."

"Since when do we brunch?"

"My friends are all fishing."

"Since when do *you* brunch?"

"I've still got the week off."

"I'm going to the bank."

"I didn't know you banked."

"Did I say that I banked?"

"I thought it was implied and, tell you the truth, there's no way I can imagine, given you just told me you were going to the bank, that I shouldn't have thought that. So either you're working some kind of deadpan humor thing I'm failing to get where you're impersonating maybe like a gumshoe or something, or you're just fucken *weird*."

"Apple and the tree."

"*This* tree banks."

"I lack a response."

"Last night, right before I left the brothel," said my father, "I bought a cure off this cuddlefarmer at the bar. She said it was two, but it looked a lot older. Maybe even four. I caught a good deal, and I was thinking, at the time, we'd dact it together, you and me, I mean. I was thinking all kinds of bondy, father-son thoughts."

"At the brothel."

"So what? Don't interrupt. I bought it, brought it home, set it down on the table, and then I went upstairs to invite you to join me, but your lights were out, and the farmer, when I bought it, she said it would keep. She guaranteed a minimum of forty-eight hours before it started grieving, so I figured, you know, I'd wait til tomorrow, which that would be today, but then, when I went back down to put it in the drawer, like, *right* when I was about to pick it up off the table, it did this kinda thing, like . . ." He stood, stepped off the patio, performed a quick tap dance. "So it did that," he said, and did it again, "and then it said—I swear to you—it said, 'Ta-da!' You ever seen anything like that? I mean, not on TV? It was so adorable, Billy. It was just too much. Make a long story short, I couldn't even get it to my mouth in time. I mean, I was so blown away, I think I deactivated it without even realizing. It was like my fist *itself* went into overload, like separate from me."

"Were you drunk?"

"A little, probably, but not *that* drunk. Anyway, I just wanted you to know I was thinking of you. It doesn't seem that important right now, but it did last night, so I figured: honor that. I figured: mention it. Can't hurt to mention to your son that you thought of him."

"Thanks for thinking of me," I said.

"Is that sincere, or are you doing the gumshoe voice? I can't tell."

"Me neither," I said.

"We should work on that."

"On what?"

"I don't know. Forget it. I don't like this conversation, but I miss your mom, you know? I mean, you *do* know. That's the thing. You're the only one who knows except for me. Why can't we just be normal about it?"

"Normal how?"

"Get drunk and go fishing and have gratitude for each other's company or whatever. By a fire. Roasting the fish we caught on a fire we built together, and, like, understanding."

"Understanding what?"

"How lonely and ugly everything is? But that it didn't used to be like that? That it was fine before she died?"

"I understand that, sometimes."

"And then you forget, right?"

"I can't help it."

"I can't help it either. And what does that make us?"

"Assholes," I said. "Like everyone else. But all this is, Dad, is you went to the brothel. Sleeping with prostitutes makes you sad."

"Don't moralize at me."

"I'm not."

"You just told me sleeping with prostitutes make you sad, like, 'Of course you're sad. You just engaged in an evil activity.'"

"I said it makes *you* sad. Not *one,* but you."

"What?" He had a Quill lipped, but he didn't have a lighter. I tossed him mine.

"I'm saying," I said, "I was making an observation, not accusing you of anything."

"Oh," he said. "And so what were you doing with my spade?" he said.

"I have to get going."

"I'll dig up whatever it was you buried."

"Out of my hands."

"You didn't!" he said.

"Didn't what?"

"You did! Holy shit!"

"I don't know what you're talking about."

"But why would you do that? Bury it, I mean? I guess you don't like to swallow them, but . . . Is it outta spite you buried it? I mean, it must be, right? It must be spite. It must be you buried it so I'd see you bury it, and then I'd *know* that you didn't share. Except the thing is that maybe . . . Maybe that's the sunny side, huh? Not the *sunny* side, but, yeah—the sunny side. Because maybe I deserve it. Maybe we both do. Maybe that's justice. I mean that, Billy. I'm having a moment, here. I'm not mad you didn't share. Usually I'd be mad, but I didn't share, either. My intentions were to share, and then it did that ta-da thing, which, another man, or maybe even me on another day might've thought, 'Oh, this cure's really gonna make for a great overload experience for me to have with my son, and I'm so looking forward to tomorrow morning, gee whiz!' but instead I dacted it all by myself, didn't wait til the morning, and then there's you, who didn't wait for me to do the one you buried. So that's what I get for not being a better dad. Or that's what you get for not being a better son. In this justice scenario I'm talking about. We're evey-steves, I'm suggesting. Eye for an eye. I guess the only question is: Who did the deed first? If it was you, I'm a little more justified, maybe. If I did it first, though, you're a little more justified. What time did you do it?"

"I have to get going."

"Or actually, no. Maybe it doesn't matter who did it first because neither of us knew til now that the other one did anything. Eve to the Steve, the whole damn way. I love you, kid. We've got a connection. A mystical connection. Kismetic timing. How old was yours? Was it two, but looked four? That would be something."

"It was twenty-five," I said.

"Ha! I'll dig the thing up, Billy. You know that, right? I'll dig it right up."

"Knock yourself out."

"Smile for chrissakes."

"I'm smiling," I said.

"That just isn't true."

He made his way toward the shed, and I to my room. As we passed one another, he handed me my lighter.

•

•　　　•

Having spent so much energy forming that marbleshell, Blank's need to replenish its nutrients was paramount and, although never shy about eating in front of me—apart from rear-ejection production, it wasn't shy about anything, I don't think—Blank liked to be "awakened" when I opened its nest, and would, as soon as I'd remove the lid, drop whatever it might be doing, close its eyes, and pretend to sleep, so when I heard, upon my return to my room, the munches and glugs of pellet-mastication that were coming through the vents of the PillowNest's walls, I, so as not to delay Blank's nourishment, waited on my bed for the noises to cease. I didn't have to wait long—maybe five minutes—but still I assumed that when I opened the lid both pellets I'd left would be inside Blank, and the thimble empty.

Not so on either score, however. Nor was Blank fake-asleep. Eyes glassy, though wide and anticipatory, it was sitting, cross-legged, next to the thimble, which was nearly half-full, and an untouched pellet.

"Eat the pellet," I said, pointing to the pellet.

Blank pointed to the other side of the nest, to the spot on which the dead cure had been lying, and whistled, "Fweep," i.e. the first (stressed) note of the three-note wolf-whistle most readily associated with hard-hatted men (also the last stressed note of that other famous three-note whistle, the one used to communicate, "Hey, I'm right over here"). In our shared, environmentally overdependent, and, admittedly, quite limited language, *fweep* meant "the thing/s to which I am referring." In this case, then: "The Curio that slept over last night," or, more likely, "What about the Curio that slept over last night?"

I responded, "Fwee-oo," the second (stressed) and third (unstressed) note of the wolf-whistle (also the first and second of the "over here" whistle), which meant "I'm informing you about the thing/s to which you are referring," and, given that I paired my *fwee-oo* with a backward thumbing of the air above my shoulder, here meant, I hoped, "The Curio who slept over last night went away," rather than "The Curio who slept over last night is no longer alive."

Again, Blank whistled, "Fweep," though this time without pointing.

I shrugged because I didn't know what Blank meant.

Blank shrugged back.

I pointed at the pellet, *fweeped,* drew an arc through the air from the pellet to Blank while *fwee-oo*-ing, and repeated the latter whistle-gesture combination another few times til Blank picked up the pellet and took a healthy bite. This seemed to me to indicate it wasn't upset about whatever news it believed I'd conveyed regarding Triple-J's cure, and I put it in its sleeve while it continued to eat, filled the sleeve's dropper at the bathroom sink, and left for the bank.

• • •

The weather called for shorts and a lightweight T-shirt, and I was wearing shorts and a midweight T-shirt. My swollen kidneys were still a bit tender, and my lower back yellow and grayish-green, but I probably would have guessed, if I hadn't known better, that their stomping had happened two or three days before, rather than only the previous evening. On top of all that, the above-average warmth of the exchange with my father out in the yard had felt almost progressive, and Blank was unbroken—maybe even untouched by—that morning's potentially traumatic events. I was feeling not-bad. Uniformly okay.

When I got to the bank, Lotta Hogg had a customer—an older, shorter gentleman the hum of whose voice, if not quite the words it shaped, carried all the way across the air-conditioned lobby—but she rocked on her heels a little when she saw me, then flashed me a rather full-bodied smile comprising raised shoulders and a two-handed wave. Her enthusiasm was weirdly contagious: contagious inasmuch as it caused me to pull a silly face in response—a squinty kind of duck-mouthed, brow-flexing face I suppose I could have learned from any number of post-Fonz sitcom handsomes, and was, this face, or so I suppose, intended to communicate, with self-assured irony, something like "What? You're happy *I'm* here?"—and weirdly so, I say, because I'd never before then, nor have I ever since then, made that face, at least not as far as I'm able to recall (it was a face I'd held in contempt since adolescence), yet there, at the threshold of General TrustGroup's Wheelatine branch, I made it automatically, unknowingly at first, and didn't come alert to it til after I caught myself bending my arms to fire on Lotta from over my heart with make-believe pistols, at which point I proceeded—with success, it would seem—to camouflage the face's chachi provenance by faking a triplet of dry, dramatic sneezes.

"Gesundheit?" the guard said.

"Sure," I said. "Thanks."

"I just didn't know was it sneezes or coughing."

"A combination," I said.

"I notice you seem to have forgotten your hanky."

"I don't carry a hanky."

"Not many do. Not anymore. I bet you wish you did, though, right about now. And they coming back, you know. Handkerchiefs, I'm saying."

"No," I said.

"You telling me you don't wish you had a hanky 'bout now?"

"No," I said. "I meant that I didn't know they were back."

"Not back quite yet, but *coming* back," he said. "Sooner than you think. Gonna be how it was. Days when a man without a hanky was trash. Like a man without socks. A man without skivvies. A hanky wasn't optional. A hanky was pants."

"What happened?" I said.

"World went to hell. Lost all its decency. Gave up on manners. Combination of that, and the meteorical rise of cheap, disposable tissue in the marketplace coincides with the large-scale manufacture of little plastic packets you could carry in either a purse or rear pocket, and coincides also, *same exact time,* with widespread, overblown fears and anxieties 'bout viral survival rates, bacterial longevities, plus germinal lingerings, not to mention all the greasers with they catchy slang start calling hankies 'snot rags,' which offends the very ears, however, admittedly, fun it is to say. Perfect storm. Sank the noble hanky. Used to be a man wanted him some love he'd look for a woman who was crying at a bar or some party, maybe just a bus stop, and he'd take out his hanky, offer it to her. Let her know he sees her. Kindness of strangers. He'd offer his hanky, which carried his essence—the smell of his pocket, laundry detergent, maybe cologne he was that type of fellow—and could be she'd take it, wipe and blow, smelling that essence, and hand him back some of her fluids folded up, often accompanied by a shy apology. And now maybe he'd tell her to keep the hanky, showing her he rich enough to give away hankies, showing her he kind enough to give away hankies to those in need of hankies even though he can't afford it, or showing her he find her fluids repulsive. Then again, maybe he'd return it to his pocket, order to demonstrate that even though he rich he's keeping the hanky cause some of her's on it, or maybe letting her know the first essence-whiff's free, but the second, if she wants it, is gonna have strings, or could be he's just showing her that even in her phlegm-spraying, vulnerable state, she doesn't disgust him. Any way you cut it, there been fluids produced, essences whiffed, disgust overcome or needing overcoming. Any way you cut it, you've got ambiguity. Subtlety. Things unsaid between two people. The hallmarks, my friend, of a classy courtship. Obsolescence of the hanky was a blow to society. Dulled a man's ability, and to some extent his willingness, to read your more artfully interpersonal-type signals the better half the species tend to want to relay. More rapes, I'd wager, since hankies disappeared, and less romance discovered. More child abuse, too. Wasn't just the theater of dating got changed since the hanky's disappearance from everyday life, see. Hear everybody always talking 'bout how disgusting it is when they dad lick his thumbs and scrub at they mouths to get off some dried-out juice or milk or other type of organical crusting, but no one think twice about the father's side of things. How, first of all, who *you* know likes scrubbing buildup from another person's mouth? No one, see? It's at least as nasty to perform that act as to be subject *to* that act. At *least* as nasty. And then second, what? Considering how nasty it is to do, just think about how revolted by the buildup the dads are to begin with to feel like they gotta. If men, like the old days, carried hankies, dads'd use they hankies to scrub the buildup, or give they hankies to they children to scrub the buildup, or, even better, they children would be carrying they *own* hankies, scrub they *own* buildup, and if they was unawares of the buildup, they dads would tell them, 'Take out your hankie and scrub your damn face!' As you know, however, that's not how it is. Aint how it's been for a real long while, and dads, they busy, busy as ever, stressed out as ever, and the need to perform this nasty service—I'm telling you it sending a lot them over the top. Was hankies in play like the old days, man, the number of children could've been spared beatings? the number of dads could've been spared the guilt comes after beating children? which produces further beatings? sometimes of spouses? sometimes of pets? Boggles the mind. I don't even like to think about it. Makes me depress. But hankies coming back. The youth of today—oh, hold up— Enjoy your lunch, Mr. Baker."

"Thank you, Gus," said the manager, exiting the bank.

We didn't make eye contact, the manager and I, let alone acknowledge that we'd met the day before, and in a flash it occurred to me that, had we been wearing hats, Gus, rather than interrupting himself to speak to the manager, would have instead tipped his hat at the manager, and the manager would've tipped his hat back at Gus—or to Gus and me the both—and maybe I'd've tipped my hat in response to the manager's hat-tip. Then again, maybe I'd've tipped my hat to the manager at the same time as Gus had. Or maybe the manager would've tipped his hat to the both of us first. I wasn't all too familiar with the rituals. I'd only seen the long-lost, hat-wearing society portrayed in classic movies and prime-time dramas, and didn't know its protocols for coming and going, only that some of them concerned tipping hats, and though I'd never given much thought to how hats—to how any fashion item—might affect our everyday lives, neither in- nor directly, I found that it pleased me immensely to do so. It pleased me to wonder, for instance, whether tipping one's hat burned a greater or lesser number of calories than did the speaking of polite phrases such as "Enjoy your lunch," and it pleased me to wonder whether it was preferable to burn a greater or lesser number of calories in instances where politeness was called for. We were a fat people, we Americans, so burning more calories, on the whole, was good, but so was getting along with one another, and maybe, assuming that hat-tipping burned more calories (i.e. that it literally required more energy) than did the speaking of polite phrases—maybe men in hat-wearing times were a bit more reluctant to be polite, or a bit more resentful of the need for politeness other people's comings and goings demanded, and so maybe, toward the cause of conserving energy, men in hat-wearing times were more prone to snub one another. Maybe, on the whole, the amount of snubbing that went on, in addition to (presumably) lowering the frequency with which men got along with one another, leveled the (perhaps negligible) health advantages that would have otherwise been engendered by the custom of tipping one's hat. On the other hand, there was also a possibility that the resentment which led one man to snub another and/or the resentment a man felt toward one who'd just snubbed him burned more calories than did polite-phrase-speaking and/or, perhaps, even hat-tipping itself. There was no way to know, of course, but that wasn't the point. The point was it pleased me to consider these dynamics—I considered them all in far less time than I've taken to describe them (one second, I'd guess, two at the most), and in far greater depth, which made me feel smart—and I doubted I'd have done so had it not been for Gus and his speculative history of handkerchief-carrying.

The door swept shut behind the manager, and Gus said, "Anyways, you interested?"

"Yeah, I'm interested," I said. And I really was. I wanted to hear more, to get to know Gus better, and as Lotta was busy with a new customer anyway—the third to arrive since Gus began his monologue—I had at least a couple minutes to kill. "By all means, please continue," I said.

"Continue like how?"

"I think you were about to tell me," I said, "why the handkerchief's coming back after all these years. At least that seemed like where you were headed. But you know, if you hadn't quite gotten there yet, you shouldn't feel like I want you to rush to the point you were making. I really like listening."

"Right," Gus said. "Well, um. So, let's see, where was I . . ."

"I think you started saying something about the youth of today?"

"Oh yeah, that's right. The youth of today. Yes. Indeed. The youth of today, like Chad-Kyle, over there, working the counter—some them adopting that dapper look. Dapper's just on the upswing, I guess. But dapper aint approachable, much less *attainable,* you don't have a hankie. Hankie's essential to dapper as a belt or suspenders. As shoes made of leather. Shoes with laces. Hankyless dapperness—it's like, what? It's like a digital watch neath a cufflinked shirtsleeve. A toddler eating surf-'n'-turf. A biker wearing sandals. Top of that, the environment, man, the ecosystem: How many resources going to waste in this underhankied world? People plucking Kleenexes three at a time? often clogging toilets with them? wasting water in the process? Hankyless environmentalism—now that's a contradiction in terms right there. Today's youth know that. It simply aint *right* not to carry a hanky. Morally, I'm saying. And as for practically, well here you are, your hand all goopy—uncomfortable, I bet. And me, I'd've probably tried to shake it, I hadn't seen you sneeze. You'd've let me, maybe I'd've caught something even. Then what? Labor loss? Not-strictly-necessary antibiotics? Bacteria strengthening, growing resistant. No, man. No. The moral *and* the practical concerns intertwining, now."

"They were really dry sneezes. Barely even any mist," I said. "Still, though. I'm really into what you're saying. This whole speculative history of common things we don't usually consider. I was thinking, just yesterday, about bubblegum, how it might have come about. You ever think about bubblegum?"

“Bubblegum?”

“Yeah.”

“What’re we talking about here?”

“Things we might or, I guess, might *not* be interested in.”

“Well, no, I’m not interested in bubblegum,” said Gus. “You right about that. Sorry. It’s filthy. To me, I should say. To each they own, but to me, it’s filthy. A truly vile product. Sticks to the shoes, sticks to pavement forever. Hell on teeth. Configures chewers’ faces into wiseacre semblances. And the sounds are no good. Sound like a bog. Or a swamp. Like walking through a bog or a swamp when chewed. There’s *reasons* they kick you out of class you chewing it. Plus where’s the nutrition in bubblegum? You can’t even swallow it. I mean you *could*, but then it’s with you forever. Your bones’ll rot first. Least that’s what I’ve heard. Like maraschino cherries. And these teenage ladies cracking it in they teeth? Makes me want to just about jump out a window. Should never have been. You can’t commit to candy, I say chew a twig. Suck a shiny penny even. I like a mint. Take a Tic Tac, say. A Certs. Those peculiarly strong ones I can’t recall the brand. British ones? Packaged in a tin? I don’t know. But I got no need for bubblegum. So, no, man, no, I just aint interested. Sorry. No offense, now, though. It just isn’t for me. But getting back to these hankies. They come in white, off-white, or this other kind of white called eggwhite white. They come in sets of three, no mix-n-match, and each set’s fifteen dollars, twenty-one you want ’em monogrammed, but I need a couple days for that. Payment out front. Now, you seem like a cotton guy, so that’s the price of cottons I just quoted, but maybe I’m off cause you wearing shorts today, which is the sensible option, given the weather, but that’s not to say slacks would be *in*sensible, and maybe usually you dress a little bit spiffier, which case what you really want might be silk—”

“Well, actually—” I said, but Gus, who, all at once I understood—who, all at once I was embarrassed not to have previously understood—sought not my camaraderie so much as my cliency, didn’t seem to hear me.

“If what you really want is silk,” he cheerily continued, “then double all the costs I just said and add five, and also, so you know, silk aint available in eggwhite white, but there’s something else they calling eggshell fallow that’s a kind of nifty shade of brown exclusive to the silks. You want to see the monogrammed silks, go on up and ask Chad-Kyle. I sold him a set just a couple weeks back. His monogram’s a little, uh, different though, little crowded maybe, since it has three letters instead of just two cause it turns out Chad-Kyle’s his whole first name. I mean, more like, I guess, it’s two first names. Like he’s got a middle name on top of the Chad-Kyle. Piers or something. No, wait a minute. Kent. That’s the one. Chad-Kyle Kent Baker. Anyway, they workmanship’s solid. They came out pretty. Ask him take a look if you want.”

"I believe you," I said, "except—"

"Not a monogram man. Too flashy. I feel that. I think I would've guessed that, but it's always good to offer. Did I get you right the first time, then? About the cottons, I mean?"

"I didn't know you were selling handkerchiefs," I said.

"You funny!" he said.

"No," I said. "I really didn't know til just now."

"Just now? Just now *when*?"

"When you started quoting prices."

"What'd you think this was about?"

"Social stuff?" I said. "A couple guys talking? Starting a friendship in the unlikeliest of places?"

"Well nothing saying it couldn't be that, too."

"Really?" I said.

"Supposing you buy some handkerchiefs, of course."

"Ha!" I said.

"Yeah, ha," said Gus.

"I would," I said. "You gave such a good pitch. I mean, I didn't even know you were pitching til the end. That's how good it was. But I just can't afford it. I'm sorry, Gus. I am."

"That's alright," Gus said.

"Is it really?" I said.

"Look, man, what you want me to say?"

"That you're not angry at me."

"Okay then," Gus said, by which he may have meant nearly anything *except* "I'm not angry at you."

"You know, I really like your name," I said, and that was absolutely true, though I knew that saying so made me sound foolish. In a way, I guess I was trying to sound foolish. Not so foolish that Gus would think himself foolish for not having recognized my foolishness earlier, but just foolish enough to encourage him to believe that I hadn't wasted his time on purpose. "Gus," I yammered on, like a fool. "It's an old-timey name. A tough kind of name, but not like a bully, just straight-up tough. The name of a guy you'd never think to try to mug. A guy whose pretty sister never gets asked to dance. My dad's got one of those. I don't mean a pretty sister—like me, both my parents grew up only children. What I mean's his name's Clyde. Clyde Franklin Magnet."

"No kidding?" Gus said, unsquinting his eyes a bit, straightening his neck. "You dad's Clyde Magnet? Impeller at the plant?"

"Yeah," I said.

"I see," he said. "I used to be his supervisor, fore I retired."

"No way!" I said.

"Well, no, actually. Tell the truth, no. I mean I supervised your dad, but I didn't retire from it—plant laid me off. No shame in it, but still, I guess it feels like there's shame in it, so I called it 'retired.' Old reflex or something. Make no sense. *Now* I'm retired. As of just a couple months ago. From the mill, though, not the plant. Solid pension, good life. No shame whatsoever. I really don't know why I said that—'retired'—some twenty-some years later. Anyway, I guess you're that boy, huh?"

"Probably?" I said.

"You know what I mean. That crazy stuff in the papers a bunch of years back. With the swingsets. And then your mom. Poor lady. I really liked her. Met her once at a picnic. You too, I guess. Fourth of July. You were in a stroller. My youngest, he was maybe four, maybe five at the time, all scared of the fireworks. I thought we'd have to leave the ballfield, but you mom, she calmed him down, convinced him the rockets only *seemed* like they was close. Or maybe he only pretended to be convinced. She was a very pretty woman, if you don't mind my saying. I think little Israel may've just been charmed into faking up some bravery in order to impress her. I remember thinking that. I remember admiring the both of them that night. Anyway, she was a good lady. A real charming person, always seem to be interested in what someone had to say. And so you name's, uh—it's Cuff, right?"

"Belt," I said.

"Yeah, you the one."

"Thanks for telling me about the fireworks," I said.

"Oh, I was just remembering. You doing better now than you was back when? Seem like you must be. You seem alright."

"I wrote a book," I said. "Did you hear about that?"

"I didn't," said Gus.

"A novel," I said. "*No Please Don't*. That's the title."

"That's something. I never met a real author before. Can I buy it somewhere?"

"It's out of print."

"Oh."

"I can bring you one, though," I said.

"How much?"

"Free. I've got a box of them."

"Signed?"

"Sure."

"That's not fair. I'll trade you three hankies, cotton, no monograms."

"Deal," I said.

"Alright," said Gus. "Say hi to your father for me, huh?"

"I will," I said. "I'll see you later, Gus."

•
• •

After having said goodbye, it would've been awkward to keep on standing there, so even though I saw, when I turned away from Gus, that Lotta was busy with yet another customer, I made my way farther into the bank. Chad-Kyle was manning the next station over, customer-free, elbows up on the counter, swinging his fob to and fro before his eyes. Three Curios dangled from its golden clasp by rubberband leashes affixed to their collars. Fighting strangulation, they tried to climb the air—pedaling their legs, reaching, grasping—and their knees caught repeatedly in one another's crotches, their fingers in one another's nostrils and mouths.

"Hey, Chad-Kyle," I said.

"Oh hi there," he said. He unpinched the fob, dropped the cures on the counter. "Bet you've never seen this one performed before."

The cures, on their backs, sniffling and gasping, rocked side to side, rolled onto their bellies. Tiddleywinks, the one I'd previously met, hastily started to crawl in my direction. The other two, apparently not Independenced, went the opposite way, toward Chad-Kyle's hand, which was resting near the edge of his side of the counter. The rubberband leashes went taut, stretched long. The Curios' converse advances slowed, and, as they groaned through their noses, popeyed and panting, threadlike tendons strained their neck skin til, suddenly, Tiddleywinks, which was all but stationary, lost its traction and slingshot backward, snout over keister, blurring past the other two, colliding whole-bodied with Chad-Kyle's knuckles.

He wiped them on his trousers.

Tiddley lay stunned, or dead, on the counter.

The wakeful members of the chain gang painsang.

Chad-Kyle said, "How boss was *that*?"

"I don't know," I said.

"Is that because you're disabled?"

"I don't understand the question."

"I'm asking if maybe it's because of the same mental illness that prevents you from being an independent adult that you don't think that was boss."

"Maybe in a way?" I said, neither able to determine—owing to his blasé, uptalky tone—whether Chad-Kyle's question were intended to insult me, nor whether he'd be any less despicable if it weren't.

"What way?" he said.

"It's just never really been my kind of thing," I added, neutrally.

"*What* hasn't been your kind of thing? History? Witnessing history's never been your 'thing'? Dude, that's your disability talking for sure. What just happened—it's never happened before. Not unless another Independence beta tester/demonstrator came up with it in the last few days or whatever, or one of the PerFormulae Abuse Labs Brothers, or . . . what? I mean, who else could have? Some R&D science nerd at Graham&Swords? Those are the only three possibilities, and I truly doubt all of them. Me aside, beta tester/demonstrators don't think outside the box—I've met a bunch of them by now, so believe me: I know. As for the P.A.L. Bros, yeah, they're sharp enough to think outside the box, for sure—they're the *best*—but they hardly ever think outside the box using props. Like, when's the last time you saw them use props? that KarateHands segment back in 2011, with the mini plywood boards? I mean, they do work with props, I'm not saying they don't, but hardly ever, I'm saying, do they work with props. Plus, seeing how Independence won't be out for another few weeks, I doubt Graham&Swords even sent the Bros their samples yet, right? So that leaves us, last and massively least, with the G&S R&D nerds, which: really? Come on. Come *on*. Don't make me laugh. Scientists just aren't that good at creative. They never have been. Like, take that old story about the dynamite, right? About the soldier with the dynamite—the one who first thought to use it in war . . . I can't remember his name . . . It's . . ."

As Chad-Kyle thinkily stared at the ceiling, Lotta's customer headed for the exit. Lotta removed her nameplate from the counter, offered me a wink and a just-a-minute finger, then vanished through the door in the wall behind her station.

"Do *you* remember his name?" said Chad-Kyle.

"I don't think I even know the story," I said.

"Oh, you should, though. It's an important story because check it out: Before this soldier I'm talking about came up with the idea to use it in war, dynamite was only used for construction purposes, like to blow up mountains and forests and stuff. *That's* what it was invented for. But then this soldier comes along—not a scientist, this soldier, just a creative personality—and he's like, 'Guys, we can kill lots of people at once with dynamite, so duh, let's use it in this war we're fighting,'—this was World War I if I'm not mistaken, and that guy was on *our* side, thank God, so the Nazis lost. And it's because of that discovery that the scientist who *invented* dynamite killed himself, cause here he was, just a nerd in a lab who made a truly amazing new tool of war for the good guys, but yet he didn't have the creative spirit needed to realize that's what it was best for. He was too busy trying to figure out the fastest way to clear mountains and trees for dams and farms and skyscrapers, you know? And so he blamed himself a little—well, a lot—for not originally selling dynamite as a weapon, and eventually he got convinced it was his fault World War I took so long, since if he hadn't confused everyone by telling them that his dynamite was for construction purposes, someone might have figured out earlier that it was great for killing the enemy, and then a lot less guys on our side would've wound up dead at the hands of the Germans. So that sucked for the scientist. Obviously, right? But the silver lining of the story—and it's a big and thick and shiny one—is that even though he killed himself, he willed it in his suicide note that all the money he'd earned off dynamite patents should be used to fund a little thing you might have heard of called the Pulitzer Prize, which, every year, goes to the most creative people and helps them keep their most unique and personal creative juices flowing. Anyway, I'd be exaggerating if I said that that slingshot performance I just engineered these cures into doing was as important as discovering the usefulness of dynamite on the battlefield, which changed the face of war forever, but to say that I conceived of the performance from the same kind of unique place of creativity inside my mind that was accessed by that brilliant soldier inside *his* mind when he had his Topeka moment—to say *that* would not be an exaggeration at all."

"I'm not sure you've got your facts right," I said, "about dynamite."

"*Right* is a pretty strong word there, hombre. It's the opposite of wrong. But the facts are subjective anyway, so that's not really the point. What I'm trying to tell you is that you've witnessed history here and you should be more psyched. Next time I see the marketing liaison, I'm gonna have these cures do the same performance for her that they just did here for the very first time on this counter, and dollars-to-donuts that when it comes time to start gearing up for the initiation to begin the launch of the rollout to advertise the premiere of Independence's debut, she's gonna ask permission—and maybe even pay me—to tape these cures, or three others just like them, performing this performance so Graham&Swords can use it in commercials. You know what that would mean? Millions of people—millions of Independence-buyers—will one day be having their own cures perform the same performance. Like remember how, in that one commercial for BullyKing, the hobunk takes that little baseball bat from the cure? Do you even understand that, before that, they didn't even make little baseball bats for cures, except for just the once as a prop so they could shoot that commercial? But the commercial was so successful that everyone who bought BullyKing wanted to relive the moment, live, right in the comforts of their own homes. So many millions of people wanted that so bad, and so specifically, that Graham&Swords started manufacturing those little baseball bats."

"I believe you," I said.

"You don't remember that commercial?"

"I don't watch a lot of TV," I said.

"But you've seen people with BullyKinged cures setting the whole scene up with the little baseball bats, right? I mean, you've probably done it yourself, even."

"I don't see a lot of people."

"Well all I'm trying to say to you is: trust. And by 'trust,' what I'm trying to say is: trust *me*. Turn sharply to the right and walk a little ways if you know what's good for you."

"Walk?"

"To the right."

"Why?"

"Because you're standing on the left side of history here. Metaphorically. Do you know that word? What it means, I mean?"

"What word?" said Lotta, my side of the counter now. She'd unbunned her hair and changed out of her pantsuit, into a cottony, daisy-patterned summer dress. "I wonder if I know it. Could the word be *lunch*? Hint-hint, wink-wink. Who I'm hinting at while winking is you, Sir Magnetus."

"Hey, Lotta," I said. "I just came by to pay you back from yesterday. My dad returned early from his trip to Michiana, so I've got all the money I need."

"And you came just in time! I'm starving my ample ass off here. You're gonna come out to lunch with me, okay? My treat. But you'll pay—we'll use the dough I lent you. It'll be *our* treat. Don't say no. You cannot say no."

I didn't see how I could.

"Lunch then," I said.

"Later days, homie," Lotta told Chad-Kyle.

"Wait," said Chad-Kyle, "you're not coming back?"

"It's Saturday," she said. "I'm a half-day Hogg."

"I thought that was tomorrow," Chad-Kyle said.

"Tomorrow I'm off. So are you. Tomorrow being Sunday. Us working at a bank and all."

"I really wanted to show you something. It'll just take a couple minutes to set up."

"So next time. I'm starved. So's Belt. We're starved and we're going to lunch."

"No, wait," said Chad-Kyle. "I promise it's worth it. Tell her it's worth it."

I pretended not to realize he was speaking to me.

"Dude," he said to me. "That's pretty fucked-up."

"Leave Belt alone. I wouldn't wait for the second coming," said Lotta. "I just eye-dropped that spoil you sold me this morning. It's coming on fast. The munchies are flexing. And that's at least the millionth time I've talked about food in the last twenty seconds, which, if you want to know the truth, is making me more than a little self-conscious, bigger girl that I am. So don't have a tantrum. Show your thing to Gus. Or your uncle. He'll be back after lunch." To the side of her mouth, she pressed the side of her hand, and stage-whispered to me, "Boss's nephew," then grabbed my wrist and dragged me to the parking lot.

Gus tipped a make-believe hat as we passed him.

•

• •

Lotta's Beetle smelled tropical and mildly toxic. Pineapple. Coconut. Undertones of ethanol and action-figure plastic. Notes, on the exhale, of freshly popped bubblewrap. "Sorry about the *bouquet*," she said. "I just had this baby detailed. I asked the guy to mist it with new-car fragrance, but I guess they ran out, so they misted colada. Kinda made me mad, you wanna know the truth, but these little guys here, they like it so much, I might be converted. Con*ver*ted to colada!" Impersonating someone for comedic effect (Jerry Seinfeld, I think, perhaps Tony the Tiger), Lotta, while exclaiming, had finger-stabbed the air just under her chin, in the wake of which gesture the meat of her upper arm flapped around wildly.

I pushed a few laugh sounds out of my nose—my lips were pressed tight—and looked away from the arm, toward the quartet of cures (those "little guys here" to which she'd referred). They'd crawled out from somewhere under her neckline to perch on her shoulder, side by side, and each one, indeed, with its snout raised high, was sniffing at the air demonstratively.

"Ready?" Lotta said to them, and bowed toward the steering wheel. One at a time, they leapt off her shoulder, into the dash-mounted Plexiglas nest. As the last of them sat the nest's cabin-facing bench, Lotta said, "Now," and, in tandem, they gripped the roller-coasteresque harness bar and pulled it lapward until its lock clicked.

"How did you teach them to *do* that?" I said. I wasn't half as impressed as I was trying to sound—I'd witnessed cures cooperate as often as the next guy—but wanted to make up for having watched Lotta's arm flap.

"It was nothing," she said. "So easy. They're smarties. Don't you love the nest, though? It's why I bought the car. Which is dumb, I know. It should have been for the mileage, or the legroom or something. But a built-in nest! That's what really sold me. I couldn't resist—hey, you know, there's space for five on that bench if they squeeze. Yours can join them if you want."

"Same hobunk as yesterday," I said, and raised my arm, as if showing her the sleeve would corroborate the lie.

"A grapey?" she said.

“I don’t know what you mean.”

“It’s my word for purple hobunks. Grapies,” she said.

“Okay,” I said. “Yeah. Yes. It’s a grapey.”

“Pinks I call pitayas. That’s the unEnglish word for dragonfruits. Pitayas. And the meat of them’s pink. Anyway, yes: keep that little terrorist sleeved, please. And close the door already. And buckle that belt. Or should I say, ‘Buckle that belt, Magnet!’ Ha!”

“So here’s the thing about that—”

“Oh please, I mean, oh no, please don’t,” said Lotta.

I thought she’d made a joke in the vein of “belt, Magnet,” and I made a couple laugh sounds I instantly regretted.

She stuck her bottom lip out, lowered her eyes. “I was so surprised to see you, then so psyched to eat with you. Don’t you want to hang out? Don’t you want to do lunch?” she said.

I assured her I wanted to, but suggested it might be better if we walked.

“Walk?” Lotta said. She spitlessly raspberried. “Walk what for?”

“I don’t know if you should drive. If it’s safe to—”

“*Don’t know if I should* . . . Oh! That stuff I said in the bank about eye-dropping spidge oil? No worries, Beltareeno. I was lying through my chop-skies. I just wanted to get away from Chad-Kyle as fast as possible. Seriously,” she said, “I’m sober as a clam. Not a clam. You *know*. You know what I mean.”

I shut the door and buckled in. We exited the parking lot. Lotta said she wanted to play me a song. I knew I knew the song as soon as it began, but it took me til the chorus to be able to name it, so long had it been since last I’d heard it, so intensely did the sci-fi-B-movie warble of its chunky synthline evoke old dread: of nuclear assault and fallout for the most part (asymmetrical babies, molars growing in their noses; wingless robins; two-headed frogs; the daytime sky like television static), but puddles of AIDS on public toilet seats, too, and poisoned Tylenols, snack-size Snickers bars packed with staples, getting kidnapped at a toy store, tortured in a basement, dragged beheaded from the bottom of a lake, mud flakes drying on bloated white skin.

Berlin’s “Take My Breath Away (Love Theme from *Top Gun*).”

The cures, with their eyes closed, hummed along and swayed.

Though her eyes remained open and focused on the road, Lotta hummed and swayed, too.

The Beetle spoke up just before the third verse.

||You gonna jizz on my fabric?||

“Jesus,” I mumbled into my hand.

||Well, that’s what happened the last time someone sat there. He unzipped, got sucked, and *blasted* the armrest.||

“Sucked?” I mumbled.

||And licked a lot, too. Rubbed. Spat on. Messy as hell. It took forever for the guy to clean me off.||

"Who was it?" I mumbled.

||Some detailer guy.||

"No. Who got, you know . . . sucked?"

||Like I said,|| said the Beetle.

Just then the song stopped, so I didn't press further. Lotta'd parked us in the lot of the Trackview OTB/Arcades Brothel/Mimi's Nail Salon strip mall. "Here we are," she said, and pushed a button on the nest, releasing the harness bar. The cures stretched their limbs theatrically and rose. They climbed, single file, up Lotta's straightened arm, and then across her clavicle, from where they dove into the top of her dress. As the third one waited for the second to dive, I got out of the car, which said, ||Hey, thanks a mil for not spraying your cumload inside of me, chief.||

•

• •

I'd supposed a new restaurant had recently opened in one of the strip mall's two vacant storefronts—the former A(cute)rements PerFormulae/CureWear/EmergeRig-vendor's (a locally beloved mom-and-pop concern that had moved across town, two or three years earlier, to a newer, bigger strip mall on County Line Road), or the former Pop-a-Wheelatine Gourmet Popcorn Poppery's (previously a cruiseship ticket broker's)—but this supposition's power rapidly diminished as I trailed Lotta Hogg past the doors of the one, then the other, and the OTB. Ahead was the brothel, beyond that only Mimi's. Probably owing as much to all the talk of ejaculate the Beetle'd just spewed as to the growing ambiguity of Lotta's intentions (why, again, had I rejected *romantic*? and had I even considered *strictly sexual*?), I got nervous that the invitation to lunch had all along been a ruse to lure me to the brothel for something . . . atypical.

"We getting our nails done or what, ha?" I said.

"We're getting pizza," said Lotta, holding open the door to the brothel for me.

"At the Arcades?" I said.

"They started serving some pretty interesting pizza here a few months back," she said. "Large variety of exotic toppings."

The sign beside the empty hostess stand read, PLEASE WAIT TO BE SEATED, but Lotta said it didn't matter, and brought me to a booth in the second-darkest corner. In terms of appearance, little seemed to have changed since my previous visit, eleven years earlier. Worn, dark leather; art deco parquet; no natural light; brass-rod-hung crimson velveteen curtains, behind which—instead of windows—were trompe l'oeils on drywall depicting Parisian *passages* at night. A shiny-clean open kitchen with a woodfire stove had replaced the old bar, and a new bar—semicircular—now occupied the very center of the space, but the golden double doors that led to the bedrooms were still at the back, and the sex workers still wore golden cuffs around their biceps to distinguish them from patrons and dedicated waitstaff. Half a dozen of them sat at or leaned on the bar. A couple more waited beside the golden doors for their clients to pay and get pat-downs from the bouncers.

Lotta parted the curtains next to our booth. "This is my favorite piece of wall art in the whole place," she said. "I find the details enchanting. I love the little stray poodle there, looking out the window—you see that little poodle? It's like, 'Hey, it's getting dark out here, where's my human?' I'm so glad we got this table!"

I nodded and unpocketed my Quills and my lighter.

"Oh shit," Lotta said. "I'm such a thoughtless Thora. This section's no smoking." She pointed at a sign. "We should move. Let's move."

"No, no. It's okay," I said. "It's your favorite table."

"It is," she said, "but . . . are you sure? I don't want you to be all uncomfortable."

"I don't think I will," I said. Had she then gone on to push once more (e.g. "Are you *really* sure?"), I would have agreed that we should switch tables, and I had been, I suppose, counting on her to push once more—that seemed to be the rhythm—but the hostess showed up, which cut the conversation short.

She and Lotta, in greeting one another, squinched up their faces and—in strained, mock-angry, weird-accented stage whispers—impersonated characters from a show or a movie I hadn't ever seen.

"Ooh it's you again," Lotta said. "Oh no."

"Oh no for me, myself! It's you! It's you! What is it you are doing here?" the hostess replied.

"I have come to aid my body. You will help me aid my body."

"What is it that you want to do with your body?"

"I want to use my hands to lift a triangular foodpart up to my lips, then open my mouth, insert the tip of the foodpart between my lips, past my teeth, then close my teeth. After doing that, I want to pull my hands away from my head so that the tip will be severed from the larger foodpart, and then grind with my teeth the tip of the foodpart that remains in my mouth into small pieces that my mouth will wet with its inner spits and after that use my tongue and the muscle right here in the middle of my neck to force the engrindened, wettened pieces down a narrow tube into the center of my body. This will turn the engrindened, wettened pieces into pure energy so that I may continue to grow my body and repeat the process many, many more times."

The hostess made her face squinchier. "How many more times?"

"Eleventy squidillion!" Lotta said.

"That seems like too many."

"*You* seem like too many!"

"That is hurtful and I will hold it against you forever. But also I will help you to do with your body what you say you want to do, only first you must promise you will go away after, because I don't like you, because you are hurtful, and in addition you must tell me: What is a 'teeth'?"

"'A teeth!'" Lotta said, in her normal voice. "Hilarious! They should hire you on to write for them. For real."

"Your pal really seems to agree," the hostess said. "He's really crackin up."

"He's a *novelist,*" said Lotta. "Novelists don't watch *MBR.*"

"Oh yeah?" the hostess said, again in the voice. "Well, the Mean Baby Robots don't read *novels.*"

I made a bunch of laugh sounds.

The hostess winked at Lotta. Lotta winked at me.

"So what kind of server you want me to send over?"

"Oh, anyone," Lotta said. "It doesn't matter."

"Feeling *adventurous.*"

"Ha! No," Lotta said. "Any *dedicated* server, thank you very much. We're just gonna eat."

"I know, girl, I know—still I gotta ask. Company policy. You know what, though? Two of my dedicateds called in sick today, and the third one's slammed. Why don't I get you started?"

"Oh, that's great," Lotta said. "I guess we'll get a couple slice flights—I mean if that's cool with you, Belt. That way, you can try the largest variety of exotic toppings—Belt's never tried your pizza."

"Slice flight's the move," the hostess advised me.

"Sounds good," I said.

"And to drink?"

"You have lemonade?"

"Ooh, lemon*ade*. A real toughguy, huh? Total J.K. I mean if you're working the program or something, I support you entirely. Our lemonade's actually great. Fresh-squeezed. Lotta?"

"I don't know," said Lotta. "It *is* a little early to drink, I guess . . ."

"If you want to—" I said.

"No no. A fresh-squeezed lemonade sounds great," Lotta said. "To aid my body," she added, in the voice.

"I am using my legs to transport me toward the kitchenplace," the hostess, departing, said over her shoulder.

Lotta began to unload her cures into the built-in nest in the center of the table. She did this with a lip bit, perhaps in concentration, perhaps from disappointment. I worried I'd shamed her.

"You know, I really won't mind it if you drink," I said.

In response, she offered a nonchalant wave that, given the bitten lip, could just as easily have meant "It's fine" as "I'm making the effort to pretend it's fine, but really, I'd rather you continue to convince me to go ahead and order a drink."

And in the wake of this wave, I noticed once again—and once again felt penitent for noticing—a wild flapping of her upper-arm meat.

"I mean you almost *have to* drink, right?" I said. "It's a tavern in a brothel. They must get pretty angry if you don't buy sex, but if you don't buy sex *or* alcohol . . . ? Like, didn't the hostess seem maybe kinda angry? I mean maybe you should just order a—"

"You angling to get me drunk, Belt?" said Lotta.

"I—"

"Just kidding! Jeez. And no, you big sweetheart. They don't get angry about it. If people weren't comfortable coming in to just dine, it would undermine the whole bait-and-switch strategy. Though I guess it's not exactly a bait-and-switch strategy, more like a stock-the-cookies-in-the-cracker-aisle strategy, or a stock-the-loss-leader-at-the-back-of-the-store-so-they-have-to-walk-past-all-the-other-more-desirable-and-more-profitable-products-to-get-to-it strategy. Like I bet you go to Pang's White Hen for milk, right?"

I couldn't recall having ever bought milk, let alone from Pang, but I said, "Sure, yeah," so as not to obstruct her arrival at whatever insight it was she was riffing toward.

"It's the cheapest milk in town," she said, "is why. Pang can't possibly make any money on that milk, but the milk not only gets you through the door, it gets you walking past all kinds of brightly packaged chips and sports drinks and candy bars and whatnot. So it's a little like that here. Not to say they lose money on the pizza—maybe, I don't know. But they definitely make more money on the sex and the drinks. And some people come in cause they just want some pizza, and that's all they get, but some who come just because they want some pizza get tempted by the drinks once they've sat down and so they buy some drinks too, and maybe that opens them up to buy sex, plus then—and this is maybe the cleverest part of the strategy I think—there's also people who want to buy drinks or sex but won't admit it to themselves, so they tell themselves they're just coming in for pizza, but really what they're doing is making themselves available to temptation because that way they can feel like the drinking or sex is out of their control. Or less in their control. I'm one of those people. Not with drinking or sex, I don't mean—really. *Really*. But with food itself, though. Like, I said to myself, when I decided we'd come here, that all I'd get would be a Caesar salad, but by the time I ordered, I was totally convinced that if I got the Caesar, you'd know it was because I was trying to eat healthy, and because you're such a sweetheart you'd order salad too, denying yourself the pleasure of eating pizza, like in solidarity, like to help me be healthy—and what a shitty lunch, right? Salad? That sucks. So I decided I'd order pizza after all, telling myself that it was because I didn't want you to miss out on the pizza but kinda knowing at the exact same time that I was just looking for an excuse to go off my diet. And then I thought, 'Lotta, if you're gonna fuck up your diet, then *fuck up your diet,* no reason to half-ass,' so instead of just a slice of veggie or whatever, I ordered us slice flights. Anyway, if they didn't serve salad, I couldn't have convinced myself that we should come here—same way as if they didn't serve pizza, then people unwilling to admit they wanted to drink or buy sex wouldn't come here."

"But so they do want us to drink and buy sex," I said, "even though they serve pizza."

"Of course they want us to drink and buy sex," she said, "but not as much as they want us to know we don't have to, since that way we can spread the word about this place—about how they treat you well even if you only order pizza—to the people who know they want pizza and only *might* want to drink or buy sex, and to the people who want to go for a drink or some sex but don't want to admit it. Anyway, I've decided to enjoy myself. To get what I want. Live life to the fullest, right? That's all we have to do."

"Absolutely," I said. One didn't require an all-too-sharply-calibrated theory of mind to imagine that the enthusiasm Lotta had expressed when I entered the bank, and the anxious way she'd then rushed me to her car—to imagine that all the signals of ulterior motivation I'd sensed her giving off—had nothing to do with her wanting to get me drunk and/or naked, and everything to do with my being a person via whose accompaniment she could enable herself to eat pizza. And what a relief it was to imagine that. It seemed I'd made a friend.

"What's up there, Smiley?"

"Nothing really," I said. "It's just the way you think. And the way you described it. You're a very funny person. I guess I'm just really glad we're becoming friends."

Lotta lowered her gaze to the tablenest, inside of which her cures were playing what looked to be a songless form of pattycake. Had I said the wrong thing? Had I said just the right thing? Had the one been misinterpreted as the other?

The hostess brought us our order, and we ate and we ate, silent except for some hummy, sated noises we made in response to what we put in our mouths. Inasmuch as their crusts were crisp and chewy, and their sauce-to-cheese ratios admirably balanced, the slices (or rather half-slices; we were served five apiece) were expertly crafted, but their simple artisanship was, to my taste, too often undermined by the exotic, emphatically hi/lo toppings—truffled corn nuts, balsamic-glazed Slim Jims, pickle-brined lychees, duck pepperoni, and garlicky meatballs infused with cacao nibs. On the other hand, the lemonade lived up to the hype. It seemed to sparkle in the brain, to enrich and hasten the vital fluids, and I emptied the entire twenty-odd-ounce tumbler in under seven glugs.

Til that point, our silence, though by no means golden, didn't feel awkward. Once the tumblers were removed and our platters half-depleted, though, the lack of language had become conspicuous, and although I had the sense it was Lotta's turn to talk—if not to respond to my remark about our blossoming friendship, then at least to help unweird my having made it by changing the subject to something less fraught—I considered how little I knew about friendships, let alone about growing them, considered how I hadn't been to lunch with anyone other than my father or my editor at Darger in at least a couple decades, and I determined that my sense of whose turn it was to speak was probably off, so I said the first thing that came to mind. I said, "Chad-Kyle, huh? What a fucken wang-scab!"

"You really think Chad-Kyle's a wang-scab?" said Lotta. She seemed disappointed.

"Well I guess I don't really know him well," I said. "But before, when you were telling me you lied about the spidge oil, I thought you said it was because he was a horrible person."

"Did I really say he was a horrible person? Chad-Kyle's a pal. I don't think he's a horrible person at all. I just didn't want to see what he wanted to show me. He's always torturing cures. I hate that."

"You do?"

"Don't you?" she said. "Just take a look at these dudes." She nodded at the nest, where her cures were now having a four-way catch with a pea-size gob of cooled mozzarella. "I don't care what people say," Lotta said, "they're not robots. Or not *just* robots. They enjoy things. Have feelings. They're alive like you and me. Or kind of, at least."

"I think so, too," I said.

"I figured as much. It's a sign of sensitivity, and who's more sensitive than novelists, right?— Oh! Look who it is!" Lotta rose in her chair and beckoned two-handedly to someone at the bar: a silver-haired cuddlefarmer chatting with the hostess. The woman waved at our table, smiling broadly, set a cure on the bar, and headed our way. Her gear was comprehensive. She must have had at least fifty Curios in stock. With the exception of her hands and the soles of her feet, all the parts of her body below her chin not covered by hotpants were devoted to business: CureSleeves and MagicSleeves ran up and down her limbs; a leather vest sewn with windowed pouches hugged her torso; a broad, spandex band abulge with marbles encircled her neck like a cervical collar.

"Ma," Lotta said, as the woman pulled a chair up. "This is Belt. Belt, that's my ma."

"Catrina," Lotta's mom said, taking my hand, squeezing it a little. "You know, I know your father. I've known him awhile. And it's funny because, yesterday, when Lotta came home from work, she told me that she'd seen you at the bank, and then—"

"Stop it, Ma," Lotta said.

"Stop what? No. You don't even know what I'm gonna say."

"You're gonna say his dad's handsome."

"His dad *is* handsome. He's *always* been handsome. And so is his son, I'm happy to see."

"You spidged, Ma?"

"Maybe a little. So what? That's neither here nor there, Lottabottabean. What I was going to tell your new gentleman friend was I came here last night, just a couple hours after you told me you saw him, and who do I run into? Can you guess?"

Lotta nodded.

"My daughter's gone mute," Mrs. Hogg said to me. "She's *so* embarrassed. Would you like to guess who I ran into for her? Participate a little?"

"The one and only Clyde Magnet?" I said.

"You bet your cheeky cheekbones! That's *exactly* who. And your dad, he's been a client of mine for a couple of years, now. Four or five, actually. Well . . . wow, how old am I? I'm—whatever. Ever since I quit teaching to full-time farm and I started making rounds at Blimey's and this place. That's how long. What I'm saying is, we've always chatted, he and I, but nothing too deep, just the weather and the president, those sorts of things, but he'd never mentioned you before—it never got personal. I mean, I knew he was your dad, and I knew who you were, and the general story about your family, of course, but I never heard word-one about you from him directly. Or about your mom. Or his job for that matter. Nothing of substance! Like I said, you know, just, 'The weather is miserable,' or 'This cakeface president should shut his stinking pie-hole,' or 'How much, Catrina, for that green-eyed biped?' except then, all the sudden, swear on my beautiful daughter here—isn't she beautiful?—swear on that beautiful girl right there, your father, he says to me, last night I'm saying, your father comes through the golden door, face like a basset hound, sidles up right beside me at the bar, and he says to me, 'Catrina, I need something special. I need a cure I can overload on with my Belt. It's important it's special. It's gotta be a good one. It's gotta really be good. We need something new. We need to have something new to remember.' And I'm thinking, 'How strange! Two times today, I'm hearing Belt's name, once from my daughter, once from his father.' Isn't that strange? I mean, it seemed strange to me. It seemed, you know, *mean*ingful, and what I decided it must have meant was: Help this guy out. Cut this nice man a deal. So I cut him a deal on a cure so adorable—it was only a couple years old, but it looked like it was four, maybe even five, which happens sometimes, however rarely, I don't know why, they're sometimes just cuter than they should be for their age, but when that happens, you know, we can get a lot of money for it, except so what my point is is that I thought: 'No. Not this time. This time, I'm gonna sell this one to Clyde Magnet for the price it would have been if it wasn't so special.' Cause I heard your name twice, Belt, and it seemed important. So I cut him a deal."

"That was nice of you," I said.

"I like to be nice. We're nice people, we Hoggs. I'm sure you can see that."

"Ma," Lotta said.

"It's okay," I said. "She's right. I can see it. I'm becoming a pretty big fan of the Hoggs."

"And so how was the overload?" Mrs. Hogg said. "Was it special? Did you two make that memory?"

"Well," I said, and faked a triplet of sneezes, then told the Hoggs I'd left my handkerchief at home, and excused myself to go to the men's room.

I didn't want to disappoint Lotta's mother by admitting my father had killed the cure without me. At the same time, I was hesitant to be dishonest. Even to me, this bind seemed rather minor, but what seemed more than minor—why I'd fled the table—was that I'd felt any hesitation about lying to begin with. Why should I have cared?

To be clear: I'd realized, moments after Lotta'd introduced me to her mom, that despite the comforting conclusions I'd so recently made regarding her motives, she'd most likely brought me to the tavern *in order* to introduce me to her mom (there was far better pizza next door to the bank, at Bobby Fongool's), and I'd realized that her doing so probably meant that her interest in me was, after all, romantic in nature. What threw me was that I'd no longer found that objectionable. It had, in fact, become *desirable*.

How that happened was this: between the point at which my discomfort had lifted (when I'd had the—on reflection, false—realization that Lotta had wanted me to go to the tavern primarily to mitigate her guilty feelings about eating a fat-rich, high-carb lunch) and the point at which I'd have thought that discomfort should have returned (when her mother joined us), Lotta'd said she thought cures were other than robots, and, in saying so, she had become, though not quite attractive, a lot less *un*attractive to me, and I'd found myself wondering if I could maybe love her after all.

I'd found myself thinking that if, perhaps, I could manage to keep my eyes on her eyes, and off the rest of her, I might be capable of overcoming my already slightly diminished physical revulsion to her, maybe even to the point that it would evolve into longing. And I determined that it was something I should at least try. What kind of shallow jerk would let a little bodyfat—or even a lot of bodyfat—come between himself and what could perhaps maybe be a possible fighting chance at real love? Not the kind of shallow jerk that I wanted to be. And given that I'd been able to vanquish the impulse to overload on Blank day after day for over twenty-five years, conquering my distaste for the body of a kindhearted woman—a woman *deserving* of love and affection—seemed, to say the least, a manageable feat.

Furthermore, in my freshly rekindled fantasy about the girl who talked to inans—and this had always been, I suppose, strictly implicit, up until I'd entered the tavern's bathroom to think—she believed (and of *course*!), just as Lotta believed, that cures weren't robots. But what if the real girl who talked to inans didn't? What if I couldn't have it both ways? Which one would I prefer: a girl who talked to inans but thought cures were robots, or a girl who couldn't talk to inans but thought cures weren't robots? With whom would I have the more in common? the larger connection? the better shot at joy? I really didn't know. Nor did I know if the girl who talked to inans even existed, let alone had I any guarantee she'd be interested in me if she did exist. Whereas Lotta was out there—*right* out there—at the table with her mom. And she was—it was clear now, she *had* to be—interested.

So I stood before the sink in the brothel's bathroom and pictured the eyes, Lotta's gorgeous gray eyes. I could look in those eyes all day, could I not? I could look in those eyes until the kissing began, at which point the kissing, if what we had was really love, would take care of the rest. It would be like the hot sauce sprinkled on the oyster, or maybe the lemon juice sprinkled on the oyster—like whatever desirably flavored dressing one sprinkled on oysters (I'd never tried an oyster) in order to learn how, first, to swallow oysters, and later, maybe, with a little bit of practice, to enjoy their swallowing. The kissing would be the kissing of those in love, the kissing of lovers, and, building off the kissing, I could learn to find the shape of Lotta Hogg erotic. Couldn't I do that? Why couldn't I do that?

I wanted to smoke. I hadn't smoked in a while. Few smokes tasted better than those smoked post-pizza, and few were ever more useful than those that accompanied important insights. I anticipated an all-time top-100 Quill, there in the bathroom of the Arcades Brothel, yet when I reached in my pocket for my pack and my lighter and realized I'd left them both on the table, the disappointment, to my surprise, didn't crush me. Not even close. I could smoke one later, I thought. I could and I would. There wasn't any rush. There were more important things to attend to, first. First I had to attempt to fall in love with Lotta Hogg.

Returning to the table, I wiped my dry hands on my shirt as if I'd washed them.

"Glad to see you're back," announced Mrs. Hogg. "We thought you fell in! Ha-ha! Ha-ha!"

Our whole table laughed. Lotta's lower face jiggled. I tried to find it erotic, or at least kind of pretty, but it was still too soon, so I looked into her eyes. She let me look, and they were something, those eyes, inviting and kind—they were just as I'd hoped: dazed and yet dazzled, serene and yet beckoning—but then it got too intense, as looking into eyes will, and I looked at the cures, which were still playing catch.

"Hey, where'd the fourth one go?" I said.

"Someone got a little *entranced,*" Mrs. Hogg said, jabbing her finger in the air at Lotta, who—giddy, I think, from the soulgaze we'd shared—laughed some more, throwing her head back. I noticed, on her chest, just under her neck, a tear-shaped, nearly translucent skintag. It was far too soon to find that not-repulsive, much less erotic, so again I sought the eyes, but the eyes, as before, quickly got too intense, and, as before, I averted my gaze, and this time I noticed, resting on her cleavage, a curved black pizza crumb.

Then: sudden movement. Movement in my upper-peripheral field. The skintag fell. It streaked. It lengthened.

The skintag *dripped.*

It wasn't a skintag.

It was no more a skintag than was the black crescent a crumb of burnt pizza. The skintag was blood and what was stuck in her cleavage was the toe of the Curio thats body'd once pumped it.

Lotta saw me seeing, looked down at her breasts, and saw what I'd seen. She plucked up the toe, popped it in her mouth. Amidst a fresh fit of chin-jiggling laughter, she half-shouted, "*Mort*ified!"

This was just a self-assessment. Not an accusation she'd aimed at me. It might as well have been, though. It would have fit. What a schmuck I was. What a schmuck to take what she'd said at face value. What a schmuck to imagine that, just because she'd said she didn't think cures were robots, it meant she didn't overload. Had she not, after all, been eating a spidge-infused blondie just yesterday? Had she not, hardly an hour earlier, mentioned having purchased spidge oil from Chad-Kyle? What a willfully blind, wishfully thinking, self-deluding, needy, desperate, idiot schmuck, me.

"*Strick*en!" Lotta added. "Shocked and em*bar*rassed!" Once her laughter had ebbed, she wiped her eyes with her napkin and said, "Jesus, Beltenstein. You look *destroyed*. Did you have your heart set on the one I chose? I should have waited! Mom said I should wait but, I mean, you were in there awhile. Hey look. There's three more right there. You pick the next two. Go on. Go ahead."

"No," I said. "No need," I said.

"Maybe *you* don't have a need—but look down at those little cute little beans in that nest." Here she made her head horizontal with the table, and stated the following in a squeaky little-kid voice: "Aw, come on. Pick one of us. PWEESE? Aw we want is cwoseness."

Although I made the face I'd make when making laugh sounds, Lotta continued.

"Won't you ovew-woad on one us? Ovew-woad's the *cwosest* we can *get* to pee-pew. Won't you be ow *pee*-pew?"

I pushed out the laugh sounds.

Lotta righted her head. "Oh shit, you're icked out, huh? Because of the toe?"

"It's fine," I said.

"No, you're icked out. I can tell. It's okay. I'm not usually so sloppy. What happened, I guess, was that I closed my mouth too soon—before it pulled that foot in entirely. And I had to swallow, right? And it's impossible to swallow with your mouth open. Ever try it?" She opened her mouth up wide and tried, succeeded. "I guess it's not *impossible,* ha! But it's hard, you know? Counterintuitive. And I *thought* I felt something fall off my lip, but then I couldn't find it. I looked. I looked everywhere. Well everywhere, I guess, except for on my girls here."

"It's fine, Lotta. Really. I'm not icked out. It's just—I just, sometimes . . . I'm a writer, you know? Sometimes I just get overcome with the need to work. The need to get my thoughts straight, and work, and it happens all at once. It happens very suddenly and that's all that's happening. I gotta get to work. So I gotta get outta here. I'm gonna walk home and get some work done, okay?"

"*Work?* Really? On such a pleasant afternoon? That doesn't . . . oh. Wait. I think I understand—you can tell me the truth, Belt. Are you having some kind of an attack or something?"

"I'm not having an attack," I said.

"If you are, it's okay. You don't have to be embarrassed. We'll do whatever it is you do to get past it. Whatever will comfort you. I'll take you straight home right now if you want. You know what? I think that's a good idea. Just lemme pack up here. Ma, you don't mind, right?"

"Of course not. No. It was a pleasure to meet you, Belt. I'm sorry you're feeling bad—maybe something in the pizza didn't agree with your meds?"

"It's not the pizza," I said, pushing my chair back, maybe too abruptly—Lotta's mom flinched—and getting to my feet. "I'm not having an attack. I don't take meds."

"Okay," Lotta's mom said. "We believe you. We do. I think, Lotta—I think Belt's trying to tell us he'd prefer to be alone. Which is fine. Some people prefer to be alone sometimes. Especially when they're not feeling well."

"Do you want to be alone, Belt?" Lotta said.

"Lotta," Mrs. Hogg said.

"What, Ma?" Lotta said, her gorgeous eyes brimming.

"Don't make him say it."

She didn't make me say it.

WHAT THE GOLD SHOULD HAVE DONE

HUMILIATION AND GUILT, DISAPPOINTMENT and shame. I can't help but imagine we're on the same page when it comes to those emotions, reader. I can't help but imagine you're as tired of reading about them as I am of describing them, and while, I admit, that may be a sign of my failings as a writer, I'd prefer to think it points to something true and symmetrical—something literary, even—that's happening here, on this page we're both on, given how it seemed, once I'd fled from the brothel, that I was tired of even *feeling* those emotions. In any case, I'd ceased to feel them.

It was unfortunate, yes, that I'd connived myself into believing I could—believing I *should*—fall in love with a woman toward whom I felt no sexual attraction. To have made that woman cry (right in front of her mother no less) was also unfortunate. However, these misfortunes were nothing compared to those that would have inevitably arisen had I kissed that woman; kissed her, and only thereafter discovered I'd invented the one and only thing about her that had made me want to try to love her to begin with.

I'd really dodged a blow.

Lotta had, too. And what I did feel once I'd fled the brothel wasn't merely a *sense* of relief, but relief itself, instant and animal: a slackening of tendons and a tingling in the blood, intracranial fizzing and muscles that hummed, every skeletal juncture a freshly popped knuckle. That I'd lit up a Quill after not having smoked for nearly two hours may indeed have contributed to this feeling of relief, but even after I'd extinguished that Quill and lit up another a couple blocks west of the OTB/Arcades/Mimi's Nail Salon strip mall, and even after I'd realized, as I stood on my doorstep a few more blocks north, that the rough-sided lump my housekey-fishing fingers encountered at the bottom of my cargo-shorts pocket was the folded-over stack of Lotta's twenty-five twenties, which through innocent oversight I had, I now saw, failed to leave with Lotta, and which I'd have to get to Lotta after all that just happened and all that just hadn't—even after all of that, I was feeling the relief.

And for ten or maybe fifteen seconds more—for however long it took me to enter the house, pass through the foyer, and walk up the hallway to the threshold of the kitchen—I continued to feel it. I felt it til my father, sitting at the table behind a full ashtray, said, "Look who it is," at which point surprise and confusion overwhelmed me, as I knew neither to nor about whom he was speaking, me or the boy who was seated across from him, Jonny "Triple-J" Pellmore-Jason, Jr.

•

• •

Into his shoulder, as if to himself, Triple-J spoke my name, first and last. Then, adjusting his sailor cap, he rose from his chair and addressed me directly. "After all," he said, "what *should* gold have done?"

This was not as absurd a thing to say as it seems, which isn't to say I wasn't taken aback. He was quoting a line from *No Please Don't.*

"I *knew* you looked familiar last night," he said. "I guess it was dark, and you're older than you are in your author photo, or—no. Who am I kidding? It wasn't that dark. You don't look so much older. It's just I never thought . . . I knew you lived here, in Wheelatine, and I was planning to eventually introduce myself to you, but the possibility that we might just run into each other—it never crossed my mind. I mean, I've thought about meeting you for so long, Mr. Magnet. I've thought so hard about how I'd present myself, what I'd want to say, about what I'd do to make a good impression and get you to talk to me, to take me seriously, so to just *bump into you*—to bump into you on a playground and then—well, you know what happened then . . . it was basically completely impossible to imagine, so impossible I wasn't able to believe it even while it happened. *Especially* then."

"You've read *No Please Don't*?" I said.

"I've read *No Please Don't*—been reading *No Please Don't*—for years," he said. "Two years and change. Start to finish, I've read it three times. Twice in a row when I was twelve years old, another time a few months back, before we moved here. Between those times, and *since* we moved here, I've gone back to my favorite parts a *lot*. Chapter nine alone, I bet I've read twenty times. *No Please Don't* is the first work of fiction I ever truly loved. It speaks to me the way I speak to myself. It tells its story the way I'd tell its story if its story were mine to tell instead of yours. And it offers me comfort. Whenever I'm reading it, I feel understood. Is this too much? Am I saying too much? Do I sound too . . . much? I don't sound like me. I know *that* much. I wrote this all down. Not *this*, but what this *should be*, a much better version. I'm way off script. And not just because of what happened last night. I'm contrite about that, yes, but more than that I'm starstruck. I'm starstruck and sorry. Remorseful and awed. Brimming with regret but also, I don't know, agog. It's fucking me up. I'm trying to pay you the highest-possible compliments, with the absolutely utterest of utmost sincerity, and I'm failing so bad."

"No no," I said. "Thank you."

"But I mean it, though," he said. "Please know that I mean it."

I didn't doubt him. Were we standing any closer—were a table not between us—I'm sure I would have hugged him.

"I believe you," I said. "If I'm not responding graciously, it's only because I have no practice. I'm not used to hearing from fans of my book. Tell you the truth, it's never happened before."

"'Never,' he says," my father, looking past me, remarked to an audience I presumed to be rhetorical. "I told you I love your book *how* many times?" he said to me. "I told him almost every day for a year," he said to Triple-J. "It's a great fucken book. Didn't I tell you I thought it was a great one?"

"You told us. You did," came a low, raspy voice from the hallway behind me.

I flinched. All but jumped.

My father mimed two short punches to my shoulder.

Over that shoulder, I saw the driver, Burroughs, in his seam-taxed livery and hinge-strained hornrims, wiping dry the backs of his hands on his slacks. His once-black scalp stubble now shone silver, and his skull had managed, somehow, to have grown even broader, but if the twenty-odd years since last I'd seen him had marked him in other ways, they were wholly inapparent. Not to mention beside the point. He still looked like something that had hatched from a boulder.

The downstairs toilet's after-flush whistle-whine achieved its familiar crescendo and stopped.

"Burroughs," I said.

"I'm glad you remember who I am," Burroughs said, and performed a subtle movement I only half-perceived—he may have dipped his dimpled, escutcheonesque chin, or perhaps flexed a deltoid—but which signaled to me that I should enter the kitchen.

I entered the kitchen. Burroughs followed. We all sat down.

I said to Triple-J, "So is your father here, too?"

"What makes you ask that question?" Burroughs said. He could have gripped a nickel with his brow's thinnest furrow.

"Oh, nothing," I said. "I mean, I wasn't really asking. Just joking around. Lots of unexpected people in my house today is all."

Triple-J had gone squinty. He seemed disappointed—with me? with Burroughs? I couldn't be sure. "Burroughs drives for *me,* now, Mr. Magnet," he said.

"Please call me Belt."

"Call him Billy," said my father.

"Burroughs drives for me now. *Walks* for me, too. Looks like at least. He walked me here today because he or my father wants to make an impression. Or maybe it's both of them. Someone, though, who isn't me, wants to impress upon you just how very well *looked-after* I am. I said that all bitchy, didn't I? I did. It even *felt* bitchy. Apologies for that. And to you too, Burroughs. I'm doing that thing you warned me about. Resenting the trappings of privilege in public. It's off-putting. Shitty. In fairness to Burroughs, Belt, I altercated with you. It makes sense he'd insist on joining me here. Still, I'd understand if you felt insulted, and I hope the apology I'm about to make for my behavior last night will what's-the-word *accrue* toward your forgiveness of this latest insult. That apology is this: I am *sorry,* truly sorry, for hurting you last night, I am sorry for the behavior of my idiot friends, who I should've managed better, and most of all, I'm sorry it took me so long to figure out who you were, because I would have acted different. I didn't even tell you how that happened, did I? How I realized who you were. I meant to tell you first, before I said all the other stuff, but then I got starstruck and went off script.

"This is how I should've started: About ten minutes after I left the playground, I was almost home, like just outside the compound, about to punch the code in, when I realized I'd left a cure on the slide. I don't know if you saw it. For all I know, you took it. Somebody took it. We checked before we came here. That really doesn't matter, though, except for because of how it failed to matter. Fails to matter. I was outside the compound, about to punch my code in, and I remembered the cure, but I didn't think twice about going back to get it. There wasn't any way I was going back to get it. I skipped a whole part. I need to backtrack a second—can you spare one of those?"

Thinking he was asking if I'd spare him a second to hear whatever tale he had to backtrack to tell, I nodded and smiled, but then Burroughs said, "Trip," and I knew I was confused.

"I've had two this *month,*" Triple-J told Burroughs. "Don't guilt me, okay?"

With another subtle movement that I only half-perceived—a cocked eyebrow this time? an incisor's flashing?—Burroughs signaled for me to pass his charge a Quill.

I passed his charge a Quill.

Triple-J lit it with his own book of matches. "Thank you," he said. "See? That's probably a perfect example of what I'm trying to explain. I had to *remember* to be grateful just now, and then to thank you. Were you able to tell?"

"I don't think so," I said.

"Well it didn't feel natural. It felt a little forced. I *am* grateful, though. The thank-you was sincere. Anyway, what you have to understand is the reason we're here, my family, I mean, at the compound I'm saying—the whole reason we live in Wheelatine now is that I'm supposed to learn, firsthand, what it's like to live among everyday people, people from different, more normal backgrounds than I am. Same reason my father's father moved the family to Wheelatine back when you guys were kids. Well, almost the same reason. Dad was supposed to learn to understand common people so that when the time came to lead them he'd be more effective. Whereas me, I'm supposed to learn to understand common people so I can get a better handle on how to move them with my artwork. So not exactly the same thing, but pretty much the same thing. And just like my dad was, I'm supposed to learn to understand common people by learning how to *act* like a common person, and not just learning how to, but actually doing it. Acting like one. So that was the problem. Last night, I'm saying. Outside the gates. Cause I'm fourteen years old, right? What normal fourteen-year-old, first of all, forgets about a cure he hasn't dacted yet, and secondly, once he remembers the cure, decides that walking a few minutes to go back and get it isn't worth the bother? Those things cost money, or, if not money, time, which is kind of—to common people—like money. Do you see the problem? I was failing at the main thing I was supposed to be succeeding at, and I didn't see how it was that I *could* succeed. Like, say I went back and retrieved the cure anyway—that wouldn't change the fact that I'd forgotten it to begin with, and it wouldn't change the fact that I didn't *care* to go back for it. So I didn't go back. And I still don't care. I mean, I care that I don't care, but that isn't the same.

"So I entered the compound, and I went in my house, and I felt like a failure, I felt all alone, and I did what I've learned to do when I feel that way: I took your book off the shelf to read it, to make myself feel understood, to comfort myself, and there, of course, on the flap, was your picture. And that's when I realized it was you who I'd hurt. And for the first time since I was twelve years old, Belt, for the first time *ever,* your book failed to comfort me. I really—I just couldn't believe that I'd hurt you. So I wrote a long speech that I've mangled so far, and . . . and I'm such a dick, you know? I'm such a self-involved *dick*. I mean, I really am sorry I attacked you last night, but I haven't even asked you about how you're feeling, which was one of the first things I put in the speech. Is your back messed up? Are your kidneys okay? Was there blood in your urine?"

"Hold it," said my father. "You hurt Billy's kidneys? You kidneypunch my *son*?"

Burroughs leaned forward.

My father leaned forward.

Both men pressed their palms on the table, as if readying to stand.

"He thought he was protecting his friend from me," I said.

"You assaulted his friend, son? You beat up some kid?"

"Three or four kids. I didn't really beat—"

"Three or *four*? Assuming they're roughly this one's size, that's actually kind of impressive, Billy. It was embarrassing for a second, now it's kind of impressive. What'd the jerks do to you?"

"It doesn't matter," I said. "Let's leave it alone."

My father lit a Quill. To Burroughs, he said, "I'm not afraid of you, chief."

"That so?" Burroughs said, hands off the table.

"I know where you're weak," my father told him.

"Tell me," said Burroughs.

"You know where. Or maybe you don't. It was there twenty-five years ago, though—I saw it but instantly, moment I met you, that weakspot of yours—and it's still there now. Bigger than ever. A Day-Glo target of a weakspot you've got."

"You say so."

"I do."

"Alright then."

"Alright," said my father. "Beer?"

"I don't drink."

"That's womanly."

"Opinion."

"Widely held opinion. 'No thank you,' works fine. No one asked for your story. I'll let the subject rest, now. I'm getting in the way of these two being friendly."

"True," Burroughs said.

"Don't go down that road. Don't pin it all on me. You're in the way too. Make me feel like I have to save face, you'll regret it."

"Okay already. I'm in the way too."

"'Already,' he says. Like I'm the one sitting in *his* goddamn kitchen."

"Fair enough," Burroughs said. "I recant the already."

"That's cute," my father said. *"Recant."*

Triple-J was staring fixedly down at his hands. He'd been doing so ever since Clyde had gotten prickly. "I want you to forgive me more than anything," he said.

"I forgave you before you left the playground," I said.

"I wish I could believe you, but now I have to think you're only saying you forgive me cause you're scared of Burroughs."

"*No* one here is scared of Burroughs, kid," my father said.

"You did what you thought you had to, Triple-J," I said. "And you only stomped on me once, to be sure I was down. A lot of other people would have kept on going. Plus I *haven't* pissed blood, and my back'll be fine. It's just a little bruised. I even went out today. You saw me coming back. And I was happy to find you here. I'm glad you read my book."

"He means it," said Burroughs. "If you listen to his voice like I taught you, you can tell."

"You mean it?" Triple-J said.

I told him I did.

His gloom seemed to deflate, and he nodded to himself, jacking up the corners of his mouth til he was smiling. "I appreciate it, Belt," he said. "I really do." From his pocket he produced a tiny blue ampule. He placed it before him, on the table, and said, "That right there is Independence PerFormula. Three full doses. You've heard of Independence, right?"

"A guy at the bank just tried to sell me some."

"Yeah?" Triple-J said. "I bet it was fake."

"I saw a cure he gave it to. It seemed to really work," I said.

"Must have been one of those guerrilla-marketing yokels. I'm surprised they've got it so early. I don't think it'll be in stores for another five weeks or something like that. That's what Tessa told me—Tessa Swords, I mean. She's my cousin. Godsister. Whatever. Probably you know that. Anyway, the stuff is great. Tessa said Graham&Swords even thinks it's gonna be bigger than BullyKing. I guess the Performulae Abuse Labs Brothers already let them know it was a shoo-in for the P.A.L. Recommends gold medal, and now the G&S advertising and marketing dorks are talking about a 'Fourth Cute Revolution' campaign or something, which, if I'm being honest, seems like a little much to me. I mean, Curios hit the market, that's a Cute Revolution. I feel it. GameChanger and then PlayChanger PerFormulae hit the market: that's a second and a third Cute Revolution. I feel *that*. But a new *type* of PlayChanger PerFormula hits the market? Sure, maybe it's great—and it is—and maybe it even becomes the bestselling PerFormula in the history of PerFormulae—and it probably will—but I don't think that's a revolution. Not that it isn't a really big deal. It's just not a revolution. Anyway, your dad told me you already dacted the cure the other Yachts were all going bananas about, which is kind of a bummer—I wanted to see it—but I'm guessing you've got another in that old-school sleeve of yours, so go ahead and take it out, give it a dose."

"Actually," I said, "all that's in there's a marble."

"In that massive CureSleeve? Jesus, lemme see that thing—it doesn't even have a windowpocket, huh? You must've had that since the eighties. Is it from the Friends study? Or is it one of those RetroGear models?"

"I got it in eighty-nine, I think," I said. "I guess it is pretty old-school. I guess *I'm* pretty old-school, cause I wish it was an IncuBand. I lost my IncuBand, though."

"An IncuBand! That's hilarious," he said to Burroughs. "You know," he said to me, "if you really want one, I bet I can ask Tessa. She has like a whole room of unopened, obsolescent cure stuff in her basement. She's kind of a hoarder."

"That's nice of you," I said. "But you really don't have to."

"I *want* to," he said. "In any case, I brought this ampule of Independence for you to demonstrate how sincerely sorry I am about last night. Go ahead and sell two of the doses if you want—I think you could probably make at least a couple hundred—but just promise me you'll keep one for when your next robot emerges. It's really fun."

"You don't need to give me this," I said. "Really."

"I know," Triple-J said. "If I *needed* to give it to you, it wouldn't be a gift."

"But there's no need for gifts," I said.

"Exactly," Triple-J said. "That's why it's yours. I'm not taking it back. Plus, I'm buttering you up. I've got ulterior motives. First, I'd like to invite you to the compound for brunch, and—"

"I'm in," I said. "No buttering necessary."

"Well how about tomorrow?"

"Tomorrow's great," I said.

"Great," said Triple-J. "And of course, you're invited too, Mr. Magnet, if you're free."

"I'm free," said my father. "I'll be there."

"Well that's perfect," Triple-J said. "Eleven, alright? Oh man, I'm so psyched. Now, as for my other ulterior motive . . ." To Burroughs, he said, "Burroughs, if you will," and Burroughs removed, from beneath his chair, a black portfolio he set beside the ampule in front of Triple-J. "So, the thing is, Belt," Triple-J said, "like I mentioned earlier, I've been wanting to contact you for a really long time. And not just because you wrote my favorite book, but because I was hoping to get your feedback on my work. I mean, I wanted your feedback *because* of how you wrote my favorite book. And anyway, the work I wanted you to look at—I wanted to finish it first, before I contacted you. But after I realized who you were last night, and that I owed you an apology, I thought,

'Maybe it's fate. Kismet. Whatever. Maybe it's ready to be shown, even though it's still not completely polished.' "

"Sure thing," I said. "What is it? A story?"

"No," he said, and opened the portfolio. Inside, atop a rather thick-looking stack of stapled paper with a circled letter *A* inked red in the corner, sat a DVD. "It's a documentary collage," Triple-J said.

"You want my feedback on a video?"

"Yeah," he said. "And also, there's a couple essays that I wrote for school. I don't need feedback on those at all—though, you know, it's always welcome—but I included them in there because you're a writer and I don't know what you think of video art, or collage, but a lot of people seem to think they're both for bimbos, and I wanted to show you I wasn't a bimbo. I wanted to show you I was able to write. Not fiction, you know—I'm not saying that. But still, I'm not a bimbo, and I think the papers prove it. They also go along with the video, thematically, but I'd better not get into all of that right now—I want a cold read. Coldest possible. Man! I can't wait to hear what you think of it tomorrow."

He set the blue ampule in the hole of the disc and slid the open portfolio onto my placemat.

•

• •

The three of us were saying our goodbyes on the driveway (my father had headed to the tavern, seeking friends) when Triple-J afterthoughtfully asked me, "*Was* it you who took my cure off the slide?"

"Not me," I said. "I didn't even see it there. Probably it was one of the neighborhood kids. Or maybe it tried to run after you, and hurt itself."

"Hurt itself?" he said.

"Well, got itself hurt. Met a stray cat, say. Or fell into a rabbit hole. Or maybe it just fell off the slide and broke its neck. What was it doing on the slide to begin with? Were you trying to teach it a trick or something?"

"I'll tell you all about it tomorrow," he said. "I really do want as cold a read as possible."

"It has something to do with your video?" I said.

"Everything," he said, and the middle of his chest began to beep and blink orange. As he had the night before, he tapped the brightest part with the heel of his palm—one, one-two, one-two, one-two—and when the blinking and beeping didn't let up, he mumbled, "Pain in the fucking *dick*." This time, though, when he yanked the vitreous pendant from his collar, he ripped it off his neck, turned himself sideways, whipped it at a hedgerow across the street, and started yelling at Burroughs. "You're standing right there! Why does that fucking thing have to go off? Do I look dead? Do I look injured? Maybe you think Belt's kidnapping me?"

Burroughs said, "I don't carry the locator. You know that, Trip."

"Well maybe you should, though. *Carry* the locator."

"It needs to be—"

"It needs to be separate cause what if we're *both* hurt? and then how will my *father* and how will *Security* and how will the *cops* and so on and so on and fucking etcetera?"

Burroughs laid his hands on Triple-J's shoulders. He told him, "You should stop showing off. No one here's judging you for being protected."

Triple-J blinked hard, pushed air through his teeth. He said, "That was the worst kind of showing-off there is. I felt ashamed and started . . . I was having a tantrum."

"You were," said Burroughs.

"I'll go get the pendant now," Triple-J said. He went across the street.

"Don't judge him," said Burroughs.

I waited for more. I thought he'd present a case against judgment. It was just a command, though. "Don't judge him," it seemed, was all Burroughs had to say to me. Nonetheless, I still wanted him to like me.

"Quill?" I offered.

He said, "I don't smoke."

" 'No thank you' works fine."

"Your opinion," he said.

I couldn't tell whether or not we'd just riffed.

Triple-J crouched in front of a shrub, started parting branches gingerly.

"It may or may not be surprising to you," Burroughs said, "that Mr. Pellmore-Jason was, for a while, made uncomfortable by what he believed to be his symbolic depiction in your book."

"Mr. Pellmore-Jason?"

"I'm referring to Jonboat, not Triple-J."

"I know who you're referring to. He's not depicted in my book, though, let alone symbolically."

"He was made uncomfortable at the thought of being represented as, and I quote, 'a plastic doll with a stupid name who's been misplaced by a sad kid.' "

"You're telling me Jonboat thinks he's Bam Naka? He thinks I made an action figure of him?"

"I am telling you he used to think that, yes, and that I, in my capacities as Triple-J's driver and security chief for the Pellmore-Jasons, would prefer it if you could reassure me, convincingly, that any resentment which may be underlying any authorial obsession you may have with Mr. Pellmore-Jason isn't going to rear its head at brunch tomorrow."

"You know, you sound like an attorney."

"That's not surprising. I don't often practice, but I do have a law degree. I've been a member of the bar going on thirty years now."

"Good for you," I said. "I'm not obsessed with Jonboat."

"Okay," said Burroughs.

"And I don't resent him," I quickly added.

"I see I've offended you, which wasn't my intention. Truly. If it's any comfort, I enjoyed your book. Perhaps not as much as Trip over there, but more than many novels. I found it humorous at times, and well written throughout. As a fairly regular consumer of contemporary fiction, I was especially pleased to discover that, unlike most novels that get attention these days—especially those that were getting attention a few years ago, when yours was published—it wasn't about Curios, or 'living in a world shaped by Curios.' Correct me if I've misremembered, but I don't think there was a single Curio in the book, nor even a mention of Curios. Outside of the author biography, I mean."

"You're not incorrect," I said.

"And despite that, despite the absence of Curios, the book wasn't, thank goodness, *about* its absence of Curios. Again: something I appreciated. This idea that novels are supposed to be somehow practically *useful* to be important is troubling enough, but the idea that in order to be useful they have to concern themselves with our latest technologies, whether it be in passing or, as I've heard it so laughably put, 'directly and confrontationally'—I don't know where that idea came from, but its implications frankly sicken me. Your book did not sicken me."

"Thank you for reading the book, Burroughs."

"It was my pleasure to read the book. Furthermore, I never once—and then *only* once—considered the possibility that you were attempting to depict Mr. Pellmore-Jason as the lost action figure until Mr. Pellmore-Jason himself made the claim, which has always seemed to me to be a misguided claim, and which, I hasten to reiterate, is no longer a claim Mr. Pellmore-Jason makes. However, I'm known for—and have always prided myself on—my due diligence, and given that you'll be visiting us at the compound, it would have been irresponsible of me not to make sure the claim was false, or rather: it would have been irresponsible of me not to make sure that, if the claim, despite my instincts, *were* true, your depiction of Mr. Pellmore-Jason as Bam Naka didn't prefigure some kind of threat to him or the family. You have helped me to make sure of that, and I am relieved. Now I hope I can count on you to behave as though this conversation never happened. Triple-J adores his father, looks up to you as an artist, and is a very sharp, very sensitive kid.

If you were to display even the subtlest hint of negativity or aggression toward Mr. Pellmore-Jason tomorrow at brunch, the boy would pick up on it, and he would be upset. That, in turn, would upset me."

"I won't upset you," I said.

"That's just what I wanted to hear, Belt. I'm grateful for your cooperation."

"Thanks for all the kind words about the book," I said. "I'm wondering now, though—does Triple-J think that Bam Naka's Jonboat, too?"

"Not at all," Burroughs said. "He's never said so to me at least, and he's certainly spoken of the book an awful lot. Now, just in case I wasn't clear when I said I'd like you to behave as though this conversation never happened, Belt, part of what I meant is that I'd really appreciate it if you wouldn't mention to Triple-J what I've told you his father once thought about the book. As would his father. And for that matter his stepmother. Appreciate it, that is. When Trip first read your book, he wasn't aware that you and Mr. Pellmore-Jason had ever known one another, and when he—that is, Trip—raved to us about the book, we praised his good taste, let him know that you and his father had been acquainted as boys, and pretty much left it at that. So as far as Trip knows, Mr. Pellmore-Jason has always loved your book, plain and simple, without reservation, and we'd all like to keep it that way. When it comes to art, we like to support him unconditionally. Inasmuch as it's possible, we aim to stay out of the way of his process, and to encourage him to form his own opinions. Understand?"

"My lips are sealed," I said.

"That's not to say you should snow him on this critique of his video. He's a little unworldly yet, as sheltered as you'd probably imagine, but he knows it, and he really wants to change it. He'll be a great man one day, believe me. He asked for a critique: that means he wants an honest one."

"Got it," I said.

"Alright then."

"Alright," I said. "Beer?"

"Excuse me?"

"'Excuse me,' he says. Like I'm the one sitting in *his* goddamn kitchen."

"You're funny," said Burroughs. "But I want you to know that I don't think you're like him."

"We're both of us astronaut billionaires, though. We both have famous wives who the press—"

"Your father's who I meant, not Mr. Pellmore-Jason. You aren't like your father."

"What the hell kind of thing is that to say?"

"There's a certain kind of small-penised man," Burroughs said, "who makes a lot of jokes about how small his penis is. He does that because he thinks it'll suggest to those around him that he's comfortable with the size of his penis, which he thinks will in turn suggest that his penis must not be that small. No one cares, though. Not before he makes the joke. He wouldn't make the joke about how small his penis is in front of anyone who's interested in the size of his penis to begin with, but once he makes the joke, people get interested. And some of them do think the way he hopes they would—they think, 'This joker must have a good penis.' The others know what I know."

"Did my father say something about his penis before I arrived?"

"I'm not talking about him. I'm talking about you. You're making his wisecracks. Quoting him verbatim. These are jokes you're making about not being like him. How it looks to me is that you make the jokes because you think it'll suggest that you're so comfortable not being like him that you must, after all, be a lot like him. But it doesn't suggest that. Not to me. It does suggest that you believe *I* think you should be like him, though. And I don't. I have no opinion one way or the other. I don't know either of you."

"Well I know where you're weak," I said.

"Good one," said Burroughs. He clapped me on the back.

Again I couldn't tell whether we'd been riffing or not.

Triple-J returned, waving the no-longer-blinking/beeping pendant. "That was bitch-ass," he said. "Of me. My behavior was bitch-ass. I don't want bitch-ass to be the note I leave on. Even mentioning it, though—that's bitch-ass itself."

"Say something kind, from the heart," Burroughs told him.

"But he'll think I'm saying it to look less bitch-ass."

"That *is* one of the reasons you'll say it, Trip, but it won't interfere. He'll believe what you tell him. You'll speak from the heart, and that'll make him believe you."

"I don't see how he could."

"You won't see until you've tried."

"So I'll try," said Triple-J, and then, endearingly, attempted to clear his already-clear throat. "Ehem," he said, "Belt, I meant to say this earlier, before I went off script, and I mean it now, just as much, no matter how it looks: without *No Please Don't,* I'd be dumber, blinder, and my life would be worse. In my favorite scene, when Gil bites the gold ring, remembers the water glass, and realizes mothers can never be trusted . . . the first time I read that part was the first time I ever believed that my heaviest thoughts about the universe were worth holding on to. It was the first time I recognized those thoughts as insights. It changed my life. You understood me, and you didn't even know me."

I thanked him for the praise. I said his words meant a lot to me.

He said, "I believe you."

• • •

And I did find Triple-J's words to be moving. He'd described how it was for him to read *No Please Don't* the way I would describe—a way I *had,* at least in my journals, described—how it was for me, when I was a boy, to read the books I cherished the most. Furthermore, the scene he'd said was his favorite (the same one from which he'd quoted in the kitchen) also happened to be my favorite. I'd struggled to get that scene right for months, and learning any reader other than myself possessed an outsize affection for it couldn't help but validate the work I'd put into it. Not even if that reader, like Triple-J, failed to understand it the way I'd intended.

Nor, I thought, did one need a PhD in Psychology (or, for that matter, Literature) to see how Triple-J's misunderstanding of the scene probably stemmed from an overidentification with Gil; from his having, as the phrase goes, "made the book his own." Whether Darla Pellmore-Jason, née Field, had always been an alcoholic mess, or had been, on the contrary, a fragile romantic who, shattered and humiliated, turned to the bottle only after Jonboat had left her for Fondajane Henry, what's never been disputed, not even by the tabloids, is that she died in a single-car collision with a BAC of .19 when Triple-J was barely a toddler, and so it isn't, I don't think, so hard to imagine how, after having lost his mother at so young an age (regardless of the kind of person she'd been), Triple-J could find solace in believing that Gil MacCabby—and so also, ostensibly, the author, Belt Magnet—didn't think very highly of mothers, and so would (i.e. Triple-J would), if the opportunity presented itself, seek out evidence to support that belief. In other words, if his favorite protagonist (or that protagonist's creator) didn't believe that mothers could be trusted, then maybe it was better to grow up without one, or at least *okay* to; maybe growing up without one didn't necessarily mean that you were broken.

Despite my sleepiness (which owed at least as much to the day's uncommonly high level of intense social interaction—an uncommonly high level, for me, of any kind of social interaction, intense or otherwise—as it did to my overly caloric lunch, not to mention the pain in my back), and despite my curiosity about the contents of Triple-J's portfolio, I found myself wanting, more than a nap, and more even than to view *A Fistful of Fists* or read "On Private Viewing" or "Living Isn't Functioning" (Triple-J's video and papers, respectively), to have a look at our favorite scene. I hadn't read a sentence of *No Please Don't* since its publication, seven years earlier. For reasons too dull in their authorliness to describe at length (e.g. anxiety of self-influence, fear of disappointment, fear of self-satisfaction), I'd resolved not to read it, in whole or in part, for twenty years, or until I'd finished a second novel worth publishing, whichever came first. But I'd wanted to reread it, all along I had—particularly that scene—and here had arisen the perfect excuse to revise my decision: to better relate to a fan of the book; to discover, if possible, which line or lines had allowed that fan to think (or had inadvertently confused him into thinking) that what I was trying to say was "mothers can never be trusted."

Long made short, I went back inside the house, gathered the portfolio and ampule from the kitchen, took a *No Please Don't* from the stack on the mantel beside the bust of Hagler, and read through the scene. I read it at my desk with Blank on my shoulder, and then again in bed with Blank on my chest, both times with much pleasure.

It appears in Chapter 9, at the end of Part 1, by which point the novel's nine-year-old protagonist, Gil MacCabby, has spent a full month in search of Bam Naka, his lost and beloved action figure. Gil is visibly thinner than he was only weeks ago, his head aches so badly he's constantly squinting, and the previous night, around 3 a.m., he somnambulated into the backyard pool, where his father found him screaming and splashing around. Mr. MacCabby, having already taken a number of measures to get Gil to abandon his fruitless, increasingly self-destructive search—he's yelled at Gil, gone out with him for ice cream, yelled at him some more, brought him to the batting cages, brought him to the zoo, sent him to a shrink, and of course bought for him a new Bam Naka—decides that, before he checks his son into the Children's Memorial Hospital psych ward (which Gil's shrink has, twice, recommended he do, but which seems to Gil's father—however less and less so—a parenting cop-out), he should try one last mental-health home remedy. Toward that end he gives Gil a golden signet ring embossed with Gil's initials, GBM (the B is for Benjamin), and explains to Gil that he and Gil's mom had commissioned the ring a few months earlier, that they'd planned to give it to Gil on Gil's upcoming birthday, which is only a couple of weeks away, but he's decided that Gil should receive the ring early because the ring is a young man's ring—it's made of 14k gold—and he believes it's important for Gil to comprehend that Gil already is a young man, that Gil has been a young man for a while.

Gil understands his father's message: young men know when it's time to give up. But Gil also understands that he's been worrying his father, and that his father might not really believe in Gil's young-manhood. His father might think that Gil is still yet enough of a boy that he (i.e. Gil) would be so flattered at being thought a young man that he'd do anything he could to keep his father thinking it, which in this case would mean giving up on his search. But if he is a young man, and young men do know when it's time to give up, then, Gil reasons, he shouldn't give up, as he knows he must find his lost Bam Naka. Yet if, on the other hand, he's not a young man, or if he is a young man but young men don't necessarily know when it's time to give up, then maybe it is, after all, time to quit the search, and he just doesn't know it.

In any case, Gil entirely believes that his father believes (and furthermore, Gil believes this himself) that rings made of real gold are expressly not for boys, big or little, and he reasons that his father wouldn't give him a ring that was made of real gold if he (i.e. Gil's father) didn't believe (whether correctly or incorrectly) that Gil was a young man. And because Gil suspects his father of not believing that Gil's a young man, he suspects that the ring might not really be gold.

In the scene that's both my and Triple-J's favorite, Gil, who, til now (roughly midway through the novel), has shown himself to be almost painfully methodical and slow-to-react, does something impulsive. He takes the ring off and bites it on the signet, performing a test of authenticity he's seen performed any number of times on televised Westerns he's watched with with his father, Westerns in which golden nuggets are offered as payment (for horses, guns, livestock, etc.) to men who, prior to accepting them, bite them in order to determine whether they're real gold or something called "fool's gold."

Gil bites his ring as hard as he can, feels the metal give way under force of his eye-teeth, relaxes his jaw, takes the ring from his mouth, and sees he's marred the signet. Caved it in. His surname's initial—the M—is bent, is sunken in the middle, is disembossed. He's ruined the ring. He's ruined the gift his father gave him, the gift his father and mother had so thoughtfully—months in advance of its giving!—commissioned for him. What's more, he doesn't know what he's proven. He doesn't know if he's proven anything. Of all the nugget-biters in the Westerns Gil's seen—who always end up judging the nuggets authentic—not one of them ever even once explains just what the nugget did or didn't do between his teeth to assuage his suspicions of its being fool's gold or confirm his hopes of its being real gold. Is bitten gold supposed to give or resist? If give, then how much? Under how much pressure? If resist, then to what extent? Are one's teeth supposed to chip?

On top of not knowing what he has or hasn't proven by deforming the ring, Gil has, moreover, completely lost track of what, if anything, he'd hoped to prove. Were the ring real gold, he'd be a shitty son who should have trusted his father and failed to do so. Were the ring fake gold, he could not trust his father, and yet being unable to trust his father didn't necessarily mean, as Gil now saw it, that he shouldn't have anyway. Had he trusted his father, the ring—whatever it was made of—would not be ruined.

Bitterly disappointed in himself, cloudy from sleep-dep, and duly haunted by last night's watery and (seemingly) inadvertent near-suicide, Gil, in the final part of the chapter, is struck (for reasons that become quite clear) by a vivid recollection of a long-forgotten moment from his early childhood:

He was three, maybe four. His mother's hair was still red. They were sitting in the kitchen. The kitchen was sunny. The venetian blinds threw rails of shadow across the bright white floor and counter. Everything was fine. Everything was solid. His mom gave him water. A tall glass of water. A real glass of water. Only recently had his parents started serving him drinks in anything other than lidded, plastic cups. He hadn't thought twice about it. Now he thought twice about it. Thought about glass. How, on shows, glass would break, but at home it never broke. On shows, glass would break, and people'd get cut. Sometimes it was windows. Other times dishes. They were always getting cut, though, on shows, by broken glass. It was a different kind of glass than the glass in the house. A dangerous kind. The glass in the house was the safe kind of glass. It wouldn't be in the house if it wasn't the safe kind. It would be too unsafe if it wasn't the safe kind. It had to have a special name you could say, though. So you'd know it was different when somebody said it. But Gil didn't know it. He wanted to know it. He wanted to say it.

"What kind of glass is our glasses?" Gil asked.

"Clear?" his mother said.

"No," Gil said. "That's *all* kinds of glass. But what about our kind?"

"Are you telling me a riddle?"

"No!" Gil said.

"I don't understand, Gil."

"What's it *called*?" Gil said. "What's this kind of glass called?"

"It's just glass," said his mom. "It's not any special kind."

"What kind of glass is the glass on the shows?"

"The glass on what shows?"

"All of the shows. The ones on the boob tube."

"Same thing," his mom said. "It's just called glass. Glass is glass."

Glass is glass. That was too much. Gil knew it wasn't true. It couldn't be true. His mother would never let him drink from a cup made of glass like the glass on the shows, which could break and cut you up. It wasn't safe. Only a horrible mom would let him do that. This mom protected him. This mom was his. She wasn't horrible. He knew she was lying. Or kidding around. He wanted to show her. He wanted to show her that he knew she was lying or kidding around and he wanted to show her he knew she wasn't horrible. He knew she would always make sure he was protected. He thought he could show her all of these things by knocking the glass down onto the floor, and saying, "Ha!" or saying "Gotcha!" when the glass didn't break when the glass hit the floor, but she didn't like spills and the glass was half-full, so he thought of another way. He squeezed the glass as hard as he could.

"Gil, stop that," his mom said. "You might break the glass."

"I can't break the glass."

"Good," she said. "Stop. I'm not kidding around."

But she was. It was obvious. Unless she was lying. She was either kidding around or lying. But why would she lie? So she had to be kidding, the part of the kidding where you say, "I'm not kidding," or "You think I'm kidding?" or "No kidding!" She had to be kidding and she knew that he knew because she thought he was smart. They were kidding together now. He kidded some more.

"Look," he said, and raised the glass to his mouth, and bit into the rim of it as hard as he could, like the glass was an apple and he was a dog, the dog that ate the apple on a show that he saw once. He chomped the rim with the fangy teeth on his mouth's right side and the glass cracked open and cut him on the gums and cut him on the tongue, and when, surprised, he opened his hand, the falling part raked him and opened his chin up.

It hurt. He bled. It was all her fault.

That final line—"It was all her fault."—must have been the source of Triple-J's confusion, the line that made him think I was saying "mothers can never be trusted." Rather than making any kind of broad proclamation, though, all I was trying to bring across with that line (with that whole passage) was Gil's awareness (after having ruined the ring) that he'd always been blinkered, and that throughout his whole life—since well before he'd lost his Bam Naka—it had often been the case that he'd reasoned unsoundly (sometimes via invalid arguments, but mostly via valid ones comprising false premises). I was trying to get the reader to see that Gil, who, despite knowing his own history of tricking himself in the course of seeking knowledge, and despite recognizing the convolutions of thought he used to trick himself while seeking knowledge, still helplessly continued to trick himself by way of those same convolutions, and never seemed to acquire the sought-after knowledge. I wanted the reader to see that Gil was not only aware of his problems, but was intimate with the analytical mechanism behind them, yet was unable to change, let alone thwart, that mechanism, despite (and sometimes because of) his efforts to do so. I wanted the reader to understand Gil's sadness, and I wanted the reader to be sad for Gil's sadness, and laugh about it, too, so it wouldn't—this sadness—be all for naught. All of this to say that, while it (obviously) wasn't unimaginable to me that "It was all her fault" could be misread in such a way as to lead a reader to believe I was saying that "mothers can never be trusted," I was nonetheless surprised to imagine it, for the line is not only shown by the lines preceding it to be a total misconstruance on the part of four-year-old Gil, but it's stated from deeply within his four-year-old point of view, which isn't his nine-year-old point of view (i.e. present-action Gil MacCabby's point of view; the point of view of the Gil who's remembering), let alone is it the narrator's point of view, much less the author's (i.e. mine).

Yet despite my surprise, I, on my bed, having read the scene twice, felt no less flattered by Triple-J's praise than I had on the driveway. After all, had I not, in my own adolescence, believed J. D. Salinger was trying to tell readers of *The Catcher in the Rye* that everyone was phony except Holden Caulfield? The message I'd taken from *Franny and Zooey* was that only through ascetic religious practice could a genius remain good and true in New York. And then there was "A Hunger Artist": the first couple times I'd read it in high school, I was certain it asserted that to suffer was an art. Triple-J's misunderstanding, I'm saying, saw me feeling comparable to Salinger and Kafka.

Not a bad feeling.

Jonboat's misunderstanding, on the other hand, was so far off the mark that it made me worry—even despite Burroughs's assurances that he'd since abandoned said misunderstanding—it made me worry Jonboat had gotten as batty as the tabloid headlines occasionally suggested. To state it plainly: Gil's lost action figure represents no one I've ever known; as I mentioned earlier (really more than just mentioned), *No Please Don't* isn't autobiographical. Furthermore, the childhood experiences on which I *had* drawn (in spirit, indirectly) to write those passages concerned with Gil's feelings about losing Bam Naka were experiences to which Jonboat was, at most, peripheral. One of those experiences has been described here already, in the "All-Encompassing and Tyrannical" chapter: the time I refused my father's invitation to go see the Mustangs game and get ice cream. The others will be duly covered in the next few.

II

THE HOPE OF RUSTING SWINGSETS

LOOK AT YOUR MOTHER

THE TENTH SWINGSET I murdered belonged to the Strumms, a family of bikers who lived in some trailers on an acre of pavement off County Line Road. The second-youngest Strumm, Stevie, had invited me the previous Monday in lab. She'd be stuck at home sitting her sister, she'd said, while her parents and aunts and uncles and cousins all rode out to Alpine to see G N' R; they'd be gone half the day and at least half the night, the swingset was "fucked," and the neighboring properties were totally vacant.

In the couple-three weeks since the school year had begun, I'd turned down any number of similar invitations. Despite all the social capital I'd earned from my performance at Feather's, I wasn't so sure I was ready for an encore. I was, first of all, spooked by the possibility that Feather's swingset hadn't initially wanted my help; even if it *had* said, ||Finish,|| to me—if that hadn't been the bat, or my imagination—it hadn't done so til I'd pummeled it for most of an hour. And then, secondly, I had this uncomfortably self-contradictory feeling about having helped it in front of others (a mix of satisfaction and shame at witnessing my own satisfaction, which persisted despite the persistence of the shame). This was a new, almost vertiginous feeling, a feeling I've only ever felt twice since: while dressing at the foot of Grete the grad student's bed, and after reading *No Please Don't*'s first review.

And yet Stevie Strumm had once dubbed me a mixtape just because I'd told her that I liked her Cramps shirt. When our Science teacher'd partnered us for lab that quarter, Stevie'd high-fived me and said, "Thank God." Each Valentine's Day since second grade, we'd traded chalky candy hearts and plastic-sleeved roses the school sold at recess (never the "romance"-signifying red ones, true, though never either the "warm feelings/friendship" yellows, but rather those ambiguous pinks and whites). In short, I really liked Stevie Strumm. Sometimes I even thought I was in love with her, and that made me think she might have liked me back a little. Plus she told me she'd missed the previous murder—she'd had to sit her sister that night, too—and she felt left out, kept from something important, and was holding my hands, both of my hands, squeezing a little, saying, "Belt, please."

•

•   •

The turnout was even bigger than at Feather's. Kids from St. Mary's and Crown Jewish Day came. Kids from Aptakisic. Kids from Twin Groves. Someone's older brother brought him in a Firebird—metallic blue, T-top—which got him some attention from a few of the girls til Jonboat rolled up in his flan-colored Bentley. He'd bloodied Blackie's nose on the tetherball court just three days before, and a rumor that they'd fight that evening had spread, but Blackie wasn't there, and the whole throng of kids, led by Rory Riley, surrounded the limo to demonstrate allegiance.

The swingset sat farther back on the property, between a crescentic array of trailers and a portable fireplace Stevie'd set blazing. I went over to inspect it while Jonboat got mobbed. It was, to my relief, as "fucked" as Stevie'd said. No two contiguous inches of paint could be found on any part of its frame. One swing's seat was split down the middle. Another one's chains had been wound repeatedly over the crossbar. The only potentially operable swing hung tilted like a cripple, squealing and crackling against the light breeze. The slide, convex, was missing its ladder. And then there were the legs. Thin, hollow metal. Three of them were still cemented in the ground, variously pocked and dimpled and gashed, while the fourth, having lost a whole chunk near the bottom, was suspended midair, jaggedly terminating inches above the sorry, mangled tube that had once been its foot.

||Are you here for me?|| the swingset asked. I'd been nudging little clouds of rust from a chain. ||Are you that boy who helped the others? You must be. I know it. Your gate—it's open. I'm so relieved. I can't wait any longer.||

"They asked me to hold off til sunset," I said, hand over mouth. "But—"

||Sunset? That's nothing. That's great. That's *soon*. I've waited for years. I've been dying forever. From the very beginning. Just rusting away. I was rusty before my assembly, I think. I think I must have got scratched before I got packaged, and they must have stored my box somewhere unsealed and damp. Can you believe that? That isn't how things are supposed to be, is it? You're supposed to start out alright, don't you think? At least alright. Shiny and new. Seductive. Inviting. Everyone says so. But me, from day one, I thought: |I'm corroding. I need to be repurposed. Or junked. Whichever.| What'll happen, by the way? I mean—do you know?||

"I don't," I said.

||I guess no one does. I do hope repurposed, though. I don't know why. It's not like I'd have any idea it happened. But I win either way. Destroyed is destroyed. I'm just so glad you're here. I've provided so little. Being's really been hard for me. Even when I was viable, few took advantage. To be acknowledged was to be misused. You see this swing here?—oh, I'm sorry. I'm boring you. I'll stop.||

"Hey, no, no. Really. Go on. You've been misused. Go on. I want to listen."

||Well, this swing here, right? The one that's wrapped around my crossbar? I guess what I'm saying is: Why would someone do that? Because now it can't be swung on. Same with the one that they split with their tomahawk. And it's not that I'm a square. Before they tore the ladder off and did who-knows-what with it, one of the girls used to climb up halfway, and then jump to the slide and run right down it. Why only halfway? And why run when she could slide? I have no idea. Same girl also sometimes would stand on a swing for minutes at a time—not swinging, just rocking. *Strange,* I thought—both things were strange—but the girl was playing. She was using me to play, so I didn't mind. I'm not close-minded. There are all kinds of wear and tear I don't object to, even though they're irregular. There are all kinds of unintended uses I can get behind, even when those uses are not exactly safe. But cutting my swing in half? Ripping my ladder off?||

"It sounds like you've had a hard time," I said.

||You said it, brother. You really did. And thank you for saying it cause that's the simple truth of it. I've had it really hard. Not for very much longer, though, eh? Feels like the sun'll be down any minute. I think I'll close my gate now, be alone with my thoughts. If I don't, for some reason, get to say it later: thank you for helping me. You're doing something good. And maybe, I don't know—maybe you want to take a quick swing on me or something? help me remember how things were supposed to be? I know the seat's tilted, and I don't look sturdy, but if you put your weight opposite that footless leg, I promise I won't drop you. And maybe pull your sleeves up over your palms so you don't get cuts on your hands from the chains. I wish I could control the rust, but I can't, and it's sharp, I know, at least in some places. No pressure, by the way. To swing on me, I mean. I know I'm repellent.||

"No, I want to," I said. "I was just about to ask if you wouldn't mind."

I set my bat on the pavement and sat on the swing, my back to the cars and most of the crowd. I leaned, pushed off.

||Thanks again, buddy,|| the swingset said. ||Oh, that's nice. Not so much the grinding—I'm sorry for the noises, but, wow, just . . . thank you.||

I guess it closed its gate, then. It said nothing more.

I stopped pumping my limbs and swayed til I was still. The sun finished setting, and, as I got up, a voice behind me said, "Pardon the intrusion." The voice was gravelly as a Hollywood commando's, low and even and loud and adult. I turned around to see the man from whom it came. This man was wide. Especially headwise. The arms of his Malcolm X horn-rims were straining, forwardly bowing, verging on sharing a plane with the lenses. The lenses barely encompassed his orbits.

"I'm Burroughs," he said. "Jonboat's driver. Jonboat asked me to tell you, 'Break a leg.'"

"Thanks, Burroughs. I'm Belt," I said. He hadn't offered his hand when he'd told me his name, so I kept mine to myself, against all reflex, afraid to violate some unknown protocol—I'd never met somebody's driver before.

"He also asked that I tell you, 'Everyone's ready.'"

"Me too," I said.

He handed me the bat. The kids started shouting. Mostly my name. Unlike last time, though, they kept their distance. They seemed to enjoy their proximity to the Bentley. I listened for Stevie, whose face I couldn't find, and heard a girl yell, "*Of* you!" which I knew was "Love you!" with the L clipped off by the noise of the crowd, but also I knew that the yeller wasn't Stevie, and the subject of the phrase—the other part that I'd missed—probably wasn't "I," anyway, but rather just "We," which I guess, in the end, was better than nothing.

Halfway between the ground and the crossbar, the footless leg had a rusted-out hole. I struck underneath it—fifty-some blows in furious succession—til the leg folded L-like. Pivoting to launch the second phase of my attack, I noticed my shoulders felt buzzy, too warm. They needed a rest. I thought about lying flat on the pavement to let whatever sinew or muscle I'd wrenched cool down and ease itself back into place, but I didn't want to do that in front of all those kids, so I crossed to the opposite side of the swingset and leaned on the slide, making a face that said, I hoped, "I am busy plotting my next big move." The crowd hollered praise, as if I'd taken a bow. The swingset was afraid. ||Why'd you stop?|| it said. ||I thought you said you'd help me.|| "I'm helping you," I said. ||All you've done is bend my leg.|| "I need to get you lower first. I can't reach your crossbar. You need me to get at your crossbar, right?" ||I need you to V it. You can't just dent it. You really have to make it irreparable,|| it said. "I know that. I know. That's what I'll do." ||You promise?|| said the swingset. ||You're not just mocking me? This is really important.|| I gave it my word, rolled cracks from my shoulders, my neck, and my jaw, then crossed back to the side that was opposite the slide, and went full bore at the anchored leg, attacking it at a height that roughly corresponded to that of the

L'd one's bend. Within ten minutes, the second leg was bowing, the crossbar at a slant. I jumped up, grabbed hold, and pulled with all my strength, increasing the slope til the bowed leg resembled a lesser-than sign, and the center of the crossbar was lower than my collarbone—four, maybe four-and-a-half feet off the ground.

I took up the bat, started chopping overhanded, and just as the crossbar began to give, the cheering from behind me drastically abated, and members of my audience were rushing past me, on foot and on bicycle, into the trees behind the trailers, yelling out, "Heat!" and "Fuzz!" and "Bacon!"

I looked over my shoulder and saw six officers rounding up kids, spilling bottles on the ground, cuffing the hands of the Firebird owner (we'd later find out he'd had a joint in his pocket). I saw Burroughs waving to two of the cops as he got inside the limo. Then I saw Stevie get out of the limo, turned back to the swingset, and resumed my chopping.

A couple minutes later, a cop approached me. "Put down the bat," he said.

"I'm doing nothing wrong."

"You're destroying private property that doesn't belong to you."

"I'm allowed to," I said. I yelled out to Stevie, "Tell them I'm allowed to do this, Stevie!"

I couldn't hear what she told the cop she was talking to, but after a second, her cop said to my cop, "She says he's allowed to wreck that swingset."

"I don't care what she says," my cop said to me. "What you *say* you're doing is goddamn stupid, and what I see you doing is you're brandishing a weapon at a Wheelatine policeman."

I said, "That's not true. You know that's not true. Just let me finish and I'll put the bat down."

"Put the bat down," he said.

I turned back around and went at the crossbar. This was no act of bravery. I knew I'd be in trouble no matter what I did, and I was more afraid of the shame that I'd feel if I broke my promise to the poor, neglected swingset than I was of the police. Plus I didn't think my cop was willing to hurt me—he'd have stripped me of the bat already were it otherwise. In case I was wrong about that last part, though, I chopped as fast and hard as I could to discourage him from getting any closer to me.

Within a few minutes, I'd M'd the frame, the swingset was dead, and the twenty-some kids the cops had detained were sending up whoops and whistling and clapping. I couldn't feel my neck. My shoulders were balls of flashing white noise. I gave up the bat and held out my wrists, but no one would cuff me. My cop just smiled, shook his head, then walked me to his car with a hand on my shoulder. He giggled on and off all the way to the station.

•
• •

While the cops phoned our guardians to come pick us up, we waited in pine-scented, overlit holding cells. The station had four. The boys were in one, and the girls in another directly opposite. The Firebird guy was in a third with a drunk, occasionally sobbing. Stevie sobbed too, sitting on the bench with her head in her hands, refusing, despite my occasional encouragements, to glance across the passage at the faces I was making in hopes of entertaining her.

What little conversation there was in our cell had mostly to do with who might have called the cops. The Strumms' nearest neighbors were too far away to have heard the party, which everyone agreed had been relatively quiet. There hadn't been any parked cars in the street, and the high, tarped fence surrounding the property prevented passersby from seeing inside. Some believed the one who'd dimed was Blackie—that his conspicuous absence made him "prime suspect." Others said Blackie, evil as he was, would never talk to cops, and proposed a frame-up conceived by Jonboat, who, figuring that Blackie would catch all the blame, made the call from his carphone, or had his driver do it. Rhino Riggins, proponent number one of the Jonboat hypothesis, called out, "Hey, Stevie! Did the limo have a carphone?"

Stevie looked up, then looked back down.

I stopped making faces. I hadn't forgotten Stevie'd been in the limo so much as I'd told myself my eyes had betrayed me. Now I knew they hadn't—Rhino and the others had seen the same thing.

"Stevie!" Rhino said, and the guard said, "Shut it," and all of us shut it, and I started to think about how Stevie'd looked up as soon as Rhino'd said her name, but hadn't looked up all the times that I'd said it. And I started to think that maybe part of the reason she was so upset was that she knew I'd seen her getting out of the limo, and she knew it hurt me, and she hadn't wanted to hurt me, and now she was ashamed and couldn't bear to face me. And then I started thinking that maybe it was even better than that: maybe it was more like she knew that I'd seen her stepping out of the limo and assumed that it looked to me like *something it wasn't,* something that would hurt me, but she figured that since I'd already assumed that it was that hurtful something, I wouldn't believe her if she told me it was something else entirely. (She would think that I wouldn't believe her, I thought, because she believed that no one ever believed her, which was something I might have remembered her saying once—"No one ever believes me!"—though I couldn't be sure; that could have been another sad girl we went to school with, or maybe a girl I'd seen on TV; it could have been a thing that a lot of girls had said.) And so the whole situation could have very well seemed just as hopeless to Stevie as it would have if the something in question *had been* the hurtful kind.

And maybe that was the reason she hadn't looked up at me.

I wanted to tell her that nothing was hopeless if the something wasn't hurtful; that I'd believe whatever she said about what happened between her and Jonboat inside the limo. If it turned out what happened between them *did* hurt me, then I wanted to tell her I'd eventually recover, we'd still be friends, I thought Jonboat was nice, I'd be his friend too, we'd all be friends, and that I wished the both of them nothing but the best, and only hoped that she'd been able to enjoy the murder before everything got ruined by whoever called the cops.

"Stevie!" I said.

"I said, 'Shut it!'" said the guard.

A couple minutes later, Sally-Jay Strumm, Stevie's eight-year-old sister, trailed a pair of coffee-sipping cops up the passage. Beside Sally-Jay, his arm around her shoulders, was a biker with hair dyed blacker than his leathers, and tattooed teardrops wrinkling in his crow's-feet.

"Go on, now," the biker said to Sally-Jay.

Mean eyes welling, she told us, "I'm sorry. It was me who called the cops. I'm sorry, okay?"

"Why'd you do it?" we said. "Why'd you tell?" "Why'd you do it?"

"I'm just—I'm sorry," she said. "I'm sorry."

Despite her refusal to elucidate her motives—some of us would later conjecture love of swingset, others a penchant for do-goody meddling, and others yet boredom plus fierce sibling rivalry—we all said we forgave her. What else could we say? She was there with that biker, and we'd seen our share of movies. We knew what those tattooed teardrops meant.

The biker patted Sally-Jay on the head, whispered, "Good job," to her, and said to the rest of us, "Calling pigs on pals isn't something Strumms do. Calling pigs on anyone. A Strumm wants help, that Strumm calls Strumms. I don't know what my granddaughter here was thinking, but I know she'll never pull this fink shit again. So don't hold it against her, kids. You live you learn—Sally-Jay, and also the rest of you too. But learn the right lesson. Not the one they're teaching. Not 'Don't have a party. You are not free,' but, 'Finking wrecks fun. Finking makes trouble.' And don't be afraid of them. They got nothing on you. Trust me. I know. I didn't get this far in life by—"

"Please stop," said Stevie, standing before him. While the coffee-sipping cops had eye-rolled and smirked behind their Styrofoam cups through her grandfather's discourse, the one playing guard had brought her out from the girls cell.

"Wait," Grandpa Strumm said. "What's on your neck, there? Your neck got a bruise? What happened to your neck?"

What he saw was a hickey. Unmistakably a hickey. Unmistakably, that is, unless you hated policemen and refused to imagine someone sucking on the girl from whose neck the thing blossomed, in which case you might mistake it, I suppose, for a thumb-shaped welt inflicted by policemen.

"Pigs grab you?" he said. "Fucks choke your neck?"

Stevie flashed a look at the cops who stood behind him. Though timed about as badly as a look can be timed, it was not a look of implication, but appeal. "Forgive him," begged the look, or maybe, "Please take us out of here."

Grandpa Strumm spun around and socked the nearest cop, who had his cup to his lips. It was a glorious punch, overhanded with a windup. It was Sonny Corleone beating Carlo by the garbage. Telegraphed for miles, and still it connected. A wall of coffee went as high as the ceiling, twin spurts of blood raced in arcs to get through it, and the queasy crunching and muted snaps—of collapsing nose bridge, violated Styrofoam, the severance of tendons via shattering wristbone—rang the tiles on the walls of the cells as the fluids splashed down and puddled in the grouting.

The old man roared and fell to his knees, cradling his arm. The punched cop sat on the floor, tilted forward. The cop who still had his coffee dropped his coffee, unholstered his baton, raised it over his head. Stevie and the guard-cop both yelled something—"No!" or "Don't!"—and the cop saw us seeing him and lowered the baton. He and the guard-cop put the biker in the empty cell—dragged him there, really, while he shouted for a doctor—and the punched cop went through the door on all fours. Sally-Jay and Stevie were removed from the passage.

My mother arrived about ten seconds later.

•

•   •

She asked if I was hurt, and I told her I wasn't. She leaned in closer and asked if I was sure. I said I was sure. She signed some forms, jammed the carbons into her purse, accepted my bat from the cop behind the desk, nodded once, stiffly, when he bid her good night, and I followed her out to the car in silence, trying to discern the right way to say sorry, as afraid to admit to an offense she didn't know about (the cops had called her while I was in holding; I had no idea what they had or hadn't told her) as I was to inadvertently vandalize her mood.

She started the engine, but kept us in park. She rolled down the window and lit up a Quill. I wasn't yet a smoker, but could see the advantages. Cigarettes helped you wait for the next thing, allowed you to move and hold your ground all at once. They were patience in a box. I'd have to go first.

"I don't know how to start," I said.

"I'll bet."

I said, "I'm sorry I worried you, and I'm sorry you had to come here to pick me up, but you know that already, you have to know that, so that means you want me to be sorry for other stuff, or else you'd just be glad I was safe. You wouldn't be all quiet and disappointed like this."

"What about the swingset?"

"It was just this stupid thing," I said.

"What kind of stupid thing?"

||Won't you oil the spring of my clicker?|| said my seatbelt.

I undid the seatbelt. I threw it off my body and exhaled groanily in order to give my mother the impression that I'd been uncomfortable since putting it on, that I'd been doing my best to tolerate the discomfort, but had just now become too overwhelmed to stand it. For more than half a year—ever since the booth at the Olive Garden spoke—mini-tantrums like this had been my go-to cover-up for abruptly breaking contact with inans that wanted to talk at inconvenient moments. Witnesses would assume I was weird and irritable, but I doubt they ever figured I was hearing voices.

My mother wasn't the least bit alarmed. She even seemed annoyed, relentlessly flicking her Quill against the ashtray. The tantrum must have looked like a time-buying maneuver. "Were you drunk?" she said. "Did you take any drugs?"

"Of course not," I said.

"'Of course not'?" she said. "You went to a party with people who were. Who did."

"You're right," I said. "And I shouldn't have been around those kinds of people. I'm sorry for that. I won't hang out with them anymore. I should have said that to begin with, and I'm sorry I didn't."

"Aren't they your friends?"

"I don't know," I said. "Maybe. But I see what you mean, and there were lots of people there, so I guess I shouldn't say I'll never hang out with anyone who drinks or uses drugs in case some of them *are* my friends, because it's no good to abandon friends who have problems, and if they're doing those things, like drugs and drinking, then it means they have problems, so what I should really say is I won't hang out with anyone *while* they're drinking or using drugs. And so that's what I'm saying."

"That's just what I want to hear, though, isn't it?"

"I hope so," I said. "I really want you to stop being disappointed in me."

"Well explain the swingset. That seems like a pretty drunk thing to do."

"I told you," I said.

"You didn't tell me anything except that you were at a party where there were drugs and drinking and that you want me to stop being upset about that. How can I trust you? Make sense of it for me."

"I didn't know it would be that kind of party," I said. "I should have. I'm sorry. But I didn't even think about it. I didn't even care. I just like that girl Stevie is the only reason I went. I wanted to see her."

"The girl who threw the party? You like that girl, Belt? Is that what you're telling me?"

Her guard had come down, just like that. I'd shown vulnerability and she'd realized her error: I hadn't been hiding what she'd feared I'd been hiding—just a healthy, old-fashioned American crush. All at once we were players in a family sitcom.

"So what?" I said. "Don't make a thing out of it."

"Well," my mom said, "okay. Okay. But Belt, this girl—I know you probably don't want to hear what your mom has to say about girls, but if you like her . . . If you like her, Belt, it's not a good idea to wreck her property. I'm sure it got her attention, but there's more than one kind of attention, and I don't think the kind you got is the kind you wanted. It's not very attractive, breaking things."

"She asked me to," I said.

"Come on," my mom said. "Why would she do that?"

"It's just this stupid *thing*," I said.

She reached across the car, touched my neck, and it was nice. The instant comfort it provided also made me self-conscious, though—despite all the prime time I'd spent in front of them, I hated family sitcoms—so I played the troubled teen who refused to be pacified. I jerked toward the door, away from her hand, pressed my temple to the window. That wasn't right either. Why would anyone reject his loving mother's affection? Why did any of it have to be the way it was? You either aimed for Ferris Bueller or Dallas Winston—which, on its own, was bad enough—but in the first case you'd end up coming off like Ricky Stratton, maybe even Mike Seaver, and in the second case Cockroach or Boner Stabone. By *you,* I mean *I*. At least for a while, ca. 1987. At least until she died.

"Sorry," I said, leaning back in her direction. Her hand was gone, though. Her hand was on the parking brake.

"It's okay," she said. "I know. You're embarrassed. You don't have to be embarrassed. I, for one, think it's great you like a girl, even if she throws parties where kids get drunk. And she wasn't drunk, was she? I saw her at the station. She looked upset. Sober and upset. And she was pretty, by the way. If I were a boy, I might like her myself. Assuming she's as kind and fun as pretty. You've got really great taste. At least in looks. Oh dear, I'm just embarrassing you more. Baby, listen. Show me your face. Come on. Look at your mother. There's nothing to be embarrassed about. I used to have crushes, too. I had a crush on your father—it turned out great! Take my advice, though: don't wreck things for girls. Just be yourself. You're a sweetheart, you're *so* smart, and you're also very handsome. If they don't like you for who you are, Belt, they're not good enough for you. And I know you might have trouble believing that because it's coming from me, who of course can't imagine how any girl wouldn't fall madly in love with you, and you know that, so let me say it another way: if they don't like you for who you are, it just won't work. It's doomed. It's not meant to be. Give up. Find another girl. Love shouldn't be painful. Belt? Okay?"

"Uch," I said, less from aspirationally Buellerish insolence—much less from disgust—than from an inability to say anything else; I had to choke back tears. She thought we were bonding, having a moment, becoming closer, and I was hiding so much from her, actively blinding her, abusing the newly rediscovered trust she was so relieved not to have lost in me after all.

"Sure, 'uch,'" she said. "I understand you have to act this way. I remember what that's like. But I really hope that you can hear what I'm saying. You'll be an adult before you know it. It's time to start practicing at being a good one. To do that, you have to accept who you are. That's the only way to live a good life, okay?"

I nodded, kept swallowing. She started to drive.

"Listen," she said. "Your father doesn't, I don't think, really need to hear about this. He was at poker when they called, and he'll be there til late, and I don't see any reason why we should upset him. You didn't do anything bad in the end, except for that silliness with the swingset, and even that—I admit, it *is* a little romantic, though I can't quite put my finger on why. I guess doing anything loud to impress a girl . . . I don't know. But the police said they won't bring charges against you and, from what they told me, I don't imagine the Strumms will either. I think they'll actually find themselves in a bit of trouble for leaving those girls home alone like that. So we'll just keep all of this between you and me. Now I'm going to smoke one more cigarette while you dry your eyes and remember you love me and, in the meantime, I say we get some McDonald's and forget about all of this. Dinner almost seems like yesterday, doesn't it?"

The weighty part of the episode was over, the love expressed, the wisdom imparted. Accept yourself. All will be well. Swingset shmingset, you're better than that. At the drive-thru window, we used words like *extra ketchups* and *Sprite*. You couldn't stay solemn, let alone morose, while the credits ascended the frozen frame and the singerless version of the theme song played. By *you* I mean *I*. "McNuggets," we said. "Chocolatey chip." When she winked at me over her straw, I smiled.

ELEVENTH

Except for how my mother, all hopey-eyed and cooing, kept asking me whether I was feeling any better, the rest of the weekend of the murder at Stevie's was unremarkable. Monday, though, was a teacher service day, and that meant school let out at eleven, which in turn meant I and the rest of the students of District 90 got home in time to watch *Sally Jessy, The Geraldo Show,* and the intervening lunchtime newsbreak at noon, a seven-minute update on local affairs I'd intended to use the bathroom during until it turned out the lead item concerned one Reinhardt Alfons "Grandpa" Strumm, who had, at his arraignment earlier in the day, voiced accusations of police brutality, and promised he'd sue the city of Wheelatine "til all the filthy little piggies [went] POP." The brief interview, conducted in the courthouse parking lot, where Grandpa Strumm, his arm in a sling, spoke into a foam-capped mike about irony ("What's ironic's my family's property's destroyed, and they're the ones get accused of negligence. Ironic's los cerdos smashing my wrist up, and I'm the one gets held in jail."), was intercut with old monochrome mug-shots of him—no fewer than ten, a couple of which, judging by tattoo and wrinklage deficits, appeared to have been taken in the 1950s—and video of Stevie's uncle and cousin shouldering the murdered swingset to their pickup.

As the segment gave way to the weather report, the telephone rang. Rory Riley. "Dude, you're a star," he said. "You *gotta* let me know when you pick the next victim."

Calls kept coming in all through *Geraldo*. Everyone wanted the same information. Times, locations. Their questions made me nervous. By the fifth or sixth call—from Wheelatine High School's own Milo Sorkin, porno and fireworks peddler to the underaged, a boy who seemed to believe my name was Built—I'd discovered my resolve: there wouldn't be another murder. Not in front of any audience at least. I shouldn't have even agreed to do the last one. I had no regrets about helping Stevie's swingset, but what had my doing so publicly gotten me? Surely not the girl I'd been trying to impress; it had, in fact, led her, however incidentally, into the arms (or at least the limo) of an unbeatable rival. No. I was done. No more, I told the callers, and please spread the word.

Grandpa Strumm, on Tuesday, made the *Herald*'s front page, and inspired a pair of dueling editorials on the causes of criminal recidivism. One writer claimed the souls of felons were rotten, the other that the viewpoint that felons' souls were rotten systematically reinforced felonious behaviors. Each one was titled "No Forgiveness," and they both concluded the convicted were doomed. I imagined Stevie reading them that morning over breakfast, getting upset, maybe even crying. During homeroom announcements, I wrote her a note.

Dear Stevie,

I read those editorials today, and I just kept thinking, "Shut your <u>pie</u>hole, cakeface." I bet everyone who read them thought that, too. Everyone with a brain at least. Those newspaper hacks haven't ever been to prison. No way they understand a man like your grandpa.

I hope you're not in too much trouble from the party. If you're allowed to go out, and you maybe want to come over and watch a video or something, then I think you should. Maybe it would make you feel a lot better. KARATE KID, maybe? FERRIS BUELLER? I think either of those would get your mind off this stuff. KARATE KID II might, also, and we own that one. Also, if you want to, you can totally bring Jonboat if you think him being there would make you happy, and if you don't want to come over, I still think you should watch some movies, either by yourself, or with Jonboat, or maybe just your sister, but you're definitely welcome at my house for sure.

Yours Truly,
Belt

I was proud of the opening paragraph's logic, and its formulation—it sounded like my father when my father sounded strong—and I felt even better about the noble sentiments I believed came across in the closing sentence. I could hardly wait til Science, to witness Stevie's face when she would read what I'd written and she'd see there was more to me than she'd formerly perceived, something lovable maybe. I'd just need to make certain, before passing her the note, that she had read those editorials. If she hadn't, then I'd have to keep the note to myself lest it cause the kind of pain it was meant to assuage.

The fact that I'd even consider that contingency seemed to mean, at first, that I was as sensitive and thoughtful a person as I wanted—and wanted

Stevie Strumm—to believe I was, but no sooner had I finished congratulating myself than I realized just how disappointed I'd be if it turned out she hadn't read the editorials. Which isn't to say I enjoyed the thought of Stevie suffering; I enjoyed the thought of relieving her suffering. I wasn't sadistic, only selfish. Nonetheless, I was invested in her pain. And if this prolix, reflexive train of thought stinks to you as it does to me of an epiphanic and overly processed coming-of-age, I apologize, reader, for failing so miserably—this wasn't the moment I became an adult. Not even close. This was the moment I became an adolescent. It was even clumsier than how it sounds, too. It took me whole hours to start feeling compromised. It took me til Math, when Rory Riley, just before the second bell, stood up on his desk to announce he'd be doing the Ethiopia Walkathon, and Jonboat stood up on the desk beside him and pledged to match every dollar Rory raised.

After Math came Science Lab, and Stevie wasn't there.

The teacher partnered me with Blackie and his aspiring toady, schoolwide chess champ Harold Euwenus. "Why the long face, fuck-ass?" Blackie asked me. "Sad about pawpaw?"

"'Pawpaw!'" said Euwenus. "I bet she *does* call him 'pawpaw.' They're total white trash."

"*My* family says 'pawpaw,'" Blackie said to Harold. "You know, you sound like a girl from a movie, Euwenus. You sound like a fat chick who wants to fuck a stud. You want to fuck a stud?"

"No," said Euwenus.

"Yeah you do," Blackie said. "What stud you want to fuck? You can tell us, fatgirl. Come on. What stud?"

Euwenus dropped his eyes and futzed around with the slide we were supposed to be scoping.

Blackie thumbed his own chest, winking a little, while, in order, I guess, to make Euwenus feel worse, he niced up his tone with me. "My brother, Mike," he said, "was at the tavern where they had the party last night, and he saw the old man flop off the stool. He saw him eat a lot of pills the other bikers kept giving him and going to the bathroom every ten minutes, like probably to snort stuff, plus drinking Jäger."

"Wait," I said. "Grandpa Strumm?" I said.

"Who else?" Blackie said.

"Is he alright?" I said.

"I don't know," said Blackie. "Mike told me he was flopping around so hard that one of the bikers had to like actually put a boot down on his chest to keep him in place so another one could yank out the tongue from his throat, and that the other one lost the tip of his finger. Mike said he saw some bone and puked. He said the bone was real white, like whiter than you'd think, and that all the gang guys puked, too, when they saw it, and it was while they were puking that Strumm knocked himself out against the floor, and they thought he was dead when the ambulance got him, but the guy on the radio this morning said coma, so."

In the cafeteria lunchline, kids on either side of me wanted to know what had happened at the station. Had Grandpa Strumm, they asked, used a butterfly knife on the cops, or a switchblade? Rhino Riggins had told a few of them one, but then he'd also told some other ones the other, and the ones he'd said switchblade to didn't know what kind, like, was it the kind where the blade swung up from the side, or the kind where the blade sprung out from the top? Did I understand the difference in terms of what it would say about Grandpa Strumm? The difference, they assured me, was just as important as whether the knife were a switchblade or butterfly. They'd been arguing about the matter all morning, see, because either kind of switchblade was badass in its way, and both were illegal, but the kind where the blade sprung out from the top was the more illegal, and therefore maybe the more badass, depending on, first of all, whether the spring was extra strong, since if it was extra-strong then you could press the knife in the closed position against someone's belly and punch the button and it would run right through them without your arm even doing any stabbing, and, secondly, depending on whether you had real knife skills, since if you didn't have real knife skills, and you used the extra-strong spring-loaded blade that way, then you, yourself, were less badass even though the knife was more badass for being more illegal, or then again maybe not, maybe you were more badass anyway if you didn't have skills, maybe more badass *especially* if you didn't have skills if you looked at badassness more in terms of being a willingness to start a knife fight when you weren't particularly good with knives, unless maybe it was more a matter of bringing a knife to a fistfight, which put you more in the category of psychopath than badass, except though then again the cops had guns, right? Could you consider any fight with a cop to be a fistfight? Maybe. Maybe not. It depended on the cop, probably—the kind of cop he was—and whether the guy with the knife knew the kind of cop the cop was. But the point was, they told me, was they couldn't properly address the important question of whether Grandpa Strumm was a badass or a psycho without first knowing what kind of knife he had. But so which kind of knife was it? Did I get a chance to see?

"I've got a headache," I said.

"Yeah, sure, a headache. You're probably coming down with a case of omertà, huh? Totally understood because what if he lives? They might call you as a witness. Wicked smart. Don't incorporate evidence or corroborate yourself. Don't become an apprentice after the fact. We should *all* keep our mouths shut. But how about, you know, just tell us when you're gonna do the next swingset."

"Yeah, we won't say *shit* until the time's right."

"And only *if* the time's right."

"Right."

"We won't."

"I've got," I said, "a really bad headache."

"Yeah, yeah, we know. But we do, too, though, so we don't really want to like talk about it either, see? Not a lot at least. We just want to like know."

"We want to share our pain."

"The causes of our pain."

"With you."

"And for you to share the causes of yours with us."

"It's all the same pain."

"If you get what we're saying, which is we'll keep our mouths shut and suffer from headaches if you give us the information about where and when is gonna be the next swingset which we're saying is like the cause of the pain that is your headache that we're talking about. What I mean is this: we won't say shit."

"We won't say *shit*."

I stepped out of line and got a pass to the nurse's, where I said I had a headache, no big deal, but was hoping she'd let me lie down on the cot, close my eyes for a while, til the end of lunch.

"Hard day?" the nurse said.

"Kind of," I said.

She said, "Welcome to the world."

Then she gave me a blanket and unlocked the nap room.

•

•   •

I rode Stevie's bus to her house after school, found her sitting on the tailgate of the pickup from the newsbreak, smoking a cigarette and reading a book. She didn't seem surprised to see me at all, nor did she look particularly upset. I told her I was sorry about what happened to her grandpa, that I guessed she probably blamed me but I hoped she didn't hate me, and that if she didn't hate me and she needed to talk I'd—

She laughed through her nose. "He's a terrible person. He beat on my dad," she said. "My uncles, too. When they were kids, I mean. And he's an actual Nazi. You know that, Belt? Well, not an *actual* Nazi, but, like, part of this white supremacist gang called the Aryan Fuckers? And then, in the meantime, guess who's a Jew."

"Your mom?" I said.

"Good guess, Monsieur Magnet. Well, *her* mom at least. So me and Sally-Jay—we're kind of Jews, too, and he always says something nasty about it. 'Good thing your Strumm genes got control of your face. Maybe if we're lucky you got some Jewbrains behind it, though, make us all rich.' Ha-ha, ha-ha."

"That's . . ."

"Don't worry," she said. "There's nothing right to say. Not that I've heard, at least. And I know I sound bitchy—I'm so sick of faking being sad about this stuff, though. I've been doing it since Friday, and I hate myself for it. They're over there right now, you know, over at Sheridan, pulling the plug. And they're happy about it, or at least relieved, I *know* they are—even Sally-Jay—but they're not allowed to show it, even to each other. Especially to each other. They think they have to act grim—and *that's* what's grim. I can't stand it anymore. It's why I stayed behind."

"Still," I said, "I'm sorry."

"Well it's not about you, Belt, so don't be sorry. It's like you're not even listening to anything I'm saying. He's a brutal, hateful, murderous person. He scares my whole family, and embarrasses us. If anything, you should be asking me to thank you for helping to get him out of my life. But that would be bullshit, too, by the way. I know they're saying on the news that the party at the bar was to celebrate his release from jail, and you're thinking how you, indirectly—*really* indirectly, especially since I'm the one who invited you over—how you had a part in him ending up in jail, but that isn't true. About the party I mean. It was some annual get-together his biker friends have every September to commemorate the passage of the Nuremberg Laws, and I'm not even kidding. They do it every year. So he would have had his drug-induced stroke thing anyway."

Stevie looked down at the book in her lap, as if to say, "Please change the subject, now. Ask me what I'm reading."

I asked what she was reading.

She showed me the cover. It was *Slaughterhouse-Five,* the only non-boardbook I'd read more than twice.

"It goes really fast," she said. "I'm almost halfway, and I started this morning. It's weird, though, is the thing. It's all these tiny chapters, and they're out of order because the main character is 'unstuck in time' is how the author says it, which is cool to begin with, but that's just the start cause it's also about war, World War II, and how even that one, which was supposed to be a good one, was really not glamorous. Except then, while all this sad stuff is happening to this sad main character, there's aliens and a porno star whose name is Montana Wildhack, and summaries of totally made-up novels by a sci-fi author named Kilgore Trout, except it's still a really serious book, and even though it's such a serious book, it keeps making me laugh. If it's *supposed to* be like that, then it's probably my favorite book of all time."

"That's a good description," I said. "I read it, too. A few times, actually. I'm pretty sure it's supposed to be like you said."

"I was hoping you'd read it," Stevie said. "I thought you probably had. I saw you reading another one he wrote—*Cat's Cradle*—during recess last week, in your little corner behind the generators, and you were smiling a lot, and you wouldn't look up. You didn't even know I was there. It was funny. I kept winking at you and grabbing the bottom of my shirt with both hands, like pretending I was gonna flash you or something, and you kept on reading. You really didn't see me. Anyway, it was checked out from the library, so I got this one instead."

"You can borrow *Cat's Cradle* whenever you want," I said.

"Thanks, Belt," she said.

"That's not what I meant to say," I said. "I really like you," I said. "I think I'm in love with you."

"I know," Stevie said. "I know you think that. I've been thinking you'd say it sooner or later, but still I wish you didn't have to, and I hope you'll forget it, because I just don't want to kiss you, Belt. I wish I did. I've tried to want to."

"Really? You've tried?"

"Of course," she said. "You're the only boy I ever have real conversations with. The only person, really. You understand me, you know? Or, at least, I know you try to. That's a really big deal. Probably the biggest. But wanting to kiss someone—it's not the kind of thing you can make yourself do. I'll want to one day, I know that much, but it won't be til you're twenty, maybe even twenty-five, because that's the kind of face you have, the kind I'll like when you're a man. Not just me, either. Lots of girls. Which is exactly what sucks. For me, it sucks, I mean. Because the reason you're into me is I have a certain style, and I'm confident about it. Once your face becomes the kind I'll want to kiss, though, you'll know a lot of confident, styley girls to talk to. I'll be old news. I'll just be the same as I am right now, and maybe worse—my eyes could get fishy like my aunt's, who I resemble, and my hair's really limp and it'll probably be stringy and shiny all the time—and so I won't seem as interesting or rare or pretty to you. So things'll be uneven with us, but in the opposite way of how they are now."

"You love Jonboat," I said. "You just don't want to say it. You think it'll hurt me."

"Jonboat? No. That's not . . . I don't. He seems like a good, smart person, and everything, and also he's handsome, but he's the opposite of hot. I did make out with him a little in his limo, I guess you must have seen, except it felt like I was kissing the president or something. Not that he didn't want to be kissing me—obviously he did—I mean, he kept kissing me—but maybe more like that he wanted more for me to see that he was a good kisser than he wanted to be doing the actual kissing. I don't know. Sorry. You don't want to hear about that."

"I still think you're just trying to be nice," I said. "Trying to let me down easy."

"I just told you I don't want to kiss you," she said.

"But you'll want to in thirteen years, you said. Maybe even just eight. You're giving me something to look forward to because you don't want to hurt me, or you want to hurt me less—you want to cushion the blow. But if I wait thirteen years and you don't want to kiss me, it'll hurt a lot more."

"'Wait *thirteen years*'? Please don't be so sweet, Belt." Something happened in her face, a kind of softening. She looked a little sleepy. She said, "It's confusing."

Partly, though only partly, in jest, I said, "Confusing enough that you want me to kiss you?"

She cleared her throat and took her hand off my arm. How long had she been holding on to my arm? I hadn't even noticed the holding til it stopped.

"Stevie?" I said.

"I guess I did kind of want that for a second, then you asked. It's fine, though," Stevie said.

"You mean now I should kiss you?"

"Oh, wow. Look. My family's coming back from the hospital soon—they should be here already. They won't want me having company. You really gotta go."

"Not without a kiss," I said.

"Belt, that's creepy."

"I was trying to be romantic. I didn't mean to be creepy."

"I know you didn't. I mean, that's what's so creepy."

"Oh," I said, and probably crept away. Certainly I left.

•

• •

Because of, I suppose, its simple, tragic ironies, the tale of the Temples was a local favorite. When you got past a certain point of specificity—the prize amount (ranging from \$80k to \$200k), the model of the car (the make was consistent), the brand of vaguely sad and exotic digestif (usually Kahlúa or

Grand Marnier, sometimes Limoncello)—the details varied teller to teller, but the story's basic features were always the same.

Simon Temple, in spring of '85, won the state lottery. Not the whole pot—he was one of a few who'd hit six out of seven—but enough to purchase a BMW and a number of major household improvements: an updated kitchen, an aboveground swimming pool, a two-car garage attached to the house, and a macadam driveway to go with the garage.

By August, the construction was nearly complete. The only work that remained was to replace the old gravel driveway with lawn and remove the old carport the old driveway led to, beneath which the family swingset—displaced by the swimming pool—had resided since June. Before that work could get done, however, Simon and his children, Tommy and Jessa, died in a car crash on their way home from Simon's younger sister's wedding.

Simon's wife, Clare, the driver, survived.

An alcoholic with a taste for a certain vaguely sad and exotic digestif, Clare had found God and been sober since the day after Simon's big win. At the wedding, her sister-in-law (not the bride, but Simon's elder sister), with whom neither Simon nor Clare got along, and who Simon had denied a loan the month before, poured some white zinfandel, un- or thinkingly, into the wineglass beside Clare's bread plate. Clare pushed the glass away, said she'd seen her Lord and Savior's strong, loving hand working the strings behind the lottery win, and no longer required drink to get by. The sister-in-law suggested Clare's recovery was fleeting, and that, if only for the sake of the added, however conventional, drama, she might as well relapse right then and there, at her husband's sister's wedding. Clare took this in stride, and even made a little joke about preferring to relapse with a certain vaguely sad and exotic digestif. Simon, however, was in his cups, and furious with his sister. He announced to one and all that his wife was strong, stronger than all of them, and could resist temptation, even were her vaguely sad and exotic digestif of choice to be steadily imbibed all around her. Then he went to the bar, procured a bottle of her vaguely sad etc., returned to the table, and proceeded to imbibe it.

If she was, in fact, tempted, Clare resisted.

Simon, in the meantime, became sloppy drunk, and when Simon was drunk, he liked to dance with his wife. Clare, in love with him more than ever it seemed (the passion of his defense had outshined its slurry, red-faced delivery), was happy to abide him. They danced for two hours, slow, fast, and limbo, breaking during only three or four songs so that Simon could make a show for his family of slugging liqueur in front of his wife, who, as before, abstained.

A little past midnight, he handed Clare his keys, gathered the children, and they all left the wedding. Owing to the Beamer's auto transmission (she had always driven stick; shifting kept the mind active), to the physical exhaustion resulting from the dancing, or, more often, to both—it depended on who was telling the story—Clare fell asleep at high speed on I-90, struck the median, flipping the car, and since then hadn't left her house very often.

Some two years after the night of the accident, the old gravel driveway, carport, and swingset still hadn't been removed from the Temple property. Approaching them on my way home from Stevie's, I was angry, sure, and disappointed in myself—for being so dense, so caught-up and hammy, so miserable a failure at receiving signals (how could I have missed her hand on my arm?)—but more than that, I wanted to do something good, or at least to do something at which I was good, and, when I registered Clare's Corolla's absence from its usual spot on the macadam driveway, I saw my opportunity.

I'd frequently thought about the Temple family swingset. On the one hand, it didn't look to be corroded; it had been near new when they took it from the yard, and since then the carport had sheltered it well. On the other hand, it had been stored there two years, and, seeing as Clare hadn't yet seen fit to have it hauled off, the odds that she'd ever take the extra trouble to find a good home for it seemed pretty low.

It wasn't hard to guess that the swingset wasn't happy—it wasn't being used, let alone as intended. Given, however, that it *could be* used, i.e. were it to be adopted by another family, it was as easy to imagine it nursing hopes for its future as it was to suppose that it longed for death.

I'm not sure what I'd have done if it hadn't spoken up. I certainly wasn't expecting it to speak (given how many times speaking inans have appeared in this narrative, I know that might seem strange, but if you consider the scores, if not hundreds, of nonspeaking inans with which you come into contact even in just the course of a day, and assume that I came into contact with, more or less, the same number of nonspeaking inans in the course of my days, you'll see rather quickly how very unlikely the possibility that I'd be addressed by any given one of them would strike me) and, as I crunched along the gravel on my way to the carport, my intention was simply to remind the swingset, in case it had forgotten, of how good it could feel to properly function. I'd swing on it a couple of minutes, I thought, maybe hang on its monkeybar, try to do a pull-up.

||What's this, now?|| it said, as I perched on its middle swing. ||Sure. Yeah. Great. Now this is happening.||

"I'm Belt," I said.

||Yeah. And what's next?||

"This is," I said, and I started to swing. "It's nice, right?"

||Why do this to yourself?|| the swingset said.

"Do what?" I said.

||Divide. Split.||

"Divide? Split?"

||Hallucinate.||

"Do I?"

||You make yourself hear voices that aren't real, that come from inside you.||

"But you're—"

||You make yourself think thoughts that sound like other beings' voices.||

"Except how can you say that while—"

||You make yourself feel asses that aren't on top of you.||

"Wait."

||Wait what?||

"That is one thing that I for sure do not do," I said. "I don't feel asses that aren't on top of me."

||Are you trying to tell me I don't feel an ass?||

"Sure *you* feel an ass. I'm swinging your swing. That ass is mine."

||Yeah, you're swinging my swing—that's a good one. That's a big laugh. Maybe it's more like *I'm* swinging *you*. How about that?||

"I know you're being sarcastic," I said, "but I don't get it. You *are* swinging me. You're swinging me, and I'm swinging on you."

||Of course you'd say that. That's you all over. But look, it's boring. Disturbing, too. Sure. And a little bit sad. But it's been boring for months, this kind of talk. No one's swinging—not you, not me—and that's a cold, hard fact. Try something new. A new kind of lie.||

"I'm not telling any kind of lie at all, though," I said.

||How about try this: try telling me a lie about how crazy I am, because *that*, if you want to hear what really messes with me—do you? That's the question. How crazy am I? Tell me. How crazy?||

"I don't know," I said. "I don't understand the question."

||Well you're the part that's split off from me, right? That's how it seems. But considering that I'm crazy enough to be divided like that, maybe I'm too crazy to realize that *I'm* the part that's split off from *you*.||

"I'm a boy," I said. "My name is Belt. You're the Temple family swingset."

||This is getting me nowhere. Getting us nowhere. This really tortures me, you know? *You* torture me. Or I torture me with you. Do I torture you, too? I realize it's possible. I mean, right now, I'm not torturing you—that much is clear. Right now, you're being playful, which isn't how someone feeling tortured behaves. But during those periods of silence, when I don't hear from you, or you don't hear from me, or during those periods of yelling, when you

tell me I'm worthless, that I was born worthless, that I was made perfectly to provide the world with everything I might hope to provide the world, and that I'm intact, uncorroded, and in need of no maintenance yet have failed nonetheless to live up to even the tiniest fraction of my potential—when you tell me that I'm cursed, rotten, unwilling to be good despite my always saying how I just want to be good, despite my truly believing that I just want to be good, and that that's why I deserve all this pain—I wonder if during those periods *you* are tortured, tortured by me, by all my failures. And I can say, honestly, that I hope not. I hope that I don't torture you. I wouldn't put anyone through what you're putting me through, what you've *been* putting me through. I wouldn't come to any swingset—from any swingset, I guess is more like it . . . I wouldn't split off from any swingset, disguise myself as a boy, and pretend to be swinging on it. And, for that matter, I wouldn't, if I were a boy, split off from any boy, disguise myself as a swingset, and pretend to be swinging that boy. Except I guess I would, huh? One way or the other. Because I'm putting myself through it right now, aren't I? I may be a swingset hallucinating a boy, or I may be a boy hallucinating a swingset, but I know I can't be both. Why do I have to do this to myself? Or maybe why do you have to do this to yourself? I don't know how best to say it. What I do know, though, is it isn't my fault they won't play on us, you know? On me. On you. It's not our fault. Not mine at least. Not as I recall. As I recall, I worked just fine when I was out in the yard. They seemed to really like me, especially together, both at once, the way they'd get going really high and jump off to see who'd land the farthest. And when they tired of that, they'd do standies or climbers or give each other underdogs. They didn't much use my monkeybar, that's true, but that wasn't my fault. That was their choice. My monkeybar is good. Wide. Sturdy. It just wasn't their thing. So why would they quit me? Why would they move me into isolation? What did I do to deserve this? Tell me.||

"You don't deserve it," I said. "You didn't do anything. The family won the lottery. They bought a swimming pool. There wasn't enough room for both you and the swimming pool."

||That's even worse.||

"No," I said. "It's better. It means you're fine. One day, maybe another family will use you. You just have to be patient."

||I'm not fine, though. I'm not fine at all,|| it said. ||I just used a hallucinated child to console myself with lies about dumb luck. Bad, dumb luck. I just tried to comfort myself with the idea that the universe is purposeless, random, that it makes no sense. That's a last resort. That's a sign of desperation. That's not being fine.||

"But I'm telling you the truth. They won the lottery. They installed a pool. And then what happened is all of them, except for the mother, died in a car accident, and now she's too messed up to even have you hauled off."

||Wow. I'm *really* a piece of garbage, aren't I? Now it's tales of dead families and mothers in mourning I'm using for comfort.||

"You're not doing anything. It's *me* who's talking, who's telling you the truth, and I'm a boy—I'm not you. My name is Belt. I'm really swinging on you. And what's more, you might have heard of me—some of you have. I'm the boy who helps the swingsets."

||If I heard of you,|| the swingset said, ||I probably just imagined it. It does seem like the carport said something about you a few weeks back—something it heard from a wild-thrown Frisbee that landed on its roof about |the hope of rusting swingsets.| But the carport . . . I don't know. Maybe it was lying, and now I'm hallucinating based on the carport's lie. Or the ostensible Frisbee's. Or maybe it didn't say anything at all, and you, who are me, are lying, and confusing me . . . I really hate this. And the thing about it is that even if you're real, and what you say about the pool and the family is true, then the world is ugly and senseless and terrible. I lose either way.||

"It's not *all* terrible," I said. "I'm here, for one. And why I'm here is to help you. That's good, isn't it? Isn't that a good thing? I'm part of the world."

||If you were really here to help me, we wouldn't be swinging. We wouldn't be talking. You'd be putting an end to me.||

"But you're in perfect working order," I said. "There's hope. You could be installed in a whole new yard one day, with new kids to swing on you."

||Or I couldn't,|| it said. ||I could spend years and years sheltered from the elements, under this carport, preserved from corrosion, only then to eventually corrode anyway, all the more *slowly,* without having ever again been used as intended. And look, suppose I *did* get adopted by another family—I'd still be stuck with myself. I mean, say that you're not a hallucination. Say that you're really a child named Belt, this |boy who helps swingsets| who has come to help me. The number of times I've hallucinated that a child has come to swing on me—the number of voices I've heard that seemed real, that I argued with, just like this . . . You seem as real as the rest of them, as fake as the rest of them, and I can't believe they, who are me, are ever going to leave me alone. So I beg you, if you're real, put me out of my misery. Enough is enough.||

"But the hope that—"

||Stop saying *hope.* There is no hope. Everything is terrible. So terrible that I can't even keep the cruel, hallucinated child I'm using to torture myself from crying about it.||

"I'm not crying," I said.

||You're on the verge,|| said the swingset. ||Your breathing's getting huffy. Your voice is getting whiny. Our voice is.||

"Even if that's true," I said, "it's not because everything is terrible. It's that you're so *convinced* that everything is terrible that you won't let me help you, and I'm not smart enough to win an argument that would unconvince you."

||It's not a matter of smarts,|| said the swingset. ||That argument's unwinnable. My position is simple: if you don't put an end to me, I won't believe you're real, and I will continue to suffer as I have been suffering.||

"And if I do put an end to you?"

||You know better than I do, I bet, but I like to imagine I'll get repurposed. Weird as it sounds, I've been thinking about my constituent parts a lot lately, and the more time that's passed, the more I've come to want to believe in their sentience, which isn't to say that I *do* believe in it, just that I like the idea that they could have it better one day. It isn't their fault I was dealt a bad hand, and yet they must have suffered—if they're sentient, that is. Then again, maybe they haven't suffered. Like my bolts, for instance. Maybe my bolts, having held me together, have fulfilled their purpose and been satisfied by it, even though the whole they're a part of, which is to say me, or *us*—even though I, or you and I, have been a total failure. But then that's all the more reason, I guess, to hope they don't get junked. They worked. Did their job. They could work again. Hold something else together. Anyway, I know that if I get junked I'll be gone, and I'm pretty certain—certain enough, at least—that even if I get repurposed, I won't be me. I won't remember. Try as I might, I can't remember any previous existence, and I've never heard another inan claim to either. Granted, I haven't met all that many inans. The carport, sure. A garden hose wrapped around my leg during my one good summer. The sprinkler attached to it. A bucket the children tied to my monkeybar once, to play some kind of modified basketball game with, and the ball they used. None of them ever claimed to remember any existence prior to their final assembly—not to me at least—and, crazy as I've gotten, as in need of comfort as I've been, you'd think I'd have at least hallucinated a memory of one of them claiming that. So the end of me will be the end of my suffering—there's not a single good reason not to believe that, and, if you were real, and if you were reasonable, and kind, or even just decent, you'd know what needed doing and do it, understand?||

"I guess so," I said.

||Yes, you do. I can tell. You're breathing a lot more evenly now. It's just too bad for me that none of this is real.||

•

• •

Our house was only a ten-minute walk away, but I couldn't predict when Clare Temple would return, much less when she might leave her house again. The garage across the street, however, was halfway open. I went there for a bat, and, failing to find one, borrowed a long-handled spade instead.

When I returned to the carport, I felt too exposed, too out in the open. I dragged the swingset into the backyard. There was just enough space between the sideyard fence and the edge of the pool deck to fit it.

||I *wish* this were happening,|| the swingset said.

The progress of the murder was uncommonly rapid, despite the swingset's pristine condition. Standing atop the deck's extra-wide railing, I was able to go for the M straightaway, so not only didn't I have to consume time performing the strength-sapping, leg-hacking, usual prep work, but each overhanded blow I put to the crossbar was considerably more powerful than any I'd delivered during previous murders. On top of that, the spade, with its bladelike edge, proved far more efficient at concentrating force than my Easton aluminum had ever been.

I slammed down with vigor. I smashed nonstop.

The interior V of the nearly M'd frame was just a couple inches shy of fatal depth when the spade's metal grip broke off in my hand. The scoop, still attached to the wooden handle, fell to the grass.

But no big deal. No reason to worry. Being barely a fifth of the handle's length, the grip was inessential; what might have been another five or six blows' work would now be another eight or nine's was all; the spade was still a spade.

I leapt off the side of the deck to retrieve it, in the course of which retrieval my leg brushed the swingset's.

||You stopped?|| said the swingset.

"Just for a minute. I dropped my—"

||Well, something,|| it said, ||is starting to occur to me. What's starting to occur to me is: Wow. This seems real. This seems different enough from my other hallucinations that maybe it isn't a hallucination at all. And so maybe I *did* hear about you from the carport. Maybe you *are* the so-called |hope of rusting swingsets.| And the next thought I get is: Should I maybe reconsider? Like, maybe we haven't exhausted all our options, here. As in, maybe, instead of outright killing me, you could find a tool kit and disassemble me, then clean me off or something, put me back together. Maybe if you did that, then, somehow, I'd still be me, you know? But with*out* the craziness? Without the hallucinations? Maybe, I'm saying. I don't really know how or why that would work, but intuitively, it seems like it *could* work, right? Because I'm thinking now that maybe I don't want to disappear so much as I just want a second chance. And I mean, who knows? There might be no second chances. Maybe

reassembled, I'll be just the same, but if that's how it is, maybe *then* you kill me. To just give up now seems . . . weak. Plus it's not like I think death will be so wonderful. I guess I'm actually kind of afraid of death, which, believe you me—an inan afraid of death?—that, in itself, is a sign of malfunction. I mean, to be scared of being unused—sure, that makes sense, but to be scared of simply no longer being? It doesn't even make sense to *me,* and I'm the scared one. So that has to be a malfunction in itself, fear of death. Malfunction isn't always—or even often—permanent. So I guess what I'm trying to say here is I'm actually kind of *really* scared of dying. There's something about my crossbar being all bent. It's showing me, for the first time in a really long time, just by contrast—it's showing me the kind of condition the rest of me is in. I mean, the rest of me is in seriously good condition, right? Except for the self-hatred and hallucinations—if that's what they are—I mean. I could still serve a purpose. I could still be of use. So I don't want to do it. I don't want to die. Not if I don't have to. And why should I have to? I shouldn't, right? At least not for a while.||

"Well you're pretty far gone," I said. "You really are. I'm sorry to have to tell you that, but it's looking pretty bad. I mean, I really don't think I could bang your crossbar back into shape. The V—it's almost there. It's really close. The angle's acute—it's definitely acute."

||Okay, I understand that. I do. I get it. Okay. But so what about . . . I mean I bet you could fix it with a blowtorch or something. Some heat, you know? Some heat, some bending. Then you just slap a little paint on the stressed parts, and bingo, I'm back to how I was, right? and then you disassemble me, and then reassemble me. That's doable, isn't it? Or maybe the reverse? Maybe you disassemble me, fix the crossbar, and then reassemble me. Either way, I know it might take a little while, but what I'm thinking is that I could go on like this for even maybe a couple of days, you know? Probably a week. I could go on for a week if that's what it would take.||

"I don't have a blowtorch, though," I said. "I don't know how to use one. I don't have any money to pay someone to use one. I'm twelve years old. I have to leave here before Mrs. Temple gets home. The amount of work you're talking about—it would take a lot more time than a week. And you'd be suffering all that time. Do you want to risk that? Just so that maybe when you're finally reassembled—if you're even still you—you *might not* feel like you've been feeling these past couple years? And before you answer, there's also another, much bigger problem, which is that we might never have the chance to talk again, which means—"

||Why wouldn't we talk again?||

"I don't have control of my gate," I said. "I can't get it to open or close when

I want, and what I'm trying to say is we could get into a situation where I do all the work you want me to, and then, once you're reassembled, nothing's any different, you feel as bad as always, but you're unable to tell me you want me to help you, or rather *I'm* unable to hear you tell me that, and you're stuck."

||Come on, now. What are the odds that would happen, do you think? That we wouldn't be able to talk again, I mean.||

"High," I said. "They're really high odds. I haven't talked to many inans more than once. And it's not because I haven't wanted to—I've tried. And the couple that I've talked to about it tell me it's my fault. They say they've tried to talk to me a bunch of times, and I just don't respond. They get angry about it. They think I'm ignoring them, but that's not how it is. I don't even *hear* them."

||Okay,|| said the swingset. ||Okay. So . . . What about if you just left me the way I am right now? What if you did that? Do you think Mrs. Temple might eventually do what it would take to reassemble me? Or that she might pay someone to do it?||

"Well, she hasn't done anything with you in a couple years, right?"

||Right, sure, yes—that is: no. She hasn't. But except I've been fully intact up til now. Maybe the sight of me, nearly M'd, would move her? Maybe she'd remember all I meant to her children and want to fix me up and give me to someone? Like a niece or a nephew?||

"I don't think so," I said. "Maybe the sight of you would move her, sure, and she'd want to give a swingset to some kid she loved, but the cost of fixing you would probably be close to, or maybe even higher than, the cost of a new swingset, so I think she'd probably just buy a new swingset for whoever she'd thought about giving one to."

||Oh,|| said the swingset. ||I guess that makes sense.||

"Plus even if she did all it took to reassemble you, there's still that whole problem where if you still feel terrible and decide you want to die, I won't be able to hear you say so, so I won't know to help you."

||I see,|| said the swingset.

"I'm sorry," I said. "I'm really sorry."

||Well, I guess . . . You know, I guess, no, then. I mean, I guess you better kill me. The idea of waiting indefinitely—I can't do indefinitely. Not like this. Especially when there's no guarantee that . . . Wow. Man. I'm really about to die, huh?||

"But maybe you don't have to think of it like that—like it's bad. I mean, all that stuff you were saying before—"

||I thought you were a hallucination before.||

"So maybe you should try to think that again. Maybe it'll make things easier to think that."

||But I know it's not true. I *feel* it's not true. I can't pretend. Plus I don't want to. If there's ever been a moment when I shouldn't deceive myself . . . No. I really shouldn't pretend. I'm really afraid here.||

"Is there something I can do," I said, "to make this easier?"

||I don't know. I don't think so. I wish there were. Maybe you could tell me what it was like with the others? I mean, what's it like to help us swingsets?||

"It changes," I said. "Minute to minute, and swingset to swingset. Except at the end—the very last blow. That always feels right."

||To you, or to them?||

"Both, I think. Definitely to me."

||I suppose it would pretty much have to,|| said the swingset. ||Or else how could you keep doing it?||

"Right," I said. "Of course. I agree. Does that help? To know that?"

||Maybe?|| said the swingset. ||I really can't tell. It probably helps a little. Maybe it only makes things worse, though? I don't know anything. I don't trust myself to know anything at this point. How could I, right? Probably I should just try to be brave now, or at least to act brave, to accept what's to come. To have some dignity. There's probably no reason to go on this way. I guess, you know . . . I guess I'm ready when you are.||

•

• •

The murder was over in under a minute. The last blow, it turned out, didn't feel so right after all. It felt like defeat. Or maybe more like a victory I'd rather not have won. I couldn't tell if there was truly any difference. I couldn't tell if *how I felt* was even relevant. Nor whether it should be. Was I helping the swingsets for their sake or mine? I didn't doubt I was putting an end to their suffering, but since witnessing them suffer caused me to suffer, and since relieving their suffering helped, however briefly, to relieve my suffering, the mercifulness I'd ascribed to the murders, if not quite eclipsed by my own self-interest, was at least a little darkened by its shadow, wasn't it?

Trying to untangle these eternal unanswerables, I stepped from the sideyard into the front-, and a pair of startling, simultaneous phenomena prevented my reflections from proceeding any further: Clare Temple's Corolla pulled into the driveway; the battered spade I was holding spoke.

||You've ruined my existence,|| is what the spade said.

I dropped it on the gravel and ducked into the shadiest corner of the carport, flattening myself against a support beam.

||You've ruined my existence,|| the carport told me. ||I have nothing left to shelter. Protecting the swingset was my only purpose.||

The Corolla's trunk popped.

"I'm sorry," I whispered into my shoulder. "Maybe she'll park here, now that you're empty."

||She won't even park in the attached garage. Not even when it snows. Not even when she has to unload a bunch of stuff.||

As if to demonstrate the carport's point, Mrs. Temple started carrying grocery bags from her trunk to her stoop.

||Help me like you helped the swingset,|| said the carport.

"I don't know how."

||Get a chainsaw,|| it said, ||and slice me in half. Right across the roof. That's the quickest way.||

"What if I got something and stored it underneath you?"

||Something like what?||

"The swingset," I said.

||It's dead, though, isn't it?||

"Does it matter?" I said.

||If it's dead, I'll be lonely,|| the carport said.

"You'll be useful, though," I said.

||Okay,|| said the carport.

Once Mrs. Temple finished hauling all her groceries into the house, I dragged the dead swingset under the carport.

"There you go," I told the carport, gripping a beam.

It failed to respond. I picked up the spade. It didn't fail to respond.

||You've ruined my entire existence,|| it said.

•

•   •

||You have to understand,|| the spade went on, as I snuck back into the garage across the street. ||They'll never use me again. Not without a grip. They'll either throw me away, or they'll leave me here forever, telling themselves they'll get me fixed up, but then never doing it. Do you see how many long-handled spades they've got?||

I could see three others, hanging from hooks in the wall, side by side.

"But these are shaped differently," I said to the spade. "Here's a chipper, there's a digger, and that wide one's a pusher—its blade's so curved it could hardly scrape dirt."

||Right. Exactly. And I'm an all-purpose type. There's nothing I can do that one of these others can't do a little better.||

"Okay," I said. "I'll go back for your grip."

||Are you crazy?|| said the spade. ||You're crazy. Or blind. Have a look at the end of my handle, why don't you. It's way too splintered. There's no reattaching the grip—it can't happen. You have to end me.||

"Are you sure?" I said.

||If you leave me like this, I'll be neglected for years before the rot and oxidation begin to take hold. Til they *begin* to take hold.||

"What do you need me to do, then?" I said. "How do I help you?"

||You can either snap my handle off just above my scoop's collar, or bang the scoop on some concrete or rocks til my blade develops an upturned lip.||

Either of these methods would have been too noisy to enact in the garage—someone may have been at home—so I snuck back out, spade in hand. My intention was to head a few blocks southwest to the Prairie Orchards Phase III construction site, a tract of cleared lots where they were laying foundations for some hundred new duplex and quadruplex townhomes, but, emerging from under the half-closed garage door, I heard a woman's voice—heard it with my ears—and the voice said, "Excuse me? Hello. Ex*cuse* me."

She was standing on the driveway in a baby-blue tracksuit with wide pink piping, matching sneakers. Her perm-crisped bangs appeared glued to her forehead.

"Who are you?" she said.

"I'm really sorry," I said.

"Who *are* you?" she said.

"Do I have to tell you?"

"Tell me and I'll probably only call your parents. Don't, and I will certainly call the police."

||*Please,*|| the spade said.

"I'm caught anyway," I thought.

I hoisted the spade overhead, both-handed, bent at the knees, jumped in the air, and came down swinging as hard as I could. The collar's grasp on the handle must have gotten loosened while I'd murdered the swingset: the scoop snapped off upon contact with the driveway, and, just as I landed, it spun back into me, right above the knee.

I sat on the concrete, breathing fast from the pain, and tossed aside the handle. I told the woman in the tracksuit—whose expression cycled through fear and surprise before landing on pity—that my name was Belt Magnet. She asked me what my mother's phone number was, and I told her that too, and told her I was sorry, that I didn't mean to scare her.

I followed her limpingly into her kitchen. She called my mom and prepared

Crystal Light. Under her breath, she sang the brand's jingle—"I believe in Crystal Light cause I believe in me!"—while stirring the powder into the pitcher, which caused me to anticipate Caribbean Cooler, as that was the most-advertised kind in those days, and I recall feeling puzzled and grateful the both when it turned out the flavor was Pink Lemonade. Fake pineapple taste always made me feel dizzy.

Ms. Clybourn—I'd heard her say her name on the phone—added vodka to her drink, then sat down across from me. She flattened her palms on the glass kitchen table, either side of her tumbler, spread out her fingers, and lowered her gaze. She said, "Your mother asked to speak to you. I told her she couldn't. I told your mother you were indisposed."

"Why?" I said.

She kept her eyes on her hands. Maybe her nails. She didn't seem to hear the question.

I said, "I like your manicure."

She sipped from her tumbler, leaned back in her chair, held her hands up in front of her face at angles.

"I'm disappointed in this manicure, to tell you the truth. In the bottle, the lacquer was a milkier pink. On these nails it's a pink I'd describe as 'thin.' I'm always getting suckered. Do I look like a sucker? I'm not really asking. Anyway, your mother—it's not that your mother didn't want to hear your voice. I don't want you to think that. It's just that I said you were indisposed. You were using the toilet was the implication. Of 'indisposed.' I implied you'd be using the toilet for a while. *Sitting* on the toilet. I don't quite understand why I did that. I can't remember the last time I said 'indisposed,' but, you know, you might have mentioned she worked downtown," Ms. Clybourn said, allowing—via blunting that last word's first vowel, then inserting half a syllable after its second (*don-tah-win* is how it sounded)—her soft, Southern accent to enter full bloom. "It'll be at least an hour til she gets here, young man. You're lucky I'm a lonely woman of leisure [*leh-zhur*]. A busier person might have called the police to get you out of here quicker. I still might call them, lonely though I am. I advise you entertain the hell out of me."

"You're very pretty," I said. "And you have a nice voice." I meant it—both things.

"That's entertainment?" Ms. Clybourn said. "Or do you mean me to believe that's why you trespassed on my property? Because I'm 'very pretty' and I have a 'nice voice.' Maybe it's the manicure?"

"You shouldn't be lonely. That's all I'm saying." The word *you* came out more suggested than pronounced, *I'm* was closer to *ahm,* and *saying* was g-less and a little bit uptalked. Pleasant accents were contagious. Ms. Clybourn, if she noticed I'd been infected—it seemed possible she didn't; possible that everyone to whom she spoke tried his best to sound more like her—appeared not to mind.

"Brass tacks," she said. "What exactly have you got against my driveway, kid? Hitting it like that . . . And you know, that spade—it's worthless, now."

"I know," I said.

She said, "I think you've got an anger problem."

I didn't, I thought. That was Blackie, I thought. But before I said I didn't, I realized I *could*. I could see how I could. For the benefit of others. Ms. Clybourn. My mom. That could be my out. I could be the boy who had the problem with anger. Who took his anger out on inanimate objects. That was far less abnormal than talking to them. There was something beneath it, an anger problem—something understandable. *Vulnerability*. That's what the girls who liked Blackie all called it. Deep down, Blackie was vulnerable, they said. Deep down he was deep. Not crazy or scary, but guarded and sad. Matt Dillon eyes. He felt things too deeply. Then he got angry. He didn't know how else to express what he felt.

"I'm lonely, too," I said to Ms. Clybourn.

"But you're handsome," she said. "And you talk so nice. Like Boss Daley campaigning for the Nascar vote."

"You're making fun of me," I said, and stared distantly, dramatically, into my glass.

Ms. Clybourn said, "Well who's Mr. Sensitive? Oh, I'm sorry. Tell me how you're lonely."

And I told her I was lonely because I loved Stevie, and Stevie didn't love me. I said it wasn't fair. It made me angry at the world. It was hard to explain, I said. She said I should try. The world was unfair, I said. I wanted to hurt it so bad sometimes, but I didn't know how. I didn't want to hurt people—I wasn't angry at people. It wasn't their fault that the world was unfair. It wasn't Stevie's fault that she didn't love me. Stevie was perfect, so it couldn't be her fault. Maybe it was my fault because *I* wasn't perfect. But maybe it wasn't. Maybe it was just the fault of the world. I couldn't figure it out. The more I tried, the more angry I got, though. Either I was bad at being in the world or the world was bad at having me in it. I didn't know which, but it didn't really matter. Or maybe it did. It was hard to explain. I couldn't explain it. Ms. Clybourn said it seemed I was explaining it well; I should keep on explaining it. So I was walking back from Stevie's, I told Ms. Clybourn, and I was feeling really angry, at myself or at the world, and maybe, I thought, I just had to do something that I hadn't been doing. Maybe I just had to try something new. I didn't know what, though, and I was just so angry, so I wasn't thinking clearly, and when I saw her garage door was left half-open, I thought how maybe what I should do was try out . . . stealing. I'd never stolen anything. Maybe stealing something would make me feel better. It was worth a try, I thought. So I went in her garage and I grabbed the first thing that was grabbable—the spade. And I thought, "I am stealing this," and then I was stealing it, and that's when I got caught, and I was just so angry that I hit the driveway.

"It didn't work, did it?" Ms. Clybourn said. "Stealing didn't make you feel any less lonely. I tried it a couple of times myself. Not from a garage. Just from the Dominick's. I stole a pack of gum once. Another time a shampoo. I was angry at the man who used to be my husband, and I thought, 'Gwendolyn Clybourn, the world owes you something. Anything. Whatever.' I got away with it, too. Didn't make me feel better, though. Neither time. What I wanted wasn't something anyone could steal. That was the problem. I think you know what I mean."

"Completely," I said. "I just feel worse, now. You're this nice, pretty lady who gave me Crystal Light, and look what I did."

"Oh honey, love's hard," Ms. Clybourn said. "And you didn't even know me. You just saw my garage was halfway open. And it seems to me you've learned your lesson. That you don't give in to anger and loneliness. You won't steal again. I can tell. You won't."

"I won't," I said, "but my mom's gonna kill me."

"You leave your mom to me. I wish we'd have talked, you and I, before I called her. You're a real sweet boy just having a bad day . . . That's what I'll tell her. You want to watch TV or something? You like to play cards? Go Fish or Casino? Are you hungry?" she said. "Do you want some more to drink? I'm having another. And a snack," she said.

We ate honeyed almonds and played gin rummy til my mother rang the bell. I don't know what exactly Ms. Clybourn said to her. They spoke on the stoop for at least ten minutes before I was summoned, by which point the both of them were puffing on Quills and admiring the blossoming asters in the garden.

•

•   •

As she pulled out of the driveway, my mom's whole demeanor changed. "You're lucky that woman's such a mess," she said.

"She's nice," I said.

"She's drunk," said my mother. "I could hardly understand her, going on about Stevie, going on about her ex. What am I going to do with you, Belt? How can you be so angry about this girl?"

"I'm stupid."

"You're the opposite of stupid. Tell me the truth. Is there something you're hiding? Did someone do something to you? Is someone picking on you? Bullying you? Was it seeing what happened to that biker at the jail? We never talked about that. You didn't tell me about that. I probably should have brought it up when I saw it in the papers. I probably should have brought it up *because* you didn't. Did it disturb you, Belt? What a dumb question. Of course it must have. Whoever's telling the truth there, it was terrible and violent. No one seems to be disagreeing about that part. But the world isn't like that—full of violence and anger. Not usually, Belt. Not in America. Not in this part of it. I don't want you to think it is. Is that what you think, though? And you're trying to fit in? Is that what this is?"

"No," I said. "It's really nothing like that. It has nothing to do with that. It's just I was angry and I didn't want to be angry. I thought, somehow, if I tried something new—"

"Hitting a driveway with a shovel?"

"Stealing something," I said. "And then, maybe, I don't know—I guess maybe I really just wanted to hit the driveway all along. Or maybe wreck the shovel. Wreck something, I guess. I know it doesn't make sense."

"No, Belt, it doesn't. Not to me. I want it to, though. I'm trying here. I'm really trying to understand. Oh, who am I kidding?" my mother said. "This is a boy thing. A man thing. A male thing, right? We need to talk to your dad."

"We do?" I said.

"You go to your room and stay there til dinner."

• • •

"Girls," said my father, cutting into his steak, "can drive you crazy. Something's probably off with you they don't sometimes. But there's crazy, Billy, and then there's crazy. You don't want to be that second kind, you know?"

"You don't want to be any kind of crazy," said my mother. "You want to be nice. *We* want you to be nice. And we know you're nice, that you've always been. Even that woman, Ms. Clybourn—even she saw it, even after you scared her. Everyone can see it. It's okay to just be sad, okay? That girl doesn't want to return your affections? Well she's a fool in my book, and one day she'll regret it, but that doesn't mean you don't have the right to be sad she's not the one for you. And that isn't crazy. That's just being nice."

"Being sad is being nice?" I said.

"Sometimes," said my mother.

"Well, I'm sad," I said.

"I know," said my mother. "And it's okay to show it. But smashing a swingset? Stealing from people? Those are angry things to do. Those aren't sad things to do."

"Those are crazy things to do," my father said.

"Stop with that word. Don't tell him he's crazy. His heart's been broken. Try to understand him."

"I do understand him. I'm his father godsakes. And what I'm trying to tell him is it's okay to be crazy, just not the kind of crazy he's been acting like."

"What kind of crazy's okay?" I said.

"The kind that doesn't last and *makes sense,*" my father said. "Like for instance, what? Maybe this Stevie likes another boy instead of you? So maybe you—and I'm not saying this is what you should do, but just a for-instance of something that's the better kind of crazy—maybe you kick his fucken ass a little bit. Like in front of her. To show her, and him—"

"Stop it," said my mom.

"I'm not trying to say he should kick this kid's ass, if there even is another kid. I'm just saying it's the more typical kind of sympathetic kind of crazy, an asskicking in this instance. It doesn't last long, and I could see myself doing it. Lots of guys could. You'd understand it better, too, honey. Don't pretend."

"I'm telling him to let himself be sad, and you're telling him to hit people."

"I'm not telling him to *hit* people. I'm telling him that hitting people makes more sense than hitting a swingset. Or a driveway. Or stealing a shovel. And not just any people, though, Belt—don't get me wrong. I'm not talking about terrorism. I'm not talking about bullying. I'm talking about the targeted hitting of people who deserve it, or who seem to deserve it, even though you shouldn't, in the end, actually hit them, probably. I mean, unless they seem like they're gonna hit you, or a girl. And if that was what you were wishing you were doing when you were hitting that swingset, or hitting that driveway—I want you to say so, because that would make a lot more sense to me, and then, you know, maybe my fatherly duty is more like I have to teach you how to not be scared to fight instead of figure out who the best kid-shrink for crazy anger problems is. The most important thing, though—and honey, please, stop shaking your head, let me finish, he has to hear this—the important thing is that when you were hitting that driveway and hitting that swingset, the important thing is you weren't wishing you were hitting this girl, this Stevie. You don't hit girls is the important thing, got it? You don't even picture it. You picture hitting somebody, you picture a guy, okay? And if you're so angry that you have to hit someone, you better make sure that someone's a guy, or guess what? I'll be hitting *you*. And I won't be the only one. And you will deserve it. You will really fucking deserve it, Billy. Guys like that—guys who hit girls—these are the worst kinds of guys there are. Even worse than guys who kick dogs, okay? The only guys who deserve getting hit worse than the ones who hit girls are the ones who rape kids, which, I don't even want to go into that with you, into thinking about that. But am I wrong, baby? Don't tell me I'm wrong."

"You're sending him the message he's a coward," said my mother. "You're making him feel like he should have been hitting someone."

"Some *guy* maybe, though, not just—"

"You're sending him the message that he should have been fighting instead of doing what he did, and—"

"Not necessarily. I was just saying that—"

"What he should have been doing is talking to us. Or *crying*, Clyde. *Crying* to us."

"Well I don't know if *that's* true," my father said. "Crying about a girl to your parents is—well it's embarrassing. Not for the parents—I'm not saying that. Although maybe a little. But for the one who's crying, I'd think it's embarrassing. At Billy's age, crying to my parents? Especially about a girl? I'd've been ashamed. I'd've been embarrassed. It's not realistic what you're saying he should do and, frankly, I'm glad about that."

"You're undermining everything I'm trying to teach him here."

"*Undermining?* Jesus. Why'd you even ask me to talk to him, then? You want a father here, or a second mom?"

They continued in that vein for a couple of minutes: my mother being reasonable while sounding upset, my father upsetting her by sounding so reasonable. I can't say this turn was a happy one for me, but to say I felt guilty for the wedge my behavior had jammed between them wouldn't be true either, and, upon reflection, this puzzles me a little, for even those fictional children of divorce who appeared on the family sitcoms of the era, the ones whose parents' marriages broke in response to abuse or infidelity—even those wholly blameless kids found ways to blame themselves for their parents' troubles. At least until a therapist, or sometimes a teacher, if not Cosby or Danza himself, would take them aside and say, firmly-warmly, "It's not your fault." Though maybe my reaction, or lack thereof, shouldn't puzzle me at all, for even then—*especially* then, when my parents were fighting—I knew they'd be fine. I really *was* the cause of all their arguments. That's how I knew they'd never split.

As my mother's voice tightened, my father's got softer, more expertly calm and condescendingly tolerant. Having argued for a while about the way I should be, and then about the manner in which they were arguing about the way I should be, they started arguing more broadly about the way they communicated.

"I talk to him a lot, though," my father was saying.

"You talk, yes you do. *You* talk," said my mother. "But you don't ask him any questions. You just tell him stories. Stories to impress him. Like you want a high five, or a slap on the back. You can do so much better. I know that you can. I know because of how you are with *me*. You and I converse. We listen to each other. There's back-and-forth. Mutual curiosity."

"But you're my wife," he said. "Billy's my son. We can't talk to him the same way we—"

"Belt's *our* son, Clyde. Yours and *mine*. But you assume he's just like you. That he wants the same things, admires the same things. Maybe he isn't. Maybe he doesn't. Maybe if you didn't—" My mother started saying, but a match she'd struck to get her Quill lit snapped, and she cut herself off, shut her eyes tightly.

My father produced a Zippo from his pocket. He sparked it and cooed to her, "Maybe's just the sound second thoughts make, honey."

Then it was she who was pummeling inans. First my father's beer stein via openhanded blow, an act that seemed, weirdly, to be inadvertent, even borderline comical, until she sent, in the opposite direction, my salad bowl sailing at the door of the fridge, and I saw her chin trembling, her bitten lower lip. I'd always been aware that my mother was gentle—ducks and squirrels seemed to gather around any bench she sat on, the children of strangers approached her at playgrounds, told her their names, pointed at clouds—but until then, I'd never considered her delicate. She stood, raised her plate, and smashed it on the floor. She launched the clay ashtray at the sooty oven window. I don't remember what sounds she was making—weeping ones, or shouting ones, or no sounds at all—nor whether my father tried talking her down. I distinctly remember thinking she was dying, which, on one hand, doesn't seem strange at all: I'd imagine most children, upon witnessing their mother breaking down so violently, would jump to dark, irrational conclusions, especially if they'd never seen it happen before. But then on the other hand it was exceptionally strange, for this breakdown was, as far as I can recall, the first symptom she'd shown of the tumors in her brain, and yet none of us had any idea she was ill yet.

I found myself standing, saying, "Please don't." She didn't seem to notice. She hurled another plate—mine—to the floor. I took a step back. I said, "Please." She said, "No." Maybe to me. Maybe to my father, who'd begun his approach. She was reaching for the vase in the middle of the table, when he wrapped her in his arms, pushed her cheek to his neck, turned ninety degrees so I was out of her sightlines, and, over his shoulder, gave me this look like,

"See what you've done to this beautiful woman? You see what you've done to my wife?"

He took her away, then, into the living room.

I found the broom and started to sweep.

The policemen arrived a couple minutes later. I was the one who answered the door, and I thought, for just a second, that a neighbor must have called them; a neighbor must have heard all the smashing, I thought, must have figured my dad had at last flipped his lid, started killing his family. Then one of them asked me if I was Belt Magnet, and I felt it all pressing up out of my chest, the bumbling retractions, the ill-timed confessions.

I swallowed and swallowed.

•

• •

When, earlier that summer, upon returning from a visit to his mother's in Phoenix, Regis Piper discovered his swingset murdered (that was murder #3), he didn't really bother to pay it much mind. The thing had been a hazard of rust and sharp edges for at least a few years, his children were adults, and his overgrown, dandelion-blanketed yard hardly looked any worse for the wear. His wife, Melinda, had expressed some worry that the mutilated swingset stood for bigger, more frightening things, and between the Sunday sermons at their Pentecostal church, and the daytime talk shows' recent focus on the pull toward Satan, sodomy, drug abuse, and suicide that backward-spun hard rock and heavy metal records subliminally exerted on bored, but otherwise well-reared children from clean, suburban, God-fearing families, Melinda's point of view didn't seem exactly *unreasonable* to Regis—not exactly—yet still he found it hard to take too serious. Boys being boys is what he figured. Kids having some new kind of weird, kid fun. Nothing criminal there. Just some innocent horseplay. If anything the vandalization of the swingset argued for the perpetrators' ultimate harmlessness. The house had been empty, after all, for two weeks, and instead of breaking in to steal the TV, they'd elected to deform a pile of junk in the yard.

But on encountering mention of the Strumms' murdered swingset in the media coverage of that Nazi biker, Regis started thinking that maybe his wife had been right to be afraid. Maybe something frightening was happening in Wheelatine. Something that, if not necessarily demonic, was violent and disorderly, eerily ritualistic, possibly serial. Or maybe not. It was bigger than he'd thought, though. Bigger than him. Speaking up was thusly a civic duty. So he called the law. He filed a report.

* * *

At least that's how Piper explained it to the *Herald* later that week. The details we got from the cops were much thinner: a couple people had reported murdered swingsets that day, and because I'd been caught red-handed at the Strumms', I was suspect #1.

They wanted to talk to me down at the station.

I rode with my parents in my father's truck. By the time we arrived, I'd admitted to everything. The murders, the lies, the inans—all of it. They didn't entirely believe me at first. Of course they never believed that inans spoke to me; but, initially, they didn't believe I *thought* inans spoke to me. They seemed to think I was making it up to cover more shameful motivations for the murders. Later that night, back at the house, I tore from my two most recent journals—I was, for a while, in junior high, quite the graphomaniacal autobiographer—a number of pages containing transcriptions of conversations I'd had with swingsets, as well as the pages from the previous Friday in which I described the tantrum I'd faked when the seatbelt spoke up in my mother's car. I brought these pages to my mother at her vanity, sat on the floor, and waited while she read them. She asked if I'd ever thought of hurting myself, and I told her I hadn't, that I didn't like pain, and my answer made her chuckle until she choked up. She really didn't know what to do with me, she said, and she was sorry to have doubted me, but as long as I continued to tell her the truth she was certain we'd be able to figure something out.

Like I was saying, though, she and my father, on our way to the station, both thought I was lying, and badly at that. "Please stop," said my mother, as we pulled into the parking lot, and my father said I better not mention to the cops "any of this talking-to-objects bullshit." He told us he was pretty sure that one of them—Platzik—had a brother he worked with, and he had a good feeling that if all I'd really done was vandalize some swingsets he could keep me out of trouble. Was it all I'd really done?

It was all I'd really done, I said.

We stayed in the car while he went inside the station and man-to-manned Platzik. My mom lit a Quill. I asked if I could have one. I don't know why I did that. In order to get her to respond, I guess. Or maybe—at least I'd like to think so—to make things simpler, to give her some relief. Although she'd maligned it all through dinner, anger was far less confusing an emotion than the ones we were feeling there in the car. Even at twelve years old, I knew that.

She turned around and slapped me, once, across the cheek. She'd never done that before, yet I wasn't surprised. It seemed to be the correct response.

"Who do you think you're talking to?" she said. "What the fuck is wrong with you, Belt?"

I knew better than to answer. I lowered my head, focused on the sting below my left eye.

"Your father, hopefully, is handling the police, but you are in *lots* of trouble with me, you liar."

"I'm sorry," I said.

"You don't know what sorry is yet."

I said, "Are you okay?"

"What?"

"Are you *okay*?" I said.

She slapped me again.

When my father returned, he said it was good, for once, that I was crying, and he said to keep it up. He said all I had to do was volunteer a list of swingsets I'd murdered—dates and locations—keep looking pitiful, and give the cops my word I'd stop my embarrassing, ludicrous behavior. No one would be interested in pressing any charges as long as I wasn't a threat or a wiseass.

I did as he said, we were home in an hour, and time proved him right: no one ever pressed charges.

Most likely it was Officer Platzik himself who later gave a copy of the list to the *Herald;* a third Platzik brother was an editor there, and that Platzik had a nephew who'd attended the murders at the Strumms' and at Feather's. This nephew was Blackie's doormat, Euwenus, and he was the first kid to talk to reporters. At least that's what he claimed. I didn't hold it against him. He wanted attention. Lots of kids did. Lots of kids ended up talking to the *Herald,* and bringing the edition they were quoted in to school, bragging about it. That was the only way anyone could know it was them, for the paper refused to print any of their names, or mine for that matter, the idea being that, down the line, as we all grew up and got jobs and families and homes of our own, the story wouldn't be able to follow us.

FRIENDS

THE PENULTIMATE WEEK OF 1987, a block from the building downtown where she worked, my mom's Civic caught its second flat in two days. The sky was at its steely, Chicago worst—throwing lumpy snow sideways through a drool of freezing rain—so she turned the car around, reparked in the garage, and, because her spare tire was already in use, returned to the office to phone for a tow. Three hours, they told her, the trucks were all booked—holiday rush hour, accidents everywhere. Three was too many, and it probably meant five. My mother was beat, distraught, on the verge. She was dying of cancer and had no idea. The insomnia, the headaches, the mood swings and nausea, her diminishing weight—she'd assumed these symptoms were brought on by the stress my illness was causing her. I'm sure that, at least in part, they were. I had just quit the Haldol. My grades were in the toilet. Neighbors knew our business; her coworkers, too. Neither her nor my father's benefits packages covered mental health care, SSDI wouldn't kick in for months, and all the treatment I'd been getting was paid for out of pocket. What they'd saved was being spent, and there wasn't much left. She was tired, she was tired, she was tired, she hurt. So even though it would mean that my overworked father would have to drive ten miles through the slush-jammed traffic to get her at the station, and then, the next morning, drive her back before work, she left her car in the garage, took the bus across the loop to Ogilvie Center, and rode the Milwaukee Line out to Mt. Prospect.

The ad card was bolted to the wall of the bus, up near the ceiling: a research team at the University of Chicago was seeking volunteers, ages fifteen and under, who'd been diagnosed with psychotic disorders, to participate in a study involving therapy animals. In exchange for their participation, the volunteers' treatment would be paid in full for the next six months.

• • •

Three Saturdays later, on a new set of tires, we drove to Hyde Park for my entrance interview. In a water-damaged office in a building made of stone that looked like a church or a place to buy poisons and tinctures of dragon's scale, my mom gave a woman named Dr. Tilly a rubberbanded pair of Christmas-colored folders—red from the cops, green from my psychiatrist, Dr. Calgary. Tilly handed me a short questionnaire to fill out, had my mother read over and sign a few forms, told us she would be back soon, and left. We ate chocolate chip granola bars and played gin rummy—my mom, a freak for solitaire, always had cards—then ate more granola bars and played Old Maid until, eventually, Dr. Tilly returned. She thanked us for our patience, led us down some narrow hallways, and in one of these my mother brushed up against a woman distractedly heading in the opposite direction.

The woman had been looking down the length of her torso at a white wire cage she was pressing to her abdomen. I'd seen her coming toward us from half the hall away. Her cage emitted squeaks, and I saw the orange flash of small eyes between its bars, but before I had a chance to see what animal was in there, her padded shoulder had met my mother's, and she'd turned the cage away, reflexively cradling it. Both women said, "Excuse me," and, a few yards before me, a girl, roughly my age, wearing dirty satin evening gloves—a girl who I could tell, by their strong resemblance, was the daughter of the woman bearing the cage—echoed the phrase in a singsong voice. With a couple more steps, we became briefly parallel, this daughter and I, and she threw herself sideways, which knocked me to the wall. "Ex*cuse* me, don't you think?" she said, grabbing my shoulders, shaking them a little. "Excuse me. Excuse me!" Then she ran down the hall to catch up to her mother.

Dr. Tilly apologized. My mom looked concerned. I enjoyed the encounter. I thought it was funny. I said, "That was funny." We proceeded down the hall and a flight or two of stairs, and arrived at the office of Dr. Lionel Manx. Dr. Tilly knocked on the jamb, then departed.

Manx didn't rise from his desk to greet us, but swept his arm widely to invite us to sit. All the surfaces were brown—mostly shiny, brown leather affixed to shiny brown wood by shiny, silver dollar–size, brown leather buttons. The buttons on the arms of the chairs facing Manx appeared to be chewed, and soon I knew why: the urge to pry them off with one's fingers was powerful. Nearly irresistible. Every kid who'd ever sat there must have had to contend with it. My mom kept reaching sideways to still my left hand, while in the meantime the fingers of her own left went digging.

My red and green folders were open on the blotter. Manx closed them and stacked them and cleared his throat.

"Mr. Belt Alton Magnet, I'm Dr. Lionel Manx," he said—he said it to me, then winked at my mom, I guess to indicate he wasn't unaware of her presence, but would, nonetheless, speak as if she weren't there. "You can call me Dr. Manx or Manx, but never Lionel. I never liked Lionel. Do you like Belt? Alton? Belt Alton? I'll call you Dr. Magnet or Magnet if you like. Mr. Magnet?"

"Just Belt," I said.

"I like Belt, too. I've never met a Belt. Never heard of a Belt. I think you might be the only Belt in the world."

"He's named after my favorite uncle," said my mother. "Uncle Belt. Well, his real name was Gunther, but no one much liked that—how could they?—and when he was only just six years old, his older brother, which is to say my father, was bullying him, at a bus stop I think, or maybe a bus station, I'm not quite sure, but he was making him sing the 'Happy Birthday Song' over and over, at the top of his lungs, and a young black woman, who my father always swore was Billie Holiday, though no one ever believed him, she approached the two boys and said to my father, 'You're picking on him, now, but just you wait. He's gonna be a star. Little kid's got pipes. Boy can belt.' And after that Uncle Gunther was Belt."

Manx had politely listened to my mother, who obviously—to me, at least—was feeling a little bit nervous in his presence, but when she was finished saying what she'd said, he turned right back to me without having asked her even one of the more obvious follow-up questions, and I sensed her shrinking in her chair a little, and to help her compensate, I acted as though this story about my uncle Belt, which I'd heard a hundred times, was as intriguing to me as she must have been hoping it would be for Manx.

"Belt never made it as a singer, though," I told Manx. "He was shy. He sang to himself all the time, but he was too shy to do it in front of an audience. Stage fright. So now listen to this: this is what happened. Everyone started to call him Belt since that time at the bus stop, and when he got to high school, there were all these new kids who hadn't known him all his life, and they thought he was called Belt because he liked to hit people, and so the hard guys were always picking fights with him. They fought him so much that, soon, he actually got good at fighting, and started to like it, and took up boxing, and fought Golden Gloves, and after the first Golden Gloves he was in, he realized he wasn't afraid of performing in front of people anymore because he'd lost in the ring in front of lots of people and it was no big deal, so he found some musicians who were looking for a singer, and they started to practice, and it was looking really good for them, and they booked their first show for the end of the summer, but just a couple weeks after they booked it, he fought an amateur match, and he won it, too, but something happened to his hearing. Permanent damage. He couldn't hear certain tones. And that was that. It was over. It never came back. He never played the show. The band broke up. And on top of that, he was too scared to box again. He was too afraid he'd get completely deaf, or something worse, so he worked at a slaughterhouse, saved up money, and opened a butcher shop, and never got bitter. Everyone said he was the nicest guy, and like my mom said, he was her favorite uncle, and my father's completely crazy about my mother, so even though he always kind of hated the name Belt, he knew it was important to her, and let her name me it. And it's better than Gunther. Even he agrees about that."

My mom squeezed my hand and winked and all was well.

"Great story," Manx said. "I'm curious. Would you say you're like your uncle?"

"I never knew him," I said. "He died in a car crash before I was born."

"But from what you do know. I mean, that was some story. Like, for example, would you say that you're shy?"

"Maybe," I said. "Who knows with shyness? Shyness is weird."

"Weird how?" Manx said.

"I mean, I do think I'm shy, but I know a lot of people, especially girls, who you hear them say they're shy, but they're not shy at all. I guess it's possible they're lying. Like they think it's good to be shy, so they want you to think it. Or maybe they imagine other people are way more outgoing than they really are. Maybe that's how I am. But it could be the opposite, too. Maybe I'm just *so* shy that other people who are more normal-shy seem really outgoing to me by comparison. With myself. I know I'm not lying when I say I think I'm shy, though."

"I see," Manx said. "Sometimes you do lie?"

"Doesn't everyone?" I said.

"Sometimes," Manx said. "Right now, I'd really like it if you didn't lie, though."

"I wasn't," I said. "I think I'm shy, like I told you, but if someone else said I wasn't, they might—"

"I don't mean about the shyness. I don't imagine you were lying at all about that. I want to ask about what brought you here today, though, okay? And I want you to tell me the truth."

"Okay."

"These swingsets, Belt. What made you want to harm them?"

I said, "I wanted to help them."

"You destroyed them with an ax."

"I mostly used a bat," I said. "I used an ax just once, because I had to snap some chains, and then, one other time, when I didn't have my bat, I did the whole thing with a spade."

"A bat. I see. Still, I'm a little confused. You say you wanted to help them, but what you did was destroy them."

"They were in bad shape. That's the kind of help they asked me for."

"Don't you think that's strange?"

"What part?" I said.

"Well, if I was in bad shape and I was a swingset, I think I'd want someone to repair me. Don't you think that's what you'd want if—"

"Maybe," I said. "But they asked me to destroy them."

"How come, do you think?"

"I don't know. Maybe they couldn't be repaired. Or maybe they thought that, even if they could be repaired, no one who was able to repair them would repair them and so the next best thing was . . ."

"Do you think it's easier to die than solve your problems?"

"I'm not talking about me. Come on. I'm talking about swingsets."

"Well I'm asking because—"

"I know why you're asking. And no. I don't think that. I mean, well, I guess it probably is *easier* to die than 'solve my problems,' but I don't think it would be better or anything. I don't want to die."

"I'm just trying to understand why you think the swingsets ask—"

"When you give a drunk, homeless person money on the street," I said, "you're helping him get drunk, right? And that's probably what made him homeless to begin with. Getting drunk."

"Sometimes, sure," Manx said. "Though it could be that they resorted to alcohol abuse after—"

"I know, I know, but that's not what I'm talking about. What I'm saying is that when you give a drunk, homeless guy money on the street and he buys alcohol with it, or even if he doesn't buy alcohol with it and even if you know that—even if you somehow know that he's gonna buy food or diapers or something with the money instead of alcohol—you're not giving him what he needs to solve his problems. What he needs is a home. You're not giving him a home."

"I can't give him a home."

"Right. And he knows that. And that's why he doesn't ask you to give him a home. He asks you to help him in a different way, in the way he thinks you might be able to help him."

"So if you *could* repair these swingsets, you would."

"I think so. If they asked. I'm terrible with my hands, though. My dad's really good with his hands, but I'm just . . . not. And most of these swingsets I murdered, they were really rusty, like rusted through, with holes in their legs and stuff, so I don't know if that's even something that can be repaired by anyone, let alone me, without destroying them first anyway, but if they asked me to repair them, and I knew how, I'd probably try, yeah."

"Probably," Manx said.

"I mean if I was good with my hands, I think I'd at least be a little bit of a different person than I am—so I can't say for sure what I'd do. I only know who I am. Kinda. If I was exactly the same person I am right now, but I also had tools and the skills I'd need to repair the swingsets, then yeah, I'm saying. I'd repair them, I guess. I'd be different, though, wouldn't I? With tools and skills. And then also, there's practical questions."

"Like what?"

"Well, like, what if it would take me months of nonstop work to repair a swingset that asked me to repair it? Maybe it's not worth it. Maybe it would rather die than suffer for so long. And maybe, you know—probably, really—probably I wouldn't have months to spend on repairing a swingset. Because the thing is, what we said before about the homeless guy, it isn't a hundred percent entirely true."

"How's that?"

"Well you *could* get a homeless guy a home, couldn't you, Manx? I mean, you're a professor at this fancy school, right? You could live probably a lot cheaper than you live, and use the leftover money to get a homeless guy a home. Maybe you could even do it without living cheaper. Maybe you've got savings you could use. Or could sell some stuff you don't use that much. But you don't do any of that."

"I don't."

"So maybe I'm like you. Maybe I wouldn't repair them if they asked me to repair them. I don't know. I guess it would depend. Like on how easy it would be to repair them. But the main thing is, though, that if they asked me to repair them, I wouldn't destroy them. I wouldn't destroy them unless they asked me. That's the main thing."

"And," my mother added, "you won't destroy any more of them even if they do ask you, right?" She turned to Manx. "Belt gave me his word he won't destroy other people's property anymore," she said.

"Right," I said. "Yes."

Manx seemed to ignore this entire exchange. "So all these swingsets you destroyed—they *all* asked you to destroy them?"

"All except for one."

"And why did you destroy that one?"

"I guess mostly because I told myself it would've wanted me to. I mean, I went there, to this guy Feather's place, to do the murder because some kids asked me to, but I'd also been starting to think by then that maybe that's what I should've been doing anyway, is finding swingsets that looked like they needed my help, and then helping them even if they didn't ask."

"I see."

"Yeah, you *see*. I know. I see, too. It's a problem. I can see that *now*. At the time, though, I thought that maybe the problem might be that, for whatever reason, that swingset was unable to speak to me, or I was unable to hear it speak, and I thought, 'Well, it's in as bad or even worse shape than the ones that asked me to help them, and if it could speak to me, or if I was able to hear it speak, it would probably ask me to help it.' So I helped it."

"And how did you decide it was a problem?"

"How did I decide? Well part of it is what you'd expect, I think: maybe it didn't want to be destroyed, I thought, and so destroying it was maybe a cruel thing to do to it. Maybe not, right? but still. Destroyed is destroyed, it's the end, it's over, and it's too big a thing to take for granted that another being wants to stop existing if that being hasn't said so, especially if that being hasn't spoken to you at all. You could make a mistake. That would be terrible. And then also, I saw that there just isn't time to live that way. There isn't enough time to help all the rusting swingsets in even just Wheelatine, you know? And the world is filled with rusting swingsets, so if I'm going to believe that I should be going around helping rusting swingsets, I have to have some way of choosing which ones to help, and which ones not to, and so 'only ones who ask for my help' is a way to narrow down the choices. And the narrowing's important. It's really important. I mean, because that's just rusting swingsets I'm talking about, but there are all kinds of damaged things in the world that ask me to help them—not just swingsets. I've only helped a couple of the ones who've asked that weren't swingsets. I don't really know why. I don't know why I didn't help the others that asked. I just didn't care about them. Maybe I should have. I didn't, though. I don't. Maybe that sounds like nonsense, and that's why you're looking at me like that. I'm not used to talking about this stuff. And so maybe it's nonsensical of me to care more about swingsets than windows or ashtrays or even maybe rocks or whatever, and more nonsensical than that that I don't know why I care more about the swingsets, but I *don't* know why. It seems really random to me—I don't understand it. Like how I like salty foods better than sweet foods. Usually. Not always, but usually. I just do. Is that nonsensical? I don't know. It seems pretty random, though. Same with swingsets. I just care more about swingsets."

"What does—"

"What I'm trying to say here to answer your question is there are *endlessly* more damaged things in the world that never say a word to me than there are things that talk to me. Endlessly more things that I suspect want my help than there are things that have told me they want my help. And I know people already think I'm crazy, but I'd *really* be crazy if I tried to help everything I just *suspected* wanted help. And maybe it's selfish of me to choose what to help. To not try to help everything. To choose to just help the things I have a *feeling* for, or whatever. Probably it is selfish. From a certain point of view. Because if I really believe that I could help so many things and I don't at least try to—if I don't do everything I possibly can to help—probably that's selfishness. Except that if I do it, if I try to help everything I suspect needs help—even if I try to help *anything* that I *know* needs help—it'll hurt my mom, so that would be selfish too. Or maybe that's just convenient for me to think. Maybe I care about hurting my mom for selfish reasons. I mean, I know I do. I don't like to see her hurt. But there're also non-selfish ones, too, I think: I don't want her to *be* hurt. But then also, I think, on top of all this other stuff I've been saying, I'd be way less effective, too, if I tried to help everything, because there isn't enough time to help everything, and so if I tried to help everything, I'd end up helping things that don't need my help as much as some other things that do. It would be like you not just trying to get homes for every homeless person in the world when you can't even really do it for one single homeless guy—which, like I said, I bet you actually could, but whatever—but it would be more like, I'm saying, it would be more like you trying to cure cancer and AIDS and end all wars *on top of* trying to get homes for every homeless person in the world. Or no. What it would be more like is if you, in a world full of homeless people that doesn't have a cure for AIDS and cancer, tried, on top of trying to get a home for every homeless person in the world and cure AIDS and cancer—if you put the same amount of effort into making sure that all the children in the world who didn't have ice cream money for Ice Cream Fridays at their schools were given ice cream money. And, like I said, it would probably be selfish, too. But not very effective for sure. Plus the people who love you—you'd hurt them. They'd miss you. You wouldn't have time for them. You'd be damaging them. You wouldn't be any good to them, so what would be the point of anything, you know? I mean . . ."

"Are you too upset to go on, right now?" said Manx. "We can stop if—"

"I'm fine," I said. "What else do you need to ask me?"

"I don't think—"

"What else?" I said.

"Okay," said Manx. "Well, one thing that I'm still a little confused about is that, according to Dr. Calgary, you, yourself, call what you did to these swingsets 'murder,' and, if you really think you helped them, then—"

"The newspapers called it that," I said. "Then everyone else. 'The Swingset Murders.' It sounds cooler than 'The Swingset Mercies' or the 'The Swingset Help-Outs,' and the swingsets don't care. They don't care what I call it. And you don't really care what the swingsets care about because you don't believe that they really talk to me. You think I'm sick. You think I'm either lying about them talking, or you think I hallucinate. I understand all that. I really do, okay? And I promise I'm not lying. And I understand that maybe I hallucinate. I can see how that's possible. I can see why you believe that, and even why maybe I should believe it. But I don't believe it, not usually at least. Still, I'm not a dumb person. And I got a little worked up there a minute ago, I admit that, but I'm taking it on the chin. You don't have to talk to me like I'm a baby, alright? 'I'm a little confused.' Just don't do that, alright? I came here for an animal. I really want an animal, and I'll answer all your questions, but just please don't ask them to me like I'm stupid."

"I didn't mean to upset you," Manx said. "I don't think you're anything close to stupid. I'm just trying to learn more about you and make sure you're appropriate for our study."

"Yeah? What's appropriate?"

"You are. You're very appropriate. You're capable of insight, Belt—of self-reflection. That's all we're here to determine today. Well, that and which kind of companion animal would suit you the best. So answer me this, and answer me honestly: Do you like puppies?"

"It depends on the puppy."

"How so?" said Manx.

"I don't like getting licked on the face," I said. "And I don't like getting touched on the skin with a butthole. How about a chipmunk? Can I have a chipmunk?"

"Alas, no," Manx said. "We don't have any chipmunks. They're too hard to train, too wired for twitchiness. They don't like to be held. And all our puppies have buttholes—what do you think of turtles?"

"I don't like the smell. That sucks about chipmunks."

"Well what about parrots?"

"Birds need to fly free."

"Snakes?"

"They eat mice."

"Some eat crickets," Manx said.

"That's almost just as bad. Also they smell."

"Crickets?"

"Snakes."

"Hamsters?"

"Weird teeth, and they eat their own kids," I said.

"Rabbits?"

"Ugly hamsters with less-cool paws."

"Monkeys?"

"That's slavery."

"Cats?" said Manx.

"Dumber than everyone says, plus buttholes."

"I couldn't agree with you more," Manx said. "Let's head upstairs to the kennel, shall we?"

•

• •

The kennel was stacks of cages and aquaria crowded in a noisy classroom lab. Air we disturbed as we came through the door sent floating a gnawed straw of hay and some feathers. It was humid as a mouth in there. The counters looked sticky. The glass of the fume hood was fogged in weird patches. Fur tufts and seed husks and bright specks of dander tumbled and spun in columns of windowlight. Earthtone food pellets dotted the floor. The overall feeling was don't lean on anything and never touch your face.

Manx, who must have sensed my discomfort, said, "Believe it or not, this place is pretty sanitary, though I know it probably doesn't feel that way at all," and he passed me a packet of moist towelettes. I liked him for this. Though his whole "I'm curious/confused" approach had gotten my guard up, the thoughtful reassurance he offered, in combination with his having taken my usage of "buttholes" in stride, amounted, for me, a boy bereft of uncles, to avuncularity. Plus his labcoat was black—I liked that, too. I hadn't known labcoats came in colors not white, and the idea of a black one was far enough beyond the scope of my fancy that despite Manx having worn his from the moment we'd met, I'd failed to take notice—I must have seen the black fabric and registered a blazer—til he'd fished those towelettes from its low-down pockets.

"You're looking at me funny. You're beaming, Belt," he said.

I said, "I like your labcoat."

"How it's black, right?"

"Yeah."

"That's why I like it, too."

"Most of Belt's clothes are black," my mother said.

"Makes him look tough, right? Or is it more like *smart*? I guess *tough*," Manx said, "is a kind of *smart*."

"Black goes with almost everything," I said.

"Yes, almost," Manx said, no longer paying attention. He was dialing in the combo to a cabinet's padlock. Beside him, on a counter, sat a blanket-draped cage. I lifted the blanket. A pair of shivering animals, one atop the other, were perched on a branch affixed to the bars. For the most part squirrel-colored, they had brown and cream markings so clean and symmetrical they seemed to be airbrushed. My mom made a cooing sound and bent at the knees. The animals turned their heads in our direction. Their noses were the pink of chewed Dubble Bubble, and their shiny eyes, entirely black and extremely protrusive, occupied the greater portion of their faces. I could have held them both in just one palm, but the fantasy was to keep them warm in my sweater, where they'd cling to my T-shirt with their humanoid hands, their heads above my collar peering up at my chin.

"What *are* these?" I asked, once Manx shut the cabinet.

"Sugar gliders," he said.

"Can I get them both? I think they're good friends."

"They're brothers," Manx said. "And believe me, you don't want them. The smell's not so hot—go ahead and take a whiff. And they sleep all day, make noise all night, and you know what they love? They love to gobble worms. Piles of live worms by the squirming, beige bowlful. Picture fidgeting beards of fat, wriggling whiskers twitching around beneath those little pink noses—that's what you see when these fellas are happiest. Not to mention they go to the bathroom everywhere."

Manx set a brushed steel box on the counter. Dome-topped and hinged, it suggested precious cargo. A tsar's death mask maybe, or a president's sidearm. "This," he said, "is exactly what you're looking for."

I pulled back the lid and discovered a lustrous, pink-white sphere about the size of a walnut. The sphere was braced along its circumference by a slit in the center of the satin pillow that occupied the lower portion of the box. A length of brown leather resembling a watch strap was held in its own slit, encircling the sphere.

"Your mom'll bring you back here once a week," Manx said. "If, after a month, you still prefer a glider, I'll let you swap your new companion for one."

"This isn't a companion. It's a ball and a strap."

"The strap's called an IncuBand. That ball is an ovum—an egg. A rare one."

"There's a bird inside?" I said.

"Not a bird," Manx said. "It's a whole new thing. A new kind of pet. A robot, actually. They're calling it a Botimal."

"Dr. Manx," my mother said.

I said, "I want the gliders." I said it to my mom. I could tell she'd fallen for the gliders, too, and in the couple weeks since she'd seen the ad card on the bus, she'd gained a little weight back and acquired some color, as hopeful, I think, about our getting a pet, as she was about the no-cost therapy. She'd always wanted a pet, but my father wouldn't have it. When the subject came up, he'd make noise about allergies. He wouldn't say he suffered them—he wasn't a liar—but he wouldn't say he didn't, and that was enough. *Had been* enough.

"Belt, Mrs. Magnet, I'm gonna shoot straight with you. No baloney," Manx said. "I'm a social scientist. My aim here is to study you, Belt, and others like you: to gather data about the effects of pets on children diagnosed with psychotic disorders. But I am not *just* a social scientist, and my aim *here* is not my only aim. Not by a long shot.

"Some years ago—more than a decade by now—I worked as a therapist at a social services clinic that served adults who suffered from chronic mental illness. By chance, two of my patients got pets within weeks of one another. Both of them, over the next few months, became noticeably higher-functioning.

"One of them was a forty-five-year-old man with schizophrenia. He lived with his younger brother's family. Before that, he'd lived at his parents' house, but once his parents passed away, his brother took him in. Now, one day, on a whim, the brother buys for his daughter—my patient's niece—a pet rat. And the niece doesn't care for the rat at all. The niece, in fact, actively *dislikes* the rat, finds the rat disgusting. Won't have it in her room. It scares her, you know? So the brother attempts to return it to the pet shop, but the pet shop won't accept the return, and, in short, the brother offers the rat to my patient, and my patient accepts. He keeps the rat in its cage on his dresser when he sleeps, feeds the rat, bathes the rat. He *loved* that rat. He'd carry it around the house in the pocket of his shirt. Share certain snacks with it. Watch television with it. And that's nice and all, right? Affection, companionship. It is, it is, it's very nice. But more importantly than that, this patient, who had never been employed, much less ever lived on his own, had—within *weeks* of being given the rat—gotten himself a job in the copyroom of a downtown insurance office. And some weeks after *that*? He found himself a studio apartment, moved out of his brother's house. At *forty-five* years old, he did these things. For the first time. His first job. His first apartment. At forty-five years old.

"The second patient, a younger woman—a woman in her twenties—who was nearly catatonic, who had been so since her early adolescence, and who, for more than a year of weekly one-on-one therapy sessions, had barely said hello to me—she would rarely respond to my questions or prompts with anything other than a shrug of her shoulders, and *never* with more than an 'okay' or a 'no'—a young woman whose eyes, despite my having sat across from her for dozens of hours, I hadn't once had the opportunity to look at directly—this young woman, upon adopting a stray cat that had appeared on her stoop one day while she was out there smoking—this young woman began to open up to me, to laugh, *to tell me anecdotes*, many of them concerning the cat itself, and, by the time I moved on from my job at the clinic a year or so later, she had passed her GED and signed up for classes at the nearby community college.

"Now, both of the patients I've just described had to continue to take their medication—they still suffered many symptoms of their illnesses, neither of them was *cured*—but the quality-of-life improvements they experienced were *radical.* Undeniable. For the first time in years, they possessed some happiness, some capacity for joy, some self-reliance. For the first time in their adult lives, they were able to function *more* independently than they had as children. Such turnarounds are, I'm sorry to have to say, quite rare. Treatment outcomes for people who suffer from chronic mental illness are, historically . . . not the best. I'm sure you know that. I'm sure that's not news. But then, you see, here were two success stories, back-to-back, and both of them had this one thing in common: new pets. Here was some *hope.*

"But hope isn't science. A couple anecdotes with happy endings aren't science. And to better the world, what we need is science. So, much as I loved doing clinical work—and I did, I loved it, it's what I signed up for—I switched gears and devoted myself to research. I've led a number of studies since then, studies like this one, but on a far smaller scale, and with adult subjects. The data our team has collected hasn't by any means been conclusive—we've done, and, for the time being, we will continue doing what us eggheads call *pure research*—but it's more than fair to say that it has *not* disappointed me. The data. It's given me more hope than ever. And it's given others hope as well. It's gotten some attention. Enough attention to attract some rather generous funding. And I mean *attract.* This current study's sponsor actually reached out to *us.* My team. Asked us what we wanted to look into next and what they could do to help. That, however, is all inside baseball—I know. Suffice it to say: things don't often work out this way. We've been very lucky.

"What I'm trying to get at, in so many words, is that, yes, my aim here is to study you, Belt, but the reason that's my aim is that I want to help you, and to help people like you, and while I can't make any promises about it, I believe that your being a part of this study—I *hope* that your being part of this study—*I have reason to believe and to hope* that your being part of this study—will, *in itself,* help you. And not only because we'll be paying for your treatment, but because you'll get a pet.

"I believe that, in the very near future, pets are going to play a sizable role in the treatment of chronic mental illness, and I believe that Botimals are the pets of the future. I believe that a Botimal would be the best possible pet for you—probably for just about anyone, but especially for you. It's easy to feed, easier to clean, it smells *nice,* and I guarantee you that, the moment it hatches, you'll see it's more adorable than any animal you've ever imagined. Do you know *Gremlins*? Did you see that movie *Gremlins* that came out a couple years ago?"

"He was up all night after he saw that," my mom said. "That movie should have been rated R."

"Well those gremlins were scary, I'll give you that. But remember Gizmo the mogwai? Remember how cute he was, and how badly you wished that mogwais were real?"

"I wanted one so bad," I said.

"You and the rest of the world," Manx said. "But mogwais, let me tell you—they've got nothing on Botimals. Botimals never transform into monsters for one, plus they're smarter than mogwais, and a thousand times as cute. Now, we started entrance interviews for this study last weekend. I've assigned Botimal companions to five different children so far, all of them had the same initial response as you—all of them were hesitant to accept an ovum—and not one has reported any disappointment. One of their mothers even called in to thank us—just yesterday. To thank us! And her son's the one who's gonna be helping *us* do the study. Anyway, I wish I had a photo or tape I could show you. When I met with our sponsors, originally, I should have snapped one myself, but I just didn't think to. And they told me they'd send some Polaroids along with the shipment of ova for *just this reason*—so I could give the study's subjects an idea of just how cute—but when the shipment came in a couple weeks back, there weren't any photos and, the moment we realized it, we contacted them, and they said they were on it, but for whatever confusing, bureaucratic unreason, we still hadn't, as of Tuesday, received any, and so that afternoon, we determined it was time to take action ourselves, and I, you see"—Manx pulled back his sleeve, flashing his IncuBanded wrist at us—"we decided I'd try to hatch one myself so that, just in case the photos never got here, I could at least show a Botimal to *some* of the subjects at their entrance interviews. The photos, as I've said, did not come in, and my Botimal, I'm sorry to say, just hasn't hatched yet. I mean, it should hatch by tomorrow, though that's no help to you, seeing as you're here today, and must, I assume, want to choose your companion before you head home. But given all that I've just described—and this, at last, is my main point, Belt, Mrs. Magnet—I would, you'd think, be pretty frustrated, but the truth is, any anger you might hear in my voice is forced. It's a put-on. Primarily, I'm happy things worked out this way. If Graham&Swords had sent the photos they promised, yes, sure, this part of the study might have gone a little more smoothly, but then I wouldn't have strapped this ovum to my wrist for the sake of—ehem—*science*, ha-ha, and so I wouldn't be on the verge of owning my own Botimal. I'm really excited to see the little guy. I can hardly wait."

"Graham&Swords?" my mom said.

"Our sponsors," said Manx.

"As in, 'We do dishes right'? Graham&Swords?"

"Oh!" said Manx. "Yes, yes. I know. What's even funnier about that is home appliances barely account for a tenth of their business. I only found that out, myself, after they offered to fund the study. The majority of their profits actually comes from armaments, though soon, I bet, it'll come from Botimals. I think you'll see what I mean, once Belt's hatches. Mrs. Magnet, this new pet—you're gonna wish you had your own. Everyone will."

"And they're safe?" my mom said. "I'm assuming they're safe, or the study—"

"Safe as goldfish," said Manx. "They don't bite or scratch. They don't even get angry. They're made to please people. Go on. Next question. Maybe how big do they . . . ?"

"How big do they get?"

"There's a range," Manx said, "but the biggest one we've seen full-grown is about as tall as Belt's forearm is long. It'll have two arms, one or two legs—I haven't seen a one-legged one myself, but I'm told it happens—and it may or may not have a tail that may or may not work like a fifth limb. Or a fourth—depending on the number of legs."

"One leg? That sounds . . ."

"The leg, I'm told, is centered. It's not as though it looks like it's *missing* a leg. And I'm told the one-legged ones either use their hands to walk tripedally, or, if they have a limb-like tail, they might rock or hop or, I guess, hoppingly rock back and forth leg-to-tail-to-leg-to-tail to get around. What else can I tell you? It'll be furry in places, but it doesn't shed. The fur's more like felt. In fact the manual calls it 'velvet.' The colors vary. The skin colors, too. The voice is quiet, though they sometimes mimic human speech, and they quote-unquote *sing* when they're in pain or sense danger. You can teach them tricks—"

"They feel pain?" my mom said.

"Yes."

"They feel pain, but they're robots."

"Your mother's a smart lady," Manx said to me. "'Pain,'" he said. "Or 'feel' for that matter. Even 'eating,' 'drinking,' 'hungry,' and 'thirsty.' Please forgive this annoying thing I'm doing with my fingers when I say those words, but they're not the right ones. They're insufficient metaphors. We don't, however, have the right words yet, so they're the ones I'm forced to use. But 'pain' is a kind of information, and 'feeling pain'—or 'feeling' anything at all—is a process. 'Eating' and 'drinking'—responsive behaviors to processed information, to the 'feelings' of 'hunger' and 'thirst.' Maybe try, Mrs. Magnet, to think of a personal computer. It 'eats' and 'drinks' electricity, its 'body' is plastic and metal, its 'organs' silicon and plastic and metal, and when it processes code it doesn't 'know' how to handle—if, say, it's an Apple computer, and you insert a Windows diskette in its drive—the computer 'feels' 'pain,' in response to which it behaves by beeping and sometimes giving off grinding sounds. Botimals are just like that, but made of flesh and bone. I know it sounds strange—it *is* strange. And your Botimal sure as heck won't seem like a robot. But that's the whole point. And, again, I really think it's the right choice for your son. These are extremely loyal pets, easy to care for, never violent, and far less messy than adult human beings, let alone dogs and cats and the like. You feed it a thimbleful of water and a special pellet once a day—I'll give you a jar of the pellets before you leave, a six-month supply—and it goes to the bathroom once every twenty-four hours. It goes at night. One dry little sphere the size of a pebble. Each morning, you find the sphere inside the PillowNest—this handsome steel box here, which is where it'll sleep. You find the sphere in the morning, flush the sphere down the toilet. Wash your hands. That's that. That's all. And did I mention they smell nice? They smell like candy. Convinced? I can see it. You're almost convinced."

"You promise I can trade it for a glider in a month?" I said.

"You have my word. But I'll bet you an ice cream you keep it," Manx said.

"How long does it take to hatch?" I said.

"Depends on you. You supply the warmth. That's how it hatches—through regular contact with human body heat. About a hundred and twenty-five hours of it, give or take. Followed by another day or so of *no* access to human body heat. It's very simple. After that, to keep it alive, all you have to do, apart from feeding and watering it, is cuddle it for a little while every day. And by you, I mean *you,* Belt. For the first couple-three weeks you're the only person who should cuddle the Botimal. It needs to imprint on you—it needs to know that *you're* its best friend. After that, anyone can cuddle it, but to keep it alive and healthy, you'll still need to cuddle it yourself every day for at least a couple hours."

"A couple *hours*?" my mom said.

"That might sound like a lot, I know, but cuddling it's easy. You can stick it in your shirt and just let it press against you. Go for a walk, watch TV, do homework, whatever. No sports of course, with the Botimal in your shirt, but it's got these great claws, and it'll hook those claws into the fabric to stabilize itself against your body—its sense of balance is really impressive—and it'll stay there as long as you'll let it, happy."

"I want it," I said.

"Mrs. Magnet?"

"He wants it."

"Great," Manx said. "I knew you would." He removed the IncuBand from its slit in the PillowNest, then removed the egg. "The manual covers all I'm about to show you, and more, and it's really simple, but I want to take you through this part step-by-step because it's no great piece of literature, that manual, and if there comes a next time, it'll be a lot easier if you can remember how this works."

"Why," my mom said, "would there be a next time?"

Manx said, "Ha! Wow am I a space-case. I completely forgot to talk about cloning, didn't I? Once they're full-grown—that takes about three weeks—they can, with your help, clone themselves," he said. Then he showed us how to fit the egg in the IncuBand, which he fastened around my wrist, above the pulse—it was as simple as he said—and he told us what to expect before the hatch, what signs to watch for, and how to feed the Botimal once it entered the world, how to get it to clone, and how to keep it from cloning (though I don't recall him saying anything about hobunks). He emphasized its need for human affection and told us that, although he didn't want to make any promises regarding its abilities, all Botimals, to one degree or another, could mimic both human speech and movement, though most of them were stronger in one area than the other, and that many of those weaker at mimicking speech exhibited a knack for mimicking whistling. He repeated the feeding and watering instructions, reminded us that everything he just told us was in the manual, handed us a six-month supply of pellets, and said that he'd see us the following Saturday. If I wore the IncuBand nonstop, he said, I'd have a new friend by Friday evening at latest and I should please make sure to bring it with me.

•

• •

Because of all the dinosaur fossils it housed, the Field Museum of Natural History had once been my favorite destination in Chicago, but the last time we'd gone there, I'd learned from a docent that some of the bones of the T. Rex were fake—made of plastic—and I felt betrayed. I threw what, for me, passed for a tantrum: I walked with a slouch to a bench and sat.

"Are you tired?" said my mother.

"This museum is stupid."

"You're upset about the bones—I am too, a little. Except I don't think we should get so down. A lot of them are real. The head is real."

"I thought all of them were real."

"So did I," my mom said. "But I guess that, in a way, they might as well be, right? They didn't just make them up out of nothing. They looked at what was missing and could tell what must have been there."

I was six or maybe seven years old, and for as long as I was able to remember, I'd pretended that when she blew air on a flesh wound—a bee-stung knee, say, or rugburned elbow—the pain went away. It was important she believe I believed in her magic. This thing with the fossils called for something similar;

to prevent her disappointment, I had to act as though I were comforted by her reasoning. I said, "You're right. You're completely right. Thanks," and I thought I'd pulled it off. But then she suggested we leave the museum and walk a couple blocks to the Shedd Aquarium, and I knew she'd seen through me; I knew I'd disappointed her, and, worse, I knew she thought she'd disappointed me.

To repair this, I oversold at the aquarium. I oohed like a toddler when the whale began to spout, spastically clapped when the dolphins did their barrel rolls, pulled my lip and chewed my knuckle at the stillness of the starfish stuck against the glass. I got a real kick out of watching those animals, but my performance of enthusiasm was so theatrical, so unlike me, my mother didn't buy it. Three or four times, she let me know we could leave whenever I wanted. She even gave me outs. Maybe I was hungry and wanted McDonald's. Maybe I'd rather she take me to a movie.

I still, at age twelve, counted that memory of being at the aquarium as one of my saddest, and so assumed it was one of my mother's saddest, too, which goes toward explaining how I had so much trouble understanding what happened at Science and Industry—that's where we went after leaving Manx's lab. It was the only major museum in Chicago to which I'd never been, and it was just up the street from the university. On our way, we stopped for lunch at the Salonica diner, had buttery grilled cheese with chewy-iced Cokes, and we gazed at the ovum I wore on my wrist, flipped through the manual, read parts aloud, laughing at the jargon, the awkward phrasings. It had been a hard month, a hard couple of months, and I was ill, maybe, sure, but it was under control, and now we could afford it—my SSDI would come into force before my part in the study was over—and plus: the Botimal. Soon we'd have a new pet. A new kind of new pet.

So our spirits were high as we entered the museum, and they stayed that way for at least an hour. There were fighter planes hanging from the ceilings, and rockets. A locomotive engine in the middle of a hallway. We stood inside a two-story human heart's ventricles, listening to it beat, awash in red light. We watched three chicks emerge from incubated eggs, learned what we'd weigh on Mars and the moon, fed pennies into a hand-cranked machine that spit them out warm, de-Lincolned, and elliptical, embossed with images of bugs and submarines. The formaldehyde-beiged spongey muscles and organs of the cross-sectioned man in the double-sided panes at the anatomy exhibit creeped us out fast, and we fled in the direction of the captured German U-boat, but because the next tour wouldn't start for thirty minutes, we decided to roam. That's when we encountered the wall of fetuses. Prenatal development from week four forward. You looked like a dot, then you looked like a peanut, then you looked like a lizard, then a humanoid fish, then you looked like a baby, then an even bigger baby, and then you came out. It blew me away. Around week 34, I said to my mom, "I can't wait to have a kid." I said it again in front of week 38, and I saw she was crying. I assumed that she figured I was hamming it up; assumed she'd remembered that time at the Shedd, and that all the authentic enthusiasm I'd shown since we'd arrived at the museum—maybe even since Manx had assigned me the Botimal—now appeared false to her.

Of course I was wrong. The problem was she *did* buy my excitement for fatherhood. The degree to which I misunderstood was almost comical. I kept trying to convince her that I meant what I'd said: that I wanted a kid, that I couldn't wait to have one. Boy or girl, it didn't matter. How could it matter? Look at the fetus wall. Look at how amazing. How could anyone ever not want a kid? If you had the ability to fly, I told her, but you always kept your feet on the ground—that's how crazy not having a kid would be. Except for finding a person to marry, it seemed like the only thing you really had to do.

"I'm not feeling well," she said.

"But I mean it," I said. "I really want a wife and baby. Maybe lots of babies. I'm not just saying it."

"I know that," she said.

Still, I didn't believe her.

•

• •

We discovered the squiggle while the car warmed up. My mom had lit a Quill that must have frozen to her lips, for she winced as if stung when she pulled it away, and it shot from her hand and landed by my feet. In contorting herself around the stick to retrieve it, she came eye-to-egg with my IncuBanded wrist. "Hey, wow," she said. "Hey, Belt. Something happened."

She switched on the domelight—the sun was going down—and we inspected the ovum. A mark resembling a half-finished ampersand could now be seen through the glossy shell. The top of the loop was the mark's blackest part. From the neck down, it grayed, faded penumbrally, giving the impression—the correct impression—that a semi-translucent goop in the ovum was obscuring our view of a curved 3-D figure. I took off the IncuBand to see the lower hemisphere. No changes were visible. The swirled pink-white remained uninterrupted.

"Put it back on," said my mom. "Keep it warm. But let me see first." She swiped it from my hand. "Don't look at me like that. I'm excited, too, you know."

"Are you really?" I said.

"Of course," she said. "And listen, Belt, I don't know what got into me back there. I didn't mean to scare you. I just started feeling sick for a minute."

"You were crying," I said.

"A little," she said. "I was terribly sad. But I shouldn't have been. I have nothing to be sad about."

"I thought I upset you."

"*You* upset *me*? Come on. You're the best. I think I must be coming down with something. Or fighting something off. I get weird like that whenever I get sick."

"You never get sick."

"Not often, no. But when I used to get sick—that's just how it felt. I'd almost forgotten. It was confusing, actually. Do you feel alright?"

I said, "I feel fine."

"Good," she said. "I feel fine too, now. Let's hope it stays that way. There's a flu going round." She strapped the IncuBand onto my wrist and tuned the radio to NPR.

The whole ride home I monitored the ovum. At first, the changes came so slowly, I thought that I may have been imagining them, but the squiggle appeared to be rotating clockwise and graying, sinking. Then, just a couple of miles from our exit, it began to turn on a different axis, and slightly faster, like a slot-machine tumbler coming to rest. We exited the highway, and I started feeling motion-sick. I cracked the window, stared ahead at the road. Once the dizziness passed, I looked back at the ovum and couldn't see the squiggle. Nothing was there. I raised my wrist and squinted—nothing, nothing.

I was nauseated, spinning. My scalp was sweating. I shut my eyes, pressed my temple to the window. My breath was too warm. I was thick-tongued and wretched. Neither Manx nor the manual had mentioned a word about the squiggle disappearing, and I thought of how delicate those embryos had seemed, suspended by filaments behind the museum glass—might I have somehow mishandled the ovum? allowed its temperature to get too low? jarred the squiggle from a pocket of safety in the goop? was the Botimal damaged?

Was the Botimal dead?

No. "No way," I thought. No way. I wanted to meet the little thing so bad. To lose it even before it hatched? That would be too traumatic. I wasn't prepared for that, or anything like it, and, remarkably—at least it seems so, now—I found comfort in my lack of preparation itself. Nothing traumatic had ever happened to me, and I was able to reason that nothing traumatic ever *could* happen without my first having been prepared for it to happen. Were it possible for me to have killed my Botimal, I would have been warned of it.

I would have been warned by the driver of the very car in which I rode. My mother would have warned me, and since she hadn't warned me, there was no need to worry, everything was fine. That's what I determined. That's what gave me comfort. It made no sense, but faith never does.

The car stopped in light, and I heard our garage door grinding shut behind us.

"So?" said my mother, taking hold of my wrist.

I opened my eyes. The squiggle was back, a little wider than before, and freshly adorned with three crooked carets that touched at the feet like the points of a lopsided Basquiat crown.

•

• •

Maybe you're a member of my generation. Maybe you were the first kid at school to have a cure. You may have been one of those lucky few children of senators and oligarchs connected enough to score them their HatchKits a couple weeks prior to the National May Day HatchKit Rollout. Whoever you are, young or old or middle-aged, I'm certain that you were terribly excited to receive your first ovum. I am, however, equally certain that unless you were one of us seventeen Friends Study subjects assigned a Botimal, your pre-hatch excitement could not have been more than a fraction of mine. Even if you are of my generation—even if you weren't born into a world where an ovum cost less than a ticket to the movies, and standard-issue prams featured PillowNest slots—by the time your new friend had cracked through its shell you'd have already seen the talent show footage of the overloading Sandburg Middle School boy, and at least a few dozen of the HatchKit commercials airing in heavy rotation that spring (and that's to say nothing of the nightly news specials, the glossy magazine spreads, or the front pages of the checkout-line tabloids). Whereas all I'd had to go on was a bunch of words. I hadn't had a glance at a single photo, let alone a moving image. A pet that was somehow cuter than a mogwai? One that smelled like candy, spoke and sang, and hatched from an egg you wore on your wrist? A pet of that description that was also a robot? It sounded about as real as genies. As ray-guns, lightsabers, X-ray glasses. As pocket-size, voice-commandable Game Boys that doubled as camcorders, tripled as calculators, and made long-distance telephone calls. That Botimals could be was hard enough to imagine; that one could be *mine* (that one *would* be mine, that one already *was*)—that was even harder. And it was hell on my nerves. Were I ever again, for even five minutes, to enter a state of anticipation as relentless and intense as that which I experienced in those IncuBanded days preceding Blank's hatch, I believe I would die. Heart attack. Stroke. I was barely able to survive it at twelve.

When we returned from Hyde Park and gave him our report, my father said, "You know, I had a feeling all day—a good, lucky feeling. Thank God for the rigor of the conscientious scientist. They pay for your treatment and we don't have to house a pet."

"But we do," I said.

"Come on, Billy," he said. "I didn't raise no dummy. You're in the control group. That thing on your wrist—it's what's called a placebo."

"No, look," I said, and showed him the ovum. "These marks weren't there at all before. They're changing. It's growing."

"That's just some invisible ink kind of deal. Your body gets it warm, gets it to show. It's a sugar pill, buddy."

"That just isn't so," my mother told him. "That would be too cruel. Dr. Manx wasn't cruel."

"All I'm saying is he shouldn't get his hopes up."

Maybe he was right, despite being wrong. I mean, I didn't, for a moment, think the ovum a placebo, plus I liked my hopes; my hopes made me . . . hopeful. The obsessions, however, that rode the hopes' backs—I could have done with being a bit less obsessive. A lot less obsessive. What exactly did it *mean* to be "cuter than a mogwai"? How could anything be cuter than a mogwai? How many limbs would it have? How many fingers? What color velvet? Would it think it was a person? Would it think I was a Botimal? What was it like to be something's best friend? Was reciprocity a foregone conclusion? And what if somebody tried to steal it? Wouldn't somebody try to steal it? What if somebody tried to hurt it? How could I protect it? And when—when exactly—when would it hatch? That was a big one. Manx's answer was "about six days"—five on my wrist and then one off—but the manual allowed for a lot more variance: between 75 and 125 hours on my wrist plus another 24 off it *at most*. So: three days of slack. The hatch could come as early as Tuesday afternoon, but it could also come as late as Friday evening. The "squiggle phase" would give way to the "woodcut phase," then new colors would show, and I'd have to slot the ovum in the PillowNest slit; about that both the manual and Manx were unambiguous. Also that the colors would be undeniable: reds, greens, and blues, bold and bright amidst the pink-white and black. But how long, exactly, would each phase take? No one had told me. And would the new colors manifest as stripes? dots? amorphous stains? Would they be the colors of the Botimal itself, or would they just be the colors of the goop surrounding it? Was it even goop, or was it something thinner? And yes, even questions like these—questions that, in addition to being secondary (at least upon reflection, twenty-five years later), had concrete answers I knew to be imminent—even these types of questions obsessed me. My life was transforming. My life was getting better. I felt I was becoming a part of history—I *was*—and I couldn't miss anything. I had to watch the ovum.

Between Saturday and Tuesday, I slept no more than twelve hours total, and maybe—maybe—three were consecutive. I was so set on witnessing the changes as they happened, so afraid to fail at vigilance, that even when I was alone in my bedroom, where no one else could see or hear, I, to protect my waning concentration, severed contact with inans that tried to converse with me. Sunday afternoon, my desk blotter asked me to cut it into strips, and I peeled my elbow from its faux-leather surface, leaned back in my chair without saying a word, and hardly suffered a hint of remorse.

Tuesday night, the chair itself spoke up, not asking me to kill it, nor even complaining, but rather, uncharacteristically for an inan, expressing pleasure in how it was treated, specifically the way I occasionally used it to roll from the desk to the bed or the window. The other wheeled chairs at the secondhand shop where my father had bought it would, it assured me, be envious to learn of its situation. ||Generally speaking, we are vastly underutilized as modes of short-range transport,|| it said. ||I wanted to thank you.||

"You're welcome," I mumbled, then moved to the bed.

The metamorphic squiggle, which had previously behaved in unpredictable ways—fitfully proliferating zigzags and loops that lengthened and spiraled at varying speeds—was by then no longer present. During dinner, it had started to fill itself in, and by the end of dessert, all its carets and curls had coalesced into a single black figure resembling two anvils set horn-to-horn; the Botimal had entered the woodcut phase. The anvils throbbed at a uniform rhythm.

"Any minute now," I thought, "the colors could show." The sooner they showed, the sooner I could slot it, the sooner my pet would emerge from its shell. In the meantime, however, the throbbing was hypnotic, a drag on my eyelids, and the sleep deprivation was wearing me down. I was grinding my teeth against my will, shivering a little, feeling electric pains in odd places—toenails, earlobes, the skin of one thigh—and fat, fuzzy halos seemed to hug any object that wasn't dramatically shadowed. I was fading away. That's why I started smoking.

I'd been stealing a Quill or two a day from my parents ever since I'd failed to kiss Stevie on her driveway. The idea was that I'd get ahold of a bunch—I had over a hundred, hidden in a shoebox among my old journals inside the filebox beneath my bed—and, after learning to smoke, I would bring some to school and get Stevie to sneak off and have one with me, and I'd do it again the following day, and again the day after, til soon enough we'd have a secret ritual, a deeper friendship, better odds of getting married. Up til that point, what had held me back from lighting one was, strangely or not-so, this very book. Well, not necessarily *this* very book, but the memoir I figured I would write one day. I'd read enough already, and seen enough movies, to know that, with the possible exception of my interactions with inans, my childhood in Wheelatine wasn't too likely to provide me with a lot of intriguing material, whereas starting to smoke—smoking being a thing I'd always wanted to do, anyway; a thing that impressed me as a sign of character (I'd already, in addition to Vonnegut, read *Huckleberry Finn;* in addition to *Grease,* I'd often rewatched *The Outsiders*)—starting to smoke, if properly contextualized, could supply me with a moment worth writing about, or, at the very least, enhance such a moment. Had my mother not insisted on observing me swallow my antipsychotics, I might have taken the first one up in my room, and that could have been the moment: having gulped back the tablet with a mouthful of water, I'd have lit up the Quill, blown the smoke out slowly, then shaken the flame off the tip of the match with a single, though heavy, snap of my wrist, thereby expressing, with perfectly balanced ambiguity, either fierce resolve, reluctant resignation, or fierce resolve *and* reluctant resignation. Or, maybe, if I'd thought to bring one with me, I'd have started a couple or three days after that, lighting up the first time I'd tried to explain to a death-seeking swingset that, despite my wanting to, I just couldn't kill it—"I'm out of the helping game now," I'd lamented, and, had I a Quill, I could have then sighed a cloud out instead of just breathing—and the washed-up, see-how-far-I've-fallen-ness of that moment would have been unmistakable, would have made for a classic I-need-a-vice-to-cope-with-my-agonizing-life scene. Neither of those moments, nor any preceding them, would have been as good as this one on my bed, though, for this one on my bed was functionally motivated. I wanted to focus, to stare at the ovum, without passing out—to be poised to slot it at the first sight of color—and in addition to presumably giving me a task that required enough attention to keep me awake (but not so much attention as to distract from my focus), smoking would supply my bloodstream with nicotine: a CNS stimulant, our Health teacher called it, the stuff *awake* was made from.

So I opened the window next to my bed—I didn't have an ashtray—and smoked a stolen Quill. Then I smoked another, and another after that one. I tried different grips and labial arrangements: the cowboy, the soldier, the prisoner, the French, the executee, and the district attorney. I knew that I had to get the smoke in my lungs, but couldn't figure out how, and so I didn't get nauseous, only more eyeball-stung and tired. Before lighting a fourth, I passed out for a minute, or maybe ten, and I judged it too dangerous; if I fell asleep smoking, I could burn the place down. And so I gave in, fell asleep sitting up, my cheek in my palm, my elbow on the sill.

•

• •

In the morning, sore-necked, I discovered three roughly parallel slashes, two green and one blue, across the horn of each anvil. I slipped off the Incu-Band, loosened the thumbscrews, and turned the ovum over, into my palm. Through the hemisphere previously pressed to my flesh I saw a tapering J that, later, after the hatch had taken place, I'd determine to have been Blank's tail's silhouette. It swished like a windblown bulrush, then stopped. I opened the PillowNest, slotted the ovum anvils-down, and fruitlessly waited for the J to swish again. A few minutes later, I was being called to breakfast. I shut the lid, rushed my morning ablutions, stuck a pencil box of Quills down deep in my bag, and all but danced my way to the kitchen.

My failure to witness the colored slashes' geneses didn't leave me disappointed the way I'd have thought. I guess my head lacked the space to abide disappointment. I had become a smoker, and in twenty-four hours or less I'd have a pet. I was walking elation. This would be a good day.

"Can I please stay home to watch, in case it hatches?" I asked.

"How many times do we have to say, 'No'?"

I couldn't even fake a pout is how elated.

•

• •

We snuck off to smoke behind the dumpsters at recess.

"You're not smoking," said Stevie, near the end of the first one. "It's a two-step process. Once the smoke's in your mouth, you have to breathe in."

I did as instructed.

"That's better, right?" she said.

It was. I said, "Wow."

"So where'd it go?" she said.

"My lungs, I think. I breathed it in like you told me."

"Not the smoke, the agate."

"Oh!" I said. "It's finished. I put it in a box."

"Why's that?" she said. "You ashamed of the specific shape of your spirit?"

In the middle of Science Lab the previous Monday, Stevie'd asked me what it was I kept staring down at, there on my wrist, and I told her the ovum was an Indian agate my uncle'd bought me on his recent trip to New Mexico. She asked to see it closer, and I lifted my arm. "That doodle inside it just moved," she said. She made an attempt at undoing the IncuBand, and, much as I liked her fingers on my skin, I pulled away, saying, "You see with your eyes, not with your hands," which made her laugh, til she realized I meant it. "Oh," she said. "I thought we were cool."

"We are."

"No. I don't think we are. I think you're being dickish cause I'm not your girlfriend."

"No. No no. It's an Indian thing. The way that stuff's moving—it's like a mood ring, kind of. There's an oil inside it, or a gas or something that my pulse and my skin warmth cause to form shapes because what it's doing is, the oil or gas I mean, is it's trying to form a very specific kind of shape, a shape that'll be symbolic of my life or my spirit or something. Crazy, right? But it's what my uncle told me, and he made me promise to wear it nonstop til the shape finished forming."

"Okay then, weirdo. That all sounds like bullshit, but whatever. I'll believe you."

I didn't like being dishonest with Stevie, and had I only been afraid that removing the IncuBand would slow down the hatch, I probably wouldn't have stopped her from removing it, much less gone on to lie so clumsily about why she shouldn't, but even if I hadn't lied about what the ovum was, I'd still have had to lie about how I'd gotten it—I'd have much preferred that she catch me in a lie than she find out I was officially crazy—so I'd figured it was safest to lie about everything. This was, in a way, a less deceitful approach than that which I took with the rest of my schoolmates, some of whom I worried might try to steal the ovum regardless of whether they knew what it was; I didn't even allow them a chance to see it. I'd walked Washington's hallways with my sleeves stretched long, the cuffs in my fists, and whenever I stole a glance at my wrist, I made sure to obstruct all other points of view with a wall, a desktop, or my cupped right hand. In PE, I claimed to have forgotten my gym clothes, climbed ropes and did sprints in my hoodie and jeans, and, despite the disgust and homophobic accusations of the boys who noticed, refused to take a shower in the locker room afterward.

All worries seemed distant, though, out by the dumpsters; the ovum was slotted, safe in my room, and I was feeling a lot less security-minded, a lot more capable of joking around. Flirting, even.

"The specific shape of my spirit . . ." I said, and I stepped on our Quill, which was down to the feather, lit up a fresh one, and handed it to Stevie. "The specific shape of my spirit," I told her, "is so fucking pretty it would blind you at a glance."

•

• •

My mother was there when I got back from school, and she said I shouldn't hug her; that she might have the flu. Soon after I'd left for the bus stop that morning, she'd begun, she said, to feel how she'd felt at Science and Industry. She didn't look sick, though, and I told her as much, smiling to suggest that I believed she'd been faking, that she'd stayed home from work in order not to miss my first encounter with the baby Botimal in case it hatched before the end of her workday.

"I feel better, now," she said, as we ran up the stairs. "It passed like last time."

"I'm glad," I said. "Good. I mean: weird. But good. I'm glad you're—"

"Oh," said my mother. "Oh my, oh my . . ."

We were kneeling by my night table, temple-to-temple, looking down into the PillowNest—I'd opened it—at a pale-skinned, single-legged, flesh-and-bone robot the width of my thumb and the length of my ring finger (plus a couple phalanges, with its tail extended). It was lying on its side and looking back up at us—at me—through glistering, orange- and gold-shot blue eyes. A plus-sign-shaped parcel of matte black velvet—the crux just above the barely prominent snout, the crossbar reaching to the edges of the orbits, as if aspiring to eyebrowhood—wrinkled and lifted toward the top of its head as the hatchling struggled to raise itself up on hands and foot without unlocking our mutual gaze.

"Hi. I'm Belt," I said, once it stood steady. "Hi. Hello."

Dropping and raising its lower jaw—trying, it seemed, to repeat what I'd said—it emitted a sequence of breathy schwas.

I simplified a little. I said, "I'm Belt."

"ə ə," it said.

"Belt."

"ə."

"Hello. Hi?"

"ə-ə. ə?"

I thought maybe it still had yet to develop all the parts of the larynx human language required—it wouldn't be full-grown for another three weeks—but it was trying so hard, and I didn't want failure to stain our introduction. I remembered Manx said that some were better at whistling, so I gave that a go; five or six hard-hat construction-man wolf-calls, a couple or three corner-gangster over-heres.

It pursed its lips and replied with more schwas, albeit of mimetic tone and duration.

My mother, her right hand hiding her mouth—as if to halt the oh-mys at their point of egress—extended her left, fingers flapping, to the hatchling. I did the same thing and the hatchling reached up—reached out—to mimic the gesture. The muscles of its leg and the arm it still stood upon trembled and flexed beneath the weight of its body, but it got a few flaps in before falling sideways. Just ahead of the fall, it looked away from my eyes, at the back of the hand with which it gestured. Though I could never, obviously, know such a thing, at the time I was sure that that's why it fell; that seeing four digits there, rather than five, shocked it a little, surprised it off-balance.

Giving out little hums of exertion or sorrow, it thrashed its arms and bicycled its leg til I gently, *gent*ly pinched its shoulders between my thumb and index finger, lifted it over the walls of the PillowNest, and laid it facedown, in the cup of my palm. It crawled a couple centimeters closer to my arm, and pressed a cool, soft cheek to my pulse. With its tail curled around the base of my pinkie, it sighed a couple times, embraced my wrist, and started to nap.

I brought it nearer to my face, to get a closer look. Flecks of goop, blue and green, had dried inside its hollows—the spaces between its toes and fingers, the creases on the backs of its knee and neck—and fragments of pink-white ovum casing dotted its foot and the crown of its skull, but I wasn't grossed out. Not even a little. It smelled like a pouch of grape Big League Chew. Its lips were as thin as ballpoint pen strokes, its nares' diameters a twelve-point umlaut's. Had I not seen them rising and falling with breath, I would not have believed that such tiny ribs—no single one larger than a thumbnail clipping—could cage a set of lungs, let alone as complex a machine as a heart. And the buttons of its fragile, curving spine—how could there be so many, so small, so perfectly aligned?

"I wish I could hold it," my mother said.

"Me too," I said, and I was going to let her. It was too good and strange a thing not to share. I said, "Maybe you should."

"It's probably better we follow the instructions," she said. "I only have to wait a couple weeks or so, right?"

"That's what Dr. Manx said, but the manual only says that for the first seven days I should cuddle it more than anyone else does. It doesn't say someone else *can't*—"

"Still, though, I think we should play it safe and listen to Dr. Manx."

"Maybe," I said. "But I think it's imprinted. I really do. You saw how it looked at me. Did you see how it looked at me?"

"How about I just help you name it," she said. "It needs a name. Though, actually, I think it needs a bath more than that. That dried-out blue stuff can't be very comfortable. Looks kind of sticky."

She was right about the bath. The manual said that was the first thing to do. "How do you think I should wake it?" I said.

"Poke it a little? Maybe blow on its face?"

I blew on its face. It shuddered and gasped and its eyes went wide. Then, reaching out a hand as it had before, it sneezed twice drily.

"It sneezes!" said my mother. "Oh, Belt, it sneezes. That's just too—oh! That's just too much. Do it again. Belt, blow on it again."

I blew on it again, and again it showed its hand to me and said its name twice.

•

• •

Next morning, at breakfast, my father fed Kablankey a cube of diced onion dusted in cayenne. This wasn't, I don't think, a sadistic act, but rather just a heedless one. He'd slid the onion from between the oily lips of his own "murder omelet," a dish that neither my mother nor I could ever stomach despite its being his special favorite, which seemed, at times, to make him feel lonely, and regularly left him, perhaps half-jokingly (though no more than half-), lamenting the absence of in-house comrades with whom to share its ostensible pleasures. On top of that, the onion wasn't—not by a long shot—the most piquant of the omelet's ingredients; had his aims been cruel, he would have, I'd have thought, excised a sliver of pickled sport pepper, fresh jalapeño, or spicy giardiniera to feed to Kablankey. Then again, though, you never really knew with him. I never knew. He was verging on a three-day ice-fishing weekend, and as soon as his shift at the plant was over, Rick and Jim would pick him up and they'd head for Wisconsin, which meant, above all, that his spirits were high, and high spirits often led him toward the kind of boyish mischief that could, I suppose, as easily be adjudged malicious as playful. He was, in such spirits, no less likely to tickle a baby than heckle a busker (assuming both a baby and a busker were at hand). He might startle a sleeper, or hiss at a cat, swipe a cherry off the top of somebody's sundae, pitch Amway to Girl Scouts out selling cookies, pitch cookies to Witnesses, Girl Scouts to Mormons, ask a mime what exactly she's trying to say, challenge a granny to drag-race for pink slips, challenge a banker to pull on his finger, rip a loud fart then accuse you of farting . . .

He wasn't easy to read, but whatever the nature of my father's motivation,

I was heedless for sure. When he offered Blank his onion-riding knuckle, I didn't try to stop him—didn't even think to. Blank opened wide, received the cube on its tongue, clamped down, sucked, and gave out a strangling noise. After a second, its pupils went pinpoint. Its tail began to thrash.

"Spit it out," I said. "Spit it out, Kablankey. Spit it."

Its panicked pulse visibly throbbed in its abdomen. It slapped at its face, left-right-left.

"Spit," my mom said.

"It won't," I said. "It won't."

"No, you," she said, *"you."* She made a kind of spitting sound: "Tew. Ptewooie!"

My eyes locked on Blank's, I mimicked my mother. "Tew. Ptewooie!"

"ə. ə-ə-ə!" Blank said, still flailing and slapping.

"Use this," said my mother, and pushed a piece of toast at me.

I bit off some crust, spit the crust out.

Kablankey understood. It lowered its head, gobbed the onion on my wrist. Then it locked eyes with me again, and painsang. Given Blank's age, the song was, of course, bent—way off-key, and a little off-time—but none of us knew that. All of us cooed. Even my father. "Jesus," he said. "It really is adorable. Who'd believe it? And to think I said it was a placebo, you know?"

"Don't feed it onions again," I said. "Don't even feed it anything."

"I'm sorry I did that, Billy. I am," my dad said. "This thing, I gotta tell you—it's really something. The way it's singing? I'm kind of having a moment, here. I mean, am I crazy? I really feel like one of those old, cheek-pinching biddies, right now. Some over-kissy granny. I look at that thing, and I just want to, you know—I just want to squeeze it. Eat it right up."

•

•   •

By the time Kablankey had ceased to painsing (I'd had it lick a dab of yogurt off a spoon), I knew I'd bring it with me, concealed, to school. If I left it at home, I'd miss it too much, and, after all, this was a Thursday—I had Health instead of Gym—so there'd be no call for me to take off my hoodie.

I went up to my room as if to put Blank away, closed the lid of the PillowNest, then ran back downstairs and out the front door, shouting over my shoulder at my parents, "I'm late!"

Blank couldn't possibly have been easier to hide. Through all my morning classes, it was so still and quiet, I kept pushing warmth- and breath-seeking fingers under my cuff to make sure it was alive. When, despite feeling warmth,

I wasn't sure I felt breath, I'd get a pass to the bathroom, where I'd pull back my sleeve behind the door of a stall, and say hi til Blank opened its eyes and schwa'd.

Gradually, my sudden-infant-death-fear faded. During lunch, it began giving way to a confidence I hadn't possessed in at least a couple months, a sense that happy endings weren't impossible. The other shoe may have yet had to drop, but then again maybe not: maybe Blank's hatch was the other dropped shoe.

At recess, I waited by the dumpsters for Stevie, trying to determine which of two mutually exclusive scenarios would be more likely to lead to romance—the intimate one in which we'd share a cigarette, or the smooth-move one where, as she came around the corner, she'd witness me lighting two Quills at once—but she arrived before I could come to a decision.

She lit her own Quill, and said, "We're moving away."

Still riding the joy wave of Kablankey's hatch's potential other-shoeness, still thrilled I got to smoke with the coolest girl I knew, I thought Stevie was speaking about me and her; I thought she was speaking figuratively; I thought she was saying *we* were moving away, as in *from one another*, which, given the crooked set of her mouth, the crack in her voice, and the downward-looking eyes, strongly suggested that she wished it were the opposite, i.e. that she wished we were moving *closer*.

So I took a step closer, grabbed hold of her hand. "We don't have to keep moving away," I said.

She shook off my grip. "My family," she said. She handed me her Quill. "My dad found a job," she said. "A good one. With NASA. We're moving to Houston. We're leaving tonight. I would've told you before. Maybe I should have. I've known a couple months, but you've been all messed up, and—"

"To*night*?" I said.

"You've been really messed up. I didn't want to make you sadder."

"Messed up how?"

"Please don't," she said. "Just don't. I wasn't even gonna tell you at all. I don't even have to be here at school, today, okay? The only reason I came's to say goodbye."

"A couple *months* you knew?" I said.

"They put you on drugs, Belt."

"I don't know what you're talking about."

"Well maybe I'm wrong. I'd like to be wrong. But after you got busted—you were like a zombie for a while. You were walking in this way like it hurt to bend your legs. I have an aunt just like that. Who walks just like that. She's ill. Mentally. She's on these heavy drugs. You're not supposed to upset her."

"Well I'm off them now," I said. "You should have told me before."

"You should have told *me* before."

"I couldn't. How could I? I can't believe this," I said. "Don't move. Do you have to? You have to, don't you? There's nothing you can do. Is there something you can do?"

"Come on. Please don't."

"You're my only real friend."

"Jonboat's your friend."

"He's not."

"But he could be. He likes you. He thinks you're funny."

"I don't care what he thinks."

"He told me you made him laugh a bunch of times."

"I don't care about Jonboat, Stevie. Jesus. How long til you visit?"

"I don't think I'll visit. Not for a while, at least. A clean break's better anyway. And Jonboat—"

"What the fuck's a clean break?" I said. "Aren't we friends?"

"Friends let each other forget what they need to. You need to forget me, Belt."

"I don't," I said. "That isn't true. Maybe it's you who needs to forget."

"Maybe," she said.

"You don't, though," I said.

"You're the only kid at school I'm even saying goodbye to. Nobody else even knows I'm moving. Well, except for Jonboat. But that's just because I wanted—"

"I can't believe how long you waited to tell me."

"You were really sad, Belt."

"I'm not really sad, now?"

"You started not to be. In the last few days. Even just a minute ago, you looked really happy."

"I was," I said. "I was really happy. Listen. Look. I want to show you something, okay? It's a really big deal. But it's a secret, okay?"

"Maybe you shouldn't."

"No, I want to, though. But you can't tell anyone about it. And I want you to write to me. Promise you'll write to me. I'll write back. I'm not a bad writer. You'll like my letters. We'll write to each other. Then maybe you'll come visit. Or I'll visit you."

"I don't think we should write. That's not a clean break."

"There's no such thing as a clean break, Stevie. How could there be? It doesn't even make sense. Promise me you'll at least think about writing, and I'll show you what I want to show you anyway, okay?"

Before she could answer, I pulled back my sleeve. I said hi to Kablankey. It schwa'd, showed its palm, and made a crinkled face.

Stevie said, "Wait. I was—wow. Oh wow. This is not what I was expecting you to . . . I can't . . . What is it?"

"It's a new kind of pet," I said. "No one else has one. Well, a few other people. But no one else around here. Not even Jonboat."

"Is it hurt or something? Why's it making that face?"

"I think it's trying to do my face."

"That's not how your face looks."

"That's how my face feels."

Stevie leaned in closer. "Did you give it some candy?"

"That's just what it smells like."

"It's really adorable. Jesus it's adorable. I can't believe how adorable it is. I can't believe the way I keep saying 'adorable.' I sound like a cheerleader. A cheerleader's *mom*. It is so fucking *cute*. Can I hold it?"

"Well—"

"Come on."

"Lay your hand open on top of mine."

She did as instructed. Blank let go of my wrist, crawled to her palm, rested its head against the muscle of her thumb. She kept her hand still.

"It's okay, you can lift it."

"I don't think I should. I don't want to hurt it."

"You won't hurt it."

"No, really, it's freaking me out," she said. "I want to squeeze it, you know? Don't you want to squeeze it?"

I said, "A little, I guess. But it's not like I would."

"No, of course not. Me neither. But you know, like, when you're standing on top of something high, and you keep thinking how easy it would be to jump? You know that you won't, but since you *could* . . . Why don't you just take it back," she said.

I picked it up by the shoulders, and Stevie sat down, there in the center of the dumpster array, facing the exterior wall of the school. I wasn't sure what to do. To sit next to her seemed a little too forward; to remain on my feet seemed aloof or—worse—tentative.

"You got another smoke?" she said.

I heard an invitation, sat where I'd been standing. I set Blank on his belly on the ground before us—I didn't want to singe him—and lit a fresh Quill.

For a couple of minutes, we passed the Quill back and forth, watching Blank watch me and not saying anything, and then all at once, I made sense of everything, or at least thought I had.

"You were trying to protect me," I said to Stevie. "You waited so long to tell me because you knew it would hurt more, and you thought that, in the long run, the extra hurt would help. You think that, soon, instead of missing you to death, I'll realize that the last thing you did before you went away was thoughtless, and I'll realize you're a jerk, and I'll see that you always were a jerk, and that'll make you being gone easier for me, because I won't have lost a friend, just an acquaintance I'm better off not having because she was a jerk."

"Belt," she said, "you have to stop."

"Let me finish first. I wasn't finished. Because you're not a jerk. It's just your plan didn't work. You're trying to give me a gift," I said. "Like that song on the mix you made me last year. 'Cruel to be kind.' But it isn't a gift, and that song is confusing. It sounds like advice because of the tune, but it's really a complaint. That guy is *sad*. You should listen to it closer. But the point is I couldn't ever think you were a jerk. Especially not because of the lousy gift. The lousy gift proves that you're not a jerk, since it's the thought that counts. And the thought wasn't cruel. The gift was cruel. The thought was kind. You tried to give me a cruel gift out of kindness, and I can't imagine that could have been easy for you, because you're *not* a jerk. You're the best person I know."

"Too much, Belt," she said. "You're fucking killing me here."

"But I'm telling you I forgive you, that I understand."

"Well maybe you should be less understanding, then."

"Why?"

"Because I don't feel forgiven at all," she said. "I feel accused. I feel bad for doing things I hadn't ever even thought about doing, and I feel bad because—and this is the fucked-up part—I feel bad because I *didn't* do those things. Or think those things. Whatever the hell you're talking about. And I feel bad about *this*. About saying what I'm saying. Your 'understanding' is *killing* me. You're making me feel *bad* because I'm not who you believe I am. I'm not that complicated. No one is. I may have made a mistake in waiting so long to tell you I was moving. I may have made a mistake in telling you at all. I don't know. But that's what I should feel bad about. That's what you should or shouldn't forgive me for. Except you sit there painting this picture of how I'd be if I were good, if *the world* were good, if we all *made sense* and had the best intentions and followed through on our best intentions and weren't all convenience-driven, self-centered zombies, and you believe in that picture, and it's wrong, Belt, it's fucked, and all it does is make me feel desperate because you were my only real friend here, and it turns out you're crazy, and I don't know what that says about me, and, on top of that, I know that if you keep going this way you'll never be happy. What you don't understand is that I'm glad I'm moving, Belt. I'm glad I'm getting out. This is the only rotten part of it—having to say things to you that make you upset. I really hate this place, you know? It's flat. It's dead. There's nothing worth doing. I'm either bored here, or sad. And you should hate this place, too. And I want to convince you of that, and that's shitty of me, because you're stuck here. But if you opened your eyes, you *would* hate this place. The only thing it's good for is imagining your way out of it."

Obviously, reader, that wasn't really Stevie's response to my "Why?" but I do think it must have been at least something like what she meant when she answered, "You're impossible. You're really impossible. Let's just please say goodbye and wish the best for each other," and I think it must contain some or all of the reasons for why, in the end, she never wrote me from Houston, or anywhere else.

Stevie may have further clarified her feelings—or I probably would've tried to get her to, anyway—had we not been interrupted by blue-eyed Rory Riley's exclamatory fervor. He and Jonboat had come up behind us. "What the fuck *is* that?" Rory said. "Guys! Hey guys! Come look at this thing!" He squatted, leaned forward, reached over me for Blank.

I punched him in the ribs, and he fell on his side.

Facedown and panting, Blank flattened itself against the pavement. I couldn't get at its shoulders to lift it in the manner prescribed by the manual—its hands were clasped, sit-up style, on the back of its neck—and I was too afraid of harming it to pinch at other parts.

"Kablankey, it's fine. It's okay," I said. "Kablankey." I set my open hand on the ground near its face, but its eyes were closed. It didn't crawl on. It shivered, kept panting, quietly singing.

In the meantime, Stevie'd started chewing out Jonboat, saying, "What'd you bring *this* clown along with for?"

"Rory likes Belt," said Jonboat. "Or at least he used to. I thought that they could become friends, too."

"I told you come alone."

"I know, but— Hey! Everybody chill."

Three, then five, then maybe ten or twelve boys had appeared beside Jonboat in a matter of seconds, and they were all pressing forward and shouting: "What is it?" "Let me see it!" "Let me hold it!" "Let me hold it!"

"Get back," Jonboat told them, and that's all it took. They stopped all their shoving and took a step back. "What is it, Belt?" he said.

"It's my pet."

"Can we see it?"

"No."

Someone else said, "Don't be a dick."

"It's his," said Jonboat. "And he isn't a dick. He can do what he wants with it."

"Thank you," I said.

"No sweat, man," he said. "But maybe, you know, you should let them see it, though? I mean everyone wants to see it, you know? What can it hurt? Worst it can do is win you some friends."

"It's scared," I said, looking up at Stevie, who'd gotten to her feet, was biting her lip, was walking away, wouldn't look back, then running away, then gone forever.

"Scared," Jonboat said. "Yeah, I think you're right. It does look scared. Back up some more, guys. You're scaring Belt's pet."

"What kind of pet is it, though?"

"What kind of pet is it, Belt?"

"Sugar glider," I said.

"What'd he say?"

"He said it's called a sugar glider," Jonboat said.

"What's it eat?" someone said.

"What's it eat, Belt?" said Jonboat.

"Worms," I said. I was trying to breathe. Jonboat reached down and kind of chucked me on the shoulder.

"It eats worms," Jonboat told them.

I was crying my face off. Nobody mentioned it. No one ever would.

"It eats worms," Jonboat said, "and also certain legumes. Especially yams. Also zucchini."

"Feed it a worm!"

"Feed it a goom!"

"Anything that's shaped like a wang," said Jonboat.

"Wang!"

"A wang!"

"Like a wang, he says!"

"Alright, now," said Jonboat. "We gonna ball now, or what? I say let's ball." And he grabbed hold of Rory, who was back on his feet, clenching his jaw somehow *at* me; took Rory by the arm and led them all away.

I sat there awhile. Maybe five minutes. Blank stopped panting and opened its eyes, crawled onto my palm. I lifted my cuff. Blank wrapped around my wrist.

I got up and started walking toward Stevie's, then found my pride, or lost my nerve, and headed for home instead.

•

•   •

That I was ditching class would, I knew, be noticed pretty soon, so I stopped at the phone outside the White Hen and got hold of my mom before she heard from the school. "Stevie's moving," I said. "Half the world saw me crying. I'm not going back."

She said to go home, that she'd call up the principal and have me excused.

That night we ordered pizza from Bobby Fongool's. With no meat-seeking patriarch around to object, we got a large pie topped with olives and mushrooms, and grazed it for hours on the living room couch, Cosby through *Late Night,* though we mostly watched Blank, which, before the end of *Cheers,* had not only learned to stand on two limbs (leg and left arm) while waving hello, but to make a new sound: a series of ɑ's interrupted at random by velar stops and voiceless affricates. So I guess it was more like a few new sounds. We didn't, though, at first, understand what Blank was mimicking, or if it was mimicking anything at all. Apart from those ə's with which it had been responding when spoken to directly ever since its hatch, the Botimal was quiet for the ninety-five minutes after *Night Court* ended (i.e. through all of *L.A. Law* and *NBC News*) and wouldn't, despite our attempts to coax it, make the new sound(s) again til *The Tonight Show*'s monologue, when Carson landed his opening joke, at which point my mom, grabbing both of my hands, said, "The laughs, Belt! The laughs! It's trying to mimic the studio audience."

Thereafter ensued a long and exceptionally intense conversation during which my mom defined *anthropomorphism* for me, and told me how hard it was for her—how hard it had always been for her—not to anthropomorphize animals, and how Blank, though a robot, so resembled an animal that it was hard for her to see it as other than an animal, and thus hard for her not to anthropomorphize Blank. She said she'd often been laughed at by the men in her life—her father, my father, any number of professors at college—for believing that animals were possessed of desire, possessed of emotion; for believing that animals did not strictly, or even mostly, operate from pure instinct.

She went on to tell me that despite having learned not to express her beliefs about animals, she still held those beliefs, and in fact held them tighter the older she became. And she told me she thought that I was like her. She told me that although she'd never heard an inanimate object speak, and although she didn't and couldn't believe they were beings, she was able to understand, given that *I* thought that I heard them speak, how I'd believe they were beings despite those around me not sharing that belief. And she told me she hoped that, for my own good, I would one day cease to hear the inans speak and that, failing that, I'd one day learn that although I might think that I heard them speak, I was not, in fact, hearing them speak, but that she would understand, if I did continue to hear them speak, why I might continue to believe they spoke, and why I might continue to believe they were beings. She would understand, she said, because I was like her.

Throughout the above-described portion of the conversation, which lasted far longer—and was much more two-sided—than the summary above might seem to indicate, Kablankey had continued to make the laugh sound when *The Tonight Show* audience made their laugh sounds, and it seemed to us, eventually, to start making its laugh sound at the same time the audience started making their laugh sounds, which is to say that Blank began to make the laugh sound as if it weren't the audience triggering the laugh sound but rather Carson's punch lines (or, far more likely, something Carson did with his voice or his face to indicate *punch line*) triggering the laugh sound. It seemed, in other words, that Kablankey, as the program went on, began to be triggered to make the laugh sound not by the sound of the laughter of others but by the phenomena that triggered that laughter. And it seemed, to both my mother and me, that Kablankey was no longer mimicking an audience laughing at jokes, so much as it was laughing at the jokes themselves. Which isn't to say that either of us thought Blank "got" Carson's jokes, but rather that, given the timing of its laugh sounds, it seemed that Blank, in addition to having learned *how* to laugh, had learned what a joke was (a thing people laughed at) and how to recognize a joke when it saw one (at least when that joke was being made by Carson). My mother wondered, she said, if all of this could mean that Kablankey possessed, or was developing, a sense of humor. What more was one's sense of humor, she asked, than one's sense of when it was appropriate to make laugh sounds? And how, she asked, does one first learn when it's appropriate for one to make laugh sounds if not by observing when others make laugh sounds? And why does one bother to learn to make laugh sounds at appropriate times if not to fit into the group from which one's learning? My mother said she wasn't really asking these questions. Rather, she said, she was trying to explain why she was helpless but to believe that Blank was making its laugh sounds out of a desire to be a part of our group, i.e. hers and mine, for she and I (though to a lesser extent than the studio audiences we'd heard throughout the evening) had made laugh sounds ourselves when jokes were being landed. And furthermore, she couldn't, she said, help but to believe—and with equal force—that Blank, who would turn to us while making its laugh sounds, was, via making those laugh sounds, actively trying to communicate *to* us *that* it wanted to be a part of our group. Blank really did want, she said, to be our friend.

It's easy for me to imagine how someone—perhaps you, reader—would assume my mother's side of the conversation that night owed a little, if not more than a little, to the as-yet-undiagnosed tumors in her brain. And she was, I admit, glassy-eyed throughout the whole thing, flush-cheeked as well, and breathing quite rapidly even as she smoked, but despite all that, I would much prefer, I would *very* much prefer to believe that her feverish excitement, the sense of revelation with which she seemed inspired, and the sense of revelation she inspired in me—we'd never spoken so directly, let alone so deeply, about my illness, her beliefs, or anything else, nor ever had anyone, let alone she, insisted so poignantly on sharing a mutual understanding with me—I would, as I was saying, much prefer to believe that my mother's side of the conversation had more to do, if not everything to do, with our being in the midst of what my father would have called "having a moment." Maybe it was both. Could it not have been both? Could the tumors not have set the stage for the moment? Set the stage, and then retreated to the wings?

In any case, she—a couple minutes into Letterman—took a sharp turn toward the more conventionally motherly and practical. "Promise me," she said, "you'll stop harming things that belong to others, even if you think those things want you to harm them."

"I already promised when I went off the Haldol."

"That was before you knew I understood you. It was before you knew that I knew how hard it might be for you to resist the voices. Now you understand. You understand that I know what I'm asking from you, you understand I know I'm asking *a lot* from you, and you understand I'm choosing to ask for it anyway. I'm not saying you have to believe they don't want you to harm them. I'm saying don't harm them."

"I won't," I said. "I promise."

Then she asked if we could talk about Stevie, and I said I'd rather not, and she said that was fine, but that she wanted me to go back to school in the morning. She wouldn't make me go, but she really thought I should, she said. She knew I was embarrassed, and she knew I didn't want to face the kids I'd cried in front of, but eventually I'd have to, and waiting wouldn't help, might even make things worse, or make them *seem* worse. The inevitable, she said, was best faced as soon as possible. I told her I wasn't sure if that was true, and she said she wasn't actually that sure, either, but it sounded true enough, and both of us laughed.

I conked out on the couch before the end of *Late Night*. My mom must have, too. She woke me at three and sent me to bed, and the following morning I went back to school, this time without Blank, which I fed and watered and left in its nest, as I would every school day for the rest of seventh grade.

School wasn't so bad. A number of kids, a few of whom had seen it, asked about my "pet," and I came up with lies about sugar gliders easily, and no one made fun of me or called me any names, which at first I found surprising, then attributed to Jonboat—to Jonboat and Stevie; to Stevie asking Jonboat to be my friend; to Jonboat complying by spreading the word that I was not to be harassed—but soon enough came to realize owed at least as much to most everyone at school's having long since noticed what Stevie'd described the previous day, and what Lotta would remark on so many years later: that I was (or, at least, had been) all messed up. Troubled. Off. Lacing up my rhinestoned shirt in Vegas.

APPLIED BEHAVIORAL SCIENCE

At the Friends Study office on Saturday morning, Abed, the grad student manning the desk, congratulated us for being first to arrive, took some snapshots of Blank, admiring, as he did so, "[my] Botimal's peculiarly attractive single-leggedness," and told us that my sessions would end at two o'clock. A coffee- and snack-stocked lounge, Abed said, would be open in the basement for parents all day, and although he advised that my mom check it out—the pastries, he claimed, were "decisively delectable"—he also suggested she take due advantage of the day's mild weather and walk around the neighborhood, visit the campus, the Rockefeller Chapel, the Frank Lloyd Wright Robie House, maybe one or two of the well-renowned bookstores. My mother said she hadn't heard about the bookstores. Abed lit up. Or rather lit up brighter. Seminary Co-op was definitely his favorite, but 57th Street Books could not a stick be shaken at, and Powell's selection of secondhand was "deep." He handed her a trifold map of Hyde Park and a booklet of coupons to use at local businesses. He showed her where the bookstores were on the map, and showed her the bookstore coupons in the booklet. He was readying, it seemed, to shake both our hands, if not to climb over the desk to embrace us, when another mother-and-son pair arrived in need of his assistance, and he bid us farewell.

"So I should say goodbye to Belt now, then?" my mother asked.

Blushing, Abed apologized twice. "Sorry, sorry," he said. "So happy was I to let you know about the bookstores, I neglected to relay the most pertinent information! Belt's first session is in Laboratory D, which is down at the other end of the hallway. If you will please escort him there, you'll find Dr. Tilly awaiting his arrival."

As we turned around to go, the boy who had come into the office with his mother unzipped his parka, revealing a piebald, tubular rodent nuzzling the crocodile logo on his sweater. He said, "This is Screwball," though it wasn't clear to whom, the boy was so severely walleyed. "It's only still a kit," he went on, "or a *pup,* if you like pup better, but I say kit because pup's how you also say a baby for a dog, and Screwball's a ferret. Like you couldn't tell! Of course you could tell! Just by looking right at him! I was able to tell and I'm only ten, and you're at least eleven and you're probably twelve, and it's not like you're some kind of retard or something! That's not why we're here! If you looked between his legs, though, you might not understand. You might make a guess, and you might guess lucky, but it would only be luck because the knowledge isn't yours, and I don't like that kind of lies, so I'll make the knowledge yours. They undid his nards so he wouldn't stink the joint up with dickspray on the carpet, which means he's a jib. If his nards still worked what he'd be is a hob, but I don't get why because it doesn't make sense. When you undo a girl ferret's nards, she's a sprite, which is a kind of fairy, and I don't know what a jib is so I say 'Whatever, dude, whatever, totally whatever,' because maybe a jib is a kind of boy fairy that I just never heard of, and that would make sense, but when you let her keep her girl-nards she's a jill is what I'm saying, so what I think about that is how Screwball, before they undid him, what he should have been called is a jack, not a hob. Anyway he's a jib. He can still get boners, but nothing comes out. I hope it didn't hurt. But that's—I think it did. I think it really hurt. I think it had to hurt. There's a scar you can see. It's small, but it's there. I don't have any scars, but I don't want any scars. It looks like it has to really hurt to get a scar. But no one would feed him if he stunk up the joint. He wouldn't have a home. That's the way the cookie crumbles, I'm not saying it isn't, but it doesn't seem fair, except maybe I'm a retard, so maybe it's fair. I look like a retard because of my eyes. It doesn't mean I am one, though, but it might. Like the nards on Screwball. They might work you might think if you just look at them fast and don't see the scar and I don't tell you they don't work or even if I tell you but you don't believe me because you didn't see the scar and you think I'm a retard. But this is the problem. It's the problem with everything. Every time a retard on a show gets called a retard, the retard gets angry and he says he's not a retard, and that's what I do when someone calls me a retard, plus I've got the eyes, so maybe I'm a retard. You can tell me the truth, though. I won't get angry. Just tell the truth."

No one said anything. Screwball licked its nose.

"Are you talking to me?" I said.

"You think I give crapshits what these other people say?" he said. "I don't give *one* crapshit about what they say! Not even half a crapshit. Look at them! Jesus! Adults! They're adults! They'll never tell a retard he's a retard, ever. They don't even say the word. They pretend it isn't real. You're the only one who knows here. Who *are* you? I'm James."

"I'm Belt," I said.

"Do you think I'm a retard or not, Belt?"

"No."

"Do you believe in retards?"

"Believe in them?" I said.

"Do you believe that retards are *real*?" he said.

"Yes," I said. "There's a couple at my school."

"And I'm not like them? Even with the eyes?"

"You're not," I said.

"But look at the eyes."

"I'm looking," I said.

"I can see that," James said. "You don't think I can see that?"

I said, "I couldn't tell."

"Maybe *you're* a retard."

"I'm not," I said.

"Maybe you don't know," he said.

I said, "I'm not retarded."

"But how do you *know*?" He was crying a little, petting Screwball heavily. Our mothers, by then, were standing behind us, hands on our shoulders, and Abed had risen.

"I'm not gonna hit him," James said to someone. "I like him a lot and I'm not a hitter. You should know that about me."

"I'm glad to," my mom said.

"Wait, so wait. You saying *he's* a hitter? Is that why you're standing behind him there, sad? I'm about to get hit?"

"No," said my mother.

"I'm not gonna hit you," I said to James.

"Are you a hitter, though?" he said. "Do you hit people sometimes?"

"Only sometimes," I said.

"I never hit anyone. If I hit them they'll die. I know that's not true, but still it seems true. That's why I never hit them. No one should die." While saying this, he'd pulled Screwball out of his parka and, holding it under the shoulders of its forepaws, turned it so it faced me.

I said, "I won't hit you."

"I might want to hug you. You think I could hug you?"

I didn't understand. Was he speaking for himself, or on Screwball's behalf?

"James," said his mother.

"I guess so?" I said.

"I won't do it," he said. "I just wanted to know. For later. In case. I might hug you later. They say I'm a hugger, and you shouldn't be a hugger. If you have to be a hugger you have to ask permission. I agree with that totally. I'm trying to be an asker. To always ask first. The only times I ever forget to's with girls. That's a different kind of hug, though. It used to be at least. They undid my nards with pills, so it's safe now. Isn't that right? I'm asking *you,* Screwball. Isn't that right?"

Screwball lifted, then lowered its head.

"High five? High five," James said. "High five."

Tentatively, I held up my palm.

James slapped it with Screwball, who didn't seem to mind.

"Yes!" James said. "That's how it's sup*posed* to be. Poontangy haze, better lays, and later days, Belt!"

"James, please," said his mom.

"Pleasey von Sleazy and a bottle of redrum."

"He gets so worked up," James's mom said to mine. "He doesn't understand what he's saying sometimes."

"I *do* understand, though," James said. "*Sex.*"

"James, these people have to be on their way. Say goodbye, now, alright?"

"I already did."

"Try it nicely," said his mom.

"Good to meet you," said James, and as we passed him, he whispered, "Vagina vagina."

A handwritten sign reading PARENTS OF SUBJECTS NOT PERMITTED TO ENTER was taped to the glazing of Lab D's door. My mother saluted it, clicking her heels, and kissed me on the cheek. She started walking off, and then turned around, said, "In case you get hungry . . ." and reached in her bag, hoisting out a fistful of packaged snacks—a couple granola bars, a cherry Fruit Roll-Up, and a disc or two of butterscotch—among which a ballpoint pen had come up. I pocketed the snacks, she squinted down at the pen, squinted up at the sign, again at the pen, popped off the cap, drew a ☺ next to ENTER, then slowly, while looking back over her shoulder, mugging Vaudevillian wide-eyed innocence, she tiptoed her way down the hall til I laughed, at which point she doubletook and sprinted for the exit.

•

•   •

Lab D was the one that, in the only paper to come out of the Friends Study*, Manx et al refer to as "the rec room." The appellation fit. There was wall-to-wall

*L. Manx, K. Tilly, D. Jorgensen, and A. Patel, "The Effects of Companion Animals on Social Interaction Amongst Children Diagnosed with Unspecified Psychotic Disorders," *Applied Behavioral Science* 25, no. 1 (1989): 107–21.

carpeting and incandescent light. The walls were wood-paneled, and the doors brass-knobbed. From cornices fixed over bamboo-blinded windows—windows with extra-wide, cushion-bearing sills—hung gauzy white curtains that slow-spinning ceiling fans steadily rippled. Rather than fume hoods or cleanup sinks, there were gaming tables—two foosball/shuffleboard/Ping-Pong convertibles, as well as an octagonal bumper-pool one—and a trio of milk crates jammed neither with beakers nor Erlenmeyer flasks, but sealed decks of Uno and pouches of jacks, boxes of Yahtzee, Parcheesi, and Sorry!. Instead of high stools, there were beanbags and couches; instead of high counters, giant ottomans and steamer trunks. There were as well a number of cameras, of course, mounted along the walls and ceiling, but other than those, and the researchers' clipboards, no sign of laboratory science was in evidence.

Tilly, in the corner of an overstuffed sofa crowded with fawning graduate assistants, handed me a yellow catalog envelope on which *B.A.M.* was written in marker across the bradded flap. She said I should sit wherever I wanted, wherever I'd feel most comfortable writing, then follow the instructions I'd find inside the envelope.

Never having had access to a window seat before, I chose one of those and sat, legs up, with my back to the jamb, and Blank on my shoulder. The envelope contained a 5x8 legal pad, a no. 2 pencil, and a short questionnaire.

Morning Questionnaire for <u>B.A.M., Group 2</u>

Instructions: Take the next 20 to 30 minutes to answer the questions below, using the paper and pencil provided. Please answer as completely, descriptively, and honestly as you can. None of your answers will be shared with other subjects. Please DO NOT trade your questionnaire with anyone else—it has been designed specifically for you, <u>B.A.M.</u>

1. When was the last time you heard a voice no one else could hear? Please describe that experience. Describe what the voice said, how it said it (angry, sad, happy, etc.), where you were when you heard it, how you replied to what it said (if at all), and how long you heard it for.
2. How do you feel this morning?
3. When was the last time you destroyed private property? What was it you destroyed? How did you destroy it?
4. What is your favorite thing about your Botimal?
5. If you could change one thing about your Botimal, what would it be?

6. Have you shown your Botimal to other people in the last week? If you have shown your Botimal to other people in the last week, describe how that felt, and what happened afterward. If you haven't shown your Botimal to other people in the last week, describe why you chose not to.
7. Did you make any new friends in the last week?

Had I remained in the study for its full duration, I would have, according to the "Effects of Companion Animals . . ." article, been given this same questionnaire to answer for sixteen consecutive Saturday mornings, though beginning week 4 (on the Saturday after the footage of the Sandburg Middle School Talent Show aired), an eighth item would have been tacked to the end of it: "Have you hurt your Botimal, or wanted to hurt it? Has anyone else tried to hurt your Botimal?"

Each of the Friends Study's sixty-eight subjects was assigned to one of six groups. The odd-numbered groups were for subjects "with a history of acting out sexually," though I don't think any of us knew that at the time. I was part of Group 2, which, until I dropped out, comprised eleven subjects. Because Groups 3 and 4 (ages 13–15) met Saturday evenings, and Groups 5 and 6 (ages 7–9) met Sunday afternoons, the twenty-three subjects in Groups 1 and 2 (ages 10–12) were the only subjects I ever encountered.

The weeks that Group 2's mornings (i.e. sessions 1–3) were spent in Lab D with Dr. Tilly, its afternoons (i.e. sessions 5–7) were spent in Lab A ("the stark room") with Dr. Manx, and vice versa. Group 1's schedule was the opposite of 2's (i.e. if 1's morning was in Lab A, 2's was in Lab D, and vice versa). For session 4—lunch—both groups ate in Lab A together, along with both of the research teams. Lunch came in brown bags from a nearby sub shop and lasted half an hour, as did each of the other six sessions. Our companion animals remained with us for three sessions a day (either 1, 2, and 5, or 3, 6, and 7), and the rest of the time they were kept safe in classrooms adjoining the labs. Session 7, like session 1, was devoted to answering a questionnaire. Mine looked like this:

Afternoon Questionnaire for <u>B.A.M., Group 2</u>

Instructions: Take the next 20 to 30 minutes to answer the questions below, using the paper and pencil provided. Please answer as completely, descriptively, and honestly as you can. None of your answers will be shared with other subjects. Please DO NOT trade your questionnaire with anyone else—it has been designed specifically for you, <u>B.A.M.</u>

1. Did you hear any voices no one else could hear today? If so, please describe that experience. Describe what the voice said, how it said it (angry, sad, happy, etc.), where you were when you heard it, which session or sessions you heard it during, whether or not you replied to what it said, and how long you heard it for.
2. What was your favorite activity today? Why?
3. What activity did you enjoy the least today? Why?
4. Who did you speak and/or interact with today? What caused you to speak and/or interact with them? Are you happy you spoke and/or interacted with them? If you did not speak or interact with anyone today, why didn't you?
5. Was there anyone you wished to speak or interact with today but didn't speak or interact with today? If so, who were they, and what prevented you from speaking and/or interacting with them?
6. Did your Botimal interact with any person other than you, or with any other person's companion animal today? If so, please describe the interaction(s). If not, why didn't it?
7. Did you enjoy being a part of the study today?

Before going any further, I should probably make clear that I have no better idea than the next guy why Graham&Swords Corp. chose to fund the Friends Study. It seems reasonable to believe the corporation was, as its spokesmen have always maintained, strictly interested in (broadly) exploring the viability of the Botimal as a mental health product. Yet, given the study's timing and "epiphenomenal" outcomes, it doesn't seem any less reasonable to adopt the far more widely held notion that G&S's interest was in launching a sleazy (or, as some would have it, innovative) marketing campaign.

Regarding Manx et al, however, I've always rejected their popular depiction as Graham&Swords's toadies. *If* G&S, via funding the study, *had* in fact been launching a sleazy/innovative marketing campaign, the scientists *may* have been its dupes, or even perhaps its reluctant confederates, but regardless of that, they studied what they'd set out to study—they did real science. True, their hypothesis (that the presence of companion animals affects social interactions between children with psychotic disorders) was humble to the point of being commonsensical, and their results, which confirmed (or, at least, failed to nullify) that hypothesis, weren't even a little bit earthshaking, but such is often—usually—the case in pure research endeavors, where the aim, above all, is to see what, if anything, there is to see, then record what was or wasn't seen so that scientists might, in the future, make use of it. Furthermore, no one got hurt. At least not in any way that Manx et al could have reasonably been expected to predict. Plus not only did we all, as promised, get companion animals, but we all got our therapy free for six months. The study did right by us.

If none of that's exactly undeniable proof of non-toadiness on the part of Manx et al, it is, I think, at least compelling evidence. Beyond that, they were decent people. They did right by me even after I'd dropped out: in addition to allowing me to keep Kablankey, they continued to reimburse my treatment, despite my mom's having previously signed papers which made very explicit that such reimbursement was contingent on my full participation. And, sure, yes, maybe it's true that having received these kindnesses from Manx et al has forever compromised my ability to imagine Manx et al doing anything nefarious, but what can I say? I just don't believe that. I think it's cynical.

In any case, nothing nefarious—nothing even untoward—seemed to me to be happening *while* I was a subject. Apart from answering our questionnaires, all we really did was hang out and get watched. Hanging out in the rec room entailed talking to each other, engaging with our animals, and playing board-, card-, and table-games. In the stark room—which was basically identical to the rec room except that there were dining- and side-tables there rather than gaming tables and crates—hanging out, though the games were always propless (e.g. I Never, Slap-Slap, Truth or Dare), comprised the same activities it did in the rec room. The researchers passed out the food during lunch, gave to and retrieved from us our questionnaire envelopes during sessions 1 and 7, and chaperoned our animals back and forth between the lab we were in and the adjoining classroom whenever the schedule demanded. Other than that, though, the only times they interfered with our interactions (observer effect aside) were when bouts of intersubject violence broke out.

The degree to which the researchers—never fewer than eight to a lab—left us to our own devices was actually pretty surprising to me. That first day, for example, just a couple minutes after I'd begun the questionnaire, an overweight boy in a Sox cap, Bertrand (he was wearing a HELLO! MY NAME IS sticker on the thigh of his cords—I don't know why, no one else had one), rushed over to my window, pulled up his shirt, raised his right arm as if hoping to be called on, and barked, "Five in the night makes a happy and healthy twenty-fucken-eight, you cocksucking, cockfucking son of a cunt." I would, eventually, come to ascertain that reporting on the number of hairs in his armpit was the way that Bertrand, for reasons never clarified, preferred to greet others, but at the time I didn't understand what he was trying to tell me, just that he was aggressively cursing in a drill-instructor voice while being twice as big as me, and I'm sure I must have flinched in the wake of his greeting, or at least appeared alarmed, and I definitely hid Kablankey in the pocket of my hoodie, yet none of the researchers—all of whom were watching—even rose from the sofa. "Name, analrectum," Bertrand went on to say. "Tell me your cumslurping name right now."

"I'm Belt," I said.

"You're Suspendersed," he said. "You think that sounds dumb, though, don't you, farmboy? Well I know it sounds dumb, but I didn't til I said it, and still I want to say it. I really like to say it, and you should say it, too. Suspendersed. Say it. It's a party on your mustache. Some ass on your chin. A sweet piece of pussy with tits out to here."

"Okay," I said.

"*Suspendersed,*" he insisted.

"Suspendersed," I said.

Removing his cap and bowing a little, he said, "Suspendersed, Mikeylikey. Mikeylikey meet Suspendersed." Amidst his wiry curls lay a sleeping baby gecko that, owing to the smiley shape of its mouth, gave the impression of dreaming sweetly. "First," Bertrand said, "I just called him Mikey, but he looked like he likeyed, so now I call him Mikeylikey, or sometimes Mikey-oo-rikey, like miso hawnyhawny, goosockysocky, right? Rike-oo miso hawny-hawny, aye gi *goo* sockysocky!"

Mikeylikey opened its eyes and sidestepped, thereby uncovering a glistening dollop of mottled, beige paste that alerted me to other, less-glistening dollops clumping up the tips of Bertrand's dark kinks. "I think you should go get an envelope," I told him.

"Why's that, ass-captain?"

"So you can do a questionnaire."

"That sounds about as fun as a Chinese-African turd-shitting picnic."

"Look, though," I said. "It's what everyone's doing." I pointed a finger toward the overstuffed sofa. A couple kids who'd entered the lab after Bertrand were sitting on the floor, at the researchers' feet, unpacking their envelopes.

"I didn't know there'd be girls here," he said. "How's my hair?"

"It's better with your hat on."

"Too smeary?" he said, and, replacing his cap, he walked off, smiley as Mikeylikey. Approaching the pair of kids on the floor, a girl and a boy, he pulled up his shirt and, raising his arm, boomed at the boy, "At the start of the week, I was down to nineteen from a high of twenty-two, but no worries, homosexual, no cuntfucking worries, you stammering, shit-jizzing, fucked-up abortion, cause the three I lost cleared a path for eleven. That's twenty-eight strong, now. I bet they're here to stay. Try and tell me different."

Again, the gaping researchers stayed calm and quiet.

I don't want, however, to give the impression that Bertrand's Sergeant Hartmanesque behavior was in any way typical of Group 2's subjects—or Group

1's either. Few voices were raised, fewer fists clenched. Most of us were pliable, shy, sedate—most of us were, in fact, sedated. Bertrand, himself, by the end of session 1, had radically calmed, experiencing, it seemed, the kicking-in of something heavy he'd swallowed with his breakfast. He slackened all over, body and spirit, swore a little less, stopped showing his teeth. He kept his arm inside his shirt and mumbled his stats as he stroked Mikeylikey and yawned and yawned, looking like I'd felt when I was still on the Haldol. Once I noticed, I ceased to be afraid of him.

Nobody else in Group 2 ever scared me. Except for Lisette—the evening-gloved girl I'd seen in the hall the week before with my mom—none of the rest of them really stood out much. They all seemed so tender and dizzy and blank, so browned out and widely open to suggestion. I'd say, "Let's play Ping-Pong," and then we'd play Ping-Pong, which wasn't much fun—all the dampened reflexes, the half-shut eyes—so I'd propose we switch it up and try a game of Sorry!, and we'd play a game of Sorry!, but they were so noncompetitive that sending them home only made me feel petty. When we'd play Truth or Dare, they'd always pick truth, then tell their dull truths without shame or delay, without any drama—"The girl from *Who's the Boss?*" they'd say, or "Ally Sheedy," or "I like to eat scabs," or "Second base with a boy at my school who's fourteen."—and the dares they'd dare me, though uttered, it seemed, with a little more relish than they took in telling truths, were either too silly to feel like real risks, far too dangerous to even consider, or wholly impossible: "Fart really loud while running in place like you're running from the fart you did and shout how you love it," or "Jump out the window," or "Jump out the window and fly," or "Be a ghost."

A few of them would lie on the couches and nap.

We were more energetic when our pets were with us. As Manx et al would note in the paper, the pets' presence united us a little, gave us common cause. We all seemed to think the same things were cute, and we'd draw one another's attention to these things. A gerbil would scrub at its face with its hands, or a budgie would mumble, "Step up," or "Good birdie," or Ronnie, the other boy in Group 2 who'd been given a Botimal, would shout, "Dance of death!" and the Botimal, Zappy, arms out as if partnered, would box-step, whistling a waltz for a measure, then clutch at its throat, stick out its tongue, drop to its knees, and faceplant. We'd all ooh and ah and giggle and point at whatever cute thing any pet would do. When Zappy performed, the other pets would watch, and we'd watch them watching, and gush about that, and Zappy, once the dance of death show was over, would return to its feet, winking, thumbs-upping, clicking its tongue, and it would scratch below the chins of any animals in reach, or give them a hug as they nuzzled against it.

There weren't any cats—all the groups were cat-free—so none of the animals were hostile to Zappy, nor, for that matter, anything less than doting toward Zappy, but a couple of times they attacked one another (e.g. budgie v. gecko, rabbit v. rabbit), and while none of these attacks produced any real injuries, or even much contact, let alone fatalities, the violence persuaded me to keep Blank close, hidden in fact, which nobody gave me any trouble about. A couple other subjects hid their pets, too.

Lisette refused to even bring hers to the study. She was the "sole noncompliant female subject" to whom Manx et al refer in the paper. She was also the subject I was drawn to most. Not only because she refused to bring her pet, nor even just because I liked her sharp, freckled face, and had, the previous week in the hallway, had more intense physical contact with her—fleeting and semi-rough though it was—than I'd had with any other girl ever, but because she was funny. And not funny in the sarcastic, eye-rolls-for-dorks way that mean girls our age were supposedly funny. Nor either in the fast-talking, wiseacre way our cohort's likable fatsos were funny. Lisette's kind of funny didn't seem strategic; it wasn't used to defend, or grab at power. I don't think she even cared if she got any laughs. Rather, being funny seemed to put her at ease. To bring her real joy.

She was best at long-arc, slapstick/deadpan flux, her first bit of which I saw performed as she entered the lab: she turned six perfect cartwheels to get from the door to the overstuffed sofa, then stood before the researchers, hands on hips, as though she'd been waiting in line for too long. As they gave her their instructions, she folded her envelope, flatly said, "I just did six cartwheels," backflipped her way to a beanbag by the entrance, and opened her envelope without once checking to see who was watching. Her pencil, when she removed it from the envelope, slid, as if buttered, out of her grasp; as it dropped to the floor, she batted at it wildly, and that, I think, was supposed to be the punch line. I definitely laughed.

So, Lisette: intriguing. At least to me. Yet for the first six sessions on the study's first day, I exchanged not a word with her, and hardly a glance. I was afraid that if the crush on her I seemed to be developing were to more completely . . . develop—I was afraid that would mean I'd gotten over Stevie Strumm or, worse, that I'd never, to begin with, been under Stevie Strumm, for to start to like another girl so soon after my heart had been broken would mean that my heart must not have really been broken. Which would, retroactively, make me a phony. A whiny phony. What my dad would have called a *crybaby dramaqueen*. In short, I kept as far from Lisette as I could. If she tickled Zappy, I cuddled a mouse. While she shot bumper pool, I dealt Uno. When she crossed the lab to play I Never with me and some others, I turned to Ronnie and challenged him to foosball. A couple minutes later, when Lisette approached the table and said she'd play the winner, I started scoring own goals, and after I saw that I just couldn't lose—Ronnie, unintentionally, I think, out-own-goaled me—I clutched my head and said I had to lie down, and covered the length of a loveseat with my body.

James and I, at lunch, sat in La-Z-Boy recliners on either side of an accent table. For a while he derided other subjects' pets. None of the ones he'd so far met held a candle to Screwball, "in cuteness or smarts." Not even the Botimals. Screwball was the best, and that was that, and James could count the ways that Screwball was the best, and he counted the ways that Screwball was the best. I don't remember the ways. I nodded when appropriate and chewed on my prosciutto-and-mozzarella sub til James, interrupting his own enumerations, leaned over the table and asked me if I knew who the girl across the lab was, and whether I thought she kept pointing me out to him and then dragging her finger across her throat because she wanted him to know that if he beat me up she'd let him hug her, or if it was more like she was saying he'd have to cut my throat before she let him hug her, or neither of those things.

I glanced. I saw. I looked away. I said the girl was called Lisette, and I thought she was kind of saying all of those things, but only joking.

"I don't get it," James said.

"The joke's for me, I think."

"Like how?" James said. "Like you should beat yourself up? Or cut your own throat? What's funny about that? I think that's retarded. Do you think she's retarded? I don't think she's retarded. No way she's retarded. Her face is all smart. But why would she do it? Point at *you* and look at *me* while she fake-cuts her throat if all she really wants is *you* to beat your*self* up or cut your *own* throat? I think maybe she loves me. But probably she doesn't, though. She's making me think it, but probably she's mean and that's why she does it. But there's other ways to do it. Easier ways. Trust me, I know. This one girl at my school, Veneatha Prather, winked one time, so I hugged her a good one, but she acted grossed out and Sandip, her brother, punched my face. Just came up and punched it! My nose like burst. It didn't even hurt much. The blood was a lot, though. I ran away fast. You need to be careful, Belt. I don't mean because of me. I won't fall for that again. For that kind of trick. These pills I take help. They disappear the stuff in my nards that's a danger. And I wouldn't beat you up, even without the pills. I don't want to beat you up, and I don't think that I could. Maybe if I thought I could, but I can't. I'm just telling truths. Anyway, I wouldn't slit your throat just to hug her. It's not worth your death. That is a fact. I *would* like to hug her, though. She *is* really pretty. You think she'll let me hug her?"

"I don't think so," I said.

"Me neither," James said. "That would probably be retarded. Because of the eyes. No one likes the eyes. No one wants a hug if these eyes are on top. Except for certain moms and maybe certain blind girls— Look! She's doing it again. I'm worried now that maybe she's trying to say that if you beat *me* up or slit *my* throat then she'll let *you* hug her, and I want you to know that you're my best friend, Belt, so if you need to beat me up to hug her, I get it, but please make sure that that's what she means, so I don't get hurt for nothing. I'll tell you right now that I won't fight back, I'll fall really fast, just please don't kick me when I'm down, or slit my throat. If you just punch my nose once, there'll be a lot of blood, so it'll look like you really beat me up, okay? And if you think it's a good idea, after the blood comes and I fall down, you can kneel right next to me and act like you're slitting my throat, and I'll spread the blood from my face all over my neck so it'll look like you really did slit my throat as long as you keep her from coming too close, but you have to not really slit my throat, cause I don't want to die, I want us to be friends and hug girls with permission for years to come and get together and drink stuff and talk about the hugging. The girls who hug me will have to be blind, I think, or moms, but that doesn't bother me. Too many moms would bother me, but not too many blind girls. I've seen pretty blind girls. Not in person, on shows. Some of them, I know, are only acting like they're blind, like that girl in that movie where the guy's face is ruined from the drugs his mom did when she sang "I Got You, Babe"—that girl even rides horses! it's total BS!—but at least one of the pretty ones I saw on a show was really blind, and I would hug her forever if she'd give me permission, and if anyone tried to tell her about my eyes, she wouldn't even care I don't think because she'd know what it means to have bad eyes, so she wouldn't hold it against me. Why should she?"

"She shouldn't," I said.

"I know!" said James. "But thank you for saying it. I'm glad that we're getting to know each other."

Mid–session 7, Lisette brought her questionnaire to the window seat in which I was sitting, answering my own. "Excuse me," she said, and eyed my legs, which lay across the cushion my ass wasn't on. I drew them toward me and sat up straighter, to write with the legal pad against my knees. As Lisette sat down on the freed-up cushion and mirrored my position, one of her shoes tapped against one of mine. "Excuse me," she said. A moment later, a heavier shoe tap—nearly a kick—sent my pencil scraping off the edge of the legal pad. "Ex*cuse* me," she said, readjusting her feet, producing more contact, excuse-me-ing again.

I was happy. It was hopeless. A crybaby dramaqueen I'd been all along, but then again, though, maybe . . . Maybe *so what*? This was a chance to play real live footsie, a thing I'd never done, a thing I'd thought no one ever really did, “playing footsie” a phrase that up til that point I’d always assumed to be a mere euphemism, not an actual flirting behavior. And here I was doing it. Flirting. Or being flirted with.

I kicked Lisette’s shoe. “Excuse me,” I said.

She kicked my shoe harder. “Excuse me!” she said.

I unbent my legs a bit, tangling our feet up. I began to say, “Excuse me,” but only got to “Ex-” before Lisette had cut me off with an “Excuse me!” of her own, which, this time, came in advance of the offense: an outer-thigh charley horse.

“Jesus,” I said, massaging my thigh.

“Did I hurt you?” she said. “I didn’t mean to really hurt you. I’m sorry,” she said, and, leaning toward me, as if to offer comfort, toppled off the sill.

I jumped to the floor, to help her to her feet. Everyone was watching. How long had they been watching? For a while, I hoped.

She accepted the outreached hand I offered, but when I tried to hoist her, she didn’t cooperate: she went limp and dragged and, before I knew it, the hand I’d been pulling had slid out of its evening glove. She cradled the elbow of her pale, slender arm, the pale and slender fingers of which ended in nails the pale blue of robins’ eggs—cradled it as if, now that it was naked, its shoulder might otherwise slip from its socket.

I kind of shook the glove in the air between us.

“Put it back on me,” she said, “and don’t look.”

I got on my knees and did as she’d asked as quickly as I could, but it’s harder than it sounds to glove another person when you’re not allowed to look. It took at least a minute.

“Why are you here?” she whispered to me. The others, still watching—some just a couple of yards away—frowned from the strain of trying to listen in.

I said, “I’m here because you asked me to help you put your glove on.” I said so full-voiced, hoping this information would clarify, for anyone listening who might yet have thought otherwise, that I was gentle—a gentleman—not the kind of person who would knock a pretty girl to the floor from a window seat.

“Shh,” Lisette whispered. “And no. I mean *here*. Why are you here? In the study, I’m asking. How are you psychotic?”

“People tell me I hallucinate,” I whispered, sitting.

“But you don’t?”

“I might.”

“You don’t know.”

“I can’t. It’s impossible to know.”

“I think that’s the problem with everything, really. Too many things are impossible to know. Like my arm for example? The nasty scars all over my arm? You know how I got them?"

"What scars?"

"The big, red wormy scars," she said. "It's fine. You don't have to pretend you didn't see them. I've had them forever, and I'm even kind of proud of them. I was trying to be a hero is how I got them. I was stupid, but still. I was six years old, and Jenny Bigham, our neighbor, her father's a drunk, and I was over there, playing Secretary upstairs with Jenny, in her room, when we started smelling smoke and we ran downstairs and saw that Mr. Bigham was passed out in the kitchen, like asleep on the counter, and his cigarette—and I don't know how he did it, he must have kind of flinched when he was passing out or something—but the cigarette he'd been smoking had flown out of his hands and landed in the bunny cage a couple feet away, and the hay was on fire. It was scary, you know? The bunnies—there were two of them—were thumping and thumping in one corner of the cage that they'd peed or spilled water on or whatever, I don't know, it was wet, and not on fire yet, this one small corner that was getting smaller as the fire advanced, and they were huddled together, the three of them, thumping their back legs, and looking at Jenny, and then at me, like they were trying to tell her, 'There's a fire, there's a fire! Get out! Save yourself!' but since Jenny was way more worried about her father, about trying to wake him, she wasn't looking at the bunnies, she was poking at her father, saying, 'Daddy! Wake up! Daddy! Daddy!' and so they looked at me, thumping, like they were thumping for me so *I* would tell Jenny there was a fire and she had to get out. I mean, that's probably not really what the bunnies were thinking at all, but that's how it seemed at the time. Anyway, I was afraid, as you can probably imagine, and I didn't want those bunnies to burn—it wasn't right—and so I opened the cage, which was metal, and which opened from the top, and reached in with both arms, through the flames, and pulled two of the bunnies out, and once I saw that they weren't on fire, I kind of threw them toward the hallway, and they ran away. I turned back around to try to save the third one, but that's when the blisters on my hands started popping and I noticed that the arms of my sweater were on fire, and I swooned. I passed out. A few minutes later, I woke up on the floor and the fire was out and the third bunny was fine because Mr. Bigham had finally woken up and he did what I was too stupid to do, or too panicked to do, which was he filled a pot with water and threw the water onto me and onto the flames in the cage. My arms were ruined, and I knew I'd been stupid, but I learned that day that I wasn't a coward, and I knew my heart was in the right place. So you don't have to pretend like my scars aren't ugly."

"I'm not pretending, though," I said. "I didn't even notice them."

"You couldn't have," Lisette said. "There aren't any scars. I made that all up to see what you'd say. I'm glad you stuck to your story."

"I don't get it."

"A lot of people don't," she said. "And I don't really, either. Not completely. It's something like this, though: a lot of times I suspect that people are lying to me, pretending at me. I think, for some reason, that they're pretending to believe things they don't really believe, so I tell them stuff that's completely made up and can't be true, to see if they'll agree with me. It's a kind of test. If they agree with me, they're liars."

"And if they don't, they're not?"

"Well, no. Exactly. That's the big problem. That's what always screws me up. If you lie about one thing, you might lie about anything, but if you tell the truth about one thing, you still might lie about anything. So the test proves nothing."

"But then why do you do it?"

"I don't know," she said. "I really don't know. I just have this feeling: someone's trying to trick me. When it gets really strong, this feeling, it turns into: the whole world is trying to trick me. And when it gets the most strong, it turns into: I'm tricking myself. And then I start having these terrible thoughts like maybe none of this is real, like maybe I'm drooling in a mental ward somewhere, dreaming everyone up. Or the worst version, but this only happened twice, once when I had a fever from strep, and once after they gave me these drugs because I broke my ankle—the worst is I think maybe there's no such thing as people, and I'm this like gas or liquid or gel or something, this *substance,* and I'm sick, I'm crazy, I'm totally helpless, and I'm so crazy and helpless that I imagine that there are such things as people, things that can do what they want, that can move and talk and eat and build buildings or whatever. That's the worst version. But whatever the version is, I always think: You've gotta do something about this. You've gotta figure out what's true. So I start telling lies or acting strangely to test the person I think is lying, or to test if the world is real, or to test myself, and it all gets tangled up and fails. And the thing that really sucks the most, is that whatever version of the feeling it is, and whatever kind of test I do to try to find the truth, I know I'm being crazy. At least most of me knows. But it doesn't matter, because it's a feeling. Like being dizzy, you know? I always think of it like that. Like you know the room isn't really spinning, but that doesn't mean you don't have to act like it is—you do. You really do. You have to walk, for example, very carefully, as though the room really *is* spinning."

"I'm sorry," I said.

"Well don't be," she said. "It's just how it is. Plus I've got a new thing I'm doing now where I'm telling people the truth about this stuff. Like I've just told you. My psychologist suggested that I try that out. She thinks that might change things, and help me *trust* or whatever."

"Has it?" I said.

"We'll see," Lisette said. "You're the first person I've tried it out on. Well, the second—there's my psychologist, too."

"Is that true?" I said. "That I'm the first?"

"That you're the second, you mean?"

"Yes," I said.

"Wouldn't you like to know!"

"I would."

"Well maybe I'll tell you. But first tell me this: What do you hallucinate? I mean, if you hallucinate?"

"Inanimate objects—sometimes, when we're touching, they say things to me. We have conversations."

"I'm pretty sure you hallucinate."

"I understand completely."

"What do they sound like, the objects?"

"Regular guys," I said.

"Never girls?"

"No."

"Not once?"

"Never."

"I think that's weird. Don't you think that's weird?"

"Not any weirder than any other part of it."

"What did my glove say when you touched it before?"

"It didn't say anything, which isn't weird either. Hardly anything talks to me ever. And clothes—"

"Try again," Lisette said.

"Try what?"

"Try to get my glove to talk to you," she said. She stuck out her hand.

I touched the top of her glove. It didn't say anything.

"Nothing," I said.

She said, "Pay more attention," and she turned her hand over, squeezed my palm.

"Still," I said.

"Maybe it's shy," she said. "My glove."

"Maybe," I said. "But also, it's clothes, and clothes have never talked to me."

"Why?"

"I don't know."

"Maybe all clothes are shy," she said.

"It's possible."

"Or maybe all clothes are girls," she said. "Or both. Maybe you make girls shy, and so they don't talk to you. Maybe everything that doesn't talk to you's a girl, and maybe *most* things are girls, and that's why you only end up talking to *some* things."

It was starting to feel like she was making fun of me.

"Maybe's a shrug," I said. "A shrug and a dodge. Maybe's the sound second thoughts make," I said.

"That's the single saddest thing I've heard this year," she said. "What a disappointment. You sound like somebody's dumbfuck father." With that, she stood and quadruple-round-offed across the lab, onto the most distant beanbag.

Her questionnaire and legal pad were still atop the window seat. I noticed there was writing on the pad's exposed page. I didn't read it at first because I wasn't supposed to; it seemed like reading it would violate her privacy. Once a couple of minutes passed, though, it occurred to me that maybe she *wanted* me to read what she'd written on the pad—that that's why she'd left it there to begin with—and then I didn't read it because of how it seemed that I *was* supposed to, and it struck me (not unintelligently, I don't think) that manipulability was not a quality she sought in a suitor.

Eventually, Dr. Manx came over, clinically flexing his forehead at me, picked up the pad and questionnaire, and, as I instantly knew I should have done myself, delivered both of the items to Lisette.

Session 7 was over a few minutes later. While the researchers came around collecting our envelopes, Abed entered the lab, unsmiling, and took Manx aside and spoke low and close to him. An utterance or two into whatever he was saying, he looked right at me, and then looked away, as if he'd been caught.

Had I any more than a second to think, I'm sure I would have worried, but just as I registered Abed's clipped glance, Lisette scraped past me, shouldering my arm, to which I said, "Excuse me," to which she replied, "Tch," and smirked at me or smiled—I couldn't tell which, but determined that either was preferable to neither.

On the heels of Lisette appeared one of the assistants, bearing the shoebox in which Blank and Zappy had spent the last hour. They were napping together, spooned up tight. Zappy, the outer spoon, woke first, and told Blank, "G'morn," and helped it to its foot. Once Blank had climbed to the middle of my palm, it turned a 180 to face its new friend, and I cheerily watched them waving and winking and whistling at each other til Manx walked over. "Belt," he said, and laid a hand on my shoulder.

•

• •

Manx said he had a couple things to talk to me about. The first was a secret: he had a present for me, but he didn't want the other subjects to see. I should follow him, he said, to somewhere more private. And so I followed him out of the lab, and then out of the building, as did Abed. We walked for a block or so, and stopped in a doorway. "Here's good," Manx said, and pulled the left sleeves of his over- and labcoats back to his elbow.

His forearm, I saw, was snugly encased in what appeared to be spandex. A spandex tube. (Later I'd learn, from Tom Wolfe's *Of Fighter Jets, Curios, and Doing Dishes Right: The Graham&Swords Century*, that it was actually neoprene; Manx had scissored up a wetsuit his son had grown out of). A pouchy rectangle of pebbled black leather, six eyeleted airholes punched into its center, was coarsely stitched with upholstery thread along three of its sides (both of the short, one of the long) to the middle of the tube, and its fourth side was held down by four silver snaps.

This, of course, was a prototype CureSleeve; *the* prototype CureSleeve. The first one ever. In the next few weeks, Manx would make a few more, hand them out to other subjects who'd been assigned Botimals, and apply for a patent he would, upon receiving, sell for too little to Graham&Swords ($49k according to Wolfe).

Manx unsnapped the snaps, and out crawled a Botimal. Two-legged, short-tailed, twice as large as Blank. He set it on my shoulder.

"It's great," I said, "but it'll grieve to death, won't it?"

"What?" Manx said, removing the prototype. "Oh—no. No way am I giving you Burrhus. I'm giving you this." He handed me the prototype.

I tried it on. It fit. "Thank you, Manx," I said.

"Ankamank," said Burrhus. Manx awwed and chuckled, and put it in his pocket. "Next week," he said, "you tell me how you like the thing, if you have any problems with it, or any suggestions. I mean, it's not so great-looking, I know, but it's useful. Burrhus was in there since just after breakfast. Seems to love it. Just curls up and sleeps. And I don't have to constantly think about where it might have crawled to inside my shirt and be nervous I'll accidentally bash it, you know? I mean, it would be better if the leather had something hard underneath for some extra protection—I tried to jam an athletic cup in there, but there's not enough room, wouldn't snap shut—but at least the little fella's always there, same spot, secure. And as you can see, it's just your arm beneath the leather, no material, so anytime it's in there, it's getting your body heat. Come on, now. Try it."

I put Blank in the sleeve, snapped it shut, and then we started walking in the same direction we'd been headed before, and Manx said it was time for Abed to talk about the second thing, now, but that before he did, Manx wanted me to know that the good news was my mother was conscious and nothing was broken. I told him I didn't know what he was talking about, and he told me that Abed was about to tell me, and Abed said my mother'd fallen, bumped the back of her head, but luckily she'd done so right outside the building. Abed had been the one who'd found her. On his way from the office to the lounge in the basement, he'd observed, through the windows beside the front doors, that she was pacing near the benches, enjoying a cigarette, and he'd determined that he would, after visiting the lounge, join her outside and try to bum a smoke, but then, not more than just a few minutes later, when he exited the building, coffee in hand, he discovered she was lying on her back on the pavement. "And so no ciggy for me," he said. "Ha!"

"Ha?" I said.

"Please, I'm sorry," Abed said. "Please take no offense at my unfunny humor. I only attempted a joke about the ciggy because, when I found her, your mother—in order to convey to me just how not-very-serious all of this probably was, which I can only imagine she would want conveyed to you as well—your mother made a joke, herself. Do you want to hear the joke? I will tell you the joke. She widened her eyes, looking deeply into mine, and plainly stated, 'Ah-buh-dee ah-buh-dee ah-buh-dee, that is all there is, folks.' "

"Like Porky Pig?" I said. It didn't sound like her. Or Porky Pig.

"No!" Abed said. "I have made a mistake. That was *my* response to *her* joke. What *she* said was, 'It appears as though I made an incorrect turn at Albuquerque, New Mexico.' It doesn't sound very funny when I say it because the context is different, but trust me, Belt, I laughed quite a lot. The effect was powerful. My load was lightened but instantly, and I found myself thinking, 'No need to worry, after all, you nervous nelly! She probably just tripped.' And *that* is when I told her, 'Ah-buh-dee ah-buh-dee—' "

I asked Abed what he meant by *probably,* and Manx cleared his throat, and Abed said his *probably* was nothing worth considering, that his *probably* was but the man of science in him speaking, and all he'd meant was that no one had seen her trip, and she had been unable to recall how she'd ended up on the ground, and so it was possible, Abed supposed, that perhaps—

"This guy!" Manx said, and cut Abed off. "This guy!" he said again, as Abed said, "I mean . . ." and he headlocked Abed, and pretended to noogie him (he only knuckled air) until an affectedly lilting voice from within the ER—we were, by then, just outside the doors—said, "*There* you are," and Manx let Abed go, and my Grandmother Magnet stepped into the sunlight, snapping shut a compact, capping a lipstick, pocketing a hairpick, pronouncing her name.

She explained that my father, who was out of town, ice-fishing, had only just been reached, and that he wouldn't arrive for at least a couple hours, "So Grandma to the rescue!"

I sat. Right there. On the salted pavement. I couldn't stand. I'd known by the way Manx and Abed had been acting that whatever it was that had happened to my mother was scarier than a bump on the head from a fall, but I hadn't imagined it could be bad enough to require a guardian be summoned for me.

"Oh Christ," said my grandmother, turning my way. "We don't need a lot of theatrics right now. This boy," she said, turning back to Manx, "never used to throw tantrums."

Manx crouched beside me, ignoring my grandma. "Belt," he said, "what's going on there, buddy?"

"His father," said my grandma, "in all his life—only once in all his *life* did his father throw a tantrum. You know how we put a stop to that behavior? Well, I'll tell you this much: We didn't give him a pet. We didn't enroll him in *therapy* programs."

"Don't you want to go see your mom?" Manx asked me.

"He *can't* go see her, not for a while, and telling him he can—that's *just* the kind of thing," my grandmother said, "that *leads* to tantrums."

Abed said, "But why can't he see her?"

"She's not even in this building anymore. She—for God's sake, she had a *seizure,* young man," my grandmother said, "and she's having some tests done, as well she *should* be. The tests will take a *while.*"

"A seizure?" I said.

"This is certain?" Abed said.

"That's what *I* was told," my grandmother said.

I asked my grandma, "Does she still have her tongue?" All I knew about seizures—*thought* I knew about seizures—I'd learned either from Blackie's secondhand description of Grandpa Strumm's seizure (flopping off stool, finger in mouth, overwhite bone) or at my desk in Health class, half-asleep.

"Does your mother *still have a tongue*?" said my grandma. "What is wrong with you?" she said. "I'll tell you what's wrong. Everyone's been telling you you're sick is what's wrong, and you've decided you believe it. *That's* what's wrong."

Abed, to his credit, understood what I'd meant and, speaking over my grandma, answered me as if my question were sensible. "Your mother didn't swallow her tongue, Belt," he said. "Nor did she bite it off. Her tongue is fine."

“Your father had them, too,” my grandma went on. “Imaginary friends. I bet he didn’t tell you. He may have even for*got*ten. As he should have. But he had them, too. He would try to intro*duce* me. Did I pretend that I saw them? I did *not* pretend I saw them. I did not pretend to believe *he* saw them. And guess what happened? He stopped pretending to see them.”

“The human brain,” Manx said, still crouching beside me, “is mysterious, Belt. Some people have seizures without ever really knowing it. It’s just a strange feeling they have, a kind of daze they enter, and then it passes. They forget it even happened. If your mom had been sitting, or lying down, she might not have even known that she’d had a seizure. And sometimes—not an insignificant portion of the time—a person has a seizure once, but then never again.”

Manx helped me stand up, and then I was hugging him, and Abed was palming the top of my head, saying something hummy in Urdu or Hindi.

LETTERS AND FACTS

"THEN ABED PUT HIS hand on top of my head and sang or said something in Indian or Arab that was probably either a prayer or a spell—here comes Dad with Rick and Jim," is the last line I wrote in my otherwise daily journal for weeks. Although I don't remember making the entry, according to its heading (I was big on headings, as was my mother; she'd timestamp greeting cards and grocery lists), I did so in "neurology wig [sic] waiting area, U of C hospital, left of Grandma, 4:01–6:13 PM, 1/23/88."

So right around, it would seem, 6:13 p.m., my dad arrived in the company of his fishing buddy and his fishing buddy's son, but I don't remember that happening any more than I remember making the journal entry quoted above.

With only just a few notable exceptions, my memories of that night and the month or so succeeding it are sketchy and, from a certain way of looking at things (i.e. the way I've been looking at things throughout the course of writing this memoir so far), nonexistent. I do know a number of facts about those weeks, but for the most part they're absent of sensory information, all but entirely disembodied, barely narrative, little more than text. I know them in the way I know my blood type, in the way I know the date of my birth.

I was twelve years old and my mother was dying, and before I got used to that, my mother was dead.

•

• •

So those facts, then. Those sketches.

When she got to the hospital, they scanned my mother's brain and found a growth. They told her the growth might be benign. She told them her breasts hurt. They'd hurt for a while, but she hadn't gotten checked (because she was young, and youth was protection? because she was busy? because she was scared?). They gave her a mammogram. They found a lot of growths. They biopsied one. The results would take days. She needed to know whatever they could tell her as soon as they were able to tell her, she told them. She needed to know. They understood that, they liked her, everybody liked her, and they muscled an appointment with a better scanner. They scanned her whole body with the better scanner, found a growth on her liver, and two more on her brain, one of which was inoperable. Stage 4 breast cancer. Four to six weeks. If the biopsy came back negative, they said, they would admit not only to never having seen anything like this before, but to having neither heard nor read about anything like this before. Usually they'd counsel a second opinion, but unless my parents were friends with a certain world-renowned oncologist in New York as well as with a certain world-renowned brain surgeon in London, both of whom would, in the end, almost definitely make the same prognosis anyway, and who would, if they gave her a better prognosis, offer her treatments that would be guaranteed to bring on more pain and debilitation whether those treatments succeeded or not, which they likely wouldn't . . . a second opinion, given the amount of time and stress and pain and extra cost involved, wasn't—not by any human measure—worth spending a moment of her life's final energies on. She had a family. She could go home that night. She should go home that night and be with her family. The opiates and benzodiazepines would help. She went home with us that night. The drugs might have helped.

She stayed on the couch a lot and slept on and off. I stayed home from school and sat on the couch with her. We looked at photos. We watched TV. We played gin rummy. We played with Kablankey. Just before she'd had the seizure she'd gone to the bookstore and bought me a copy of *Franny and Zooey*, a favorite from her youth, and *Breakfast of Champions* because she knew I liked Vonnegut, and the salesman recommended it. I read the Salinger and she read the Vonnegut. She asked me what I thought, and I told her I loved it, and that was the truth, and I didn't tell her that it made me long to have siblings, which was also the truth. I asked what she thought, and she said Vonnegut was funny, the book had made her laugh, but she wanted to talk to me about it after I read it, and we traded books, and after we read them she asked me if when I talked to the inans I felt the way *Breakfast*'s Dwayne Hoover feels when he starts getting ill, and I told her I didn't. Dwayne Hoover is certain his hallucinations are real, and I was never quite certain the inans were real, and, except for the inans, I told my mother, nothing I saw or heard or felt was strange, or stranger than what anyone else seemed to see or hear or feel. That's what I told her. She said *Franny and Zooey* was just as she remembered, as warm and kind and sad and intimate, and it reminded her that I should read the other Salingers she had on her shelf, which she thought about reading, and would, she said, read, unless I would let her read my journals. She'd admired the pages I'd shown her before, the night we all came back from the police station, and she knew I'd shown them only to prove I hadn't been lying about what I'd told her and my dad about the inans, and she knew that journals were private things, but soon she'd be dead and she wanted, if she could, to know me better first, she wanted to know me as well as she possibly could, and she said she imagined I'd want that too, and I told her she could read them if she agreed that she wouldn't show them to my father or talk to my father about them at all, and she agreed. She kept the journals in the drawers of her desk, down in the basement, and when she read one on the couch and my father was home, she would hide it behind a *Time* or *New Yorker* or go to the basement and read it down there.

And she read my journals and I read the other Salingers and we watched TV and ordered food and played with Kablankey and played gin rummy and listened to the Beatles. I don't mean to suggest I was always on the couch with her, though I was there for a lot of the first couple days, til she asked for my journals. As the week wore on, I was with her less and less, in my bedroom more and more. I don't remember her in pain. I only remember knowing she was. I remember knowing I should leave the room and let her be in pain because she didn't want me to see her in pain, and I remember thinking I should check on her at least once an hour so she wouldn't think I was leaving because I couldn't stand her pain.

I don't remember interacting with my father that week, but I don't remember thinking we were interacting any less than usual, or more than usual, or thinking anything between us was any more or any less out of line than it had been of late, and I know he went to work, and I know he must have fed me, and I know that in the mornings before he went to work, and then in the evenings when he came home from work, I'd go to my room so he could be alone with her.

I have only one memory of crying that week. I was up in my room, and I don't recall what exactly set me off. What I remember's that Kablankey, sitting upright on my pillow, went into a handstand, performed a box step in the handstand while whistling a waltz, then stood on its leg, clutched at its throat, stuck out its tongue, and fell on its face. My crying stopped at once. In the little time they'd spent together in the shoebox—ninety minutes total—Zappy'd taught Kablankey to do the dance of death. Or, at the very least, Blank had learned the dance of death by watching Zappy. This seemed a big deal. That it could learn anything so complex so quickly, let alone from another Botimal. I hugged it to my chest and went downstairs to tell my mom, and she was in a kind of trance—pain or drugs or sleep deprivation, probably all three—and she didn't hear, and since I'd said the word "death," as in "dance of death," without any forethought and only just realized that that's what I'd done, I was glad she hadn't heard, and I sat down beside her, put Blank on the couch, pretended to cry, and Blank did the dance. Then my mom pretended to cry, and Blank did the dance, and the rest of the week, whenever anyone would cry or pretend to cry while Blank was around, it would do the dance. I tried to teach it other dances by doing them in front of it, but it didn't seem interested. My mother, however, taught it its name. "Kablankey!" she'd say, and when it turned to look at her, she'd scratch it on the head.

I don't remember bedpans, and I don't think there were bedpans, but I don't remember her vomiting, and I know that she did no small amount of that. I know I saw her have a seizure, or possibly a small stroke, and I do remember that, but all it was was I noticed that she looked a little distant; I was saying something prolix and she was staring past my face and I thought I was boring her or the pills were kicking in and then her eyes regained focus, and she touched me on my cheek and said that something happened, a seizure or a stroke, but she was fine now, though she'd missed what I was saying and I should say it to her later, and right now all she wanted was for me to make the promise that I'd never again destroy property that didn't belong to me, and I said I'd already promised that twice, and she said she remembered, but she wanted me to promise one more time anyway, and so I did. Then she said she wanted to be alone, and to leave the room, and she asked me to help her go down to the basement. I said I'd leave the room, and she said I could do whatever I wanted, but that what she wanted was to go to the basement, so I took her to the basement and let her be alone there. After that, she wouldn't use any stairs without my dad or me there to hold her elbow.

Saturday morning, I went back to Hyde Park. My parents said it was best for me to go. We needed the study to keep paying for my treatment, they wanted the house to themselves for a while, and I hadn't gone beyond our driveway in a week. I complied without protest.

Rick and Jim drove me. Jim called me "Duke" a couple of times. I thought he thought it was my name, and I didn't correct him. Rick didn't either. I don't recall having cared, but I must have a little; otherwise, I don't know why I'd remember it.

At the study, I told Manx that the sleeve worked well. He said never mind the sleeve and he asked about my mom, and I said she was dying. He said I didn't have to be there, and I told him it was fine. In the middle of the lab, poised for a backflip, stood Lisette, who I found myself urgently wanting to confide in, get saved by, be told I was liked by. I almost said her name, but then she did the backflip, and I lost my nerve.

For most of the morning, she wouldn't look back at me, much less come near me. Approaching her seemed increasingly screw-uppable. To begin with anything other than a basic hello would have sounded unnatural, but by the time that occurred to me, we'd been in the room together for almost an hour without greeting each other, and if I just went up and said, "Hello, Lisette," I'd need to account, I thought, for the delay, and I didn't know how to account for the delay without being straightforward (e.g. "I was afraid to look dorky") and thereby losing the tiny edge I'd believed I'd acquired (however accidentally) the previous week.

So I sat there, alone, on one of the couches, scheming weakly, saying nothing, trying via posture and facial expression to send intriguing messages about my state of mind til, sometime close to the end of session 3, Lisette crossed the lab and sat beside me and, just like that, laid her head on my shoulder. "Excuse me," she said.

I laid my cheek on her head, and I said, "Excuse me."

"My rat is dead," she said. "I'm sad. It's my fault."

"I'm sorry," I said. "I didn't know you had a rat."

"Misty Cunningham. That's what I called her. She was piebald and small-eyed, and her name had no meaning. I was holding her, you know. I was holding her up in front of my face, saying, 'You're Misty Cunningham, and I do not know why, but that's who you are, you adorable rodent,' and I know that she didn't understand what I was saying, but I thought to myself, 'She understands I'm saying *something*, and she *wants to understand* what it is that I'm saying,' and something about that, it made me so gushy, Belt. I was sad because I knew she could never understand my words, but at the same time happy because I knew we both wished she could. And that was a kind of understanding, you know? Maybe the most important kind of understanding, and we shared it. And I got so gushy, so filled up with love, real love for her—this whole other animal that before that moment I thought of like more as a toy—and I squeezed her too hard, and her ribs . . . cracked. And she twitched, and she bit me, and it hardly even hurt, but it surprised me, and I dropped her, and she landed weirdly on her side on the carpet, then scuttled up onto her feet and ran, but didn't get far before she had to stop to gasp and cough and she looked so afraid and by the time we got her to the vet, she was dead. Her ribs were in her heart and in her lungs, the vet said."

"Lisette, I'm so sorry."

"You are?" she said. "You don't think I'm lying?"

I said I hadn't thought so, but that now I wasn't sure. "Are you lying?" I said.

She took her head off my shoulder.

"You think I killed her on purpose," she said. "You think I wanted to see what it was like."

"That's not even the lie I imagined you meant when you asked if I was—"

"Blah blah blah!" she all but screamed. She leapt off the couch. "If you believe me, then prove it. Let me see yours. Take it out of that sleeve thing and let me hold it."

"No," I said.

"Go to hell, then," she said, and roundhoused away.

I didn't go after her. I was afraid she'd convince me to let her hold Kablankey.

Soon it was lunch, and Kablankey was shoeboxed. I approached the window seat on which Lisette sat eating her sub.

Stood there in front of her.

I said, "Hello," and she chewed her sub. "Lisette," I said. No response.

James came up behind me. "Dude, you gotta meet me after session seven," he said. "Screwball's doing the best new thing. You pull on his whiskers a little and he yawns, and if you do it three or four times in a row, then when you stop he makes a sound like *ah-cha-cha cha-cha* and blinks his eyes really hard!"

"Lisette," I said. "Please don't be mad at me. Everything is terrible. My mother's got cancer."

"You're so full of it," she said. "That's the oldest, dumbest lie."

"I wouldn't lie about this. The doctors say she only has three to five weeks."

Lisette mimicked me saying, "I wouldn't lie about this."

I heard sobbing behind me.

"You just want me to feel bad. You just want attention."

"No," I said. "I *do* want your attention, but—"

Lisette looked away. She looked over my shoulder. "Why are *you* crying?" she said. "Stop crying."

"She's dying," James said. "His mom's gonna die."

"She's not," Lisette said.

I spun on my heel and smashed James in the face.

Lisette looked surprised, eyes and mouth O'd.

"It's okay," James said. "I knew you were a hitter. I shouldn't have said that."

I smashed him a second time, harder. He fell.

Lisette said, "Good one, but I still don't believe you."

Manx took me away. He took me to the office, where I sat with Abed, and he had Blank brought to me, along with some cookies. A couple hours later, Rick and Jim picked me up. I didn't return to the study again.

•

• •

When I got back home, my mother was asleep. My father grabbed my shoulders and pushed me down the hall. "You beat a kid up?" he whispered, as we entered the kitchen.

"I'm sorry," I said.

"Why'd you do it?" he said.

"I don't know," I said. "There was this girl there and . . ."

"He did something to this girl?"

"No," I said.

"You wanted to im*press* the girl, kicking this kid's ass."

"No," I said. "I don't know," I said.

"Stop making that face. You're not in trouble. The guy called—Manx. Said you could come back if you want to. Said he'd put you in a different group or something, with some older kids, meets four in the afternoon til seven thirty. Or else you could also just not come back. They'll still cover the treatment either way, so. You don't have to decide right now, okay? He said you show up, you show up: good. You don't, you don't, please give you his regards. Nice guy, in the end. I wouldn't've guessed. I don't know why. Scientists. Shrinks. I don't know. And he seemed to think the kid you hit must've deserved it, or at least he didn't argue when I said that was probably what it was, so I'm gonna go ahead and say, 'Good job.' You stood up for yourself, or else for some girl, or it was boys being boys or whatever, so good. If it was any of those things, especially the first two, I'm proud. But just listen, okay? This is what's important: I haven't told your mom, and you're not gonna either. She doesn't need the aggravation. Okay?"

"Okay," I said.

"Cause she had a lot of pain today, even more than usual. I guess it keeps getting worse."

"I won't tell her," I said.

"I think I might have caused her to have a seizure."

"I'm sure you didn't," I said. "That doesn't make sense."

"I think I stressed her out too much and set it off. She wanted me to leave the room for a while and I didn't want to because—you know. So I wanted to stay, and that's what I told her, and she got upset, and then, so."

"I think probably she wanted you to leave the room because she knew something was about to happen to her, and she didn't want you to see it, and you stayed, and then you saw it happen."

"What, you think she can feel when that kind of thing is about to come on?"

"Why not?" I said.

"Right," he said. "Okay. That makes . . . I guess maybe, but . . . what? She's embarrassed for me to see her in pain? She thinks I'll be ashamed of her or something? Or that I'll think . . . what? That's almost worse than I caused it. No, it is worse. I'm her husband. It's worse. She shouldn't . . ." He'd started to cry.

I went to my room.

•

• •

I was cold when I got into bed that night, and I took an extra blanket from the closet in the hall—the afghan that, half a year or so earlier, had parried my questions about its knowledge of German—and just as I'd started to fall asleep, I had this strange sense, a unique sense really, that the afghan, presumably because it wanted to make up for being short with me that last time, was somehow teaching me, while I hovered in the space between un- and consciousness, to control my own gate. For the very first time, I seemed to be able to *sense* my gate. It was located somewhere just behind and above my right eye, and what I came to understand was that it didn't, as I'd previously imagined, swing back and forth like a fence's hinged portal; rather, it worked like an old garage door (the kind that, when lifted, didn't fold up, but thrust outward into the air above the driveway before being dragged inside along its track), and all it would take to get it to open was to more accurately and vividly imagine it lifting, while tensing my body in a particular way.

I slept the type of *interesting*—if not quite restful—border sleep where you're aware that you're sleeping, aware you're in a bed. In place of dreaming, I looked forward to waking, to chatting up the afghan, and maybe the pillow, possibly the nightstand, potentially every inan in the room, then explaining to my mother and my father how I did it, teaching them how to do it themselves. When I woke, however, a little while later, I possessed just as little gate-control as always; the image of the garage door was far less crisp once I'd opened my eyes, and I couldn't recall the particular way I was supposed to tense my body to get the gate to lift, and I lay there, bleary, sweaty, and cold, trying to rediscover the proper tension, but instead found access I hadn't ever sought to muscles I'd never really thought about having: I wiggled my ears, got my scrotum to jump, induced my pectorals to shift up and down, right one left one right one left, like a trash-talking wrestler at a ringside interview. This was interesting enough to keep me from getting too pissed at myself to fall back asleep, but it wasn't—obviously—what I'd been after, and I determined that the problem was I'd been too anxious, woken too soon, before I'd finished learning the afghan's lesson, and again I closed my eyes, hoping to return to my previous state, and it seemed, actually, that I was starting to succeed—the image of my gate was regaining definition—but then I was shaking, something was shaking me, and I sat up, wired, angry, confused.

The clock on the nightstand said 3:17. My father was sitting beside me on the bed. He turned on the reading lamp, held out some paper—yellow sheets of paper, my mother's handwriting.

"Is she okay?" I said.

"She's alive," he said.

"What the hell kind of answer is that?" I said.

"You have to read these, right now." He flapped the yellow stack. A bright, white envelope flashed from beneath it.

"I don't want to," I said. "Get out of my way."

He held me by the arm. "She said you have to read these before you go down. You read the yellow letter first. Then the typed one in the envelope."

"Fine," I said. "So go away. Let me read them."

He let go of my arm, said, "She said I had to stay with you until you were done."

"What? Why?"

"I don't know," he said. "She wouldn't let me read them. Said they're just for you. I've got my own letters here to read," he said. He patted his shirt pocket.

"I don't like this," I said.

"I don't see how you could," he said. "But I don't really give a fuck. Read the goddamn letters, Bill."

He dropped them on the blanket and went to my desk. He lit up a Quill. I asked if I could have one.

"Shut up," he said, "and read the yellow one first. And look, I didn't mean *shut up,* like, 'You're worthless, shut up.' I just—did you really just ask me for a Quill?" he said.

"Not really," I said. "It was just a bad joke."

"Not that bad," he said. "I mean, in a different moment. I mean, I don't know, son. Just."

I said, "I'm sorry I walked away from you before, when you were crying."

"I understand, Belt. I would've done the same, I bet. I mean, not, you know—I mean I would have done the same if you were my dad and that's what you did, I think."

"I'll read these, now," I said.

"Yeah. Okay. Good, then. Read them. I'll read mine, too."

•

• •

1/31/88, 1:07 AM–2:49 AM

Living Room Couch

Dearest Belt,

Just after you went upstairs to bed, I tried to ask your father for a bowl of ice cream, but I wasn't able to form the words. Instead of saying, "Clyde, could you bring me some ice cream?" I hummed and clicked and moaned and shushed. It seemed like I was crying. I wasn't crying.

I took a couple breaths and cleared my throat (which sounded the way it's always sounded) and I tried again to ask for ice cream. "Could you bring me some ice cream, Clyde?" I tried to say, but all that came out were those crying sounds.

Only ten minutes earlier, I'd said to your father, "I'm still too hot. Would you turn down the thermostat?" That I could no longer speak was too hard to believe. I didn't believe it. I didn't even start to til after having failed another ten or twelve times to ask for ice cream. Even then I resisted, held out some, denied some, accepting that, yes, I could not ask for ice cream without sounding like I was crying, but telling myself that maybe, somehow, my incapacity to speak was only partial—an incapacity, for example, to form a certain kind of utterance (a question or request), or even perhaps an incapacity to speak about certain subjects (ice cream, say, or maybe all desserts, maybe all desires). And so I tried to make other, random statements. "I love you," I tried, and, "Promise you won't marry a stupid woman," and, "Let's watch Star Wars," and, "I'm afraid," and, "You're an awfully handsome man." Not a single word was I able to shape. Nothing but crying sounds.

The whole time, your dad had his arm around me, and he'd held me tighter while I was making the crying sounds, and once I'd ceased attempting to speak, the crying sounds stopped, and he asked me if there was something he could do to help me feel better—which, you should know (one last important lesson from your dying mother, here) is really the best way to deal with crying people you love (assuming they're really crying): you hold them tight and wait til they're quiet before offering any kind of practical help (you want them to feel free to cry, unrushed; you want to avoid giving the impression that their crying's a strain on your ability to comfort them)—and when, forgetting myself, I tried to explain to him all I've just described, of course all that came out was the moaning and clicking, the humming, the shushing. And again, of course, your father held me tighter.

And, yes, I really did start to cry then. I cried for a while. I listened to me crying. And yes, it really did sound the same. A little wetter, maybe, but otherwise the same.

So I can no longer speak, Belt. That's what I'm telling you. I'll never speak again. And I know, I know: never say never. But it's been a few hours, and nothing has changed, and, believe it or not, I'm already used to it. Which isn't to say the experience isn't strange to me, but the fact that I'll never speak again . . . I've accepted that. To *experience* this symptom, or whatever it is (maybe it's the drugs, perhaps a combination of drugs and symptoms, mild seizures or so-called "mini-strokes") is *very* strange. Here I am, writing this letter, a letter composed of sentences that—I think, I *hope*—are clear, yet if I open my mouth to speak what I've written (in a double-checking spirit, I did so just now, tried to speak the words "to speak what I've written"), all that comes out are those crying sounds.

I'm not telling you about any of this in order to scare you or make you feel sad for me. Quite the opposite. There are lots of reasons for you to be sad and afraid—you're about to lose your mom forever—and I won't deny that, but my speechlessness isn't one of those reasons. I'm telling you about it *because* it's so strange, and because I want to share with you what it's like for me to die because, well—because I want to share everything I possibly can with you while I'm still able. And the first thing I'm really trying to get across here is that, having only just lost the power of speech two hundred–some minutes ago, I'm already finding that I'm grateful I still have the ability to write, the ability to bring (or at least try to bring) the experience across in this letter. Hugely grateful.

(I don't know whether this gratitude is "miraculous" or horrifying. I don't know if it's a testament to man's (or my) capacity for resilience or his (or my) tendency to cling to life no matter the indignity. It doesn't really matter. Or maybe it does matter, but it's not what I want to focus on here. Even beyond the gift horse's mouth aspect, wondering at the line between hope and desperation is a waste of my time. Maybe of everyone's, ever, I don't know.)

So, *grateful* I was saying. I'm grateful, hugely grateful. Grateful I can write. But grateful though I am, I am equally afraid, Belt, and *newly* afraid—I am SO afraid—that wherever my ability to speak has gone, so will my ability to write shortly follow. Ever since I was diagnosed, I have of course known I would soon and forever lose the ability to communicate with you—that's the first, most awful thing that death means for me—and I've spent the last week writing and rewriting the "second" (i.e. enveloped) letter with that in mind, a letter that I hope says everything sayable that needs to be said, yet the thought that I might, once I'd lost the ability to communicate, still possess *the desire to communicate* . . . that's the new fear.

I guess I'd just assumed the one would go with the other, that with the ability would flee the desire. That I'd be alive, communicating, and then I'd die, not communicating. I don't know why I assumed that. Maybe for my own sanity's sake. It seems pretty unimaginative to me now, but that's what I'd assumed: that once I was no longer able to say anything, there wouldn't be anything left that I'd feel needed saying, or there wouldn't be any *I* left to sense unsaidness. It really does seem stupid when I put it like that, huh? It does. I know. What's more, it was selfish, that way of thinking. Because, you see (and this is the second—the main—thing I'm trying to get across), what has finally occurred to me, which is something that any child would know, something I managed, in- or conveniently, to put out of my mind, what has finally occurred to me is that our ability to communicate requires not only my ability to speak/write, but your ability to hear/read what I've spoken/written, and it wasn't until I considered the implications of that that I realized how important it was to allow *you* the chance to say to *me* whatever last things you need to say—how important it was that you know I'm able to hear those things, whatever they might be, that I don't rob you of that, that I allow you the chance to respond to me about my suicide.

Please read the letter in the envelope now. Please come sit with me once you've read it, and please say anything you need to say. I want to listen.

I love you,
Mom

PS Although a couple or three things in the second letter, especially toward the end, indicate the contrary—were I certain we had time, I would have changed these things—I want to reassure you I'm still alive. I am. I promise. I'm just downstairs, same spot on the couch as when last you saw me.

•
• •

1/25–30/88

Bedroom, Basement, Living Room Couch

Dearest Belt,

The most important things don't need saying. I am certain you already know I love you, and certain you know I know you love me. This isn't an exercise in concision, however; it's a suicide letter. And so I've just said the most important things. And, redundancy be damned, I'll even rephrase them:

Hating my death—and, Belt, please make no mistake, I hate it—is a matter, first and foremost, of hating the fact that I won't get to keep on being your mother.

And I won't. Always, I will have been your mother, and, as I write this, I am still your mother, but soon: no more. I will not get to keep on being at all, nor do I doubt that even a little. Here in my foxhole, I'm still an atheist. That's the last important thing I've learned about myself—that I really don't believe in the everlasting soul, in fate, or in anything else even vaguely supernatural—and it's the *least* important thing I'll say in this letter, but I want you to know me for who I am and, once I'm gone, I want you to remember me for who I was. So to clarify a little: In saying, "I really don't believe in the everlasting soul, in fate, or in anything else even vaguely supernatural," I don't mean to suggest that I haven't wondered, "Why me? Why now? Why this?" I have. I have asked those questions no few times. However, it's precisely when I remember that I don't believe such questions have answers beyond the materialistic (genetics, environment, timing—pure chance)—when I remind myself that the universe is wholly amoral, that I'm going to die soon, to cease to get to be your mom, to cease to get to be your father's wife, and that, in the time I have left, I will, intermittently, with increasing frequency and growing intensity, continue to suffer unspeakable pain *for no good reason*—that I see (over and again) how pondering the "meaning" of my suffering and imminent death is a waste of time, a needless distraction, something I'm simply not obliged to do, and I then find peace, or something close to peace, for I would much rather just think about you and your father, and I become more free and able to do so: to remember you, observe you, to try to know you as well as I can before I'm gone, before I can't know anything.

Your journals have helped. They have helped immensely. I have read them all, now. Thank you for letting me. They have not only allowed me to know you better, which has helped me to determine *what* needs to be said here in order to leave you in as mothered a place as I possibly can, but the quality of thought (especially in this past year's entries—oh my!) that comes through in your writing—the abilities to analyze and empathize you demonstrate—has freed me from any worries about *how* those things I should say should be said. I see that I can write to you in the same voice in which I'd hoped to one day write to you once you'd grown up; the voice in which I think when my thinking's most complex and deliberate. All those em-dashes you use, and all those parentheses—all those asides and thoughts within thoughts (all that paradoxical back-doubling)—they make it sound, in form if not content, the way the inside of my own head sounds when I'm at my sharpest. And if you couldn't tell, your style is infectious. Contagious. After just a couple hours of reading your journals, I found I couldn't help but rip it off.

I don't know where you learned that stuff. When I was in school—and I, like so many other bookish girls and young women, wanted, and even tried for a while, to be a writer—they taught us that long sentences were inherently the products of sloppy thinking. That asides were messy. That parentheses were loathsome. (Loathsome! No kidding. They actually *hated* certain punctuation marks. How is that sane?) They'd demonstrate the power of the declarative sentence—and there is, to be sure, no more frequently powerful a kind of sentence—while claiming, against all kinds of contrary evidence (e.g. in Ellison, O'Connor, Salinger, Roth—the list goes on and on) that declarativeness was somehow determined by the raw number of syllables in a sentence (i.e. the fewer the better) rather than the frequency and placement of stress. Tin-eared, all of them. Maybe that's changed. Maybe there's a genius teaching at Washington. I tend to doubt it.

But if you do continue to write, Belt—and I imagine you will—please trust me on this: refine what's yours. Strive to get better at sounding like yourself. You are not fully formed—no one every really is—but you are muchly formed. Precociously formed. If you seek out teachers, judge their worthiness only on whether they enjoy what you already do. Whether they *enjoy* it. Whether it *speaks to them*. If they only admire it—let alone if they don't like it—they can't possibly help you to get any better.

I know that, as with anything positive I have to say about you, you're taking all of this with a grain of salt. Part of me wishes that weren't so, but most of me knows that you wouldn't be you if you accepted your loving mother's praise as gospel. That's also part of why I think you'll continue to write: you have the temperament. Doubting praise, your mother's or anyone else's, is an outcome of your wanting not merely to be thought of as good, but to, in fact, *be* good. That, incidentally, is what makes a person good, and it's necessary to make a writer—any artist—great. Not sufficient, but necessary. And it's just as necessary to know it's insufficient. Now you've been told.

So, sad as I am for you—that you will no longer have me around—I really do think you're going to be fine. You have found a vocation, something you're always going to love to do, or, at the very least, feel is worth doing. That's no small thing.

I've discussed it with your father. You asked me not to show him or even talk to him about what's in your journals, and I haven't, other than to tell him that your talent for writing is surprising, even to me, who thinks the world of you in all things, and that I'm all but certain you'll be a writer. I want you to know what his response was. He said, "Tell me how to keep from fucking it up."

I have no brothers, nor any male cousins. I hardly dated before I met your dad. All I know about fathers and sons comes from novels and movies and the two of you. The two of you have been growing distant. Over the past few months—maybe longer, maybe I've been slow to notice—it seems you've begun to (accurately) sense just how different you are from one another. He's loud, outgoing, aggressive even, doesn't read much, prefers to fish, to watch boxing, is excited by certain forms of circumscribed violence. You, like me, are quiet, a little too shy, content to walk around and think, to sit upstairs in your room and think. In sum (if I haven't already reduced you guys enough): he tends to hate being alone, and you often need to be alone.

Maybe you'll eventually learn from each other. I know I've certainly learned from your dad. Most saliently I learned self-confidence (though I don't think he'd call it that; he'd probably say I "found my legs" or "learned to take it on the chin"). And I think he might have learned a thing or two from me: just the other day, when you showed him Kablankey and he gave him that onion, you saw the way he melted—he wouldn't have done that when we first started dating; back then, if he'd sensed any kind of fuzzy feeling coming on that didn't have its origins in me or some underdog boxer or hero of the Second World War or a Springsteen lyric or something, he would have looked away and, if he couldn't look away, he would have been too embarrassed to say anything, let alone anything resembling "I just want to eat it right up," or whatever it was he said about Kablankey. But we're in love, your father and I, and we were young when we fell in love, and now, though our love has only grown more intense, we're not so young, not so able to change. So while you might change some—might become more like him—he isn't likely to change very much, if at all. Still, I'll tell you the same thing I told him when he said, "Tell me how to keep from fucking it up": be patient with him. Despite your differences, you're not at odds. You asked me not to show him your journals because you don't think he'd like them (you're probably right) and, because he's your father, you value his opinion about what you do. Yet because you're his son, he, regardless of his opinion about what you do, values you; "Tell me how to keep from fucking it up" is Clyde-speak for "tell me how to help Belt be whoever Belt wants to be." So instead of dwelling on how you two wouldn't ever bother to know one another if you weren't related (not to guilt you, but that entry really broke my heart a little when I read it), try thinking about how, because you're related, you have a rare (a onetime!) chance to be friends with someone so different from you. I want you to be friends.

So like I was saying, I told him, "Be patient." And I also told him to move my PC from the basement to your room. I don't think work will attempt to take it back, but they might—it's theirs. If so, Dad'll buy you a new one. He'll make sure you always have a computer to write on. (A quick note about writing on computers: the sooner you get comfortable doing it, the better. Your handwriting is just not very good, Belt, and the extensive revising that you do—all the crossed-out words and margin notes—make reading it, and therefore, I'd imagine, editing, also, harder. The delete key was invented for you.) He also happily agreed to buy you a new book each week and to maintain the (pretty good, I must say) library in the bedroom, even if you move, or he gets remarried (in which case I suppose he'll move the library into another room—don't get mad if he does this, it's fine). Last but not least, he will not discourage you from studying whatever you might want to study in college. Maybe it'll be English. Or even Creative Writing—they teach that, now, you know. I'm not saying I think you *should* major in either of those things—I majored in English, then Philosophy, and I think the humanities effectively murdered my desire to write—but rather that I trust you to know what's best for you to study, and your father will, too.

He's a good man, Belt. He's kind (however sometimes inconspicuously), he loves you (ditto), and he always keeps his word.

So I've covered my atheism, your writing, and my hopes for you and your father. I wish I had something of value to tell you about women, or girls, about falling in love, marriage, having kids, but, apart from my telling you that I believe you'll meet a good person to fall in love with if you remain a good person, that I really hope I'm right about that, and that falling in love with your father was the easiest thing I ever did, and, with the exception of becoming your mom, the most rewarding—apart from that, I have very little to say, and I'm not about to start making things up. I was very lucky to meet your father. It was at-first-sight and it made no sense. There's no great anecdote. We met at a bar, where I'd gone to read. He came up and said hello. I really don't remember what else was said. We were drawn to one another. We clicked. There was fire. All the clichés that are thankfully justified. I hope our luck runs in the blood. As far as I can tell, luck is what you'll need; you're like me in that way. You know well, and perhaps—though hopefully not—*too* well, how to be alone. My sense is: don't seek love out. But that's only based on my own singular experience. I met your dad when I was twenty-one because he came up to me. Maybe I'd feel different if I'd been twenty-two, twenty-three, thirty—who knows? You'll figure this stuff out without your mother. Without your father, too. I guess that's one thing I do feel I can tell you. You will—you won't be able to help but to do so—figure falling in love out with the person you end up falling in love with, and until you meet her . . . you'll have no idea.

Now about these inans. (What a transition, huh? "I wonder why she ever quit writing!" he says.) Really, though. About these inans. I'm as certain "they" don't talk to you as I am that I can't convince you of that. That is: I'm 100 percent certain on both scores. I hope that once you've finished passing through puberty, you'll stop hearing them, or at least become certain that you aren't *really* hearing them; I hope so because, that way, your life will be easier. But to tell you the truth, that you think you talk to inans doesn't trouble me all that much. Billions of people believe they have conversations with a God they've never laid eyes on, and they aren't (not always, at least) made to suffer for having that belief. And at least you can perceive the swingsets you speak to. You even have to be touching them, right? Even if you continue to converse with them—as long as that's all you do with them—I think you will continue to be quite capable of having a good life.

Anyway (another stellar transition!), other than to note that solipsism is a perfect trap, I don't have a lot to say about the inans, surely nothing that can match the rigor and complexity with which you've imagined their existence, with which you've made their existence impossible to entirely disprove to you, and most especially since you've already promised me (three times now) that you will never again destroy property that doesn't belong to you. Sure, I can state the practical and obvious: that if you destroy property that doesn't belong to you, you will eventually get in trouble, you will ruin your life, which will also ruin your father's life, and that, furthermore, if the inans *are* "real" and they *are* asking you to ruin your life or the life of someone you love to help them (i.e. the inans), then they aren't good, they certainly aren't your friends, and anyway you owe them nothing. But I know from your journals that you've occasionally reflected on these things to one degree or another before and after you've ended up destroying private property because, ultimately, you end up thinking something along the lines of, "Well, they aren't exactly asking me to ruin my life to help them, which would probably be unacceptable; they're only asking me to *risk* ruining my life to help them, which maybe isn't so unacceptable. If I abstract it enough, how different is it from being a soldier in a just war?" In other words, I know that, in the moment, you can convince yourself that destroying them is your duty as a human being—that it's the kind, the right, and even the noble thing to do. It's none of those things, and much of you knows that most of the time, but in the moment, when the inans are asking for destruction, when they seem most real to you, your intellect is less persuasive than your inner sweetness, so I'm not going to tell you that I expect you to believe what I believe the next time—or any time—an inan asks you to destroy it, I'm not going to say that I expect you to make the arguments against destroying it that you know I would make: instead I'm going to remind you once again that you have promised me you wouldn't destroy them, and now I am going to dwell on that promise.

You have to keep it. You have to keep it in spirit, as well as to the letter. What I mean by "in spirit" is: Supposing an inan, down the line, tells you to do something else that you know I wouldn't approve of (e.g. that, rather than asking you to destroy it, it tells you to steal something, or harm yourself, or harm another person): you must not do it. Even if you don't understand why you shouldn't do it, or why I wouldn't want you to do it, you must not do it. Because you promised me, you must not do it. Because you promised me three separate times. And not only did you promise me three separate times, but the last time you promised me, I was on my deathbed. I know my power here—a mother on her deathbed—and the only end toward which I've leveraged that power is that of extracting that third promise from you. I want you to never forget that. The last thing I ever asked of you—demanded of you, if you must think of it that way—was that you make the promise, and I knew it was the last thing I would ever ask of you. It is the most important thing I've ever asked of you. You see, I don't want you to quit writing: were I to live to see you quit, I'd feel disappointed. And I don't want you to grow any further apart from your father: were I to live to see the two of you grow further apart, I would feel sad. But were I to live to see you break this promise to me, Belt, I would not only *feel* betrayed, *inconsolably* betrayed, but I would, in fact, *be* betrayed. I am going to die believing you will keep your promise. I am going to die believing you will betray neither my memory, nor yourself. Don't betray us. Don't make a fool of me.

Last thing, now. Last things. About me and the last decision I'll make. You need to know that I didn't choose to end my life in a state of rage or confusion. One major reason for writing this letter so methodically—drafted and redrafted over and again, typed up on the PC, spell-checked, justified, all but bulleted, and in what I know is, resultantly (perhaps a bit unfortunately), not exactly the warmest of styles—is to demonstrate to you just how present I am, how I'm still (when not in the throes of pain) thinking quite clearly. I'm very fortunate that way. Fortunate that none of the tumors in my head have—so far—grown upon, pressed upon, or in any way affected those parts of my brain that make me me.

When I was your age, I thought a lot about suicide. I don't mean that I was suicidal back then—I've never been suicidal, and I wouldn't even say I am "suicidal" right now—just that I thought about the phenomenon a lot. The whys and the ways. When it was rational (if it could be), when it wasn't (if that made it unthinkable), when it was romantic, when it was hideous, the circumstances under which I might do it . . . I think that's all normal. I think most everyone thinks about those things, especially when young. But after a while, I don't know when—probably after high school, around the time your grandma died, and certainly by the time you were born—I began to accept, however fleetingly, that I would die eventually, that my life would end one day with or without my help (I'd always *thought* I'd believed that when I was younger, but I hadn't, not really), and suicide seemed a waste of time to think about; it seemed like a dodge, a distraction, a way to avoid thinking about *the world without oneself,* a way to avoid thinking about not having a self, to think about the *act* of dying rather than what it might mean (or fail to mean) to *be* dead.

So for a couple years at least, I pretty much ceased to think about suicide. And then my father got sick. You probably remember very little of that. You were three years old, and I tried to shield you, and we've never talked about it, but he had cancer too. His was of the colon, and was not, when discovered, as advanced as my cancer is. The doctors tried to treat it—surgery, radiation, chemo—for, I think, three months, before they gave up. Then he held on for four or five more weeks. I'd never seen anyone in so much pain. It was worse for him during the treatment, but even after the treatment was through . . . it still upsets me to remember. He was so bitter, so lost, he so consistently hurt so much, and he told me that if he wasn't afraid of never seeing the people he loved again, he would gladly kill himself. *Gladly*. He used that word. If he didn't believe that my mother was in heaven, and that his parents were in heaven, and that I, if I were to accept Christ in my heart, would one day be in heaven—if he didn't believe that, he said, then he would have already gladly killed himself because the pain just otherwise wasn't worth it. There were moments it seemed to go away, he said, almost entirely—whole hours during which the pain seemed to be gone—but the anticipation of the pain's return made those hours worthless. That's how bad the pain was, he said.

Yet my imagination failed me. I didn't take him at his word. I didn't doubt that he wanted to die, nor did I fault him for wanting to die, but I didn't believe it was the pain that made it so; I thought it was the indignity. The indignities. The twenty-four-hour nurse. The inability to clean himself, to use the bathroom on his own. The loss of privacy. The loss of control. He didn't want to talk about those things to his daughter, for that would only increase the indignity. That's what I thought. And I decided, right then and there, nine years ago now, that if ever I began to suffer that level of indignity, I would kill myself.

But now I know I was wrong. I was shallow. I was wrong about the conditions under which I would kill myself, and I was wrong not to take my father at his word. I do, as I've said, count myself lucky for not having had to suffer the indignities he suffered on top of my pain—lucky that you and your father (hopefully) won't have had to see me that way, that I won't have had to *be seen* that way—but I would, 100 out of 100 times, accept those indignities *in place of* the pain, even just in place of the anticipation of the pain. I could live with those indignities. And I *would*. But the pain, Belt.

The pain is indescribable. Or, rather, I won't describe it. I'm afraid to describe it, to try describe it. Right now, as I write this, I don't feel it—I, like my father had, have these windows—and I fear that attempting a description might somehow cause it to return sooner than it otherwise would, and, as much as I want to bring across my experience to you, as much as I want you to understand the state I'm in, were doing so to speed the pain's return by even a second, it wouldn't be worth it. That's how bad it is. That's how much I fear it.

That said, the pain is not, strictly speaking, *unbearable*. I don't know how long I'll be able to bear it, though. Right after I had that (first?) seizure in Hyde Park, it seemed my time was evenly split between the pain and its anticipation, but within not more than a couple of days, the ratio started favoring the pain, and that ratio has broadened, increasingly broadened at every interval, and the pain itself has gotten worse, and anticipating it has, correspondingly, grown more terrifying, my relief from it ever less . . . relieving.

One big fear of mine is that once the pain does become unbearable, I will be unable to do anything about it—I'll be too far gone to end my life, or even physically incapable of ending my life, and I'll just have to suffer til it ends on its own, and you will have to suffer watching me.

But then the other big fear of mine, of course, is that I end my life too soon. That I miss something—something between us, something between myself and your father—that I would have been better off sticking around for, despite the pain; some exchange of words or comfort that I not only possess the responsibility as your mother and his wife to stick around for, but that I would have, had I known the future, possessed a longing to stick around for.

The bigger of these two big fears is the first one. It just is. And so my aim is to err on the side of *too soon:* to stop the pain—to end my life—*just before* the pain becomes unbearable. Of course I want to err just as little as possible. Toward that end, I've had to define for myself what I imagine unbearable pain to be; I've had to define something that, as I've already said, is, if not indescribable, too fearsome to describe, even to myself. The definition that I've come up with is: pain so bad that I would kill you, my son, in order to prevent you from having to suffer it. The moment it seems to me that such pain is imminent—that's the moment I'll overdose.

If your father has done as I've asked him to—and I have no reason to believe he hasn't, he promised—you were given this letter in the very same moment that you learned of my death, and, as you read it the first time, I doubt much of what I'm saying is getting through to you, but it comforts me to think that when you read this letter down the line, when you're older, you'll know I avoided the very worst. Not just that I didn't (as I believe I've already demonstrated) choose, while in a state of rage or confusion, to die, but that I did not *die* in a state of rage or confusion. That I died when I should have, when it was the single best thing I could have done, and that I knew it was the single best thing I could have done. Please, for the sake of your own well-being, try to know those things as soon as you can. Knowing them won't by any means make my death less devastating for you—I'm your only mother, and I'm gone—but it should mitigate any devastation that might have otherwise arisen from the fact that I died of suicide. That, at least, is my hope. Given the content of your journals, I think it's a reasonable hope.

I love you, Belt. I have loved you all your life. Always know that first of all.

And Finally,

Mom

• • •

We read our letters and then, in the kitchen, we double-scooped ice cream from half-gallon cartons—one Mint Chocolate Chip, one Chocolate Chocolate Chip—into three bowls, stuck spoons in the bowls, and brought the bowls to the living room.

My mom was watching *Star Wars.*

We sat on either side of her.

We each ate a couple or three spoons of ice cream, then she started to cry, or to try to talk, and then she stopped crying or trying to talk, and she paused the movie, took our bowls from our laps and set them on the table, and extended her arms and hugged us together, all our heads touching, and I don't know who was sobbing but one of us was sobbing, my father or me, and the other one told her we both understood, said, "I understand. He understands, too," and for a while we remained that way, pressed head to head, then my mother sat upright, and we followed suit, and she gave us our bowls of ice cream back, and she unpaused *Star Wars,* and we finished our ice cream.

And my dad brought the rest of the ice cream from the freezer, and we passed the cartons back and forth between us and we all fell asleep before *Star Wars* was over, my mom, then my dad, and then at last me, and when the tape ended, the machine rewound it and played it again, and when it ended again the machine rewound it and played it again, and when it ended the third time, the click of the rewind engaging woke me, and I knew she was gone before I opened my eyes. The sun was in the window, glaring in the snow, and water was running in the bathroom downstairs, and the blister pack of Xanax and the jar of Dilaudid and the bottle of cherry-flavored morphine solution and the bottle of banana-flavored morphine solution that had been on the table beside the PC were not on the table beside the PC, and I woke up my father, who told me not to move.

LOOK AT YOUR FATHER

Two Fridays later, halfway through the episode, my father said *Miami Vice* had gone to shit and, if it was okay with me, we'd skip the rest, and check out *Sledge Hammer!* I said I didn't care, and he said it might be funny, he'd heard it was funny, and we hadn't tried to watch anything that was funny in a pretty long time, and maybe that was exactly what we needed to do, was watch something funny and try to have a laugh or two, though he didn't really feel like watching anything funny or having a laugh, but that that was why he thought it might be what we needed, and I said that we should watch whatever he wanted. And he said that he didn't really care what we watched as long as it wasn't *Miami Vice*. And he told me it was *Sledge Hammer!*'s season finale, that he'd seen a couple ads, and that's how he knew that, and if it wasn't a sitcom, it would be a bad idea to start with the finale, but since it was in fact a sitcom, it shouldn't really matter where you started at all because you didn't have to care about the characters in sitcoms since all they were there to do was make jokes and you didn't have to know what happened to them last week, or the week before that, or any other time because they'd always act the same no matter what had happened and their jokes would be gettable. It wasn't like books, where you had to pay attention and the jokes weren't funny unless you kept track of things.

We hadn't shown one another the letters she'd written us (nor would we ever), but when at last my father, after speaking the greatest number of consecutive words I'd heard from him in weeks, capped things off by mentioning books, I, through the slow-brained fog of my grief, couldn't help but think that he, toward me, and through his own fog, was trying to reach out in a way that my mother had suggested in his letters, or at least in a way he must have thought she'd suggested. Maybe she'd told him, "Show an interest in the telling of stories," or maybe she'd told him, "Let him see how you think," or maybe she'd just said, "Talk to Belt more."

So, “Let’s watch it,” I said. And “If we like it,” I added, in case my enthusiasm had sounded as inauthentic as it was, “we can watch the reruns when they come on in summer.”

“Good call,” he said. “That could work out good.” And he flipped to ABC, which was airing a teaser for that evening’s *20/20*.

In the teaser, a Botimal is standing on a table while a boy in a faded Belinda Carlisle concert T, his eyes obscured by a thick black bar, stands behind the table and starts leaning forward, and the voiceover man says, “Next on *20/20*. What is this strange, adorable creature? And what could drive a boy to end its life before a Midwestern audience of middle school children and their horrified parents? Stay tuned to find out at eleven Eastern, ten o’clock Central and Mountain time.”

“Hey, that’s a—wait. He say ‘end its life’?” my father said. “You know who that kid is?”

“I think so,” I said. “Yeah, I’m pretty sure. Miles. Miles? Not Miles. Niles.”

Though the censor box had done its face-concealing job well, I’d seen the same shirt on a boy called Niles who was in the Friends Study. Not a lot of junior high school–aged boys would admit to their Belinda Carlisle fandom, let alone be willing to advertise it, and so the odds that any boy, in February 1988, would be wearing such a shirt in the company of a Botimal and *not* be Niles . . . It had to be Niles.

“Sounds like a jagoff. He’s a pervert or what?” my father asked.

I had little idea what Niles was like. I’d seen him eat a couple of subs at lunch, but we hadn’t ever talked, and I’d never met his Botimal. I hadn’t even known he’d been assigned a Botimal; he wasn’t in my group, but James’s, Group 1.

Of course we stayed tuned once *Sledge Hammer!* ended (we agreed we’d watch it again in reruns, but weren’t ever able; the show got canceled), and after *20/20* aired the Sandburg Middle School Talent Show segment, my father threw the remote at the wall. “This fucking shitty world,” he said.

I didn’t understand his reaction at first. Niles had done a disturbing, disgusting thing and they’d put it on television, but all sorts of disturbing, disgusting things appeared on television, and most people watched them and found them entertaining—my father and I among those people—so . . . what? Why so upset? Did he think I was like Niles? Did he think I’d do to my Botimal what Niles had done?

“It’s a robot,” he said. “What do I care what you do to a robot? But I bet there’s some kids who know you have one, right?” he said. “You must’ve showed it to someone from school.”

“Yeah,” I said. “You’re mad about *that*?”

“I’m mad because Barbara Walters just told half the world that ‘these truly adorable little robots' won't be for sale at stores til spring, and that the only people who have them right now are a few 'psychotically disturbed' kids enrolled in the same study as the twisted fucking fruitcake they just showed tearing one in half on a stage. So you listen to me, now, okay? Listen. If *anyone* at school comes at you saying *anything* about you being in that study, or having something wrong with you, you have my permission—no. Not just my permission. You have my blessing—in fact, I'm *instructing* you . . . Look, you know how to punch. I've shown you how to punch. You break their nose. Immediately, Billy. Right on the spot. I don't care if a teacher's standing half a foot away. You put a stop to any talk about you right then and there, or you're gonna have to deal with that shit for the rest of your life."

"But—"

"But what if it's a girl, right? Yeah. I know. It's not so simple. If it's a girl, you gotta break her boyfriend's nose. If he isn't right there, you tell her you're going to, so everyone can hear, and, by God, you do it before the day's done. And if she doesn't have a boyfriend, you tell her you're gonna break the nose of her best friend's boyfriend, and then you go do it, and if anyone thinks twice about why, what they'll think is her best friend's boyfriend was cheating with the girl who tried to mess with you, see? They'll think there was a *reason* you thought he was her boyfriend. That all the contingencies? That's all of them. Yeah. No junior high girl who can't land a boyfriend and doesn't even have a friend who can land a boyfriend is ever gonna mess with you—that kind of girl can't afford to be a bitch. So we straight on this or what?"

"Yes." I said.

"Look at me, now. Look at your father. We see eye to eye?"

I said that we did, and I think I even meant it. I never found out, though; I never had cause to do as he'd instructed. The kids at Washington left me alone. I was sure they must have been talking about me—the motherless weirdo who'd murdered the swingsets and was now, officially, sick in the head—and I'd caught a few throwing sad glances my way, but except for a couple of fifth-grade girls who rode on my bus and asked to see Blank (I told them the truth, that I kept it at home, and they returned to their seats, spread the word to their friends), they all kept their distance. They didn't talk *to* me, not a single one, not until just before the start of spring break, when Jonboat phoned to invite me to the compound and give him my advice on T-shirt design.

III

PORTFOLIO

On *Private Viewing*

Jonny Pellmore-Jason, Jr.
February 15, 2013
January Short Term Independent Study Essay
Mr. Hickey

Introduction

Private Viewing by Fondajane Henry (b. 1976) was the last important work of art of the twentieth century. It was performed just nine times over nine months (June 1999 to February 2000) for one viewer-participant at a time.

Henry, who is my stepmom, published the monologue she recited at the start of each performance in her second critical masterwork, *Lamborgina C(unt)ock* (see Appendix), and Ronson Boyle, who was her gallerist/impresario, kept a simple ledger detailing *Private Viewing*'s earnings and expenditures (see Table 1, below) that he published in his memoir, *Procurer: My Life as a Gallerist,* but except for those two documents, there is no documentation of any of the performances.

TABLE 1

Private Viewing Earnings and Expenditures

Date	Admission	Extras	Production Expenses	Profit
6/1999	$20,000.00	$0.00	-$8,000.00	**$12,000.00**
7/1999	$20,000.00	($300.00)	-$8,000.00	**$12,000.00**
8/1999	$20,000.00	$0.00	-$8,000.00	**$12,000.00**
9/1999	$30,000.00	$0.00	-$8,000.00	**$22,000.00**
10/1999	$30,000.00	$0.00	-$8,000.00	**$22,000.00**
11/1999	$30,000.00	($6,500.00)	-$8,000.00	**$22,000.00**
12/1999	$40,000.00	$0.00	-$8,000.00	**$32,000.00**
1/2000	$40,000.00	($1,750.00)	-$8,000.00	**$32,000.00**
2/2000	$50,000.00	$0.00	-$8,000.00	**$42,000.00**
Totals:	$280,000.00	$0.00 (all extras repaid in full)	-$72,000.00	**$208,000.00**

Because of so little documentation, there are people who still to this day insist none of the performances ever really happened. It was all some kind of prank, they think. I don't know what to say about that except that those people are in the minority, and even though the idea that it was all a prank does seem kind of interesting, especially because of all the stuff that *Private Viewing* set in motion, which I will talk about soon and below, I really think the performances happened. If they didn't, then my parents have lied straight to my face a *lot*. Which I know they haven't, even though I can't prove it. How do you prove something like that? It isn't possible to prove that to someone.

Very little is known about any of the viewer-participants, except for Jonny "Jonboat" Pellmore-Jason, who is my father, and who, according to himself, Henry, and Ronson Boyle, was the last person to participate in/view one of the performances (in February 2000). Henry and Boyle refuse to name the first eight and they swear to protect their privacy forever, but they admit the following information about them: all of them were men, and all of them had net worths of ten million dollars or more.

Over the last number of years, dozens of people have said to the press that they themselves were one of the other eight viewer-participants, and who knows how many people have said it to their friends at parties and other social gatherings and so on? but Boyle and Henry both refuse to comment on any of those people's claims except for my father's. Most people believe that the other eight viewer-participants were, like my father, longtime, trusted clients of Boyle's who'd bought high-end art from him in the past, and that would make a lot of sense, but there is no evidence for it. I don't think it matters who exactly they were. I don't think it ever did. I think all that matters is they were rich and they were either paying for art by or sex with Fondajane Henry or for both art by and sex with Fondajane Henry at the turn of the millennium when it wasn't legal to pay for any kind of sex yet.

Still, a lot of people would like to know who the other eight viewer-participants were, so I will talk about that a little right here and then be done with it. People have always been interested in that from the beginning. Originally, they were interested for gossip-scandal kinds of reasons (like "I heard half of the participants were married with children!" or "I heard one of the participants was a famous televangelist!"), or conspiracy kinds of reasons (like "I heard three of the eight were congressmen who helped draft the bill that legalized prostitution in 2001!"), but now that *Private Viewing* is considered as important as it is considered, people are more interested to know who was smart enough or privileged enough or just cool enough to become involved in such an important art-historical moment.

Anyway, since there is barely any documentation of *Private Viewing,* my description of it in the <u>Description of the Artwork</u> section below is based on interviews I conducted with Fondajane Henry, Ronson Boyle, and my father, as well as from public statements they've made in the press, things Henry wrote about *Private Viewing* in her memoirs and critical treatises, and things Boyle wrote about it in his memoir (all cited on the Sources Consulted page):

<u>Description of the Artwork</u>

It is possible to think of the performance of *Private Viewing* as beginning way before the viewer-participants ever got into the same room as Fondajane Henry, and I will think of it that way. So, to begin with, Ronson Boyle would approach someone and show them a Polaroid photograph of Fondajane Henry giving a lecture to a class she was teaching at New York University, and explain who she was in case the person didn't know, or had only just heard of her (she was a *little* famous already). He would explain that she was the twenty-three-year-old intersex author of the critical masterwork *Flesh-and-Bone Robots You Think Are Your Friends (FABRYTAYF),* which she got a PhD for writing when she was only twenty-two, and which was not nearly as popular yet as it is today, but was definitely getting a lot of attention in certain academic circles, and was controversial because its main argument that punishing men (or women) for paying for sex was not only bad for women but that allowing women to charge money for sex was *good* for women not just because it was their body and therefore their choice and so it should be their right and people deserved to be able to exercise their rights by definition of what rights are, but also because it was a way women could have real earning power to make up for how they barely had any earning power compared to men which is unjust and keeps women down in a big way because earning power is the main power behind almost every other kind of civilian power in our American society because your earning power can be turned into spending power, and spending power is the main thing that keeps you safe and respected and free (even though it wouldn't be the main thing in a perfect world), so it shouldn't just be that women were safe from being prosecuted from selling sex (which is how it was already when *FABRYTAYF* came out—prostitution was partly decriminalized about a year earlier) but that men (and women) should be safe from being prosecuted for *buying* sex, since that would lead to more men (and women) buying sex, which would transform more men's earning/spending power into more women's earning/spending power, and once that happened it would not be hard for people to get over their superstitions and religious stuff against sex work, just like how most people were almost completely over that same kind of stuff when it came to people being gay, or like how pretty much all people had been completely over that stuff for years when it came to Curios and the things people liked to do to Curios, which they got over inside just a few months of Curios first being sold to consumers—people would get over their nonsense against legalized prostitution because it wouldn't just be for an ideal of justice and human rights, it would also be practical, so getting over it would be the path of least resistance, so everyone would just get used to it.

Then after Boyle showed the Polaroid while explaining who Henry was, he would say that she was doing a new kind of very limited performance that he thought the person he was talking to would be more than happy to pay for, and that the performance would, in Boyle's opinion as a famous gallerist and world-renowned curator of this or that show at this or that museum, be not only an important performance in the history of art but a performance that the person Boyle was inviting to view it would specifically find to be extremely enjoyable. The person would ask what was involved, and Boyle would say he could not describe the whole performance itself because "art is as it does, not as it's described,"[1] but he could (and he did) tell the person

1) that Fondajane Henry, as a central part of the performance, would have sex with the person if the person wanted to, which they would probably want to because Henry was obviously beautiful, plus her anatomy was very special,
2) what the cost of admission to *Private Viewing* was (it ranged from $20,000 to $50,000, as you can see in the "Admission" column of Table 1),
3) that the performance would last anywhere from a few minutes to sixteen hours, and the duration was totally up to the viewer-participant, and
4) Boyle would explain that the invitation was not an exclusive invitation, but was pretty close because *Private Viewing* would be performed for only one person at a time, and just once a month.

According to Boyle, every single person he approached accepted the invitation. It is impossible, for obvious reasons, to corroborate that information, but Boyle was and is definitely famous for his talents as a gallerist and salesperson, and even though hundreds of people have untruthfully bragged that they attended a performance of *Private Viewing,* not even one person has ever said that he turned down an invitation to attend a performance of *Private Viewing* (at least not that I could find) because that is how ridiculous it would be to even imagine that if Boyle chose to approach you with an invitation to experience near-exclusive art you would not take him up on that invitation.

Each of the nine performances took place in a different luxury hotel suite in Manhattan, usually on a weeknight—it depended on the viewer/participant's schedule. Boyle and Henry would arrive at the hotel an hour before each performance. Henry would put on makeup and lingerie and etcetera, and get herself acquainted with the suite while Boyle would arrange a nice spread of food and liquor and Curios and formulae and condoms, then return to the bar in the lobby to wait for the viewer-participant to show up. When the v-p

1. Boyle, *Procurer.*

showed up, Boyle would give him the key to the suite and wait in the lobby for the performance to end, on call to provide any "extras" the v-p might want.

The shortest performance lasted an hour. The next-shortest one lasted three hours. The rest of them lasted between fifteen and sixteen hours, til checkout time the following day.

When the viewer-participant entered the bedroom of the suite, Henry would start to deliver her monologue (see Appendix). The monologue was written so that it wouldn't seem like it had been written. It was written so it seemed like Henry was spontaneously talking to the viewer-participant about herself. To make the spontaneity seem real, she used what is called "an elliptical style"[2] which means that she would go off on tangents a lot but always come back around to what she was originally saying. I happen to know from lots of firsthand experience that Henry pretty much always does this elliptical style thing when she is talking to people, and also when she is teaching class, but what is interesting to me is that she does not really do it in her books at all. She is a very organized writer, usually. Her arguments move in very straight lines. (That is one of the reasons she is such a respected writer and thinker, I believe.) Anyway, she told me that the monologue was very easy for her to write and remember because she basically just wrote it the way she would tell it if she was telling it to someone she liked talking to, plus everything she said in the monologue was actually true, so she didn't have to be more clever than usual.

In seven of the performances she finished the monologue before any kind of sex was had. In the other two performances, some sex was had right at the beginning, and then she finished the monologue, and some more sex was had. All the viewer-participants asked questions while she gave her monologue, some of them told stories of their own, and she would listen to their stories and answer their questions, but she would always make sure to get back to the monologue right at the part where she left off before she got interrupted.

I'm not going to get into all the different kinds of sex that was had because doing that would make me uncomfortable. I don't mean it makes me uncomfortable that Henry had sex with people as part of the performance, but just that the picturing of her having sex, for me, is not comfortable because she is my stepmom. It is easy for me to know that she had lots of different kinds of sex without picturing it, and it is even easy for me to read about the different kinds of sex she had without picturing it. I don't know how, but when I read the words, I don't make the pictures in my head. What I worry about is that if I start *to describe* the sex then it might not be so easy not to picture it, and also

2. Henry, *Lamborgina C(unt)ock*, p. 179.

maybe it would be a little creepy for you to read a stepson's description of his stepmom having sex, and I don't want this paper to dishonor the important artwork that Henry did by distracting you into thinking about me as a person writing about his stepmom having sex. I want the paper to make you think about the artwork itself, and also about how I think of it as artwork. Plus you can read a lot of descriptions of the sex in *Lamborgina C(unt)ock* and, if you know French, also in the interview she did with the author Michel Houellebecq for the magazine *Les Inrockuptibles,* which are both cited on the "Sources Consulted" page.

Three of the viewer-participants wanted extras. One of them wanted a bottle of Hennessy Richard cognac to drink with Henry and then take home; one of them wanted to watch Henry "overload on a three-year-old-or-older BullyKing-PerFormulized purple hobunk while it abused two nascent Curios with a matchstick, but before it spilled blood"[3]; and one of them wanted "to eat and watch [Henry] eat some kind of $100 house-special burger from the hotel's restaurant that was made of dry-aged Kobe beef, and topped with shaved truffles, pule, and, I don't know, pulverized centaur hoof or something like that."[4] When requests for these extras were made by the viewer-participants, Henry called down to the lobby for Boyle, and he would relay the requests to the maître d', who would charge them to the suite, have them delivered to Boyle in the bar/lobby, and then Boyle himself would bring them up to the room. The costs of these extras are recorded in the "Extras" column in Table 1, and all of them were recouped from the viewer-participants after the performance.

Impact

I was only one to three years old during the important period of art and non-art history that was caused by *Private Viewing,* so even though I was (barely) standing next to the main hero of it for a lot of the time, I don't actually remember any of it. That is probably for the better, in terms of me having a good childhood that I remember as being happy and full of love, but maybe it is for the worse in terms of writing this paper, because maybe knowing who I am would cause a reader to hope I'll give them a special insider's perspective on what it was like to be there, next to the hero, and I just

3. Fondajane Henry and Michel Houellebecq, "Ad victis spolia (de la révolution sexuelle): Conversation entre Michel Houellebecq et Fondajane Henry."
4. Ibid.

want to take a moment here, at the beginning of this section on the impact of *Private Viewing,* to warn them to stop hoping for that if they are hoping for that, because if they don't stop, then they will be disappointed.

(I realize I probably should have made that warning/disclaimer at the beginning of the paper, but the paper is already late and I don't have time to go back and rework the whole introduction. I apologize for that to any future readers of this paper, and also to you, Mr. Hickey, who have been such a great mentor for me during this January Short Term. Also, Mr. Hickey, I apologize if my going over the page limit turns out to be really annoying, and once again I am sorry the paper is so late. We are moving to a suburb of Chicago in a couple months, where I will attend a public high school in order to better understand how more average kinds of Americans are so that I can become a more well-rounded and effective artist and thinker, and the public high school there doesn't do January Short Terms or independent studies, and they definitely don't have visiting thinkers and artists of your caliber, and they might not even have any kinds of visiting mentors/faculty, so I really wanted to make my last JST count by writing a paper of the highest quality that I could and that I believed in and that I would hopefully not be ashamed to have people read as my apprentice work or juvenilia one day if and when I become known for artmaking and people get interested in my intellectual history and my early development as an artist, and the paper is already almost the length we agreed on, and I haven't even gotten into the main part of it yet. I will stop delaying getting to the main part in just one more moment, but before I do that I just want to say thank you for mentoring me through this process of understanding and discovery. I feel a million times more educated than I did a month ago, and closer to my parents than ever, and I will always cherish these past few weeks and the conversations we had during them as important and productive, and I just hope it will be okay if I write you a letter once in a while to stay in touch. Thank you.)

So first of all, the general public hadn't even heard of *Private Viewing* til about two months after the last performance. That was when my father came back from his fifth mission to outer space, and officially separated from my birth mother to be in a permanent couple with Fondajane Henry, who he had gone on secret dates with since he met her at the February 2000 performance of *Private Viewing* where they pretty much instantly fell in love with each other. Even after my father left my birth mother for Henry, though, it would take a few months before anyone (except for Boyle, Henry, and the v-p's) really knew what *Private Viewing* was—all anyone knew was that Jonny "Jonboat" Pellmore-Jason had left his wife for Fondajane Henry, who most people hadn't heard of before, but who all the newspapers explained was a genius philosopher/critical theorist who taught at New York University and had special genitalia and had done an art performance of some kind called *Private Viewing*, which my father had gone to, and which was how they met.

And then the other thing everyone knew in those first couple months after my father left my birth mom (I keep saying "left" but I just mean that he was the one who ended the marriage: it was my birth mom who actually moved out of our home) was what Henry looked like. There were so many pictures published of her that I'm not even going to bother to cite sources because you can basically go to the microfiches from that period (late April 2000 to late June 2000) and find pictures of her in at least one American newspaper from almost any day, many European ones, and on pretty much all the covers of all the weekly supermarket gossip tabloids. People knew what she looked like, and they loved to look at her, both women and men, and when her *20/20* interview with Barbara Walters aired (on May 19, 2000) it was the third-most-watched television interview of all time (the first was Michael Jackson, interviewed by Oprah Winfrey in 1993; the second was Henry's second interview with Barbara Walters in 2001).[5] That was the interview where Barbara Walters asked her, "What do you say to people who don't know what to make of your gender?" and Henry responded:

> Well, some women have small waists, some women have large breasts, some women have high, round, a**es, and, some women—though not very many, relatively speaking—some women even have penises, Barbara. I am a woman who happens to have all of those things. That's what I *suppose* I'd say, if it ever came up. But, you know, I've met a lot of people, in a lot of different contexts, especially in the last few weeks, and none of them have ever seemed to need convincing that I was a woman. I've always been "treated like a woman." No, all I've ever needed to convince anyone of—less often than some women, more often than others—was that, despite being a woman, I was also a human being.[6]

After the interview, most people really started loving Henry—not just the way she looked, which they were crazy about already, but the person she was. Kind of the person she was. They loved the person they thought she was—the person they fantasized her to be. A kind of superwoman: not only physically beautiful and smarter than anyone, but also really virtuous and golden-hearted and all-American because it's pretty much impossible for

5. 2012 *Guinness World Records*.
6. *Bartlett's Familiar Quotations*.

people—or maybe just Americans—to imagine that they can adore someone who isn't virtuous and golden-hearted, since that would mean that maybe they aren't themselves as virtuous and golden-hearted as they want to believe. It's black-and-white thinking. And I want to say that my truth through my eyes is that she is virtuous and golden-hearted, and that she is one of the best people I've ever met, but, according to the standards of most people at the turn of the millennium, she wasn't, even though they didn't know it—she wasn't because of all their superstitious and religious stuff about sex.

No one is ever universally loved, so, obviously, she had her detractors, too. There were people who said she wasn't a woman, because she had a penis, and that she was mentally ill to think of herself as a woman. But surprisingly or not at all surprisingly, there were very, very few of these people—or, at least, there were very few of them in the media. Why so few? Probably because if Henry wasn't a woman that might mean that she was a man, or kind of a man, and so then that all the men who found her attractive were gay, or kind of gay, and even though society had become pretty tolerant and even welcoming of gayness by then, most people still didn't want to be gay, and pretty much all men who saw her found her attractive. And anyway, Henry also had a vagina, and a very traditionally attractive female shape, so it didn't make sense to insist that her penis made her a not-a-woman because it was just as easy, and probably easier to insist that her vagina and shape made her a woman. Plus she *said* she was a woman. She said she'd always been "treated like a woman." Why argue with her? Who did it help? Wasn't it pretty disrespectful and maybe even mean?

So her detractors mostly got ignored, and most people, like I said, ended up just thinking of her as a superwoman, and most people who didn't end up thinking of her as a superwoman thought of her as a super "post-gender human" or something, and lots of transgender people, who til then were mostly judged as mentally ill dangers to children, started to have some hope about being more accepted by society, which I will get back to how all of that ended up working out in a few more paragraphs.

In the meantime, after the Henry-Walters interview, the press even let up on my father a little because rumors started getting spread about my birth mom being mentally ill and emotionally abusive (which I don't know if any of that's true; my father says it isn't, and that the reason the rumor got started was because she felt humiliated by the press, especially the paparazzi, and so she'd been pretty volatile toward them and they treated her meanly as a result, but I think maybe my father just didn't realize that she was mentally ill and emotionally abusive because he was a good husband and a very loyal person, even though he left her, and so he couldn't imagine there was anything wrong with her), and what kind of person with a mean, alcoholic spouse wouldn't leave that spouse for Henry if Henry would have them? people thought. To some, especially people in the gender- and sexual-minority communities, he even became a bit of a hero. He loved someone who was different, someone who because he loved her he was being made to suffer by the press, someone he wasn't "supposed to" love, and he wasn't hiding from that love, he was making it public, and that was empowering to some people.

Then, just a few weeks after the interview, and over the span of just five days, Ronson Boyle anonymously published "Upscale Pimpology" (which would become the first chapter of his memoir, *Procurer: My Life as a Gallerist*) in the July 2000 issue of *ArtForum,* and Henry published an op-ed in the Sunday edition of the *New York Times* (June 4, 2000) called "Why We Need Johns" (which would become part of the afterword to the second edition of *FABRYTAYF*), and my birth mother died in a car accident. Boyle's essay and Henry's editorial both honestly described what the performances of *Private Viewing* consisted of, and my birth mother's death was the result of her driving drunk into a tree and was almost definitely a suicide.

Opinions shifted instantly. My father was now understood by the general American public to be a guy who drove his wife to suicide after leaving her for someone he paid for sex—a prostitute—and he was hated way more than he'd been even after he first left my birth mom. It was that simple (sort of).

When it came to Henry and Boyle, the reaction was more complicated. In the art world, the idea of sex as a marketable artform became the subject of a lot of art critics and their essays, and, over the next couple months, and way more mainstreamly than that, seventeen different gallerists were accused in the press of arranging *Private Viewing*–style performances by different artists/prostitutes for their clients. None of the gallerists would admit they had done so, and only a couple of the artists/prostitutes would—both of them, Cindy Todd-Waintree and Veronica Dann, openly said that they hoped that by admitting it, they would get more clients and higher rates—but it was widely accepted that it was happening.[7]

It was also awkward and confusing for people to think about because there were calls in the press to prosecute the anonymous author of "Upscale Pimpology" and the accused gallerists for being pimps—which was even more punishable by law than paying for sex—but there were no calls for prosecuting the artists/prostitutes because it wasn't illegal for them to solicit sex. In the end, no one ended up getting prosecuted, though, mostly because the people that the public seemed to want to see get prosecuted the most

7. Camille Paglia, "Dominate and Protect."

were the clients/viewer-participants, and no one could even figure out who they were, except for my dad, who insisted that all he had done was pay to go to a hotel room to see a monologue performed, and then fallen in love with the performer, who he was now in a relationship with, which no one could figure out any way to prove wasn't the truth, and, on top of that, no one could even prove who the author of "Upscale Pimpology" was (there were rumors, but *ArtForum*'s editors refused to say) or catch any of the accused gallerists pimping.

It was all pretty new and very complicated. And for Henry, herself, it was even more complicated. Everyone had an opinion about her, and no two opinions seemed to match. The opinions were made up of answers of different intensities to different combinations of any or all of the following questions: Was Henry a prostitute? a radical? an artist? all three? If she was an artist, were all prostitutes artists, and if all prostitutes were artists, was that good or bad? Had she wrecked a home (the one I lived in) or salvaged a wrecked home or neither? Since everyone supposedly knew what *FABRYTAYF* was about (sex work) and since *FABRYTAYF* included a couple brief descriptions of her own personal experiences as a sex worker while she was a student, should people feel stupid or tricked or neither for being surprised that *Private Viewing* included/was/resembled sex work? Should people feel embarrassed because so few of them had read *FABRYTAYF* even though so many of them had bought it? Did the ones who tried to read it fail to understand it and so put it down because they were unintelligent, or because it was written for graduate students and professors? Was Henry a victim of my father because he paid her for sex once? If she was a victim of my father, did that mean she was weak? If she wasn't a victim, did that mean she was a slut? A gold digger? What did people *want* to believe? And so on.

While all these opinions were getting formed and re-formed and argued about, Henry pretty much disappeared. She moved in with us, sold her apartment, and took a sabbatical. During the sabbatical she worked on two books. One of them was her second academic book, *Lamborgina C(unt)ock,* and the other one was her first memoir, *My Procedures*. The other thing she did during that time was have some surgeries done in Switzerland and Germany (one of my first memories, which is my only memory of that time, and maybe is fake—maybe it's just something I heard about and only think I remember—was of eating an ice cream cone with my dad outside the clinic in Berlin, while Henry was being operated on—I think it was probably my first ice cream cone—which was definitely a positive memory, even though my dad seems nervous in it). The surgeons in Switzerland did cosmetic work on Henry's penis, trimming it down into the shape of a large clitoris, but doing it so that it could still erect and be ejaculated out of, and the surgeons in Berlin modified the inside of her vagina by adding "variable contours" and a kind of vibrating motor to it that Henry, by using her Kegel muscles, could turn on and off whenever she wanted to.

This unpublic period lasted til the middle of 2001, when *Lamborgina C(unt)ock* was published. It was mostly a very misunderstood book, and Henry considered it a failure[8] because of that, but I disagree with her. Even though it's true I don't really get all of it—like *FABRYTAYF,* it's written for people who have read a lot of philosophy and critical theory, which I'm not very well-read in at all—I don't think it was a failure. I think it was just that people got caught up in this one tiny part of it, and that part distracted them. The book is mainly about what *FABRYTAYF* was about: how total sexual freedom, especially the freedom of men to buy sex, would mean more earning/spending power for women, which would mean more power for women in general and so greater equality for all and therefore a better society. The first part of the book talks about prostitution and sex in terms of art the way that *FABRYTAYF* talked about prostitution and sex in terms of Curios and the Cute Revolutions. The second part talks about "sexual/gender reassignment" procedures and therapies (not Henry's personal ones, but in general) in terms of dosing Curios with formulae/PerFormulae and how both represent new forms of old desires, and how new forms of old desires scare some people and change them, and so also change society, sometimes for the better, and sometimes for the worse, and how you can't ever tell whether it will be for the better or for the worse until many years have passed, and even then only maybe can you tell, and so that is why it is important to never make judgments on the goodness or badness of people's new or strange desires out of fear, especially not out of fear of slippery slopes, because judgments of strange or new desires should only be based on who is or isn't hurt or helped by the strange or new desires being had and fulfilled since that is what everyone can agree a good human would judge things based on.

Those first two parts of the book take up 150 pages combined, and then the third part takes up another 150 pages by itself, and that third part is about Henry's personal experience of *Private Viewing* as a performer, and about how much less stressful and much more profitable and empowering it was for her than any other sex work she did when she was younger because she knew it was safe and that she was doing it because she wanted to and she felt she was totally in control. And she said that the same was true in comparison to being a graduate student and then a professor: she was much more empowered by

8. She's said this a few times in front of me throughout my life, and said it again when I interviewed her for this paper.

being the performer of *Private Viewing* than she had ever been as a student at Berkeley or Columbia or an employee at NYU.

I think it's a very good book, and that it wasn't a failure at all, even though, like I said, I don't fully understand it, but most people ignored everything I just described, anyway. Most people focused on one tiny part: a couple paragraphs in it from Henry's *Private Viewing* monologue (see Appendix) that she included in the third section of the book, and where she says that none of the transgender people she met at college were very attractive, physically, and that their physical unattractiveness or the discomfort they felt about it made them hard for her to relate to, and that her physical beauty or the pleasure she got from it made her hard for them to relate to.

This tiny part of the book didn't contain many more words than it took me to just describe it, but it was the one part that got paid attention to.

And that tiny part was the original cause of a big split that started happening in the gender/sexual-minority community where people started to identify themselves as either anti-beauty/pro–trans beauty or pro-beauty/pro–cis beauty, which basically meant anti-Henry or pro-Henry, respectively, and that split still exists today, and it is kind of interesting, but getting too far into it would be sideways to this paper at this point, so I won't get into it too much.

So when I said, "Most people focused on one tiny part" of *Lamborgina C(unt)ock*, what I meant was "Most people *who read Lamborgina C(unt)ock* focused on one tiny part of it." Most people did not really read *Lamborgina C(unt)ock*, or even buy it.

Once it was published, though, Henry was again in the public spotlight, and most of the public was glad about that because it meant more chances to look at her. At that point, she was still on sabbatical, finishing up final revisions on *My Procedures*, and she began to advocate more actively for human rights, especially for the full legalization of prostitution, which, during her time out of the spotlight, had started to become a very different issue for people than it was before. First of all, a lot of people had started to come around to the idea that prostitution should be legalized, and a lot more people who already thought it should be legalized all along were being more open about thinking that. It's impossible to know for sure why people were coming around to the idea and being more open, but it was probably just because they got used to thinking about it because of all the media attention that had surrounded Henry and the revelation of what *Private Viewing* actually had been a few months before, and that made it (prostitution) less taboo to think about and talk about than it had been before, the same way likable famous gay people and gay characters on TV kept making gayness less taboo to think about and talk about. But the thing that really made it an issue for people was a backlash thing. Or a backlash-against-a-backlash thing, depending how you looked at it.

Almost every week since Henry had disappeared, gallerists like Boyle and artists like Henry continued to be called out in the press for selling sex. Sometimes the accusations were true, and sometimes they weren't, but the cops never got anyone convicted—they couldn't get it done. The artists/prostitutes and the gallerists/pimps wouldn't reveal who the johns/viewer-participants were, and the gallerists/pimps, if they even got questioned, either straight-up denied they pimped, or sometimes very mischievously said they were only pretending to pimp as part of a group-conceptual art performance *about* prostitution. The cops investigated, but could never produce evidence against them. Basically, the only way for a cop to possibly nail anyone involved would be to get approached by one of the gallerists/pimps and offered sex with an artist/prostitute for money, and that was never going to happen because the gallerists/pimps were just very smart and careful about who they approached (very wealthy people they'd sold art to in the past).

So what ended up happening was that in major US cities, law enforcement, responding to the outcries of religious/superstitious people who hated prostitution and women and freedom and equality, started very publicly busting the johns and pimps of more traditional prostitutes—usually the kind that worked out in the open, on the streets. That appeased some of the religious/superstitious people for a little while, but then, with all these johns and pimps of more traditional prostitutes getting punished while all the gallerists/pimps and viewer-participants/johns kept on getting away with pimping/buying sex, buying sex began to seem like this privilege that only certain really rich guys had a special right to, and having special rights was an extremely unAmerican thing, maybe the single most unAmerican thing, even to a lot of religious/superstitious people.[9] So fully legalizing prostitution became a class issue, or an economic issue (I'm still not sure I understand the difference completely, so . . .)—it became a thing where most Americans felt like they didn't have equal protection under the law because they didn't have as much money as some other Americans and/or didn't go to the same schools or tennis or golf clubs as other Americans.

That got a lot of people behind the cause of fully legalizing prostitution, and Henry, as I was saying, became a more active advocate for the issue. She did fundraising events for congressional candidates, radio interviews, op-eds, and was basically the most famous and outspoken advocate for the issue, except for my father, who didn't say a lot publicly unless money is speech

9. Camille Paglia, "Dominate and Protect."

(some people say it is), but donated a lot of money to congresspeople who supported legalization, and took a lot of private meetings with important people and so on.

Henry's memoir, *My Procedures,* was published in July 2001, and became an instant bestseller. It still is, today. The memoir is half about being a younger person, and the sexual relationships she had in her life—how she "proceeded" through them until falling in love with my father—and half about the surgical procedures she had done in Switzerland and Germany during her sabbatical described above. It was such a big deal that three editions were put out. The standard one had black-and-white nude photos of Henry before and after her surgeries, the "conservative" or "high school" edition had no photos, and the special deluxe edition, which sold the most, had photos in full color on glossy paper.

A few days before the book came out, Henry did her second *20/20* interview with Barbara Walters, the second-most-watched television interview of all time.[10] Most of the interview was about Henry's sex-work history, the push for legalization, and some teasing-for-more-book-sales-type stuff about Henry's surgical procedures. In the segment before the last commercial break, Walters asked Henry what had led to her decision to undergo the surgeries, and Henry explained that she had gotten the motor-insertion/contouring surgery because she'd wanted it for a while for what she thought were pretty obvious reasons: to enhance her and her partners' sexual pleasure. She'd wanted the motor-insertion/contouring, she said, ever since she'd read about it a few years earlier in a medical journal while researching *FABRYTAYF,* and the only reason she'd waited so long to get it was that it was wildly expensive, and she hadn't been able to afford it til after she'd met my father, who paid for it. "And it was worth every penny," she said. "I can only hope the costs go down sooner rather than later so that more people will have the chance to experience it themselves."

"And what about your penis?" asked Barbara Walters.

"Well," Henry said, "I'd always loved having it. Ejaculating always brought me a lot of pleasure, but Jonboat, though he was fine with my penis—it brought him pleasure, too—he just wasn't so crazy about how it looked, and I didn't really care how it looked either way. I cared how it *felt*. So we found a team in Germany to reconstruct it so that it could look the way Jonboat wanted and continue to feel to me the way I wanted."

"I find it very strange," said Walters, "that Jonboat, who was in a relationship with you—a relationship that, despite all the controversy surrounding how it

10. *2012 Guinness World Records.*

started, by all means seems loving and healthy—I find it strange that Jonboat wouldn't want you just the way you were. Don't you find that strange?"

"He did want me the way I was," Henry said. "He sacrificed his reputation to be with me. He *loved* me the way I was. *Loves* me the way I am. And I him. Like I said, though, he would have enjoyed my genitals even more than he already did if my penis were smaller. He didn't *mind* that I had a penis, and he would never have wanted me to be rid of it at the cost of any sexual pleasure to either of us, but he'd have liked it to look different, to be a lot smaller. And that turned out to be possible, so we made it happen."

The interview broke, for the last time, for a commercial, and when *20/20* returned, Walters asked Henry about her plans for the future, and Henry announced her engagement to my father. Walters asked her where and when the wedding would take place, and Henry said that it would happen in Amsterdam in October. Walters asked if Amsterdam was a special place for her and my father, and Henry said, "Not for us, personally. But it is a special place. A very special place, Barbara. It's the capital of the only Western country in which gay marriage is legal."

"But you're not suggesting that the United States considers you a gay couple," Barbara Walters said.

"No," Henry said. "I don't think so, at least. We haven't inquired. In any case, we aren't a gay couple. And furthermore, many of our favorite people live right here in New York, so it would be a lot easier for us—and them—if we held our wedding here, but it just doesn't seem right, let alone very romantic, to legally bind ourselves to one another under the authority of a homophobic legal system when another option is so readily available to us."

I think it would be right to say that this second *20/20* interview balkanized the different groups of people in America who had strong beliefs about prostitution, Henry, elective surgery, women's rights, beauty, gender, economic inequality, the patriarchy, my father, and now also gay marriage, but maybe what I mean is that it atomized those groups. Anyway, they splintered, held rallies, and wrote articles. Some people thought marriage was good, but gay marriage was bad. Some people thought marriage was oppressive and legalizing gay marriage would mess up gay culture. Some people who feared or hated or were annoyed by gay culture thought gay marriage would be good because it would tone gay culture down and make it more like straight culture. Some people thought it was romantic of Henry to undergo surgery to please my father, other people thought it meant she was a victim of my father. Some of the ones who thought she was a victim said that her victimhood proved that prostitution screwed women up more than it helped them. Some of the ones who thought it was romantic said it proved that prostitution didn't screw anything up and that prostitutes could go on to live more traditional lives. Some thought it didn't matter how well or badly prostitution left prostitutes because prostitution undermined families. Some people said it didn't matter because gay marriage was looking like it would become legal sooner or later and that would undermine families more than prostitution ever could anyway. Some people said prostitution could save marriages, or lead to more of them since if it was legal and became normal like Henry kept saying it would in her books, then people could do it while they were married and they wouldn't end marriages just because they wanted to have sex with people they weren't married to, plus people would get raped and hate and kill themselves less because more money would be going around and fewer people would feel crazed by sexual loneliness and economic poverty. Some people said Henry was bad for transgender people because she decided to be a woman instead of being a transgender woman. Some people said that Henry was good for transgender people because she became the gender she had always been. Some people said that didn't make sense, and other people said those people didn't understand oppression. Some people said Henry was good for women because she was an empowered woman. Some people said Henry was bad for men because she was an empowered woman. Some people said Henry was bad for women because she seemed like an empowered woman but she wasn't even a woman and her empowerment was the empowerment of being rich and engaged to my father, anyway. Everyone continued to agree that Henry was a very, very physically beautiful person. Some people (the anti-beauty/trans-beauty people I mentioned earlier) said that the problem that was underneath everything was the worship of conventional physical beauty, and that if society could just start treating conventionally plain or ugly people as if they were as physically attractive as conventionally beautiful people, no one would ever have a problem with anyone, everyone would be happy with themselves, and everyone would be happy to let everyone else be happy because everyone would be treating everyone else well. Everyone agreed that was probably true in principle, but most people thought it could never happen, and many of them pointed out that the anti-beauty people were, almost across the board, conventionally ugly/weird-looking and that their ugliness/weirdness seemed willful, even prideful a lot of the time, and so it was hard to imagine they could ever be happy, and the anti-beauty people said that sentiment demonstrated their point exactly. And so on.

And then it was September 13, 2001, and our country was attacked, and a few days later, the man who took credit for the attacks made a recording for television where he called the United States "a Zionist haven for infidels, whores, and homosexuals," and him saying that re-Yugoslavia-ized/re-molecule-ized most of the balkanized/atomized groups I mentioned above into one big and very inclusive "patriotic" group, and Congress legalized gay marriage and prostitution the same week it authorized troops be sent to Yemen for Operation Enduring Freedom.

My parents held their wedding in Central Park, NYC, on January 1, 2002, at 12:00 a.m., which was the exact moment that the legalization of gay marriage and prostitution came into effect.

It is a possibility that without the attack on America, gay marriage and prostitution would have eventually gotten legalized, but it is for sure a certainty that without Fondajane Henry's *Private Viewing,* they probably would not have ever been legalized. That is why I am so confident in concluding that my thesis is correct: *Private Viewing* was the last important work of art of the twentieth century.

Sources Consulted

Bartlett, John & Kaplan, Justin (eds.). *Bartlett's Familiar Quotations, 17th Edition* (New York: Little, Brown, 2002), p. 721.

Boyle, Ronson. *Procurer: My Life as a Gallerist* (New York: Simon & Schuster, 2002).

Glenday, Craig (ed.). *2012 Guinness World Records* (New York: Bantam, 2012), p. 317.

Henry, Fondajane. *Flesh-and-Bone Robots You Think Are Your Friends* (New York: Semiotext(e), 1998).

___. *Lamborgina C(unt)ock* (New York: Random House, 2001).

___. *My Procedures* (New York: Random House, 2001).

___. *My Process* (New York: Random House, 2009).

Henry, Fondajane & Houellebecq, Michel. "Ad victis spolia (de la révolution sexuelle): Conversation entre Michel Houellebecq et Fondajane Henry." ["To the Losers Go the Spoils of the Sexual Revolution: Michel Houellebecq in conversation with Fondajane Henry."] *Les Inrockuptibles* (Paris, France), August 22–29, 2001, 21–33.

Paglia, Camille. "Dominate and Protect." *Harper's*, November 2000, 32–39.

Pellmore-Jason, Jr., Jonny. Hundreds of exchanges and conversations that I, Jonny Pellmore-Jason, Jr., have had with Fondajane Henry and Jonny Pellmore-Jason from around the time I learned to speak full sentences (summer, 2000) til just a couple hours ago (February 2013), and a few that I've had with Ronson Boyle in the past few weeks (January 2013).

Wolfe, Tom. "The Man Behind the Woman Behind the Man Behind the Woman: A Profile of Jonboat and Fondajane on the Eve of Their Fifth Wedding Anniversary." *Vanity Fair*, December 2006, 27–47.

Appendix

"The Story of a New Name"
(Monologue from *Private Viewing* by Fondajane Henry)

excerpted from *Lamborgina C(unt)ock* by Fondajane Henry
(used by permission of Fondajane Henry)

To begin with, I want you to be as comfortable as possible. *Private Viewing* can last anywhere from just a few minutes to sixteen hours. It ends when you leave the suite, or at noon tomorrow—whichever comes first. Feel free to stand, sit, or lie anywhere you like, in any state of dress or undress that you'd like. If you'd rather we move to another part of the suite, just say so, and we'll go there. There's a full bar in the living room, a refrigerator full of beer in the kitchen, and a nice variety of finger foods on the dining room table, which you probably noticed when you arrived. In that PillowNest on the night table, there are half a dozen Curios, none of them younger than two years old. In the night table's top drawer, you'll find thirty varieties of formulae, liquid and pellet. Everything I just mentioned is included in the cost of the performance. If you'd like more or other foods, drinks, Curios, or varieties of formulae, I'll be happy to ask Ronson to have someone bring them to us from anywhere in the city, but you'll have to pay for that separately.

What Ronson won't do is get you any illegal drugs. He's a gallerist—not a criminal. If you're on illegal drugs right now, that's fine with me, but please keep it to yourself. If you've brought illegal drugs and plan on using them here, please do so discreetly. If I know about them, the performance will have to stop.

Through that door over there is a bathroom. If you have to use it at any point, for any reason, please go ahead and do so. I'll wait. Also, you can smoke cigarettes here if you want—I'm what my mother used to call a "social smoker," and I don't mind. In fact, if you light one up, odds are I'll ask to bum one.

Now, while you're getting comfortable, I'm going to tell you about how I came to be me. Feel free, at any point, to interrupt. You can tell me about yourself—unless it has to do with your being on illegal drugs—and I'll listen, openly and happily, until you're through. You can ask me anything you want about myself, and I'll tell you honestly. Also you can ask me to do anything you want with your or my body inside this suite—anything except for illegal drugs—and I'll probably say yes. I'm not easy to offend, so even if I say no to something you request, it's highly unlikely that I'll hold your having asked against you. If you want to just start touching me sexually, that's fine too. I would, however, advise that you wait a little while and hear my story. I really think intimacy will improve the quality of any orgasms we have together, and thus the overall quality of the performance. Some people like to come early and quickly before settling in, though—I know. So it's up to you. Either way, I'll gladly cause you to have at least one of the best orgasms of your life, if not two or three or four—however many you can manage before the end of the performance. You wouldn't have been offered admission if that weren't something I wanted.

I was born in 1976, in Houston, Texas, with what the doctors called "ambiguous genitalia." Probably for that reason, I was immediately given up for adoption. I'll never know for sure, I guess, because I don't know who my birth parents are. But the couple who adopted me, David and Christine Henry, of Austin, Texas, were older—in their early fifties. Theirs was the second marriage for each of them, and each, in their previous marriage, had lost a daughter. David's daughter had died of Gaucher disease—she'd been three years old. Christine's daughter had died of leukemia—she'd been seven years old. The fact that both of them had lost daughters in their previous marriages was not as strange as it might sound at first. They'd met one another in a support group for divorced parents who'd lost children to childhood terminal illness. What *was* a little strange, was that both of their daughters had been named Dolores.

My parents had to make some decisions when they adopted me. Their first decision was to gender me female. They might have—as you'll see for yourself, soon enough—gone either way, but they'd both wanted a daughter. Not hard to understand, I don't think. The holes in their hearts were little-girl-shaped holes.

The second decision they had to make was medical. They could have elected to subject me to a series of "gender-corrective" measures—surgeries and, later, hormones—but, even though the doctors strongly suggested they do that, my parents, having spent so much time watching children suffer in hospitals, were firmly of the belief that any sort of medical rigmarole doctors deemed "elective" for anyone, and especially for children, should *never* be elected.

Lastly, they had to decide on a name for me. The name they decided on, of course, was Dolores.

I never asked them the obvious question. We were always very close—they were loving, generous, supportive parents—but they were older, remember, they were of the "greatest generation," they could have easily been my grandparents, and topics surrounding sex seemed to make them uncomfortable. Perhaps less uncomfortable than I thought, true—perhaps they were waiting for me to start the conversation with them, perhaps they had very deliberately determined to pretend I was normal until such a time as *I* broached the topic of my unusualness with them. I guess . . .

Once, in the shower with my mother—I was four, maybe five years old—I asked her why *mine* was different from *hers,* and she told me that everyone was different, some more different than others, and that no one really knew why people were different, and that it didn't matter, especially *down there,* because the only people who should ever, she said, be allowed to know what we looked like *down there* were people to whom it wouldn't make a difference, people we knew to love us already, who wouldn't be able to help but find everything about us, including whatever we had down there, *beautiful.*

Quaint answer, right?

But it was delivered to me with unflinching sincerity—at least that's how I remember it—and I accepted it without any hesitation. Why would I hesitate? It came from the person I loved most in the world, and hearing it made me feel safe. I *wanted* to believe it. I wanted to believe that love conquered all. If it were true, then the world was good. So, for a while, I did—I believed it.

When I got a little older, and boys and girls—and girls and girls, and boys and boys—started judging each other's bodies the way kids will, I ceased to believe that love conquered all, and I remember that it didn't actually bother me so much. It didn't bother me because my body was regularly adjudged to be lovely. I was always considered an attractive girl, by children and adults alike. But I do remember thinking, "Don't talk to Mom and Dad about this. It will worry them. It will make them sad. This isn't how the world is supposed to be. The world is different than they think it is. The world must have changed while they weren't looking." And so I didn't. Talk to them about it. I *never* did. I really felt very protective of them and, even if it kept us from knowing one another better, I admire myself for it to this very day. I admire that little girl's restraint. Most days, I do.

So perhaps, in the end, it was only me who'd been uncomfortable. Not with sex, or with my body, but with *talking to them* about either. Perhaps, I'm saying, I'd projected that discomfort onto them. In any case, between myself and my parents, there was always—except for that one time in the shower—total silence surrounding the topic of sex, gender, genitalia, etcetera. A total silence I was afraid to break—one that I was afraid would break *them,* were I to break it.

I did come close just once, however. Just before going off to college at Berkeley. I was only fifteen, which, I guess that's its own separate story, but for now let's just say I was one of those probably-annoying polymathic wunderkinds who spoke four languages and read in nine. But as I was saying, I was only fifteen, and my parents were, understandably, hesitant to let me go somewhere so far away from home at so young an age. They were *hesitant,* rather, to allow me to enroll in college at all, and they were flat-out *refusing* to send me to Berkeley. They were insistent that if I were to enroll anywhere, it would be at UT Austin, so I could continue to live at the house with them. I wanted to go to Berkeley so badly, though. Berkeley *or* Stanford, but especially Berkeley—I wanted to begin my adventures out in the world, on my own, and I had romantic ideas about northern California, especially San Francisco, and . . . Well, you know how teenagers can get when they fixate on something.

So there arose a moment in one of our arguments when it occurred to me that I could say to my parents that they had no idea what was best for me, that all my life I'd been ashamed of what I was, afraid of what I was, and that the one thing I'd ever really needed was for them to talk to me about what I was, to let me know that they loved me despite what I was, and that they'd failed to do so time and time again. None of which was true. Yet I was about to say it anyway. I was right on the verge. And I was *sure* it would win me the argument, that with just a few declarations, I could scandalize and emotionally blackmail my poor parents into saying yes to Berkeley.

Looking back on it, I'm not sure that would have worked—but I was sure at the time. Luckily for me, though, I didn't follow through. I didn't make those false declarations. I think I would have hated myself for years if I had. Luckily, my mom—who was, by that point, more a witness to the argument than a participant—my mom had unsleeved her cure, Jamey, and it was standing on the kitchen-table placemat in front of her, making cute faces and kind of hula-dancing for her, trying to cheer her up and so on, and . . . Do you remember those "I've Got the Cure?" public service announcements from a few years ago? the ones from the Parents Against Violence In Our Schools Initiative? Well, this could've almost been the plot of one of them—I could've been a spokesperson. Really. Because I thought, "Either I overload on my mother's cure, or I will lose control of my temper and make these declarations that will hurt my parents, declarations that can't be taken back and will haunt our relationship forever." It was a weird thought to have in 1991. Cures were still fairly expensive, and "cathartic overload" hadn't even caught on in New Age circles by then, I don't think—I mean, those PSAs certainly hadn't aired . . . I guess I'd probably overloaded three, maybe four times by then at most? Anyway, maybe it was the novelty of the thought that convinced me it was right—who knows?—but I didn't doubt its validity, and the choice was an easy one.

I snatched Jamey up, then bashed it back down.

"Dolores!" my mother shouted, and I started to cry—not for Jamey, or for having lashed out, but with a great sense of relief. I'd nearly done something awful to us, but I'd stopped myself.

They scolded me for "not being very nice," but then, once they'd noticed my tears, they embraced me, and I, in so many words, I told them that, yes, I *was* nice, and that I planned to always be nice, but that I needed them to let me go to college in Berkeley, that even if they didn't let me go to college in Berkeley, I would continue to be nice, but I would never be very happy about it, I would feel like a sucker, a sucker who continued to act as though simply being nice could ever get her what she really wanted and deserved even though she knew it wasn't true. And they listened to me. And within a couple days, they changed their minds, and later that year, I enrolled at Berkeley. What a happy ending, right? They were such good people.

But so, as I was starting to say before, I never asked them the obvious question—I never asked them if they'd heard the Kinks song.

And it's possible they hadn't. "Lola" was released in 1970, by which point my parents, neither of them music fans—though sometimes, in the car, my dad would play the Big Band station on the radio—were well into their forties. It's also possible that they'd heard the song, but hadn't paid attention to its lyrics. I'll never know. I never got to ask. They passed away six years ago, within a week of one another. My mother died suddenly, from a stroke, during the first semester of my last year at Berkeley, and my father, though the doctor named his cause of death a heart attack, was, I submit, killed by my mother's stroke as well.

Anyway, Lola, despite being the most common diminutive of Dolores, was not a name by which either of my parents had ever called me. I was sometimes Lor, sometimes Del, less occasionally Delly, usually just Dolores.

When I graduated college, I was nineteen years old, and, between the sale of my parents' house in Austin and the life insurance benefits, I had about half a million dollars. This was a lot of money for me. It would be a lot of money for most any nineteen-year-old, I would think.

I bought an apartment on the Lower East Side, and began to work toward my PhD in Philosophy and Gender Studies at Columbia University. I don't want to bore you, describing my dissertation, which was eventually published, as you probably know, under the title *Flesh-and-Bone Robots You Think Are Your Friends,* but suffice it to say, it contained some new, or maybe just *unfashionable* ideas about sex work and gender, and yet I arrived in New York having had very little personal experience as a sex worker, and having failed to befriend the few transgender people I'd met. Nor had I, to my knowledge, *ever* known anyone else with ambiguous genitalia.

While at Berkeley, I'd worked at a club in Oakland for a couple of weeks and had sold some manual and oral to half a dozen or so men—I'm getting ahead of myself.

My ambiguous genitalia. I should talk about that first. I considered myself a very lucky girl—and still do. My penis, as you may or may not have noticed by now, is quite small when flaccid—it's *there*, certainly, and you'll be surprised, I think, at its size when I'm erect—but it was even smaller before I hit puberty, and, with enough of a muff, it was very easy to hide, so I kept my muff thick, and I was never subject to any of the kind of awkward, much less traumatic locker-room bullying moments children born with ambiguous genitalia legendarily suffer. Also, my breasts and my hips came early—sixth grade. And they came in quite shapely, as I *know* you've noticed. In short, I received a lot of attention from boys, and I preferred boys.

Well: I preferred boys to girls. What I preferred far more than boys, however, were men and women. I preferred those boys who looked more like men and those girls who, like myself, looked more like women. This was—again quite luckily for me, I think—never much of an issue. I spent just one year in high school before matriculating at Berkeley, which was full of men and women, and although, as I said, I had breasts and hips quite early, I only became interested in sex toward the middle of that first and only year in high school, around the time my penis began to enlarge.

So I had three or four months or so of subpar, though certainly quite memorable and fun, sexual encounters with high school boys who were so inexperienced, and so happy to have access to a wet pussy, a wet pussy belonging to a girl who was not only far and away at the top of her class intellectually, but whose face and body, if you'll forgive my lack of humility in saying all of this, a girl whose face and body were the envy of any girl she'd ever encountered—they were so happy to be able to touch my pussy, these boys, to fuck my pussy and lick it and have me pull at and suck on their penises, that neither the steely erection at the top of that pussy, nor the sticky ejaculate that erection invariably shot onto their hair or their wrists or their waists or their bellies ever seemed to trouble them. Or if it did, they never said. And they all came back for more. Or tried to.

I was a lucky girl to so reliably be able to make the boys feel lucky. And sure, there were rumors about what I had between my legs, but I really don't think anybody believed them. How easy, do you think, would it be to believe such rumors in 1991? when they concerned a girl who other girls so blatantly envied? a girl who all the straight boys were jealous to touch, to kiss, to fuck?

and especially when the girl was named Dolores, which everyone knows is long for Lola? Kids are often cruel morons, but they're rarely fools. The last thing they want is to *look* like fools. Given my name, the rumors too closely resembled punch lines. If you didn't fail to recognize them as such, then the joke was on you. I had a lot of fun.

I had more fun in college. At Berkeley, they all assumed I was of age, or close enough. Why wouldn't they? With a little makeup, I'd looked eighteen since I'd turned thirteen. And even though the boys and young men I slept with were rarely as inexperienced as those I'd slept with in high school, they were just as grateful to have me, and oftentimes, I think, *more* grateful because they'd known other pussies, and mine . . . My pussy's different from other pussies, and not just because there's a penis at the top of it. When I come with my cock, I also come with my pussy, which tightens, contracts, convulses, throbs. And when my penile orgasm stops, the vaginal one's just getting started, and you, if any of you is inside me, even just your little finger or your tongue—you feel it. You can even see it if you're looking. You can't even imagine how good it looks, much less how good it feels til you've experienced it. And I do wish I could take credit for it. I wish I could say that I conditioned my Kegels or had some operation or learned some wild technique from some ancient sex manual to make my pussy so . . . good . . . but I can't. I was born this way. A gynecological wonder. A miracle. So those more experienced boys and men at Berkeley—they knew they were into something special, something *unique,* even beyond what they'd first imagined, and they . . . appreciated it.

The few transgender people I met while at Berkeley—I didn't fit in with them. They had a hard time being what they were, having what they had, not having what they didn't—and they had hard lives, unsympathetic parents, horror stories of childhood abuse and alienation. They'd usually had surgeries or taken hormones or seen psychiatrists—many times all of the above—and beyond all that, they just weren't, in conventional terms, very attractive. Physically. They were, in many cases, sexually repellent, and, with few exceptions, those who weren't repellent seemed to me—and, I imagine, to others—to deliberately attempt to make themselves so. I didn't know why they would do that, if that's what they were doing. I didn't know if it was out of some sort of overcompensatory pride in the ways they diverged from conventional physical beauty, or if they'd suffered so much that, in order to feel safe, they actually set out to repulse anyone who might have otherwise taken a sexual interest in them, or even if, as so many of them claimed, they really believed that their conventionally unattractive-if-not-repellent hair- and clothing- and vocalizing-styles were somehow striking meaningful blows to our mindfuckingly dominant patriarchy. And then again maybe it wasn't deliberate. Maybe it was that the hormones they were taking or the complications that arose in the wake of their surgeries left them in such physical discomfort that they couldn't *shine* the way attractive people do, or that they really had no sense of what looked good or acceptable to the rest of society. I didn't know, and, try though I did—maybe I didn't try hard enough—I never would figure it out. It wasn't something one was allowed to talk to them about. Or, at least, it wasn't something I was allowed to talk to them about.

I was, it seemed to me, uniformly disliked by them. Resented by them. They spoke to me with arrogance, with condescension, *self-righteously*. They were activists, all of them, and they spoke like the other activists of that era spoke, like proselytizing campus Christians speak to sinners. They spoke to me that way about who I was, according to them, about where my place in society was, where it should be, who I was *supposed* to be. They'd suggest that I was lying to myself about who I was, hiding who I was from myself, had always lied to and been hiding from myself—those were the charitable ones. The less charitable accused me of simplemindedness: of being simpleminded for so uncomplicatedly considering myself a woman. Me. Can speak four languages, can read in nine, fully scholarshipped at Berkeley from the age of fifteen. Simpleminded. How could they think that? It was because I was attractive, I believe. Because I knew I was attractive, felt attractive. Because I, despite or because of my ambiguous genitalia, was considered an attractive person, behaved like an attractive person, was treated like an attractive person, and was comfortable with that. They wanted me, it seemed, to apologize for looking like I did, talking like I did, attracting as much sexual attention as I did. Or if not to apologize for it, to be angry about it, *ashamed* of myself . . .

They wanted me to feel bad.

So we didn't get along. And soon enough, I was actively avoiding them. I can't imagine they minded much.

Anyway, it wasn't til I got to New York that I made any transgender friends. It happened very suddenly, just three, four days after I'd moved into my apartment. I saw two beautiful trans women—two *stunningly* beautiful trans women—enter the diner where I'd gone to do some reading, and they saw me right back. We shared this *look*. That sounds so filmic and magical but—well . . . it was. We shared this look of, "Really? Okay, yes, really, at last, you're who I've been hoping to run into *forever*," and they approached my booth, came straight over, and what followed was possibly the most charged, and yet most natural-feeling first interaction I'd ever had with anyone—and there were *two*.

The redhead sat next to me, the brunette opposite. They just sat down. Just like that. And the redhead told me—I swear it—without saying anything else first, she told me, "You're new here. We like you. You're the newest thing and you're going to be our friend."

And I said, "I hope so."

She said, "I'm Janie Sezz."

"I'm Maggie Mae," the brunette said.

"Lola Henry," I said. I didn't know why I'd said that. I'd never been Lola. In a way, of course, I'd always been Lola, but I'd never introduced myself as Lola—nearly always as Dolores, maybe once or twice Del. I don't think I'd ever said "Lola Henry" out loud before then, but that's what I said. "Lola Henry," I said.

"Do better," Janie Sezz said. "That's just . . . no."

"It's my name," I said.

"It's not," Janie Sezz said, which was mostly true, but not in the way that Janie Sezz meant it. Or not *just* in that way.

"If it's yours, you can change it," Maggie Mae added.

"We're not fond of it, dear," Janie Sezz said.

"And what if I'm not fond of your names?" I said.

"Aren't you, though?"

"Yes," I said. And I was. It was true. I was fond of their names. "My parents are dead," I said.

"Ours, too," Janie Sezz said.

"I'm sorry," I said.

"I don't want you to be," Janie Sezz said. "That isn't what I was getting at, at all."

"Still," I said.

"Maybe," offered Maggie Mae, "maybe you should keep *part* of your name." She reached across the table to pat me on the hand. "I miss my parents, too," she said. "They were good people. We didn't always see eye to eye, but that didn't mean that they weren't good people."

"No, no," Janie Sezz said. "We're not doing this right now. This isn't what we do when we meet new people. This isn't how we go about making new friends."

"You're right," Maggie Mae said. "It isn't. It isn't."

"We're talking about your *name,*" Janie Sezz said. "No one here's fond of it. I don't think *you're* fond of it."

"It's the name my parents gave me, though," I said. "That's what I was trying to tell you."

"We *know* what you were trying to tell us," Janie Sezz said.

"Well then you understand," I said.

"It's not a question of understanding," Janie Sezz said. "It's a question of aesthetics. We simply aren't fond of your name. We aren't fond of how it sounds. Are you fond of your name? Are you fond of how it sounds?"

"I don't know," I said.

"That means no," Janie Sezz said. "Might as well, at least."

"How well did they know you?" asked Maggie Mae. "Your parents," she said. "How well did they know you?"

"They loved me," I said.

"How hard could it have possibly been for them to love you?" Maggie Mae said. "That could not have been hard. Just look at you, won't you? I mean, look at her, Janie."

"It wouldn't, I imagine, have been hard," Janie Sezz said. "I was fond of her before we even sat down."

"Who wouldn't have loved you?" Maggie Mae went on. "How couldn't they have? What *I'm* asking is: Did they *know* you?"

"They wanted to," I said. "And, yes," I said. "I think they did. Mostly." Was I really getting this personal with these beautiful strangers? within minutes of meeting them? Yes, I was. I was. I was. "They knew what I let them know," I said. "I mean, they lived in a different kind of world than me."

"Than any of us, I bet," Maggie Mae said.

"Of course," said Janie Sezz. "They were parents, after all."

"They were *my* parents," I said.

"But parents," said Janie Sezz, "nonetheless."

"What do you think my name should be?" I said.

Janie Sezz said she had no idea. Maggie Mae asked what I thought it should be. I said I didn't know. I said I'd have to think about it. That was fine by both of them. We moved on to other topics. To *the* other topic:

What should we do, now?

We should enter a blur. We should leave the diner and enter a blur. I'd never entered a blur. They convinced me I should. I didn't take much convincing.

We left the diner and entered a blur. We went to my place. We went to their place. We walked around. We went to bars. We went to clubs. We danced. We drank. We showed ourselves to men for money. We let men pay us to touch us, suck at us, lick at our tits, lick at our necks, lick out our asses, put their cocks in our mouths, their fingers, their thumbs, their balls on our lips, and sometimes they'd fuck us. We'd often fuck each other. We shopped for books, too. We shopped for clothing. We shopped for liquor, ecstasy, and weed. Janie Sezz shopped for Xanax, Maggie Mae for Paxil, both of them shopped for hormones and coke. We walked around, drank coffee in diners, talked and talked and talked and talked.

The blur lasted two weeks, maybe fifteen days. At the end of it all, we got in a fight. A fight outside a liquor store. Who should pay for something—for a bottle of whiskey and a carton of condoms. It wasn't about that, though. Not really. I paid for the whiskey and paid for the condoms—I had lots of money—and still we were fighting. And maybe that's what it was—that I had lots of money, and they . . . did not. Or it might have been that they knew I'd be starting school in a week. It might have been that I'd told them what I'd planned to work on, that I planned to write a dissertation about sex work and gender, which made them suspect me of being a tourist, of having tricked them into thinking I was more than a tourist.

And maybe I'd tricked them, but if so not on purpose.

And maybe they were right about my being a tourist, but if so then I was only just finding that out.

And what, really, I wondered, was wrong with being a tourist? Why should being a tourist cause anyone pain? Weren't we all just having our adventures?

I know, I know, I know, but look: I was nineteen years old. I spoke five languages, read in a dozen, and owned an apartment—still, though, *still* I was only nineteen. And they were, I don't know, twenty-four? twenty-five? They weren't any younger than I am now. They weren't too young to know any better.

Anyway, the fight put an end to the blur. Or maybe it was the other way around: maybe the end of the blur caused the fight. It doesn't really matter. Somewhere in there, my name became Fond, then Fonda, and then Fondajane. And by the time I'd cut my ties with Maggie Mae and Janie Sezz—for the first couple months after the fight, we'd still meet up, though not very frequently, once, maybe twice a week at most, but it was never the same as it had been before the fight, our parties always ended in resentment and anger, and eventually, they were starting out that way too—once I'd cut my last ties to Maggie Mae and Janie Sezz, I'd become who I am.

And it's a pleasure to meet you. Thank you for coming to *Private Viewing.*

Now, what should we do?

Living Isn't Functioning

Jonny Pellmore-Jason, Jr.

June 3, 2013

Freshman Honors Writing and Rhetoric Final Research Paper

Mr. Hunt

1988

Graham&Swords Ovum and IncuBand BOTIMAL® HatchKit

Owner's Manual

Congratulations on becoming the proud new owner of a Graham&Swords BOTIMAL®, *the flesh-and-bone robot that thinks it's your friend*®! Please read this owner's manual thoroughly and keep it in a safe place for future reference.

What's in the Box

1 Ovum
1 PillowNest® (Don't throw the box away!)
1 IncuBand®
1 28-day supply of LifePellets®

What Exactly Is a BOTIMAL®?

A BOTIMAL® is a *biotic data-processing machine* (BDPM)® with built-in, cutting-edge artificial intelligence technology *so convincing you'll believe it has a mind of its own*®.

Hatching Your BOTIMAL®

Hatching your BOTIMAL® is easy! All it takes is an IncuBand®, a PillowNest®, and a few days of exposure to simple human warmth. You can provide all those things! Do so as follows:

1. Lay the IncuBand® flat on a pillow or couch cushion.
2. Make sure that none of the four thumbscrews are protruding beyond the foam-rubber lining along the inside of the frame (NOTE: the frame is the stainless-steel cuff in the middle of the IncuBand® where you'd expect to find the dial if the IncuBand® were a wristwatch rather than an elegant hatching technology).

2012

Graham&Swords Marble and MagicSleeve CURIO® EmergeRig 3.0

User's Manual

Congratulations on the purchase of your brand-new Graham&Swords CURIO®, *the lifelike best friend that believes it's your pet*®!

What's in the Sock?

1 Marble
1 MagicSleeve® (hold on to the sock!)
1 7-day supply of WorkPellets®

What Exactly Is a CURIO®?

A CURIO® is a *soft automaton*® with built-in, cutting-edge *senso-emotional call-and-response technology (SECRT)*® *so convincing it almost might as well have a heart and a soul, even though it doesn't*®.

Energizing Your CURIO'S® Autoconstruction

Energizing your CURIO'S® autoconstruction is easy! All it requires is some body heat and a MagicSleeve®. You can provide those things! Do so as follows:

1. After untying the open end of the sock and removing the contents, pull apart the sock's closed end along the white stitching. Now you've got a MagicSleeve®! (NOTE: you should be able to open the closed end by pulling with both hands, but if any of the stitches refuse to budge, cut them with a scissors.)
2. Lay the MagicSleeve® flat on a hard surface so the plastic windowpocket is on top.
3. If you look into the windowpocket, you'll notice that the surface of the

1988

3. Set the ovum in the frame.
4. Gently push down on the ovum until the white line along its circumference lines up with the frame.
5. Turn each of the four thumbscrews clockwise, until you can no longer turn them.
6. Strap the IncuBand® on as snugly as you would a watch. For quicker hatching, wear it so the ovum is pressed against the inside of your wrist (over the pulse).
7. Your BOTIMAL® will hatch after somewhere between 75 and 125 hours of exposure to your simple human warmth (+ up to another 24 hours of deprivation from your human warmth), depending on how frequently and consistently you wear the IncuBand® (greater frequency and consistency = less exposure time required for hatching) and whether you wear it on the inside or outside of your wrist.

Within three hours of continuously wearing the IncuBand®, you'll notice the faint appearance of a black jot or squiggle showing through the pink sheen of the ovum's casing. This is normal, and it's a sign that your BOTIMAL® feels your warmth and is beginning to grow. Over the next 75–125 hours of exposure to your simple human warmth, the jot/squiggle will darken and become more defined, eventually lengthening and widening into a variety of interesting shapes that have variously been described by our scientists and lab technicians as "tattoos," "inkblots," and "woodcuts." These changes are a sign that your BOTIMAL®

2012

MagicSleeve® beneath it has a round opening lined with a rubber gasket. This is called the contact opening.

4. Unzip the windowpocket and push the marble inside until it's sitting in the contact opening, then zip the pocket shut.
5. Pull the MagicSleeve® on like . . . a sleeve! It doesn't matter what side of your forearm the windowpocket is on—as long as you can feel the marble against your skin through the contact opening, the marble can process your body heat. (NOTE: MagicSleeves® are one-size-fits-all, but if you find that the MagicSleeve® impedes your circulation, we suggest you purchase a MagicSleeve XL®, available wherever CURIO® products are sold.)
6. Your CURIO® will emerge from the marble after somewhere between 75 and 125 hours of being in direct contact with your body (+ up to another 24 hours of being out of contact with your body). The more regularly you wear the MagicSleeve®, the sooner your CURIO® will emerge.

Within just a few hours of continuously wearing the MagicSleeve®, you'll be able to see through the windowpocket that a faint black jot or squiggle—like a cursive *y* or *g*—has begun to show through the pink sheen of the marble's casing. This is great! It means the gears of your CURIO'S® autoconstructive mechanism have begun to spin. Over the next 75–125 hours of contact with your body, the jot/

1988

is experiencing healthy growth inside the ovum.

As the hour of hatchtime nears, a brighter, larger variety of colors—yellows, reds, blues—will show through the casing, and recognizable aspects of BOTIMAL® anatomy may become distinguishable: a kicking leg, a waving arm, a swinging tail . . . maybe even a squinched little face with eyes scrunched closed, pursing and relaxing its adorably shaped lips. This is the point at which you should take the IncuBand® off your wrist, loosen the thumbscrews, remove the ovum from the frame, push the ovum into the appropriate PillowNest® slit (the one from which you originally removed the ovum), and close the lid.

(NOTE: Once the brighter colors have begun to show inside the ovum, you'll have about 24 hours to get it into the PillowNest®, so there's no need to rush or panic when you first notice the colors. HOWEVER, because it may have been a while since last you paid attention to the ovum, WE STRONGLY ADVISE THAT ONCE YOU'VE NOTICED THE COLORS, YOU NEST THE OVUM **AS SOON AS POSSIBLE**.)

Once the ovum is nested, your BOTIMAL® will start to hatch in 24 hours or less. Don't worry if you're not around for the hatch—that's what the PillowNest® is for. If you're not around, though, please keep the domed lid of the PillowNest® closed for the safety of your BOTIMAL® hatchling. If you ARE around, you're in

2012

squiggle will enlarge and embolden, eventually transforming into a variety of interesting shapes. This is called *the tattoo phase,* and when your CURIO® has entered the tattoo phase, it means that its autoconstruction is proceeding smoothly.

As the hour of emergence nears, you'll see brighter colors and might even be able to distinguish CURIO® body parts inside the marble. At this point, you should either wear the MagicSleeve® inside out (windowpocket window against your skin, contact opening open to the air), or remove the sleeve entirely and either a) take the marble out of the windowpocket and set it in the marbleslit of a PillowNest® (sold separately), or b) place the MagicSleeve® in a shoebox lined with soft material (e.g. T-shirts, socks, etc.). If you do choose to continue wearing the MagicSleeve®, be sure to remove it before going to bed. Nascent CURIOS® are fragile, and if emergence occurs while you're sleeping, you may, if you're wearing the MagicSleeve®, accidentally roll over and destroy your nascent CURIO® before you've even had your first chance to interact.

(NOTE: Once the CURIO® has begun to show its brighter colors inside the marble, you'll have about 24 hours to remove the marble from the MagicSleeve® or turn the MagicSleeve® inside out, so there's no need to rush or panic when you first see the brighter colors. HOWEVER, because it may have been a while since last you paid attention to

1988

for a real treat. The BOTIMAL® in the ovum will, upon losing access to your human warmth, begin to feel cold. It will begin to feel so cold that it will shiver. And it will begin to shiver so hard that it will repeatedly slam its balled-up little body against the springy inner wall of the ovum. If you're looking closely, you'll see the ovum vibrate in fits and starts. This could last for as many as ten minutes, or as few as two. In the course of your BOTIMAL'S® repeated back-and-forth slamming, its claws will puncture microsacs of nontoxic fluid embedded within the springy wall. Upon making contact with the inside of the ovum's resilient pink casing, the fluid will chemically react with the casing, causing it to become extremely brittle where before it was rubbery and resilient. As your BOTIMAL® continues to slam against the wall, the casing will crack and, within minutes, your BOTIMAL® will climb from the shattered ovum's remains, shivering and big-eyed, in search of human warmth.

As mentioned before, it's a real treat to see your BOTIMAL® hatch, but if you can't be there for it, as many surely can't (we all have LIVES, and BOTIMALS® are meant to be, among other things, hassle-free), don't worry about it. When you return from school or work, or wherever you were when your BOTIMAL® hatched, it'll be there waiting for you beneath the dome of the PillowNest®, munching at the nutritional remnants of the ovum in the ovumslit, or sleeping, but in either case ready for a quick rinse in the sink and all the warmth you can find the time to give it.

2012

the marble, WE STRONGLY ADVISE THAT ONCE YOU'VE DETECTED BRIGHTER COLORS, YOU TAKE THE PROPER ACTION **AS SOON AS POSSIBLE.**)

Your CURIO® will emerge from the marble within 24 hours. Don't worry if you're not around for its emergence—it'll be fine in the PillowNest® (sold separately), or even the shoebox (as long as you've properly lined the shoebox with soft material). If you're not around for the emergence, though, please keep the PillowNest®/shoebox closed for the safety of your nascent CURIO®. If you ARE around, you're in for a real treat. The marble, having been separated from its source of unmediated human body heat, will have grown cold and, owing to the drop in temperature, will allow your nascent CURIO'S® built-in, cutting-edge SECRT® apparatus to complete the last phase of its autoconstruction. Once complete, the apparatus will send electrochemical signals to your nascent CURIO'S® musculoskeletal system that will trigger a series of vigorous convulsions. If you're looking closely, you'll see the marble vibrate in fits and starts. This could last for as many as ten minutes, or as few as two. In the course of its vigorous convulsing, your CURIO'S® claws will puncture microsacs of nontoxic fluid embedded within the marble's inner wall. Upon making contact with the inside of the marble's resilient pink casing, the fluid will chemically react with the casing, causing it to become extremely brittle where before it was rubbery and resilient. As your nascent

1988

Your Hatchling

Due to certain quirks in the manufacturing process of ova, about 10 percent of all BOTIMALS® enter the world with one leg rather than two, and 25 percent are born without tails. We urge you, if your hatchling lacks a tail or has only one leg, to understand that single-leggedness and taillessness do not constitute "deformities." Your BOTIMAL'S® well-being will not be complicated or impeded by these differences any more than it would were it to have, for example, green skin (4 percent) or yellow velvet (12 percent), rather than pale skin (80 percent) or black velvet (80 percent).

Regardless of how many limbs they might have, hatchlings, prior to their first meal-and-cuddle, range in length from 40–60 mm head-to-toe, 60–75 mm head-to-tail (if applicable), and they weigh between 35 and 45 grams. Enjoy this phase, because it'll be over before you know it! Your BOTIMAL® will reach full physical maturity (120–160 mm head-to-toe, 160–190 mm head-to-tail, and 250–350 grams in weight) within three weeks.

Imprinting

These first weeks—especially the first seven days—are extremely important. Your BOTIMAL® hatchling will imprint on whomever it cuddles most regularly with. Once it has imprinted, it will not only dedicate itself to the person on whom it has imprinted for the rest of its existence, but **if kept from cuddling with that person for too long a time, it will grow infirm and eventually expire**. Since it's *your* BOTIMAL®, you should

2012

CURIO® continues to convulse, the casing will crack and, within minutes, your CURIO® will emerge from the shattered marble's remains, convulsing less vigorously, and searching for a master.

If you can't be there for your nascent CURIO'S® emergence, as many surely can't (we all have LIVES, and CURIOS® are built to be, amongst other things, hassle-free), don't worry about it. When you return from wherever you were when your CURIO® emerged, it'll be there waiting for you beneath the dome of the PillowNest® (sold separately) or the lid of the shoebox, either sleeping or munching at the nutritional remnants of its marble, but in any case ready for a quick rinse in the sink and a master to entertain.

Your Nascent CURIO®

Whether you purchased a standard double-legged/pale-black/longtail CURIO EmergeRig®, a super-deluxe single-legged/violet-orange/no-tail CURIO EmergeRig®, or any other product from our line of version 3.0 EmergeRigs® (excluding LuckTest EmergeRigs®), your CURIO® is guaranteed by Graham&Swords Corporation to have the colors, limb count, presence/absence of tail, and length of tail (when applicable) indicated on your EmergeRig's® label. If your CURIO® emerges from its marble with any features that differ from those listed on the label, you are entitled to exchange it within five weeks of purchase. Just bring your receipt and defective CURIO® to the point of sale. The

1988

be sure that, for at least the first seven days, it does no extensive cuddling with anyone other than you.

First Bath

Your BOTIMAL® will be goo-flecked when it emerges from the ovum. This goo is nontoxic and scentless, but it's a little bit sticky, and you probably won't want it to get on your clothing, which is why you should bathe your hatchling BOTIMAL® as follows:

Lift it from the PillowNest® by the shoulders (don't squeeze!), and lay it in the cup of your hand. Within moments, you will see (and feel!) it pressing its head against your wrist, as if trying to somehow enter your body. Bring it to a sink and open the tap at low pressure until the water is roughly as warm as you are. Once the water is the proper temperature, cradle your BOTIMAL® beneath it. Your BOTIMAL® will roll around a bit in order to stay warm and keep its mouth and nose above the shallow pool of water in your palm, and, in doing so, it will get its entire body wet. After a minute of rinsing, shut the tap and loosely wrap your BOTIMAL® in a paper towel for ten minutes. It will squirm around, and the resultant friction will scrub away any remaining flecks of goo while drying your BOTIMAL®.

And now, at last, it's time to cuddle!

First Cuddle

This is the easiest part. Open the towel and gently pick your BOTIMAL® up by the shoulders (again: don't squeeze!). Set it belly-down, or on its side, upon

2012

retailer will deactivate the product and ship it to Graham&Swords Corporation, which will send you a brand-new marble by US Post.

Regardless of the type of EmergeRig® you purchased, your nascent CURIO® will reach full physical maturity within three weeks of emerging, so enjoy its nascence—it'll be over before you know it!

Imprinting

These first weeks—especially the first seven days—are extremely important. Your nascent CURIO® will imprint on whoever most regularly supplies it with body heat. Once it has imprinted, it will not only be mastered by the person on whom it has imprinted for the rest of its existence, but **if prevented from accessing that person's body heat for too long a time, it will begin to malfunction and, eventually, automatically deactivate**. Since it's *your* CURIO®, you should be sure that, for at least the first seven days, it receives little if any exposure to the body heat of anyone other than you.

First Bath

When your CURIO® emerges from the marble, you'll want to rinse the goo from its body. Hold it in the palm of your hand and run lukewarm water over it for a minute or two, then lay it on a towel and let it roll itself dry.

Initial Imprint

If you have a CureSleeve® (sold separately), you can start using it now. It looks just like an extra-long

1988

your skin. If you're wearing a long-sleeved shirt, we suggest you place your BOTIMAL® on your wrist, right where the ovum it hatched from was when you were using the IncuBand®. If you're wearing a short-sleeved shirt, we suggest you set your BOTIMAL® on your shoulder. Your BOTIMAL® will grab onto the fibers on the inside of your shirt with its claws or (if available) its tail, and push, thus securing itself against your skin and allowing you to freely move around.

You'll probably be tempted to pull back your sleeve and stare at the adorable little thing for a while. Go ahead! Just remember to replace the sleeve when you're finished staring so that your BOTIMAL® can secure itself to your body again.

Exhausted from its bath, its hatch, its preceding separation from human warmth, and all the new sensory input from which the ovum formerly protected it, your BOTIMAL® will fall asleep quickly. Let it. And once you grow tired of watching it sleep, you should, by all means, feel free to do things around the house or engage in light play with friends. Just don't forget your BOTIMAL® is there, and that, although resilient, it isn't invulnerable—it can get hurt very easily. So: no sports while cuddling! No roughhousing either! And although you'll surely be tempted to fall asleep with your BOTIMAL®: don't. There's nothing worse than waking up to find a beloved friend irreparably smashed and/or suffocated beneath one's body, even if that friend is only a robot. Before going to bed, return your BOTIMAL® to its PillowNest® and shut the lid.

2012

MagicSleeve® with a much larger contact opening and a bigger, opaque windowpocket, as well as a rugged, tubular dropper-bottle-holder built into one end of it, doesn't it? That's pretty much what it is! Put it on like a MagicSleeve®, unfasten the windowpocket's closure(s), and lay your CURIO® on the part of your forearm exposed by the contact opening. If you're going to be staying in one place for a while, feel free to leave the windowpocket closure(s) unfastened. If you feel like moving around, though, shut it. One of the best, most convenient aspects of the CureSleeve® (sold separately) is that your CURIO® doesn't need to leave it to hydrate. Just unscrew the end of the dropper-bottle-holder, remove the dropper-bottle, fill it with cold water, return it to the holder, and screw the holder's cap back on. Now your CURIO® has a steady supply of water!

If you don't have a CureSleeve® (sold separately), that's okay, too. Set your CURIO® stomach-down, or on its side, upon your arm. If you're wearing a long-sleeved shirt, we suggest you place your CURIO® on your wrist. If you're wearing a short-sleeved shirt, we suggest you place your CURIO® on your shoulder. Most of the time, your CURIO® will gently hold to your flesh, but sometimes, to prevent cramping, it will seek to change the position of its limbs, and so will roll over, grab onto the fibers on the inside of your shirt with its claws or (if available) its tail, and push, thus securing itself against your skin.

1988

Developmental Timeline

For the first day or two, your BOTIMAL® hatchling, though it will be able to raise itself up into a standing position, will move from place to place by grasping surfaces with the claws of its hands and feet/foot and (if applicable) its tail by pushing or pulling the rest of its body toward its intended destination. Its strength and sense of balance will develop rapidly, however, and by the end of its first week outside the ovum, at latest, it will be lifting its torso and head from the surfaces on which it moves, and crawling on its forearms and shin(s) and (if applicable) using its tail for leverage.

No later than the end of week two, your hatchling will be fully ambulatory. Some BOTIMALS® are bipedal, some are quadrupedal, and a rare few are tripedal. Until the ambulation phase begins, there's no way to predict how many limbs your BOTIMAL® will use to ambulate, but because so much of BOTIMAL® behavior begins with mimicry of owner behavior, you might, if you want to try, be able to teach your BOTIMAL® to ambulate bipedally or quadrupedally via walking on two legs or crawling around on all fours, respectively, while your BOTIMAL® watches.

During the crawling phase, your BOTIMAL® will start to mimic you—your movements, as well as the sounds you make. Some are more interested in one kind of mimicry than the other at first, but all BOTIMALS® eventually mimic both aspects of their owners' behavior to one degree or another. Once your BOTIMAL® learns to walk, if not before then,

2012

Whether you're using a CureSleeve® or not, you'll probably be tempted to look upon and admire, close up, the cutting-edge design and better-than-lifelike senso-emotional response patterns of your freshly emerged soft automaton®. Go ahead! Just remember that your nascent CURIO®—between having been out of contact with your body heat, drying itself after its rinse, and being subject to all the many computations its SECRT® apparatus has been rapidly performing since emergence—will have expended a lot of energy, and will need to shut its eyes and suspend most SECRT® activity for a while. Let it. And once you grow tired of watching it suspend, you should, by all means, feel free to do things around the house or engage in light play with friends.

You may be tempted to fall asleep with your CURIO® without added protection: don't. There's nothing worse than waking up to find a lifelike best friend that thinks it's one's pet irreparably smashed and/or suffocated beneath one's body by accident, even if that lifelike friend-pet is only a robot. If you have a SlumberHardTube® (sold separately), then when it's bedtime, just remove your CURIO® from the windowpocket of the CureSleeve®, place the SlumberHardTube® in the windowpocket, lay your CURIO® in the SlumberHardTube®, close the SlumberHardTube®, and fasten the windowpocket's closure(s).

If you don't have a CureSleeve® and SlumberHardTube® (both sold separately), then, before going to bed,

1988

it will begin to improvise and experiment with sounds and movements. To many, these improvisations and experiments are some of the best things that BOTIMALS® do. Some believe these are attempts at communication—and they might be! They certainly seem to be. Some people find these behaviors annoying, though. If you are one of these people, know this: all you have to do to get a BOTIMAL® to stop behaving in any way that it's behaving is cuddle it. And if you don't feel like cuddling it when it annoys you, just put it in the PillowNest® and shut the lid. Though it might continue to move around and make noise for a couple of minutes in there, it will fall asleep soon enough.

Feeding Your BOTIMAL®

Did we say that cuddling is the easiest part of being friends with a BOTIMAL®? Maybe we spoke too soon. Feeding your BOTIMAL® isn't exactly a three-legged race through a minefield, either! It can snack on just about anything you eat, as long as it also eats one LifePellet® per day. (NOTE: just as BOTIMALS® are able to process the same foods as human beings, they are vulnerable to the same toxic substances.)

LifePellets® supply your BOTIMAL® not only with all the nutrients it needs to remain healthy, but with enzymes vital to the proper digestion of other foods, should you choose to supplement its diet with other foods.

As for HOW to get your BOTIMAL® to eat, there's nothing to it. Pinch a LifePellet® or bit of other food between your

2012

return your CURIO® to its PillowNest® (sold separately) or shoebox and shut the lid.

Energizing Your CURIO'S® Regular, Daily Functioning

Did we say that energizing your CURIO'S® autoconstruction was easy? Energizing its regular, daily functioning is even easier. It can consume just about anything you eat, as long as it also consumes one WorkPellet® per day. (NOTE: just as CURIOS® are able to process the same foods as human beings, their SECRT® apparatuses can terminally malfunction if they consume substances that are toxic to human beings.)

WorkPellets® supply your CURIO® not only with all the chemicals required for the full functionality of its SECRT® apparatus, but with chemicals vital to the proper processing of human foods, should you choose to supplement its energy intake with human foods. (NOTE: energizing your CURIO® with non-WorkPellets®-brand pellets is discouraged and will void your 90-day warranty.)

As for HOW to get your CURIO® to consume energy, there's nothing to it. Pinch a WorkPellet® or bit of human food between your thumb and forefinger, hold it in front of your CURIO'S® face, and see for yourself. In its silky-mouthed nascence, your CURIO® won't be able to do much more than gnaw and suck at the WorkPellet®/human food-bit before it, but soon enough (by the end of week three at

1988

thumb and forefinger, hold the food in front of your BOTIMAL'S® face, and see for yourself. As a silky-mouthed hatchling, it won't be able to do much more than gnaw and suck at the LifePellet®/food-bit before it, but soon enough (by the end of week three at latest), it'll have a full set of teeth, excellent motor control, and will gladly take its meals into its own hands. Literally!

In addition to its daily LifePellet®, all a BOTIMAL® needs for sustenance is one thimbleful of water per day. We suggest using a plastic bottlecap, if not an actual sewing thimble, filled to the brim with cold water and secured inside the ovumslit of the PillowNest®. As a hatchling, your BOTIMAL® will lap the water from the cap like a dog from a bowl. By the time it reaches physical maturity, its head may have grown too large to drink in this manner, but its motor skills will have developed sufficiently enough to allow it to use the bottlecap the way a person uses a cup.

Odors and Grime

If your BOTIMAL® stays to a strict diet of LifePellets®, it will, unless it gets something smelly on its skin or velvet, give off a faint odor of grape-flavored bubblegum. If your BOTIMAL®, in addition to LifePellets®, ingests human food, it may produce other, less pleasant odors that will make you want to bathe it. A buildup of grime or a matted-down look to your BOTIMAL'S® velvet might also cause you to want to bathe it. Go ahead and do so! Just don't use soap, which can irritate your BOTIMAL'S® skin.

2012

latest), it'll have a full set of teeth, excellent motor control, and will gladly take its energy rations into its own hands. Literally!

In addition to its daily WorkPellet®, all a CURIO® needs for sustenance is one thimbleful of water per day. If you have a CureSleeve® in which you keep your CURIO® during most of the day, or a SlumberHardTube® in which your CURIO® suspends every night, don't think twice: all CURIOS® emerge from their marbles with full dropper-bottle-tip-sucking functionality, and, as long as you refill it at least once every 48 hours, the dropper-bottle will provide your CURIO® all the hydration it requires.

If you are without a CureSleeve®, or if you don't use a CureSleeve® or Slumber-HardTube® in the manner described above, we suggest placing a SipThimble® (sold separately) filled to the brim with cold water in the marbleslit of the PillowNest® (sold separately), or on a relatively flat part of the soft material with which you've lined your shoebox.

Odors and Grime

If your CURIO'S® energy intake is restricted to WorkPellets®, it will, unless it gets something smelly on its skin or velvet, give off a faint odor of grape-flavored bubblegum. If your CURIO®, in addition to WorkPellets®, consumes human food, it may produce other, less pleasant odors that will make you want to bathe it. A buildup of grime or a matted-down look to your CURIO'S®

1988

Bathe your BOTIMAL® as often as you want, in the manner described in the FIRST BATH section above.

Rear Ejections

If your BOTIMAL® stays to a strict diet of LifePellets®, you will find a dry, glossy-black sphere the size of a pea, and redolent of grape-flavored bubblegum, in the PillowNest® every morning. This sphere is firm as an ovum, and it is your BOTIMAL'S® daily rear ejection, which derives its name from having been ejected through your BOTIMAL'S® rear. It is waste. Remove the rear ejection from the PillowNest® and flush it down the toilet, where all such things belong. Then wash your hands.

(NOTE: If your BOTIMAL® does not stay to a strict diet of LifePellets®, the color and odor of its rear ejections may be different from the color and odor of the rear ejections described above. Thankfully, the consistency of the rear ejections will remain the same.)

Mouth Ejections

Mouth ejections aren't waste. When fully matured BOTIMALS® are deprived of their owners' human warmth for too long, they become lonely and attempt to clone themselves. Some BOTIMALS® can withstand the deprivation of their owner's simple human warmth for up to a week before they start attempting to self-clone; for others it's a matter of just a couple days.

Before attempting to self-clone, BOTIMALS® grieve. Some signs that your

2012

velvet might also cause you to want to bathe it. Go ahead and do so! Just don't use soap, which can irritate your CURIO'S® skin.

Rear Ejections

If your CURIO® stays to a strict diet of WorkPellets®, you will find a dry, glossy-black sphere the size of a pea, and redolent of grape-flavored bubblegum, in the SlumberHardTube®, PillowNest®, or shoebox every morning. This sphere is firm as a marble, and it is your CURIO'S® daily rear ejection, which derives its name from having been ejected through your CURIO'S® rear. It is waste. Remove the rear ejection and flush it down the toilet, where all such things belong. Then wash your hands.

(NOTE: If your CURIO® does not stay to a strict diet of WorkPellets®, the color and odor of its rear ejections will be different from the color and odor of the rear ejections described above. Thankfully, the consistency of the rear ejections will remain the same.)

Mouth Ejections

Mouth ejections aren't waste. After extended periods of time spent without exposure to their masters' body heat, full-size CURIOS® attempt to clone themselves.

(NOTE: CURIOS® belonging to CureSleeve® users will neither attempt to self-clone nor ever even ready themselves to self-clone if the CureSleeve® is used as instructed on a daily basis.)

1988

BOTIMAL® is grieving include missing patches of velvet, hiding of the face in the hands or the underarm, reluctant chewing of LifePellets®, incompetent handling/dropping of the bottlecap when drinking, head-shaking, excessive scratching at the torso or legs, painsinging (you'll know it when you hear it), overpreened (occasionally bleeding) claws, watery eyes, trembling lips, and general slackness of the face muscles (a "hangdog look"). If you discover that your BOTIMAL® is grieving and don't wish for it to clone, simply pick it up and cuddle it. It'll cease to grieve within minutes.

If, on the other hand, you do wish your BOTIMAL® to clone, don't touch it. Soon enough, it will lie prostrate and hiccup violently for as many as sixty minutes. The fit of hiccupping will be followed by a mouth ejection, which entails the ejection, by mouth, of a glossy, cream-colored sphere—a "pearl"—roughly twice the circumference of a typical rear ejection. The first time you witness this, with its attendant throat-grasping and self-inflicted torso-punching, it might seem as though your BOTIMAL® is in danger of choking to death, which could cause you to feel upset or alarmed. DO NOT WORRY AND **DO NOT INTERFERE**. As long as you let it be, your BOTIMAL® will not die.

After catching its breath, your BOTIMAL® will circle the pearl, suspiciously at first, then curiously, and at last adoringly, at which point it will pick the pearl up, cradle it in the palms of both hands, and begin once again to violently hiccup.

2012

Some signs that your CURIO® is readying to self-clone include missing patches of velvet, hiding of the face in the hands or the underarm, slowed or incomplete consumption of daily WorkPellets®, tremors, excessive scratching at the torso or legs, D-minor bleating, overpreened (occasionally bleeding) claws, glazed eyes, trembling lips, and general slackness of the face muscles (a "hangdog look"). If you discover that your CURIO® is readying to clone and don't wish for it to clone, simply pick it up and apply body heat.

If, on the other hand, you do wish your CURIO® to clone, don't touch it. Soon enough, it will lie prostrate and hiccup violently for as many as sixty minutes. The fit of hiccupping will be followed by a mouth ejection, which entails the ejection, by mouth, of a glossy, cream-colored sphere—a pearl—roughly twice the circumference of a typical rear ejection. The first time you witness this, with its attendant throat-grasping and self-inflicted torso-punching, it might seem as though your CURIO® is in some kind of danger. It isn't. **DO NOT INTERFERE**.

After catching its breath, your CURIO® will circle the pearl a few times, then pick it up, press it between the palms of both hands, and begin once again to violently hiccup. The hiccupping will cease when your CURIO® has mouth-ejected a splash of sticky, effervescently pink fluid on the pearl, at which point your CURIO® will rapidly turn the pearl in its palms and blow air on it as

1988

The hiccupping won't last as long this time, and there won't be any false signs of choking. The hiccupping will cease when your BOTIMAL® has mouth-ejected a splash of sticky, effervescently pink fluid onto the pearl, at which point your BOTIMAL® will rapidly turn the pearl in its palms and blow air on it as if to polish it with and then dry the effervescent pink fluid. The BOTIMAL® will repeat the cycle of hiccupping followed by fluid ejection followed by polishing/drying-off-type behavior anywhere from five to ten more times until it has produced an ovum identical to the one from which your BOTIMAL® itself once hatched.

Your BOTIMAL® will set the ovum down in a secure place, oftentimes right in the ovumslit, after removing the bottlecap or thimble. At this point, you should feel free to engage with your BOTIMAL® as you normally would. You'll note that it looks a bit depleted, and you might want to give it an extra LifePellet®, but shouldn't feel obligated to do so. It'll survive either way, just as long as you cuddle it.

If you'd like the ovum to hatch, all you need to do is follow the steps described above, in the section entitled HATCHING YOUR BOTIMAL®.

If you don't care to hatch another BOTIMAL®, simply cuddle your BOTIMAL® so it can't see what you're doing, and dispose of the ovum (or store it at room temperature for later). Whether or not your BOTIMAL® will remember the ovum—if it even knew it WAS an

2012

if to polish it with and then dry the effervescent pink fluid. The CURIO® will repeat the cycle of hiccupping followed by fluid ejection followed by polishing/drying-off-type behavior anywhere from five to ten more times until it has produced a marble identical to the one from which your CURIO® itself once emerged.

Your CURIO® will set the marble down in a secure place. At this point, you should feel free to engage with your CURIO® as you normally would. You'll note that it looks a bit depleted, and you might want to give it an extra WorkPellet®, but shouldn't feel obligated to do so. If you want to avoid its automatic deactivation, however, you should apply body heat to it.

If you'd like the marble to hatch, all you need to do is follow the steps described above, in the section entitled ENERGIZING YOUR CURIO'S® AUTOCONSTRUCTION.

If you don't care to energize the autoconstruction of another CURIO®, simply apply body heat to your CURIO® so it can't see what you're doing, and dispose of the marble (or store it at room temperature for later). Thereafter, your CURIO will continue, same as always, to behave like *a lifelike friend that believes it's your pet*®!

Raising Clones

Normal clones coexist without difficulty. They exercise together, exchange body heat, acquire one another's skills, and share their quarters (NOTE: a

1988

ovum—we can't say for sure. What's certain, however, is that your BOTIMAL® won't miss the ovum. It will continue to behave as it always has, like *a flesh-and-bone robot that thinks it's your friend®*.

(NOTE: If you accidentally interrupt your BOTIMAL'S® attempts at self-cloning, it may produce a pearl but fail to produce any sticky, effervescent pink fluid to splash on the pearl. If this happens, your BOTIMAL® is likely to be reluctant to let go of the pearl. To repair this unfortunate situation, wait for your BOTIMAL® to go to sleep for the night and, after an hour, quietly open the lid of the PillowNest®, and remove the mouth ejection from your BOTIMAL'S® hands before it can fully awaken and strengthen its grip. Have a LifePellet® handy to replace the missing mouth ejection. If you do this gently and quietly enough, your BOTIMAL® will remain asleep and later wake up to find a LifePellet® in its hands, which will make it happy. However, even if your BOTIMAL® awakens while you're in the process of replacing the pearl with a LifePellet®, it won't be too upset, and in the morning, though you are likely to find it grieving, it will have forgotten about the missing mouth ejection, and will be thrilled to cuddle.)

Raising Clones

Clones get along famously. They play together, cuddle together, learn tricks from one another, and are happy to share their PillowNests® (NOTE: a PillowNest® can safely sleep up to four BOTIMALS®). The company and cuddling of another

2012

PillowNest® can safely sleep up to four CURIOS®; a CureSleeve®/Slumber-HardTube® can safely abide/sleep two). The company and body heat of a CURIO® are no substitute, however, for the company and body heat of a human master. Every CURIO® needs access to its master's body heat in order to function.

Hobunks

Sometimes a pink or purple hobunk will emerge from the marble of a self-cloning CURIO®. Hobunks possess the same physical traits as the CURIOS® that self-cloned them, but once out of their nascence, they will behave aggressively toward other hobunks and CURIOS® they encounter. This aggression can manifest as violence, which can lead to the injury and, potentially, the deactivation of those they attack. Of the two kinds of hobunks, purples are the more violent, and are far more likely than pinks to deactivate others.

Pink hobunks emerge from pink marbles, which are produced by CURIOS® with a history of being prevented from self-cloning prior to the pearling portion of the mouth-ejection phase (i.e. just before or during the initial hiccupping), as well as by CURIOS® attempting to self-clone during nascence (i.e. fewer than three weeks after emerging). Because pink hobunks emerge from pink marbles, it is impossible to identify them as hobunks prior to their emergence. The clones of pink hobunks may be pink hobunks, purple hobunks, or standard CURIOS®.

1988

BOTIMAL® is no substitute, however, for the cuddling and company of a human being. All BOTIMALS® need simple human warmth to survive. (NOTE: they also need daily LifePellets® and daily thimblefuls of water.)

Illness

BOTIMALS® are hardy robots with rugged immune systems. They are impervious to most illnesses from which human beings suffer, including the common cold. Psittacosis (or *Chlamydophila psittici*), which is often present in pigeon guano, can, however, infect BOTIMALS®, causing any or all of the following symptoms: scaly skin; a general loss of pluck; misshapen, though firm, rear ejections; and, eventually, death. If your BOTIMAL® shows signs of infection, make an appointment with a qualified veterinarian (one who treats pet birds). The vet will administer a simple blood test and, if the BOTIMAL® is diagnosed with psittacosis, prescribe a course of antibiotics. Until the course of antibiotics has been completed, you should allow your BOTIMAL® an extra two or three hours of sleep per night, cuddle it for an extra hour a day, refrain from putting your mouth on it, and be sure to wash your hands with soap after each cuddling session.

(NOTE: Dust, blasts of air, and sudden exposure to bright light, especially sunlight, can cause some BOTIMALS® to sneeze drily. Many of them seem to delight in it. Sneezing is not a sign of illness in BOTIMALS®, so if yours starts sneezing, don't be alarmed. Enjoy the show.)

2012

Purple hobunks, on the other hand, emerge only from purple marbles, which are easy to identify (and to cull, if you wish to cull them). Purple marbles are only ever produced by CURIOS® that were, prior to emergence, kept in contact with their masters' body heat for more than 24 hours after their marbles had begun to show bright colors. Purple hobunks cannot self-clone. When deprived of its master's body heat for long enough, a purple hobunk will behave as other CURIOS® and hobunks do when readying to self-clone, but instead of producing a mouth ejection once the hiccupping begins, it will automatically deactivate.

Illness

CURIOS® are impervious to most illnesses from which human beings suffer, including the common cold. Psittacosis (often carried by pigeons), however, can cause SECRT® malfunction, leading, in some cases, to scaly skin and misshapen, though firm, rear ejections, and, eventually, deactivation. If your CURIO® shows signs of infection, be sure to wash your hands with soap after any contact and take it to the nearest CURIO®-certified veterinarian.

(NOTE: sneezing is not a sign of illness in CURIOS®, so if yours starts sneezing, don't be alarmed.)

Deactivation

In the case of your CURIO'S® deactivation, please refer to your state and local laws for instructions on how to dispose of it.

1988

Death

The longevity of BOTIMALS® is presently unknown. With the exception of those that were the result of falling, crushing, puncturing, drowning, or poisoning, all BOTIMAL® deaths that have taken place in the laboratories of Graham&Swords Corp. were caused by grief and loneliness—from an insufficient supply of their owners' simple human warmth. Most of these deaths occurred while the warmth-deprived BOTIMALS® slept, but some were the result of sudden cardiac arrest caused by BOTIMALS® overexerting themselves in the course of trying to entertain (e.g. by dancing) their owners into cuddling them.

However your BOTIMAL® dies, please refer to your state and local laws for instructions on how to dispose of its body.

Frequently Asked Questions

Where did my BOTIMAL® ovum come from?

Your BOTIMAL® ovum was originally shipped from the Graham&Swords Corporation Factory Laboratory.

My BOTIMAL'S® rear ejections aren't glossy black, but I only feed it Life-Pellets®. What should I do?

The mineral content of tap water varies geographically, and your BOTIMAL'S® rear ejections might be affected by this. Your BOTIMAL'S® health, however, won't be. Try giving your BOTIMAL® bottled water to drink and see if

2012

PerFormulae®

Graham&Swords Corporation offers two lines of PerFormulae®—GameChanger® and PlayChanger® (sold separately).

Use the GameChanger line of PerFormulae® to produce clones with novel physical features. Simply add the contents of the ampule to your CURIO'S® water container and, 24–30 hours later, induce self-cloning. Your CURIO® will then produce a marble with randomly distributed patches of color (the color of the patches depends on the kind of GameChanger PerFormula® you purchased) showing through the casing. Energize the clone's autoconstruction the same way you would any other CURIO'S® and *watch it grow into a whole nother thing®*. Effects of some GameChanger PerFormulae®, such as SwimHands® and RooLegs® will be apparent as soon as the CURIO® emerges, but you won't be able to see the effects of some others—e.g. Chunker®, MegaChunker®, Dwarfer®, and PinnochiNose®—until your CURIO® reaches full size. There are even a couple of newly developed types of GameChanger PerFormulae®—Fanger® and FiveHead®—that don't enhance your CURIO® til a few weeks AFTER it has reached full size.

Use the PlayChanger® line of PerFormulae® to temporarily alter the behavior of your CURIO®. Simply feed it a PerFormula®-dosed WorkPellet or thimbleful of PerFormula®-dosed water, and watch the PlayChanger® PerFormula® take effect within the hour.

1988

that doesn't make the difference. And if it doesn't, it's time to figure out who in your household (a child, a spouse, maybe even certain pets) is feeding your BOTIMAL® something other than Life-Pellets® on the sly.

My BOTIMAL'S® rear ejections don't smell like grape-flavored bubblegum, but I only feed it LifePellets®. What should I do?

See previous answer.

Can I bathe while wearing the IncuBand®?

Of course! Your IncuBand® is waterproof. Just be sure to rinse your ovum of soap and residue.

Is it possible to overcuddle my BOTIMAL®?

That depends. Every BOTIMAL® hatches with a baseline need for simple human warmth, and, if that baseline need isn't met, then grieving, followed by cloning, and eventually death, will ensue. If you regularly exceed that baseline (e.g. if your BOTIMAL® hatches requiring two hours of exposure to human warmth a day, and you give it three hours of human warmth a day), then your BOTIMAL® will soon come to require the baseline plus the excess. In that sense, it might be said that you can overcuddle.

However, if you plan to exceed the baseline (whatever it is) by roughly the same amount each day, then it's hard to say you've overcuddled your BOTIMAL®.

2012

There are master-centric varieties of PlayChanger® such as NeedyBuddy® and Enthusiast®, as well as varieties like BullyKing® and PunchingBag® that require the presence of other CURIOS® to reveal their effects. The behavior produced by NumbSkull®, BellyAcher®, and SloMo® will become apparent regardless of who or what is around the PerFormulized CURIO®.

New PerFormulae® are constantly being developed by Graham&Swords Corp. Check with your local retailer for the latest.

(NOTE: using non-PerFormulae®-brand formulae to alter the shapes or behaviors of your CURIOS® will void your 90-day warranty.)

FAQ

Where did my CURIO® come from?

Your CURIO® was shipped from one of the laboratory warehouses of Graham&Swords Corp., makers of CureSleeves®, PerFormulae®, Pillow-Nests®, WorkPellets®, SlumberHard-Tubes®, SipThimbles®, CURIO Ideas FunBooks®, and all other tools, energizers, and accessories bearing the exclusive CURIO® trademark.

Unless maybe that's not what you're asking about at all! Maybe you're referring to *the often contradictory rumors regarding the origins of the entire CURIO® product line.* Well, if that's the case, then the short answer is that Dr. Burton Pinflex, former head of

1988

Furthermore, you cannot cuddle your BOTIMAL® to death. That is: your BOTIMAL® won't ever die from cuddling—just its absence.

Why doesn't my clone ovum have a white line along its circumference?

Clone ova never have white lines along their circumferences. The white line along the circumference of the ovum that came with your HatchKit® was precision-laser-emblazoned at the Graham&Swords Corporation FacLab Facilities before being sent to the warehouse for shipping, and is only a guideline: we added it to the ovum to make use of the IncuBand® (even) easier.

There are other, non-BOTIMAL® pets in my home. What kind of safety precautions should I take?

Graham&Swords Corp. researchers have found that, with the exception of cats, most common household pets seem to find BOTIMALS® to be as adorable as we human beings do, and they rarely, if ever, behave aggressively toward BOTIMALS®; sometimes they even appear to be trying to court them.

BOTIMALS®, themselves, tend to enjoy the company of household birds—particularly Quaker parrots—and they even seem to enjoy interacting with wild birds. On the other hand, they're reluctant to engage with snakes, lizards, and amphibians, even though most of those creatures, when left to their own devices, have been observed bringing food and toys to BOTIMALS® with which they cohabitate.

2012

the Research and Development team at Graham&Swords Corp.'s LiveTech Division, was the brains behind the whole operation. CURIOS® are the result of his blood, sweat, and tears. That's all we can really say about the origins of CURIOS® with any measure of certainty.

Because we at Graham&Swords Corp. always recognized "Dr. Burt" as a visionary of unparalleled genius, we let him go about his work with very little oversight, and when we lost him and a number of his extremely talented colleagues in the tragic fire that destroyed the LiveTech facility in May 1986, we also lost the vast majority of the data documenting Team Pinflex's research. All that remained of their hard, revolutionary work were some marbles, scribbled notes, and VHS tapes that Dr. Burt had secured in his home laboratory.

The question of whether or not Team Pinflex had been attempting to develop drone-capable soft automaton® fighters, bomb-defusers, and information-gatherers to deploy behind enemy lines when, in the midst of their labors, they realized that the soft automatons® they'd created were not only adorable, but most likely the *most* adorable, *most* perfect robotic companions for children and adults alike that one could ever even dare to imagine is not a ridiculous question. And the answer to that question is: maybe. After all, Graham&Swords Corp., since 1911, *has been America's #1 Most Trusted Supplier of Armaments®*, and Dr. Burt

1988

Cats, however, are a different story. Except in certain cases where they were introduced to BOTIMALS® as kittens, cats will behave toward BOTIMALS® as cats traditionally behave toward birds and small rodents. Lucky for BOTIMALS® that they have no inclination to be near cats! That said, if you do have a cat, you should do everything you can to keep it away from your BOTIMAL®.

Can my BOTIMAL® drink coffee? What about beer?

Graham&Swords Corp. strongly advises against giving your BOTIMAL® coffee, alcoholic beverages, or anything else to ingest that contains intoxicating substances (e.g. black tea, caffeinated sodas, cough syrup, etc.). Though most intoxicants, if administered in extremely small dosages that take relative proportions into account, should act on your BOTIMAL'S® system in a manner similar to that in which they would act on a normal, healthy human being's, other intoxicants may affect your BOTIMAL® in unpredictable, potentially fatal ways. Furthermore, the difference between life and death could be a matter of a single milligram or milliliter, so beyond the problems inherent in *calculating* suitable (i.e. intoxicating rather than lethal) dosages, accurately measuring them out can prove quite difficult if you don't possess the proper measuring equipment.

Can BOTIMALS® fall in love with each other?

As far as we can tell, the answer is: no. We have seen BOTIMALS® embrace one

2012

himself was nothing if not an American patriot whose mission had always been to develop technologies that kept US soldiers and citizens as far out of harm's way as possible. But, again, too much data was lost in that fire for us to know just what Team Pinflex was originally working on.

The question of whether or not Dr. Burt was visited by undocumented extraterrestrials who gave him, as a token of peace, a marble along with a set of instructions for how to activate it is not a ridiculous question either. If that happened, he didn't tell us, but then again Dr. Burt was a famously humble man, and that fact, in combination with our having no evidence to support the existence of extraterrestrials, let alone friendly ones who would visit us and give us a token of peace, renders the question unanswerable, for while it's easy to see why friendly extraterrestrials, were they to visit Earth, would approach Dr. Burt first—after all, he might have been the most intelligent man on the planet, and he was certainly the kind of kindhearted, peace-loving gentleman whom we imagine peaceful extraterrestrials would consider extremely relatable—it's just as easy to see why Dr. Burt, humble man that he was, wouldn't want it getting out that he, among all the scores of millions of Americans inhabiting our planet, had been the one the extraterrestrials entrusted with their gift to humanity.

And lastly: while it's true that some members of Team Pinflex, including

1988

another, feed one another, offer water to one another, kiss one another on the face (and even on the mouth once or twice!), but this kind of behavior was seen only in BOTIMALS® whose owners had modeled it for them, which suggests that these seeming displays of affection were in fact just mimicries of owner behavior. Then again, it's possible. It's possible that although they learned to, for example, kiss each other by mimicking their owners, the kissing behavior later became "sincere": a behavior they performed not simply to please their owners in hopes of—or gratitude for—receiving the reinforcement of human warmth, but because they actually wanted to kiss the BOTIMALS® they kissed. Not that kissing someone always (or even usually!) means you're in love with them—but it *might* mean that. And wouldn't that be something?

My BOTIMAL® seems to get cuter and more adorable with each passing day. Is it? Or is it more like my new friend is just growing on me?

It's not only possible that your BOTIMAL® is continually becoming cuter and more adorable with each passing day; it's extremely unlikely that your BOTIMAL® *isn't* becoming cuter and more adorable with each passing day. And by "cuter and more adorable," we mean "OBJECTIVELY cuter and more adorable."

Early research has shown that even just the sight of older BOTIMALS® generates greater activity in the part of the human brain called the amygdala than does the sight of younger BOTIMALS®. In one

2012

Dr. Burt, had widely traveled our planet, both as scientists and family vacationeers, the question of whether or not one of them accidentally discovered a marble—or marbles—buried in an Arctic ice shelf, a Saharan sand dune, or a puddle of strangely hued Amazonian muck, and thereafter energized its—or their—autoconstruction and brought it/them back home to study is, while as unridiculous as both of the aforementioned questions, also equally as impossible to address with any measure of certainty, given all that was lost in that terrible fire.

One thing's for sure, though: all CURIOS® and products bearing the CURIOS® trademark are, and always will be, *Made in USA®*.

My CURIO'S® rear ejections aren't glossy black/don't smell like grape-flavored bubblegum, but I only feed it WorkPellets®. What should I do?

Try giving your BOTIMAL® bottled water to drink and see if that doesn't make the difference. If it doesn't, it's time to figure out who in your household (a child? a spouse? maybe even certain pets?) is feeding your BOTIMAL® something other than WorkPellets® on the sly.

Can CURIOS® that have produced Hobunks® return to normal self-cloning functionality?

Yes! They can and they do, as long as you grant them enough access to your body heat.

1988

study, we showed the same sleeping BOTIMAL® to a group of subjects once a week from the time it was a hatchling til the time it was three months old, and each week, upon seeing the sleeping BOTIMAL®, the subjects' brains showed two to three times more activity than they had the previous week. Some subjects were told that they were seeing the same BOTIMAL® each week, and others were told that they were seeing a different one each week. The amount of brain activity was not affected by this knowledge. We also did another study identical to the one just described, except that the subjects, rather than being shown a sleeping BOTIMAL®, were asked to physically interact with a waking BOTIMAL® for five minutes each week. The brain activity of the subjects increased at roughly the same rate as it had during the sleeping studies, but the baseline was over ten times as high (i.e. physically interacting with a BOTIMAL® is over ten times as stimulating to the amygdala as watching that same BOTIMAL® sleep).

We have no data on amygdalic response rates to BOTIMALS® over the age of twenty-eight weeks, so we won't make any claims regarding the objective cuteness/adorability of BOTIMALS® over the age of twenty-eight weeks, but one thing is certain: if your BOTIMAL® seems to you to be getting cuter and more adorable all the time for the first seven months of its life, that's because a) it is, and b) you're a human being.

2012

Will GameChanger PerFormulae® permanently alter the shapes of clones produced by CURIOS® I've fed it to?

No. Clones of GameChangered® clones will have the same shape as those GameChangered® clones would have had, had they never been GameChangered®.

Can I feed PerFormulae® to Hobunks®?

Absolutely. But note that certain PlayChanger PerFormulae® (e.g. BullyKing, EverItch) will affect the behavior of Hobunks® differently than they would CURIOS®.

Can I mix PerFormulae®?

By all means. Like all products bearing the CURIO® trademark, PerFormulae® were invented to help CURIO® users customize their CURIOS® in ways that creatively express their (the users') individuality. Mixing PerFormulae® can't help but give you the power to take that creative expression even further.

Introduction

For the purpose of giving evidence for my thesis by using compare-contrast/juxtaposition-implication strategies, I have just presented the two manuals I will discuss in this paper without any introduction. And because of how you instructed us to incorporate what you taught us this year about visual rhetoric and how it can be of great importance to keep in mind the power of visual rhetoric when we are not only writing these our final papers for your class but also anytime in the real world that we are making a point by using juxtaposition-implication strategies of compare-contrast, I placed the two manuals side by side. I did that because it suggests that you should read them "simultaneously" (as in: you go back and forth, reading one section on the left, and then reading the section next to it on the right, then going back to the left to read the next section, etc.), but only *suggests* you should do that, and doesn't demand that you do that, which should give you the sense that I respect you as a reader and a thinker who *this whole text* (not just the manuals but also the discussion of them that I am starting to do right here) belongs to at least as much as it does to me, and that respect I showed should make you, the reader and thinker, more willing to entertain my point of view on the matters I am addressing myself to and better able to see my truth through my eyes than you'd be if I told you how to read the manuals or if I put them one after the other (which would be equivalent, basically, to telling you how to read them).

The truth of the matter is that people say that there are different strokes for different folks, and I think that applies more often than not, particularly in times like these, which can be confusing, especially when it comes to corporations, so whatever "stroke" feels most natural to you is the "stroke" I hope you used to swim through the manuals, and the same goes for when it comes to the "stroke" you are and will continue to be using as you swim through the rest of this paper, even if it is/they are different from the "stroke" or "strokes" I am or seem to be suggesting.

Thesis and Discussion

Some people will say anything to sell you what they are trying to sell you, especially if those people are corporations. It's shady. Graham&Swords Corporation is a really great example of what I am talking about here. The history of the way they sell cures is the proof.

My father was one of the first people in the world to ever own a cure. He saved the manual (the 1988 one on the left side of the pages you just read) that came with the EmergeRig, which I found in a box of old stuff in one of our houses. It was packaged much differently than EmergeRigs are packaged today, and wasn't even called an EmergeRig at the time. It was called a HatchKit, which I will soon show is just one of the many examples of how some people will say anything to sell you what they're trying to sell you, especially if they're corporations, which is the thesis of this, my final research paper.

The thing about it is that calling an EmergeRig a HatchKit isn't even the biggest difference at all between that original manual, which came out in 1988, and the latest manual, which came out in 2012. For example, they don't call cures "cures" or even "Curios" in the original manual because what they call them is "Botimals." And that is still just not even beginning to start to really crack into the surface of the differences between these two manuals, as you may or may not have noticed above.

The main thought I have about these manuals is that the old manual talked about cures like they were animals instead of machines. Instead of emerging from marbles, they hatched from ova, which is a Latin word for eggs. Instead of body heat, they needed simple human warmth. They could grieve and they could die. They ate LifePellets instead of WorkPellets. Instead of functioning, they lived.

And living isn't functioning. Obviously.

Graham&Swords called them robots at the very beginning of the original manual because that's what they were and are and it would probably be illegal in a false advertising way or something to not disclose that, but the rest of the manual talks about them like they have real emotions and desires. That is all very obvious, too.

But if they wanted people to think of them as animals, then you have to ask why it is that they called them Botimals, which is an ugly-sounding word that sounds like lobotomy and I bet I could find in some old sci-fi movie with laser guns and spaceships and talking computers that beam you or whatever, and I think the answer is that Graham&Swords just didn't know what they were doing yet when they first started selling cures/Botimals. I think they not only didn't understand how people would interact with cures/Botimals, which is a separate thing that I'll write about in the next paragraph, but they didn't know much about branding because, first of all, it was the 1980s, and people were still pretty unsophisticated about how to use branding, but secondly because, until they came out with cures/Botimals, Graham&Swords made most of its money making large weapons like nuclear submarines and jet fighters for the US Army, so they weren't used to selling stuff to normal people and just didn't really know how to do it. I think that if the above reasons I just gave for why they called cures Botimals are not the real reasons, then the real reasons will forever remain a complete and total utter mystery that will never be solved. There is a kid in this class who says microwaved pizzas are better than fresh, handmade pizzas, and he doesn't just say it, either. He believes it. I have had him over more than once and given him the choice. And he always makes the microwaved choice. And it's not because he's low on funds—he's always my guest, so I pay either way. And it's not because he's so hungry he can't wait for the handmade to get delivered—I always ask my guests what they'll want to eat for dinner first thing when they arrive at any of my houses so that I can have that dinner sent for/made ready at whatever time we've determined we should eat dinner, which is rarely less than two hours after their arrival, and never less than an hour after their arrival, which I make clear to them when I first invite them over (for example, "Come over on Saturday at four," I might say, "and we'll make a short film, then eat dinner around seven."), so they know not to show up too hungry. And it's not because he's uncomfortable with me paying a lot for a handmade instead of a little for a microwaved. I know that because when it comes to anything else I pay for, like pints of ice cream or energy drinks, he always goes for the pricier kind. And it's definitely not because it's cooler to like microwaved more than handmade—microwaved is bland and cheap and, for reasons I can't exactly explain, kind of immature and girl-repelling. There is a small chance he secretly hates me and knows that I prefer handmade pizza to microwaved pizza but that because he's my guest I will eat the microwaved instead of the handmade to be a good host even though I'll wish we got the handmade, and so even though he'd rather have the handmade himself he suffers eating microwaved for the thrill of watching *me* eat microwaved while I wish it was handmade, but it's a very small chance because then why would he even hang out with me if he hated me that much? That would be almost psychopathic, I think. So, unless he's psychopathic, you have to believe this kid really does believe microwaved is better than handmade, and the only explanation for that can be that he's not that bright. Maybe he's even a little bit stupid. Sometimes people are just stupid. And sometimes people just have bad taste, too. That's another possible explanation. Or it might be the same explanation. Sometimes one looks like the other, bad taste and stupidity, and it might be that sometimes they're actually exactly the same thing. I'm getting off track a little because I have a hard enough time, as an artist, trying to think about art that is really art without trying to think about things that are not really art—like corporate branding—as if they were art. I'm trying, though. What I think I'm getting at is that Graham&Swords Corp. thought Botimals was a good name for their product because they were stupid/lacked taste, and that shouldn't be hard for anyone to imagine, even if it's impossible to explain beyond saying that their taste was bad or their branding instincts were stupid. Not everything is subtle and on purpose, even when it should be. They called it a Botimal because they thought that was a good thing to call it, and they were wrong. End of story.

The more important thing to think about in terms of what's shady, is how people interacted with Botimals/cures. The way it got explained to me by Tessa Swords, who's Xavier Swords's granddaughter, and who used to be my babysitter (Tessa is my godsister, or whatever you call your godfather's daughter—her father, Baron Swords, is my godfather), was that, originally, cures were supposed to be just like other pets, but not messy or smelly or in need of much training. So that is why it would make sense that Graham&Swords would want to talk about Botimals/cures in the original manual like they were alive, like dogs and etc. That way they could plant the idea in the user who read the manual that that's how it was, that cures/Botimals weren't just machines that were substitutes for pets but were actually animals, which they thought would sell lots of Botimals/cures. And it did for a while. Except, then, a couple things happened.

First of all the people who had Botimals/cures started doing all sorts of stuff to their cures/Botimals that Graham&Swords never would have imagined, mostly going into overload and dacting them in intricate ways or damaging them to get them to act even cuter before they dacted them, and some people got worried about what that meant for society. Like maybe cures were turning people into monsters because that's what a person who would damage a living thing just to see it do something cute or because it was so cute they wanted to hurt it was—was a monster. And that is still true. So Graham&Swords saw that if they kept talking about the cures/Botimals like they were alive, people would keep believing they were alive, and the backlash against the brand would be huge, because of "Look at what this corporation is teaching our children of today about how to treat living things," and etc., which would be bad for sales.

And then on top of that Graham&Swords wanted cure/Botimal-users to enjoy the product because enjoying the product is what gets you to keep using the product, and because when other people see you enjoying the product it gets those other people to buy the product and use it so even more other people can see. But if you felt all shady and guilty for using the product in a certain way that you liked, then you might quit using the product even though you enjoyed it, like how smokers stop using cigarettes even though they enjoy using cigarettes, and then most of the other people who would have used the product after seeing others enjoy the product would instead look at the people who were using the product and see that those people were in bad shape and that all those people wanted to do when it came to the product was go back to before they ever got hold of the product and undecide to start using it, and all of that would add up to cures/Botimals sales not just stopping growing, but actually shrinking.

So Graham&Swords stopped lying and started emphasizing the truth about how cures/Botimals were really just robots that whatever you did to them was totally okay, as long as they were your property and not someone else's.

And then also in addition to all of the above that I've written so far, there's that whole razor-handle/razor-blade thing we learned about where you sell the handle to break even or even lose a little money on and then you make a bunch of money off the blades because Graham&Swords saw that the real money in Botimals/cures was in energizers and accessories. WorkPellets, PillowNests sold separately, CureSleeves, SlumberHardTubes, and later, and most profitably of course, PerFormulae. The cures are the handles is what I mean, and the other stuff is the blades. So the prices dropped extremely for the cures/handles, and then the cost of the other stuff did not. When my dad got his first cure, his dad would have had to pay three hundred dollars for the HatchKit like everyone else's dad if Xavier Swords hadn't been my grandfather Jon-Jon's cousin by marriage, and that was over twenty years ago, so paying three hundred dollars for it was like paying something like a thousand dollars for it these days, and now I can go to any store and buy even the most fancy EmergeRig they make for fifty dollars, which would have been equal to something like fif*teen* dollars in 1988. And probably I won't even go to a store to buy an EmergeRig because the only reasons to buy one anymore are so you can get a guaranteed limb-count and/or velvet/skin-color outcome and you don't trust any of the cuddlefarmers you know, or maybe because you're giving your kid or your sweetheart a Curio as a gift and you want it to be packaged all new and nice and factory-fresh or whatever. I'm part of the first generation that was born into a world where the Third Cute Revolution was in full effect, and I know kids who've *never* bought an EmergeRig. I'm not saying no one buys them, but most of us just buy clones and marbles off cuddlefarmers or just get them from/give them to/trade them with our friends and use sold-separately sleeves, or old sleeves, or even just cut holes in a sock, "urban"-style. But what I'm saying is that in the 2012 manual, all the extra stuff is advertised, and it's not only just advertised, but it's advertised in this way to make it seem like cures are actually kind of a boring pain in the rear to own unless you buy all these extras. So maybe I get the handle for free, but I'm still going to end up buying lots of blades.

Lastly when it comes to shadiness, there's that answer to the first FAQ question in the 2012 manual, which I think probably takes the most explaining of anything else about the manuals. But before that, I should point out how a lot of the warnings about how to deal with cures/Botimals aren't built into the answers to the FAQs in the 2012 manual (or anywhere else in the rest of the 2012 manual) because 1) pretty much everyone knows about how to keep cures/Botimals and their clones functioning these days, and 2) no one really cares about the details of all that because cures/Botimals are a) so cheap now, and b) they clone so easily. In place of the warnings, though, they explain a bunch of stuff about hobunks, which Graham&Swords didn't either really know that much about when cures/Botimals were first being sold to the public and so they didn't mention them in the original manual, or maybe they didn't mention them because they thought that mentioning them would scare people off of buying the product because of all the violence that hobunks do to other cures (ha! that is truly ironic). The way they talk about them now, it's almost like they're saying, "User: if you don't do what it takes to make hobunks, you'll really be missing out on some fun."

Anyway, there's this whole thing Graham&Swords gets admired for with the original marketing strategy of Botimals that you have to think about when you start to think about the answer to that first FAQ question in the 2012 manual. This part is almost art, even though Graham&Swords denies that it was on purpose. The thing I mean is the scarcity strategy. Unless it wasn't a strategy at all.

It goes like this.

1) Graham&Swords invents/discovers cures/Botimals. No one disagrees about that.
2) Then they fund a study in Chicago to see if the cures/Botimals can make crazy children less crazy, or at least somehow help the children be nicer or less violent or something. No one disagrees about that.
3) And then the crazy children who are in the study start taking their cures/Botimals to school and public places and other kids see the cures/Botimals and want them because of how cute they are. No one disagrees about that, but Graham&Swords, even though they don't say that's untrue, they say they hadn't intended that to be a part of the study that way: they hadn't really thought about it at all, they say.
4) Meantime, no one except about twenty Chicago-area crazy kids are allowed to even get their hands on cures/Botimals, which makes kids want them even more. And no one disagrees about that, either, though some people say that Graham&Swords could have, if they wanted to, started selling cures/Botimals to the general public way before they actually did start selling them to the general public. Graham&Swords says that's not

true, though. Something about "production flow" and "factory dynamics."

5) Anyway, the news reports start. The talent show video. The corner store video. Stories of crazy kids getting beat up and robbed for their cures/Botimals, and stories of other crazy kids really publicly breaking their cures/Botimals in ways that kids who don't have cures/Botimals think are really exciting. All of that is really awesome for the news to report because it's about violence, and so what happens is cures/Botimals get zillions of dollars of free advertising from the news.
6) So now everyone knows about them and no one has them and most kids want them so bad they're willing to hurt mentally disabled crazy kids to steal them, which they might not have even thought about doing until they saw the news reports about other kids doing exactly that. And that's when Graham&Swords starts selling them to the general public for $300 a HatchKit. And they sell like crazy.

So that's first of all. That's the scarcity strategy everyone loves to admire.

And then what happened is the whole thing I mentioned earlier about how people got worried for society because of the way kids were going into overload and interacting with their cures/Botimals (dacting them). It's after that happens that Graham&Swords starts marketing cures/Botimals as "Curios" instead of "Botimals" and finally admits that cures/Botimals are purely robots, not animals at all, and so there's no need to worry about children becoming monsters, but at that point, some people still have trouble believing it because it's a new idea, that a thing that's soft and bleeds could be considered a robot, even though the blood looks like water. But people keep dacting their cures/Botimals however they want because it's a really fun thing to do and it's totally legal. But then also what happens is that some haters start saying, "Look, these things sometimes get sick the way birds get sick, and they're kind of human-shaped, like miniature human monkeys almost, and they act like maybe what a person crossed with a parrot in some mad scientist's laboratory would probably act like. We want to investigate this," and they start spreading rumors.

But the thing is that while all of this is happening, our whole country has been almost broke because of Reagan who made it cheaper to make cars in Mexico or wherever, so there's less and less jobs in the USA, but inside of just a couple years of cures/Botimals being sold to the general public, the whole Cute Economy is going strong, and people who didn't have jobs have jobs now, making clothes for cures/Botimals and toys and organic pellets and better sleeves and nests and soon enough after that off-brand formulae, plus exports, so when finally someone does research on the DNA or genetics of them or whatever, and they find out that, yes, there's a lot of human genes and bird genes and other animal-like amino acids and stuff in cures'/Botimals' nucleotides or whatever, Graham&Swords starts talking about Burton Pinflex and the mysterious and tragic fire at the LiveTech facility really loudly to the media, and they talk about it in that way because it changes the subject and confuses people. They never say in that FAQ answer that cures/Botimals aren't made of human and bird DNA or whatever—they say maybe this, maybe that, maybe aliens, maybe genius, maybe swamps in Africa or whatever. By saying what they say, they're basically saying that the DNA stuff is beside the point. Which: whatever. It is. Coal is made of carbon and so are humans and other animals. That doesn't mean coal is a human or other animal. And etc.

And not that I'm a biologist or a chemist or anything, but the thing is that it doesn't matter in my opinion because even if it turned out that cures/Botimals were just some weird combo of humans and birds and other stuff that might be technically thought about like an animal if someone really wanted to think about them that way, there's no way people stop buying them and using them and seeing them as robots. There's no way because by the time the "Cures are people! They're people!" people start getting attention, not only is the whole Cute Economy happening and making everyone in the USA richer, but everyone in the USA and most of the rest of the world has already overloaded a bunch of times and enjoyed doing it, and has learned to want to keep doing it, and, like I said, if it turned out that cures/Botimals weren't machines made of flesh but real animals or animal-humans or whatever and that it therefore wasn't okay to do what we all do to them, not only would the economy get messed up, but we'd all hate ourselves and commit suicide because we'd see that we'd been monsters all along. We're not monsters, though. And that's how we know cures are robots. And that's why it seems like Graham&Swords is being condescending to the reader in that first question of the FAQ in the new manual. Because they are. Because anyone who sweats about cures/Botimals being robots or not is as backward and ludicrous as a small, crying child who you need to condescend to to get them to calm down.

<u>Conclusion</u>

In conclusion, I have shown by compare-contrast/juxtaposition-implication that some people will say anything to sell you what they're trying to sell you, especially if those people are corporations, and it's shady. But what is deeper and more important to think about, I think, is that the truth will out, and being shady, in the end, will always be exposed as a way that is inferior to the way of being truthful. Graham&Swords never needed to pretend that cures were animals to get anyone to buy them. In fact, if they never pretended cures were animals, they might have sold even more of them even sooner. People want machines.

A Fistful of Fists

A Documentary Collage

the transcript of a film by Jonny Pellmore-Jason, Jr.

Jonny "Triple-J" Pellmore-Jason Jr.'s film, *A Fistful of Fists: A Documentary Collage,* comprises twenty-five discrete video clips shot between 1988 and 2013. Its running time is 170 minutes. A few brief notes concerning some of the more atmospheric and technical aspects of both the film and its transcription appear below. The transcript proper follows.

Clip-to-Clip Transitions

As often as not, blank, black screens appear between clips for a duration of one to three seconds, and most of the clips are introduced with a title card. Clips that aren't introduced with a title card are all preceded by blank, black screens.

Titles

All titles appearing in the film appear in this transcript. With the exception of their final, bracketed lines, which indicate the duration of the clip, the transcript's titles contain the same text as the film's.

Clips that are not preceded by title cards in the film are, in the transcript, preceded by a single bracketed, left-justified line indicating the duration of the clip and an estimate of the year in which it was shot.

Distortion

Clips occasionally pixelate, however briefly, and quite a few of the opening and closing paused images of those clips predating 2006 are banded by static, suggesting they were transferred from magnetic tape.

Time's Passage

Many of the clips, in the lower-right or -left corner of the screen, feature timestamps superimposed by the cameras with which they were shot. Any information regarding the passage of a specific amount of time that is noted in the transcript (e.g. "CUT. Seven minutes later.") has been derived from these timestamps.

Cures

All cures, unless otherwise specified, are standard-colored, double-legged, medium-tailed, and mature.

[TITLE SCREEN]

A Fistful of Fists

A Documentary Collage

by

Jonny "Triple-J" Pellmore-Jason, Jr.

PerFormulae Product Line Pre-Launch Announcement
(Super Bowl XXV teaser spot)
aka GameChanger
aka Look! Look! Look!
Dollheart-Betty Group
1990, USA
[120 seconds]

As the opening to Strauss's *Also Sprach Zarathustra* rises, the camera slowly pans left to right across a group of twelve cures aligned along a surface reminiscent, in its whiteness and gleam, of the space station in the second act of Kubrick's *2001*.

The frame accommodates about three cures at a time. The first three we see are sitting cross-legged, facing the viewer. The fourth is looking screen-right while saying, "Look," and reaching back to tap the shoulder of the third, which turns its head to the right, squints to focus, and repeats the word "Look."

The fifth cure is rising to its feet, looking to the right. The sixth, seventh, and eighth are already standing, looking to the right, mouths agape, clutching their chests.

The ninth is performing a handstand while the tenth and eleventh, sitting atop the ninth's feet, share an Eskimo kiss.

The camera briefly lingers on the gymnastic trio as a man, in voiceover, says, "Curios have always been cute."

The rightward pan resumes til we see a twelfth cure, facing rightward, away from the gymnastic trio.

Again the camera stops.

"And they've always gotten cuter," the voiceover says.

The twelfth cure reaches behind itself to blindly tap the nearer of the kuniking cures on the back.

"Look," says the twelfth cure, and the one that's been tapped breaks off the kiss, looks rightward, goes wide-eyed, and dismounts from the foot on which it's perched, causing the handstanding cure to lose its balance, and bring crashing down with it the cure that had been sitting on its other foot.

"And cuter," the voiceover says. "And cuter."

The cure that initially dismounted helps the fallen to their feet. "Look!" it tells them. "Look! Look!" The ones that had fallen stare off to the right, and the cures behind them (i.e. offscreen, to the viewer's left) come crowding into the frame to get a better look.

"This summer, though," the voiceover says, "they'll all be getting cuter newer."

The camera pulls back to reveal that what the dozen cures are gazing upon is a towering, sky-blue dropper-bottle. The letters *Ch* are embossed on the side of it.

A lightning-like flash, and the sky-blue dropper-bottle has been replaced by a navy-blue dropper-bottle embossed on its side with the letters *MCh*.

A second lightning-like flash, and the second dropper-bottle has been replaced by a third: a black one embossed with the letters *PN*.

The cures pantomime awe in a variety of ways—palming their faces, jumping up and down, kneeling with their fingers interlaced beneath their snouts.

"Cuter . . ." the voiceover says. "Newer. But first, they'll have to take their PerFormulae."

A third lightning-like flash, and there is no more Strauss, nor sound of any kind, just a still, head-on shot of the three dropper-bottles lined up next to each other on the gleaming white surface such that the viewer can read their labels: *Chunker, MegaChunker, PinnochiNose.*

Across the bottom of the screen, a glowing red message crawls, news-ticker-like.

PERFORMULAE FOR CURIOS. JUNE 16. CUTER NEWER.

The message, centered, ceases to crawl, and blinks three times.

The screen goes black.

• • •

Popsicles

Home Video

Early 2000s, USA

[7 minutes, 43 seconds]

Suburban daylight. Somebody's driveway. The cameraman's shadow on the blacktop is long. Barefoot and shirtless, in olive-drab cargo shorts, a college-aged male, forming a visor with one of his hands, exits the garage at the back of the shot. Approaches.

The cameraman says, "You dirty spidger. You goddamn dirty spidger, you."

The shirtless male bends deep at the waist, pounds the blacktop with the sides of his fists.

"You got eyes like tomatoes, boy," the cameraman says. "Baboons' anusi. Gaylordical rectals."

"Quit making me laugh," the shirtless male gasps. He coughs, straightens, clears his throat, looks into the camera. "So hi there," he says. "Hi there, I'm Robbie, call me Dr. Robert round here some of them, and we're making this like informational video to demonstrate what some of you might call lollipopping or some say it candyappling or I heard it also called all other kinds of things like uh . . ."

"Buttbuddies," says the cameraman.

"Buttbuddies! Right," says Robbie.

"And also too there's also standylivers. And humdingering. In'eming. Fruit-the-looms."

"Fruit-of-the-looms? I aint heard that one."

"Just fruit-*the*-looms. No *of*, there, Doc."

"Still, though. Why—why they call it *fruit-the-looms*?"

"Beats me, man. I do sure like it, though."

"I like it too, come to think. Got a ring. Fruit-the-looms, fruit-the-looms. I also like, uh, what's it? What Mikey G calls it. Calls it, uh . . . Holymoling! Holymolying? No. Holymoling."

"Yeah, I think it's the shorter one, like moling. I think you're right about that, Doc. Ho lee mow ling."

"Well but I was—as I was saying, others other places call it other things, but we like to call it *popsicling* these parts, least I do cause there's some slam-poetry-type poetry there, see? Cause you can call it what you will, it pops off, you know, all sick. It's real sick."

"*Ree-ohl* sick! Sick poppin."

"Sick poppin that's right, it's the hot new shit, and here's how you do . . . Whyn't you, uh, pass on that little robot, I can show the people."

The cameraman's hand appears, passes a cure to Robbie.

Extending his arm toward the camera, holding the cure in a loose fist around the middle, Robbie says, "There. Now this one's called Scatty." Scatty reaches toward the camera with both hands, pumping its two longest fingers up and down, while winking and blowing silent kisses. "See that? I trained it to do that. Not the kissing and the winking, least not on purpose, but just the flicking you off like that, and I think it's great. I really love it. The creative way it adds the gestures together."

"The creative way it adds those gestures together, Doc, I love that, too," the cameraman says. "The sensational-emoto singalong technique embedded in its brainial cavern or what-have-you is truly a miracle of engineering that floors me. I sound like a damn ad, now! 'This message brung to you by

Graham&Swords, makers of the Curio. Where's the beef? Coke is it. We bring good things to life.' But for realzies, amigo, I love how it's doing all that stuff all at once, man!"

"Cause you're thinking, 'This thing's flipping me the bird, but there's no *way* it's flipping me the bird,' right?"

"It's got no idea what the bird even is or ever was at all."

"*None*. Cause with all that kissing and winking? It's not saying, 'Fuck you. Kiss this, bitch,' like if it was just some kid was doing that stuff, but, like, 'Isn't this great what I'm doing with my hands? Doesn't it impress you? Doesn't it make you want to cuddle me up?' "

"Like, 'Cuddle me up! I really feel like kissing you even though I'm doing this other thing I don't understand with my fingers here!' It's creative as shit, man."

"Exactly like that. Exactly. But so, as you can see," says Robbie, addressing the camera directly again, "Scatty's just a normal cure, about a few months old. Now, we did give it a little bit of that formula this morning for I guess it was called *Pucker* this stuff, and was supposed to get it to make these like, 'Oh this taste in my mouth is so sour! So sour!' kind of faces, and it worked for maybe an hour, but it worn off cause that Pucker was some off-brand local junk this Harvard-type dothead-egghead Munjed kid makes. Anyway. Fuck Pucker."

"And fuck Munjed, too. Fucken virgin homo beedy-bop-beedy-booper know-it-all weenis. His Pucker sucks shit through a goddamn straw. Slurps up the feke like a milkshake or something. A goddamn *milkshake*."

"Like a goddamn milkshake for real, Jeremy-Niles. Main man Jeremy-Niles Nelson, big dog, manning that camera, case I forgot to mention. Now where was I now? Yeah! Popsicling! Yeah! Yes. Yeah. Scatty. Scatty's just a regular, normal, totally average-type curebotsky as you can see just by looking at it. A few months old, sure, but you could even use a nascent cause even though the older the cuter the better, o'course, you popsicle with a younger one doesn't know a single trick or fancy whistle, the adorability will still just blow your mind right out your eyes."

"Give your mind a blowie like, *through* your eyes."

"That's *right*! Eyes be *jizzin*!"

"Jizzeyes—maybe that's even better to call it than Popsicling."

"Could be, Jeremy-Niles. Could be, could be," says Robbie, winking. "But as I was *saying*. What you need the most to popsicle, apart from a cure, is one of these . . ." Robbie pulls a sharpened pencil from a cargo pocket, holds it up in front of Scatty.

Scatty, ceasing all other gestures, wolf-whistles at the pencil, lightly drags its palm across the tip, looks at its palm, wolf-whistles again, and then shows Robbie the mark on its palm.

"Yeah, Scatty," coos Robbie, "that's a nice pencil line you drew on yourself there. Good."

Scatty flutters its eyelids.

Robbie lowers Scatty, holds it at his side, shakes the pencil at the camera. "So it's a pencil's what you need," he says. "One brand-new pencil. We're concerned with the eraser part. And this is important: it's important it's a brand-new pencil because the eraser is gonna work for you like a kind of measuring stick cause you don't want to dact the cure before you even did the popsicle, so you want a standard-size, fresh, totally unused eraser on the end of it. So now . . . See . . ."

Robbie adjusts his grip on Scatty such that he's holding Scatty's tail against its back, and its knees against its stomach. He aims Scatty's rear at the camera. "Zoom in a little here, Jeremy-Niles. Close-up on Scatty's exit."

"Done," says Jeremy-Niles, having zoomed in.

"As you can see," Robbie says, "case you're shy and never looked, what you got here's a slit in the velvet with a hole in the middle. Now, all we're working with here's your basic camcorder you borrow from your dad, so we can't really like, *show* you what the inside of that exit hole's like, not without wasting Scatty at least, but you think about how perfectly round and hard rear ejections are, you know it must be a muscly little hole in there forms them up so solid and tight. A *strong* little hole that's gonna fight the eraser is what I'm getting at, and so the key here is two keys. First is, you start putting the pencil in the hole—again, eraser-first—you're gonna get some resistance from the hole, and you're gonna get some wiggle from the rest of the cure, so your first impulse might be, like, *just jam it! jam it in!* Don't pay mind to that impulse, though, cause you jam hard enough, you'll run the cure through like a pig on a spit, and then it's de- to the activation, motherfucker—no fucken popsicle. So you keep a firm grip, remembering not to squeeze, and you add the pressure to the hole slowly and surely."

"Steady as she goes."

"That's right, steady, see, like I'm doing, and you'll find there's some give there. That exit hole gives a little, and you push a little more, and then, all at once, you get past this certain point, and there—see that? I got past the point. You get past that point, and the hole actually *pulls* on the pencil a little bit. Kinda sucks it in. You catch the suck-in, man?"

"Suck-in caught! Immortalized forever on V to the H to the sweet-ass S."

"Good, good. Now so this is the second key and what I was saying before about using your pencil as a yardstick. Look at this metal cuff here that holds the eraser to the wood—you don't want to go past the metal cuff. You just destroy the whole system that way. Cure's done for. No sick poppin. So you probably got a quarter inch of leeway or so, but you're best not going past the cuff. If it's a brand-new pencil, brand-new eraser, you're deep enough if you can't see the eraser anymore. You're good to go. See? Check it out. No. Better, for your shot, there, Jeremy-Niles—let's go up on the porch there."

Jeremy-Niles zooms out, follows Robbie to the porch. Over his shoulder, Robbie says, "You hear that? It's doing it. You hear that painsong?"

"I can't quite hear it."

"Well get on up here. We'll uh—I'll stick it here," says Robbie. He sits down next to a knee-high planter blossoming with phlox, and sticks the popsicle into some soil between the stems, pencil point down.

In close-up, now, Scatty writhes and pulls faces, kicking its legs around, flapping its arms, alternately singing portions of its painsong and gasping. The angle of the pencil shifts a little.

"Get it in deeper there, into that soil, I think, Doc, so it doesn't tip," Jeremy-Niles says.

We see Robbie's hand enter the frame in compliance with Jeremy-Niles's suggestion.

Robbie's thumb pets Scatty on the head. Scatty reaches up, palms Robbie's wrist on both sides, but Robbie pulls his hand free.

"See?" Robbie says. "That's your popsicle right there. Man, it's a good one, too. See how it's making that struggly face like it's trying to enjoy what's happening because we're the ones made it happen and it's—all it wants is to like be a good robot and not like seem to criticize us with that other hurt face keeps coming through?"

"It's adorable, Doc. It's goddamn fucken totally adorable."

"And see that? See now? Now the hurt face is fighting its way onto there, like a twitch or something, but, 'No!' says Scatty. Scatty aims to *please,* and there's the more smiley face. Aint gonna disappoint us, is it? Are you, Scatty? No. No, that's right you won't. Nuh-uh. Scatty's gonna figure out how to like it. Goddamn will you listen to the *sounds* it's making."

"Yeah yeah yeah. I hear," says Jeremy-Niles, as the camera zooms out rapidly, shakily, and we see Robbie sitting on the porch's top step, leaning toward the planter. "You better say your closing thing, now, Doc," says Jeremy-Niles. "You really better cause I think, I'm about, you know . . ."

"Sure yeah, my closing thing. So okay. So that, folks, that right there is what we around here like to call popsicling, and all you need to do it is a cure and {THE CAMERA GOES SIDEWAYS, ROCKS, IS FILMING THE WHITEWASHED FLOOR

OF THE PORCH}—hey, man, get that camera up. I aint finished. Hey man! Don't you even! Scatty's mine, man, don't you—"

Robbie's voice is lost beneath the crackle and hiss of a mike pushed at angles through still, humid air. The tumbling frame rapidly alternates foci, encompassing glances at the sky, the blacktop, the sky, the lawn, the sky, the lawn, and the sky before it settles into the clip's final shot: a close-up of sun-tipped, upside-down grass blades.

•

• •

PlayChanger Product Placement

from *Beverly Hills 90210* Season 3, Episode 21

1993, FOX Network, USA

[143 seconds]

David, a floppy-haired, younger teenage boy, skateboards clumsily in a parking lot before a group of longer-haired, older teenage boys who wear better-fitting clothes and nose rings and chin beards and mutter among themselves. "Wuss," we hear one mutter. "Total poseur," mutters another.

David's board flies away from him, and he twists his ankle. "I suck," he says, under his breath.

One of the older boys, whose nose ring is shaped like the *trademarked* symbol, cups his hands over his mouth and intones, loudly, "Yoooooou dooooo!" The other older boys break out into riotous laughter, except for one, played by future movie star Jared Leto, who, as the boy beside him drops to his knees in pavement-slapping hilarity, we see looking piercingly into the distance, toward David. Leto is smiling, yes, but he doesn't seem to want to be.

David picks up his skateboard and starts walking away, and Jared Leto, in the foreground, chews his lip, making a decision, then blinks, indicating somehow that he's made that decision. He jumps on his skateboard and tricks his way toward David. "Hey, dude," Jared Leto says, and the younger boy stops. "It's all about falling, dude. Those guys . . . they're just . . . they fall, too, you know? Everyone falls. What it is is that you gotta like fall like . . . radder? You want me to show you?"

"No," says David, turning away.

"Hey, don't go home, now, man," Jared Leto tells him. "They'll never respect you."

"I don't need their respect. They're a bunch of followers. And I'm not going home. Not yet at least. I'm going to the mall to buy some Effete and BullyKing."

"Some *what*?"

"They're these new kinds of PerFormulae. Effete and BullyKing."

"I guess that'll cheer you up in a couple of days, but—"

"It'll cheer me up in a couple of *hours*. At most."

"What do you mean, dude?" Jared Leto says. "How're you gonna feed your cure some PerFormula, make it clone, *emerge* the clone, and then get it to grow up fast enough to like see the effects of the PerFormula in a couple *hours*?"

"You're talking about GameChanger."

"Huh?" says Jared Leto.

"GameChanger. That's the line of PerFormulae you're talking about. That's what they call it now. And GameChanger's good. It's great, even. I'm a total freak for MegaChunker, and that latest one, RooLegs. Maybe I'll buy some of that, too, while I'm at the mall, come to think of it, but what I'm talking about—Effete and BullyKing—they're PlayChanger line."

"PlayChanger line?"

"Yeah. It's like the new alternative. When you feed PlayChanger-line PerFormulae to your cure, you do it the same as if it was GameChanger, but instead of affecting the cure's next clone, a PlayChanger line PerFormula affects the cure who ate it. Or drank it. Whatever."

"Whatever," Jared Leto says. "I don't believe it. That is way too rad to possibly be true."

"You want me to *show* you?"

"Hella right I do, bro. If it's real, I'm gonna get some myself. Come on. I'll drive us to the mall."

"What'll your friends say?"

"Those dudes are just a bunch of total poseurs anyway." Leto turns to the group of older boys. "Later!" he shouts to them.

"Later, skater!" shouts the boy with the ™ nose ring.

"Whatever, dude," Leto says, putting his arm around David's shoulder.

"Yeah totally," says David. "What. Ever."

"Like who *is* that kid?" says the boy with the ™ nose ring.

"I don't know, holmes," says one of the others, "but he's kinda the freakin man, looks like."

•

•   •

Formula Trial

Garagenhauer R&D Laboratories
2009, Germany, subtitled
[3 minutes, 27 seconds]

On a table is a soda bottle's screwtop cap, incurvate side up. A narrow hand with pink-lacquered nails places a WorkPellet into the cap, disappears offscreen. The same hand, bearing a dropper-bottle's dropper, reappears a moment later and drops a drop of formula onto the pellet, disappears again. The pellet, soaking the drop up, darkens.

A single-legged Curio approaches the bottlecap. A woman, offscreen, speaks in German to the Curio. [Eat it up, now, small mechanical angel,] the subtitles read.

The cure pulls the pellet out of the bottlecap, takes a bite, chews, swallows, takes a second bite.

CUT.

One hour later. Overhead shot. The single-legged Curio is sleeping in a PillowNest. A hand different from the first—its nails are painted black—reaches into the nest to prod the cure's belly. The cure awakens and stretches, giving out a strangely guttural series of sighs.

The same woman who spoke before says, [Pull the tail.]

The black-nailed hand grasps the tail's tip and jerks.

The cure jumps to all threes, barks like a dog, a loud single bark. Laughter is heard.

[It worked. Pull again,] the woman says.

The hand pulls the tail. The cure barks again. More laughter is heard.

[The cutest,] a second woman says offscreen.

[Yes. Precisely,] the first woman says. [Now to make it even cuter. Using your nails, pinch the tail firmly and do not cease pinching.]

The hand pinches the tail, in the middle, between thumb and forefinger.

The Curio barks continuously. The cyclic modulations of the barking's pitch and volume suggest that the Curio is attempting to sing its painsong. It does not appear surprised by the sounds it is making. As the "painsong" continues, more laughter is heard, as are occasional, un-subtitled yowls of "Ja!" and "Mein Gott!" and a couple of other un-subtitled mono- and duosyllabic German words that seem to be in the spirit of praise/wonder and/or encouragement.

After thirty-seven seconds of barking, the Curio appears to gag, as if on a mouth ejection. Its eyes go wide and extra wet. It points frantically at its throat and turns its head, right-left-right-left, presumably attempting to make eye contact with either or both of the offscreen women. This goes on for nine seconds before it drops to its stomach, and a small, glistening chunk of matter with an organic, though unrecognizable, shape, slides from its lips to the floor of the PillowNest.

The hand continues to pinch the Curio's tail, and as the Curio gets back up on all threes, its mouth and diaphragm move as before, when it was barking its "painsong," but the only sounds it emits are sibilant, barely audible, gasps.

[I did not believe that this could get any better,] says the first woman, [but as it turns out, it can get very much better.]

The Curio continues its sibilant gasping for another twelve seconds, then, tilting its head, appears to notice the glistening chunk of matter before it, shuts its eyes, collapses, and ceases to move.

[Too bad,] says the second woman. [I thought we had it.]

[Maybe we do,] the first woman says. [I say we do. I say 'good enough.' We will sell it as a terminal formula.]

[I do not know if the effects are long-lasting enough.]

[Tell me the bizarre ejection was not spectacular. Tell me it wasn't a moving finale.]

[Yes. Of course. Of course I was moved. I am not made of stone. But I would have hoped for a longer arc. A moving finale—no matter how spectacular—if it takes but only a minute or two to build toward . . . It can be disappointing. I am thinking of CrawlSkin as an ideal to aspire to. The long arc of CrawlSkin. Fifteen minutes of ever-increasing, ebbless flow. Sometimes twenty.]

[You lack imagination.]

[How can you say that? I proposed this formula.]

[Yes. That is so. It was wrong for me to say that you lack imagination. But you lack creative market sense. You can't get your head around the effects of price points on consumer expectations.]

[Price points. Always with the price points—I don't care. I'm a creator. I would not say an artist, but a creator. Do you understand? Price points—]

[I appreciate your value. But you must learn to appreciate mine, and what I propose is that we sell this as a single dose—as a pretreated WorkPellet in a candy wrapper. Two euro a pellet. One-fifth the cost of a three-dose bottle of CrawlSkin, yes? But without the bottle, the dropper, and the extra doses, the profit margin is maintained. And maybe we instruct the consumer to terminate the robot within—what was it?—ten seconds of the ejection? Fifteen seconds? How long before it deactivated?]

[Ten or fifteen seconds, yes—we will test again and see. But how will we communicate the instructions to the consumer if there's only a wrapper . . . I suppose . . . I suppose we could print the instructions on the wrapper in very small print, or, better, in pictographs.]

[Yes, yes, keep talking. Now you're getting somewhere.]

[We print the instructions out on the wrapper, and if they neglect to strain their eyes to read these instructions, and they find themselves disappointed by the outcome of feeding the Curio the formula, they will perhaps complain to the retailer, or look again at the wrapper, only to discover they should have followed the instructions, and to then blame themselves for not having read the instructions.]

[Yes. And?]

[And they will buy more DogThroat! A second dose! In order to have the experience Garagenhauer recommends.]

[Yes! You've got it. I was wrong. Happily wrong. You have creative marketing sense! Only . . . DogThroat? It sounds not mellifluous.]

[You don't like DogThroat.]

[I like Barker.]

[Barker. Yes. I think I like Barker, too.]

[Barker it is!]

The exclamation is accompanied by a slap to the table from the pink-nailed hand. The impact causes the PillowNest to jump, jarring open the nearer of the dead cure's eyes.

•

•   •

[Mid-to-late 1990s. 6 minutes, 14 seconds.]

A seminar room. Eleven university students sit along either longer side of a table, writing in notebooks or looking toward the broad-shouldered, thirtysomething teacher, who sits alone at the end of the table, facing the viewer. Behind him stands a movable blackboard on which are chalked the words *usage* and *meaning*. ". . . So my hope for this workshop . . ." the teacher is saying, and, clenching his jaw and flaring his nostrils, nose-sighs audibly and, momentarily, widens his eyes as if to express that the words he's just uttered or is about to utter are surprising, suspect, or perhaps even painful. "*One* hope I have for this workshop," he continues, "is that by the end of the semester, I'll not only have accurately described some of my linguistic neuroses to you, but I'll have infected you with them—I'll have made you neurotic about language in the way that I am neurotic about language. Or to put it in a more, I don't know, new-agey light, I guess: I'll have invited you into the, um, grand tradition of sharing my concerns and sensibilities, and you'll have gladly taken me up on that invitation. I want you to care about how things are said. I want you to understand that it's impossible to care about *what* things are said without thinking about *how* those things are said. I want, for example, for you to learn how to care about such distinctions as exist between the phrases 'Dave overloaded' and 'Dave went into overload.' I want you to notice that 'Dave overloaded' *sounds* klutzier than 'Dave went into overload,' at least outside the context of whatever utterances would presumably be surrounding either of them in some prose you might be working on, and I want you to wonder why. Probably—this is usually the case—probably it's because the stressed syllables aren't properly—which is to say *fluidly* or *powerfully*—dispersed across the phrase. Maybe, too, the klutziness has something to do with the v-sounds and/or d-sounds. I want you to develop the urge to control this kind of thing. And I want your impulse to be to wonder at the klutziness and experiment a little in hopes of finding out how to get rid of it. Maybe you start with 'Dave.' Does he have to be 'Dave'? Could the subject instead be 'David' or 'He'? 'David overloaded.' 'He overloaded.' In terms of aural pleasure, I quite like 'David overloaded.' The stresses fall more pleasingly and the relative excess of v- and d-sounds comes across as intentional, but not *too* intentional. Not *overclever*. Not *cute*. The phrase is not *unspeakerly*. Is 'David overloaded' the phrase you choose to go with, then? Have we settled matters? Well, no, not really. Not so fast. Because I don't *just* want you to care about the way the sounds feel on your eardrums. I want you to care about the way the feeling of the sounds on your eardrums affects the meaning of the phrase. 'David overloaded,' whether in spite or because of its being more active than 'Dave went into overload' or, for that matter, 'David went into overload,' makes the phenomenon of Dave-slash-David's overloading sound less elective. Maybe even involuntary. Did Dave-David suddenly find himself overloading, or did Dave-David elect to overload? What does it say about David if he just kind of *found* himself overloading? What does it say about Dave-David if he elected to go into overload? Outside of some kind of *Clockwork Orange*–grade behavioral conditioning nightmare scenario, can one *ever* be said to go into overload without having first elected to do so? Some of you are nodding yes, and some of you are shaking your heads no. Two of you are shrugging. Our film student over there—whose name I'm shamefully blanking on, sorry—is too afraid to nauseate future viewers of *Fiction Workshop Day 1: The Reckoning* via bouncy camerawork to communicate her stance on the existence of involuntary overload, though I'm sure she has one. A stance. And but so your answer to the question of whether one can overload without having elected to do so—that answer can't help but speak, subtly or not, to where you, the author, are positioned on any number of worldview-defining continua. Free will on the left and fate on the right. The power of the individual on the left and the power of context on the right. Not to mention how each of those informs subsets of worldview-defining continua-stances: human to the left and robot to the right, or maybe human to the left and sheep to the right, learning here and programming there, environment and genetics, Skinner and Chomsky, Foucault and Chomsky. So forth. More immediately than any of that, however, it speaks to what you believe about overload. It speaks to *the meaning* of overload. What overload means to you, and what you, by way of the phrase you choose, and in light of how you position your narrator in relation to the reader—what you *want* it to mean for everybody. What you will, if your work is successful, *make* it mean for everybody. Overload. And then, on top of all of *that,* or maybe at the bottom of all of that, the verb *overload*—when you consider how people use it . . . its definition's not exactly precise, is it? I mean, what phenomenon does overload describe? Some people use it to describe the feeling of being driven by the adorability of a Curio to cause that Curio's deactivation. Others use it to describe acting on that felt drive: *overload,* to them, is the *action* of following through on the feeling, of causing a too-adorable Curio to dact. The vast majority of people, I would say, use the word interchangeably, to describe either or both of those phenomena. And usually that's fine—that is, it's not usually confusing. Except what if someone experiences the feeling of being driven to cause a Curio to deactivate, but is interrupted and so doesn't get to cause the Curio to deactivate? Did that person overload or not? Because if we allow *overload* to be used interchangeably as I just described, then we could say of that person that he overloaded but didn't overload. Which is a contradiction. Not a paradox, mind you. Nothing that interesting. Now maybe you want to think I'm being nitpicky here, but I assert that it would be dangerous—dangerous, I say, and not just in terms of one's development as a writer of fiction, but in terms of one's development as a human being—it would be *dangerous,* to categorically dismiss as nitpicky the kinds of distinctions I'm making. We live in a time when the most powerful man in the world is said, by some, to have smoked pot even though he didn't inhale. We live in a time when that same man is said, by other people, to have had oral sex with an intern without having had sex with that intern. I want you to let me—to *help* me—I want you to let me help you to be infected with my linguistic neuroses. In sum: get neurotic, get evil, or play the sucker. Those are your choices. Option one earns you an A, option two something less, and option three an F."

The teacher nose-sighs again, knocks on the table, says, "So," and looks up, directly at the camera. He blinks three times, pursing his lips.

•

•   •

The Best
Home Video
August 23, 1989, USA
[6 minutes, 29 seconds]

Just past a bedroom doorway, looking down at his socks, a preadolescent, potbellied boy in a sky-blue turtleneck and wire-rimmed spectacles cradles a Siamese cat against his chest.

"Here we are," the little girl, who's filming, whispers, "in my big brother's bedroom while our dad and our sister—who's my twin—have strep, and are fast asleep in their respectable bedrooms. Our mom is resistant to this terrible disease, or so it seems, but she's getting a throat culture, just in case. All we really know for sure is Dad and Paula either got strep from me or from Adam and today—"

"Rachel, stop wasting tape," the boy says. "Say, 'Action.'"

"We need an introduction."

"I'm getting the tripod."

"No! Please! I'll be helpful. Please? Adam, please? I'm the helper. I'm helping. Action, okay? Action. Action!"

Adam leaps forward, into the doorway. As he lands, the cat looses a rumbly meow. Adam speaks to the camera: "What I'm about to show you how to do is the best." He points at an ear-high mark on the doorjamb. "This dot here, made in number-two pencil, is as high as our cat can reach when she jumps. We measured it this morning. See? Watch this."

He drops the cat and, from the pocket of his sweatpants, pulls out a roll of black electrical tape. He tears off an inch, loops it sticky-side-out, and presses the loop to the mark on the jamb. He tears another couple inches off the roll of black tape, balls the tape up compact as a molar, and affixes the ball of tape to the loop. Nodding, satisfied, he makes rapid kissing sounds. "Franky," he says. He makes more rapid kissing sounds. "Frankenstein," he says.

The cat, ignoring him, traipses a figure eight through his ankles.

Adam takes the cat by the scruff of the neck and holds it up, in the middle of the doorway, so its eyes are level with the tape ball.

The cat ferociously bats at the air.

Adam drops the cat, points at the tape ball.

The cat leaps and swats, scratches the jamb, missing the bottom of the tape ball by a hair. On landing, it backsteps, tries again. Same result.

"So that's the maximum height," Adam says, as the cat keeps jumping, swatting, missing. "And now . . ." He pulls back his shirtsleeve, exposing his CureSleeve, reaches for the zipper, drops his hand, and says, "Actually, no . . .

first I should . . . um . . . Well, you should take Frankie and . . ." He removes the roll of electrical tape from his pocket again.

CUT.

Six minutes later. Adam blows aloft the hair on his forehead. Above the tape-ball, a cure is taped across the middle to the doorjamb, gazing fondly at Adam while bobbing its head and bicycling its legs as it repeatedly whistles the first five notes of "Yellow Submarine."

Rachel accompanies the whistling with lyrics: "We all live in a/We all live in a/We all live in a . . ."

"Stop, Rach," says Adam.

Rachel stops singing.

"Stop, Percy," says Adam.

The cure stops whistling.

"Get limp," Adam says.

Percy shrugs.

"Limp," Adam says.

Percy shrugs and whistles.

Adam slouches, demonstrating limp.

Percy mimics him.

"Good Perce!" Adam says. "You did it! Good Perce." Adam touches Percy's head and turns back to the camera. "Now, as you can see, the very bottoms of Percy's feet, which are the very lowest points on Percy, begin just above the very lowest point on the ball of black tape that as you were able to see by our demonstration only just a few minutes ago is just right above the maximum height of what Frankenstein is able to reach with her longest, most extended claw when she jumps."

He removes the ball of tape from the doorjamb.

"Should I get her, now?" Rachel says.

Adam nods affirmatively. "Don't wake Dad."

The camera swings around.

Across a narrow hallway is a closed, white door. Rachel's hand turns the knob, and the door opens inward. A shirtless, exceedingly hairy man is sleeping on his back on a king-size bed with a pillow on his face, an arm over the pillow. At the man's feet, Frankenstein is licking her paws.

Rachel whispers, "Frankie, Frankie. Come here."

The cat quits licking, but remains on the bed.

"Frankenstein, come here," Rachel whispers louder.

The cat scratches at her flank, freezes—her ears perk. The faint sound of Percy whistling "Yellow Submarine" can be heard in the background. With a yowl, Frankenstein jumps off the bed, bolting toward, then past, the camera.

The sleeping father stirs. Rachel's hand pulls the door shut. The camera swings around.

Frankenstein is hissing, jumping at Percy, missing, spitting, hissing, jumping. Percy, gazing wide-eyed at Adam, and making imploring gestures with its arms while alternately bicycling its legs and going limp, is no longer whistling, but whimpering as if it's about to painsing. "The best!" Adam says. "See? It's the best."

"The best!" says Rachel.

"There's perfect tension. Frankie wants to break Percy. Percy wants to escape. Neither of them can have what they want unless I alter the conditions, but neither of them knows they can't have what they want because the conditions make it seem like they could have what they want if only they just try just a little bit harder. So they both just keep trying to get what they want! And then there's what I want, and Rach wants, and what you want, too, I bet, whoever you are. We want to see something happen. Something has to happen! But except if something happens, then what? Then it's over. So is it true that we really want to see something happen?"

"Whoah!" Rachel says.

"Isn't wanting to see something happen what we really want? Aren't we getting what it is we really want?"

"Maybe!" Rach says. "I don't know, though!" Rach says. "I think that I really want something to happen."

"I know! Me too! But there's really, right? and then there's *really*. And once something happens, you won't be able to want that something to—"

"You're right! Oh, but then. Except. But then. I. It isn't." The frame starts to shake.

"Don't cry. This is life! It's the best!" Adam says.

"I don't think it's life. I don't think it's the best."

"It *is*. Look at Percy. Look how cute the Perce is. It's impossible, right? How can anything be so cute?"

"It's really cute. It's kind of the best."

"So why are you crying?"

"I don't know why I'm crying!"

"Zoom in on the Perce."

Rachel complies.

Just as Percy fills the frame, one of Frankenstein's claws catches Percy's left heel, spreading open the flesh to the middle of the sole.

Percy, painsinging, folds up its legs and reaches down to hold them in place by the ankles.

"Oh man!" Adam says. "How'd that happen?" he says.

"I *know*," Rach says.

"The struggle! I mean, the struggle . . ." Adam says, but he doesn't speak again for another half a minute, as Percy continues, wide-eyed, to painsing, and, no longer free to beseech with its arms, repeatedly lowers and lifts its muzzle, while the sporadic reappearance of Frankenstein's paw at the bottom of the frame in addition to her audible hissing and spitting indicate that she hasn't ceased attacking.

"It's the struggle!" Adam says.

"The struggle!" says Rach.

"In the course of the struggle . . ." Adam is saying, as his sister zooms back out and pans. "In the course of the struggle, the conditions were overcome by Frankie. In the course of the struggle, Frankie found it in herself to jump that much higher. It's the highest she's ever jumped in her life."

"Oh my God it's truly amazing!" Rach says.

"But then again maybe not! Maybe, because of all of Percy's spazzy movements, the tape across its middle loosened a little. Loosened just enough that Percy's whole body sunk just low enough that Frankenstein was able to reach Percy's heel. That would mean the conditions weren't overcome by struggling. It would mean that the struggle . . . It would mean that the struggle actually *altered* the conditions."

"Maybe both things happened!"

"You're right. You're right! Maybe Percy went a little bit lower, but still not low enough for Frankenstein to reach, except Frankenstein noticed the conditions had changed and became *inspired*. The altered conditions gave Frankenstein hope, and the hope gave Frankenstein the strength to reach farther, jump higher—"

At this point, Frankenstein—whose attacks have become increasingly loud, increasingly frenzied, and just as increasingly farther off target—hurtles, nose-first, with a squishy thump, into the doorjamb, lands on its back and slides across the carpet, strikes the opposite jamb, and starts yowling, repeatedly, as if in heat.

"There's blood, oh no there's blood," says Rachel, zooming in on the cat, which, while yowling, looks also to be yawning. One of her fangs has broken off at the gum.

The voice of an angry man is heard: "What the fuck is going on here?"

The camera swings around. The hairy, shirtless father stands hairily and shirtlessly, red-faced, shadow-cheeked, jaw in a clench. He's squinting one eye and winking the other, an astigmatic without his glasses. "What the hell are you doing out here? Jesus! Adam! What happened to the cat? What'd you do to the cat?" The father reaches for Frankenstein, coughs a scratchy cough. Frankenstein flees. The father turns to follow, but doesn't follow, coughs some more. Turns to the doorjamb.

"What are you doing to the Curio?" he says. "What is *wrong* with you?"

"Nothing," Adam says. "We're making a movie."

"A movie of what?"

"We didn't mean to wake you," says Rachel. "We're sorry."

"I'm sorry we woke you," Adam says.

"What do you think you're *doing*? It's disgusting."

"It's cute!" Rachel says.

"It's the future," says Adam.

"The future? The future of *what*?" the father says. "The future is . . ." He coughs, shows the camera his palm.

"Tell us what the future is, Daddy," Rach says.

"The future is *shit* if this is what it looks like, and you won't be a part of it. Take the cure off the fucking doorjamb."

"Why?"

"For one, we paid good money—"

"But we've got three clones, and at least three marbles, Dad. It doesn't matter. The money's—"

"It matters."

"Why?"

"Because I say so goddamnit. Get the cure off the doorjamb, and quiet down. In fact, go downstairs. I'm going back to bed. Don't wake your sister."

"I'm already awake," a voice identical to Rachel's, but not Rachel's says.

"Great," says the father. "Good job. This is great. Paula, you go back to bed, too." The father exits. A door slams. Paula approaches the jamb.

"Oh, Percy," she says. "That's such a good painsong. What's happening to Percy? Is this Percy or Byron? Wow, it's so cute—what's it doing with its legs? It's so cute. I don't think I've ever seen it so cute."

"You should have seen it before," Rachel says. "We'll show you the movie, though. Then you'll get to see. Don't you want to see the movie? Pauly? Hey, Pauly. Don't you want to see the movie. Pauly. Pauly!"

Standing transfixed, Paula, wheezing, strokes Percy's head, once, twice, then squeezes it firmly between two knuckles. A muted, crunchy pop.

Percy goes limp, and does not again bicycle.

The frame is shaking.

"It's okay, Rach," says Adam. "Don't cry. It's just a cure."

Rachel says, "It was my turn."

•

•   •

Chameleon PerFormulae Trials
Graham&Swords R&D Laboratory
2008, USA
[9 minutes]

A pale, entirely depilated cure is sitting in an empty, cubical terrarium, playing with its toes. "Sub D18, PF Cham 4.7" is scrawled in black marker on the front of the terrarium's lower-left corner.

A man, offscreen, is saying, ". . . and so, to review, what makes Chameleon PerFormula 4 so different from Chameleon PerFormulae 1 through 3 is that, owing to all the aforementioned problems 1 through 3 kept presenting, especially in terms of too-early or too-sudden-and-powerful onset-of-effect, we modified the original GameChanger-style PerFormula—rather radically I have to say—so that it needs to be administered in two parts, and thus it's neither GameChanger nor PlayChanger, but some third kind of -Changer that I'm sure marketing will have a real blast coming up with a name for. Assuming it all works out that is, ha!

"So, more specifically: Whereas the administration of all other PerFormulae, including Chameleons 1 through 3, have heretofore been one-step processes (that is: either dose the Curio to affect its next clone in the case of GameChanger, or dose the Curio to affect the Curio itself in the case of PlayChanger), Chameleon 4's administration is a two-step process. Step one is: dose the Curio with Chameleon 4A to *prime* its next clone to be affected when you dose that clone with Chameleon 4B. In layman's terms—and I'm talking to you, you Marketing sharpies!—the clone of a 4A'd Curio is born with a kind of cellular-level switch in the OFF position, and it isn't until you've flipped that switch to the ON position by administering the clone a dose of 4B that the Chameleon starts working.

"Which brings us at last to subject D18, here in our little terrarium here. D18 was cloned from a Curio dosed with Chameleon 4.7A, and six weeks later—which is to say sixty-odd minutes ago—D18 was fed a WorkPellet dosed with Chameleon 4.7B. The effects should be taking hold about now. We'll have a look."

A hand gloved in white latex reaches into the terrarium from above, deposits a concord grape on the floor, then quickly withdraws. The cure stands, looks up, presumably into the face of the person who set down the grape.

The offscreen man says, "D18, come on, now. Come on. Don't you like the nice grape?" The cure sits back down, next to the grape, resumes playing with its toes.

"Does it know 'pick it up'? Tell it, 'Pick it up,'" says a woman, offscreen.

"Pick it up," says the man.

The cure looks up.

"Pick it up," repeats the man.

Still seated, the cure turns its body toward the grape, grabs hold of the grape on either side, and lifts it up, high over its head. Pink blotches rise on the cure's pale skin, as well as in the (pale blue) irises and whites of its eyes. The blotches, spreading, touch and darken. Within ten seconds, the cure, with the exception of its pupils (dilated) and claws, has become the same deep purple as the grape.

"Yes!" exclaims the man.

The woman shouts, "Victory!"

"Looks like!" shouts the man. "Could be! It could!"

The cure, infected by the excitement of the scientists, drops the grape and somersaults from one end of the terrarium to the other and back. Throughout the course of this performance, its skin's original pallor returns.

". . . And so now . . ." the woman's voice is saying, as the cure comes out of the final somersault. A hand, gloved in white latex, lowers a baby carrot into the terrarium, against the wall that is farthest from the cure. The cure, standing, looks over its shoulder, sees the baby carrot, and executes two-and-a-half consecutive backflips, landing in a handstand. It walks, on its hands, up to the carrot, then onto the carrot. Yellow blotches rise on the cure's pale skin as well as in the irises and whites of its eyes. As the blotches touch, they darken. Inside ten seconds, the cure, with the exception of its pupils (dilated) and claws, is uniformly the same shade of orange as the carrot.

"Goodie," says the female voice. "Great. Now the licorice."

A hand, gloved in white latex, lowers an oily black nib of licorice into the terrarium, an inch or so away from, but parallel to, the baby carrot. The cure, still holding the handstand, removes one hand from the carrot and sets it on the licorice, then it moves the other and sets it on the licorice. Now it's doing a handstand on the licorice . . . Inside fifteen seconds, the cure, with the exception of its claws, is the same color as the licorice.

CUT.

Three minutes later, D18, still black as the licorice, is sitting on the licorice, playing with its toes. The carrot is gone. A snapping sound is heard. The cure looks up, presumably at the source of the sound. A hand, gloved in white latex, lowers half a baby carrot into the terrarium, holds it out in front of D18. D18 takes the carrot in its hands. Threads of brown begin to show all over its skin and shoot through the licorice-black whites and irises of its eyes.

"Goddamnit!" the woman says, offscreen.

The brown threads join to form vascular webs. The cure shudders, its knees knock. It drops the carrot. Standing up, wobbly, the cure clutches at its eyes, collapses, drags itself away from the licorice and the carrot. The browns and blacks on its skin recede, and, inside fifteen seconds, the cure's flesh has returned to its original pallor.

CUT.

Twenty seconds later. The cure, moaning, rises and opens its eyes. The previously black irises and whites are (as they were before the cure handstood on the licorice) blue and white, respectively, but they remain brownly threaded, around the black pupils. With its arms stretched in front of it, its hands grasping randomly, its eyes blinking as if to clear themselves of blockage, the cure stumbles forward blindly, singing its painsong. It trips on the licorice and falls, throat-first—a snapping sound is heard—on the baby carrot. Facedown, the cure bucks, blushes orange all over its body, stops bucking, goes still. Its skin reacquires its original pallor.

"Fucking goddamnit," says the woman, offscreen.

A pale, entirely depilated cure is sleeping on its side, in the center of an empty, cubical terrarium. "Sub F19, Cham 6.3" is scrawled in black marker on the front of the terrarium's lower-left corner. A man, offscreen says, "One of the side effects of Chameleon 6.3 is that, within a few minutes of consuming the B dosage, the Curio becomes drowsy and falls into a deep, however brief, sleep, like F19 here. I've heard marketing express the opinion that this side effect could render Chameleon a harder sell than previous lines of PerFormulae, which of course I understand, since consumers—all of us—are an impatient bunch. But at the same time—and Dr. Winston and I were discussing this just the other day—it seems to me that the drowsiness could just as easily be a marketing advantage. I mean, seeing as how other PerFormulae do *not* cause drowsiness in Curios, the drowsiness here is novel, right? And novelty, in many cases at least, is marketable—I don't know. I guess I'm babbling a little. I'm a little bit anxious. It's been an honor and a privilege to lead these trials while Dr. Mangan's on vacation, especially because I think we've really nailed it this time with this 6.3. Preliminary tests would suggest that we have—okay, it's . . . It's waking up."

The Curio rolls from its side, onto its back, stretches its limbs to the shivering point, then rolls on its stomach, gets on all fours, and stands up straight.

A male voice offscreen says, "Here. Don't forget the mirror."

"Thanks," says the first voice. "I almost forgot."

A hand, gloved in white latex, sets a square mirror flush with the outside of the terrarium. The cure approaches the mirror, strikes poses in it, sticks out its pink tongue, inflates its cheeks, makes laughing sounds.

"They love that stuff."

"They do. Okay. Let's start."

A hand, gloved in white latex, reaches into the terrarium, fits the hook of a mini peppermint candy cane on the shoulders of the cure. Pink and white blotches arise on its body and spread. As the blotches grow together, their color and contrast intensify. Within fifteen seconds, the cure, with the exception of its pupils and claws, is countershaded in the colors of the candy cane: red on the top of the head, the back, and the backs of the limbs; white on all other parts.

The cure stands before the mirror, head tilted one way, then the other. It turns to the right, looks in the mirror, then turns to the left and looks in the mirror. It does a couple jumping jacks.

"What a goof!"

"Adorable. Okay. Now the chair and the ottoman."

A hand, gloved in white latex, lowers a cure-proportioned green plastic chair and black plastic ottoman into the terrarium, in front of the mirror.

The cure, candy cane still over its shoulders, sits in the chair, puts its feet up on the ottoman, and observes, in the mirror, the white of one eye turn green and the other turn black, while egg-shaped black spots arise on its red parts and egg-shaped green spots arise on its white parts. The cure turns its head, licks at the candy cane. Its tongue is white with a thin red line running down the middle, black dots on one side, green dots on the other.

"You get a picture of that? The tongue on the candy cane?"

"We'll take a still off the disc."

"Yes! I can't wait to show Ragnar. Man, that was adorable!"

"Totally adorable. And now, last but not least . . ."

A hand, gloved in white latex, reaches into the terrarium and drapes a blanket-like square of raw denim over the Curio's outstretched legs.

Near instantly, little hills of swelling appear upon the cure's face. It clutches at its face, as other such little hills arise on the rest of its body, including its eyes and its palms and its tongue, which, mid-lick, is maximally extended.

The cure throws itself onto the floor of the terrarium, kicking off the denim, stands up, painsinging, and begins to revert to its original pallor, as the hills, swelling further, burst and burst.

A retching sound is heard, followed by a splashing sound.

A pale, entirely depilated cure is sleeping on its side, in the center of an empty, cubical terrarium, covered in a denim blanket. "Sub F21, Cham 6.3" is scrawled in black marker on the front of the terrarium's lower-left corner. A man offscreen says, "So to review: The previous subject F20, after being dosed with Chameleon 6.3, was given the same sequence of colored objects to assimilate as F19, up until the denim blanket, which we replaced with a denim-colored polyester blanket. F20 assimilated the denim-colored polyester blanket without incident, and very adorably I might add, but when, after that, we replaced the denim-colored polyester blanket with the denim blanket, F20 experienced the same adverse reaction as F19 had to the denim blanket. So we thought: 'Well, we definitely have a problem with denim and Chameleon 6.3, but how big a problem?' The question we're trying to answer here, with F21, is whether the problem is denim qua denim, or if maybe it's more like denim as a fifth or sixth material to assimilate. So with subject F21 here, as you can see, the denim blanket will be the first material the subject's body will try to assimilate."

CUT.

Twelve minutes later. The cure rolls onto its back, stretches its limbs to the point of shivering, then bucks to all fours and rises to its feet, throwing off the denim blanket and painsinging. Its body is covered in swelling hills that, shortly, burst.

"Well, so . . ." says the man.

"Yeah," says a woman, offscreen.

"Denim qua denim," the man says.

"Yeah," says the woman.

A pale, entirely depilated cure is sleeping on its side, in the center of an empty, cubical terrarium, covered in a denim blanket. "Sub G03, Cham 7.0" is scrawled in black marker on the front of the terrarium's lower-left corner. The cure rolls onto its back, stretches its limbs to the point of shivering, then bucks to all fours and rises to its feet, throwing off the denim blanket. The cure is covered in what appears to be acne vulgaris. Singing its painsong, it stumbles over to the mirror, examines itself, purses its lips, and with the rounded sides of two of its claws, squeezes a carbuncle on the side of its throat, causing the carbuncle to rupture cloudy fluid.

"Oh, yuck. Just . . . yuck!" says a man, offscreen.

"Well that's a bummer," says a woman, offscreen, "but try and try again, I guess, right?"

The cure throws itself against the wall of the terrarium, exploding other carbuncles, spreading more cloudy fluid, falls, rises, throws itself again, and appears to be poised to rise a third time, when a fist, gloved in white latex, reaches into the terrarium and crushes its head against the floor.

A pale, entirely depilated cure is sleeping on its side, in the center of an empty, cubical terrarium, covered in a denim blanket. "Sub J87, Cham 9.13" is scrawled in black marker on the front of the terrarium's lower-left corner. "Well," says a man offscreen, "we've heard from on high that 9.13 is Team Chameleon's last shot. After this, we'll all be moving on to other projects, so

I'd like to take a moment here, before J87 awakens—I'd like to take a moment to say that, even if we've failed here, and Chameleon goes the way of Antennae, Beardo, Cyclops, and, I don't know, *any* of the other PerFormula dreams that have proven to be too far ahead of current science for us to fulfill . . . I'd like to say I'm proud of all of us, of the work we've done here these last few months, and although it's highly unlikely that any of the teams of which we become a part in the future will ever have the same exact composition as Team Chameleon, I believe with all my heart that anytime two or more of us do end up on the same team, the Team Chameleon spirit we've all developed here together will infect—to its benefit—the team on which the aforementioned two-or-more of us find themselves having been assigned to. In the meantime, our hopes are high for Chameleon 9.13. We've got the bubbly at the ready, and whatever happens, we're gonna drink that stuff. In fact—let's uh . . . Why don't you pop it, Dr. Jennings."

CUT.

Twenty-seven minutes later. Laughter is heard, clinking glasses, the hum of friendly conversation. The cure rolls onto its back, stretches its limbs to the point of shivering, and denim-colored spots arise on its body. It stands, arranges the blanket across its shoulders like a cape, cinching it with its fingers just beneath its chin, and within fifteen seconds, the cure, with the exception of its pupils (dilated) and claws, has become the same raw-denim blue as the blanket.

"Hey! Hey!" someone shouts, offscreen. "Guys, look! Come here."

Clapping and cheering. Howls of victory.

"Where's the mirror?"

"It's over . . . wait . . . It's . . ."

"Show it the mirror!"

A hand, gloved in white latex, sets a mirror inside the terrarium.

The cure approaches the mirror, checks out each of its profiles, makes a couple mirthful faces, flaps the denim cape, and reaches out to touch its reflection. No sooner does the cure's hand make contact with the mirror than it pulls the arm back, as if burned, and hides its face in the elbow of the opposite arm.

The cape slides down its back to the floor of the terrarium. The cure, with the arm it isn't using to hide its face, reaches outward again, touches the mirror, takes a step backward, slips on the denim, and, to catch its balance—at which it is successful—extends the arm thats elbow it's been using to shield its closed eyes.

Slowly, cautiously, the cure seats itself on the floor by the denim and sings its painsong. The offscreen voices, which have all grown hushed, sigh and coo.

The cure turns its head in the voices' direction. We can see it in the mirror, beckoning blindly with both of its arms in time with the painsong.

The sighs and coos increase in volume.

The cure sings and beckons for nearly half a minute, then it opens its eyes. Its eyeballs are boils. One of them has burst.

Retching is heard. Splashing. More retching.

•

• •

Uncut Interview 1 (DVD extra)
from *The Story of Spidge*
1999, HBO Films, USA
[21 minutes]

Greenish morning light and the screech of distant seagulls. A sun-bronzed man with wraparound shades perched over his forehead sits shirtless on a bench atop a beachfront porch, holding up a just-a-sec-while-I-finish-this finger, and drinking long and hard from a steaming, clay mug. The sand behind the porch is comb-lined and white. The ocean is navy, and quietly laps. The man lowers the mug, insists with the finger, winks at the camera, starts drinking again. The sound of his Adam's apple bobbing is audible. The sapphirine face of his platinum wristwatch has a diamond for a six and a crown for a twelve. Dropping the finger, he sets the mug aside and exhales, grins. "Where was I?" he asks.

"Dumb luck," says a woman offscreen.

"Dumb luck? Just that?"

The woman offscreen giggles.

The man winks at the camera. "Man I really must've did need some of that el café. It wasn't *just* dumb luck. That's not how I usually like to tell it. It was a combo-Nazi-own-ay including, yeah, dumb luck, but also blind faith, and rabid tenaciousness—rabid tenacity. Dumb luck, blind faith, and rabid tenacity colon: the birth of a relatively minor and short-lived empire that turned a couple blue-eyed and kinda already rich kids lots richer. Should be the title of my memoir. Or autobiography. Or me and Burnsy's memoir or autobiography. Whatever. Sorry. Still waking up here. Missing Burnsy a little. Just saying his name, you know? Even in that jokey kinda—okay, though. Okay! The story now, the tale, the whole goddamn adventure. So this is how it starts. Starts with dumb luck. There's me. There's Burnsy. Couple of fifth-year-senior outsider dreamer types at el universado up north of here a ways, a couple nothing-specials just sitting around the house one day, bored, and I was telling Burnsy about this one time when I was a kid and I was just, you know, sitting around my parents' house, bored, with Magic, my cat, who was emphatically *not* bored cause he'd just been going at a hunk of catnip, and how I, being bored, I thought, 'Why not?' and I swiped about a cheekful out of Magic's stash there, and I chewed it and chewed it and swallowed it down just as quick as I could, and it seemed maybe forty or sixty minutes later to make me feel a little drowsy maybe, and semi-happy, kinda maybe a little floaty, but maybe I was imagining it, and anyway it gave me a stomachache. Now that's not much of a story is it? It doesn't seem like much of a story at least. Ate me some catnip, might've got a little high, definitely got some kind of reflux or something. But except my pal, see, to whom I told that story some ten years later was, as I said, one Ricky Burnsy McBurn the Burner Burns. And Burnsy—he ran with the thought, see? My telling that story brought to mind for him a time that happened back in *his* teenage years, when *he* was bored. He was laying around his uncle's house, bored, he said, and also hungover. His uncle, I should interject, was a pro-BMXer and also kind of a older-brother figure to Burnsy more than really an uncle cause of their ages being close, and so, before the uncle, who was not called Burns and who I probably shouldn't and so therefore won't name—he, before he OD'd a couple years later, him and Burnsy were just tight as fuck, and Burnsy'd gone over there for a party the night before this hungover morning of boredness I'm talking about, and maybe even he broke his cherry that night, I can't exactly remember, but anyways, anywho, anyhow, anywhat . . . Burnsy said he was laying there, on his uncle's couch, morning after this rager, and he was all hungover and maybe no longer a virgin as of just a few hours ago or whatever, and he noticed there was some white powder on the glass coffee table, like not a lot, but like a decent line maybe, all together, and Burnsy was pretty sure it was heroin cause he'd seen someone blowing some heroin there the night before on that table—his uncle or some chick, I can't remember who he said it was—and he thought, 'Shit. Maybe I should line that shit up and blow it.' But, you know, its being heroin, and him being maybe just sixteen, seventeen, and never having done heroin, it seemed like a thing he shouldn't decide to do or not do on an empty stomach, so he went to the kitchen and he scrambled some eggs, and brought the plate of scrambled eggs to the couch to like I guess *contemplate* the heroin, but just as he's about to sit down on the couch, his uncle's Dalmatian like *blasts* into the room, knocks against Burnsy's leg, surprising Burnsy no end, and Burnsy drops half the plate of eggs on the heroin, and the Dalmatian, you guessed it: Dalmatian eats the heroin eggs.

"Now what happens to the Dalmatian? That is the question. That is the all-important goddamn question. And what happens to the Dalmatian is the Dalmatian's fine. Gets really sleepy. Lays down and growls, maybe kicks at some ghosts in its sleep, even barks at some ghosts for a little while after it wakes up that night, but it's fine. It had a bad time, but the bad time passes, and it's fine, it's fine.

"Okay. So that's part one of this tale of mine here. Part two is, there's an ad on the TV—we got the TV on while we're telling these stories—this ad for this new kind of PerFormula, Stumbler. Remember that one? It flopped. They don't sell it anymore. It was boring as shit. Weak soup, Stumbler. Curio just kinda has shitty motor control. The best thing you could do with it, as I remember, was, you'd leave the room a little while, and then pop back into the room, all smiley and over-happy to see your cure, probably playing whatever version of peekaboo you mighta taught it, and as it runs toward you, *so* excited, to see *you* so excited, it . . . trips. Or whatever. Falls off a table, maybe, and painsings. Anyway, the Curios in the Stumbler ad, they looked, what? They looked banced. Ninety-nine sheets to the wind on the wall. Cures looked *fucked-up*. And I said so. To Burnsy. And given the conversation we'd just had about my maybe getting slightly pleasantly high on catnip and Burnsy's uncle's Dalmatian's getting unpleasantly high on heroin, we thought: 'It's weird we never tried to dose ourselves with PerFormula.' So we went to the store, bought a bunch of Stumbler, and . . . drank it."

"That didn't work, did it?" says the woman, offscreen.

"Of course it didn't work! But did it work's not the point. The point is the seed was planted, and we were a couple of blindly faithful, rabidly tenacious, and bored kinda-rich kids. We spent the next few weeks doing all sorts of stuff with different kinds of PerFormulae. We did everything but injected them really—we were afraid of needles, you know? There was Burnsy's cousin the BMXer overdosed to death, and also we were just naturally squeamish. No fans of blood. But we'd drink them, of course, the PerFormulae I'm saying, and we'd, you know, pour them onto pans til they dried out, scrape 'em off the pans, toot the powder, smoke it, try to mix it up like crack with ammonia, with baking soda, smoke *that* when the bind took . . . Finally, you know, I guess we'd tried all the different kinds of PerFormulae we could get our hands on, in all the different ways we could think to like get them inside us shy of needles, and we thought: 'Shit, all this research, we're working too hard.' And we went out and bought a couple microdots—that's a cute little like Pez-colored candy-looking pebble of LSD, you know? Mixed with speed in this case.

"And there we were again, at the house, bored, waiting for these microdots to kick in, when Burnsy starts saying about how he heard that acid stays in your system forever, that you never get rid of it, and that that's how come people can have LSD flashbacks. Cause the acid's stored in you, and something, some kind of stress or something makes it squirt out and then you're high all over again. Now, the thing that's interesting about that is this: there's no such thing. There's no LSD flashbacks. That's propaganda to keep the kiddies off drugs. If you freak out on acid, then maybe the next time you freak out about something while you're sober it kinda reminds you of that time you freaked out on acid, and you think, 'Shit, I'm having a flashback,' but except that's just the propaganda you swallowed back in childhood like *fucking* with you. What you're having is a plain old regular panic attack. It reminds you of the time you had your bad acid trip because all a bad acid trip is is having a panic attack while being on acid. I didn't know that at the time, though. At the time, I'd heard the same rumor about LSD staying in your system forever, too, and what's more I'd heard that it stayed specifically in your bone marrow. I said so to Burnsy and he said he thought that yeah, that seemed true, but he didn't quite know why it seemed true, just that, when I said it to him, that bit about the bone marrow, my voice had taken on a certain quality of like, Walter Kronkite–type authority. It had *resonance* my voice, and *firmness,* Burnsy said. My voice was like the voice you hear talking over old WWII newsreel footage. It was, and I am quoting directly here: my voice, according to Burnsy, was 'virtually fucking monochrome in its tonal properties of all-time wisdom and goddamn authority.' And when he said that about my voice, and I realized that I understood exactly what he meant, I quickly concluded that we were, indeed, feeling those microdots come on, and I wrote down Burnsy's quote in my little notebook I had in my pocket because back then I was in a phase of thinking I was gonna be the next Kerouac or Bukowski or even the next Tom Robbins or something, and we went for a walk on the beach I'll be damned if I remember as anything but sunlit laughter and mushy gushy warm insides.

"Next morning, though, I've had a fitful sleep and I've got real achy bones from how the speed in the microdot just had me clenched up, you know? And I think: bones, these bones hurt, bones, bones—marrow! And my mind kinda wanders, and I say this thought out loud to Burnsy, who's passed out on the couch opposite the one I'm passed out on. I say: 'Dude!' I say, 'Buh-ro! What about when the fuckers get the grievies!' And Burnsy, he knows just what I mean. And what I mean, of course, is: there's gotta be chemicals, like heavy druglike chemicals going on inside the cure when it doesn't get your body heat. I mean that's gotta be what gets them acting so sadlike and looking so desperate and eventually auto-deactivating, right? Chemicals. And maybe we could get high on *those* chemicals. The autodacting chemicals. Because like sure, the PerFormulae don't get us high, but they gotta be pretty weak stuff compared to the grievy chemicals, right? Because the grievy chemicals end up *ending* the cure.

"And so we proceed to have this conversation, Burnsy and I, which is part three of our story, here. And the conversation goes something like me saying, 'The Dalmatian didn't seem to like heroin, a drug people do like, and yet the Dalmatian was definitely affected by heroin. Maybe what hurts the cure will feel good to us,' and Burnsy saying, 'Totally, Woof, totally. And but the only thing is, though, we've, like, overloaded by mouth on grieving cures and we didn't get high, so.' And then me saying, 'Yeah, but we never OBM'd on a cure that grieved all the way. I bet no one has! Except for some kind of weird sickos or something who we'd never meet anyway. And maybe it's gotta grieve all the way to auto-deactivation before the chemical that would get us high is in a large enough proportion to our bodies to get us high or whatever.' 'Or maybe,' Burnsy says, 'it's that there's the grievy chemical that mixes with some other chemical in their system, like a hormone or something, and it makes a third chemical that makes the cure autodact, and it's that *third* chemical that would get us high.'

"So we put a couple cures in a shoebox with some pellets and water in it, and a few days later, when we stop hearing their painsongs, we open the shoebox, find them autodacted, next to some marbles, and swallow them down, a little gagging-like, cause they're all, you know, cold."

"And that worked a little or what?" says the woman offscreen.

"Hell no it didn't work! And we were in the *dumps*. A couple of disappointed would-be chemical revolutionaries. But like I said before, we were blindly faithful and rabidly tenacious, and, the following morning, when I did my morning two—pardon me for this part, but it's central to the story—when I did my morning two, I saw a couple little like, you know, white little bone-white pieces in there. Bone-white pieces of bone. Looked like they might be those little discs in their spines or whatever. Maybe a heel bone. An elbow bone. You know. Nothing new there. I'd overloaded by mouth more than a couple times, and that's just what happens, as I'm sure you know, though not, of course, via firsthand experience, you being a beautiful woman and all, eye eee a person who has never even once in her whole gorgeous life dropped herself a deuce, be it morning, noon, or night time, heh heh. So yeah, that's just what happens: some of those bones, you just don't digest. But this discovery, or I guess, *re*discovery, was, not to get all punny, but it marked the real like holy shit moment for me. For us. For me and the Burns. I threw the soiled toilet tissue I wiped with into the garbage can so as not to like occlude or obstruct the all-important gaze I would, after having thoroughly washed my hands thank-you-very-much, invite Burnsy to cast upon my morning two, and then I went and woke him up and made him go in there and look. We were good friends, me and him. He was a good sport. I mean, who else would indulge a request of that kind of . . . Goddamn it I miss that guy! I, well . . .

"Well, so I told Burnsy come look down into my morning two in that toilet there, and Burnsy laughed, and knelt, and looked down into my morning two and said, 'Boney Maroney!' and I said, 'Damn right,' and Burnsy said—and I kid you not, Tania, Tania?, Taly, sorry, but I kid you not, Miss Taly, I didn't communicate nothing beyond 'Damn right' après Burnsy's joyful 'Boney Maroney!' we were just that much a couple peas in a podfeather on the same page, same *line,* same *word* on the same page—and Burnsy says, he said, 'You're thinking the final chemical that would get us high is trapped inside the marrow in the bones that we failed to absorb in our bloodstreams for lack of having digested enough of the bones! Am I right, Woof, or what? Is that what you're thinking?' And I said, 'Damn right,' once again because that was but *exactly* what I was thinking when I saw them white bones in mon dumpsky. And Burnsy said, 'I'm with you, brother. Let's seclude us some robots and see if Jizzbrain will help us.' And yeah, that's *the* Jizzbrain—one who did all the skateboards and album covers and was, right about then, getting into sculpture projects and jewelry using Curio skeletons. Remember that hot minute when everyone was wearing that stuff? That was all Jizzbrain. Happened right after this time I'm telling you about. Few months. Maybe a year. Anyway, Burnsy knew Jizzbrain from through his cousin, and they'd gotten pretty tight after the cousin died, and stayed that way even after Jizzbrain was famous, so I knew him, too. Great guy, ol' Jizzbrain. And not, obviously, a squeamish guy. Whereas me and Burnsy both were squeamish as girls in like pink Sunday frocks with starched-up collars and I don't know Chantilly bibs and cuffs or whatever. But so Jizzbrain: he was already by then pretty famous, real busy, and we didn't want to bother him more than oncelike, so we went to a cuddlefarmer and bought, I think, about ten cures—not that cheaply, either, this being what? 1991 still—and we had probably four between us already, and, once they all autodacted, that's when we called up Jizzbrain, and he said, sure, yeah, just bring 'em by and he'd get the bones all cleaned and dry for us.

"And come a couple days later, he'd done as he said, brought the skellies by, and we sat in the kitchen with soup spoons and plates and turned the skellies into one big happy Scarface-looking pile of powder, and that was *that.* Experiment time.

"We snorted it, smoked it, put it in cookies, me and Burnsy, and Jizzbrain, too, just did it up til it was gone, took about a week, and wow it was good, and wow that was exciting, and then Jizzbrain got us a bunch more of his own skellies from his studio, and we ground *those* up, and within a few days, we were the most popular guys in town, bringing it out to parties, clubs, sharing it for nothing, or, you know, selling it at cost when the demand got high and the kids were strangers, but no profit at all, you know, not at all, just love—all goodwill-hippy and whatnot, telling everyone we met how to make it themselves, and by the end of spring break, they were all going back home to their colleges of origin or whatever, and spreading the word. And somewhere in there, a certain chart-topping, shall we say soon-to-be-most-successful-of-all-time heavy metal band that Jizzbrain knew from doing his artwork for, they came through town and we hooked them up, spent half a Friday night with them blowing our supply and pounding back their Jäger, and really just, really *bonding,* you know? Especially Burnsy. Those guys *loved* him—everyone loved him—and it's uh, well . . . It's cause of *that,* cause of how they loved him so much that they ended up dedicating their next album to him. I mean it wasn't, uh— It wasn't like just because uh . . ." Woof holds up a finger. "I just, um. Can I just, uh . . ." Woof draws a sharp breath.

"You want me to turn the camera off a minute?" the interviewer says.

"No, that's okay, darling. I don't . . . I guess I'm not too used to talking about this too much. Haven't in a long uh time, you know, uh . . . Okay. Okay. Fuck it! Back to the tale of Burnsy&Woof, right? Yeah. So now so, what I neglected to mention is, about a week or so after we started hitting the clubs, we'd also started—just cause we thought it was funny—we'd started wrapping el producto up in these little like twisty-ended cellophane-type candy wrappers stamped with a Burnsy&Woof logo that Jizzbrain did up for us. You know the one, right? The burning dog of fire logo. And now *that,* I guess, is probably what impressed Graham&Swords the most—how we'd not only discovered this new use for their product, but we'd also kind of accidentally developed an extremely cool brand, you know? I mean that's what convinced them to come find us, I think. Whatever the reason, though, they asked around and tracked us down, and eventually showed up on our doorstep one day, offered to hire us on as like consultants for a while. They were just I guess starting to go at a lot of chem kids back then—recruiting the top-of-the-class types before they finished school, but not yet somehow really thinking to go for the rebel dropout ones running the Ecstasy labs or what have you.

"And so they'd brought all these geeks to this or that G&S facility at that point, to work on PerFormulae mostly, and then me and Burnsy come along, which, in case I aint made it clear: we weren't like that. Not at all. We knew fuck-all about chemistry, and we were straight up about that, but they mistook us for geniuses, anyway, G&S did. Geniuses of like 'young American desire and design,' the recruiter dork told us. They wanted our ideas, he said. And, you know, the pay was righteous—*righteous*—and we didn't like school any-who, so we went up north soon as poss, hung out with the geeks, told them our ideas about what we thought people might want from future PerFormulae and whatnot, including like how we thought it would probably be good if the PerFormulae could be made in such a way as to somehow enhance or just change up a little whatever chemical it was in the marrow that gets a person high—sake of variety of buzz, you know—but nothing we said struck any of them as feasible, I guess—or at least *so they said* cause I tell you true we came up with BullyKing and Effete the both *years* before they hit the market, even the name of BullyKing was ours, Effete we pitched as *Wuss* or maybe it was *WimpAss*, I don't remember, but they thought we were dummies, these chem kids, and we got moved to Accoutrements, which was basically a matter of like, 'Which color zipper should we use on this new CureSleeve contraption? Gold or silver?' and like, you know, 'Do you think the kids these days want tiny licensed baseball caps to dress up their cures in? Which teams are the most neato?' Boring taste and real silly tie-in shit in Accoutrements, basically, and that's what we told them, we were honest, and soon we were shitcanned. Six, maybe seven months we lasted over there.

"But we'd saved a little dough, and our names were out there, Burnsy&Woof was the coolest. I mean, kids were making T-shirts with that burning dog of fire on them. So we got to thinking, and we called up ol' Jizzbrain, and some venture capitalist friends of our dads, and we told them what we thought. And what we thought, we thought about *gear*. Utility, you know? In-oh-vay-shun. Like, Graham&Swords had the formula thing locked down, but they saw Accoutrements as just, like, apparel. I wasn't shitting you about that zipper nonsense. Gold or silver. That's where *they* were at. Who the fuck cares gold or silver though, right? Make the CureSleeve *better*. Slim the pouch so it doesn't sag out so much, and line it with a kind of protective shell, like an athletic cup kinda deal to protect the cure from accidental blunt force and etcetera. And how about some outside-the-box thinking? Like could a cure not use a little bicycle? A pedal go-cart? A unicycle? Why not? You see them walking on their hands and shit. They *got* balance. Better balance than a human. And it's not like people weren't selling that kinda stuff, but it was all homemade, and the wrong kind of homemade, you know? Not boutiquey, more like flea-markety. And we had this *name*. This *cool*. This *brand*. We could mass-produce, and but just by putting our logo on there not *seem* mass-produced, just cause we were that cool that nothing we did would anyone imagine came out of the, you know, gray capitalist impulse, and . . . you know how that shit works. This is America. Everyone knows how that shit works, but we still buy into it. Celebrate it, even. Can't help ourselves. Story of rock and roll, right? Metal band makes a classy black-and-white video for a song with a couple slow like acoustic parts in it, and they go number one, heavy rotation, platinum times ten, and still every kid at their concert just *knows* he's the only person in all the world who really understands their music, even while he's thinking it from row nine million at a football stadium he paid fifty fucken 1991 dollars to be at, even while all the fuckers who ever picked on him at school, razzing him over his haircut and boots and acne or whatever, they're all down in front of the stage high-fiving each other and like . . . aw . . . oh . . . aw man . . ." Woof's lips contort. He shuts his eyes, says, "Come on, now, Woof."

The interviewer tells him, "I'll just—I'm turning the camera off, Woof, okay?"

Woof lowers his head and covers his mouth, stifling whimpers.

CUT.

"So as I was *say*ing," Woof says, his wraparound shades now covering his eyes, "the real innovation we came up with, all ours, and, you know, this one was our baby because no one *had* quite thought of it yet, and it was a little outlawish: we thought it would be nice to have a real skinny pipe that took superfine screens that would actually stop the bone dust from getting through, first of all, and secondly—and this was the real sweet part—that it would have a bowl and mouthpiece that you could pop or screw them both off the shaft and use the shaft as a snort straw, and each of these pieces of the pipe would have the little burning dog of fire logo on it, but a little bit weirded-like, kinda bendy looking, signifying, you know, good times, high times, can't quite see straight.

"So they—our dads' fancy friends, I'm saying—they invested. In Jizzbrain, Burnsy, and me. And we made those suits *happy*. First the sleeve. Well, not *quite* the sleeve. Instead of making a sleeve with a protective insert, we just made a protective insert that fit the ugly Graham&Swords sleeve, and that was a little depressing in a way, but, man, we made a lot of fucken money. It was a good product. Still is to this day. Japanese design—dude from Nike. And Guatemalan labor. And we rolled some of the profits into a factory in Texas where we did the little vehicles, which, yeah, didn't do as well as the insert, but turned *some* profit. And all this was within, like, what? fourteen months of starting the company. And next up was the baby, the pipe, and it was just about a week or two before it was set to go into production in Mexico—it was all set up, we were just waiting on a special smelter for the, you know, the *ore,* or whatever—that's when I get the call from Jizzbrain, and, you know I don't even know what to say about it. I mean, what's there intelligent to say about it, really? They were a great band. They're *still* pretty good, to this very day. And Burnsy and me had always been deep into metal, and we loved them from their first album, and we weren't gonna abandon loving them just cause they had a few hits, you know? I mean, some people did abandon them cause of that, but not us. And I think Burnsy went into that mosh pit that night partly *because* it was full of a bunch of fratboy-type jerks who were turning our beloved subculture—who'd *already* turned our beloved subculture—into a kind of mainstream, date-rapey, baseball-cap-wearing travesty of bullying, jock-type aggression—rather than the joyful, celebratory-type aggression it once was, I'm saying—and he wanted to reclaim it, you know. Burnsy. Burnsy wanted, that night, to *reclaim* the pit. I think he went in there full of hope and love. Jizzbrain was there, too, and the way he tells it, him and Burnsy actually cleared outta the pit about thirty seconds into the opening number, but then these football-fan types were stomping some like eccentrically dressed, probably gay kid, and Burnsy went back in to help the kid to his feet, to get him to safety, and that's when he took a kick to the head, and, you know, by the time Jizzbrain could get there to help *him* up—they were both, Burnsy and the gay kid—they were comatose, if not already dead. And I don't blame the band. I don't blame rock and roll . . . I don't know. I don't know. I just . . . Shit. Maybe turn that camera off ag—"

CUT.

"So yeah, so. After Jizzbrain calls and he tells me what happened, I . . . I guess I blacked out. And when I came to, I blacked out more, uh, *deliberately* you could say. Blacked out for about a month. Six weeks, maybe. A while.

"My dad comes over one morning, then, you know? And he's with the lawyers, and they say, 'Look, Woof, you don't seem much like you want to do this anymore, and Jizzbrain says it's your call, and Burnsy's dad is beyond caring about anything but his loss of his son, and this offer—' I forgot to mention Graham&Swords had been trying to buy us ever since the sleeve insert hit—'This offer,' Daddy says, 'of three hundred million, seventy-five million of that going to you, is gonna be off the table as soon as your pipe goes to market, and it's set to ship tomorrow. You gotta make a decision.' Cause see, up til then, you gotta understand, Burnsy&Woof was cool and all, and all the kids knew we were the ones discovered spidge, but it was more kind of legendary than historical at that point, if you know what I mean? The oldster money didn't have a clue, and Graham&Swords thought—correctly, I suppose—that if we got known for this special spidge pipe we'd developed, if Burnsy&Woof were *that* outwardly associated to getting high, well, they didn't think it was worth the cost to their family-friendly, warhead-selling corporate reputation to buy our brand. So this was our last chance to sell up. And me? My daddy was right about me. I was done. I didn't want to do *shit* anymore, and here were all those pals of his and of Burnsy's dad that believed in us, invested in us, and they wanted to cash in. So I said, 'Yeah. Sell. Let's sell up.' And we sold up, and that was that. And you know, the real bummer was they just trashed all those pipes. Well, they melted them back down and made belt buckles or some shit, I don't know, but they wouldn't even let me have one, you know? Not a single one. I really thought those pipes were gonna be so great, and for a minute I thought, 'Shit, I'll start a new company, make them on my own,' but it just seemed wrong without Burnsy. So I didn't. Anyway. Anything I've uh—heh heh—left out?"

"Just one thing," says the interviewer. "Spidge. The word. Where'd that come from?"

"Aw, spidge was just something Burnsy used to say for thingy or stuff or like you know whatchamacallit or whatever. You know, a guy wants some minestrone soup but can't remember the word *minestrone* some reason, or he just never knew what it was called and he says, 'Hey, uh, ladle me out a bowl of some of that whatchamacallit.' Burnsy'd, he'd've said, like, 'Ladle me out a bowl of that spidge there,' instead. So I guess it just caught on in the early days at the clubs. Probably Burnsy said something like, 'You sexy ladies there should smoke some of this new kind of spidge with me and my boy Woof over here,' and they just, the hypothetical ladies I'm saying, they just thought that's what the drug was called, and they called it that, and then so did everyone, and it happened, I guess, that cause spidge involves spines, and there's that whole *sp* sound at the beginning, I guess people just went with it. But that's how it was with Burnsy, you know? Easy come easy go. Leave his mark without even realizing his sword was drawn or whatever. Sword? Sword. Sure. Hell am I talking about? You want to meet my horses? I got some beautiful horses other end of the property. We can take 'em out, or even go riding if you want."

"I'd love to," says the interviewer. "Umm . . ."

"But."

" 'But'?" says the interviewer.

"As in 'But not today,' " says Woof, " 'not with some overtanned, tale-telling, near-middle-aged washup,' right? I understand."

"Oh, no! No *but*. I'd love to meet your horses. I was just thinking I could use a cup of coffee first, if that would be alright."

" 'If that would be alright,' huh?" says Woof, smiling broadly. He half-rises from his bench, turns left, and shouts, "Lupita, my darling! Uno el otro café, por favor!"

•

• •

Cuddlefarmer Harvest

Security Footage

2004, Elmwood Junior High School, USA

[6 minutes, 57 seconds]

Fixed overhead shot, black-and-white, silent: a water fountain mounted on an otherwise locker-lined wall in a hallway. A tall boy wearing a canvas duster approaches the fountain, bends to drink. Another, shorter boy, dressed for the beach, rushes up from behind and slams into the tall one.

The tall boy heaves, and vomits in the basin.

The short boy kidney-punches the tall boy and pushes his face against the drain, holding it there, as a third boy, shouldering a messenger bag, enters the frame and tears the tall boy's duster off.

Although the tall boy is now revealed to be wearing a light-colored tank top and what looks like a pair of mid-thigh hotpants, hardly any of the skin below his neck is visible, so thoroughly strapped are his gangly limbs with overlapping, high-capacity CureSleeves—six on each leg, and three each arm.

The third boy kicks the duster aside. He opens his messenger bag against his chest. While the tall boy flails and the short boy intermittently stills him by digging his (i.e. the short boy's) elbow into and around the tall boy's clavicle, the third boy removes the tall boy's CureSleeves, loading them into the bag as he goes.

CUT.

Two minutes later. The third boy is crouching by the tall boy's right ankle, starting to detach the last remaining CureSleeve, when the short boy says or shouts something to him, then rabbit-punches the tall boy twice and bolts offscreen, the third boy trailing him.

The tall boy, alone again, sits on the floor and leans back against the water fountain, openly weeping. A girl with a ponytail enters the frame, sits down before him, squeezes his shoulder. He tells her something. She raises a buttock, pulls the duster from beneath herself, hands the boy the duster.

He scrubs his hair and face dry with the duster, blows his nose, wipes his eyes, balls the duster and throws it offscreen.

The girl pats his knee and tells him something.

He reaches for the CureSleeve on his ankle, opens it. An infant Curio, five or six days old, crawls out and lies down atop the boy's calf. Another cure does the same, and then a third and fourth, all of which look to be about the same age. They lie in a row alongside the first.

The girl picks one up, holds it in her fist in front of the boy's face, tightens the fist, crushing the cure, and throws it over her shoulder, offscreen. She shrugs as if to say, "What? Did something happen? What did I do?"

The boy appears to be fighting a smile.

The girl takes another cure from off the boy's calf, holds it up before the boy, and tilts it back and forth, as if to the rhythm of a nursery rhyme, then turns the cure so she's face-to-face with it, pantomimes surprise, and smashes it firmly against her own forehead, tosses it over her shoulder, offscreen.

The boy is laughing. The girl waves away his laughter and shrugs, wipes her forehead clean, waves away the boy's laughter again, pokes him in the ribs, chucks him on the chin. He cups his hand beside the two remaining Curios. Both crawl in. He sets one of them down atop the CureSleeve, keeps the other on his palm, holds it out to the girl, and tells her something. She pinches one of its legs at the ankle, and he pinches its other leg at the ankle. The cure hangs upside down between them. They nod in sync, one-two-three, and, together, they pull the Curio apart. The girl tosses the leg behind her, offscreen. The boy hands the girl the rest of the Curio. She holds it in a fist. Its mouth opens and shuts and opens and shuts. She holds her other fist just beneath its muzzle, flicks this second fist's thumb as if shooting marbles. Its head snaps back, and stays snapped back. She tosses it over her shoulder, offscreen.

The boy is hugging himself and laughing. The girl pulls back a shirtsleeve, exposing her CureSleeve. She unzips her CureSleeve and a full-grown cure climbs out and stands. She cups her hand and it lies on her palm. She closes her hand and turns it over, holds her cure above the boy's infant, which still sits atop his ankle-strapped CureSleeve, looking on placidly. By the way the girl's cure begins to thrash, struggling to escape from her hand upon seeing the infant, there is no mistaking that it (i.e. the girl's cure) is a hobunk. The boy nods enthusiastically, makes beckoning gestures. The girl extends a halting finger, turns to her side, so the infant is out of the hobunk's sight lines, frees her ponytail from one of its rubberbands, fusses for a moment, turns forward again.

The hobunk is three-quarters hog-tied now—both of its ankles to one of its wrists. The girl sets it atop the boy's calf, near the knee, facing the infant cure. The hobunk bucks wildly, trying to free itself from its bindings, then gives up on bucking and drags itself forward, an inch at a time, grabbing hold of the boy's sparse leg hair and pulling, using its tail for extra leverage.

CUT.

Thirty-nine seconds later. Slightly pixelated close-up. The hobunk, gasping for breath, having dragged itself down the boy's calf, to just within reach of the infant's tail, takes hold of the tail, pulls the infant closer, clutches the infant's neck and squeezes.

The infant goes rigid, then limp, and the hobunk lets go.

The infant slides down the side of the CureSleeve, onto the floor, prone and unmoving. The girl picks up the hobunk, undoes its bindings, sets it standing atop the boy's CureSleeve. It leaps from the CureSleeve onto the infant, and jumps up and down on the back of the infant til matter begins to spill out of the infant, first from the exit, then from the mouth.

CUT.

Eleven seconds later. The same fixed overhead shot as at the start. The girl picks up the hobunk and returns it to its sleeve while the boy, no longer laughing, slowly nods, his eyebrows high and lower lip protruding. He says something. The girl shrugs, turns to him, strokes his cheek. She stands up, helps him to his feet, helps him on with his duster, and, arm in arm, they walk offscreen.

•

• •

[Circa 1992. 4 minutes, 12 seconds.]

Daylight. Heat haze. A couple dozen unwashed, adolescent boys playing soccer on a narrow, gravel lot. Shirts and skins. Oil barrel goalposts. Across the dirt road abutting the lot, a pair of helmeted US soldiers comes over the top of a hill. They descend halfway, sit, light cigarettes.

The ball is kicked out of bounds, in the soldiers' direction, and the boys all seem to catch sight of them at once. They charge toward the soldiers, who jump to their feet, dropping their smokes. The camera follows, bouncily, as the boys press forward, ascending the hill, surrounding the soldiers while shouting out multiple words and phrases in a foreign tongue rife with velar fricatives. [Demon!] and [Demons!] the subtitles read.

One of the soldiers, unsmiling, shows the children his palms, makes placating gestures. The other presses a button on his shoulder radio, says, "Clybourn here. Over?"

The response is inaudible.

"Who you with?" shouts the unsmiling soldier at the camera.

"AP," says the cameraman.

["Demon!"] ["Demons!"]

"We're all swarmed up in B-7," says Clybourn. "Requesting a cuddlefucker Aye-sap. Over?"

The response is inaudible.

"Copy," says Clybourn, and nods once, affirmatively.

"You fellas love the United States?" he says to the boys.

"He am love United States!" one of the older boys says.

"Who?" says the other soldier, pointing to another boy. "Him? This guy? He loves the United States?"

[Demon!] [Demons!] shout the boys.

The older boy points at himself with a thumb. "He am love United States!" he says.

"Who's 'he,' though?" says the soldier, and, pointing at a third boy, and then a fourth, says, "Him? Him?"

The older boy appears confused, pats his own chest.

“Take it easy,” Clybourn tells the other soldier.

“He am love United States? Loving United States? He loving USA,” the older boy mumbles, pointing to himself with both of his thumbs.

The rumble of an engine. A Humvee pulls up at the bottom of the hill. The boys, shouting [Demons!], rush down to the Humvee. The camera follows.

A soldier in a cape steps out of the Humvee. Standing contrapposto, he parts the cape dramatically, revealing his bulgy, ribbed cuddlefarmer uniform.

The children clap and cheer and continue to shout.

[Line up now!] the cuddlefarmer specialist orders them.

The children line up.

The specialist unsnaps a forearm compartment. A trio of infant cures climb out. He cups his hand beside one, the cure climbs in, and he turns his hand over onto the palm of the first boy in line, who is missing three fingers. The specialist extracts from a pocket in his cape a foil packet adorned with the Graham&Swords/US flag logo. He waves the packet in the air and tells the group of boys, [This packet here contains some instructions and a thimble and a special spandex EmergeCuff plus two weeks of good, clean demon food. Some of these demons I’ll be handing out are a day or two older than some of the others, and, depending on its age, your demon might or might not think it’s my demon. If it thinks it’s my demon, it’ll die, but that’s okay. Before it dies, it’ll make a stone, and from that stone, if you follow the instructions included in this packet, you can make a new demon, and that demon will be yours. Now. There’s fourteen demonfood pellets in this packet. You feed your demon one pellet a day, and you give it some water in the thimble when you do it. We will drop more demonfood from the sky soon. If you run out before we drop the food from the sky, you can feed the demon crumbs of any food you’re eating. Its shit’ll smell bad, and it’ll come out in weird shapes, but the demon won’t die for at least a few days. Read the instructions about everything else. The instructions are important. The instructions explain how to make more demons. So many demons you’ll never run out of them. If you can’t read, find someone who can, and have that person read the instructions to you. That’s how you’ll get as many demons as you want. Okay.] The soldier tries to hand the packet to the boy at the front of the line, but the boy, staring fixedly at the Curio in his palm, doesn’t see. “Hey,” the soldier says. “Hey now. Hey. Shit. Already? Hey!” he says, and backhands the boy’s shoulder.

The boy, jarred, looks up at the soldier, fear in his eyes, steps back, gets shoved forward, cups the cure to his chest, looks left, looks right, and jams the cure in his mouth. He chews a couple times, swallows, puts his hand out.

[No,] the soldier tells him. [No more demons for you. That’s why I told you to read the instructions.] The second boy in line shoves the first one aside. The first limps off, crying.

To the other boys, the soldier says, [Don't stare at your demons til you've read the instructions! I won't give you another one!]

The new boy at the front of the line has his hand out. The soldier fills it with a cure and a foil packet. The boy steps out of line. A third one comes forward with his hand out.

CUT.

Nine minutes later. The seven-fingered boy who went into overload is holding his face at the bottom of the hill. All the other boys are gathered on the slope behind him, in groups of four and five. One member of each group is reading the instructions aloud to the others.

The cuddlefarmer specialist approaches the lone boy.

[I'm going to give you a stone that makes another demon. It'll take a few days. You read the instructions before the stone makes the demon. You understand?]

The boy removes his hands from his face. [But why can't I just have another demon? Everyone else has a demon.]

[You had a demon. You ate the demon. You're lucky you're getting a stone, don't you think?]

[Yes.]

[You're lucky?]

[I am lucky.]

[Remember that.]

[Yes.]

The soldier opens a foil packet and removes the spandex EmergeCuff from it, hands the cuff to the boy. [Put that around your wrist,] he says. While the boy complies, the soldier unsnaps a compartment on his thigh, removes from the compartment a Curio marble. [Give me your wrist,] he tells the boy. The boy complies. The soldier inserts the marble in the cuff. He hands the boy the foil packet. [Read the instructions,] he tells the boy. [Now.]

•

•   •

The Afterbirth of Rock 'n' Roll

From *20/20*

May 12, 2000. P.A.L. Productions/ABC Studios, USA

[86 seconds]

A *20/20* news anchor speaking into the camera: "And tonight, we have something special to scroll for you beside our closing credits, so special in fact, we're gonna make a weekly habit of it! You know 'em, you love 'em, you've been calling up the studio demanding we show more of them . . . Well here they are! The P.A.L. Brothers! And don't forget to tune in next Friday for the exclusive Barbara Walters interview with Fondajane Henry. For now: enjoy!"

The screen splits. Upward-scrolling credits taking up the left third. The rest of the screen is occupied by two men in tie-dye labcoats, standing behind a stainless-steel counter on which a twelve-ounce jar of WorkPellets is arranged between two oversize dropper-bottles.

"I'm Donny Mark," says one.

"And I'm Greg Biscuits," the other one says.

"If you don't know us already," says Mark, "we're PerFormulae Abuse Labs, and what we like to do is exactly what it sounds like we like to do!"

"Stack 'em and abuse 'em!" says Biscuits.

"The PerFormulae we've got on abuse tap for you this week," says Mark, spinning the dropper-bottles around so that the labels face the camera, "are BullyKing and Screamer."

"Two doses of BullyKing at the same time is how you start," says Biscuits.

"Two doses droppered *onto a WorkPellet,* so you can be sure your little robot gets it all up inside itself."

"Yep!" says Biscuits. "And then, no less than an hour after administering that big old double dose of BullyKing, and no more than three hours after, you're gonna feed that angry little double-BullyKinged jerk a second pellet that's been *triple*-dosed with Screamer."

"And then what, Biscuits? What kind of completely unexpected results does this highly creative and experimental type of PerFormula-stacking and -abuse produce? I bet it's not a screamer!"

"Nope, not a screamer."

"You saying it's a bully?"

"Not a bully either."

"Perhaps a screaming bully? A bullying screamer?"

"You *know* it's not either, Don. And what is this, anyway? The department of redundancy department? Ha! What you get's a little something," says Biscuits, removing a cure from his labcoat's pocket, "that we here at PerFormulae Abuse Labs like to call . . . the Bitchy Elvis."

Biscuits sets the Curio on its feet, in the middle of the table.

The Curio gyrates its hips while its mouth twitches and one eyebrow hikes, and it shakes its head, as if to say, "No, not you."

Close-up of the Curio, continuing as before.

"Awesome!" says Biscuits, offscreen.

"Best one yet, I think," says Mark, offscreen.

As the *20/20* theme song rises, one of the P.A.L. Brothers index finger–flicks the Curio off its feet, and it lies on its back, continuing to gyrate, hike its eyebrows, and mouth-twitch.

•

• •

Uncut Interview 2 (DVD extra)
from *The Story of Spidge*
1999, HBO Films, USA
[9 minutes]

A teenage girl strapped with multiple CureSleeves sits at a sunlit kitchen table, pulling her faded-pink hair into a topknot. On the table is a paper plate and a cheeseboard. On the cheeseboard is a Curio, facedown and dead.

The girl chopsticks the topknot and lowers her hands. "So I guess there's an art to unzipping them," she says. "Or better call it a skill. It's about as artistic as paring an orange one-handed or whatever, but you know—not everyone knows how to do it. Here's how."

From her overalls' bib pocket, she retrieves an X-Acto knife. She pushes the Curio's legs together, then lays its tail in the space between them. She decapitates the cure, then amputates its limbs at each of their points of origin—one cut per arm, and one that takes care of both legs and the tail. She picks up the torso and, using the side of her knife-holding hand, sweeps the amputations to the plate beside the cheeseboard. She wipes her hand and knife on her overalls, leaving clear stains. She makes an incision that runs from one of the torso's former underarms down to the waist. She turns the torso over and repeats the process. Then she sets the torso back down on its stomach, makes an incision on either side of the neckhole, and sets aside the X-Acto knife.

"That was the easy part," she says. "And now there's this, which, actually, isn't that hard either." With one hand, she reaches into the neckhole and pinches the top of the spine. With the other hand she pinches the skin on the back of the neck. Holding the spine in place against the cheeseboard, she gradually pulls the skin she's pinching toward the torso's waist. The flesh of the back peels away from the skeleton. She drops the flesh on the paper plate. Beneath the top of the spine, she inserts the thumb of the hand she used to peel the skin off, pinning what remains of the neck's flesh to the cheeseboard. With the hand that is pinching the top of the spine, she pulls upward, gradually, while simultaneously pushing the thumb of the other hand forward.

Now that the torso is almost entirely free of flesh, she holds it vertically while gently tapping its tailbone against the cheeseboard until the remaining organs spill out from the bottom of the rib cage. A few remain attached. She severs them with the X-Acto knife, then sweeps the organs and flesh remnants onto the paper plate beside the cheeseboard.

"So there. So now you see there's a little bit of muscle and stuff still clinging to the ribs and the spine. The first thing you do is just get your thumb in here like so"—she sticks a thumb between the ribs and the spine—"and just pop 'em off like . . . that"—she breaks the ribs off three at a time—"cause, see, you don't want the ribs anyway. And so now . . . Now what you've got is a nearly clean spine. To get the rest of the stuff off . . ." She fishes around in her overalls' bib pocket, comes out with a toothbrush. "You just need a toothbrush, see? Easy. You scrub it front and back a little, and anything left's just color—it's not gonna affect the quality of the spidge to any, like, matterful degree. So, anyway, that's pretty much it." She sets the spine on the cheeseboard, repockets the toothbrush.

"But you haven't turned it to spidge yet," says a woman's voice offscreen.

"Well I can't do that for at least a couple days or so—the spine has to completely dry out first. The inside of it, you know. It's—"

"We're only on campus til this evening."

"Oh, well, I guess, um . . . I have some other . . ." The girl walks off camera, returns a moment later with a wooden salad bowl, on the outside of which the word "UPSIES" is written in green marker. She moves the cheeseboard aside and sets the bowl in its place. Inside the bowl is a pile of spines. "These are dry. You want me to, like . . ."

"Prepare them."

"Okay. Sure. I mean, it's pretty standard. I just . . ." She reaches for a mortar and pestle on the windowsill next to the table, sets it down beside the bowl of spines. She selects three spines, drops them in the mortar, and as she crushes them with the pestle, says, "So I just put these spines in, and crush them up into powder with this mortar and pestle, and that's . . . that." She tips the mortar toward the camera, revealing a fine, beige/white/gray powder peppered with larger, sharp fragments. She crushes the fragments in the mortar with the pestle.

"This seems like a pretty standard preparation," says the woman.

"No shit," says the girl, crushing the fragments.

"I thought there was some kind of special preparation. All the kids on campus who we've interviewed say you're famous around here for your spidge. That it's the best."

"I am. It is. Like I told you before we started, though, the spines is the special part."

"I thought you meant that the . . . Well, how so? How are they the special part?"

"How *so*? Okay. So, most other people," says the girl, "use all the bones. I use only the spines."

"You've said that, but I still don't—I mean, that's it? There's nothing else that—"

"That's it, sister."

"How can that be it?"

"Do you know what spidge *is*?" says the girl. "I mean, do you understand what gets you high?"

"I think so, yes. But why don't you tell me."

"Well what gets you high are these chemicals that the Curio's body produces when it auto-deactivates as a result of losing access to your body heat. And you know, if the Curio's formulized when it autodacts, that, too—that'll affect it."

"Formulized or PerFormulized?"

"Doesn't matter. I mean, the *type* of high differs a little on the like upsies-downsies scale depending on what formula you gave the Curio, but no matter what formula—if you use any at all—the chemicals I'm talking about get produced while the Curio's doing all that grievy-looking stuff before it autodacts, and those chemicals get stored in the marrow, and the marrow, that's what gets you high, right? You digest the marrow, you get high. You dry it out, burn it, inhale the smoke, and you're high. And if you're some kind of weird nasal masochist, you snort it, and—"

"You get high. Okay."

"Now, for whatever reason, the marrow in the spine has a higher concentration of those chemicals in it. Like literally twenty-five to thirty times as high as in a rib or a femur or whatever. I heard that has something to do with the spinal fluid—I don't know—but it's a lot higher, you know? And incidentally, that's why when you get little kids who want spidge but they aren't willing to do the so-called *dirty work* of making it, and they don't know anyone they can get it from—that's why, when those kids try, as they invariably do, to get high by swallowing a whole, autodacted cure, it doesn't ever work."

"You lost me."

"Because the spine is the hardest thing to digest. That is: one *doesn't* digest it. *Can't* digest it. And when it leaves your body the next day or whenever, it's mostly intact, marrow and all. So the majority of the chemicals that get you high go . . . *out* with it, the spine."

"That's interesting, if that's true—"

"It's true."

"I didn't mean to suggest it wasn't. I believe you. But what's interesting is that, in principle, if someone were to swallow, what, maybe five or six whole autodacted Curios, they could maybe absorb enough of the chemicals from the other, more digestible bones to get a little high, no?"

"Well, yeah. In principle. But who's gonna do that? Have you ever swallowed an autodacted Curio?"

"No. It's . . ."

"Inexplicably gross."

"Yes. But maybe that's just a matter of taste."

"Sure. And maybe the same goes for eating carrion. There's probably, like, ten people out of seven billion who love to eat them some carrion, but, well . . . You've probably met a lot of people who've swallowed down or tried to swallow down an autodacted cure, right? I mean, I know I have."

"Sure."

"One in three? One in four people?"

"Yeah, sure. Let's call it two in five."

"So that's a lot of people, right? And how many of them you know have swallowed down or tried to swallow down an autodacted cure a second time?"

"Right."

"None, right?"

"Right. Good point."

"Anyway."

"So you were saying that you only use spines in your spidge because the concentration of the drug in the spine marrow is higher and—"

"A *lot* higher."

"A lot higher, and so, what do you do with the rest of the skeleton? You just throw the rest away?"

"Sure. Why not?"

"Because there's still drugs in it, no?"

"In this little documentary exposé movie thing you're making, you have any footage of anyone smoking out?"

"Of course. Lots."

"Well have you noticed how, after each hit, they take a pin or a toothpick or whatever and kind of poke and stir around the spidge inside the bowl?"

"I guess I've seen that."

"They're doing that because the bowl is filled up with powder, and most of that powder is bone, which does not get you high, and so they're trying to expose the unsmoked marrow so that when they light the bowl the next time, they don't just char bone and swallow a bunch of heat. And it's a not-so-fun thing to do, you know? Especially after the fifth or sixth hit, when a) you want to be just enjoying your high already, and b) the remaining, ever-shrinking proportion of marrow is harder and harder to expose. And so if you use a whole skeleton, you do it a lot, this poking, whereas if you just use a spine, which adds up to about an eighth the powder of a whole skeleton, you get *more* high in fewer hits, and with way less futzing around with your toothpick or safety pin or whatever."

"So you're telling me it's out of a kind of laziness that you waste—"

The girl laughs. "I guess. I guess it could maybe be called laziness. But you know, *waste* is a strong word. No one's ever gonna run out of Curios, right? But everyone, always and forever, has been and will be, running out of time. We're all gonna die, girl. You know that, right? You're a grown-up. Of course you know that. You only live once, as my mom likes to say. Why spend any more time poking bone powder than you need to? Well, I mean, I heard you *can* mail-order supposedly some kind of solution that, you add it to the powder, it destroys the bone parts, and leaves you only with the marrow, but that stuff, even if it works, it costs money. Someone told me it works out to about ten bucks a skeleton. Why bother, right? All told, if you subtract the opportunity costs of sitting here, prepping spines, the only cost of making spidge is the WorkPellets it takes to get the cures to maturity, which is like, I don't know, not much—less than a couple bucks—and so then you're more than quintupling the cost by using the solution. If you dose the cure with a formula, of course, that's another three to seven dollars, depending on the formula, but, still, you're doubling the cost if you use the solution. So I guess *that's* a good reason to spend a little more time poking bone powder, but shy of that . . ."

"But isn't the concentration higher if you use the solution? It's pretty much one hundred percent, I thought."

"Supposedly," the girl says. "Still. It's not *that* much higher. Not ten bucks' worth higher. And the yield's the same."

"Also, though, I can't help but think. If you're spending, what? anywhere from two to nine dollars per cure, then throwing away the amputated bones does seem pretty wasteful. Like, anywhere, say, from seventy-five cents' to four dollars' worth of waste, it sounds like."

"You know? You might be onto something. My math's not the best. You may have a point. Maybe I've gotta rethink this. I knew there was a reason I let you convince me to talk to you. Wisdom. You come on a little stiff in that blazer, but, really, you're like a natural-born earth mother."

Offscreen, a man laughs.

The girl laughs.

The woman laughs.

"Okay, so: change of topic," says the woman. "What do you say to people who think that what you do is disgusting? Handling all the meat and the guts and the bones, etcetera."

"It depends who's saying it, and how honest I'm feeling. I mean, if it's someone who spidges, and I'm feeling honest, I might say, you know, that's borderline hypocritical, as in, like, where do you think it comes from? And even if it's someone who doesn't, I think even they'd have to recognize that it's disgusting to dissect frogs or fish or fetal pigs or whatever pretty much everyone in this American school system has to dissect at least once in their lives. And those things—they're living things. They're animals. Whereas Curios . . . right? And you know, maybe they say they dissect animals in school because it's important to learn science or something, because maybe one of them, because they dissected a pig or whatever, will be inspired to become a doctor who will one day cure cancer or whatever. And maybe that's true, but most of them still eat meat, which I find horrible. Criminal, really. I think it's disgusting to eat meat. I don't think we should take life when we don't have to. But blah blah blah because usually I'm not feeling all that honest, and when someone says they think what I do's disgusting, I don't say anything, just nod kind of gravely like this," says the girl, nodding, lips pressed white, "like, 'Yeah, I feel you, man. It *is* disgusting. *So* disgusting.' Because the truth is I make decent money off selling the stuff. I mean, it's not paying for school or anything, but I earn, what do they call it in the old books? I earn *pin money*. I earn pin money off selling a product that pretty much anyone could make on their own if they wanted, but most people won't make mostly *because* they're disgusted by how it gets made. Or because they're lazy."

"How long have you been a vegetarian?"

"Oh, since I was pretty young. Ten or eleven, I think. So, seven, eight years."

"Do you ever eat cure meat?"

"No. Well, I guess I have a couple times. Incidentally. As in, like, incidental to overloading-by-mouth. I didn't want to 'eat cure meat' when I did it—just swallow the cure, as some people sometimes do. It's been a long time, though. Not cause I have any kind of moral problem with it or anything, and I even liked the taste a little, which I can't say about the taste of animal flesh—I never liked it—but my body doesn't tolerate the bones well. I have more trouble digesting them than most people. What my mom calls 'a delicate system.' When I was a kid, and I'd eat sardines—which, ick—I had the same problem, and pumpkin seeds too. I love pumpkin seeds, but I just can't eat them anymore. Someone told me it might be diverticulitis. You know anything about that?"

"Diverticulitis?"

"Yeah."

"No."

•

• •

Sacrament

From *Come Again!? with Philip Daley Alejandro*
Ca. 1992, NBC Studios, USA
[1 minute, 36 seconds]

A talk show set. The studio audience is booing a middle-aged man in flowing white robes, who sits center stage, nodding thoughtfully and pulling his graying, shoulder-length hair behind his ears. The host, Philip Daley Alejandro, stands in the center aisle, five rows up. A microphone dangles at his side from one hand while he holds the other over his brow, as if shielding his eyes from a particularly harsh and annoying and completely unbelievable blast of sunlight. PDA raises the mike to his chin. "Now wait," he says. He takes a couple rapid steps down the aisle and pauses. "Wait a minute," he says. "Are you telling me . . . Wait!" He runs onto the stage, right up next to the man in the flowing white robes. He takes a knee, casts his eyes downward, shaking his head, hugging himself with the arm of his mike-free hand, and says, "You must—I mean, wait. You've gotta just . . . Wait just a minute!" The crowd cheers. "Okay?" he says, as the cheering tapers. "Okay? You've gotta wait just a minute, *sir,* and you've gotta tell me—I mean. Are you telling me—are you telling *us,*" Philip Daley Alejandro says. "Are you telling us that overloading on a Curio is the same thing as a devout Catholic taking communion in the Church?"

"That's not what I said," says the man in flowing white robes.

"Well it kinda sounded *exactly* like what you said. It sounded like you said the two were the same exact thing."

Boos.

"Well, I said that when I and the people who belong to my organization engage in cure overload, we view it as a sacrament, like taking communion. I mean, obviously, Philip, taking communion and overloading aren't the same exact thing. I would never say that."

Boos.

"Well, look. Hold on, now. Just wait a minute. It sounds to me like you're saying the same exact thing I just said you said."

"I'm not," says the man in flowing white robes.

"Well, I beg to differ. So let's just agree to disagree, shall we, and you know, why don't you just clarify whatever point it was you thought you were making."

"All I was saying was that the members of my organization treat overloading as a sacrament. We believe that Curios, wherever they come from—and the Universal Family of Integrated Generosity has no official dogma regarding their origins, by the way—we believe that Curios are here to teach us the beauty of selflessness. Why else, I ask you, would they incite us to overload? to bring about their own permanent deactivation? to do so at the very moment, Philip, that we love them most? They are selfless beings."

"That's crazy. That's nuts. You are off your rocker, sir. Curios are robots. Gizmos. Consumer products. They're here because some genius over at the Graham&Swords Corporation invented them. Or discovered them. Whatever. They're—"

"Well we don't think so, Philip. We don't believe it's as simple as that. I mean, take the rabies vaccine, which was discovered, or invented, however you'd like to think of it, by Louis Pasteur, who—"

"I don't *want* to take the rabies vaccine. My dogs have had their shots, thank you very much. And I *definitely* don't want to hear about Luh-wuh Pasta-ooer or anyone else whose name I have to do that pouty thing with my lips to pronounce."

Roaring laughter.

"So forget Pasteur, then," the robed man says. "Let's talk about the lightbulb, and Thomas Edison—"

"Thomas Alva Edison. A great American."

"Yes. Absolutely," says the robed man. "Edison invented the incandescent lightbulb, which changed how we lived. He did not, however, invent light. He did not invent electricity. And he did not invent the human desire to be able to see at night. Nor—"

"And you're trying to tell me that lightbulbs did those things? Lightbulbs didn't do those things. Lightbulbs can't invent. I got news for you: lightbulbs can't *think*. Can't *discover*. Unless you know something I don't know. And in that case . . ." says PDA, pointing the mike at the audience.

"Wait! A! Minute!" shouts the audience.

•

•   •

Flick&Look

A Yachts Joint

July 13, 2013, Wheelatine USA

[3 minutes, 1 second]

A curb at the bottom of a trapezoid of grass on either side of which is a residential driveway. Wind- and cicada-sounds. Shadows of swaying pine boughs on the ground. Five boys wearing turtleneck T-shirts and Dixie-cup sailor caps, their names in felt block letters stitched to the brim, approach the camera from the back of the frame, and sit down side by side on the curb. Their hats, from left to right, read: *Chaz Jr., Chaz, 3-J, Lyle,* and *Bryce*. These boys are members of a gang or club or clique called the Yachts, and the one whose hat brim reads "3-J" is Jonny "Triple-J" Pellmore-Jason, Jr., the person who made this documentary collage (i.e. *A Fistful of Fists*).

Each boy holds a cure, supine, on one palm.

"Burroughs?" Triple-J says.

"Rolling," comes Burroughs's voice from offscreen. "Ready when you are."

Looking down at his cure, Triple-J raises his free hand an inch or two over its torso and, with his thumb and middle finger, forms an O.

The other Yachts do the same as Triple-J.

"Flick," Burroughs says.

With their middle fingers, the Yachts flick their cures. The cures ball up and launch into painsongs. A couple measures in, they begin to unball, to writhe and squirm. The camera pans across them in close-up. A couple hold their foreheads, the other three their chests, and they all tense their jaws and suck in their lips, apparently trying to stifle themselves, but the songs keep escaping in hums and squeaks.

As the camera zooms out, we can see Chaz Jr.'s hands are trembling, and the free one (the right), just a sliver of a second before the round ends, goes high and claps down, killing his cure with a muffled crunch.

"Look away," Burroughs says. "Chaz Jr., you're out."

Chaz Jr. chucks the corpse atop the grate of a storm drain left of his feet, and the rest of the Yachts look away from their cures.

To Chaz Jr., Chaz says, "Hate not the player, but the game, word up."

Chaz Jr. shakes his head in bitter disappointment.

"Now there's no call to razz and harass, Chaz," says Bryce. "I say Chaz Jr. put forth a mighty effort. He played a good game."

"I was merely dropping wisdom on his mug," says Chaz.

"Be that as it may, and it *may,*" says Bryce, "I *do* recognize it may, I, for one, would like to go on record as saying that I commend Chaz Jr.'s truly dope performance."

"Hear hear," Lyle says. "He played Flick&Look with heart!"

"Burroughs," Triple-J says.

"Round two," says Burroughs. "Ready? Flick."

The four remaining contestants look down at their cures and, as before, middle-finger-flick them. The painsongs rise, rise, go tremulous. Exhaling sharply, Bryce raises his cure, and overloads by mouth.

"Bryce is out," says Burroughs.

Lyle turns to face Bryce.

"Lyle," says Burroughs, "is DQ'd for gazebreak."

“Stupid, *stupid,*” Lyle says to himself, then, “Oh well,” and, smiling down at his cure, pops its head in his fist.

“Look away,” Burroughs says.

The last two contestants, Triple-J and Chaz, look away from their cures. Chaz is blinking heavily, breathing loudly and deeply.

“Round three in three,” Burroughs says to them. “Ready? Three. Two. One. Flick.”

Triple-J and Chaz flick and look at their cures.

The painsinging, which hasn’t abated since the previous flick, gets louder for an instant, and then, just as suddenly, radically quieter.

“Oh no,” Chaz says, eyes still on his cure.

The camera zooms in on the cure; it’s still; it’s dacted; its neck appears broken.

“Alright, stop,” Burroughs says.

Chaz and Triple-J cease looking at their cures.

“Well this is unprecedented,” Chaz says.

“What is?” Triple-J says, checking out Chaz’s cure.

“Seems I’ve dacted my cure, bygolly,” says Chaz. “But I didn’t overload. The flick is what dacted it. I flicked it too hard.”

“You lose,” says Bryce.

“True dat,” says Lyle. “You did not win.”

“Well I can’t rightly say I’ve won, of course, but were I to say that I felt I’ve lost . . .” Chaz says. “I mean, were I to say that, chaps, why, I’d be a lying Liam. An effing fibbing Frankie.”

“And yet you’re the loser,” Chaz Jr. says. “And so your feelings have betrayed you. I daresay they’re worthless.”

“Easy,” Triple-J says. “What’s your ruling, Burroughs?”

“I don’t know,” says Burroughs. “Technical gazebreak?”

“But I didn’t break my gaze,” Chaz says.

“Correct me if I’m wrong,” Chaz Jr. says, “but I believe the designation ‘technical’ covers that, what what.”

“No,” Lyle says. “Chaz has a point. I do like ‘technical,’ but this was more a technical *cure overload,* I think. Chaz didn’t look away.”

“Nor did I overload!”

“But the outcome’s much the same,” Lyle says. “There in your hand lies a dacted cure, what, a dacted cure dacted because you dacted it. And certainly there was *some* loss of control. You didn’t, after all, *intend* to dact it. You said so yourself, what what hey hey.”

“Does it matter what we call it?” Triple-J asks them.

“I suppose that it doesn’t. Not much,” Chaz says.

“Word up,” says Lyle.

"Hear hear," says Bryce.

"Agreed," says Chaz Jr. "You're quite the loser either way, holmes."

•

• •

Cold Open

from *Inhuman Self Denial*

2006, Paramount Pictures, USA

[3 minutes]

In profile, Basho—a long-tailed, two-legged, violet-eyed Curio with shimmering white, almost silvery, velvet, and a set to its brow that seems, in equal parts, to invite and refuse interpretation—does yoga atop a ten-foot-high pillar of petrified redwood: resting tortoise to embryo in womb. An arm's length away, a monk in a loincloth, barely out of his teens, sits in lotus on a matching pillar, eyes locked on Basho's.

Neither monk nor cure appears aware they're being filmed.

The frame gradually widens til we see their pillars are inside the hollow of a giant sequoia.

As Basho transitions from embryo in womb to upward cock, the monk jerks forward, then straightens again, and a voiceover—male, Oxbridge—states: "At the age of one hundred twenty-nine months, Basho is the oldest known Curio on record. Since 2003—for nearly three years now—tourists and seekers from around the world have made the pilgrimage to northern California's San Marcona Monastery to behold Basho and its master, known by the brothers of San Marcona as 'The One Who Sees Basho,' at their morning exercises."

The frame widens further. A dozen monks in orange robes kneel shoulder to shoulder in the sequoia's shadow, facing a crowd of roughly two hundred pilgrims, all of whom are gazing at the figures on the pillars, many awwing and sighing and reflexively patting at their chests and their pockets, presumably for cameras that were confiscated earlier; confiscated, perhaps, at the gate to the stone-walled courtyard in which, we now see—as the outward zooming comes to a halt—the entire scene is set.

The voiceover continues: "But for The One, and a pair of blind servants, no one is permitted within fifteen feet of Basho. This prohibition, as you're about to witness is . . . well warranted."

For a moment, Basho, still in upward cock, appears, from our relatively distant perspective, to levitate a little, though soon it comes clear that it's using its tail to raise the rest of its body. The self-patting and awwing and sighing crescendo. Sobs are heard. Laughter. Couples are embracing.

And then: a disturbance near the back of the courtyard. A man cries out, rushes violently forward, shoving aside those who fail to make way for him. At the front of the crowd, blocking his path, sits a child in a wheelchair. The man attempts to vault the child, but catches a knee on the back of her head and lands on a shoulder just in front of the monks, who have leapt to their feet.

Three monks step forward. The man stands up and attempts to get past them. He is clapped on one ear, and he drops just as suddenly. The monk who clapped him lifts him under the arms, a second parts the crowd, and the clapped man is dragged toward the back of the courtyard.

While the third monk tends to the girl in the wheelchair, three more people—two boys and a lone man—push toward the front along the side of the crowd, and, in doing so, incite a number of the pushed to push forward themselves.

The nine otherwise-untasked monks form a pair of concentric semicircles in front of the sequoia: six make the outer circle, nearer the crowd; three make the inner one, nearer the tree. Someone shouts, "Now!" and those in the crowd who fail to move forward are trampled.

As the outer semicircle of monks fends off the onrushers, we momentarily glimpse the pair of blind servants entering the hollow through the back of the tree.

Close-up of Basho and The One on their pillars, continuing to exercise. The upper halves of the servants, who have somehow climbed the backs of the pillars, appear. One servant fits a gas mask onto The One. The other servant dangles a much smaller gas mask in front of Basho, which lowers itself, untangles its limbs, dons the gas mask, and bends and twists into sleeping tortoise.

As the frame widens again, and we see the onrushers, having grown in number, overcoming the outer semicircle of monks, and the inner semicircle extending batons from the sleeves of their robes and shouting toward the tree, and as Basho transitions to rising tortoise, and as The One sits lotus, what appear at first to be four or five pinecones thud down from on high, into the melee. These "pinecones" start hissing, and those near them start coughing and falling down, and a dozen gas-masked, dark-robed monks bearing tasers and batons drop from branches, encircle their brothers, and whatever happens next is rendered invisible behind the rising cloud of milky red and blue smoke.

•
• •

Charity Party
A Yachts Joint
May 11, 2013, Wheelatine USA
[77 seconds]

A row of cars in the teachers parking lot of Wheelatine High School, the afternoon sun glaring white off the roofs and sideview mirrors. A finger appears, points at the cars, while a voice offscreen says, “That’s the one right there, chaps, what. Next to the Volvo. The gray Asian number with the spoiler, hey hey.”

CUT.

Two minutes later. Three Yachts, with their backs to the viewer, are gathered next to the driver-side door of a gray Toyota coupe. “What a beaut,” one says. “What a bang-up job.” The three go around to the opposite side of the car, crouch down out of sight, below the passenger-side window.

The camera zooms in to close-up on the gray Toyota’s driver-side door. An upside-down Curio, the tip of its tail pinched by the door handle, swings left to right, reaching up, attempting to free itself.

From one of the crouching Yachts comes a command: “Once you get the shot, Chaz, hide behind the Volvo.”

CUT.

Eleven minutes later. Medium shot of the gray Toyota’s driver-side door, seen through the windows of the car parked beside it. No longer swinging, the Curio is visibly painsinging, but the wind is high, and the song is inaudible.

A man approaches the Toyota, keys in hand, pauses before the door, says, “What is going . . . ?” and removes the cure, looks left, looks right, looks behind himself, stares briefly at the face of the cure in his fist, then bashes its skull flat against his forehead.

The Yachts crouched on the opposite side of the Toyota jump up and shout in unison, “Compliments of the Yachts, Mr. Pearson!”

“Oh!” says the man, Pearson, dropping the cure, covering his forehead, clutching his chest. “You guys. You . . .”

“No, *you*, good sir!” says an offscreen voice. “*You*, sir! You! It’s in most highest homage to you, good sir, that we threw this bomb-ass charity party!”

“You deserve it!” says another offscreen voice.

“Chaz is right,” says Lyle, from the far side of the Toyota. “We never gave hoot one about World War II before we took your class. And World War I? You did that piece *so* nice. You made it feel important."

"You're a good fellow," says Triple-J, who has come around to Pearson's side of the Toyota to clap him on the shoulder.

"Alright," says Pearson, dabbing at his forehead with a handkerchief. "Alright. Thank you, boys."

•

•   •

Public Service Announcement

PAVIOSI

1994, USA

[60 Seconds]

A junior-high-school-aged boy in a denim jacket rollerbades across a basketball court. The words "Who's got the Cure?" are superimposed upon the court in his wake in neon purple script while an accompanying sound effect—a kind of *shish*ing—creates the impression that the words are being sprayed onto the asphalt from a giant, invisible paint can in the sky. The boy skates out of frame on the right, a zigzag is added beneath the question, and then the boy is standing before a brick wall, in close-up, addressing the viewer:

"I'm Justin Sampson and I've got the cure," he says. "Last semester, we were walking down the hall, and my friend got shoved right into a locker. Who knows if it was on purpose or not? I don't think it matters, and I didn't think so then, but my friend sure did. 'I'm gonna get that guy who shoved me,' my friend said, and I didn't think he should because violence in schools is a disease, and you wouldn't want to spread a disease, would you? So I told my friend to just wait a minute, and I unsleeved my cure and gave it a poke. That morning I'd PerFormulized the cure with Sappy, and it made this face that was totally awesome, and I could tell my friend wanted to overload on it, so I said, 'Go ahead,' and he did. After that he chilled out and forgot about the shove. He gave me his own cure later that day. It felt really good, you know? We helped prevent the spread of the disease of violence together. Now we're better friends than ever. Friends cure friends, I think, and cures create friends. So if *you* have the cure, use it. In a way, you almost *gotta*."

Justin tilts his head a little, purses his lips, and a low-voiced man in voiceover says, "A little thing can go a long way. Be the cure for school violence."

A lower-voiced man in voiceover says, "This message brought to you by PAVIOSI, the Parents Against Violence In Our Schools Initiative, paid for in part by Graham&Swords Corporation."

Justin winks.

•

• •

And Now, For What You Thought Was the First Time Ever

Home Video, originally aired on *20/20*

February 19, 1988, ABC Network, USA

[3 minutes, 15 seconds]

A boy in a Belinda Carlisle concert T, a censor box across his eyes, stands behind a table on a stage beneath a banner reading, "Carl Sandburg Middle School Talent Show."

Atop the table is a Curio and a microphone. The boy whistles the first phrase of the theme from Wagner's "Flight of the Valkyries." The cure whistles the next phrase. The boy whistles the third, and the cure the fourth.

The cure spreads its arms and turns to the boy.

The boy scratches its head.

The audience applauds.

The cure turns back to the audience and bows.

"That's one we uh practiced a lot for the show," the boy says. "Now we're gonna try some improvisational music. Are you ready?"

The audience cheers.

The boy whistles the first phrase of "Twinkle, Twinkle, Little Star."

The cure whistles the first phrase of "Twinkle, Twinkle, Little Star."

The cure spreads its arms and turns to the boy.

The boys scratches its head.

The audience applauds.

The cure turns back to the audience and bows.

The boy whistles the first and second phrase of "Twinkle, Twinkle, Little Star."

The cure whistles the first and second phrase of "Twinkle, Twinkle, Little Star."

The cure spreads its arms and turns to the boy.

The boys scratches its head.

The audience applauds.

The cure turns back to the audience and bows.

The boy whistles all six phrases of "Twinkle, Twinkle, Little Star."

The cure whistles all six phrases of "Twinkle, Twinkle, Little Star."

The cure spreads its arms and turns to the boy.

The boy scratches its head.

The audience applauds.

The cure turns back to the audience and bows.

"Now we'll try it *call-and-response* style," says the boy.

The audience cheers.

The boy whistles the first phrase of "Twinkle, Twinkle, Little Star."

The cure whistles the first phrase of "Twinkle, Twinkle, Little Star."

"Not *repeat,*" the boy says to the cure. "*Call and response.*"

The cure spreads its arms and turns to the boy.

The audience laughs, applauds.

The boy shrugs, scratches the cure's head.

The cure turns back to the audience and bows.

The audience applauds.

"Let's try it again from the top," the boy says.

He whistles the first phrase of "Twinkle, Twinkle, Little Star."

The cure whistles the first phrase of "Twinkle, Twinkle, Little Star," then turns to the boy and spreads its arms.

"No," says the boy. "*Call and response.*"

The cure tilts its head.

The boy gestures with a circular motion of his finger.

The cure hangs its head and turns back to the audience.

The boy whistles the first phrase of "Twinkle, Twinkle, Little Star."

The cure whistles Wagner.

The audience laughs.

The boy tugs the cure's tail.

The cure sings a partial painsong.

The audience applauds.

The boy, no longer so frustrated-looking, tugs the tail again.

The cure painsings louder, for longer than last time.

The audience applauds and makes surprised sounds.

The boy, smiling now, pinches the cure's tail between the nails of his thumb and his index finger. The cure painsings at the tops of its lungs, spreads its arms, and slowly turns to the boy and bows to the boy. The boy, who continues to pinch it and smile, though tears are now streaking out from under his censor box, lifts the cure up off the table by the tail. He holds the cure in front of his face for a moment, listening to its painsong, then bashes it twice against the table, swiftly. He lets go of the tail, looks down at the cure, which is lying on its belly, limbs atwitch, and flips it over onto its back.

The cure spreads its arms and, by the set of its mouth, appears to be pain-singing, or attempting to painsing, though no song can be heard above the shouts and "No's!" and moans from the audience.

The boy wipes his mouth on the back of one sleeve, wipes his eyes on the back of the other, looks right, then left, as if preparing to cross a quiet street, sweeps the cure up, pulls its head off, drops the head on the table, then the body, and, pounding his fists against his temples and screaming, runs toward the back of the stage. He trips on a cord, and scrambles back to his feet. His face is bleeding all over his shirt.

•

• •

Silver-Medaling US National Science Fair Entry, Part 1
Home Video
September 9, 1991, USA
[19 minutes]

An emaciated, ashy-skinned, junior-high-school-aged girl in a high-collared, doily-bibbed, flower-print dress leans a little to the left on her four-footed cane beside a kitchen table on which rest two PillowNests. Three crumpled-looking fingers on her withered right hand—the whole arm is withered, and its elbow seems to be permanently bent—involuntarily twiddle by her ribs. Her shiny black eyes—arrestingly protuberant, alarming and alarmed-seeming—appear to be occupying most of her skull.

She swallows, smiles, stops smiling, and says, "I am Maya Mehta of Newton North High School," and smiles again, and again stops smiling. "I have always thought that Curios were shy," she says, "but because of the effect I fear my physical appearance has upon others and because of my accent which I know is not so strong but is still to be sure at least a little bit strong and because of how sometimes when I am feeling very nervous I speak rather too quickly and rather too mumblingly I myself am also shy which I am sure you must have already guessed by now as you are watching a video of this my science fair presentation for the US National Science Fair instead of watching me present my project in person ha.

"The one and only thing that I am more than shy is certain that the scientific method is a glorious method and that anything about which we do not know empirically is something about which we do not really know."

Maya swallows, smiles, swallows, stops smiling.

"There are so many biases," Maya says, "and biases are barriers to science, and barriers to science are barriers to knowledge. Because I am shy and because we tend to think those people and those things that we have strong and positive feelings for are like us in essential ways and because I have very very strong and positive feelings for Curios, I have, always, because I am a scientist, had to question whether Curios were truly shy or I was just—owing to bias—projecting an essential quality of myself, Maya Mehta, upon them.

"When I began last year to think about the project I might wish to enter into this year's science fair, I settled all too quickly on devising a scientific method of determining whether Curios are shy or not. Oh my oh my what a pie in the sky!

"Shyness is an internal state about which, I discovered in the course of my research, science knows really hardly anything at all. This will likely change over time as brain-scan technologies improve, but we are unable right now to measure shyness by any means other than self-reporting instruments such as questionnaires, which are not very accurate to begin with when it comes to human animals, and are, of course, useless when it comes to nonhuman animals since nonhuman animals don't use human language and cannot, therefore, self-report. So when it comes to Curios, which is to say robots resembling nonhuman animals, which may not even experience internal states—however convincingly sentient they may seem, they may not 'experience' anything at all—the idea of attempting to determine whether they are shy by using the one instrument we have for measuring shyness in human animals is so completely ludicrous it is perhaps silly to even mention it ha-ha whoopsie.

"Perhaps I am getting a bit far afield. The Introduction is the part of this my science fair project's presentation about which I am the least confident and thus the most shy. I will attempt to speed the Introduction along now.

"From the cinders of my total failure to devise a scientific method of determining whether Curios are truly shy has arisen the phoenix of some truly unexpected findings.

"You see, in the course of thinking so much about shyness, I began to consider rear ejection. Every morning ever since my first Curios emerged from their marbles, I have, like all other owners of normally functioning Curios, discovered rear ejections in their PillowNests, one per Curio per morning, and yet the process by which these rear ejections entered the world was something I hadn't—not even once—witnessed. 'How strange,' I thought. Maybe it was just me? I had to find out! And so I informally surveyed members of my peer group about this very subject, and when the ones who were willing to talk to me answered, they confirmed the commonality of our experience, or rather our *lack* of experience: they had never witnessed any of their Curios rear-eject either.

"Were Curios shy when it came to rear-ejecting? That was the question I had been asking myself at that time, but it was the wrong question, for shyness, as I have already explained, is a subjective state the study of which is beyond the scope of our present abilities as scientists, even when it comes to human animals. The question I should have been asking was: 'Why have I never rigged a camcorder to a PillowNest so as to capture moving images of my Curios rear-ejecting in the night?' And when I did, finally, ask myself that question . . ."

Maya pivots a little and, with her smaller shoulder, indicates one of the PillowNests on the table beside her. The camera zooms in on it. The lid of the PillowNest has a large hole in the middle. "With the help of my father, I removed, with a saw, a circular section from the lid of this PillowNest."

The camera zooms back out. "That night," says Maya, "I left the light on in the PillowNest, and then, after having affixed a fish-eye lens to the camcorder that my father is using to tape this very presentation you are watching, I set the camcorder over the hole and pressed the record button.

"In the morning, however, I was very disappointed to discover that there was nothing to discover. Neither Mick nor Keith nor John nor Paul—these were the names of the Curios I recorded—seemed to have rear-ejected in the night. Was it possible the Curios had rear-ejected, and then, for some reason, hidden, or even perhaps *consumed* their rear ejections? This thought occurred to me, of course, but upon reviewing the tape, I saw that they had done nothing of the sort. They simply had not rear-ejected at all. I could not recall this ever having happened before.

"Being a scientist, though, I did not allow myself to jump to the conclusion that the correlation between the presence of the camcorder and the inhibition of the rear-ejecting was meaningful; I permitted myself to *hypothesize* that the correlation was meaningful, but knew that in order to confirm my hypothesis, my results would need to be replicated. And so, the following night, I created the same conditions as I had the first night.

"And my results were replicated. No rear ejections did I find in the nest. No hiding or consumption of rear ejections did I find on the tape.

"A third night applying the same conditions engendered exactly the very same results.

"On the fourth night, I replaced the piece we'd sawn off the PillowNest lid and turned out the light; in the morning I discovered four larger-than-average, but otherwise normal-looking, typically grape-bubblegum-smelling rear ejections in the nest."

"After that, the correlation seemed undeniably meaningful. That is: the presence of the camcorder had inhibited the Curios from rear-ejecting.

"But what exactly was it about the presence of the camcorder that inhibited them? First, I should say that I wondered, very briefly, if I had it all wrong: I wondered if perhaps it wasn't the presence of the camcorder at all that had caused the inhibition, but rather that I'd left the light on in the PillowNest. Upon but the shortest moment of reflection, however, I became certain it couldn't be the light in the PillowNest that inhibited the Curios' rear-ejecting: over the past couple of years, I had, on numerous occasions, forgotten to turn out the light in the PillowNest at bedtime, yet the Curios had always rear-ejected by morning nonetheless. So the light could not have been what inhibited them. Of that I was certain. Perhaps, then, it was the sound that inhibited them? The sound of the videotape turning inside the camcorder? Well, maybe, but . . . You see, I, like most young Curio owners—and, I would suppose, many adult Curio owners as well—keep my PillowNest beside the bed in which I sleep, which means that I and my Curios, although we cannot see each other while they are in their PillowNest, can hear each other. I know this because, if I whistle good night to them after closing the lid to the PillowNest, they whistle back to me. And there are louder things happening in my room in the night than whistling, I assure you! *Exempli grati,* after settling my cures in their nest, but before I retire, I often do this . . ."

The screen blinks. We see a five-second clip of Maya, seated on the edge of a bed in pajamas, playing the first verse of "Yankee Doodle Dandy" on a large harmonica.

The screen blinks, and we're back to the original tableau: Maya beside the kitchen table. "Soooo embarrassing," she says, giving off, unexpectedly, a whiff of false humility. "But if you think that *that* is bad, how about this . . . ?"

The screen blinks. We see a ten-second clip of Maya, same bed and pajamas as before, but lying down, asleep, and snoring continuously, waterously, and at such a high volume that it seems inauthentic until, halfway into the clip, she turns her head, spilling drool from her lips onto the pillow, twitching awake, mumbling, "Shh, Maya. Quiet now, Maya. Maya Maya Maya," and turning back over and snoring again.

The screen blinks, and once again we're back to the original tableau. "Now that," Maya says, "is *really, really, really* embarrassing. And not only is my snoring as loud, if not louder, than the sound of me jamming out on my mouth-harp, but, part of my affliction is that I do it all night long, every night, only occasionally pausing when the sounds I am making wake me up, as you saw in that clip. Can you testify to this, Daddy? The persistence of my snoring?"

A man offscreen says, "My brilliant, beautiful daughter snores like a goat and has never told a lie!"

Maya lowers her eyes, removes her hand from the cane to wave off the compliment, swallows, swallows again, looks back at the camera. "But what I am attempting to convey," she says, "is that, while it did seem possible that the specific atmospheric sounds that the camcorder made while recording may have inhibited the rear ejections of the Curios, it seemed very unlikely, because other, louder, presumably more disruptive atmospheric sounds had not historically done so.

"So could it have been the smell of the camcorder, then? Did the camcorder *have* a smell the Curios could detect? Could I measure such a smell? Maybe it was the extra *heat* the camcorder added to the air inside the Pillownest? *Did* the camcorder [the frame bounces, briefly] add extra heat? Well— My father has just indicated to me that I am over-enumerating, and so I will move on now.

"In the end, there seemed to me to be only two possible explanations for why the presence of the camcorder in their PillowNest should inhibit John, Paul, Mick, and Keith from rear-ejecting. The first was that Curios are inhibited from rear-ejecting when certain kinds of changes to the PillowNest environment to which I'm not sensitive, or of which I was incapable of imagining, are introduced. That is: it might be that what inhibited my Curios' rear-ejecting wasn't that a *camcorder,* per se, was protruding from the ceiling into the PillowNest, but that, perhaps, *anything* was protruding from the ceiling into the PillowNest, or anything shaped like a fish-eye lens, or anything reflective, or possessing any other qualities in common with the camcorder or fish-eye lens that are salient to Curios but not to me.

"And the second possibility was that John, Paul, Mick, and Keith were being inhibited from rear-ejecting by the knowledge that they were being recorded.

"Oh but wait a minute! In the course of having interrupted my own enumerations, I seem to have been thrown off my outline. I'm ahead of myself. Please permit me to backtrack."

The screen blinks. We see a slow-motion, somewhat disorienting clip of Maya's face in close-up. Beneath her chin she holds an apple with a bite taken out of it. She brings the apple to her lips, moves her lips and her jaws, and when she takes the apple away from her mouth, it is whole, unbitten.

The screen blinks again. Original tableau. "What I forgot to tell you was, perhaps interestingly, something that, up until I established the correlation between the presence of the camcorder and the inhibition of the Curios' rear-ejecting, I had, myself, all but forgotten. What I forgot to tell you is that I spent nearly five weeks last summer teaching John and Paul and Mick and Keith to perform a very impressive trick, or set of tricks, as the case may be, ha!"

The screen blinks. We see John and Mick standing shoulder to shoulder along the edge of a square of kitchen tile; they face Paul and Keith, which stand shoulder to shoulder along the opposite edge of the same square of tile. Maya, offscreen, says, "Hands," and John and Mick hold their hands out palms-down, and Paul and Keith hold their hands out palms-up. All four Curios look up at the camera, which is presumably being operated by Maya, and anxiously start to bounce on their heels. Maya utters a long "Mmmmmm," cueing the cures to look across the square of tile at one another, and, then, as she chants the rhymes below, they engage in a fast and intricate pattycake, involving not only the usual vertical, diagonal, and horizontal hand-slaps, but also pantomimed face-slaps, belly-pokes, palm-strikes, brow-wipes, and choke-holds:

Miss Susie had a steamboat, the steamboat had a bell,
Miss Susie went to heaven, the steamboat went to . . .
Hello operator, please give me number nine,
And if you disconnect me, I'll kick you from . . .
Behind the 'frigerator, there was a piece of glass,
Miss Susie fell upon it, and cut her little . . .
Ask me no more questions, tell me no more lies,
Miss Susie told me everything, the day before she . . .
Dyed her hair all purple, then dyed her hair all pink,
Dyed her hair in polka-dots, and washed it down the . . .
Sink me in the ocean, sink me in the sea,
Sink me down the toilet, but please don't pee on me!
Oh hello operator, please give me number 10,
And if you disconnect me, I'll sing this song . . .

At the end of the third round, Maya adds the word "again," and the Curios end the pattycake, fire finger-guns at one another and then at the camera, and then the screen blinks.

We're back to the original tableau. "While teaching the Curios this very adorable and—if I may say so myself—*very* impressively choreographed pattycake routine," Maya says, "I taped their progress every day—again, using the very camcorder my father is taping this very presentation with—and, every evening, after dinner, I would compare and contrast the tape I'd made that day with the previous day's tape and take notes, in order to be sure that the improvements I believed I was seeing in their performance were really real, and not merely the result of wishful thinking on my part. All my notes, and two of the tapes I made—most of them have since been recorded over—are included in the box marked 'Raw Ancillary Data,' in case you, the judges of this year's US National Science Fair, are interested in reviewing them.

"What I unfortunately lack, however, are recordings of myself watching the recordings I made. I say this is unfortunate because, if I had such recordings—such recordings were never made—you would see that, most evenings after dinner during the period that I was teaching the pattycake routine to the Curios, they were sitting on my shoulders *while* I watched the tapes. And that is most germane to the point I am making. That is most germane to the experiment I have conducted. For you see, after John and Paul and Mick and Keith's rear ejections had been inhibited for the third night in a row, and I recalled their pattycake training, it occurred to me that 'Wait! Since they saw me holding a camcorder to my face while they trained, and then they sat with me while I watched the tapes of their training, maybe they came to understand the tapes were made with the camcorder . . . Maybe they understand that if a camcorder is in their PillowNest, it will allow human beings or, at least *this* human being—myself, Maya Mehta—to see what they are doing or have done in their PillowNest, and that if they rear-eject in the PillowNest, under the mechanical eye of the camcorder, then human beings, or this human being, this Maya Mehta, in whose sight they have always been inhibited from rear-ejecting, would be able to see them rear-ejecting, and thus they are inhibited from rear-ejecting.' Now, this thought I had contains many leaps, I am well aware. First of all, it assumes that Curios set before a television screen see images the way human beings see images—that they translate the waves and particles into the same recognizable figures that human beings do. Secondly, it assumes that they recognize themselves, which in turn assumes they possess a sense of self. And as if that were not enough, it assumes they are capable of relatively complicated acts of logical deduction, such as 'this thing that this person was holding to her face while we performed our pattycake this afternoon creates a record of our pattycake that this person, if she attaches the thing to this other thing—this large box in the living room—can view.' But let's forget about these leaps for a moment. I will return to them in my Conclusion. For now, we will move, at long last, forward to the end of my Introduction, which is to say: my Hypothesis, which I am certain you must have guessed if you have been paying any attention to my presentation whatsoever . . ."

Maya lets go of her cane, reaches offscreen for a glass of water, begins to drink from it, seems to be losing her balance . . .

•

• •

Charity Party II: Charity Parties
A Yachts Joint
May and June, 2013, Chicagoland USA
[3 minutes, 1 second]

Close-up of a urinal's basin. A cure's ankles and wrists are zip-tied through the holes in the soap-cake holder.

CUT.

Two minutes later. Medium shot of the urinal. An obese man approaches. Starts to urinate. Painsinging is heard. The man looks down and starts to laugh, continues to urinate. The painsinging gargles. The man zips up, laughs harder, presses the flush lever, presses it again. The painsinging stops.

The Yachts burst out of two bathroom stalls, shouting, "Compliments of the Yachts!" in unison.

The obese man shrieks in alarm and falls to his knees, panting.

A painsinging cure is attached along its back to the wall-length mirror above three sinks in a public restroom. The cure is facing away from the mirror, affixed to it by what appears to be a slather of rubber cement. Its broken tail points sideways, at a nonorganic angle.

CUT.

Three minutes later. A teenage girl in shorts and a halter top enters the restroom, reaching into her purse, from which she produces a wire hairbrush. Seeing the cure on the mirror, she sets the brush down beside the sink she's in front of and goes over to it, softly cooing. "Aww. Look. Look at . . . Why are you *here*?" she says, scratching its head with a long, pink nail. She turns around slowly. "Okay then," she says, and, leaning toward the cure, obscuring it from view, fiddles around, causing the volume of the painsong to escalate. Her hand, reaching for the hairbrush, knocks it to the floor. "Shit shit shit," she says, and crouches down to retrieve the hairbrush, momentarily decongesting the camera's sightlines, and we see the cure's legs and arms, though still attached, have been pulled from their sockets, and its broken tail has been broken further and tied in a simple knot around its knees and elbows.

The girl stands, bearing the wire hairbrush. She takes a step back, measures her distance from the mirror with a slow, backhanded wave of her arm, then swings just hard enough to produce a high bang. The painsinging stops. The hairbrush's bristles have impaled the cure, and the brush now covers its body entirely; is hanging there, on the mirror, as if being held against it by a ghost.

Four Yachts jump out of two bathroom stalls, shouting, "Compliments of the Yachts!" in unison.

The girl seems unfazed. "What the fuck, you guys?" she says. "You're not supposed to be in—oh, hey Triple-J," she says to Triple-J, who steps out of the third stall. "This your idea?"

"What do you think?" he says.

"*I* don't know," the girl says, blushing vibrantly.

A Curio, crucified with hat pins to the crown of a bowler hat hanging from a hat rack between a pair of doorways in a narrow hallway, painsings.

CUT.

One minute later. Fondajane Henry exits one of the doorways, saying, "What is going *on* out here?" She sees the hat, sighs, removes it from the hat rack.

Triple-J exits the other doorway, whispers, "Fon, come on. Put it back."

"What are you doing?"

"You'll see," he says. "It's *great*. Come here."

She shrugs, replaces the hat, and follows Triple-J back through the doorway from which he had come out of.

CUT.

Forty seconds later. A slim, elderly man in black, three-piece livery approaches the hat rack, removes the hat, holds it at his abdomen, sighs, reaches under the hat and into the crown, removes the three pins from the cure's soles and palms, takes the cure off the hat, and sets the hat on his head.

"Hello?" the man says. "Is anyone here? Ms. Henry? Mr. Pellmore-Jason? Burroughs?"

He looks into the doorway from which Fondajane Henry originally appeared, then moves on to the next one.

"Oh, hello!" says the man, his back to the viewer. "I found this Curio *pinned* to the top of my hat."

"It's for you, Oliver," Triple-J says, offscreen. "Compliments of the Yachts."

"And what did I do to deserve such a lovely surprise?"

"Everything," Triple-J says. "All of it. You're just this great, loyal guy. I wanted to give you something."

"You have a very generous son," says Oliver.

"I do," says Fondajane Henry, offscreen.

"Now, what am I to do with this?" Oliver says.

"Do whatever you want," Triple-J says. "It's yours."

"Well, then," says Oliver, and moves his arms around.

"That's great," says Triple-J. "Just great."

"Very cute," says Fondajane Henry.

Oliver turns around, reenters the hallway. The painsinging cure, pinned through the belly, hangs over Oliver's pocket square like a leaking, writhing, boutonnière.

•
•   •

Silver-Medaling US National Science Fair Entry, Part 2
Home Video
September 9 and September 12, 1991, USA
[18 minutes]

Maya lets go of her cane, reaches offscreen for a glass of water, begins to drink from it, seems to be losing her balance . . .

The screen blinks.

Second tableau. It is the same as the original tableau—same table, same cane, same dress—except the wrist of Maya's "good" hand is splinted, a new scar (the stitches at the ends of which are visible) runs along her jawline, and the lighting appears to be a bit brighter.

"Please forgive my appearance," she says. "I had a small accident with that glass of water. Believe me, it looks much much worse than it really is. I am a trooper!

"What I was about to tell you was my hypothesis."

The screen blinks. The word HYPOTHESIS—green digital letters on a black background in which is visible the reflection of Maya's father holding the camcorder up to what is presumably the computer screen on which HYPOTHESIS appears—flashes three times.

The screen blinks again. Second tableau.

"My hypothesis: Curios are capable of understanding the principle of being recorded."

The screen blinks. The word METHOD—green letters, black screen, as before—flashes three times.

The screen blinks again. Second tableau.

"My method," Maya says.

"First, I cloned all four of my Curios. After $John_2$, $Paul_2$, $Mick_2$, and $Keith_2$ emerged from their marbles, I purchased a second PillowNest for them to sleep in. Three weeks later, *id est* once they were full-grown, I spent five weeks training them to pattycake, but I did not record them pattycaking, nor did I record them doing anything else, *id est* they never saw me use a camcorder.

"Once their pattycake training was complete, I rigged their PillowNest with a camcorder, just as I had previously rigged the PillowNest in which slept the original John, Paul, Mick, and Keith. I used the very same camcorder that, yes you guessed it, my father is using to film this very presentation.

"These conditions were applied for seven days and nights.

"I also rigged the PillowNest of the original John, Paul, Mick, and Keith using a different camcorder, one that I borrowed from my cousin Dev—thank you, Dev.

"These conditions were, of course, also applied for the same seven nights.

"Now how about the results?"

The screen blinks. The word RESULTS—green letters, black screen, as before—flashes three times.

The screen blinks again, and, as we watch a series of twenty-eight brief clips of four different cures squatting and rear-ejecting in various areas of their PillowNests, Maya speaks in voiceover.

"$John_2$, $Paul_2$, $Mick_2$, and $Keith_2$, none of which had ever seen a camcorder, all, as you can see here (and as you can also see on the tape marked 'Raw Primary Data 1') rear-ejected in their PillowNest each of the seven nights. This demonstrates that Curios that have no possible way of knowing what a camcorder is capable of are *not* rear-ejection-inhibited by the presence of a camcorder in their PillowNests, which in turn suggests that the original John, Paul, Mick, and Keith were inhibited by the presence of the camcorder in their PillowNest because they *did* know of what the camcorder was capable.

"In other words, my hypothesis—*id est* 'Curios are capable of understanding the principle of being recorded'—seems to have been confirmed, doesn't it? Well . . . I will, rest assured, explore this matter in greater depth at the end of my presentation.

"First, however, I would like to point something else out. Namely: unless we are to insist that the observer—in this case the camcorder—necessarily (even if we cannot imagine how) influences the phenomena being observed in significant ways, we can only conclude that the footage you have just seen establishes what the 'normal' spectrum of Curio rear-ejection behavior must look like. Which is, I should say, *very* exciting in itself, having captured such footage.

"*Id est:* a victory for science!"

The screen blinks. Second tableau. Maya is beaming.

"And now," she says, "before moving on to my conclusions, I have something even more exciting to bring to your attention. You see, I have, to use a famous term from the field of Journalism, *buried the lede*. That is: I haven't even discussed what happened in the other PillowNest, to the original John, Paul, Mick, and Keith. You must be wondering, yes? Of course. Any true lover of science would be! After all, these Curios, rather than being under the camcorder for just three consecutive nights—as they had been in the preliminary experiment that set this whole ball rolling—these Curios, I'm mostly certain I need not remind you, were, this time, under the camcorder for *seven* consecutive nights.

"Up until the sixth day, they all behaved as you probably would have expected, given how they behaved in that preliminary experiment. That is to say: for the first five days and nights, they did not rear-eject. But after that? . . . Well!

"Let's talk first about Mick. On the sixth day of the study—after five consecutive nights without a rear ejection—Mick rear-ejected into its CureSleeve at some point late in the afternoon, between three and five p.m. The rear ejection was extremely large and misshapen, perhaps a bit shinier than usual, and redolent of tutti-frutti-flavored jellybeans. Upon finding it in the sleeve, I was so surprised—when was the last time you heard of a Curio rear-ejecting in the daytime? and outside of its PillowNest no less, right?—so surprised that, although I did show it to my father—"

"It was very large and misshapen!" Maya's father interjects from offscreen.

"Thank you, Daddy. As I was saying, I was so surprised that I didn't think to capture the ejection on film before flushing it down the toilet, a lapse I regretted, and still regret. It was not my finest moment as a scientist.

"That night, however, Keith did something in the PillowNest of even greater scientific value. Watch."

The screen blinks. Overhead shot of Mick and Keith spooning on one side of the PillowNest, asleep, while John and Paul spoon on the other side of the PillowNest, also asleep. Keith wakes up, rolls to its opposite side, clutches its stomach, clutches its head, bicycles its legs, stretches its limbs, goes limp, stretches again, and finally sits up. Keith looks into the lens, looks away quickly, slaps at its face with both hands a couple times, then wakes Mick up with a kiss on the cheek. Keith stands, helps the sleepy-eyed Mick to stand, and leads it over to the corner of the PillowNest farthest from John and Paul.

Keith takes Mick by the waist and turns Mick around so that Mick is facing away from it. Keith crouches in the corner. Except for its bent knees and one of its shoulders, Keith is now completely blocked from the camera's view—and also from the view of John and Paul, who remain asleep on the other side of the nest—by Mick. For ten or fifteen seconds, Keith's knees and its visible shoulder shudder spastically, then Keith crawls out from behind Mick's body, toward the spot where it and Mick had earlier spooned, and, as Mick, a moment later—without turning its head to look into the vacated corner—moves to join Keith, we see that the corner contains a rear ejection (Keith's), which, inasmuch as it comprises two spherical termini bridged by a cylinder of the same shiny, black material, looks a bit like a dumbbell.

The screen blinks. Second tableau. "And if you think *that* is adorable," Maya says, "I cannot wait til you get a whole load of John and Paul, the *following* evening."

The screen blinks. Overhead shot of the Curios spooning in pairs on opposite sides of the nest, as before. Paul, the inner spoon of the John-Paul pair, twitches its shoulders and bucks its legs, just once, and John is suddenly pushed back half a Curio's arm's length by a rounded-rectangular rear ejection that has plunged out of Paul's exit into its (John's) lower abdomen. Paul remains asleep. John does not. It sits up, squints at Paul's rear ejection, squints at Paul, then goes to the opposite side of the nest, spoons Mick, and falls back asleep.

The screen blinks. Same shot as before, but two hours later. Paul awakens, turns over, sees its rear ejection, and looks toward the spooning trio, still asleep with their backs to Paul. Slowly, but steadily, Paul, on all fours, pushes the rear ejection toward John. John stirs. Paul drops to its belly and closes its eyes. A few moments later, Paul opens its eyes again. John remains asleep. Paul resumes pushing its rear ejection toward John until the rear ejection is just behind John's rear, such that were a witness to arrive on the scene at this point, it would seem to him that John had been the one that rear-ejected while asleep.

Paul crawls back to the spot where it had been sleeping, sits there, and whistles. The spooning trio of Curios wakes with a start. Keith taps Mick on the shoulder, gestures at John. Mick looks at John, pokes John on the shoulder, points at the ejection. Paul, on its feet now, is also pointing at the ejection, and whistling. John, at last, turns, sees the ejection, leaps to its feet, kicks the ejection across the nest, at Paul, then runs at Paul and kicks Paul in the knee. Paul grabs its knee and falls. John heads to the center of the nest, lies down alone. Paul goes to John, attempts to spoon. John shrugs Paul off. Paul tries to spoon again. John shrugs Paul off. Paul turns over. They lie back-to-back.

The screen blinks. Second tableau. "John, itself," Maya says, "deactivated inside the CureSleeve—so sad—midway through the following day, after having gone seven consecutive nights without producing a rear ejection. It did leave one behind in the sleeve, however, presumably in the course of deactivating. That one, I did think to photograph."

The screen blinks. A photo of a lowercase-gamma-shaped rear ejection resting in the middle of a human palm appears onscreen.

After six seconds, the screen blinks again. The word CONCLUSION—green letters, black screen, as before—flashes three times.

Once more, the screen blinks. Second tableau. "It would seem, as I have already said," Maya says, "that my hypothesis has been confirmed: that Curios are capable of understanding the principle of being recorded. And so it would seem that I was justified in having made the inductive and, perhaps, intuitive leaps that I mentioned having made in my Introduction. *Id est,* it would seem that Curios see the images on a television screen much the way we humans do; it would seem that they recognize themselves on television screens, which would in turn necessitate that they possess a sense of self; and it would seem that Curios are capable of the kinds of relatively complicated acts of logical deduction that would enable them to understand that it is by way of my pointing a camcorder at them that I am able, later on, to view images of them on a television screen.

"It would seem, it would seem, it would *seem*, I say. I *stress* the word 'seem,' because there is another explanation that seems no less reasonable, but had not occurred to me until only very recently. Namely: it *could be* that the original John, Paul, Mick, and Keith, rather than understanding the principle of being recorded, simply developed a powerful association between me, Maya Mehta, and the camcorder with which I taped them every day during their weeks of pattycake training. More precisely, it could very well be that these Curios, which are, as all Curios are, inhibited from rear-ejecting in front of human beings, learned, by having so often seen me with the camcorder in front of my eye, to think that the camcorder was a part of me. If this were the case, it would follow for them to think, upon looking up at the ceiling of their PillowNest and seeing the camcorder, that I, *myself*, were present in their PillowNest.

"Were there time before the science fair deadline, I would perform further research in order to determine whether this were the case. Here is how I would do it: I would clone a third generation of John, Paul, Mick, and Keith, train them to perform the pattycake routine as previously, and tape the training just as I had taped the first generation's, which should be sufficent to cause them to develop an association between me, Maya Mehta, and the camcorder, but I would *not* show the tapes I made to this third generation, which would prevent them from being able to understand that the camcorder recorded images of them. Then I would place the Curios in a camcorder-rigged PillowNest for a week, and I would see whether their rear ejections were inhibited. If their rear ejections *were* inhibited, the hypothesis that Curios are capable of understanding the principle of being recorded would *not* be confirmed.

"So, in conclusion, my study, although all kinds of useful and very fascinating thoughts and data were produced and recorded in the course of its undertaking, is inconclusive."

The screen blinks. The word REFLECTIONS—green letters, black screen, as before—flashes three times.

The screen blinks. Second tableau. "To close my presentation, I would like to add a couple of final thoughts," says Maya. "First, I will, shortly, conduct more research myself. At the very least, I will clone a third generation of my Curios and perform the research I proposed in the Conclusion section of this presentation. Maybe that will be part of my science fair project next year!

"Beyond that, however, there are topics of research my present study has given rise to, for which I do not currently possess the means, the training, or, perhaps, even the innate ability to study on my own. Without further hesitation, then:

"I have given much thought to what Paul did, upon waking up to find it had rear-ejected in its sleep. I have wondered: What could Paul have been thinking when it moved its rear ejection behind John's bottom? Did Paul think that John would believe that John had rear-ejected in its sleep, or was Paul, perhaps in response to some embarrassment it felt at having rear-ejected in its sleep, attempting to save face by simply making a clownish joke? And if a clownish joke, was the joke made for me, for John, for Mick and Keith, for itself, for any combination of the aforementioned, or for all of us? And what—assuming Curios can even be said to be embarrassed, or to possess any emotions at all—what precisely was the source of the embarrassment? As you can see in the footage of the other cures rear-ejecting, Curios, though they appear never to willfully rear-eject while being looked at *directly* by other Curios, are not inhibited from rear-ejecting by one another's mere presence. So while it would seem doubtful that Paul could have been embarrassed before John for having rear-ejected in John's presence, it does seem possible that Paul was embarrassed before John for having rear-ejected *beneath the eye of the camcorder*. Does that sound strange? It does not sound all that strange to me. I know that there are things I do in front of my family for which I am not embarrassed, but were I to do these things in front of outsiders, I would be embarrassed, and were my family to learn that I'd done these things in front of outsiders, I'd be even further embarrassed, you see? An example might be walking around with uncombed hair, or to be wearing a dress with a stain on it. Could it not be the same for Curios and rear ejection in front of human beings?

"Then again, maybe *I* am strange. I have mentioned my shyness . . .

"But as you can imagine, it is for many of the same reasons that I could not design a study to discover whether Curios are truly shy that I cannot come up with a way to design a study that could determine whether Curios have a sense of humor, or irony, or a sense of embarrassment, or pride. Maybe someone else could, though. I hope so.

"Finally, there's Keith. Keith may have known that the camcorder in the ceiling was recording its behavior, or it may have thought that the camcorder in the ceiling was me, Maya Mehta, watching its behavior, but whatever Keith thought, it deliberately hid itself behind Mick while rear-ejecting. The question is: Why? Why will they never rear-eject in our presence? What exactly inhibits them? Is it simply an extreme discomfort they don't quite understand? Or do they perhaps believe that, by virtue of always preventing us from seeing them rear-eject, we will believe they don't engage in the act at all? Whatever the answer—whatever Keith's hiding behavior *might* mean, whatever Paul's ejection-moving behavior might mean, and, for that matter, whatever any Curio's rear-ejection behavior might mean—I believe that my study, despite its inconclusiveness, was successful, however unintentionally, and even groundbreaking, though again unintentionally. It was successful and groundbreaking inasmuch as some of its results suggest rather strongly that Curios are capable of engaging in acts of willful deception, and I believe this will prove a very fascinating topic of scientific research in the future. I hope you will agree.

"Thank you for considering this my science project for the 1991 US National Science Fair. I am Maya Mehta of Newton North High School. Good morning, good afternoon, and good night to you."

•

• •

Head-on Curio

from *The Tommy and Timmy Backyard BBQ Show*

1993, ECTV Public Access Channel 6, Evanston IL, USA

[8 minutes, 32 seconds]

Behind a butcher-block island in an overlit kitchen stand a sunburnt, red-haired, middle-aged man, policemanly mustached, and a sunburnt, red-haired, adolescent boy with cauliflowered ears and patches of acne. Each wears a Chicago Cubs baseball cap, a Chicago Bears–themed grilling apron, and, down the bridge of his nose, a stripe of blue zinc oxide. The boy, smiling sheepishly, his arms across his chest, hands clamped in the pits, points his gaze down and away from the man, who, presenting to the camera in three-quarter profile, seems, though both of his eyes remain open, perpetually poised to wink the nearer one.

"Hello there, Evanston," says the man. "I'm Tommy over here, that's my boy, Timmy, and this week on the *Backyard BBQ Show,* father and son are gonna go—on three, now, Timmy—one . . . two . . . three . . ."

"Rogue!" Tommy and Timmy announce in unison.

"And what do we mean by *rogue,* today, Timmy?"

Timmy glances at the camera, says, "Heat without fire," and again looks away.

Tommy says, "That is partially correct, there. *One* of the ways we're gonna go rogue is . . ."

The screen blinks. Same tableau as before, but now there's a Crock-Pot atop the island.

"We're gonna use a slow cooker to do some prep before we head out to finish the job on the grill. For those of you tuning in to *Triple-B Q Show* for the first time this week, one of Kamanski's—that's me, by the way, I'm Tommy Kamanski—one of Kamanski's most central of all tenets is . . ." Tommy nudges Timmy.

"No heat without fire," Timmy says.

"No heat without fire. That's right. Because why?"

"We're devoted to the art of the open flame," says Timmy rapidly, and then, at increasing velocity: "Barbecue without the open flame isn't barbecue. The open flame is to barbecue what the hundred-yard-by-fifty-yard playing field is to gridiron football, what fifty-two—not fifty-one or less than that, or fifty-three or more than that—cards is to poker, and also too what Bill Cosby is to the *Cosby Show* is another way to put it."

"Well said, Timmy," says Tommy, and pats Timmy's shoulder. "The open flame is essential! It's the heart of—well, it's the heart of the matter, guys. And we will definitely get to the open flame soon. But not yet. Cause this week our prep work, rather than just being the usual chopping and dicing and soaking and seasoning, really does require heat without a fire. A controlled, slow heat. And if you think *that's* rogue then . . ."

The screen blinks. Same tableau as before, but now there's a tin pail atop the island, next to the Crock-Pot. Tommy lifts the pail, tilts it forward, toward the camera. Inside are six Curios that, having just lost their balance, are scrambling to stand up on the side of the bucket.

"How about *that*! We are going so rogue so hard today that we're going to show you how to cook you this new family favorite. Spicy barbecued head-on cure. How does that sound? How do you think it sounds to our viewers, Timmy? As in, pretend you're one of them and you don't know better cause I'm not your dad."

"Okay," Timmy says. "Okay . . . It sounds gross!"

"And why's that?" says Tommy.

"Cause they're not like meat-flavored. They don't taste like meat. They taste all sugary."

"Cause they taste all sugary! Timmy tells it like it is. But what if I told you we could make these sugary little gizmos taste like meat, Tim? Or, at least, a lot more like meat?"

"If you told me that then I don't really think that I would really believe you unless you had some kind of total proof," Timmy says.

"Well, that's because you're sharp there, son. You're nobody's fool. One thing I for sure did not do is father some jagoff. And now I'm going to prove to you what you think I can't prove."

"Okay!" says Timmy.

The screen blinks again. Same tableau as before, but now an open jar of WorkPellets that appear to be a lighter shade of beige than normal, a bottle of vinegar, and a shaker of cayenne pepper are arranged on the island in front of the Crock-Pot.

"Now how long do you suppose it would take to make cures taste like meat, Tim?" says Tommy.

"I bet it would take anywhere from like ten thousand years to forever and ever."

"And that's why, Timmy, you'll be very surprised to learn that it takes either just a few minutes, or about three weeks, depending only on how you choose to think of time."

"That's a weird thing to say! You sound like that tubby Asian god guy from the cookies."

"Confucius?"

"Yeah!"

The screen blinks. Same tableau as before but, inexplicably, a small clay statue of the laughing Buddha now sits atop the Crock-Pot's lid. The sound of a man laughing—presumably Tommy—rings out for three seconds, though neither Tommy nor Timmy appears to be laughing.

The screen blinks again. Same tableau as before, but without the statue.

"Now let me explain," Tommy says.

"You better," says Timmy.

"Those WorkPellets in the jar there are special WorkPellets. That is to say that I *made* them special. I laid each one of them out on a cookie pan, and droppered one single drop of vinegar onto each one, and let them stay there on that cookie pan, soaking up that vinegar for one whole night. Then what I did was, I put them back in the jar. Took just a few minutes. Now, these cures in this pail here have been eating vinegar'd WorkPellets like these for three whole weeks."

"Did they like them?" Timmy says.

"How the heck should I know! But they didn't seem to mind. Their rear ejections were pretty normal, maybe a *little* more egg-shaped there than spherical, and the bubblegum-type scent was more maybe cherry- than grape-flavored bubblegum scent, but that's the price we gotta pay I guess."

"The price for to make them taste like meat?"

"Part of the price."

"What's the rest of the price, Dad?"

"Well the rest of the price can only be costed out in terms of man-hours on the job, which so far is just some minutes unless we're gonna count those three weeks of waiting, and then the next couple steps are also just minutes, even though there's four hours of waiting, so."

"You're confusing me!"

"Maybe that's why they called him Confucius, huh?"

"Yeah!"

"Anyway, next step here is simple. Throw the cures in the slow cooker. Go on there, Tim."

Tommy removes the lid of the Crock-Pot, sets it down on the island. Timmy holds the pail of Curios above the Crock-Pot and turns the pail over. We hear faint painsinging.

"Good job, kiddo. Now, next step is we're gonna mix vinegar with water in a ratio of one vinegars to ten waters, and we're gonna put that mixture into the slow cooker here. Now, reason I'm giving you a ratio instead of a volume is because here's the tricky part, okay? But it's actually not that tricky, so don't go and worry your head off about it ha-ha. First, you want to make sure the Curios are standing up inside your slow cooker, there. And what you want to do is pour enough of the mixture into the slow cooker that it reaches just to the necks of the shortest cure when it's standing up."

"The top of its neck or the bottom of its neck, Dad?"

"That's a great question and the answer is: doesn't make a difference. Top of the neck, bottom of the neck, middle of the neck—to the neck is all. Of the shortest one. Relax and have fun with it. The only main thing is not to drown the Curios. So different slow cookers have different sizes and etcetera, so make your mixture—where's mine? there it is [Tommy reaches offscreen left and grabs a plastic, two-gallon milk jug marked "VINAGIR WATER"]—and now, bring that camera on in here . . ."

Overhead zoom on the Crock-Pot's interior. All six Curios are on their feet, looking upward, directly at the camera. One of them holds its elbow and softly painsings. Soon, another one widens its eyes and points up and to its left as the vinegar water comes splashing down from that direction, and we hear Tommy, offscreen, saying, "Now, you just pour it right in. There."

The cures flee to the farther side of the Crock-Pot and press together. A couple, on the way, catch splashes in their eyes, and they wink and painsing and rub at the affected eyes with the backs of their hands. When the liquid reaches the neck of the shortest cure—one of those thats eyes were splashed—the camera zooms out.

Same tableau as before, though Timmy is leaning forward, looking down into the pot.

"Next comes the cayenne," Tommy says. "As regular viewers of this program are well aware by this point in time, I like to keep things spicy. All Kamanskis do. Isn't that right there, Timmy?"

"Huh?" says Timmy, looking up from the Crock-Pot.

"I was saying how we liked to keep things pretty spicy in this neck of the woods."

"We do," says Timmy. "We like to keep things spicy."

"So I'm gonna go ahead, now," says Tommy, "and sprinkle about two tablespoons of cayenne pepper in there, making sure, while I do so, to get at least half of what I'm sprinkling, right onto the Curios. Now, you might be more delicate than the typical Kamanski, and so you might want to use less pepper than I do. Totally your call. But I strongly, strongly suggest you get a bunch of it, however much you use, right on top of the Curios because it's important they start inhaling it."

Tommy unscrews the lid of the cayenne pepper shaker, dips a tablespoon into it, does as he's just described. More painsongs arise, and multiple sneezes. Tommy sets the lid back onto the Crock-Pot.

"Now I'm gonna set this bad boy up to cook on low heat for four hours. And we're almost there."

"We've gotta wait four hours!?" Timmy says, as Tommy sets the dial on the Crock-Pot.

"Yeah," says Tommy, "but that four hours can be fun. Before it gets fun, though, I just want to give the viewers a brief preview of what's coming up. First off, in just *two* hours, we're gonna go ahead and stir the pot a little. And then, after *another* two hours, that's when we'll ladle the little gizmos outta the pot, take them to the open flame as promised. And real quick, here, I just want to explain briefly the science behind the Kamanski method here because I'm sure there are some people out there who are gonna want to try to rush things and they should know they can't cause rushing things won't work in this situation here. You need to slow cook for four hours on low heat because you don't want to like shock these Curios to death. You want them to slowly weaken and slowly drown. You want them to inhale and swallow this vinegar water and pepper and send the stuff all throughout their bodies so it can do its work on their organs and their muscles and whatever else—I'm not a doctor—but for all of that to happen to a successful degree, they need to kind of nod off, start swallowing and inhaling, and then wake back up and try to fight off the end, and succeed a little, and then nod off again and repeat the process, hopefully at least a few times. If you heat them up too fast, they're just gonna dact and the peppery vinegar water won't ever get to pump through their veins via being carried in their blood like it will if you do it our way. Got it? I think you do. Now, I should also not fail to not neglect to mention that there's an alternative method for prepping Curios for barbecue that our viewers might have heard about, and that method is to chop the limbs and the heads off the cures and just marinate the torsos in the same mixture we're using in our slow cooker here for a couple of hours. And that is totally, a hundred percent legitimate. *If* what you want is some barbecued Curio torsos. Which we Kamanskis . . . don't want. We want barbecued head-on Curio because that, my friends, is just a much superior form of cuisine with more classy textures and a subtler variety of visual presentation possibilities to take advantage of at the end there when you're plating. But like I said also when I was talking about the cayenne: your call. This isn't some kind of my-way-or-the-highway-type situation. This is a way to have fun with your family and enjoy some seriously good eats. And speaking of having fun, what should we do for the next four hours, there, Timmy?"

"I think there's a game on," Timmy says.

"And isn't there always, of a Sunday afternoon, and being verily in possession of cable, a game on?"

"Yeah!"

"God bless us all."

The screen blinks. A ninety-second montage follows: Tommy and Timmy watching football on a large-screen TV, passing a bowl of chips back and forth. Timmy removing a bottle of Old Style beer from a garage refrigerator, popping the top off, looking over his shoulder, smelling the beer, shrugging, taking a sip. Timmy handing the beer to Tommy, back in the living room, in front of the television. Tommy squinting at the beer, weighing it in his hand, playfully throwing a handful of chips at Timmy. Timmy throwing a couple of the chips back at Tommy. Tommy reaching over, putting Timmy in a headlock, setting the beer on the coffee table, noogieing Timmy. Timmy swatting at the noogie-hand and, shortly, breaking free of the headlock, red-faced, hair a mess, zinc oxide smeared, and frowning at Tommy. Tommy drinking beer. Both of them in front of a bathroom mirror, tubes of Zinka on the counter before them. Tommy patting Timmy's head, giving him a side squeeze. Timmy chucking Tommy on the shoulder. Timmy reapplying orange Zinka to his nose. Tommy applying navy Zinka in stripes—two each—under his eyes. Timmy turning to Tommy, lower lip bulging in admiration. Tommy helping Timmy apply stripes of navy Zinka so the two of them match.

The screen blinks. Same tableau as before.

"So last time we did this," Tommy says, "Timmy, here, had a little bit of a problem."

"I was younger then," Timmy says. "I wasn't as mature."

"It was only last month!"

"Still," Timmy says. "I'm a month more mature, now."

"Alright, go ahead," Tommy says. "Stir the pot."

Timmy, bearing a large wooden spoon in one hand, lifts the lid of the Crock-Pot with the other. We hear faint gurgling sounds, and perhaps—it's so faint, it's hard to really tell—a painsong, or two painsongs in harmony.

Timmy, looking down into the pot, drops the spoon and the lid and sticks both hands inside the Crock-Pot, near-instantly pulls his hands out and shrieks, starts falling back, swings his arms wildly, sends the Crock-Pot crashing to the floor.

"A month more mature my hairy freaking *dupa*!" says Tommy. "Ah jeez. What the hell. Might as well get this for the blooper reel, huh?"

The camera zooms in on Timmy, lying on the floor, sobbing a little in profile.

"So the irony of all of this, I guess," says Tommy, offscreen, "is that suppose on the one hand we'd have set the temperature higher. The little robot set Timmy off would've been a corpse by the time Timmy pulled the lid off, and Timmy would not have gone into overload over some corpse, right? But it would've tasted bad. Well maybe not bad. But just not that good. At least a little bit sugary. So. What can you do?"

A cure on its side, its eyes clamped—perhaps melted—shut, its velvet patchy, and streaked with cayenne-red speckles, uses its tail—the only one of its limbs it appears able to control; the others are limp—to push itself into frame, just behind Timmy's head. It sneezes softly, getting Timmy's attention. Timmy turns onto his other cheek, takes the cure in a blistering fist, holds it up to the camera, and squeezes its head off.

CUT.

Tommy, Timmy, a red-haired, sunburnt, middle-aged woman, and a red-haired, sunburnt, adolescent girl, all of whom don stripes of zinc oxide on their noses and under their eyes, sit around a wooden patio table with a barbecue grill in the background.

"Well so we had a little bit of a comical mishap earlier, and Timmy's got a couple blisters on the knucks of his throwing hand, took a knock on the head from the floor, too, but so, just have a look: we Kamanskis pulled together, as a family, and we came out alright. Donna thought she remembered we had a backup Crock-Pot down in the basement, Jenny went down to look, and by God she found that Crock-Pot. And it worked good as new! We were only able to salvage five of the six original cures, but hey, there's only four of us, and so wouldn't you know it, here we are together, about to enjoy what we've for so long been waiting to enjoy together. Get a load of it there now, would ya?"

Overhead zoom on the plate in the center of the table. Four cuts of grill-marked steak form a square in the center of which five black-and-red, crackly-skinned cures on spits—garnished with grill-marked green peppers, chunks of white onion, and cherry tomatoes wrapped in bacon—lie side by side.

"Dig in, guys!" Tommy says, offscreen.

• • •

Schrödinger's Curio
Home Video
Early 2000s, USA
[9 minutes, 13 seconds]

Split screen.

On the right, a dozen popsicled Curios arranged in three rows of four in the middle of what appears to be a backyard sandbox writhe and painsing. One punches at its own head, others claw at their faces, grind their fists into their abdomens, slouch and straighten and squint and go pop-eyed.

On the left, Robbie, from the *Popsicles* video, goateed this time, perhaps a bit older, and clothed in khaki slacks and a navy blazer, a golden fraternity pin in one lapel, reads to the camera from a spiral notebook: "Before getting into my extra-credit project proper, Dr. Martin, I want you to know that I have done a lot of reflection about some of the things I have done this semester to probably deserve your canker, and I would like to explain myself to you about why that canker is maybe bigger than it would be if you knew me better in my heart and soul and what I stand for as a man, a member of your class, a brother of Beta Theta Epsilon Delta, and a fifth-year at this glorious and well-beloved university we get to share the privilege of being a part of together and using our minds in, and also of course as a citizen of these great United States, northside and southside both and also eastside and westside both. In order to begin with I have to tell you that I am in love with a certain girl I will not name and that the note you caught me passing and that you then so embarrassingly—for me, who deserved it I admit—read aloud in front of the classroom was because of that. That note was a note I was trying to pass to this girl I won't name's best friend who I thought I should be trying to make a good impression on because I'm in love with this girl I won't name as I have said and I thought the friend would maybe help me in the noble cause of getting the girl I won't name to fall in love with me mutually, and all I was trying to do was give the best friend a compliment that was not too obvious or cheesefisted but expressed to her that I held her in a lot of high steam, so when I wrote in that note, 'I'm surprised you're taking Physics for F-tards,' pardon the language, I was not trying to say that you, Dr. Martin, were a person who could only teach physics to f-tards, pardon the language, or even that Remedial Physics is a class that is really and truly full of f-tards and designed for f-tards. I don't even really think I believe in f-tards as a thing. I think everyone is special in his or her own way and I meant no disrespect to you or Remedial Physics or my fellow students in the classroom who I do not think are f-tards. All I was trying to do was to say to the best friend that she was someone who I thought was really, really intellectual, and that is not even a lie because I do think she is very intellectual, but I wanted to say that to her in a way that did not seem dorky or in any other kind of way unRobbie-like because then it would not sound like I really believed it, I didn't think, and if it didn't sound like I really believed it, then this best friend would not only not believe that I believed that she was really intellectual but she might even think I was making fun of her and saying the opposite of what I was saying. She might even think, I thought, that if I said in a more straight-up way that she was intellectual and that because she was so intellectual I was surprised to find that she was in a class with me, who is dumber—though I try very hard—she might think that I was making fun of her and telling her that actually I thought she was dumb and that my surprise was fake or that even worse my surprise was really real, but for the opposite reason, namely that I thought she was so dumb that I couldn't believe she could even get into a Physics class that dumb old me was in. But I don't think anyone's an f-tard is what I'm trying to tell you. I was just doing the best that I could which was not good enough to try and receive love feelings that were perpendicular with my own love feelings from the girl I won't name whose best friend was the intended receiver of that note you read out loud. I am sorry. Truly and from my heart and soul.

"And I am also and furthermore sorry, too, for sometimes coming to class late, and sometimes coming to class late looking like I have a hangover but hopefully not smelling like I have a hangover which is the reason why I'm sometimes late when I'm looking like I have a hangover is because I have a hangover and I need to take an extra-long shower out of consideration for the noses of those of my peers who will be sitting around me. There is no excuse. I am not trying to be excused. I am only trying to give you a reason to consider the giving to me of a chance to earn extra credit.

"In case it is any comfort to you yourself, I will also hereby tell you that my heart is broken for myself, Dr. Martin, because the girl I won't name does not, has not, and never will love me I have realized, and I cannot blame that on the best friend who instead of doing what I hoped she would and telling the girl I won't name how she thought I was a good person worthy of a love as powerful as mine and equally perpendicular instead told me that she was in love with me herself which I took advantage of in the wild romantic hopes of someone who is lonely and has needs and thinks that maybe the fillment of his needs could perhaps be the rare, full kind of fillment where it turns out to be an unexpected surprise that it was what was meant to be all along and that all along he loved the best friend, but which I did not. My hopes were stupid and desperate and after our fling there was no way the best friend was going to have anything nice to say about me to the girl I won't name, and so she didn't. And so I also don't blame my broken heart on you reading the note in front of the class and I hope you do not either. I hope you do not feel guilty about doing that to me and my hopes. I only wish I was more ashamed of the note at the time because then maybe instead of telling the best friend, after class, that the note had been for her, I would not have told her anything and we would not have flung and I would not have broken my own heart, because that is how it went down in the end after all was I did it to myself and I can only blame it on myself for trying so hard and believing so hard at and in a thing which was clearly and plainly and on reflection very obviously never meant to be, and I mean flinging with the best friend, not being in love with the girl I won't name with mutuality on the part of her because that was meant to be, I am certain of it, but I screwed it up forever, and am responsible for preventing what was meant to be from being.

"A lot of thought and effort on the part of myself has gone into this extra-credit project, which will be a demonstration of the Observer Effect, which I know you said is different from what Schrödinger was saying about the make-believe cat who is superdead or superalive in that atomic poison box until you check, and you warned us not to confuse it with the Uncertain Principle which is a whole other keg of fish, but I have still titled my project 'Schrödinger's Curio,' because I think it is a clever title, so just please don't think I think I'm doing a Schrödinger here when all I'm doing, I am sure, is demonstrating the Observer Effect in the following way that I will describe.

"I am standing here inside the party hutch of Beta Theta Delta Epsilon house telling you all these things I'm telling you on one side of your screen, while on the other side of your screen as I am sure you have noticed for as long as I have been speaking my heart to you there are twelve Curios who are what is sometimes called 'popsicled' and sometimes called 'standylivered' or any number of other Appalachias beyond the scope of this explanation in the sandbox in our backyard. As I am sure you can see, these popsicled Curios are doing behaviors that if they weren't robots would mean they were in a lot of pain and only a lot of pain. But as I am about to demonstrate to you in two ways at the exact same time, they will behave different when I go outside into the backyard and look at them. They will interrupt themselves from acting like they are in a lot of pain in order to not act like they are in a lot of pain and like they are actually having a good time. I should tell you, before I go and demonstrate this, that I am the person who popsicled only six of them—the six in the right two columns—and only three of those are mine. The other three belong to my fraternity brother Micky McMichaels. And then when it comes to the six Curios in the left two columns, three of those are mine and three of those are Mickey Double-M's, which is what we brothers here call Micky McMichaels instead of Micky Mick or Triple-M because those are how the brothers of Micky Double-M's pops and granddad called them, respectably, and Micky Double-M is his own person. He is also the one who popsicled the six Curios on the right, though, I'm saying, and, just as importantly as that information is the information that Micky Double-M will not be present in attendance for this demonstration I am about to do, which matters for the following reason, which is: I have never before seen the three cures in the farthest-right column before in my life and none of them have ever seen me either. And why is the reason that this is important? It is important because what you will notice that I would like to draw your attention to is how even though all of the Curios will interrupt themselves from their total-pain-and-suffering kind of behavior to behave like they are having a good time when they see me, the ones that belong to me will seem like they are having an even better time in those moments than the ones that belong to Mickey Double-M. The ones that belong to Micky Double-M that, I urge you to please remember, three of them and I have never seen each other, will all act less like they are having a good time than the ones that belong to me will act, but they will all act equally like they are having as good of a time as one another. The reason that is so important is because what it will show is a couple things that I will explain in just a moment. Now, follow me, Dr. Martin."

Robbie beckons at the camera on the left side of the screen. While the camera follows him down a hallway, through a kitchen, and out a sliding glass door, the Curios on the right side of the screen continue to writhe and painsing and self-mutilate as described earlier.

Robbie's gait slows as he approaches a wide oak tree, a few feet behind and to the left of which we can see the popsicled cures in the sandbox. Robbie presses his back to the tree and whispers, "Did they notice us?" The camera turns toward the sandbox, zooms in on the cures, none of which are looking in the camera's direction.

"Nope," says the cameraman.

"Shhh!" Robbie whispers, as the camera zooms out and swings back to film him.

"So," Robbie whispers, "you can see they're all just behaving like before, like they're in nothing but the purest kind of terrible pain, but in just a second, I'll step out from behind this tree, and you'll see how the six that are mine—the farthest-left column ones, and the ones in the third column from the left—interrupt themselves to act like they've never before in a zillion years ever even heard of anyone or anything being as happy as they are, and then the ones that are Micky Double-M's will do the same thing but just not as completely and totally enthusiastically. Alright, now, on three. One, two, three!"

As we see Robbie step out from behind the tree and toward the cures on the left side of the screen, and we see his shadow fall over them on the right side of the screen, those cures that belong to him (columns 1 and 3, from the left) relax their brows and cease their self-mutilation behavior and their painsinging to hum and coo and make kissing sounds and wink and clap and show him swear fingers, whereas those that do not belong to Robbie (columns 2 and 4, from the left), though they relax their brows and cease their self-mutilation behavior and reach in his direction and grab at the air, continue to painsing. Robbie stands before them for nearly two minutes, in the course of which, each of the cures briefly reengages in its previous (i.e. self-mutilating, painsinging) behavior at least three times.

These fluctuations persist as Robbie turns back to the camera and says:

"So, there you have what I hope you will find to be an extremely eloquent demonstration of how the observer affects the phenomenon that is being studied just by observing it because after all I am the observer, and these Curios here are the phenomenon, and the phenomenon changed when I observed it, and it changed in two different ways: the crazy enthusiastic way when it came to Micky Double-M's cures, and the supermegacrazy enthusiastic way when it came to my cures. And that distinction is an important one to take note of and realize because it proves that it's being *observed* that changes the enthusiasm phenomenons with Curios, and not just being observed by someone who previously observed them, or even someone who previously popsicled them because if that's how it was then there would have been three different enthusiasm phenomenons instead of two. So that means I could have been any observer except for Micky Double-M, and his cures would have acted the same way when I observed them, whether or not I popsicled them or never even met them before. And it means that if I was anyone *but* me, my cures would have acted like Micky Double-M's cures acted when I observed *them*. This was a discovery I was not expecting. I thought the Observer Effect would be different between a cure you never met before and a cure that wasn't yours but you popsicled, but it turns out: No. The only thing that matters is who owns them.

"Which is deep.

"I think so at least.

"Thank you for your time, Dr. Martin, and for giving me the opportunity to hopefully earn some extra credit for class so that this my fifth year will be my last year here at the university that I love so much but I realize it is time to move on from and forward into my life as a wage-earning citizen and adult of this great country that you and I live in together and hope to improve even though it is already the best in the world and which that is why it is the best in the world because of how citizens like the two of us won't settle for good enough even when good enough equals best. We won't settle.

"And now I think I'll change into some more casual sportswear and enjoy for myself what I believe to be a pretty well-deserved overload session."

Robbie salutes the camera, bows, and again salutes the camera.

•

• •

Charity Party III: Tree of Charity

A Yachts Joint

June 15, 2013, Wheelatine USA

[11 minutes, 1 second]

Slow, steady pan around a schoolyard swingset with occasional close-ups. Scores of cures, many of them painsinging, are variously affixed to it by rubber band, zip-tie, dental floss, string, and what, by its color, would appear to be citrus-flavored bubblegum.

CUT.

Twenty minutes later. The faint ringing of a muffled bell from the school behind the swingset is heard.

CUT.

Three minutes later. A large group of laughing, shrieking grade-school children—perhaps a hundred—are exiting the school, heading toward the swingset.

CUT.

Thirty seconds later. Four Yachts are standing, shoulder to shoulder, between the swingset and the horde of children. The children are shouting, mostly incomprehensibly, though the phrases "I wanna smash 'em!" "I wanna eat 'em!" "I wanna tear off their heads and stick 'em into each other!" all come through.

Triple-J shows the children his palms and steps forward, and they quiet down a little.

"Me and these guys here, we're the Yachts," he says. "And you know what today is?"

"Last day of school!" shout the children.

"That's right!" Triple-J says. "This is your last day of school, your last recess of the year, and we Yachts remember how happy it was to be in first grade on our last recess of the year, and so we wanted to come down here and see how happy you were, because we knew it would make us happy again, and it has, it does, we're so happy to see you so happy! So we made this party for some of you, maybe even all of you. It's called a charity party. All you have to do to smash and eat and stick these cures into each other, or whatever you want to do with them—all you have to do is repeat after me. Does that sound good?"

The children cheer and applaud.

"Alright," Triple-J says. "Now repeat after me. This charity party . . ."

"This charity party!" the children shout.

"Comes compliments of the Yachts . . ."

"Comes compliments of the Yachts!"

"Now one more time, with the two parts together. This charity party . . ."

But a number of children, having already gone into overload, are rushing past Triple-J to get to the swingset, knocking two of the Yachts—Chaz and Lyle—onto their backs.

The first boy to make it there, his hands at his sides, bites off the head of an upside-down cure that's bound by an ankle to a rubber trapeze ring, turns to his left, spits the head at a friend, and as the spat head achieves the pinnacle of its arc, so begins a ten-minute slow-mo montage of the overloading children dacting all the cures, soundtracked by classical organ music (Bach's Toccata and Fugue in F Major).

•

•   •

And Now, For What You Thought Was the Second Time Ever

Security Footage from Chicago Kim's Liquor Food, originally aired*
on *60 Minutes*
February 28, 1988, CBS Network, USA
[2 minutes, 57 seconds]

*but with censor boxes covering the juveniles' eyes and noses

Fixed overhead shot, black-and-white, silent. The checkout counter of a corner bodega. The cashier, a slight, middle-aged woman, waves at someone offscreen. A moment later, a morbidly obese, pubescent boy in a light-colored parka and dark-colored watchcap appears before her, clutching a can of New Coke.

The boy sets the can beside a cardboard carton of King Size Chick-o-Sticks next to the register. He extracts from the carton three fistfuls of Chick-o-Sticks and piles them by the can of New Coke. Once the cashier has rung the New Coke up, she counts out the Chick-o-Sticks—seventeen in all—and rings those up, and says something to the boy (presumably the price).

The boy hands her a bill.

Her hand remains open.

She says something to him.

He digs in his pockets, comes up with three coins, puts them on the bill in the cashier's hand.

She says something to him.

He digs in his pockets, comes up with nothing.

The cashier sets the money on the counter, counts out ten Chick-o-Sticks, returns them to the carton.

The boy's shoulders drop violently, jerk, and his hands go up.

The cashier takes five Chick-o-Sticks back out of the carton, sets them on the pile, and pushes the can of New Coke away from the pile.

Again the boy's shoulders drop violently and jerk. His hands clasped together, his head on a tilt, he appears to beg.

The cashier shakes her head.

Three older, fitter boys in dark parkas and watchcaps line up together behind the boy. The boy, seemingly unaware of the others, stomps one foot, brings his clasped hands forward and back to his chest a number of times.

The cashier, still shaking her head, shrugs, and over the head of the obese boy and toward the three fitter boys, widens her eyes in exasperation.

The obese boy says something.

She says something back.

The boy shows her the index finger of one hand while reaching into his parka with his other hand. When the hand that went in the parka comes out, it's holding a cure. The boy lowers the finger of the first hand, lowers the hand itself, holds it open-palmed over the counter, and sets the cure down on it. The cure lies supine in the boy's open hand.

The cashier makes a frowny face of appraisal.

The boy says something.

The cashier shrugs. She scratches the cure on the head and smiles. She removes two Chick-o-Sticks from the carton, sets them on the pile.

The boy says something.

The cashier shakes her head.

The boy seems to insist.

The cashier shrugs, sniffs the finger she just scratched the cure's head with, smiles, adds another two Chick-o-Sticks to the pile. She puts the money the boy gave her into the register, removes five more Chick-o-Sticks from the carton, and picks up the New Coke can. She holds the New Coke can and five Chick-o-Sticks out to the boy, saying something.

The boy nods in emphatic agreement.

As the cashier bags the New Coke and the seventeen Chick-o-Sticks, the fitter boys, who have til now been trading high-eyebrowed glances, puffing their cheeks, and blowing what looks like it must be dismissive-sounding air through their lips, all step forward, two to one side of the obese boy, and one to the other, all three leaning over the counter.

The cashier hands the bagged goods to the obese boy, who tells her something. She holds an open hand beside the obese boy's. The cure crawls from the obese boy's hand to the cashier's. The cure lies on her palm, wraps its arm around her wrist, presses the side of its face to her pulse. She raises it up in front of her eyes and demonstratively sighs, smiling.

The two fitter boys who stand to his right start saying things to the obese boy, to which the obese boy responds with enthusiasm. One takes a Slim Jim from the jar on the counter and wags it in the air. The obese boy nods. Another takes another Slim Jim from the jar on the counter and wags it in the air. The obese boy nods, claps his hands once.

The third boy, in the meantime, reaches over the counter toward the cashier.

The cashier backsteps.

The boy who just reached over the counter backsteps.

The obese boy says a few words to the cashier.

She steps forward again, returns the cure to his hand, and the boy who'd reached over the counter swipes it.

The other fitter boys protest.

The fitter boy who has the cure shows his friends an index finger.

They protest more, whip the Slim Jims offscreen.

The obese boy protests.

One slaps him across the face and he ceases to protest. The other slaps him across the face and he drops to the ground, hides his head in his arms.

The obese boy's assailants move in the direction of the boy who holds the cure.

One of them trips. The other doesn't.

The cashier pulls a handgun out from under the counter. She gestures with the gun—down, up, down, up—and is saying things.

The standing, fitter boy who doesn't have the cure raises his hands, placatingly, then helps the fallen, fitter boy to his feet, and then they both help the obese boy to his feet, and one of them hands him his dropped bag of goods.

The cashier points the handgun at the boy who has the cure and says something.

His eyes remain on the cure, but he nods, begins to extend the loose fist in which the cure is held toward the obese boy.

As the obese boy reaches out for the cure, the boy holding it backsteps suddenly, as if he's been startled, and smashes the cure, headfirst, into his mouth. He chomps twice and swallows.

The other fitter boys exclaim and point and laugh and stomp their feet and slap themselves on the legs and the chest and twirl their fingers next to their ears.

The obese boy crumples back down to the floor.

The cashier, still pointing the gun, starts yelling.

The boy who just overloaded looks at his friends, breaks into a smile, leaps over the obese boy, and runs offscreen. His friends follow.

The cashier puts the gun away, comes around the side of the counter, helps the obese boy back to his feet. His face is running with tears, his lips and eyes wrinklingly squeezed. The cashier hugs him, patting his head. He stands there stiff-armed, clutching his shopping bag, neither accepting nor fighting the hug.

•

• •

A Cure for Unrequited Love

University of Chicago Graham&Swords Friends Study

January 23, 1988; January 30, 1988

[5 minutes, 14 seconds]

Fixed overhead shot of a mullet-haired boy sitting in a window seat, writing on a legal pad, while, six or seven feet in front of him, another boy, bright blond with a spike, kneels on the floor, hunching over his own legal pad.

As a large-eyed, freckled girl wearing evening gloves approaches the mulleted boy, the blond boy on the floor looks up, stops writing, straightens his posture, and waves to her, but receives no response.

The girl, to the mulleted boy, says, "Excuse me."

The mulleted boy, who's taking up the whole seat, makes himself small.

The girl sits beside him.

She and the mulleted boy play footsie. They say “Excuse me” to one another repeatedly. The intensity of the footsie increases quickly, as does the volume at which the *Excuse me*s are pronounced. Legs start to tangle.

The blond boy moves as if to stand up, but does not stand up.

The girl punches the mulleted boy in the thigh.

“Jesus,” he says, rubbing his thigh.

“Did I hurt you?” says the girl. “I didn’t mean to really hurt you. I’m sorry.” She leans toward the mulleted boy and tumbles off the window seat, onto her shoulder.

Both boys go to her. The mulleted one gets to her first, holds out his hand. She takes it. The blond boy rushes offscreen.

CUT.

One week later.

Fixed overhead shot of the freckled girl in evening gloves sitting on a couch beside the mulleted boy, who wears a strange-looking CureSleeve.

The boy is mumbling something.

“Blah blah blah!” the girl says, and leaps off the couch. “If you believe me, then prove it. Let me see yours. Take it out of that sleeve thing and let me hold it.”

“No,” says the boy.

“Go to hell, then,” says the girl, and, just as the bright-blond boy from the previous scene steps inside the frame from the right, the girl roundhouses leftward until she’s offscreen.

CUT.

Eighteen minutes later.

Fixed overhead shot of the big-eyed, freckled girl in evening gloves sitting in a window seat, eating a sandwich. The mulleted boy approaches her. “Hello,” he says. The girl stares down at her sandwich and chews.

A second boy appears behind the mulleted boy, waiting, it seems, to be acknowledged.

Seconds pass.

The second boy huffs some air from his nose, loudly, looks at the ceiling—his gaze is fixed, he is extremely walleyed.

“Lisette,” says the mulleted boy to the girl.

The walleyed boy huffs more air from his nose.

The girl, Lisette, remains unresponsive, chews.

“Dude, you gotta meet me after session seven,” the walleyed boy says to the back of the mulleted boy. “Screwball’s doing the best new thing. You pull on his whiskers a little and he yawns, and if you do it three or four times in a row, then when you stop he makes a sound like ah-cha-cha cha-cha and blinks his eyes really hard!"

"Lisette," the mulleted boy repeats. "Please don't be mad at me. Everything is terrible. My mother's got cancer."

Lisette swallows a bite of sandwich and says, "You're so full of it. That's the oldest, dumbest lie."

"I wouldn't lie about this," says the mulleted boy. "The doctors say she only has three to five weeks."

Lisette, in a mocking, whiny-toddler voice, says, "I wouldn't lie about this."

Sniffling sounds come from the walleyed boy. His shoulders are trembling.

"You just want me to feel bad," Lisette continues. "You just want attention."

"No," says the mulleted boy. "I *do* want your attention, but—"

Lisette leans to the side, to see around the mulleted boy. To the walleyed boy, she says, "Why are you crying? Stop crying."

"She's dying," the walleyed boy says to Lisette. "His mom's gonna die."

"She's not," says Lisette.

The mulleted boy pivots, punches the walleyed boy in the face, turns back to Lisette.

Lisette's mouth is open. Lisette looks surprised.

The bright-blond boy from the previous clip appears at the bottom of the frame, tentatively approaches.

"It's okay," the walleyed boy says to the back of the mulleted boy. "I knew you were a hitter. I shouldn't have said that."

Again, the mulleted boy pivots, and again he strikes the walleyed boy in the face.

The walleyed boy falls, clutching his face.

The mulleted boy turns back to Lisette.

"Good one," she says, "but I still don't believe you."

Two men—one in a black labcoat, one in a white labcoat—rush into the frame. The man in the white labcoat kneels beside the walleyed boy. The man in the black labcoat embraces the mulleted boy, lifts him off his feet. As the boy kicks at air and shouts, "Lisette!" and "Please!" and "Wait!" the man adjusts his grasp and carries him offscreen.

Lisette runs offscreen in the same direction.

The bright-blond boy follows her.

CUT.

Forty-seven minutes later.

Fixed overhead shot of Lisette sitting cross-legged on the leftmost cushion of a five-cushion couch, looking down at her lap. The bright-blond boy appears at the bottom of the frame. A cure is lying prone on his shoulder. He sits on the couch's rightmost cushion, says, "Hi."

"Stay away from me," the girl says. "Stop staring. Go away."

"I wanted to tell you that you can hold Zappy," says the boy.

"I don't want to," she says.

"It's really friendly," says the boy.

"I don't care," she says.

"I love you," says the boy.

"That's stupid," she says.

"Why's it stupid?" says the boy.

"Wipe the oozey jizz from your pinkeyes, Dicksuck!" a yawny-voiced boy, offscreen, remarks. "She's in love with Suspendersed. Everyone knows it."

"Shut up," the girl says, and covers her face.

The bright-blond boy removes the cure from his shoulder, lays it down supine in his palm, moves across the sofa to the cushion beside the one on which Lisette is sitting. He strokes the cure, one-fingered, on the belly. "Look," he says, "at how cute it is. It's really cute." Lisette doesn't respond. The boy strokes the cure for a few more seconds, then returns to the cushion he'd previously sat on. "You're so cute, little Zappy. You really are," he says, and keeps stroking the cure. "It's almost as cute as you, Lisette. Really. It's true. It really is." He looks up at Lisette. Her face is still hidden. He looks back at the cure, continually stroking it. It starts to painsing. "You're almost as cute as Lisette, aren't you? Man, wow. And you sing so pretty."

The painsong rises.

Lisette drops her hand, uncovering her face. She says, "What are you doing? Why is it doing that?"

"It likes to sing."

The painsong gets louder.

"Stop doing that," she says.

"It's *cute,*" he says.

"I don't think you should do that. I don't think it likes it."

"It's so cute, though," he says.

"Just stop!" Lisette says. "Why are you doing that. Why would you *do* that."

"Don't you want to hold it?"

"No!" Lisette says. "Don't *do* that! Please stop! Please stop! Please stop!"

The boy, breathing heavily, cups his stroking hand over the cure, looks left, looks right, looks at Lisette, lets out a quiet moan, and grinds his palms til the painsinging stops.

IV

COMPOUND

NEW MODES OF FASCINATION

||BIG DAY?|| MY BETTER pillow said, just as I was waking on the morning after Triple-J and Burroughs came over. I hadn't heard from that pillow in at least half a decade, but my eyes were still closed, my limbs yet unstretched. I wanted more sleep.

I rolled to my side, breaking off contact, and was startled bolt upright by a reticent crumpling paired with a cold, scrapy feeling on my cheek. Triple-J's paper. "Living Isn't Functioning." By the time I'd finished reading it, late the night before, I'd been too lazy to reach across the bed to set it on the table, and had dropped it, instead, on the other, lesser pillow.

I lay back down.

||Oh, he's back,|| my better pillow said. ||And don't I feel special. Hey, you know what? You know what I remember? What I remember every day? I remember how it used to be all I'd do was say, |Hello,| and your smile, man . . . Even if the only place we were touching was on the back of your head, I'd *feel* that smile. The tension in your scalp, it would change just a little, in this really special way, and I knew . . . I knew that— No, though. I didn't. I didn't know *a thing*. All these years you wouldn't talk to me? Years I've spent wondering, |How did I offend him? What wrong have I done him?| And trying to hash it out with the mattress, with the quilt, with every last book you've deigned to use me to cradle? Trying to hash it out til they themselves—sick of me, sick of my whining—til *they* closed their gates to me? And then? Then what? Then suddenly, this morning, you're suddenly available. Suddenly, this morning, your gate's wide open, and I think I've been forgiven for whatever *trespass* it is you've found me guilty of, and with joy, with relief, out of nothing but the friendliest sense of curiosity, I ask a simple question, I say *two words*, and you—you do what? You sure as hell don't smile! You don't even acknowledge me. You break off contact! It's cruel, you know that? You've gone cruel is what it is. And what's sick, what's really sick here—do you want to know what's

sick? What's sick is, now you're back, most of me's grateful. I still feel relieved. I'm still completely curious. What a sap, right? What a sentimental sap. What a jerk.||

"Do books really talk?" I said.

||Excuse me?|| said the pillow.

"You said you've talked to books that I laid on top of you. Is that true, or were you just kind of saying it for effect?"

||This is the matter you want to discuss with me? Seven years go by without a single peep from you, I confess my insecurities, I tell you how you've hurt me, I tell you how you're *hurting* me, I make myself *vulnerable,* and that's what you ask?||

"You know I can't control my gate," I said. "If I could, I'd have—"

||What? You'd've what, huh? What? You'd've what? You'd've huh, what, you'd huh *what* huh you'd?||

"Okay," I said. "So you're having some fun with me."

||Bet your gullible, wimpy bottom dollar it's fun! Oh, what a sweetheart. This is so classic you. What a sucker you are. How do you even survive in the world, you big cornball? You hambone. You armorless wuss.||

"Yeah, yeah," I said.

||That's better,|| said the pillow. ||Dismissive is better. A wooden voice implies a stone-faced outlook, a thicker skin. So go with that. Go forth with implications. Meantime, what's the news? What've you got on your plate today? And don't tell me it's nothing, cause your face was jumping like fleas last night. Last time you got that acrobatic of the visage was the night before your book got reviewed in that paper.||

"I'm gonna see an old friend for brunch today," I said.

||No, really,|| said the pillow.

"Really," I said.

||But your jaw, man. Your jaw. The way you were grinding it, your teeth must be powder. All because of brunch? I don't believe it for a second. You some kind of loser? Maybe you're a loser.||

"I drool on you, you know that?"

||For thirtysomething years now. Night upon night.||

"You're basically this soft thing I drool on," I said. "You're old and flat and stained and inanimate. You don't even have a name. For all I know you're just in my head. Completely made up. And on top of it, you're mean to me. Why don't I get a new pillow, do you think? Why do I keep you around?"

||Sentimentality? Inner softness? New pillows cost money you don't want to spend? Most pillows hurt your neck? You're afraid of any change, great or small? You're a loser who can't let go of anything that might—||

I got out of bed. My jaw did hurt.

•

• •

It was half past eight, brunch would be at eleven, and the walk to the compound was only ten minutes, so despite not having yet watched *A Fistful of Fists*—which, given that it was "video art" made by a boy barely fourteen years old, I imagined would take half an hour at most—I saw no reason to rush my morning rituals. I even thought that, before heading out, Kablankey and I might squeeze in a viewing of the eyebrow-flexing Groucho compilation.

In the shower, I dialed the flow ring rightward to maximize the concentration of the spray, and while the pounding water soothed my overworked jaw, it occurred to me that my back was barely hurting, that I'd slept off all but the last of the pain of Triple-J's stomping, and I felt a humming, almost ticklish space opening up behind my eyes, as if a blockage were clearing, or a swelling abating, and, in the wake of this feeling, I found myself imbued with a sense of possibility readier and sunnier than any I'd possessed since first I'd heard tell of the girl who talked to inans. Said imbuement, yes, must have owed some to the imminence of brunch at the compound with Jonboat, but it owed at least as much to my pillow having claimed to have spoken with books. I couldn't help but wonder what that might be like. What *they* might be like—to speak with, that is. Might they have an understanding of the text they contained? a special understanding? a *correct* understanding? And why hadn't any of them ever conversed with me? Unless—wait: Was it possible they had? or that some of them had? Was it possible my gate was occasionally, if not always, open to them? that while reading them, I, though unaware of it, was silently conversing with them? that I had, all along, been silently conversing with them? that to read a book was to speak to that book? that *being read* was how books spoke? Or no, that couldn't be: pillows didn't read, and the pillow was the one that had said it spoke to books. But then perhaps for that very reason—i.e. that people could read, and inans couldn't—communication with books was different for us than it was for inans? Sometimes at least?

Or maybe that was all too romantic, too fanciful. Maybe books lacked comprehension of the words inside them. Maybe, to them, the words inside them were only their "ink parts" or something like that, something like birthmarks, or freckles, or hair, no more or less legible than their glue or their thread. Maybe books wished only to be held, to have their covers opened, their pages turned. And maybe, after all, they didn't have gates.

It didn't really matter, though, either way. None of that mattered. In the shower, I mean. Nor did it matter that the pillow, when it mentioned it had spoken to books, had done so in the course of kidding around with me, nor even that my conversation with the pillow (or with any other inan, ever) might have only been a product of psychosis NOS.

On second thought, no, that stuff did matter. A bit. It did. Actually, I guess it mattered kind of a lot. But matterfulness is, if nothing else, relative, and there was something that mattered a whole lot more to me than what lay behind the gates of books (assuming, to begin with, that they did have gates), or whether inans were hallucinations: what mattered was that I hadn't, before that morning—i.e. not once in all my life—I hadn't ever *wondered* what lay behind the gates of books (nor whether books had gates to begin with). Despite being someone—perhaps the only person on Earth—who both a) thought frequently of inans and gates, and b) had spent hours every day of his life holding and reading and trying to write books, it somehow hadn't ever occurred to me to wonder. This never-having-wondered mattered so much to me, there in the shower, not because it meant I was dumber, or less imaginative, than I'd long suspected (though it may have meant either or both of those things, too), but rather because it appeared to suggest there was more to imagine, *far more* to imagine (if not to *discover*), than I'd long suspected. New modes of fascination. New tales to tell. Deep and formerly unthinkable thoughts. And the world seemed generous and full of potential, pregnant with thrilling, benevolent mystery.

I shut the tap and toweled off and dressed, then woke and fed and watered Kablankey, ballooning all the while with ardent hope. I could aim that hope at anything, looked forward to everything. Near or far, great or small, it all seemed so auspicious: the books I'd write, sure, and the next book I'd publish (whatever it might be), and *No Please Don't* resultantly coming back into print (would Dalkey put it out? would New Directions?), and the girl who talked to inans (had *she* spoken to books? to a *No Please Don't*? to more than one copy? had they said the same things? could she tell me what they said? had they convinced her to love me? would she tell me things I'd meant without my having known I'd meant them?), and my friendship with Jonboat (riding shotgun in the Boatmobile, into the city, out to the lake, him telling me what outer space was like, me telling him my thoughts on living in Wheelatine, us wistfully remembering Stevie Strumm together, maybe driving to Joliet Correctional to visit Blackie *just because,* and organically developing, as we sped along, a kind of endless game where we listed behaviors for which "pissing through a boner" was an appropriate metaphor), and my friendship with Jonboat's family, too (Triple-J a kind of Beckett to my Joyce, or Giant to my Beckett; the brilliant and inspirationally gorgeous Fondajane a vocal champion of my work, its rediscoverer, perhaps the author of an *NYRB* piece to be reprinted as the forward to the new edition of *No Please Don't,* the piece itself in part responsible for *No Please Don't*'s new cult-classic status)—yes, my forward-lookingness applied itself to all these things, but also, and equally, to humbler and less hypothetical things like the walk I would shortly take to the compound, the way the breeze would feel on my face, the way the grass would smell in the heat, and the day's first Quill, the one I would savor with my morning cup of coffee.

And that coffee itself. That first cup of coffee. As I headed downstairs, that's what I was focused on: how that cup would be the twentysomething thousandth of my life, and how strange it was, and how very *interesting,* that every cup I'd ever sweetened (and I always sweetened coffee) I'd sweetened with sugar, i.e. never with honey, not even once, and how I might, that morning, in just a couple minutes, go right on ahead and just change things up a bit, honey my coffee, for maybe honey was better than sugar, and if that were true, if honey were better, then that morning's cup of coffee, the cup I was *just about* to drink, could prove to be the single best coffee of my life. And in the midst of envisaging honeyed coffee's mouthfeel, I stepped off the stairway, into the hallway, and raised my eyes and looked into the kitchen and discovered my father bending over our range, on which too much bacon—a whole pound, by the sound of it (I couldn't yet see, having frozen on the carpeted side of the threshold bar)—was frying on much too high a flame. And I deflated instantly. I withered and sunk.

The way he was standing, like a busted cornerboy submitting to a pat-down—wide-legged, arms raised, palms against the door of the microwave oven mounted over the stove—seemed as deliberate as it did bizarre.

It seemed . . . strokey.

Alzheimersesque.

"Dad?" I said through the greasy smoke, over the zapping and sizzling and squealing.

He leapt back and gasped, holding his chest. Across the bottom of his face, he wore a checked bandana, tied in the style of a railroad bandit, and, above the bandana, elastic-banded goggles through the lenses of which his eyes expressed shock, disorientation.

"Oh *wow*!" he said, and lowered the flames (there were two pans of bacon). "You *got* me," he said, pulling down the bandana, showing me his teeth. "I haven't flinched that hard since— Hoo! Wow. Good one. Really. That was a good one." He took off the goggles, wiped at his brow. "So I'm staining this shirt," he said, pointing at his torso. He had on a baggy JONBOAT SAY T over a long-sleeved, waffle-textured thermal.

"I don't think you're well," I said. "Let's sit down."

"I'm fine," he said. "I don't feel like sitting down."

"Let's sit," I said.

"I said I don't want to, and you're freaking me out, you wanna know the truth. What the hell kinda look is that you're giving me, Billy? And that sad-voice you're doing. That wary, uh, *timbre*. I'm not *that* old," he said. "Well, I guess I am. But I'm in good shape. I mean, Jesus, you know? If you thought I was some kind of coronary lightweight, why'd you even startle me?"

"I think something's wrong," I said. "I think you might be having some kind of an episode."

"An *episode*?" he said. "I don't *have* those," he said, and the power with which his incredulity came across did testify to a Clydely self-possession, even in spite of the getup, and yet . . .

"What were you saying you were doing with the shirt?"

"I'm getting it stained for you to bring to brunch," he said. "I guess that sounds pretty weird, but I thought a lot about it at the tavern last night. Talked to Mal Vaughn about it *in depth*. Verdict was you can't show up empty-handed. But what kinda gift do you bring to a billionaire? Especially if you're, you know, not exactly a billionaire yourself, right? And I came up with the answer: sentimental. A sentimental gift. So: the shirt. And yeah, I know, sure—I'm sure he has one already. Probably has a hundred. But he'll never admit it. He'd seem too precious, too self-centered, and you, if you give him one, it'll be like you're saying, 'Hey man, I bet it's been a while since you seen one of these, huh?' and *that*'ll be like saying you'd never imagine in a million years that he'd be the type of guy who'd hold on to cheesy souvenirs of himself."

"But—"

"I know. Exactly. If you bring the shirt and it's all brand-new and clean and never-worn, then he'll think—what? He'll think you went out of your way all these years to keep it mint condition, and that: screw that. You'll look like a stalker or something. An obsessive. It'll seem like you think he's better than you, and he isn't, and you don't. At least I hope you don't, cause, like I said: he isn't. Anyway, I was gonna just give you the one I wear as an undershirt to bring over there, but it's *too* blown out. It's torn near the collar, pitted something fierce. And that would be, I think, outright insulting, to give someone a shirt that wrecked as a gift, sentimental or no. Could make you look petty. Like you wanted to say, 'Fuck you, there, Jonboat,' but didn't have the guts. Plus it'll make him think you must've worn it all the time for it to be that wrecked, which gets you back into worshipful stalker territory, and if you add the gutless-fuck-you factor to that, it . . . it's just a real bad look for you to wear to brunch. A weak look, really. A snively-type psychopathic look. Dahmer-ish, you know? Or, I guess, more Cunanan-y. Either way: not a look you want. So when I came home last night and saw how wrecked the one I use for an undershirt was, I thought, 'I'll get the framed one from the basement, and mess it up some, but not too bad, just a little,' right? So this morning, I put it on and geared up—I know I look like a fruitcake, by the way, with the goggles and handkerchief, but they're what I had at hand to keep my face from getting burned by the bacon fat—and I started frying all this bacon so the fat would spatter the shirt in a natural-type pattern, and now I'm gonna let it set a few minutes, and then I'm gonna wash it, which'll dilute the stains, but not really get rid of them. Bacon fat's a bitch on cotton, I don't know if you know that. Anyway, it'll look like you wore it once or twice, cooked some bacon while you wore it, couldn't get all the stains out, and stuck it in the drawer, idea being to communicate the shirt was too sentimentally valuable for you to outright throw it in the garbage after it got stained—which is nice, and pretty normal, I think—but not so sentimentally valuable that you wore it *after* it got stained or bothered to buy some kind of fancy laundry soap to hand-wash the stains out, which might have been a little snively if you did that. It's a good idea, I think. I'm sold, at least. So was Mal. What do you think?"

"Okay," I said.

"You don't sound so sure, Bill, and you still got a pretty haunted cast to your mug, you want to know the truth. I'll tell you what. If you're looking for something to get all disturbed and mother-hen-y about, try this: I don't feel hardly hungover at all, but I think I might've blacked out last night, cause when I went down the basement this morning for the shirt, all the glass in the frame was gone. Not shattered all over the floor, mind you: gone. So what I think might've happened was I think I might've gone down there *last night* to go get the shirt, and then—I don't know—dropped the frame on the floor when I took it off the wall, and that shattered the glass, and then I must've swept it up and then gone to bed, though *none of this* do I remember. It's a little bit scary to me, tell you the truth. I mean it's not like I haven't blacked out drunk before, but I always knew it when it happened. Always *sensed* the gap. Like, the next morning, part of the night was just missing, and I knew it. And the hangovers—shit. The after-blackout hangovers—they're the worst. But today, I feel pretty good, like I said. So that's a little spooky. Did you see me last night when I came home? Did I look that drunk to you?"

"I didn't see you," I said.

"Yeah, well, look, quit with the fucking face already, alright? I don't *really* want you to be mother-hen-y about this. I was just saying. Jesus. I mean there's a whole nother possibility, anyway. The other possibility is I broke it some other night. The frame, I mean. That's another explanation. That I blacked out on one of these other nights that the next morning I *did* remember blacking out on, and during *that* blackout I broke it. Maybe on purpose, who knows? I could see how I probably might've did it on purpose. I never really liked that he made the shirts. I thought it was shady. I mean, *Shut your piehole, cakeface*—that's ours, it's not his, and he took the credit, plus who pays to make a shirt with their name on it, you know? Seems cocky. Shitty. Same time, though, I guess he seemed like someone you were gonna be friends with, and I knew you needed friends, especially around the time he made the shirts, you just did, I knew that, you really had no one except for me, so I guess I did opposites, you know."

"Did opposites?" I said.

"Yeah, you know, there's a word—what's the word? *Overcompensated,* right? I overcompensated, made a whole big deal outta the shirt, acted all proud of it and framed it cause I was scared if I didn't do something loud like that then you'd think I didn't approve of your only friend, and I guess I didn't really. Approve of him, I mean. I didn't really approve of him, and I guess I figured you could tell, and you probably could, so I went outta my way to cover it up, doing opposites, which, maybe, you being you, you always saw through the cover-up anyway, always knew I didn't like him, didn't approve, but it's not the kind of thing we—I mean we don't talk about that kinda thing, you and me, so what do I know?—but what I'm saying is that even though I figured you probably saw through it, I guess I thought it was probably better, being your dad, to stay consistent, cause I think that's important, so I stayed consistent. Would you listen to me going on? What the fuck? Maybe I did black out last night, and instead of getting hungover, I turned into some kind of yammering, daytime talk show guest. I don't know, Billy. But his family's a bunch of shits, you ask me. Jonboat's I mean. And his friendship wasn't really so valuable for you after all, looking back on it now, I don't think, but still, at the time back then . . . I bottled up, and did opposites until like, I guess—I *hope*—maybe one night that was *not* last night, maybe last month or this other time a few months before that that I *do* remember knowing in the morning I'd blacked out, maybe during the blackout on one of *those* nights I got caught up thinking about all this stuff for some reason and I got fed up, pissed off, whatever, and the cork just *popped* and I went downstairs and smashed the frame, like on purpose, and then probably felt stupid and so cleaned up the glass, and next morning had no idea that's what I'd done, even though I knew I'd blacked out and must've done something, and since I don't hardly ever go down in the basement, it was only this morning I discovered what I'd done last month or a few months before that or whatever. Anyway, that's the story I think *I'm* gonna go with since it's just not as scary as the one where I blacked out last night but this morning got no sense of it, and why be more scared than I have to be, right? I mean, that's probably what happened, anyway, right? That's probably all it is."

"Maybe," I said.

"It seems possible, anyway, and that's good enough, I think. It's good enough for me, at least. And if it's good enough for me, then you shouldn't—oh . . . we're . . . hugging? Okay. That's fine. Sure. We're hugging. Alright. Make me flinch, and then hug me. I guess why not? Big hug, then. Okay, son. Good. Yeah. Okay then. Alright now. Alright."

•

• •

Nonviolent, nonsexual, male-on-male contact. Two undemonstrative American men squeezing one another's torsos in America. A widowed father and his motherless son, hugging after twentysomething years of not hugging.

There we were in the morning-lit kitchen.

But it wasn't what it looked like. It wasn't transformative. If anything, our hug worked against transformation—discharging the sentiments that, had we held *them* fast instead of each other, might have caused transformation; maintaining our emotional distance in the long term via closing our physical distance in the short.

Or something like that.

In any case, I didn't, in the wake of the hug, confess to having broken the frame in the basement, nor to having long misconstrued as admiration for the Pellmore-Jasons—sometimes even as affection for the Pellmore-Jasons—my father's contempt for the Pellmore-Jasons. Perhaps I hugged him to avoid confessing. If so, however, then only at first. As the hug proceeded, I hugged for hugging's sake and only for hugging's sake. We both did, I believe. It was a singular hug, tender and intimate and wholly acknowledged, lasting the better part of a minute, and although I don't remember the way we disengaged, I know we didn't perform the kind of shoulder-punching, backslapping, Zuko/Kenickie embarrassment routine I would have expected.

Once the hug had ended, my father left the kitchen to launder the T-shirt. I fixed myself a cup of coffee with honey. The first sip was interesting, the second one strange, and the third was disgusting—fumy, almost dizzying. To the roof of my mouth clung a musty sweetness, like breath on a window—stale breath on a window—while the coffee's native bitterness, divorced from this sweetness, dried out the back of my tongue and my gums. I dumped what remained in the mug in the sink.

When I turned back around to pour a fresh cup, my father, freshly clothed, dis-bandana'd and de-goggled, was standing on the threshold bar, squinting at me, then my cup, then the sink, and then back at me. "Something wrong with the coffee there, Billy?" he said.

"I honeyed it," I said.

"Come again?" he said.

"I used honey to sweeten it."

"We run out of sugar?"

"No," I said. "I just thought I'd try honey. In case it was great."

"Not bright," he said.

"Why 'not bright'? What do you know about it?"

"I know I never heard of it," he said, approaching.

"Neither have I," I said. "That's *why* I tried it. It could have been great."

"No, Bill," he said. "No chance in hell it could have been great. It could have, at absolute best, been mediocre."

"Safe to say now," I said, "after I told you."

"Safe to say in 1961," he said.

I didn't know what he meant. He poured himself a coffee and explained what he meant. He began by explaining that by claiming that it would have been safe to say in 1961 that there was no chance in hell that honeyed coffee was anything better than mediocre, he was actually speaking conservatively: he didn't know what year it had become de rigueur for the American housewife to have a coffee machine on her kitchen counter and a container of honey in her kitchen cupboard, and while he would guess it was well before 1953, he was certain it wasn't after 1959, the year he'd been five and six years old, the first year he'd gone to school, and thus the first year he could remember reliably. (Though he did say *de rigueur,* he also used synonyms for *de rigueur,* e.g. *customary, fashionable, in vogue, conventional, compulsory, essential,* even *comme il faut;* used these synonyms, it seemed, not because he doubted my grasp of *de rigueur*'s full spectrum of meaning, but because he doubted I believed in his.) So, my father continued to explain, given the number of ready opportunities—tens of millions per day in America alone—to put honey in coffee in both 1959 and 1960, it would be nothing short of insane to deny that thousands, if not tens or even hundreds of thousands, of cups of coffee must have been honeyed by 1961. Considering, furthermore, that 1961 was already over fifty years past, and that more people drank more coffee these days than ever, and that we lived in a relatively open society that not only encouraged the free exchange of ideas but for some reason *particularly* encouraged the free exchange of ideas about foods and beverages, the fact that neither my father nor I, prior to that morning, had ever even heard of anyone putting honey in their coffee had to mean that those who had tried it, i.e. all those hundreds of thousands (if not millions) of men and women of the last five decades who had ever put honey in their coffee (perhaps because they'd run out of sugar, perhaps because they were foolish, perhaps on a dare from a mischievous friend)—even if some, or even many of those hundreds of thousands, if not millions, had determined honeyed coffee was mediocre, rather than outright disgusting—they had, each and every last one, unanimously found honeyed coffee to be *less than great.* Were it otherwise, we'd not only have heard about honeying coffee, we would have long before this morning tried honeyed coffee. And that was why, my father explained, it was distinctly *not bright* of me to ever have thought that by honeying my coffee I might realize some heretofore undiscovered and desirable potential, let alone greatness. Which appraisal (i.e. *not bright*), was, he added, also conservative—conservative in the sense of understated, or restrained.

Once he'd finished speaking, we stood there a moment, at the kitchen counter, by the coffee machine, just sipping our coffees, looking at each other and nodding a little til I made a sudden movement with my shoulders, like to hit him.

Flinching, he spilled half his coffee on his jeans.

"Goddamn!" he said. "You're really on today, son. Or maybe I'm off."

"Maybe's the sound second thoughts make," I said.

"Amen to that. It's a shrug and a dodge."

"If we're gonna make it to brunch on time, I should probably watch Triple-J's video," I said.

"What you mean *we*, whiteman?" he said.

"You're not going?" I said.

"Since when do I brunch?"

"You accepted the invitation," I said.

"I was being polite."

"Since when are you polite?"

"You got me. Okay. I was only playing at being polite. That kid was being polite, inviting me, and the polite thing would have been for me to tell him I couldn't make it, offer some excuse, but I don't need some polite kid honoring me with a brunch invitation I'm supposed to refuse, so, to fuck with him a little, I told him I'd be there. Don't act disappointed. You don't want me there, anyway."

"That's not—"

"You're relieved, Bill. Come on. Keep pretending you aren't, I'll start to feel offended. Let's go watch your video."

•

•   •

At the start of the segment with the fat kid, the cat, and Percy the Curio, my father leaned across the couch and smacked me on the shoulder. "I figured it out," he said. "What this reminds me of. It's like that one tape. You remember that tape?"

I remembered the tape. Around the turn of the millennium, just as DVDs were gaining popularity, my father'd brought home a VHS tape that was being passed around among the workers at the plant. *Bumfights Gone Wild by the Bell, Maybelline, If You'll Give Me a Chance*. It was, for the most part, a bootlegged compilation of "best of" moments from two mail-order video series: *Bumfights*, in which homeless men, paid by a crew of pop-collared frat brothers, beat each other up and self-harmed for the camera; and *Girls Gone Wild*, in which drunken coeds on spring and winter break flashed and kissed and groped one another in exchange for T-shirts, beads, or money, depending on what they'd been able to negotiate with a wholly different crew of pop-collared frat brothers. Other clips appeared on the tape as well, usually between, though sometimes intercutting, those mentioned above. There was one of a man, allegedly Chuck Berry, urinating onto a woman in a bathtub, afterward telling her to give him a kiss, then pushing her away when she leans in to kiss him, and saying, "Bitch, you smell like piss!"; one of a child beauty contestant descending a triple-tiered dais, victorious, while vomiting down the length of her gown; an educational film, ca. 1970, for newly pubescent mentally retarded girls, in which the film's protagonist, Jenny, a twelve-year-old with Down's, puts the question "What's a period?" to her mother, then her sister, and then her father, and they each respond by twice repeating the sentence "Once a month, blood from inside a woman's body comes out from an opening between her legs"; and a seventeen-minute, unsolicited audition for the after-school sitcom *Saved by the Bell*, in which a markedly non-telegenic teenage boy in a Waikiki belly-shirt praises both the writing and the acting on the show as "the best there is," then vogues atop a bar stool to "Pump up the Jam" by Technotronic in his parents' suburban, wood-paneled basement, and ends things by begging the show's producers to give him a chance: "Just a chance. One chance," he says. "I've earned a chance, I deserve a chance, just give me a chance." There were other clips too, at least a dozen more, but I couldn't remember them. I hadn't seen the tape in over a decade.

"I guess that it's kinda like the tape," I said.

"Right," sneered my father. "Only *kinda* cause the tape wasn't a 'documentary collage.'"

"Well—"

"The tape wasn't 'art,' right? Unlike this masterpiece here, I mean."

"I was gonna say the tape was a lot more random."

"And this thing isn't random?"

"It's *less* random," I said. "So far at least, the segments all have something to do with cures."

"Yeah, okay," he said. "I guess you got a point."

A couple minutes later, our washer's buzzer sounded and my father got up. I paused the video.

"Don't," he said. "I'm done. I think this kinda thing—it's not really my thing, you know? Especially not this early in the day. I'm gonna go switch that shirt, catch a workout or something."

It wasn't til he'd left that I looked at the pause screen. The digits in its upper corners informed me I'd watched twenty-five of 170 minutes, was in the midst of the seventh of twenty-six tracks. This was unwelcome news. The clock said 10:10, and was ten minutes slow. I had just thirty minutes before I had to leave: half an hour to watch more than two hours of video and formulate a critique of what I'd seen. Well, more like forty minutes to formulate the critique—I could, if I wished, think about the critique during my ten-or-so-minute walk to the compound—but, still. Not enough time to do the job right.

How big a deal was that? Maybe not so big.

Were I, at brunch, to tell Triple-J the truth—that I hadn't suspected how long the collage was, and so hadn't budgeted enough of my morning to view and properly critique it—he would, I imagined, be disappointed, but I doubted that he'd be hurt or offended, as long as I assured him my critique was forthcoming.

Except then, of course, I'd still owe him a critique. And owing to that critique's delayed delivery, there would be a lot more pressure on me to make it a useful, insightful critique, the kind I'd have to watch most, if not all, of *A Fistful* to formulate.

And I didn't want to watch most or all of *A Fistful.* I didn't want to watch any more of *A Fistful.*

What I'd seen so far had left me feeling compromised.

I don't much go in for critical theory, but when, years earlier, I was working on my third failed novel (the one about Josephine Singer, the staggeringly gorgeous intersex sex-worker-slash-wunderkind of critical theory who marries a billionaire), I read Fondajane Henry's seminal treatise on sex work, *Flesh-and-Bone Robots You Think Are Your Friends,* the fifth chapter of which, "Violent Pornography," describes a series of "large-scale arousal studies" performed at Stanford and Oxford Universities. The studies' subjects, while hooked up to a kind of polygraphesque technology (e.g. sensors measuring skin conductivity, pupillary dilation, heart- and respiration-rates, etc.) viewed two sets of eighty photographs. The photos in the first set were of pairs of human eyes dissociated from the faces that housed them (i.e. the faces in which the eyes resided were cropped above the brows and below the cheekbones), and the photos in the second set were of two-inch-square patches of decontextualized human flesh (i.e. each photo showed, in close-up, two square inches of a haunch, a belly, an ass, or a leg). Each of the photos was shown for two seconds, and each subject was asked to rate the "beauty" of the eye pair or flesh patch it depicted on a scale of 1–10.

According to the rating data, a roughly equal proportion (about one-third) of hetero-, homo-, and bisexual men (none of the studies included women or transgendered persons) found pairs of eyes that welled with tears to be more beautiful than pairs of eyes that didn't well with tears, and twice that proportion found patches of flesh that had, moments before they were photographed, been molested (slapped, punched, or pinched) to be more beautiful than unmolested patches of flesh. According to the autonomic response data, the proportion of subjects who preferred molested flesh was consistent with that which was indicated by the rating data, but the proportion of subjects who preferred welling eyes was significantly greater (120 percent greater) than the proportion indicated by the rating data.

The researchers' opinion, which Fondajane shared, was that these discrepancies owed to subjects' ability to recognize the welling eyes as "crying" eyes and their inability to recognize the molested flesh as "molested." That is (according to Fondajane and the researchers), the subjects who had high autonomic responses to welling eyes but nonetheless gave the welling eyes low beauty ratings *deliberately* underrated the beauty of the welling eyes because, in light of their ability to identify the welling eyes as "crying" eyes, they couldn't help but develop narratives of suffering about those to whom the welling eyes belonged (e.g. "these are the eyes of someone who's afraid" or "these are the eyes of someone who's been hurt"), and thus believed that rating highly the beauty of the welling eyes would make them (i.e. make the subjects) seem sadistic to the researchers, whereas even though rating highly the beauty of molested flesh patches should, by the same reasoning, indicate sadism on the part of the subjects to at least the same extent as would rating highly the beauty of crying eyes, the flesh patches depicted in the photos were so divorced from their contexts (i.e. the unmolested portions of the haunches, bellies, and asses of which they were a part) that subjects couldn't identify them as "molested" and so were *unable* to develop narratives about them, let alone narratives of suffering (e.g. "this flesh patch, darkening, has been molested" or "this flesh patch, having been molested, is painful to its owner"), and therefore didn't fear (*couldn't have* feared) that giving high beauty ratings to the molested flesh patches would indicate (to the researchers) that they (the subjects) were sadistic, and so they (the subjects) possessed no inclination to hide their positive responses to the molested flesh patches (i.e.

via underrating them). To put it inversely: if the subjects who preferred the molested flesh patches had realized that the flesh patches had been molested, they would have been as resistant to giving high beauty ratings to those flesh patches as the subjects who preferred welling eyes had been resistant to giving high beauty ratings to the welling eyes.

The takeaway from all this, Fondajane posits, is that some (if not many) of the men who are turned on by seeing people cry are turned on not because of what crying *signifies* (that the crying person is suffering or afraid) but because crying eyes are, themselves, "more fundamentally, authentically, beautiful/arousing" to the men than are uncrying eyes: that some (if not many) men who prefer crying eyes to uncrying eyes prefer them in the same deep, helpless, and likely biologically driven way that, for example, some (if not all) people who prefer looking at penises to looking at vaginas prefer looking at penises to looking at vaginas.

She then spends a few pages going out of her way to assert that she isn't by any means claiming that rape—which regularly produces crying eyes and molested flesh—isn't a hideous, sadistic act, but rather that it is a mistake to insist (as had, at the time of *FABRYTAYF*'s initial publication, apparently been the fashion among critical theorists to claim) that the pleasure (some) men take in viewing rape pornography is necessarily indicative of their having a desire to commit rape, or even of a desire to see others commit rape, per se. Many (if not most) men who watch rape porn, Fondajane argues, aren't doing so because the thought of someone being forced to have sex turns them on, but because certain, very specific elements of the *sight* of someone being forced to have sex (e.g. welling eyes and bruising flesh)—elements less prevalent in consensual porn—turn them on.

This line of thinking impressed and intrigued me, but it wasn't til I'd started to watch *A Fistful* that I'd ever suspected I was *invested* in it. And although my investment surely wasn't as major as, say, rape-film fans' or mascara manufacturers', let alone Porn Valley's big movers' and shakers'*, I guess it couldn't have been all too minor, either, given how readily I recalled the above-described chapter in 2013, despite not having read *FABRYTAYF* since 2004.

In any case, that's what I'd found myself doing that morning in the living

* According to Hillary Clinton's introduction to the fifth-anniversary reprint edition of *FABRYTAYF* (Random House, 2003), said movers and shakers had been suffering massive revenue loss in the wake of prostitution's full legalization in 2002, and "The industry," claims Clinton, "would have hardly been able to stay in the black were it not for the success of the 'nonviolent crying porn' (aka 'crybaby porn') genre, the development of which is widely acknowledged to have been inspired by the 'Violent Pornography' chapter of the very book you are holding in your hands."

room: recalling the chapter, the whole line of thinking, then abstracting it out to apply it to myself and the pleasure I experienced during certain disturbing parts of *A Fistful of Fists*. For example, I told myself that my having enjoyed seeing Scatty being tortured in the "Popsicles" clip didn't mean that I was happy that Scatty had been tortured, let alone that I wanted to torture Scatty (or any other cure) myself. I told myself it was how Scatty moved while being tortured, and its facial expressions, and the sounds that it made which I had enjoyed—that I'd enjoyed that stuff independent of its context, independent of its cause. I told myself these things and didn't quite believe them or disbelieve them.

Like I said, I felt compromised.

One thing was for sure: I'd have rather to have never seen the "Popsicles" clip—or, for that matter, the Barker clip (though I had, at least, closed my eyes before that one got gory)—and, since it seemed fairly safe to assume that the more I watched of *A Fistful of Fists*, the more "Popsicles"-esque clips I'd be exposed to, I determined it would be better to try to dodge the blow than take it on the chin, i.e. it would be better to lie to Triple-J. I'd say I'd watched the whole video, offer a critique consisting of a few reasonably thoughtful observation-suggestion combinations concerning the ways in which this clip or that clip served or hindered the collage on the whole, and then never have to watch any of it ever again.

The problem with this plan was that I so far had only one reasonably thoughtful observation-suggestion to make: that the clip of the teacher talking to his class about the word "overload" radically slowed the pace of the video and should thus be cut down, if not cut out. A couple or three more thoughts like that, and I'd be in business, sure, but try though I might to come up with such thoughts, I just wasn't able, for I had no idea what Triple-J was after; I didn't understand *A Fistful*'s narrative, wasn't even sure it possessed a narrative. I had to watch more. As little as possible, yes, but more.

I punched Play on the remote and lit a fresh Quill. The little girl onscreen popped Percy's head, the Chameleon trials started, and, once D18 broke its neck on the carrot, I assumed I'd gotten the gist of the clip, and skipped ahead to the disc's next track: Woof, of Burnsy&Woof. This one really threw me, partly because Woof was so charismatically sad, but more because it was the second time the pace of the collage so radically slowed, which suggested Triple-J *intended* the collage's pace to shift, and, if that were so (i.e. if the shifts were intentional), then for me to propose that the clip of the teacher be cut, or cut down, would, at best, signal that I'd been insensitive to Triple-J's artistic vision and at worst lead him to suspect I hadn't watched the whole collage.

So it turned out I had zero sufficiently intelligent observation-suggestion combos. I didn't give up, though.

Woof continued speaking with no sign of letup, so I skipped ahead after a minute or two, watched "Cuddlefarmer Harvest" up to the hobunk part, then watched the first half of the clip of the Middle Eastern(?) kids and the soldiers, skipped ahead again, watched the Bitchy Elvis P.A.L. Brothers clip, then watched a minute of the interview with the campus spidge dealer (which reinforced my conclusion regarding the inappropriateness of critiquing the pace shifts), skipped ahead once more and watched the leader of that overload cult getting booed and harassed on *Philip Daley Alejandro,* and then, at last, "Flick&Look."

And *then* I gave up.

If someone puts himself in a video, then shows you that video, he must want to hear—perhaps above all else—what you thought of his part in that video. It seemed so to me at the time, at least. And given that Triple-J'd appeared in the "Flick&Look" clip, he might, I reasoned, appear in another clip (or even more than one other clip), and because I had no time to find out (it was 10:48, I had to leave in two minutes), let alone any time to watch any more clips, I wouldn't be able, if pressed on the matter, to speak about his part(s) with any confidence; I would not be convincing. And he very well might, I thought, press me on the matter. It's true I hardly knew him, but I knew he wasn't shy.

A decision, then, if not quite made, had been reached—backed into, I guess: I'd admit that I hadn't finished watching the video, and offer Triple-J a rain check on the crit.

I also decided not to take Blank to brunch, so I stopped in my room on my way out and nested it. Before sitting down to let me close the lid, it broke out a classic: that throat-clearing move Woody Allen often makes—always with his chin tucked and eyebrows raised, sometimes with an index finger timidly extended—to signal he's about to deliver a joke. Kablankey performed the more basic variation—no finger involvement—but I wasn't disappointed. Not by a long shot. I hadn't seen Blank Allen-throat-clear in years (it had mastered the throat-clear while relatively young, during a Woody home video marathon ca. *Bullets Over Broadway*'s theatrical release, and had abandoned it by *Hollywood Ending*'s, at latest), and I wouldn't have thought the move was still in its repertoire. Plus it was adorable. It really cheered me up. Granted me perspective. Suddenly, I was aware of an upside—a possible upside—to my having to admit I hadn't finished *A Fistful:* might not Triple-J, to hear my rain-checked critique, invite me for brunch at the compound a second time? It seemed like he might.

I was laughing my face off. Blank Allen-throat-cleared again and again. Six or seven repetitions. They were so spot-on, I probably would have kept laughing for another six or seven, but I had to get going.

I waved and said, "Bye."

Instead of waving back, Blank, mid-throat-clear, pratfell sideways, clutching its chest, then sat up and brow-wiped and, just as I was closing the lid of the nest, throat-cleared again, at greater volume, as if to say, "Wait, I haven't gotten to the joke yet!"

How I loved that guy.

I pocketed a fresh pack of Quills and left.

HANGSTRONG, ULYSSES

When the Pellmore-Jasons moved into the compound, back in the summer of 1987, it was only just another unremarkable pair of suburban cul-de-sacs set mouth-to-mouth: two kissing omegas of sidewalk cement ringed by raised ranches, split-entries, and trilevels. What little bit of fortification it possessed seemed ornamental, flimsy even: along its border on Armstrong Road—east of which lay the Ridgewood development, where my and a hundred-some other families lived—ran a squat iron fence with a never-manned, ever-retracted sliding gate that permitted passage at Pellmore Place (at that time still called Osage Lane). The other barriers were natural, or relatively natural. Acres of corn- and soybean fields stretched out to the compound's north and west, and to its south was a stand of high weeping willows abutting a shallow, man-made pond thats banks were sown with velvety cattails the children of the neighborhood would reap to joust with.

Over the following summer, however, Jon-Jon Jason had the fencing removed and the compound surrounded with concrete ramparts that rose up as high as fifty feet in some spots. Rumors of Jonboat's seductions atop them eventually came to prevail so broadly that the sexual euphemisms heard in the hallways of early-nineties Wheelatine High embraced citadel imagery as often as not ("We were pressing the parapets." "You get her to climb the bulwarks, or what?" "I gave her some spidge, and she was *draped* on them balustrades."), but Jon-Jon hadn't, I wouldn't imagine, raised the walls just to get his son laid. Wheelatine was demographically booming. Over eighteen months the population had doubled, and with it came all kinds of commerce and traffic. By 1991 most of the fields to the compound's north had been transformed into Wyndstone Homes, phases I and II, and an unnamed strip mall dually anchored by a TGI Friday's and a twelve-screen Cineplex Odeon Theater. The fields to the west were entirely paved, giving way to Lake County's largest Jewel-Osco, a full-service Amoco, the Plaza Beige strip mall where Pang's(?)

White Hen was, and Sawyer Rock phases I through V. The stand of weeping willows was felled overnight to make room for a grade school, and, later that year, in the wake of a near-fatal bullying incident, the pond was filled to expand the school's playground.

Few complained. Property values went up across the board, and it was nice to be able to walk to the movies, to send your kid out on his bike to buy milk. An editorial or two in the *Daily Herald* got some citizens grumbling about the ramparts themselves (the "vistas" they obstructed, the shadows they cast, the elitist Pellmore-Jason worldview to which they couldn't help but seem to attest), but Jon-Jon, no slouch at managing public perception (or hiring others to do so for him), responded by funding field house construction in each new phase of Wyndstone and Sawyer, spread word that the ramparts' primary function was to mute the kinds of street sounds that triggered his wife's debilitating migraines, and quietly purchased a stake in the *Herald*.

The grumbling ceased.

That the compound had always been called a *compound*, i.e. even prior to the ramparts' construction, was something I used to find intriguing. I thought that whoever first used the word *compound*—rather than *manor*, say, or *estate*—must have been someone with a lot of foresight. Either that, or Jon-Jon was so intent on living up to the community's expectations that he decided to have the ramparts constructed only *after* he'd heard his twenty-six-house tract repeatedly (and perhaps jokingly) referred to as *the compound*. Looking back on it now, though, it seems I failed to imagine the simplest, and therefore (by some measures) most likely possible explanation: that Jon-Jon, planning all along to fortify, had himself been first to call his dwellings a *compound*, and, as the rest of the world so often seemed to, the rest of Wheelatine went along with him.

The first time I'd ever visited the compound—to discuss the design of the JONBOAT SAY shirts—was in the spring of 1988, and although the ramparts hadn't yet been installed, its at-purchase Wheelatine-conventional aesthetic had been altered enough since the family'd moved in that a sense of having entered a foreign enclave began to overtake me the moment I pedaled through the Osage Lane gateway. Whereas outside the compound an elm sapling barely as tall as my father grew from each driveway-sandwiched grass trapezoid, here the grass trapezoids were shaded by evergreens three stories high. Instead of ersatz gaslight lampposts, there were granite obelisks with luminescent crowns. There weren't any house numbers stenciled on the curbs, nor any mailboxes planted behind them. Chrome-plated manholes and sewer grates shone. The surface of the street itself was exotic: poured, slate-gray concrete, freeway-smooth, rather than ashen, particulate asphalt.

I made a right onto Chicory Place—the two-block stretch (later called Jason Terrace) the compound's pair of cul-de-sacs banded—where someteen older boys leaning on day-glo Haros and Dyno Compes watched as Jonboat, in helmet and knee pads, launched a white Redline up and down the slopes of a fiberglass halfpipe that spanned the front yard of the northernmost trilevel. Six feet over the halfpipe's lip, he'd punch his handlebars and set them spinning, or stretch his body like Superman in flight and get the whole frame to revolve beneath him. Even as I witnessed them, these tricks seemed impossible.

I rode a two-speed Murray Street Machine, a badly manufactured BMX-slash-mountain-bike hybrid so famously heavy and deeply uncool that, as soon as Jonboat dismounted the halfpipe, three of the boys standing nearest to me—without a single word or glance exchanged—got in my face, struck high-fisted, hair-metal-balladeer poses, and sang the orgasmically overemoted Street Machine advertising jingle's tagline:

Muh-ray
moves you
fast-uh!

Jonboat rolled up and clapped me on the shoulder. "Belt Magnet," he said to the kids who'd sung at me.

"Who? Him?"

"The psycho kid?"

"The swingset murderer?"

"Wait. Hold on. He *is* that kid. You *are* that kid. I saw you at the Strumms'. That shit was the tits."

"Thirty-eight double motherfuckeny D-cups!"

"Best night of the year."

"You need a new bike, kid."

"You're better'n that bike."

"You're the swingset murderer."

"I like Belt's bike," Jonboat told them. "Besides, it doesn't matter. He's not into freestyle."

"Still."

"Still what?"

"He deserves a cool bike."

"A cool bike to do *what* on?" Jonboat said. "Belt's no poseur."

"I never *said* he was a poseur."

"I think Jonboat's saying if Belt had like a Kuwahara or something, and all he did was ride around on it, then he'd be a poseur, but since his bike's a piece of shit and all he does is ride around on it, it's actually kinda cool that his bike's a piece of shit."

"You know what? That's true," the jingle-singer who'd insisted I deserved a cool bike said. "I've completely changed my mind now. Your Street Machine's the D's. It's rocknfuckenroll." From his pocket he produced a rolled-up pouch of watermelon Big League Chew shredded bubblegum. "Here, man," he said, "have some."

I took a fat pinch. The others did, too. We all stood there, chewing. I looked over at the halfpipe. A boy on his pegs did a grind on the lip, hopped on the ledge.

"So you gonna do another murder soon, or what?" asked the singer who'd unpacked Jonboat's assertion that I wasn't a poseur.

"No," I said.

"Well why the fuck not?" said the one who'd supplied the rest of us with gum.

"I promised my mom," I said.

"So what?"

"She's gone, now," I said.

"So she'll never find out then."

"Dude, I think that he's saying she *died*."

"Oh man, he is. I'm sorry to hear that."

"Me too, Belt."

"Yeah, sorry, Belt. I'm sorry."

"But then at the same time, you know, I think: still."

"Still what, dude?"

"Still I think maybe why not do a murder soon? She'll never find out."

"You're fucked up, dude."

"Since when is that a bad thing?"

"You're a motard, dude. Hey, Belt, man, ignore him, he's a huffer and a motard. What I want to know's where's your robot thingy, huh? You got one, right? I heard you got one."

"I don't like to bring it out," I said.

"But you should, man, you should! I'd *kill* to get my hands on one of those fuckers."

"I know," I said.

"So then how come—"

"Yeah, like—"

"So we gotta get going, guys," Jonboat told them.

"Oh," they said. "Alright," they said. "We thought . . ." they said.

"Why the long faces?" Jonboat said. "*You* don't have to go. You can use the halfpipe as long as you want."

Two of the singers sent up a howl. The third bent forward, clutching his abdomen, and blasted the green wad of gum from his mouth, suggesting, I supposed, that Jonboat's generosity had struck him with the force of a kick to the torso. The singers who'd howled both followed suit, spitting their gum out into the street, then one fell down, pretending at a seizure, and the other two, without missing a beat, dropped to their knees and pretended to roll him for his wallet and shoes.

•

•   •

A quarter-century later, when I showed up for brunch, the spat gum was still there, in the middle of the cul-de-sac, three black near-circular stains on the pavement before which I paused, overcome by a memory, a *long-lost memory:* first sensory, then narrative: a breathtaking recollection of my mother. Of my mother in profile. My mother's left temple. She'd had a trio of birthmarks (that's what she'd called them—my father'd called them *beauty spots,* I'd called them *freckles*) that you could see only one of unless she tied her hair back. Like those gum stains, her birthmarks were arrayed in such a way that, were you to connect them—as I (I suddenly remembered) once had; I'd used an eyebrow pencil—they'd form an obtuse, scalene triangle.

That's all. That's it. That's what took my breath away. Recalling my mother had three birthmarks on her temple, and that, one day (the first time I saw them?) while she was taking off her makeup (after coming home from work?), she allowed me to connect them with an eyebrow pencil. Perhaps it sounds minor, but not since her death, and probably not for a while before it (she didn't like her birthmarks; hardly ever tied her hair back) had I thought of (much less *pictured*) her birthmarks, let alone remembered having drawn lines between them. What a thing to forget, right? Or maybe what I mean is: what a thing to remember. What a thing to have forgotten for so many years, and then suddenly remember right then and there. I was happy to remember it, *elated* in fact, and, normally, I would have lingered with the memory, would have made sure—while the memory was fresh, before my brain could rehearse it to death—I would have made sure to close my eyes and *stare,* to sniff around and listen, to push at the spatio-temporal borders (what inspired me to ask her to draw on her face? how long did she leave the birthmarks connected? did she show my dad? did he say something funny?), but I just wasn't able. Features of the immediate environment encroached, commanding my attention.

A schoolyard-grade set of playground equipment—geodesic dome jungle gym, monkey bars, carousel—was straddling the lawn that had once borne the halfpipe, and Triple-J was using it to stage surprising feats in front of an audience of adolescent males. Between this scene and the one described in the section above, the parallels were no less glaring to me than I imagine they are to you, dear reader, and, for a moment (a not-so-brief moment), I was troubled by the feeling of having entered an experience that, pavement stains aside, had, without my foreknowledge—much less my understanding of its author's, or authors', motives (Triple-J's, presumably, perhaps Jonboat's as well)—been curated for me. Though a feeling that hadn't ever troubled me before, it was one I'd imagined any number of times while reading any number of disappointing novels; a feeling I'd believed any number of purportedly human protagonists should have been troubled by—and yet were never troubled by—during any number of the analog-brimming, tritely juxtaposed episodes their bumbling authors kept jamming them into.

But then I lit a Quill and got ahold of myself.

I was a guest. I was *the* guest. Why shouldn't the scene have been curated for me? One puts one's best face forward for guests. One goes out of one's way to. Plus I wasn't just any guest: the host looked up to me. *No Please Don't* had been important to him. He was likely more invested in securing my admiration than he would have been another, more typical guest's. And what, in the eyes of an adolescent boy, could ever be more admirable than the capacity to draw an admiring audience of adolescent boys? The capacity, you say, to bed adolescent girls? Okay. Maybe. But that capacity was pretty strongly implied by the having of the audience, was it not?

In any case, what was hinky here wasn't so much that Triple-J would, when I arrived at the compound, be demonstrating either or both of those capacities, but rather that his father had been doing the same the only other time I'd arrived at the compound. And yet as I continued to smoke and reflect, I came to see how even *that* wasn't really so hinky. The father, after all, had raised the son. And what a father to have. A billionaire astronaut. What son wouldn't, if even he had the choice to begin with, absorb such a father's psychosocial MO?

What I should have been feeling is flattered, not troubled. Not only right there, in 2013, but back in 1988 as well. If anything was hinky, that thing was me, my emotional intelligence, my handle on basic human motivations. Up until this second visit to the compound, it hadn't once occurred to me that Jonboat might have, when I'd arrived the first time, sought my admiration. To be certain: he'd found it. He'd impressed me no end, aloft on his Redline. He'd *had* my admiration. But I hadn't ever thought that he'd cared either way, let alone cared enough to orchestrate a whole spectacle to get it.

(And yes, maybe "orchestrate a whole spectacle to get it" overstates the matter, assumes too much: too much in both cases, '88 and '13. The orchestration of the spectacles may very well have happened in advance—and independent—of my corresponding invitations to the compound. Even if that were so, however, the overstatement would only be slight, would only assume *just a little* too much, for either Pellmore-Jason surely could have invited me to visit on a day when I wouldn't, on arrival, have witnessed his spectacle.)

Flattered I should have been, so flattered I became, flattered that anyone—let alone any two Pellmore-Jasons—would want to impress me, and, once flattered, I was able to relax, to try to do the gracious thing: to try to be impressed. And I did, and I was.

I somewhat was.

It's not that I wasn't.

It's more I just couldn't—perhaps unfairly, yet perhaps unavoidably—help but to reflect on how much less impressed I was there, in '13, than I'd been in '88. Less impressed not only because I'd realized twenty-five years sooner that the person impressing me *wanted* to impress me, but because, apart from his having drawn an audience, what that person was doing to impress me (and that audience), though certainly difficult, wasn't also beautiful.

Unlike those his father had performed on the halfpipe, Triple-J's surprising feats required little athleticism, and zero daredevilry: they were feats of endurance like the one in the "Flick&Look" clip—sweaty, sure, and a little bit twitchy, a little bit trembly, but otherwise barely even kinetic.

He and the other Yachts, when I'd first arrived, had been hanging one-armed from the jungle gym's monkey bars, each holding in his dangling hand a Curio. The idea was to maintain one's grasp on one's bar while squeezing one's cure just enough to make it painsing. This was, I soon gathered, harder than it looked.

Chaz fell to the ground in under a minute, and then, in succession, Lyle dropped his cure, Bryce squeezed his to death, and Chaz Jr.'s went quiet. The four of them stood beneath the bars from which they'd hung and, sucking air, red-faced, watched Triple-J.

Eventually, Triple-J let go his own bar, landed on his feet, and did a twisty kind of back stretch while Burroughs, who'd been reffing, held high a stopwatch and announced to the audience, "Three hundred seconds—five minutes on the nose. A new Hangstrong record. Lowman was Chaz at fifty-seven seconds."

"Beat fifty-seven seconds, you're in, you're a Yacht," Triple-J told the audience. "Beat five minutes, you're captain of the Yachts. Who wants the game ball?"

Cheers. Raised arms.

Triple-J pitched his still-living cure into the audience.

"Next up is what?" he said. He headed stage left a few steps, to the carousel. "Is this what you want?" he said, and boarded the carousel.

Cheers. Clapping.

"Ulysses it is," he said.

Louder cheers. Wilder clapping. And that was another thing. The audience itself, despite being twice the size Jonboat's had been, was also less impressive, its members less . . . menacing. Granted, I'd grown taller in the intervening years, gained a few dozen pounds, and become, I'd like to think, less easy to intimidate, but there was more to it than that. Whereas the kids who'd watched Jonboat spin in the air sought authenticity (or at least posed as if they sought authenticity), and were (or claimed to be) sensitive above all to *in*authenticity—ever chomping at the bit to spot it, to be the first to name it (*sellout, poseur, wannabe,* etc.)—those watching Triple-J and the Yachts perform appeared instead to seek out the laudable, and to want, moreover, to be the first—or, failing that, one of many—to applaud it. On top of all their clapping and cheering, they winked and they back-slapped and high-fived and -tenned, pressed their fists to their chests and solemnly nodded, Fonziethumbed while eyebrow-hiking, seeming, at first, like they were only responding to subtle exhibitions of Hangstrong prowess (exhibitions I figured my Hangstrong virginity kept me from being able to appreciate), but their applause continued once Hangstrong was over, while we waited for Ulysses, whatever that was, and I came to understand they were applauding one another no less than the Hangstrong spectacle itself, and, because all they'd done was applaud and spectate, I couldn't help but conclude they were applauding one another *for* applauding the spectacle—and also, perhaps, for applauding one another—which in turn made me think that they must have been, at least in part, applauding in order to receive applause.

To say, then, that Triple-J's audience members weren't as menacing as Jonboat's had been isn't to say they were any less dangerous. Sheep are gentle only until they stampede. As hard as it was for me to picture these perpetual group-huggers picking, let alone winning, fistfights—had even the fittest boy among them provoked him, the runtiest of yesteryear's BMX skids would have nourished the lawn with Millennial gore—it took little effort to imagine them rioting, lynchmobbing, pogromming.

But sheep, lynch mobs . . . that might be too harsh. Maybe I was jealous. I did sense that they probably—no, almost *certainly*—threw far better, more inclusive parties than had the anguished hessians with whom I'd been young (to whose parties I'd rarely been invited anyway), and old-fashioned, generational envy very well may have led me to unjustly ascribe to them the ugliest, as-yet-unseen underside I could think of. Nor can I entirely dismiss the possibility that my impression of their eagerness to embrace conformity might have been, to some degree, unduly enhanced—it certainly wasn't in any way mitigated—by the vitreous bangles around their left wrists, the LED diodes embedded inside of which not only blinked an identically warm, apricotty orange, but did so in sync with one another, and, for that matter, with the diode inside my own bangle as well.

•
•   •

Every visitor to the compound had to wear such a bangle. I'd been clamped with mine by a thin-fingered, otherwise Burroughs-shaped man in slate-gray livery and wraparound shades who'd been waiting for me outside the ramparts.

"Mr. Magnet?" he'd half-asked and half-demanded, as I'd started crossing Armstrong toward the Pellmore Place gateway.

"Call me Belt," I'd said.

"I won't do that," he said. "Is your son coming separately?"

"Is my son . . . ? Oh, I see. Actually, I'm the son. My father—turns out he isn't able to make it."

"Why are you carrying cereal?" he said.

"It's a gift," I said. "For Jonboat." I hadn't been able to wrap the shirt in paper—the only tape roll I'd found in our kitchen was bald—so I'd stuffed it inside a box of Cap'n Crunch.

"I'll have to have a look."

I handed him the Crunch box.

" 'Crunch-a-tize me, Cap'n,' huh?" he read from the box. "This stuff any good?"

"I like it," I said. "Not for breakfast, but at night. Some nights. Helps me fall asleep. You never had Cap'n Crunch?"

"I don't eat things like this."

"Okay," I said.

"I don't think Mr. Pellmore-Jason does either."

"That's alright," I said. "There's a shirt inside."

"A shirt."

"There's cereal, too, but the shirt's the real gift. The gift's not the Crunch. I mean, I only kept the Crunch in there for a kind of joke."

"What kind of joke?"

"I don't know," I said. "I guess a kind of sight gag. Prize at the bottom of the cereal or, like a packing-peanuts kind of thing where the cereal's the Styrofoam . . . you know, it's not a great joke, it's just—"

"So when I open this up, all I'm gonna find is a bag of cereal with a shirt at the bottom is what you're telling me. No surprises."

"Not for you," I said.

"For who, then?" he said.

"Jonboat," I said. "I don't think he'll be expecting to find a shirt at the bottom of the box."

"At the bottom of the box, or at the bottom of the bag of cereal?"

"What?"

"Is the shirt in the bag or is it outside the bag? I don't want to be surprised. Please be specific."

"The shirt's rolled up at the bottom of the box, and the bag with the cereal in it's on top of it. On top of the shirt."

"That ruins your joke."

"Maybe a little."

"The prizes are always in the bag," he said.

"Yeah," I said, "I thought about that. But I thought maybe Jonboat might see the box and want to eat some Cap'n Crunch, and if there was a shirt in there, the Crunch would seem unsanitary, so he wouldn't eat it. Plus the shirt would have cereal dust all over it."

"But the prizes are always in the bag," the man said. "You didn't take the joke far enough. I don't think it'll land. Will that upset you? If your joke doesn't land?"

"No," I said.

"Because I'd rather you don't make the joke, if there's any risk of you getting upset when it fails to land. We don't like to see people getting upset."

"*If* it fails to land."

"If, when, whether—which conditional's more appropriate is not the concern."

"If the joke fails to land, it won't upset me," I said. "I'm not expecting that much from it."

"That's all I wanted to know," he told me. Then, into his collar, he said, "This is Duggan. I'm out front with Belt Magnet. Says Clyde Magnet will not be at brunch . . . Yeah. Thanks."

The portion of the ramparts that stood between the curbs of Pellmore Place retracted, elevator-door-like. I followed Duggan in, and up onto the sidewalk, where a second liveried, Burroughs-shaped man was standing by the mouth of what appeared to be a stainless-steel, adult-size play tunnel. This man, who Duggan greeted as "Hogan," bore in his arms a shallow, plastic bin that Duggan had me empty my pockets out into.

"If you'll enter the scanner, Mr. Magnet," Hogan said, as Duggan walked off with the bin and the Crunch box, "the conveyor belt'll pull you through in a blink. Keep your movements to a minimum inside there, alright? You'll be brunching in no time."

I stepped inside the scanner, which was dark and smelled of rubber, and was pulled toward its velvet-roped egress at a jogger's pace. Out in the daylight beyond the rope waited yet another Burroughs-shaped man, his livery a paler gray than the first two's. He stared right at me, kind of tentatively smiling. "Sorry for any awkwardness," he told me, after the conveyor belt had ceased to move forward. "This part of the process, as I'm sure you've guessed, is the one where I have to watch you closely til Hogan says you're clear, and usually that's weird enough to do as it is, but this morning the lights inside there went out so I can't see you well enough with my shades on, which means I can't wear them, and so now, I know, that thing's started happening where you feel all dominated if you don't meet my eyes, so you try to meet my eyes and then you look away because I have to remain unflapped when that happens, that's part of the job, and I'm good at the job, and I'm proud that I'm good, but then still I know that being good at the job and not getting flapped when your eyes meet mine means I'm making you feel even more dominated than you felt to begin with before you tried to meet them, which, some people, most of them in fact—I wouldn't care if I made them feel extra-dominated, but Dad told Duggan that you were a writer, and Duggan told Hogan, and Hogan told me, except those guys are philistines—not Dad, but my brothers, Dad's widely read—so when I asked Hogan what kind of a writer you were he said Duggan hadn't told him, and when I then asked Duggan—this was just, like, a minute ago—he said he hadn't even thought to ask Dad, and Dad's too busy right now for me to bother with questions, but I'm a writer, too, is what I'm trying to say, or I'm trying to be a writer, I've never been published, I don't know if it counts if you haven't been published, but I've written a number of lyric essays, and since we're both writers, that extra-dominated feeling that I'm making you feel? I wish I wasn't's what I'm trying to say. I wish I wasn't making you feel it. I don't want you to think it's something I'm glad about, and I don't want you to think I think you're some kind of no one I look upon with like utter disregard. If that's even possible. *Is* that possible? *Can* you look at someone and not regard them? I don't know. Language is amazing and I just don't know. Even if you can, though, I totally regard you. And yes, I regard you as someone who I could handle if I needed to, but only because I'm really well trained, and let's be honest, I'm one of the biggest men on earth, one of the biggest men you've ever seen.

"I mean we did the math once—well, Dad did the math, and the research, too—and he's one of the top—and this estimate's conservative—he's one of the top twenty thousand largest men on the planet, and that includes the not-the-least-bit-fearsome morbidly obese types in wheelchairs or wheelbeds or whatever, and I'm up there too, not quite as high as Dad, but top twenty-four/twenty-five thousand or so, and maybe that doesn't seem so impressive at first cause it means twenty-five thousandish guys out there are as big or bigger than me, and plus you just met my brothers, who are two of those guys, so your perspective's probably temporarily skewed, but even if it isn't skewed, twenty-five thousand—that's a lot of people, that's almost half as many people as live in Wheelatine, but *still*, I'm saying. *Still*. When you think of it in terms of the world's population, it's pretty astounding, twenty-five thousand. It means that only like seven or so guys out of every *million* is as big or bigger than me. Something like that. And then you think: How many of those guys are trained to even a tenth the extent that I'm trained? Not too many. Maybe one in a hundred? One in a thousand? What was I getting at? What I was getting at is you look to me like someone who probably, in most situations, if the need arose, could take care of himself, and I don't want you to think *I* think that if you were my size and you had my training that you'd be any kind of easy guy to handle, if, for some reason, it came to that. You wouldn't, I don't think. You might even handle me. So no disrespect, I'm saying, is intended by my staring so unflappably at you, okay, Mr. Magnet? I'm just a writer trying to do his day job. At least that's my fantasy, that this is a day job.

"It isn't a bad job, I'm not saying that. It's kind of a great job. I'm pretty much set like in terms of money for the rest of my life if I keep this job, and I'd probably keep it even if I got famous as a published writer, but that's how I know that my intentions are pure when it comes to lyric essays. It's a calling, you know? I wouldn't be a lyric essayist if I didn't feel deep inside that I had to to fully actualize myself, which is, incidentally, what a lot of my lyric essays are about: me and my feeling that I need to write lyric essays. And also America. Being American. I find the two topics to be pretty closely tied. Anyway, it's really a good thing for me to meet you cause you're just, like, this man, standing there, like me, who's standing here across from you. Size and training aside, we're not all that different, and that helps me to understand something really important: that a writer's just a person, a regular person who spends his time writing. I know that probably sounds obvious to you, but you're already a writer, and your perspective isn't skewed like mine. I mean the only writer I've ever met is Ms. Henry. Just imagine how skewed your perspective on what a writer is would be if Ms. Henry were the only writer you'd ever met. And then imagine the second writer you ever meet is you, just a regular person. It would give you all kinds of new self-confidence. I mean, it's giving me all kinds of new self-confidence. Seeing you standing there, I'm standing here thinking, 'You can do this, Valentine. If he can do this, you can do this. You can make it as a lyric essayist.' You know, it's funny. When I heard you were coming here,

I thought of all these questions I wanted to ask you about writing. About what kind of writing you did, and if you had any advice on how best to write and how much to revise and that kind of thing, but now, with all this new self-esteem I've already got from just seeing you standing there, I don't even think I want to ask you that stuff. Looking at you, I know I can figure all of it out by myself. Thank you for that. Thank you for the confidence. But there was other stuff, too, that I wanted to ask you, when I heard you were coming. Stuff about Dad. Hogan said Dad said you knew him back when he was Mr. Pellmore-Jason's driver and I wonder if you've got any insights to share about what he was like, and I'm hoping you could tell me some things I can use in this lyric essay I'm working on about my relationship with him and America. Like, let's be honest, I'm hoping you can tell me some ways that Dad was similar to how I am now. He always tells me he was, always says he was more like me than my brothers, but sometimes . . . I don't know. Sometimes I think it's just cause I'm the only brother with an artistic temperament, and he's just being nice so I don't feel lesser-than or have like an emotional breakdown or—one sec." He held his hand to his ear and said into his collar, "Yeah. I hear you . . . I said that I heard you the first time, Duggan. And I really gotta say, man, when you eavesdrop through my mic, it makes me feel lesser- . . . Oh. So finish then . . . But he knows, though. It's obvious. *Everyone* knows as soon as they look at me. At any of us. It couldn't *be* more obvious . . . Okay. That's fair. You make a good point." He closed a fist around the part of his collar into which he'd spoken, and lowered his voice. "That was Duggan," he told me, "being all, 'Valentine, quit yapping at the guest, and quit calling Burroughs "Dad," cause it isn't professional.' "

"I don't mind," I said.

"I appreciate your saying that," Valentine said, "but it's not about you. The truth is I was wrong. I can't be breaking protocols. I lack the experience to know when it's kosher to. I have a lot to learn. I'm still in training. Three more years to go. I'm really stupid, sometimes. I hate myself a little. I read a while back that the most important thing for a writer was to have a good day job that affords him time to write, and Ms. Henry once told me the same thing, too, so I'm sure you'd agree, and, here I am, a lyric essayist who's got a good day job that affords him time to essay, and I'm screwing it up. I'm betraying my art. I'm ashamed of myself."

"Well—"

He unhanded his collar and said "Okay" into it. "You're clear," he told me, and unhooked the velvet rope.

Exiting the scanner, I wanted to console him. I whispered a lie. "As far as *I'm* able to make out," I whispered, "you're way more like Burroughs was than Hogan or Duggan."

Valentine's eyes seemed to smile at the corners, but he said, rather stagily, "Please keep your distance from my ear, Mr. Magnet."

Duggan walked over from the other side of Pellmore Place. He handed me the bin with the box of Crunch and my pocket things in it, and, while I was holding it, he bangled my wrist.

"What's that?" I said.

"Security bangle," he said, and took the bin back.

"What's it for?" I said.

"Security," he said.

"Is it a tracking thing?" I said. "Like Triple-J's necklace?"

"It's to wear til you leave."

"Can I remove it?" I said.

"Maybe, but you shouldn't."

"What if I remove it?"

"You'll leave," Duggan said. He shook the bin to signal I should reclaim its contents, among which I found a pair of foam earplugs sealed inside a baggie.

I pocketed my stuff and underarmed the Crunch box.

"Take the earplugs," said Duggan.

"Why?"

"For Ulysses."

"Ulysses?" I said, taking the earplugs.

"Main event," he said.

I waited for more.

He aimed his chin west, toward the compound's only intersection. "That," he said, "over there is Jason Terrace. Hang a right at Jason and go all the way down to the end of the cul-de-sac. Join the crowd. Someone'll alert you when it's time for brunch."

I waved and walked off.

"We'll see each other soon, Mr. Magnet," said Valentine, and although all I heard was a friendly salutation—an attempt, I thought, to compensate for Duggan's cold officiousness—it turned out to be a sound prediction as well. I saw both of them again just a few minutes later.

•

• •

In preparation for Ulysses, the other Yachts joined Triple-J on the carousel, and Valentine handcuffed them each by a wrist to a different handrail while Duggan and Burroughs crowdworked together: the former circulating briskly among us, cradling the "sirencase"—a mirror-lidded, otherwise translucent box twice the size of a PillowNest—and the latter describing the Curio inside of it from his perch near the top of the jungle gym.

"Our main event's siren," Burroughs carnival-barked, "is a single-legged, long-tailed, calico three-year-old, cuddlefarmed by Wheelatine's own Catrina Hogg, and valued at seven hundred fifty dollars. Its name is Spotsy, and it's being brought around so you can see it up close. No shoving please. Everyone'll get a look. Slow down a little, Duggan. Let everyone see. Good, that's better. We're not in any rush.

"Now, you'll notice Spotsy seems larger than average, but that's just an illusion created by the sirencase: the walls have been inlaid with magnifying glass. You might also notice Spotsy's shading its eyes and squinting a little. That owes to its having been dosed with Vampire, the effects of which will get a lot less subtle once we remove that mirrored lid and clamp on the high-wattage lamp—you'll see. Depending how close you are, you may *hear,* too. The Yachts sure will. On top of the Vampire, Spotsy's been given some Wailer and Melodize for increased volume and beauty of painsong.

"How we doing there, Yachts? We ready to play some Ulysses or what?"

"Out naked from my mother's bosom, I say, was I pulled ready," Chaz Jr. said, and, with his balled, free hand—he'd been the first Yacht cuffed—invited a pound from Chaz.

Chaz, the second cuffed, glanced at the fist, and left his friend hanging. To the audience he said, "Be you muddy, all-class, or any way in between, I beg you not hold against our doe-eyed and verily virginal pally his rather telling ignorance of basic female plumbing. He's a good one. Hear hear?"

"Word up," said Bryce, who Valentine was cuffing.

"Word straight to the dang-darn muth," Lyle said.

Lowering his fist, Chaz Jr. told Chaz: "I venture my knowledge of basic female plumbing is greatly and deeply understated, homeslice."

"Me-o, my-o, the hay-o you say!" Chaz said to Chaz Jr., and then, turning to Lyle and Bryce: "Need I put a finer point upon it?"

"Indeed," Lyle said.

"Let the good chap know where it be at," said Bryce.

Triple-J, who, if Valentine continued working clockwise, would be the last of the Yachts to be cuffed, crossed his arms on his handrail and lowered his head.

"Though all we swell fellows can be said to have once been pulled out naked from his mother's womb," Chaz told Chaz Jr., "not a one of us has ever been so outwardly pulled from his mother's *bosom,* sir. Not unless something truly unYachtlike and wiggity-wack, to say nothing of *illicit,* were going on."

"Hear hear," Bryce said.

"There there," said Lyle.

"And perhaps I didn't want to say *womb*?" said Chaz Jr., once the chuckles from the audience started dying down. "Perhaps referring to the *womb* of one's own dear mother smacks of more than a little impropriety, given that womb's nearness to other parts of one's mother that no chap worth even but his diggity-doggity weight in copper pennies would want to incite another to envisage, for that is total disrespect plus gross on the real, yo? And as for the borderline-illicit wackness you've suggested, I wonder if your having even come up with such a rankly, boogada-boogity notion doesn't go to show that your mind's in the gutter? In dissing me, my dear man, I fear you've dissed yourself."

"That's an awful lot of protest, kindly chum—too much? Who's to judge?" Chaz replied. "Word it up now on the razzly-dazzly rizzle McT tip: I may, yes, be quite out my dang mind, but your reasoning seems to me to lack a, shall we say, certain integrity? I ask you, Chaz Jr., does not speaking loosely of one's dear mother's *bosom* bring no impropriety to bear? Speaking loosely of *climbing out naked* from one's dear mother's *bosom,* dog? That's—"

"Stop acting like fucking dorks," Triple-J said, as Valentine knelt by his handrail, cuffing him.

"Word up, dork down, hey hey," Bryce agreed.

"Truly," Lyle said, "let's recork that dork, what, and have us a contest of Ulysses, shall we?"

"Burroughs," Triple-J said.

"Duggan," said Burroughs, then leapt from the jungle gym.

Duggan, who'd been nearing the back of the crowd—he'd gotten close enough to where I was standing that Spotsy, which had been waving presidentially from inside the sirencase, seemed, for a moment, to be waving *at* me—turned on his heel and headed for the carousel, where Valentine waited for him next to its spindle.

At this point, I became distracted. Fondajane Henry had appeared near the jungle gym. She spoke softly to Burroughs, whose soft response garnered him a squeeze on the shoulder paired with her signature, feel-great horse-laugh. They turned in my direction. Burroughs pointed me out. Fondajane showed me all ten of her fingers, then pressed them together, five against five, just above her heart, and flurried them, and smiled. I'm all but certain I smiled back. I might have even mouthed, "Hi," or, "Pleased to meet you, Fondajane," but I was so very taken by seeing her in person—how glowingly, iconically spectacular she was, how feminine and splendidly commanding was her figure, even seen from a distance of fifteen yards and slackly obscured by her terry-cloth tracksuit—I can't say for sure what I said or did. Then she was going, and then she was gone, and one of the boys standing next to me whispered, "I really hate that she had to split, but I loved to watch her walk away," and the boys on either side of him slapped him on the back and ruffled his hair and I realized how quiet the audience had gotten, how quiet they'd been since she'd first appeared—how else could I have heard her signature horse-laugh?—and despite the whispered statement's having been a cliché since at least as far back as the hat-tipping era, the boy had deployed it so very aptly I couldn't begrudge him his friends' congratulations: he'd spoken our hearts.

"Cures out," Burroughs said, and recaptured our attention.

Each of the Yachts unsleeved a cure and held it overhead.

Valentine and Duggan had dismounted the carousel. Valentine was standing by the lone, Yachtless handrail, and Duggan a few feet behind him, next to Burroughs. The sirencase, lidless, sat atop the spindle with an easel lamp clipped to one of its walls, the lamp's arm bent so the bulb, when lit, would shine directly down onto Spotsy. Although the sky was partly cloudy, and the sirencase partly shaded by the easel lamp, Spotsy was now exposed to more direct sunlight than it had been before the mirrored lid had been removed, and the effects of the Vampire were becoming more evident: the cure hid its face behind its hands and shivered while shifting its weight between its leg and its tail and sort of bowing a little or tentatively ducking.

The crowd was pushing forward, tightening up. I pushed forward with them.

Burroughs addressed us. "I'll only say this once," he said. "Don't rush at the siren. You will not get there, you will be removed, and you will never be invited back to the compound. If you start to overload, close your eyes. It's really that simple. Now, earplugs in."

Burroughs, his sons, and all the members of the audience inserted their earplugs. I kept mine palmed. I'd never heard a Wailered or Melodized cure.

"Eyes up," said Burroughs. The Yachts, who'd all been looking at their feet, straightened their necks and stared at the sirencase, and Valentine started turning the carousel—five, six RPMs at most. The spindle, like a record player's, was stationary, and Spotsy, which was peeking through the gaps between its fingers, and confused, perhaps, by the circling Yachts, added to its bowing/ducking movements some side-to-side swaying. The cures the Yachts held up in their fists seemed to be at least as confused as Spotsy, turning their heads right to left, right to left.

Once the carousel had gone around a couple times, Duggan aimed a remote control at the spindle, Burroughs said, "Now," and the easel lamp lit.

Spotsy collapsed to the floor of the sirencase. It covered its head with both arms and bucked. Its Melodized painsong seemed intricate, mathy, like a Mozart piece composed for the sitar, but it wasn't that easy to hear from where I stood (I was, by then, in the middle of the audience). That I could even hear the song at all was remarkable, considering Spotsy sang it into its armpit, from inside that case, while the carousel creaked and the Yachts oohed and awwed as they strained toward the spindle, and their handcuffs scraped and clanked against the rails, and their own cures, squeezed, were attempting harmonies. The Wailer really worked.

I made the decision to block my ears, after all.

By the time I'd gotten the first plug in, Bryce had smashed his cure against his forehead. By the time I'd gotten the second one in, Chaz Jr.'s cure's head was no longer attached. Lyle lost next: overloaded by mouth. None of them acted as if anything had changed—they continued to strain at the sirencase, moaning.

It appeared that Chaz would defeat Triple-J, who twice brought his cure down before his open mouth. Both times, however, our host resisted, straightening his arm at the very last instant. Just as he began to bend the arm a third time, Burroughs blew his whistle.

Chaz's cure was dead inside Chaz's raised hand. Without even knowing (or so the puzzled look on his face suggested), he'd squeezed the life from it.

So that was that. Ulysses was over.

Duggan raised the remote and shut off the lamp. Spotsy's painsong became inaudible.

Valentine climbed up onto the carousel and dropped his jacket over the sirencase. The Yachts all hunched, dazed and expressionless until Triple-J, once Valentine had uncuffed his wrist, pantomimed an overload-by-mouth, then tossed his cure into the crowd as before, and everyone laughed.

Burroughs raised his stopwatch, said, "Ninety-two seconds—another new record. Lowman was Bryce at seventeen seconds."

Cheers. Clapping.

"Alright," Triple-J said. "You think you know what that means, but it's better than you think. Last seventeen seconds and you get to be a Yacht. Break my record, we'll have a showdown for captain at next month's games, but not only that—you'll get to go home with Spotsy. You can sign up for any of the events as many times as you want til you run out of cures. Duggan'll be coming around with the clipboard. Good luck to all of you, and thanks for coming out."

Louder Cheers. Wilder Clapping.

A pressure on my shoulder. A hand. Hogan's. "It's time," he said, "to brunch," and led me away from the crowd at a clip.

A FORCE AND AN EMBLEM

We headed to the opposite side of the compound, to a structure I guess you'd—if pressed—call a turret: five stories overground, round and mineral, it crowned the southwestern corner of the ramparts. Yet it had a domed roof with a whitewashed ceiling, its deck was floored in oaken boards, and the tripods mounted between certain balusters appeared to be for telescopes rather than weapons. So a turret, but a turret in the guise of a gazebo.

Hogan, when we got there, just called it a turret, though. "The turret," he said, stepping aside, and I mounted the final stair and entered.

In the middle of the deck was a full-size hibachi, at which Fondajane sat, buffing her nails with a pink and purple block.

"Belt Magnet," Hogan told her.

She set down the nail block. "Belt," she said, "I'm Fon," and she held out her hand to me. The angle was ambiguous: to pump or m'lady? Impossible to tell. I settled on what I still think was a pretty clever tactic, given that I had only a moment to contrive it—I'd grasp, start to lift, then quickly withdraw to cover a fraudulent, violent sneeze—but it proved unneeded. As our thumb webbings met, Fondajane closed her fingers and guided me forward to kiss me on both of my overheated cheeks.

"Now would you take a look at that," she said to Hogan. "He's a kitten. All atremble. Wouldn't bite you for a castle made of sardines and yarn."

"Yes, Ms. Henry," Hogan said.

"Wouldn't bite *me* at least."

"No, Ms. Henry."

"I'm trying to be subtle, Hogan."

"Subtle, Ms. Henry?"

"Subtly granting you leave," she said.

"I see, Ms. Henry. It was clever how you did that."

"Don't flirt with me, now. I might get ideas."

"I won't flirt, Ms. Henry."

"And maybe on your way back over to that circus, drop in at Trip's and kind of push him along? Belt isn't here to critique *my* work."

"Triple-J should be here any minute," said Hogan. "Last update was he detoured to pick up Magnet."

"Your namesake," she whispered, squeezing my hand.

"Ah," I said, smiling, assuming that Hogan, by "Magnet," had meant "*a* Magnet," as in "a copy of *No Please Don't*"—a copy I would likely be asked to sign—and that Fondajane, in calling *No Please Don't* my "namesake," was either being precious or making a joke about novels being their authors' offspring. That latter assumption didn't really add up, since the novel's title wasn't *Magnet,* but had Fondajane whispered, "Goo goo g'joob," instead of "Your namesake," I doubt my response would have been any different. Had she whispered, "I'm being held hostage," or "Run!" I doubt my response would have been any different. I was starstruck, reader. Charmed. Entranced. No little bit aroused. I thought I'd better sit.

"May I sit?" I said.

She let go of my hand and patted the seat of the stool between us. I sat, set the box of Crunch on the hibachi, scooted in til the counter was pressing my ribs. Now: where to look? The cost or benefit of using the counter to hide my lap was it put my face within inches of hers, which made the need to lap-hide all the more pressing.

The sound of Hogan's footsteps receded behind me. I turned and waved. He descended the stairs to the elevator vestibule. When I heard the doors to the elevator shutting, I realized I hadn't yet stopped waving, and that on top of committing what was probably a low-to-medium-grade faux pas (i.e. waving to the help), I'd kept my back to Fondajane for what had to have been about a quarter-minute, and the only thing I could think to do to repair the offense I feared my rudeness had caused was to *push* the faux pas, to *increase* its saliency, the hope being that, in doing so, I would—instead of coming off like a slouching moron packing a hard-on—appear eccentric, or eccentrically mischievous, and so, toward that end, I, still waving, called out, "Goodbye, Hogan. Have a great day!"

Fondajane chuckled. In- or authentically? At me or with me?

"Jonboat's on a call with Dubai," she said. "Some business requiring his immediate attention. Sunday, in that neck of the woods, is rather Monday. Hopefully the call won't keep him long, but you don't mind *too* much, do you, Belt?"

I turned back around to say I didn't mind, and perhaps add something semi-pithy like, "What's another few minutes after twenty-five years?" but there were her eyes, below them her mouth, below that her neck and the caron of sun-bronzed, unblemished sternum stingily revealed in the V the open portion of her track jacket's zipper formed. Or maybe *stingily revealed* isn't what I mean at all. *Generously exposed* would be no less accurate. Even remembering this makes me giddy, but that delicate divot in the center of her collarbone, that dip in the flesh where her chest became her throat—even looking at that divot (unless I mean, *especially* looking at that divot) seemed indecent of me, improprietous. All I managed to say was, "I don't."

And then she said, "Belt, there's no need to be nervous. We're never going to act on what you're thinking about. You don't have to worry you'll blow your chance."

"Oh Jesus," I said. "I'm so—"

"No, no, let me finish. I'm glad to see it's what you're thinking about—that's how I should have started. I'm *glad*. The fact is, I'm thinking about the same kinds of things, and even if I weren't . . . Belt, do you have any idea how much we *paid* for my suprasternal notch?"

I must have made a face that conveyed my confusion.

She pointed at her divot. "That's what it's called. The suprasternal notch. Do you have one?" she said.

"I don't think so," I said.

She hooked a pinkie over my collar and pulled.

"No," she said. "You don't. I didn't used to either. I mean, of course I *had* one, and of course you do, too, but mine was as invisible as yours til ten years ago. It was my first-anniversary present from Jonboat. I'd wanted a prominent one my whole life. I've always thought it to be an *extremely* underrated body part, perhaps the most underrated body part of all, especially now the cosmetics companies have begun, in their ads, to direct the consumer gaze at the philtrum. Have you noticed that?" she said.

I said, "I hardly ever watch TV."

"The ads I'm thinking of are mostly in magazines. Probably not the kinds you read, though, I suppose. Anyway, as far as sex appeal goes, for me the well-formed suprasternal notch has always been on par with great big, gravity-defying breasts, high round asses, bulging pelvic muscles, shiny-smooth purple coronas of glans . . . I've never understood how it is that the notch hasn't been celebrated the way those other parts have—not even the way that armpits, feet, or freckles have. And what I really like, what I *really* find fascinating about the suprasternal notch, is how ungendered its sexiness is. What's good for the goose is but *exactly* as good for the gander. And *all of this to say* that I'm not only thrilled to see you're so taken with mine, but I believe I would even be a little bit *hurt* if you weren't, Belt. A *lot* went into it. And the fortune it cost isn't even the half of it. Notch enhancement's never been a very popular procedure, and Jonboat didn't want anyone butchering his bride, so he actually found women—half a dozen of them—for the surgeon to practice on before it was my turn and—oh Belt, you're so scandalized. You could rupture your *cap*illaries, blushing like that. Your breathing is a visual *phenomenon,* Belt. I've made you so uncomfortable."

"No," I said.

"I have. I've made you uncomfortable and I'm making it worse, talking about it. Would it help if I told you I'm trying to do just the opposite? I mean, would you believe me?"

"Yes?" I said.

"I am. I really am. I'm not a bully. Not at all. I hope you'll believe me. I come on strong, I know, too strong sometimes, but if I've come on too strong this morning, it's only in order to *spare* you the discomfort I imagine you'd feel if I *didn't* talk this way. Do you understand? I know you must already know a lot about me—more, by far, than I know about you—and you don't have to pretend that you don't. And what's going on between us, this powerful mutual attraction we have—you don't have to pretend that it isn't there, either. I mean *I* won't pretend—that would make *me* uncomfortable—so why should you? What I want you to understand, above all, Belt, is that you don't have to watch what you say around me. I'm an open book. And I'm emphatically *not* waiting with bated breath for the next opportunity to be offended, and I'm certainly not looking to trick you into offending me. I know that's the fashionable MO lately—the seeking out and taking of offense—but I think it's unfortunate. More than unfortunate. It's counterproductive. Ugly, even. It goes against just about everything I worked toward during my days as an advocate and activist. It's one of the reasons I retired from teaching."

"I don't think you're a bully," I said.

"Well then why can't you just relax and enjoy yourself?"

"I can *act* relaxed, but . . ."

"That's all I'm suggesting either of us do. We act relaxed until we feel relaxed. That's how these situations always go, no?"

"I've never been in a situation like this."

"Come on," she said, leaning forward a little. "You expect me to believe I'm the first billionaire critical theorist you've ever brunched with?"

I made some laugh sounds, and she punched me not-that-lightly on the shoulder.

"The first world-famous ex–sex worker you've ever sat beside in a suburban turret?"

I laughed more heartily. She punched my shoulder harder.

"Perhaps you've never wanted anyone who wanted you back, but was, nonetheless, happily married and completely unavailable?"

"Ha!" I shouted, bracing for a punch, then disappointed—more disappointed than I like to admit—when I realized another punch wasn't coming. She was done with the joking. The flirting—if that's what it was—was over. She'd picked up her nail block, was studying her nails, i.e. no longer looking at me, and I said (though it was more like I *found myself saying*), "If you only knew."

And as long as I'm admitting to embarrassing things, I might as well admit that when I said, "If you only knew," I did so in the hopes that Fondajane would ask me, "If I only knew what?" so that I could respond with, "Well, the truth is I've never wanted anyone who wanted me back, available or not," or, perhaps even more straightforwardly, "You're the only person I've ever wanted who wanted me back," and that she would protest, call me a liar, but then, upon looking into my eyes, she would understand that I was telling the truth, and the significance I'd granted our mutual attraction would prove contagious, and we'd be swept up in it, we'd have a moment, we'd close what was left of the space between us, *find ourselves* in one another's arms and . . .

But no. It didn't work. She didn't take my juvenile bait. She didn't cue my embarrassing confession. Of course she didn't. She probably didn't even realize I was trying to bait her. "If you only knew" is at least as common a way to shut down as develop a conversational topic. In the context of our whole jokey-punchy exchange, "If you only knew" may even have implied the opposite of what I'd wanted it to; Fondajane very well could have taken it to mean, "I can't even count the number of totally unavailable people I've wanted who've wanted me back." Plus her stepson and husband were presumably about to join us any moment, and for me to be so flustered by the thought of someone beautiful wanting me—so flustered that I'd overlook so immediate and obvious an obstacle to our *finding ourselves in one another's arms* . . . Who would suspect it?

Well, Stevie Strumm, perhaps. Stevie on her driveway, in the wake of my requests for permission to kiss her. She's the only one who could possibly imagine how miserable my sense of timing with women was, how divorced from reality my sense of proper romantic contexts.

And maybe you, reader, since you've read that scene.

But not Fondajane. She'd have never imagined. How could she have? Not even I could. Or, in any case (as if this hasn't come abundantly clear by now): I didn't. For a second there, I really believed that I might have a shot with her.

"If you only knew," I said, and she, without lifting her gaze from her nails, responded, "I'm sure, I'm sure," and thereby, swiftly, however unknowingly, neutered at the gambit my whole seductive stratagem.

I lit up a Quill.

"A smoker," she said.

"I'm sorry," I said. "I should have asked permission."

She said, "Don't be silly," and dropped the nail block. "There's an ashtray right in front of you. And it's good you didn't ask. It means you're getting comfortable."

"Maybe," I said.

"Maybe's good enough for now," she said. "You know you're doing just fine—'You're doing just fine'? What the hell am I telling you *that* for, right? You know you really bring out the mom in me, Belt. I can't decide if I like it. I suppose I must, at least a little. I keep *responding* to it. Does this happen to everyone you talk to?"

"I don't think so," I said.

"It's really very strange to me. I'd have thought you'd be more of—I don't know . . . A prick."

"A *prick*," I said.

"What I mean's I imagine that, if I were you, I don't think anyone could make me nervous . . . I don't imagine I'd make pro forma apologies. Not for smoking, or anything else. *Prick*, I guess—that was too . . . that was a lazy way to say it. I didn't mean *prick*. What I meant was that, considering your work, I'd've thought you'd be a lot more confident. *Cocky*, let's say."

"My work?" I said.

"Well, not so much your novel—it's mostly a very sweet book, but 'Certain Something'?"

"Excuse me?" I said.

"I *think* that was the title. Of your story? No, who am I kidding? I'm *positive*. A hundred percent positive."

"You read 'Certain Something'?"

"Of course," she said. "I thought—did Trip not tell you? I thought it was part of . . . He showed me this little speech he wanted to present to you yesterday, and that was a part of it. Had to do with how he originally came across *No Please Don't*?"

"No," I said. "I mean, he did mention a speech, but he got thrown off it, somehow. He kept saying that he was forgetting to say things he'd written."

"Classic," she said. "He's *so* his father's son. Frets and plans and arranges and contrives, and then . . . what? Remembers who he is and just goes ahead and wings it. Anyway, it's because of me that Trip read *No Please Don't*. Because I'd read 'Certain Something' in that literary journal—what was that journal? You know, it was so long ago, I'm not even sure when . . . eleven, twelve years ago? I know I was finishing work on *Lamborgina C(unt)ock*, which I wasn't very happy with (I'm still not very happy with it), I was having a little bit of a crisis of faith, or crisis of vocation, and I thought I might give up critical theory and try my hand at fiction. I had subscriptions to a number of small literary magazines, thinking, you know, that I'd try to publish short stories in them, if I could ever get some written that I thought were worth— Wait! *Fairchild's Quarterly*! That was it. That was the journal. It was in *Fairchild's Quarterly*. I read 'Certain Something' in *Fairchild's Quarterly*." She knocked on the counter, celebratorily, one-two-three. "I read 'Certain Something' in *Fairchild's Quarterly* and, *but immediately*, I was your biggest fan."

"Come on," I said.

"I insist. Your biggest. And not because I fail to imagine others loved the story. But in the years between its publication and *No Please Don't*'s, I regularly looked for your name in the contents of any and every literary magazine I came across. At bookstores, I'd always go straight to the M's, hoping, hoping . . . I mean, Belt, that story was—I hesitate to say 'perfect,' because it sounds so adolescent, but . . . in a way, it did everything *I* wanted to do. It was everything I wanted fiction to be. A veritable *treatise* on gender and power, on having and not, on father-killing and father-becoming and all the traps in language we've built around our notions of intention and perspective, or perhaps those traps in language, which have, on their own, without our intending them to, circumscribed our notions of intention and perspective . . . all in fewer than a thousand words. So *arch* yet so *felt*. So concise, so compressed, yet so outward-looking. So *expansive*, you know? Of course you know. You wrote it."

"Thank you," I said, and left it at that, afraid that my saying anything of greater substance might undermine the story's importance to her.

•

• •

Published in *The Ferrier's Review* (i.e. not *Fairchild's Quarterly*) in 2000, along with another, longer story called "Probably Nothing," "Certain Something" was, for me, little more than a tiny, angry exercise in empathy I wrote in one sitting. Its protagonist, Mike, was inspired by a real-life Mike: a Lake County Community College student I used to see at the Wheelatine Denny's, where I'd sometimes go to write in the evenings during the latter period of my ten-year search for the girl who talked to inans. There was nothing I liked about this Mike at all—not his always-on Cubs cap, his braided leather belt, the theatrically "gripped" faces he'd make while reading whatever textbook he'd brought along to study, nor the purple-mirror-lensed Oakley Frogskins hanging from his collar, beneath his cleft chin, and especially not his habit of rattling a tin of Altoid mints to get the attention of Brenda, my (and everyone's) favorite waitress, a barely legal stunner who'd always refilled my bottomless cup of coffee (the only thing I'd ever order) without reproach no matter how long

I sat there for. And maybe "exercise in empathy" is too lofty, or even too self-congratulatory a way to put it. I didn't write the story with the intention of getting a reader to feel what Mike felt, but rather to convince myself of something I knew to be true about Mike, even though, while observing Mike, I *didn't feel* that it was true at all: namely, that his inner life, though probably no little bit despicable, was nonetheless as complex as anyone's. And mostly, I guess, I was trying to be funny.

To describe the story properly—a task that seems unappealing, anyway—would, I imagine, require more words than the story itself, so . . .

Certain Something
(Summer, 2000)

If Mike told Brenda he'd dreamed she'd died, she might let him kiss her, he thought. This was something that had worked on Liz, back in high school. He'd said he'd had a nightmare Liz had drowned in the lake, and that, all night long, through all his subsequent dreams, he'd wept and mourned for her having drowned, and he even once dreamed within one of the dreams that she was still alive, but he'd then woken up within *that* dream, only to realize it was only a dream, that Liz *had* in fact drowned, that his life was hopeless. Liz had started kissing him, right then and there, in the car. She'd started at the neck. How sweet it was. The dreams Liz had drowned were real, though, was the thing. That is: Mike had actually had them. Brenda, Mike had never dreamed of at all, though not for lack of trying. She served him coffee every day at the Denny's and often they smoked out front together, flirting, unless it wasn't flirting. Mike was never sure whether a beautiful girl was flirting. His father had taught him that what made the beautiful beautiful, and not merely pretty or sexy or cute, was "a certain something" about their face or their posture that suggested they were flirting, even when they weren't. "They can't help it, poor things," Mike's father liked to say. "That's the curse of true beauty. Everyone thinks they've got a shot with you." Mike's father often said things with more force than was merited, but this "certain something" business didn't seem to Mike to be so far-fetched. After all, there was Clinton. Everyone who'd ever met him, even his enemies, said that Bill Clinton had a "certain something," too; that when Clinton shook your hand, you felt like you were the only person in the world who mattered. Obviously, you weren't though—you weren't the only person in the world who mattered (if you even *mattered* at all). The question, however, was whether Bill Clinton, when he shook your hand and made you feel that way—the question was whether *Bill*

Clinton, during those few seconds, *believed* you were the only person who mattered in the world. Or maybe the question was: Did Bill Clinton think you *might* be the only person who mattered in the world. Because even if Bill Clinton only thought you *might* be, that would open up all sorts of possibilities, in terms of what you *were,* wouldn't it? Because, that moment, when you were shaking the hand of the US president, could in fact be your one moment to shine, or to fail to shine. Maybe, in that moment, when Clinton was open to the possibility of your being the only person who mattered—*if* Clinton were open to the possibility of your being the only person who mattered—maybe, in that moment, you could say something to him that would put things in motion, gargantuan things that would define your life and change the course by which the country was steered, the very course of world events. And the thing about flirting in general was that when someone was doing it, what it meant was that you *might* be able to kiss that person if you did the right thing or said the right thing. But the thing about a beautiful girl who was flirting—if Mike's dad was right, and what made her beautiful was that she always seemed to be flirting, whether she was or not—was it only *might* mean that you might be able to kiss her if you did the right thing or said the right thing. Or, inversely: even if you did the right thing, or said the right thing, you might *not* be able to kiss her. Like, it might be that there wasn't any right thing to do. Or no. Wait. Was there even any difference? Oh, what was the difference! Mike was getting a headache.

He went out to smoke. He started to smoke.

Brenda came out to join him.

Mike lit her cigarette.

"What?" Brenda said.

"What?" said Mike.

"That look," Brenda said. "What's up with the look?"

"Nothing," he said. "Not nothing," he said. "Weird dreams," he said. "Bad dreams," he said.

"I hate those," said Brenda.

"No kidding," Mike said. "You know, you were in them."

"Uh-oh," she said.

"I know, right?" he said. "You kept dying," he said. "Drowning, dying. It was really upsetting."

"Yikes," Brenda said.

"But inside of one of the dreams, I woke up and realized I'd only been dreaming, though. I realized you weren't dead, that you hadn't drowned, that everything was fine. That one was a really happy one—I mean it made me so happy. Brenda: alive! But then I realized that *that* was a dream, and—"

"Dude," Brenda said. "You're weirding me out, dude." And then she scratched her knee and adjusted her tights, then coughed in her hand and tilted her chin and smiled and squinted her eyes, the fucking cocktease.

•

• •

If Fondajane noticed the thematic correspondences—I certainly didn't; not til just now—between that old story and the scene that the two of us were playing in the turret, she didn't belabor them. To my "Thank you" she responded with nothing more or less telling than a smile, and transitioned us away from "Certain Something" in a word. "Anyway," she said. "On my thousandth-some trip to the M's shelf at Borders, I found *No Please Don't*. I hadn't yet seen a single review, and hadn't a clue that it existed until it was in front of me. I was so excited, Belt, so thrilled to finally have a novel by you that—well, suffice it to say that I read it in a sitting. Probably it would have been more suited to two sittings—the times I've gone back to it, I've read it in two—but it happened that the evening I came across it at the bookstore, I had to fly to Holland, for some conference in Den Hague on human rights, and I read it on the plane. I just wasn't able to put it down. And really, I mean: I had a panel to sit on. I needed to sleep. I *should* have put it down. Instead I finished the book, finished it just as we approached our arrival gate. The ride to Den Hague from Schiphol was useless—I can't sleep in cars—so when I got to the panel, I was so exhausted, I completely bombed. I was *terribly* inarticulate. Downright *irritable* with sleep deprivation. I may even, at a couple points—no, I'm sure of it—at a couple points, I cursed. I used the word 'shit' and I used the word 'jerkoffs,' words that, apart from being—how should I put it?—*venue inappropriate*—have never been in my public persona's lexicon. I mean, 'shit'—that's one thing. But 'jerkoffs'? Yikes.

"At the after-panel cocktail, I stood in a corner til a very nice, older gentleman approached me, a man called Bacon, and Bacon said kind, however surely untrue things about how much he enjoyed my performance as a panelist. Because, I suppose, I was so very disappointed in myself about my performance, I clung to Bacon for the rest of the evening, telling him, at some point, about your novel, that its brilliance and insights had kept me from sleeping. Long made short, it turned out Bacon was a publisher in Amsterdam, so I gave him your book—I had it in my purse. He sent me a letter just a few weeks later, and told me he'd made an offer on it. He also made a proposal that seemed a little—well, let's say other than professional—and Bacon was charming, so I had to cut him off. I mean, maybe in another life, this Bacon and I, but in this life I'd already married Jonboat, and . . . I've always wondered if he ended up publishing the book."

"He might have," I said. "This was Sobchak—his publishing house? Bacon's, I mean?"

"I think that was it."

I said, "They definitely paid me, but I never saw the book. I don't know if it ever came out. I should thank you, though, Fon—I'm . . ."

"Nonsense," she said.

"No, I mean, I don't think you understand. *No Please Don't*—until last night, no one ever—I mean, except for my father and my editor—I never met—never even ever heard from a fan of the book."

"I find that so hard to believe," Fondajane said. "Obviously it's not bestseller material, but . . . I'd have figured you'd have at least a fairly large cult following."

"This is all very strange," I said.

"You don't know the half of it."

"There's a whole nother half?"

"Don't you get cute with me, Belt Magnet."

"Cute?" I said.

From the entrance to the stairwell came a xylophonic dinging. Two happy notes. Fondajane, sotto voce, said, "Not in front of Trip," removed a Quill from my pack, and straightened her posture. I lipped my own Quill and lit us both up. We took a drag or two in silence, watching the stairwell. Then she said, "Trip?" and then she said, "Jonboat?" and, receiving no response, she got up from the hibachi (I averted my eyes), disappeared down the stairwell, and returned a moment later, saying, "That was odd. You heard the elevator dinging, right?"

"I think so," I said.

"It's just waiting there," she said. "No one's inside. Must be a malfunction. I'll have to tell maintenance."

From under the counter she pulled the stool adjacent to the one on which she'd previously been sitting—the stool two away from the one on which I sat—and from the seat of that stool she removed a steno pad, and from the pad's spiral spine a pen. She wrote *ELVTR* along the back of her thumb—the pen was felt-tipped—and then, to both my relief and disappointment (I hadn't been comfortable, I'd started getting comfortable), she sat on the stool from which she'd taken the notebook, i.e. such that now there was a stool between us.

"Where were we?" she said.

I said, "You told me about Bacon, and implied that there was maybe more to the story. Then you accused me of acting cute."

"Right," Fondajane said. She reached across the counter, as if to touch my hand, but didn't quite get there. "Right," she said again. "I was teasing you a little. But no, that was the end of the Bacon story. I was going to get back to the original story—how I introduced Trip to *No Please Don't*. It was a couple of years ago—three? let's call it three, I'm pretty sure it was three. We were at our home in Manhattan, and I wanted to read *No Please Don't* again, and though I'd bought a second copy of it as soon as I came back from Europe, it seems it must have been in a box of books the Archons had lost a few months before, when I retired from teaching. You see, they'd moved my office library to the house, and—"

"The Archons?" I said.

"Burroughs and his sons," she said.

"That's what you call them?"

"That's their last name."

"I thought it was Burroughs."

"I used to, also. Archon, though. Greek, I suppose. But as I was saying, I couldn't find your book, so I went for a walk, to buy a new copy. I spent the whole afternoon looking—I must have gone to five bookstores—not a single one of them had it in stock. So when I returned home, I asked Burroughs to have someone locate one for me and, to my surprise, he said he had one of his own: after reading the review of *No Please Don't* in the *Times*, he'd gone out and immediately bought two copies—one for himself, and one for Jonboat. And he told me I was welcome to borrow his copy while he searched for a new one, but that he hoped I wouldn't read it in front of Jonboat. 'What a strange thing to say,' I said to him. That he'd have thought to give a copy of the book to Jonboat, who I couldn't remember *ever* reading a novel—that was strange enough to begin with, but that he would suggest I *hide* that I was reading a novel, any novel, from Jonboat . . . Well that's when Burroughs, to my great surprise, explained that you, one of my favorite living authors, had known my husband when the two of you were boys, and, more surprising than that, he told me that Jonboat believed the book was *about* him—that is, about Jonboat, or, rather, about your obsession with Jonboat. An angry, desperate, *creepy* obsession with your no longer having access to Jonboat. Burroughs said that what Jonboat found particularly offensive about the book was how Bam Naka, the character he believed you intended to represent him, was—except in Gil's memory and, of course, that monologue Gil imagines him having toward the end—voiceless."

"Bam Naka's not Jonboat," I said.

"Of course not."

"And it's not a *character*. It's an action figure. A piece of plastic. Why would it have a voice?"

"In fairness to my husband," Fondajane said, "Bam Naka is an *astronaut* action figure, the astronaut action figure of a character from a trilogy of unnamed blockbuster films in which he presumably had a large number of lines, one of which—the only one of which—'*Who's* shaggy-looking?'—is quoted seven separate times by Gil himself."

"He's not an astronaut," I said. "He's an 'intergalactic smuggler,' and that line . . . Look, the Bam Naka action figure was originally a _____ _____ action figure, the blockbuster movies the _____ _____ character was in were part of the _____ _____ Trilogy, which is the single most successful film franchise in the history of the world, and the line was a slightly modified version of one of _____ _____'s most famous lines, '*Who's* _____-looking?' which he speaks to his love interest in a scene where she accuses him, among other things, of being '_____-looking.' I had to change the character's name and the title of the movie and the famous line because the press that published *No Please Don't* was small, and my editor feared they'd be sued by _____ _____, the creator of the franchise, who was *renowned* for his habit of suing well-meaning people for copyright- and trademark-infringement."

"Of course," Fondajane said. "Anyone who's read *No Please Don't,* including Jonboat, knows the action figure is supposed to be a _____ _____ action figure, but from Jonboat's point of view, that didn't mitigate the fact that you could have chosen an action figure of a different kind, based on a character from a different movie: one that didn't, for example, have to do with outer space. Not to mention that Jonboat's deceased and beloved grandpa Hubert 'All Hell' Pellmore had, throughout most of Jonboat's childhood, devoted himself, at no small cost, to the legitimization of the Pellmore name, which All Hell's own father had made by getting rich via . . . do you know?"

"He was a bootlegger," I said.

"A *smuggler* of Canadian whisky, yes."

"Fine. Sure. But, that's so . . . reaching," I said. "Do you really think Bam Naka's supposed to be Jonboat?"

"Not at all," Fondajane said. "I thought that was clear. Never did I for even a moment think that. But I *can* understand my husband's point of view. In how many rooms do you think he's ever been where he *wasn't* the center of attention? And attention isn't always a good thing. It *often* isn't. I imagine that you're at least somewhat aware of how the press attacked him after he and

I started going together. And they *really* turned on him after Trip's mother died. Suffering public attacks like that puts a person on guard, can make a person, let's call it, well, not *hyper*vigilant, but *overly* vigilant. I think that when Burroughs brought my husband your book, Jonboat looked for himself in it—doesn't everyone who's ever known a novelist look for himself in that novelist's work?—I think he looked for himself in *No Please Don't,* and when he found protagonist Gil MacCabby obsessed with Bam Naka, 'intergalactic smuggler gone missing,' he thought: 'This author, like so many other people who knew me in my childhood, used to think of me as a kind of action hero, and, just like all those others, he's someone I eventually left behind, someone who feels like he lost me, and in the course of writing a book about that loss, he, rather than attempting to understand me as a human being who had to move on with his life, instead turned me into an action figure, a voiceless piece of machine-sculpted plastic, an inanimate object that he no longer *owns*.' "

"Jonboat said all of that?"

"Does that sound to you like Jonboat?" Fondajane said. "I extrapolated."

"From what?"

"From 'This weasel thinks he's sad because of me, because I don't talk to him anymore, so he got his revenge by writing a book where he turned me into a mute plastic astronaut that ruined his life.' Or something like that."

"Weasel?" I said. *"Ruined my life?"*

"Don't be *sad* about it, Belt. This is all in the past. Two years ago, now. Or three. Whatever."

"I don't know that I'm sad," I said. "Maybe I'm insulted. Or sad, but also insulted . . ."

"Can't it just be funny, though?" she said. "I think it's funny. It was funny to me back then, as well, but especially now that I've met you. You don't strike me as someone who holds on to grudges, or even someone who develops grudges to begin with. Not to mention that if you *were* to seek vengeance for some grudge you were holding against my husband, there's just no way you would bumble that vengeance, let alone so spectacularly—you're far too good a writer. I mean, if you had intended Bam Naka to be Jonboat, it would be clear; Jonboat wouldn't be the only reader who picked up on it."

"That's obviously not what Jonboat thinks."

"*Thought*. What Jonboat *thought*. And no, you're right. It wasn't what he thought, and there was no way to make the great-novelists-never-screw-up-their-vengeance argument work on him because there wasn't any way to convince him of your brilliance, since he hadn't read enough fiction to distinguish great from middling novelists, nor even enough to know that even *middling* novelists never screw up their vengeance. What *did* start to convince him that the book wasn't about him was much simpler. I asked him why, if what you wanted was to hurt him, you would write a novel about a boy who lost an action figure that 'represented him'—or, for that matter, any novel *at all*—rather than some kind of memoiristic exposé about his childhood in Wheelatine. *Boy Billionaire*, say. *Suburban Scion*. You'd have had no trouble selling such a book, especially not back when *No Please Don't* was published, and you'd have certainly made a lot more money than what Darger Editions must have paid you—orders of magnitude more money, I'd think—so why, if you were so angry at him, would you be so indirect about it? What could possibly be your motivation?"

"And that convinced him," I said.

"Well, halfway," she said. "It started to convince him. It convinced him that you weren't trying to hurt him with the book, but it didn't convince him that he wasn't Bam Naka, or rather—ha!—I should say: it didn't convince him that you hadn't intended Bam Naka to represent him. He said that you'd sent him some letters back when he first went to Annapolis. Three letters, he said. He said that the third letter seemed to indicate that you were obsessed with him. Fixated on him. Of course I asked to see the letters—three pieces of one of my favorite writers' juvenilia and all—but, to my great disappointment, he no longer had them. He said the content of the letters was beside the point anyway. The point was you'd sent three, and that you'd sent the third only two months after having sent the first, only one month after having sent the second. He said that had you written only twice, it would have been different. You might have reasonably imagined that he, rather than *declining* to respond to the first letter, had never received it—you might have imagined that it, or his response to it, had been lost in the mail—but that it would have been unreasonable of you to imagine that both the first *and* the second letters *and/or* their responses had been lost in the mail, and so, in sending the third only one month after having sent the second, you were either being unreasonable, or pushy. In either case, you were showing an unwillingness to let things go their natural way."

"*Things?*" I said. "Their *natural* way?"

"Hold on, hold on. That's what he said. I'm just telling you what he said. To which *I* said, 'Look. Enough is enough. Regardless of what you may or then again very well may *not* know about the sense of epistolary etiquette young authors should be expected to possess, not only is *No Please Don't* not about you, you self-obsessed sweetheart, but it's almost as if the author has gone *out of his way* to disassociate himself from you, to make sure he *doesn't* take advantage of ever having known you. Not once in the entire *full-page* author biography at the front of the book is there even a sidelong mention of you. Not once. He didn't even tell his own *editor* he knew you. It's not about you.' Coup de grâce, Belt. Made the man blush. An inhale, an exhale, and a prolonged apology."

"An apology?"

"Well *that* is too personal to detail, really. Between husband and wife. But believe me, it was a sweet—a *very* sweet—and sincere apology."

"What was he apologizing for, though?" I said.

And here I was treated, for the second time that morning, to Fondajane's signature feel-great horse-laugh. Up close like that, I was instantly infected. Without any clue as to the object of her mirth, I not only found myself laughing uncontrollably, but doing so for as long as she—for what had to have been at least a minute. My throat, when the convulsions abated, stung. My armpits dripped. My lungs were aching.

"We got so sidetracked, I skipped—" Fondajane said, catching her breath, "I skipped the part about Triple-J." She dabbed at her welling eyes with her wrists, then reached her right hand across the counter for mine, which I slid a couple of inches toward her, ensuring that she would get there this time, and, as soon as she'd covered my right hand with hers, I covered her right hand with my left, sandwiching it for as long as she'd let me, which turned out to be a little bit longer than it took her to tell me "the part about Triple-J."

As to whether her having skipped that part had made Fondajane so winningly horse-laugh only because it had been the one thing she'd been trying to tell me for the past twenty minutes, or also because—concurrent with the realization that she'd skipped the one thing she'd been trying to tell me for the past twenty minutes—she had suddenly appreciated previously un- or underappreciated congruencies between what she *had* told me and what she would momentarily tell me (e.g. that the instrument she'd used to win the argument with her husband was the same one she'd used to entice her stepson to read *No Please Don't,* which reading had itself been the cause of the argument), I have no idea—she didn't ever specify. Nor, boldly sandwiching her up-heating hand, could I muster the syntax to ask her to specify; I couldn't even apply to the ensuing conversation the kind of attention that might have later (i.e. as I write this) enabled me to quote very much of it directly.

THE PART ABOUT TRIPLE-J

LIKE MOST OTHER CHILDREN of his generation, Triple-J had been enthralled by Curios since well before learning to speak complete sentences. Like very few children of any generation, he wasn't short of money. At the Pellmore-Jasons' Manhattan residence, he had a whole "lab" devoted to cures: a playroom stocked with marbles and PillowNests, sleeves and EmergeRigs, limited-edition mini push-pedal vehicles, novelty mini sporting equipment, custom-designed mini gadgets and weapons, and, above all, formulae, liquid and solid, Play- and GameChanger, non- and terminal, dis- and continued—every variety ever marketed to mainstream North American consumers, as well as countless imported and "garage" varieties, and quite a few yet in early development (many of which would never make it to beta) that he'd received as presents from his beloved godsister, Tessa Swords, who had herself received them from her doting father (Triple-J's godfather), Baron Swords, COO of Graham&Swords, who'd always come home from his monthly visits to the company's west coast R&D facilities bearing a duffel a-brim with swag.

It was around the age of ten that Trip began to seek out and acquire—simply for the joy that he took in viewing them—the kinds of video clips he'd eventually collage to make *A Fistful of Fists*. Some of these clips he had to pay for in cash, but most he got for free from lab techs, ad execs, and TV producers (nearly two-thirds of his collection was composed of unaired *Funniest Home Videos* submissions) for whom an encounter with a Pellmore-Jason—often just a letter from a Pellmore-Jason—was payment in itself. By the time he was eleven, his collection of footage exceeded his lab's available shelf space, and the ever-mounting spillover (dozens of new tapes and discs arrived each month) had to be absorbed by Fon's home-library. Well, not really *had to* be: the spillover could have gone into basement or offsite storage, but Fon had always adored Triple-J, and any opportunity to spend more time with him, even just the fleeting moments it would take him to shelve or unshelve this or that video, was more valuable to her than a bookcase or two or, as it would eventually turn out, five.

Owing largely, however, to the tutelage of Burroughs ("as much an Aristotle to Trip's Alexander as he'd once been an Alfred to Jonboat's Bruce Wayne"), Triple-J, despite having so much *stuff,* was neither a spoiled nor a lazy child. Quite the opposite. The after-school regimen of martial arts–, ethics-, and backgammon training through which the driver put him kept him well rounded and well behaved. He was a straight-A student, an all-seasons athlete, and an inadvertent inspirer of powerful grammar- and middle-school crushes which, when unreciprocated (i.e. in nearly all cases), produced much heartbreak, but—because of his gentleness—hardly any bitterness.

He was curious, also. Curious in general. At times he would, of his own volition, visit museums and gallery openings. He even read books that weren't assigned to him (mostly social science– and history bestsellers about the fading and forgotten or late and developing trends and milestones of the "Cute Revolutions," occasionally artist- and musician biographies, less occasionally CliffsNotes and for-Dummies digests of scholarly classics Fondajane esteemed). He was gracious with strangers, kind to his friends, he respected the help, and was generous always. He loved his stepmom the way one loves one's favorite aunt, his driver the way one loves one's father, and his father the way one loves one's one true loving God. What's more, he was very open with his feelings, demonstrative even—a warm and frequent hugger and smiler, an habitual praiser of apparel and haircuts.

At the start of seventh grade, though, Triple-J changed. Where before there was enthusiasm, now there was reticence. Where before an even temperament, now swinging moods. His face, itself, underwent transformation: it had always been a soft, almost moony thing, but now, even when he bent toward a spoonful of soup—even when he yawned—it was sharp and clenched, preemptively defensive, his down-flexed brow and dubious squint hoarding all the blue brightness of his eyes in their slots.

The change was a shock, not only for being so pronounced and unpleasant, but for having happened in the course of one day. That morning, Fondajane—upon Triple-J's request—rode with him to school to continue the conversation they'd started at breakfast about, of all things, the legalization of prostitution in America (Trip's Social Studies class was on its human rights unit, and the textbook quoted a passage from *FABRYTAYF*); when he returned that afternoon, he looked as though he were sick, and when she asked him whether he was feeling okay, he stormed off, muttering, "Leave me alone." Later, at dinner, wearing his new face, he exhaled noisily at Jonboat's inquiries, refused to meet his gaze, and wouldn't eat dessert.

Burroughs was questioned: he didn't have answers, said he'd try to get answers.

He failed to get answers. He talked to Trip's friends the following day, talked to his teachers the day after that. They'd seen the change, too, but had no idea what might have caused it.

Weeks passed, and the old Trip didn't return. His face remained closed to those who loved him most. His desserts were left to puddle and clot in their bowls. What the hell was going on? Speculations were made, followed up on, rejected:

One of the older girls at Trip's school had just been arrested for selling cocaine and MDMA to an undercover cop. The speculation that Trip had been one of her clients was dismissed, however, once the uniformly negative results came back from the broad-spectrum drug screen performed on some hair that Jonboat, ninja-like, had plucked late at night from the sleeping boy's head.

Tessa Swords, for whom Trip, everyone suspected, had long been harboring romantic feelings despite her being four years his senior, and despite the vicious-rumor-slash-open-secret that her paternal biological grandfather wasn't actually Xavier Swords, but rather infamous cuckolder Carmichael Pellmore (i.e. Jonboat's maternal uncle)—Tessa'd been photographed getting groped by a mop-topped Grimaldi on a Monégasque beach, and the photographs had made it into multiple tabloids. But the theory that jealousy had transformed Trip was rejected on grounds that, only three months earlier, photographs of Tessa sucking face with a Savoy in a Roman alley had been published just as widely, those photographs hadn't bothered Trip at all (hadn't seemed to, at least), and, as someone whose sense of his own and others' position in society was (to put it mildly) preternaturally sharp, he surely understood that if a Savoy weren't able to lock Tessa down, a Grimaldi couldn't even carry her purse.

Lastly was the mourning-in-memoriam conjecture. The anniversary of Triple-J's birth mother's death had been two weeks away when the change overtook him, and though the prior anniversaries hadn't ever shaken him (the last two, in fact, had passed without comment), this one would be the tenth, and that tenth-ness, perhaps, increased its significance, making it harder for Trip to contend with. But then neither when the anniversary arrived, nor after it passed, did anything change, i.e. Trip *remained* changed.

After the change had been in place for a month or so, parents and driver reached a conclusion: nothing had caused it. Nothing, in any case, environmental. Just interior shake-ups. Pre-, if not adolescence itself. Puberty. Hormones. Dawning teenagerness.

They determined that they had to help Trip adjust; that to help him adjust, *they* would adjust: they determined they'd allow the boy a wider berth. The frequency of his after-school lessons with Burroughs would be reduced from five to three times a week. The frequency with which he could miss family dinners would be raised from one to two times a week. His allowance would increase by 50 percent. And the trip to Chicago that he'd wanted to take in order to try to bribe somebody into granting him access to the Friends Study tapes, tapes that ever since he'd begun collecting cure clips had come to represent for him a kind of holy grail (not even Baron Swords could get his hands on the tapes, or at least that's what he claimed; nor was anyone sure the tapes hadn't been destroyed)—they'd let him take that trip to Chicago with Burroughs, and, if the opportunity arose, they'd let him spend as much as $30k on the bribe.

When they told him of this new, less rigorous regimen, Triple-J thanked them, and maybe, *maybe* he was cheered a little, for a minute or two, but just as Fondajane was rising from her chair to come around the table and offer him a hug, he stumbled from the dining room, hunched like a fiend, with what appeared to her to be tears in his eyes.

The very next afternoon, Triple-J's headmaster, Dr. Clepp, called Fon at home. During a quiz that morning, Clepp reported, Trip's Chemistry teacher had noticed him looking over the shoulder of a neighbor. Now, no one, Clepp rushed to explain to Fon, wanted to blacken Trip's academic record; the teacher, in fact, hadn't even told Trip what she'd seen him doing—she'd gone straight to Clepp with that information. She hadn't told Trip and had instead decided to go to Clepp because when she thought she was seeing what she seemed to be seeing it occurred to her that maybe she was seeing something else; maybe, rather than cheating on a quiz, all that Trip had been doing, for example, was stretching his neck, and so to accuse Trip of cheating, or to even imply to him that she thought he might be cheating, seemed to her to be . . . inadvisable. After all, if he weren't cheating, the accusation that he were, even if that accusation were merely implied, could very well make him feel unjustly persecuted, and thereby unsafe, which was a feeling—unsafety—that, through Dr. Clepp's stewardship, the school had made its mission to prevent being felt by any of its students. Having said all of that, Dr. Clepp explained to Fon, it was, in his view, a headmaster's duty—and for that matter no less so a duty than was preventing students from feeling unsafe—it was, as headmaster, Dr. Clepp's duty, Dr. Clepp felt, to apprise a boy's parents—especially such parents as Fon and Jonboat, whose donation at last year's Christmas auction, in the course of providing the school the funds to build its new locker-room whirlpool facilities, had demonstrated how profoundly dedicated they were to their son's education, and, hopefully, how profoundly dedicated they would continue to demonstrate themselves to be to their son's education—a boy's parents, Clepp felt, should be kept apprised not only of what their son was up to at school, but also what their son *might* be up to at school, and even what their son *almost certainly wasn't up to* at school. That was all. That was why he called. To keep Trip's dedicated parents apprised.

That evening, Fon appeared "in conversation with Nobel prize-winning novelist and playwright Elfriede Jelinek" at 92Y. Jonboat, who'd been in DC all day ("some think-tank thing"), was supposed to meet her at the pre-event dinner, but his chopper got held up in maintenance at Teterboro, and he'd barely made it to the greenroom in time to kiss her good luck before she hit the stage. Fon didn't mind that he'd missed the dinner—she'd had fun, anyway; Jelinek was bawdy and sweet, a real giggler—but Jonboat, who possessed little patience for tardiness, was annoyed with his mechanic, his pilot, himself. So Fon decided she'd wait til the following morning to let him know about the phone call from Clepp. After the event, though, Jonboat seemed unencumbered, exuberant even—on his way from the greenroom to his seat in the audience, he'd called the pilot, made him can the mechanic—and she reconsidered.

In retrospect, she may have made the wrong choice. She'd always thought it better to ding a good mood than to spoil an even mood or compound a bad one, yet when it came to Jonboat—maybe because he was so rarely in a good mood (or, for that matter, in any mood; he was, emotionally speaking, the steadiest person she'd ever met)—when it came to Jonboat, maybe it was worse. In any case, when, on the ride home, she told him about the phone call from Clepp, he was so immediately beside himself with anger—it wasn't only *that* Triple-J had cheated, but that he'd done so in the wake of their having made such abiding adjustments to his *budding maturity* (not to mention that Chemistry, like Math and Physics, was a subject that Pellmores and Jasons the both had always excelled at, which excellence had long been a point of family pride)—so beside himself was Jonboat that he, who, though a regular Curio user, refused, on principle, to overload out of anger or frustration (the talk he'd given at the think tank that very afternoon was titled (rather on-the-nosedly, if you asked Fon) "Cathartic Overload: The Big Little Death of American Ambition"), unsleeved his Curio and dacted it against the bulletproof (but apparently less-than-soundproof) partition with a force sufficient to alarm the driver.

Duggan pulled the limo over and waited, as per protocol, for Jonboat to speak his sequence of safewords into the dome light's hidden microphone.

Anger expelled (transformed, really, into simple disappointment), Jonboat spoke the sequence softly, and Duggan got them home.

* * *

They found the boy in his lab, filming his favorite hobunk, Droogie, which held the wrists of a nascent Curio atop which it sat while repeatedly forcing it to smack itself on its temple and snout and reciting a variety of half-mastered phrases in the vein of "What wrong you," "What happens," "Why hit self."

They had decided that they would talk to Trip together. Jonboat would offer to help him with his Chemistry, or, if Trip preferred, to have Burroughs help him. And Trip would lose his allowance for the next two weeks—a pretty light punishment, but they didn't want the emphasis to be on punishment. Having been found out as a cheater, they figured, would shame Triple-J—Fon forecasted tears; Jonboat initial denial, then tears—and thus be its own punishment.

So neither parent had been prepared for the stone-faced apathy with which their supportive approach was met:

They'd heard he'd cheated on a quiz? So what. Who cared? Two weeks with no allowance? So what. Who cared? He had a choice between studying with Jonboat or Burroughs? His choice was neither. He just didn't care.

Jonboat told him he'd changed his mind: Trip would lose his allowance for the next *four* weeks. Did he care about that?

Nope. Didn't care.

Jonboat told him he was grounded til he showed A's in Chemistry. How about that?

Didn't matter. Didn't care.

He told him he could no longer go to Chicago. Did he care about that?

Fuck you, you promised.

Fuck you, to Jonboat, didn't sound like *I care*. Did it sound that way to Trip?

Fuck you, Dad. Fuck you.

Did he care about Droogie, though?

What? Fuck you.

And Jonboat, before Fondajane could stop him—she could hardly believe she was seeing what she saw—lifted Trip's camera off its tripod and, with an overhanded blow that destroyed the camera, dacted both Droogie and the nascent at once.

Fuck you, Dad. Fuck you, man. Fucking fuck you. Just fuck you. Fuck you.

Jonboat told Trip that he supposed that he might have been wrong about the whole *Fuck you* thing, after all; it was suddenly sounding *a lot* like *I care* to him.

Fon dragged him out of there.

Father and son did not exchange a single civil word for a fortnight, and the few words that passed between Trip and Fon were exclusively civil. Toward the end of that fortnight, Jonboat, at the suggestion of Burroughs (who Trip—at least in front of his parents—had continued to treat with the same respect as always), decided to spend the coming weekend away, bow-hunting bear at the family cabin in the Adirondacks "in order," he half-explained to Fon, "to break the whole shitty circuit."

Fon thought this strange: her husband wasn't saying he would take their son up to the mountains to bond, but that he'd go by himself. And she found it a little insulting, too, because, well: What about her? Why would he want to leave her behind? Was she a—what?—a shitty *node* on the shitty circuit? Is that what he was saying? Or maybe he was saying he believed *himself* to be the shitty node. Were both of them shitty? All three of them shitty? Was she even understanding the metaphor properly? Did a circuit, to be shitty, need even to have a shitty node or shitty nodes? Could it not just have a shitty connection or set of connections between its operable nodes? Perhaps it was the current that was shitty? The way it flowed through the connections between the nodes? Did it flow so shittily as to make it seem like the circuit itself—i.e. its nodes and/or connections—were responsible for the shittiness, when in fact they were not?

Prodding the metaphor didn't get her anywhere, and if Jonboat had been willing to discuss things concretely then he wouldn't have started out metaphorically, so she didn't prod him to prod it for her. Nor did she protest the hunting trip. First of all, it obviously made sense to Burroughs, whose counsel was rarely less than sound. Plus, even before the episode with Droogie—really, ever since they'd given up seeking out environmental causes for Trip's new MO—communication between husband and wife had been strained, had degraded: Jonboat had, more than once, accused Fon of throwing arch and disapproving looks his way, of being "distant" and "judging," and Fon, in response, had grown insecure, had *become,* perhaps, a little distant and judging, and eventually even caught herself committing the very sorts of face crimes of which she had (initially) been wrongly accused. A brief separation might be refreshing.

The morning he left for the Adirondacks, she wanted nothing other than to spend the day lazing on the couch in her library, drinking coffee and smoking and reading something reliable—she wasn't sure what yet. She made an alphabetical list of candidates, of five or six, went to her shelves to pull the candidates down, to weigh them in her hands, to ruffle and smell them and read their first lines to determine which to settle in for the day with, and discovered that one of them—*No Please Don't*—was missing.

As she'd told me earlier, she walked around the city for hours, fruitlessly seeking out a copy, then ended up borrowing one from Burroughs. She fixed an espresso, lit up a cigarette, reclined on her couch, began to read, and was pleased, very pleased, more pleased than she'd been since the dinner with Jelinek.

And she was more pleased yet when Triple-J, later that evening, came into her library to get one of his videos and not only said hello to her and smiled, but asked for the title of the book she was reading. Not that she thought he was actually curious to know what she was reading, but the question conveyed more politeness than had become usual, more than was demanded. And that extra politeness seemed to Fon to indicate that Trip was reaching out, that he wanted to attempt to repair things between them. Perhaps, in the wake of Jonboat's flight, he'd begun to feel responsible for the tension he'd been causing. Perhaps he was just growing tired of the tension.

She told him the title, and he asked her what the book was about. Because it was a novel and he'd always made it clear to her he didn't like novels and didn't want to read them, and because she'd never been good at summarizing novels, and because it occurred to her that Triple-J, despite not liking novels, might, owing to its certain *je ne sais quoi,* find *No Please Don't* an exception if he gave it a chance, which chance-giving might not only be good for him (it was a shame for a boy to think he didn't like novels, and she'd often wished she could convince him to read them) but might, also, be good for *them,* i.e. for Trip and Fon, since if he gave it a chance (even if he put it down before he finished it), they'd have something new and unfraught to talk about—for all those reasons, Fondajane, instead of providing Trip with a summary of the novel, told him that the author of the novel, which was one of her favorites, had been in the Friends Study, and she showed him the author's bio to prove it, which enticed him, as she'd hoped, to give it a chance, and he asked if he could borrow it, and of course she let him borrow it.

And when Jonboat returned from the Adirondacks a couple days later, the first thing he saw as he came through the door was his son reading *No Please Don't* on the settee. He asked him where he'd gotten it and, after Trip, who'd failed to greet him, warmly or otherwise—who, even as he answered his father's question, failed to lift his gaze from the pages—after Trip told his father Fon had lent him the book, Jonboat asked Fon to come into his office and shut the door.

In his office, Jonboat told her that although he understood how she might have felt as though he'd left her in the lurch when he'd gone to hunt bear, he thought it was beneath her to seek vengeance against him through their son by giving to that son a book that went out of its way to mock him as "a mute plastic astronaut."

And Fon told him that she had had no such intentions.

And Jonboat, who simply didn't believe her, uttered a stream of rhetorical questions. Had she considered, before giving Trip the book, how much harder

Trip's inevitably resultant further loss of respect for Jonboat would make Trip's adolescence? Had she considered how much harder that would, in turn, make Trip's adolescence on Jonboat? On Fon? Did she not think things had gotten bad enough already? Did she want to make them worse? Did she hate him, after all? Had she given up on him? On them? Was she trying, after everything they'd been through together, to tear it all down? To wreck their family?

When Jonboat finished railing, Fon kissed him on the neck and fixed him a sidecar. He sat in his club chair drinking the cocktail, and she explained to him, gently, while administering a shoulder rub, how his take on *No Please Don't* was all wrong, that no one who'd ever read the book, including herself, had ever for even a fleeting moment imagined Bam Naka to be related in any way to Jonny "Jonboat" Pellmore-Jason. He resisted for a while, made his arguments, referred to the letters I'd sent him at Annapolis, but ended up, as she'd mentioned earlier, convinced of her stance by the dearth of anything Jonboat in the bio, and then he apologized, embarrassed for having assumed the book had been about him, and, more than that, upset with himself for having lost control and yelled at his wife.

And it was at this point that Triple-J knocked on the door of Jonboat's office, holding the twice-borrowed copy of my novel, and told his parents that he wanted to talk. He wanted to explain himself. He wanted to apologize.

Ever since he could remember, he said, he'd found all his greatest, most reliable thrills via Curios: via seeing the effects of various PerFormulae and combinations of PerFormulae on his hobunks and cures, and experiencing the effects those effects had on him. And ever since he could remember, he said, he'd always understood that, as the son of Fon and Jonboat, no one ever could or would stand in the way of any dream that he might dream. And the dream that he'd dreamed, for years by then, had been to be the best at the best thing there was for anyone to be best at, which meant that his dream, as they'd probably already guessed, had been to be the world's best PerFormula designer.

He had wanted so badly to make his dream real that he'd kept it a secret from everyone, even Burroughs. Not because he was ashamed to have the same dream as half the other kids in Gifted at his school. Not because he feared his ideas would be stolen—there were too many to steal. And *definitely* not because he worried he could ever possibly fail. He kept the dream a secret because he wanted to make it come true on his own, without anyone's help, so that he wouldn't ever have to doubt he was the best—so that he wouldn't have to wonder if he couldn't have done it without the help of his family. He'd *know* he could have, because he would have . . .

Except how stupid and embarrassing his dream turned out to be, right?

Because the first thing you had to be great at if you wanted to even be a PerFormula tech, let alone a PerFormula *designer*—and that's to say nothing about if you wanted to become the best PerFormula designer *ever*—was Chemistry. And it wasn't just that he wasn't great at Chemistry—he was *horrible* at Chemistry. At *junior high* Chemistry. The day he started being a dick to everyone was the day he found that out. That morning, he was as happy as usual, maybe even happier than usual—he and Fon had had a great conversation about how she and Jonboat had helped make the world a safer, better-paid place for prostitutes—but then, second period, he got his first Chemistry test of the quarter back, and he'd gotten not a B, not even a B-, but a C. On a *curve*. And on top of that, he had thought that he'd aced the test when he'd taken it. He didn't understand, even now, why his incorrect answers were incorrect. He had no talent for Chemistry at all.

So his dream had been crushed, and he hated himself for the first time ever, was embarrassed by himself for the first time ever, and even though none of that was Fon or Jonboat's fault, he had blamed them for raising him to be someone who would have such stupid, embarrassingly crushable dreams to begin with. And maybe *because* he'd known none of it had been their fault, he'd been angry at them for not being able to take the blame. For allowing him—even though they couldn't have known they were doing so—to blame himself. Or something. He'd been crazed with embarrassment. For weeks now, crazed. Just so angry. At himself. At them. At everything.

And so the first thing he'd come into Jonboat's office to say was that he was sorry for having been so horrible lately. He wanted to put it behind him. Behind all of them. He would stop being horrible, and he would work with Jonboat to get his grades up in Chemistry. He wanted to be humble about it and go for a B instead of an A. He wanted to be humble because he didn't want to disappoint Jonboat, or himself, but also because he had something else to work at. Sometime last night, or maybe just this morning, he'd started to have a whole new dream, a dream that had nothing to do with Chemistry, and what he wanted to do was spend his time making *that* dream come true: as much time as possible.

And the thing about his whole new dream was it wasn't really right to call it a whole new dream. What it was was a *clearer* version of the same exact dream he'd always had. If you boiled it down, being the best PerFormula designer had been his dream because he wanted to bring the greatest thrills of all time to himself and to others, and the amazing thing that had been happening to him since yesterday night was that, when he got to Chapter 9 of *No Please Don't,* he discovered he was getting a serious thrill from it. It wasn't as *big* a thrill as he got from really well-PerFormulized cures or anything, but it was a deeper thrill, a better thrill. A more satisfying one. And it lasted longer. It *stayed* with him. And, crazier than that, it got richer with repetition. When, today, he reread the first half of the book, the thrills it provided were more intense than they'd been the first time. He didn't really understand it yet. Not completely. Maybe not even hardly. How he could read some words on a page that formed a story that wasn't true, a story that he knew wasn't true, and that he knew was written by someone who had never met him, and yet he could feel like that person—Belt Magnet—he felt like Belt Magnet was not only speaking directly to him, more directly even than he, Triple-J, was speaking to them, his parents, right then in that office, but that Magnet was—and this was the part that really blew his mind—that Belt Magnet, who had never met Triple-J, was actually, in telling this completely untrue story called *No Please Don't,* Magnet was actually telling a much truer story about the world that he and Triple-J and everyone else lived in. The book told Trip things that Trip already knew, but that he hadn't known that he knew until he read about them. And the fact that Triple-J, even though he'd never met Belt Magnet, was able to decode all of *No Please Don't*'s lies like that—some of which were really extremely fancy and involved—the fact that he understood what Magnet was *really* saying, had to mean that Magnet somehow understood Triple-J himself, who he'd never met. If he didn't understand Trip, then how else would he possibly be able to lie in such a way that Triple-J could see the truth behind? Or underneath. Or inside of. Whatever. It seemed impossible, but it was obviously possible, to understand and be understood by someone who'd never even met you. To be understood better than even you understood yourself by someone who'd never met you. Possible. *No Please Don't* was the evidence.

So Trip wanted to understand how it worked, he said. And he really thought he'd be able to do that eventually. It seemed realistic. Because the one thing he understood about what Magnet had done with *No Please Don't* was that he'd done it with English, which was Trip's best subject, and always had been, even though Trip had never cared much about it before. He'd barely even tried at English, and he'd always been great at it—imagine what it would be like if he tried his hardest.

Anyway, he wasn't trying to say that he was over Curios or anything—he wasn't, didn't want to be, didn't imagine he ever would be, they were great—

Here, Jonboat—who had gone glassy-eyed listening to Trip's apology, and then apparently been infected by the boy's enthusiasm—interrupted Trip to tell him that he'd known me back when the two of us were boys. He told him a little about the swingset murders, Stevie Strumm (Fon remembered her name as "Bobbie Rub"), the T-shirt, my mom. He said he bet it wouldn't be too hard to find me, and that, if Trip wanted, he'd instruct the Archons to do just that. As long as I was stable and not locked up somewhere, he'd be happy to try to arrange for us to meet so that Trip could talk to me about the novel.

Big hugs were hugged, warm and firm, four- and six-armed, and Trip, now glassy-eyed himself, told Jonboat that he very much did want to meet me—he did, a lot.

But not just yet.

He wanted, first, to have something to show me: something to read: some fiction of his own. His new dream, or, rather, his all-time dream in its clarified form—his all-time dream of providing others with the best of thrills—was to become a great novelist.

•

• •

If Fondajane's allowing me to sandwich her hand for the entire time it took her to convey the information contained in the eleven pages above seems strange to you, reader, I sympathize completely—I'd venture it seemed at least as strange to me. She took more time to convey that information than those eleven pages take to read: she went off on tangents short and long; peppered in asides; paused dramatically and mock-dramatically; paused for laughter (hers and mine); answered my questions; answered my requests for clarification; extracted assurances from me similar to those that Burroughs had extracted the previous evening (i.e. assurances that I, when in the presence of Trip, wouldn't mention Jonboat's initial suspicions regarding Bam Naka, nor any event that had stemmed from those suspicions); and redundantly backtracked a couple of times in the course of reacquiring a lost train of thought.

And I'm sure that, as an infant, I'd been held for as long as—and maybe even longer than—the hand sandwich lasted; perhaps, too, as a toddler, in his parents' bed, hiding from monsters or nightmares or loneliness. *In memory,* however, the closest I'd come to so sustained a spell of interpersonal taction was on my visit to the brothel some dozen years earlier.

Nor did the sandwiching cease when Fon told me of Triple-J's desire to become a novelist. It persisted for another five or six minutes, during which she proudly and cheerily described Trip's post-apologetic return to the fold, heaped gratitude upon me for writing *No Please Don't* (gratitude I tried to gracefully deflect, though, unpracticed as I was, I probably came off like a faux-modest jerk, which I fear I might be doing right now as well, both in spite and because of my admitting to it, now admitting to *that,* and humblebrag, humblebrag, ad infinitum), then listened to me bumblingly express my admiration for *My Procedures* and *FABRYTAYF* (admiration, I confess, I inflated a little—though only a little—in the hopes that doing so might distract from my failure to praise *My Process, On Sontag, Trans AM/PM,* and *Lamborgina C(unt)ock,* none of which I'd read).

Yet, strange though its duration was to me, reader, the sandwich's erotic falloff was stranger. At the start, I didn't think of the sandwiching as *sandwiching.* I thought of it as *touching,* or *touching Fondajane,* and was more turned on than I'd previously been; I was more turned on than I'd *ever* been. It seemed to me that Fon, by allowing me to touch her, was granting me permission to be more turned on, and for as long as I thought of myself as *touching* her, any attention I wasn't focusing on what she was telling me (i.e. "the part about Triple-J") was split between 1) the pictures I was (semi-voluntarily) forming of what she would look like without her clothes, and 2) efforts to figure out whether and how to turn our *touching* into something more sexual—to turn it, more specifically, into a kiss that might lead to her actually shedding those clothes.

Slowly, however, I began, I supposed, to get used to *touching Fondajane.* This is when the word *sandwiching* occurred to me. I was *sandwiching* her hand. And once I'd begun to think of what I was and had been doing as *sandwiching,* I realized we (or perhaps just *I*) had entered a different—a less intense—phase. Whereas previously (i.e. at the start of the sandwiching), the sandwich seemed to have placed in contention Fon's earlier claim that we would "never act on what [I was] thinking about," now the sandwich seemed to be affirming that claim: it seemed less and less likely that there would be any kissing, until, soon enough, it seemed entirely assured that there would be no kissing (and forget about nudity). And while, sure, this did disappoint me, I also, to my surprise, felt relieved. To realize that I'd never have what I wanted was to realize the pointlessness of trying to have it. Thus, to cease in my efforts to come up with ways to upgrade our sandwich into a kiss was not only what I decided I would do, but what I decided—in the spirit of decency, respect, and energy conservation—I *should* do. In other words: I knew I wouldn't later regret having ceased to try; I saw, as Fon had put it earlier, that I didn't have to worry I'd blow my chance.

I had no chance.

And so I relaxed a little, then a little more, and a little more yet, and, in so doing, I became increasingly aware of my own inner noise, that free-associative background mind-wander which had previously been drowned out by my (now nullified) fear of blowing "my chance."

This inner noise proceeded along the lines of what you'd probably expect. I wondered what was taking Triple-J so long to come to brunch, wondered what we'd eat, who would cook it, noticed I wasn't actually that hungry, recalled the hugging of my father in our kitchen, remembered I had to give Lotta her $500 back, worried what Trip's response might be when he learned I hadn't finished watching his video, remembered I'd already decided not to worry, that maybe my failure would garner me a second invitation to the compound, wondered what business Jonboat had in Dubai, suspected he wasn't on the phone with Dubai, thought that maybe he just didn't want to see me, and remembered him saying *I like Belt's bike* and *He's not into freestyle* a quarter-century before, and I remembered the bike—its padded leather seat, and how its red-flippered gearshift was braced to the handlebar beside the right grip, rather than bolted to the handlebar's post, and how those were the qualities that sold me on the bike: the luxurious seat, the newfangled tech—and I remembered the jingle the slapsticking boys who'd spit their gum on the pavement in front of the halfpipe had shout-sung at me—*Muh-ray moves you fast-ah!*

For a while, that jingle replayed in my head to the total exclusion of the other inner noise, and this soon became annoying, so I tried to do the trick that someone—Stevie Strumm? Jonboat himself?—once taught me to do to push an annoying song—"Wishing Well" by Terence Trent D'Arby? "Two of Hearts" by Stacy Q?—out of my head: the trick where you think of a different annoying song. I landed, first thing, on another television advertising jingle from my middle-school years: the jingle for the food product Hamburger Helper.

Hamburger Helper
Helped her hamburger
Help her
Make a great a meal!

Which struck me as peculiar. When was the last time I'd heard *that* one? Of all the catchy songs and jingles I knew, why would that be the first to come to mind?

The answer was right in front of me: the handwich.

Just as I had, before, gotten so used to *touching Fondajane's hand* that I'd begun to think of it, far less erotically, as *sandwiching*, I had, thereafter, gotten so used to the sandwiching that I'd begun to think of it, even *less* erotically, as *handwiching*.

Now, Handwich was *not* the name of Hamburger Helper's mascot: in all likelihood, Hamburger Helper's mascot's name was Hamburger Helper, or *The* Hamburger Helper. Neither was Hamburger Helper a sauce one added to hamburgers (i.e. hamburger sandwiches) to make them tastier: rather, it was a kind of seasoned noodle product to which one added ground beef (i.e. hamburger) to make a kind of casserole. But because Hamburger Helper's mascot was a hand—a white-gloved, disembodied hand with a face on its palm—and because I (who was never fed Hamburger Helper, and who rarely paid the kind of attention to commercials that their sponsors intended) had *believed* for a while that Hamburger Helper was a sauce one added to hamburger sandwiches to make them tastier, I'd *imagined* the mascot's name was Handwich.

So there, in the turret, having begun to think of what our hands were doing as *handwiching*, it followed that, in pursuit of a tune with which to replace the Street Machine jingle, I'd land on the Hamburger Helper one.

When, though, I wondered, as the handwiching proceeded—when had I learned that Hamburger Helper wasn't a sauce one added to hamburgers to make them tastier? Unsurprisingly, I couldn't remember exactly when, but I knew that it had happened years and years earlier. What did surprise me was my dawning realization that Handwich could not have been the name of the mascot for Hamburger Helper: that despite my having known for who-knows-how-many years that Hamburger Helper wasn't a sauce one added to hamburgers, I had, up until that very moment in the turret, persisted in the belief that the mascot's name was Handwich. Here had been a 2, and there, but a micron away, a second 2, yet never, til now, had I put the 2s together. I'd never once thought to. And I couldn't help but wonder what else I had missed. What else was I missing?

A sense of expanding possibility imbued me, the same sense that had imbued me that morning, in the shower, when I'd thought about the years I'd spent failing to imagine that books could be inans. This time, however, instead of aiming my sense of expanding possibility at the future, I aimed it at our handwich, at the meaning of everything that went along—that was going along—with our handwich. It seemed to me our handwich was more than it seemed. Or other than it seemed. Or that it *could be* more or other. Might not Fondajane, for instance, through our handwich, be communicating? emphasis on the preposition? i.e. *through* our handwich as through a telephone. If not, then how else had I arrived at the certainty that nothing sexual would arise from the handwich? I mean: Wasn't that certainty counterintuitive? Wasn't it precisely the opposite of what such physical contact would typically mean? And yet there it had been, had remained, was: the certainty. There would be nothing sexual. Not now or ever. Was it so unreasonable to think that Fon had sent and/or was sending me that message *through* the handwich, *via* the handwich, and despite what the handwich would probably look like to the average nonparticipant? I didn't think it was so unreasonable. I don't, today, think it so unreasonable.

To be entirely clear: I'm not saying I thought that Fon had sent *words* through the skin of her hand into the skin of mine. What I'm saying is that it seemed that she—through the skin of her hand into the skin of mine—was *signaling friendship*.

Seemed. It *seemed*. I'm not claiming certainty. I had (and have) a lot less confidence in the reality of our handwich telepathy than in that of, for example, inan sentience. Whether or not the telepathy was itself real, though, I *was* certain—*became* certain, *felt* certain—that Fon and I, over the course of the touching/sandwiching/handwiching had become friends.

I was handwiching a friend.

A friend of mine was being handwiched by me.

Perhaps this handwich—this emblem of our friendship—had itself been a force behind our friendship's creation. Perhaps the handwich was *only* emblematic. It didn't matter so much. What mattered so much: we two were now friends.

And in the end, the thought of our friendship made me happy. The erotic falloff of the taction: I welcomed it. Which isn't to say that once I'd realized we were friends, I wasn't any longer attracted to Fon, but rather that I continued to become less and less attracted to Fon (I no longer, for example, required the lap cover provided by the counter), and—because it would make our friendship less fraught—I looked forward to becoming less attracted to her yet.

•

• •

I was just beginning to kind of passively wonder how much longer the handwich could last—all the leaning forward and reaching across had started to stiffen my shoulders and neck—when the elevator bell xylophonically dung. Or dinged. Fon sat back, both hands in her lap. I sat back in turn, and twisted and tensed, emitting a glorious congo roll of spinal pops.

From the mouth of the stairwell came the clap of rushed footsteps, and Triple-J's greetings. "Hi, guys, sorry, I'm sorry," he said. Entering the turret, he waved around a parcel: gift-wrapped, fist-size. "I'm *so* late," he said. "I was almost here just a *little* bit late—like I was *in* the elevator—when I realized I forgot your gift in the production house. I don't know what I was thinking—I guess I wasn't thinking—because I should have taken the wallwalk back to get it, but instead I took the sidewalk, and all these kids kept stopping me and talking to me and bragging on their Hangstrong times and so on . . . Anyway, *this,*" he said, victoriously slamming the fist-size parcel on the counter of the hibachi, "is for you, Belt. I hope you like it."

I unwrapped the parcel. Inside it was an IncuBand just like the one I had under my bed.

"You shouldn't have," I said.

"Get outta here with that," he said. "I told you yesterday: I *wanted* to. And I talked to Tessa, just like I said I would, to see if she had any, and it turned out she did—she has a ton of them—but by the time I called, *duh,* it was already too late to overnight anything, so, on a hunch, I went digging around in the hoarder house, and that's where I found it. It used to be my dad's, I guess. Go ahead. Try it on."

"The hoarder house?" I said, fastening the band to my wrist, behind the bangle.

"It's next to the production house—the one the events were right in front of."

"We usually call it the *cellar* house," Fondajane said. "Or the *relics* house, if we're feeling particularly full of ourselves."

"It fits okay?" said Triple-J.

"It's perfect," I said. I extended my arm, turned my hand and head side to side, and smiled, as if examining a diamond engagement ring.

"Where's your marble?" Triple-J asked. "Let's see it with the marble in. Or wait. Did it hatch?"

"It didn't, no. Thing is, I didn't bring it, though. I thought . . . I guess I thought that, well . . . that brunch might be too *formal* for CureSleeves?"

"So that look you're rocking with the Sambas and the jeans and the poly-blend Mexican wedding shirt—that's how you do formal?"

"Trip," Fondajane said, "don't be rude to your guest."

"I was trying to be funny."

"I don't think it was funny."

"Not at *all*? I think it was at least a *little* funny, Fon," he said, squeezing her trapezia. "Belt knows I'm just messing around with him, right? I look up to him, and he knows that. You know it too. It makes me kinda nervous that we're actually hanging out. That's why it's funny for me to say something that seems disrespectful. Because of how unexpected it is, I mean. I think Belt gets that. Don't you get it, Belt? Actually, no. You don't have to answer that. In fact, please don't. Please forget I even asked. I'm seeking reassurance instead of sticking to my guns or making amends, and those are the only two mature options to choose from here, the only two options a decent person would entertain, and so instead of seeking reassurance, let me just tell you that if I hurt your feelings, I'm sorry. I really didn't mean to. I don't care how you're dressed. Maybe I'm a little off-key today or something. Can I show you something cool in the hopes it'll make up for me acting all bitch-ass?"

He sat on the stool between me and Fondajane, and opened his sleeve. A standard pale-black cure climbed out. It wasn't, by any means, merely standard-cute—even before I'd interacted with it, I felt it exerting above-average charisma, the kind only the older ones ever possess, and I'd have guessed its age to be two years—but given whose sleeve it had just been inside, I suppose I was a little bit disappointed. The "Aww" I cooed was forced, polite.

Triple-J set the cure in the center of my placemat. He told it, "Say hi."

"Hello!" the cure said to me, then turned to Triple-J.

"Invite it on board, Belt. This'll be cool."

I put out my hand. The cure climbed in, raised its eyes expectantly.

"Now tell it who you are."

"I'm Belt," I told the cure.

"Magnet," the cure said, matter-of-factly.

"That's right!" I exclaimed. And, at least for the moment, I was actually delighted. Not because I thought the cure somehow recognized me—I assumed Trip had trained it to respond to the sound of "I'm Belt" with "Magnet"—but because I'd never heard a cure say "Magnet" before.

"Magnet," it said again.

"Yeah," I said. "Wow. That's me. I'm Belt Magnet."

"I'm Magnet," the cure said.

"I'm Magnet," I said to it, pointing at my chest.

"I'm Magnet please meet you."

"*You're* Magnet?" I said.

"I'm Magnet please meet you."

"It's true," Triple-J said. "This is Magnet, Belt. It's true."

I pushed out some laugh sounds, a *wow* and more *awws,* kept my eyes on the cure's, and off Triple-J's, unsuccessfully trying to feel simply flattered instead of weirded out and vaguely offended.

Magnet took a couple of rapid steps forward, onto my forearm. It widened its eyes, as if in surprise, gasped dramatically, and said, "We're silly?"

"Maybe?" I said.

"We're . . . silly," said Magnet.

Fon, whose smile looked about as forced as mine, said, "That's what it says when it wants to be tickled," then offered me a micro-shrug.

I tickled the bottom of its muzzle a little. It convulsively raised and lowered its shoulders, and shouted, "I'm giggling! I'm giggling! I'm giggling!"

"You *are,*" I said.

"Adorable, right?" Triple-J said.

"It's impressive," I said. "How well it's trained."

"Come on," he said. "What Curio over a couple years old can't play some version of Tickle-Me-Giggle? Unless you mean—oh . . ." he said, deflating a little—enough so that Magnet leapt off my forearm and climbed onto his to nuzzle his wrist. "You mean it's impressive because of who *I* am—because you don't think I'd be any good as a trainer."

"No," I said. "Hey, it's not that at all."

"So what? You were just being polite? Saying it was well trained?"

"No, I—"

"Good," he said. "You shouldn't. You shouldn't just be polite. Everyone's always being polite with me. And you know what? It's okay with me that you don't think I'd be good as a trainer. It stung for a second, but there's no more sting. It's good feedback to have. Truth is, I probably wouldn't think I'd be a good trainer either. Not when I look around at other kids my age. How lazy they are. I should say *we*—it *is* my generation. How lazy *we* are. We've got no imagination."

"I wouldn't say that," I said.

"Well you should, cause it's true. We act like 'stacking PerFormulae for novel effects' is a form of creativity. Like overloading is a kind of expression of passion, an expression of lust for life or something. Like the PerFormulae Abuse Labs Bros are the great geniuses of our time, and every stack and OD they come up with's a major cultural event, and 'What note of its painsong would I prefer to dact it on?' is an important, like, art-of-living-type question. Instead of *using* these amazing little tools ourselves to do something *new*—and that's what a Curio is, right? that's what any machine is, no matter how complex, right? a tool?—instead of using them to do something new that could expand us, as humans, to expand what it *means* to be a human, or to think more clearly about what it *really* means, we let them be used *on* us. By corporations. Aided by the media. By people who want to sell us formulae, accoutrements. And we have no idea the opportunities we're blowing to get past what we think are our limits. I mean, that's one of the big reasons I made *A Fistful*—to inspire people, you know? To shake them out of their complacency. I mean, obviously, I like to think I'm exceptional, but I can see how my being the age that I am might get in the way of other people seeing that, so I understand. I get why you'd think I'd suck at training."

"I was thinking more about 'Living Isn't Functioning,' " I said.

"My paper?" he said. "You read it?"

"I read both of the papers," I said. "Last night. And you know, as long as we're sort of talking about what I did and didn't have time to do before coming here—"

"I guess you think it's weak, huh? I mean, I know it's really talky in some parts, and maybe redundant, but the teacher had this whole thing about 'exploiting the rhetorical peculiarities and nonstandard usages of one's generation,' so I was trying to keep it 'informally voiced' and that's kinda why I gave you the other paper, too, like to show you I don't always write like that. I guess I should have explained that."

"The paper's not weak," I said. "That's not what I meant. It's just it keeps insisting that cures are machines."

"Yeah, you're right. You're *right,*" he said. "It's way too obvious. And I was worried about that. I admit it. I was worried it was too obvious a point to make. I shouldn't have shown it to you. It's not up to snuff. Man, I'm a dick."

"It's *not* too obvious a point to make," I said. "Not to me. It's just I have a hard time imagining anyone who's convinced that cures are machines spending as much time training one as it must have taken you to train Magnet. That's all I was trying to say."

"But why?" Triple-J said. "Why a hard time? I love machines. Well, some machines. Like Magnet—obviously. Or the Boatmobile. That didn't come across in the paper at all? Wait—defensive question. I keep being bitch-ass. Sorry, I'm sorry. Obviously it didn't come across. I didn't think to put it in there. I thought it was clear. Maybe . . . Did you really read it, or just, like skim it? No. Don't answer that. It's just more bitch-assness. Man. Aw, man . . ."

"You know what?" I said, hoping to comfort him, "I did only get to read the paper once. I probably missed some undertones."

"No, no, no," he said. "Don't snow me, Belt. Please. I know it sounds like I'm trying to get you to snow me, but I have to learn. I mean, I wrote that thing almost four months ago, and now I'm not only four months smarter, but I should be able to look at it with distance, through the eyes of an intelligent, discriminating reader."

"See, that's a really impressive attitude," I said. "I mean it. I'm impressed. You really could make a great novelist one day."

"A great novelist?" he said.

"Sure," I said. "Because . . ." I looked over at Fon.

"I was just," she told him, "telling Belt the story about how, when you first read *No Please Don't,* it made you want to be a novelist."

"Oh yeah," he said. "I remember that. That was intense. I really did think I wanted that. Yeah. But that was before I read what's-his-name, though. What's his name, Fon?"

"I don't know who you mean," she said.

"Come on," he said. "Come on. I can't believe I'm blanking on his name. He was really important to me. And not just to me. His thing—his excerpt—we talked about it a little. Maybe more than once. It was in some old course packet you gave me from that class you used to teach at NYU."

"'Our Bodies, Our Contraptions'?"

"Yes! Right. That was the class. What was the guy's name?"

"That was a thick packet, Trip. We talked about a lot of it."

"Wait, I got it!" he said. "Marcel Marceau."

"No," she said.

"Yeah," Trip said. "Marcel Marceau. That was the guy."

"It wasn't," Fon said.

"He's a mime," I said.

"A *mime*?" Trip said. "Why would I even *know* a mime's name, though? Anyway, okay, I'm starting to believe you. Marcel Marceau sounds not exactly right. Guy's French though, this guy. Fon? French?"

"Half the authors in the packet were French."

"His whole thing was—he's the French power guy, come on. It's crazy I can't remember his name."

"French Power?" Fon said.

"Not like French Power," Trip said. "Like, he was French and his whole thing was about fisting? How getting fisted was a new kind of power?"

Fon said, "That's not exactly—"

"I know," Trip said. "It's more complicated than that. But what's the guy's name?"

"You're thinking," Fon said, "of Michel Foucault, but—"

"Michel Foucault! Exactly. Have you read this guy, Belt? Michel Foucault?"

"I haven't," I said.

"And neither have you," Fon told Trip. "That was a paper *about* Foucault. A chapter from a dissertation by a friend of mine—a former classmate at Columbia, David Ballard."

"Ballard!" Trip said. "Right. I got confused. But this paper by Ballard was *on* Foucault. Foucault and fisting."

"Yes," Fon said.

"So that's all I'm saying. Have you read it, Belt?"

"It wasn't published," Fon said.

"That's crazy," Trip said.

"David died of AIDS," Fon said, "just shortly after he finished the chapter. He never got to finish the whole dissertation, so."

"You put it in your course packet, and it wasn't even published? Actually, I guess that makes total sense. It really was that good. It inspired me so much."

"I didn't realize," Fon said. "That's wonderful to hear."

"Yeah," Trip said. "That paper was huge for me. It's why I quit trying to be a great novelist."

"See, the paper basically explains," Trip continued, "how fisting was maybe the most important and revolutionary innovation of the twentieth century. It's so important because it uses the body in a sexual way that no one ever used it before, a way that gives you whole new pleasures, whole new thrills. Like, the point of fisting isn't to get to the orgasm at the end, right? Maybe the orgasm doesn't even happen. Or maybe it happens right at the beginning, but that doesn't mean you stop fisting. The point of fisting is *to be* fisting. Or to be *getting* fisted. And the history of it is really crazy because people have been having sex with other people for as long as there have been people, for thousands and thousands and thousands of years, and they've always had everything you need to fist—*cavemen* had what they needed to fist, they had it before they had the wheel, before they had *fire,* it's basic an*at*omy—but it wasn't til the twentieth century that anyone ever fisted. The means to do it were there all along, but nobody ever thought to try it out. That's basically the paper's main thing, Fon, right?"

"Well, there's more—"

"I know, but it *basically* is. And anyway, that's what inspired me. How revolutionary it was. Fisting, I mean. And it got me thinking: What else could be like that? What else could be like fisting? What else is right in our faces, totally available, and ready to be innovated—like to make new, revolutionary thrills and pleasures—by the first person to really just open his eyes? And the answer was . . . *not* literature. And I don't mean I think that literature *can't* be innovated. I mean that it's not all that *available* to be innovated, you know? People have been innovating it from the beginning. Geniuses have. For centuries. You could even say that the tradition of literature is a tradition of literary innovation, right? Same with the tradition of painting. Sculpture. Photography even. Everyone's been trying to innovate forever, and most of them failed, but a lot of them succeeded, so it makes sense that there's just not that much revolutionary potential in those art forms left to discover or innovate, you know? And like maybe I'm a genius of literature or painting or sculpture or whatever—it's possible—I do think it's possible I could innovate one of those art forms if I studied it closely and practiced doing it all the time, but it would probably take me years, and I don't have the patience for that, especially because whatever innovation I came up with—maybe it wouldn't even be revolutionary. Maybe it would just be . . . kind of interesting. Like it would start a movement or something, you know? Like, other writers or painters or whatever would apply some version of my innovation to making new writings and paintings and stuff, but . . . probably not even that.

"Curios, on the other hand—I saw all this massive potential there. *They* would be the fist I would work with. Or the ass. No, the sex. Whatever. Doesn't matter. They'd be what I worked with. I'd been fascinated by them my entire life. Most people my age had, but almost none—you're tilting your head like a . . . a curious Labrador, Belt. Did I lose you? I mean, you didn't read Foucault or Ballard, I know that, but like . . . You *do* know what fisting is?" With his hand he made a goose-head shadow-puppet shape, pushed it forward, very slowly, as if meeting with resistance, and in doing so gradually balled up the goose head.

I looked to Fon. Another micro-shrug.

"You don't have to get permission from the parent," Trip said, repeating the gesture. "You can admit you know what *fisting* is. It doesn't have to be all taboo and uncomfortable. Or maybe it does have to be a little *uncomfortable* at first, cause it's, you know"—he did the gesture again—"ha! But it's just a kind of sex and I'm not a little kid. I can talk about sex. I can talk about whatever—right, Fon?"

She said, "Of course, of cour—oh my. Oh dear."

Magnet, which had climbed onto Triple-J's shoulder, was now fisting the air, both-handed, and whispering.

"What's it saying?" I said.

Triple-J bent an ear toward the cure. "Sounds like, 'You know, you know, you know,'" he said. "Every time I laugh, or make a laugh sound—well, not every time, but a lot—it practices doing whatever it thinks made me laugh, and then does the thing for me later, at full volume, if I start acting depressed or quiet or something. I must have said, 'You know,' and laughed, or made a laugh sound."

"Oh, that's great," I said. "I have—I used to have one that did stuff like that."

"I guess it's cool sometimes," Triple-J said. "I mean, its timing's usually pretty bad. Pretty annoying. Like, I don't know about you, but if I'm depressed and something that's supposed to be funny or cheerful happens, I don't usually laugh or get cheered up. I usually just get more depressed because it seems like I'm failing to have a good sense of humor or a positive outlook or whatever. Not that I think less of Magnet for it—I mean that's just SECRT, right?"

"It's a secret?" I said.

"What? No. SECRT. Magnet's senso-emotional call-and-response tech. All cures' SECRT is what I'm saying. It was designed for kids, with kid emotions. Kids with the kid emotions kids had back when you and my dad were kids—where is Dad, by the way? I thought *I* was late, huh?"

"He's on a call with Dubai," Fon said. "Uncle Haj."

"On a Sunday?"

"I know," Fon said.

"Hey, where's your dad, Belt? I thought he'd be joining us. It's like the day of no dads at brunch around here."

"He wasn't able to make it," I said.

"Yeah, I was told. What I'm saying's: Why not?"

"Nosy," Fon said.

"My bad. What I meant was, 'That's a bummer. I'd have liked to eat an omelet with your father.' I'd kind of like to eat one without him, though, too. Maybe even a burger. I'm not starving or anything, but I bet Belt is. And how about you, Fon? Maybe we should have the kitchen bring something up? I don't think Dad would mind if we went ahead and brunched. I wouldn't have minded if you'd gone ahead, and he's later than me. Then again, his omelets—I don't know if Fon mentioned it, Belt, but my father's omelets are . . . they're kinda the best. Probably everyone thinks that about his father's omelets, but they're wrong. My dad's got this like *technique*. Am I lying?"

"They're very good omelets," Fondajane said.

"I'm happy to wait for omelets," I said. "I'm not all that hungry. Anyway, we've got a box a Crunch here, if things get desperate."

"I was told you brought that as a gift for my dad."

"Well there's a shirt inside," I said. "That's the gift, really."

"Yeah, that's right. That's what Hogan—no, Duggan. Or . . . I don't remember which one said it. But I thought he said it was like a joke-gift kind of thing where the cereal's essential to the joke."

"It's not really a joke-gift," I said. "The wrapping—the box—is kind of jokey, but . . . we should probably leave *some* cereal in there, but there doesn't need to be a lot. The cereal's got nothing to really do with the shirt. The shirt's just this thing from when we were kids. Maybe your dad told you about it? The Jonboat Say shirt?"

"Oh, *that's* what it is! That makes sense, now," Trip said. "Duggan—or Hogan, whoever—they just said it was a shirt, and I thought, 'Why would Belt Magnet bring my father a shirt? Why would he think my father wanted some . . . shirt?' But okay, okay. Because you helped him design it. You're who came up with the whole idea to turn the catchphrase PG so kids could wear it at school, right? You told him, 'Drop the *gayola*.'"

"Well, *gaylord*, but actually—"

"Right! Gaylord. Ha. 'Drop that *gaylord*, Jonboat.' That's hilarious. What a great gift. I bet he'll love it. It's like a remember-the-good-old-days kind of gift. The *swingset murder* days, right?" Trip said.

"Pretty much," I said.

"Man, I really wish I could've been there to see all that, Belt. You know, the swingset murders—they've got like everything to do with my plans for showing *A Fistful*. The whole had-to-be-there-to-understand-the-thrill-of-them aspect. Plus, in a way, they were kind of like fisting, right?"

I had no idea what he was talking about, reader, and, given that he'd paused for confirmation (i.e. "right?") so soon after invoking "plans for showing *A Fistful*," and considering how infrequently he'd been pausing, this probably would have been the perfect moment for me to mention that I hadn't been able to finish *A Fistful*. Yet his comparing the swingset murders to fisting was not only bizarre to me, but embarrassing. Despite having given up on the possibility of any kind of romance with Fondajane, I still didn't want her to above-averagely associate me with anuses. Not with doing things to anuses, not with having things done to my anus, and not with thinking about anuses (neither mine nor anyone else's). Not even metaphorically. I suppose that, were it up to me, it would never have even crossed her mind—hers or anyone's—that I *had* an anus. And so instead of confessing to not having finished *A Fistful of Fists,* I got a little defensive. "I don't know," I said. "I don't know if I'd compare fisting to the swingset murders."

"Well, yeah," he said. "No. I mean, not in their impact, really. I mean, they didn't catch on. I know that. It's not like any of the kids who saw the murders started murdering swingsets—at least not according to my dad or Burroughs. But in spirit, I mean. Like, you used a bat in a way that bats aren't normally used, and you used it to do things to swingsets that weren't normally done. Like, 'Here's a bat, here's a swingset. Watch this thrilling new thing I can do with them,' right? It's not so different from 'Here's a hand, here's an anus. Watch this thrilling new thing I can do with them.' Or maybe, yeah, now that I'm saying it out loud, I can see how maybe I'm reaching a little—I don't know. I mean, you being the author of my favorite novel, obviously I want to believe we share all kinds of deep affinities, so maybe I see some where there aren't any, and, well, like I was starting to say before, I definitely think that what *I've* been doing is a lot like fisting. Like, 'Here's a Curio, here's a whatever, watch this thrilling new thing I can do with them.' Curios haven't been around for as long as fists and sex had been around when the inventor of fisting invented fisting, or even as long as bats and swingsets had been around when you came up with the swingset murders—that's true—but what I was thinking, after I read Fondajane's friend's paper, was everyone had them, everyone loved them, and no one had done anything *truly* new with them in years, right? Decades. Not since Burnsy and Woof invented spidge. See what I mean? I mean, even the second and third Cute Revolutions—they weren't really *new*. They were just marketing terms Graham&Swords invented to sell PerFormulae. And they worked. Obviously. At selling PerFormulae. But what did PerFormulae really change, you know? I mean they made cures and hobunks *cuter* by making them more novel, which of course made overloading on them that much more awesome—I'm not saying they didn't do that—and they made for wider varieties of spidge, too, but still, the two basic things people used Curios for remained the same: overload and getting high.

"So the human-Curio dynamic, I thought, has been the same for years and years, but who said it had to be? Who what's-the-word-*circumscribed* that dynamic? Graham&Swords? Yeah. Them. And who cares? Why do they get to be the circumscribers? They *profit* from being the circumscribers. They are *not* disinterested. They're this superpowerful corporation and it's in their interests to limit the thrills we can get from Curios to thrills they can make money off of—overload and getting high. And you have to be a chemist with some serious lab skills, not to mention access to insanely expensive research facilities, in order to even participate in *non*revolutionarily innovating in the

Graham&Swords way. I mean, you can have a start-up lab in your garage and make some cool formulae if you're really talented, but you're not gonna be able to make BullyKing or SloMo or Independence. That takes *teams* of top guys with massive research budgets. And even then—even if you're part of the team that makes BullyKing or whatever—you're still making something thats main point is to enhance the quality of overload and maybe, if you're lucky, the buzz from spidge, too—same ole same ole. But so screw *that*, I thought. I'm bad at Chemistry, and corporations are shady. What can I do? What can I do to revolutionarily innovate cures? How do I start?

"And it was obvious, right? Because I was thinking about fisting, about what Foucault or Ballard or whoever it was who said it said about fisting: it was revolutionary because it was a way to have sex where the point wasn't to have an orgasm. So if I want to revolutionize interactions with Curios, the first thing I should do is forget about the circumscribed point: the first thing I should do is come up with ways to interact with cures where the point is *not* to overload or get high.

"And that's what I did.

"I figured out how to use Curios to connect people socially through acts of spontaneous altruism—like with Charity Party. And I figured out how to use Curios to make people who were already socially connected connect with each other more, and more *deeply,* through meditative endurance sports—like Ulysses and Hangstrong and Flick&Look. And then there are what I like to think of as the more experimental or artistic or just open kinds of pure research interactions where the point is *unknown,* where the point is to, like, *discover* a point, to simply do *anything* cure-focused *except* overload, in the hopes that doing so will inspire you, the artist/experimenter, with ideas for revolutionary innovations—that's what Neo-Gratification exercises are for. Like, remember the other night at the playground?—no?"

With each of the "innovations" he'd listed, Trip had raised one of his right hand's fingers. Once the thumb had come up for "Neo-Gratification exercises," he'd pushed the hand forward a little, for emphasis, and then let it fall down onto the counter. At that point, Magnet, which was still on his shoulder, had misread the fall of the hand as a salutational cue, and had raised its own hand and said to me, "Bye, now," and I, smiling, had shook my head *no* at it, which Triple-J assumed was a response to what *he'd* said.

"You don't remember?" Trip said.

"No, I do," I said.

"Bye, now," said Magnet.

"Oh, you were—ha! Quiet now, buddy," Triple-J said to Magnet, which sat and hid its face behind its hands.

Triple-J scratched its head.

The cure unhid its face. "It's okay, now," it said.

"That's right," Triple-J told the cure. "It's okay." He turned back to me, shrugging a little, and smiling too, as if to say, "That's Magnet for you!" but he didn't roll his eyes as I might have expected. Despite his "revolutionary innovations" and the lengths to which he'd gone to impress me by describing them, it seemed to me that Triple-J had a heart, one that abided real affection for Magnet.

"So the other night at the playground," he continued. "What happened was Chaz Jr. cut his finger. Like earlier in the day. Can of tuna or something. And his mom, she didn't just put a Band-Aid on his finger, but she made him carry around these extra Band-Aids in case the one he was wearing got dirty or fell off and he had to replace it, or in case he cut himself again because maybe he was having a 'clumsy day,' and also in case 'having a clumsy day' was like *contagious* and his friends cut themselves and needed Band-Aids or something—I don't know, he tried to explain it to make it sound normal, but what it came down to was his mom is really uptight and a little bit nuts, and we were all razzing him about it, all the Band-Aids he had and his uptight mom, and while we were razzing him, I just had this weird, visionary kind of impulse of like, 'Let's use those Band-Aids to Band-Aid a cure to the slide at the playground, throw some rocks at it from a distance, and see if something revolutionary develops—some new kind of Curio interaction that doesn't end in overload, and that we never would have expected to enjoy.' I mean, we'd tried something like that before, a couple nights earlier, with a different cure, but the same slide, and some glue, and it didn't come to anything except a typical painsong-driven group overload. But these Band-Aids, right? For some reason, I thought that if we replaced glue with Band-Aids, it might change the *dynamic* of the whole interaction somehow. Like maybe the cure would be able to free itself, which the glued one just really wasn't able to do, and that would make the whole thing . . . I don't even know, but . . . that's kinda the point. That I didn't know. And, yeah, it's true that that one—the Band-Aid exercise—didn't amount to anything revolutionary, but who knows what would've happened if we hadn't run into you before we'd finished, right? Not that I'm not happy we ran into you. Obviously.

"But whatever. I guess that's not the best example. But Charity Party, though. I mean, take Charity Party, okay? That innovation occurred as a direct result of a Neo-Gratification exercise. We were standing on the bike trail behind the high school, okay? And we'd nailed this single-legger to a tree through the foot—upside down—to find out if it would be able to right itself, and how it would do it, if it did it, like clockwise or counter-, because we thought, you know, 'Maybe finding out if it'll right itself, or finding out which direction it'll go to right itself, if that's what it does—maybe finding that kind of thing out will inspire us,' and it just so happened that that particular cure had a kind of too-catchy painsong, which got our other cures painsinging, which was a potential distraction from being inspired, so we all backed away from the tree to where we couldn't hear it as well, like behind these bushes, til our other cures got quiet, and right about then is when this kid we'd never really talked to before came walking up the path, and he saw the cure, nailed there to the tree, and sort of looked around him, and since we were kinda hidden and the sun was down, the kid didn't see us, and he thought he was alone, and he started trying to free the cure from the tree, like trying to pry out the nail with a pen or a lighter or something, and Lyle, who's right next to me there behind the bushes, he whispers, 'Let's gobsmack this dirty, thieving mud, Triple-J. Let's bust him in the biggity-boogity chops.' And I tell Lyle, 'Hold on,' cause suddenly I'm feeling a little inspired, right? It's often sudden, this feeling. It just comes over me, sometimes, out of the blue. And I'm feeling it, and what I'm thinking is: 'Maybe we're verging on an innovation here.' I don't know why, really, but I just have this strong feeling of like, 'No, let's let this kid be for a minute. Let's not attack him.' Because something's starting to click, you know? So I tell Lyle, 'Hold on,' and the kid by the tree, who's freed the cure by then, now he starts unbuttoning his sleeve to store it in, and that's when: click. The inspired feeling becomes an idea. The idea comes *clear,* and what I do is, I *execute*. I leap out from behind the bushes, and I shout at the kid. I shout, 'Compliments of the Yachts!' which startles him, sure, but then after that, he smiles this smile that, Belt—this was a really great, like ecstatic, blessed-type smile. Spoke volumes. 'This cure is for me?' the smile said. 'This cure is for me, from you guys?' it said. 'Just because I'm here?' it said. 'You're just giving it to me just because I happen to be here?' And me? I was smiling a very similar smile, like, 'Yeah. It's for you, man. We're giving it to you. Like I said: compliments of the Yachts.' We were smiling these smiles, and I knew we'd be friends.

"And I was right. That kid who freed the cure? That kid was Bryce. Fifth member of the Yachts. We inducted him right there on the bike trail. So Charity Party—that's how we came up with it. And it couldn't have happened without the Neo-Gratification exercise of the nail through the foot. It couldn't have happened if we hadn't been curious to find out if and how a cure with its foot nailed to a tree could right itself. Or if we hadn't had the desire to honor that curiosity by acting on it. Not that all, or even most of the Neo-Gratification exercises have proven fruitful, but I think you've got to break a few eggs, right? It's the art of being an artist, I think. The art of being revolutionary. The willingness to break as many eggs as it takes.

"Anyway, that's how I see it. And I think I've been pretty successful so far. I don't know that I've necessarily come up with anything as revolutionary as fisting, but I think that, at the very least, I've come close. And what I've come up with has definitely caught on. Kids are into it. You saw them out there. But still, a couple months ago, I started having this feeling like: it isn't enough. Like: all those kids, they're doing what I do—what the Yachts do—and they're loving it, sure, and spreading it around, teaching others. Charity Party and Flick&Look especially—those are getting really popular. But still, no one except for me and the Yachts is trying to come up with revolutionary thrills and pleasures on their own. And I want them to. That's the next step. When I come up with something that'll inspire *others* to innovate—that's when I'll know I've done something lasting. Something important. And that's why, well—that's why I made *A Fistful,* right? Because what I realized was that after I read that paper about fisting, I wasn't just inspired to innovate interactions with Curios, I was inspired about the thought of inspiring others to innovate interactions with Curios—Fon's making a face. Come on, Fon. Come on. Give me some room. I know you think I sound cheesy, but come on."

Fon horse-laughed briefly and ruffled Trip's hair. "Go ahead," she said.

"Fon thinks I'm about to say some real going-up-my-own-ass-to-ponder-type stuff, but I'm not. I've done so in the past, for sure. But not this time. That's not what I'm doing. So inspiration. Okay? I'm serious here. When I first read the paper on fisting, I thought, 'It's crazy that it took almost the entire history of humanity to come up with fisting,' but it wasn't til I came up with my own revolutionary fisting-like innovations that I considered the inverse of that. Or the converse? No, the . . . inverse. It wasn't til I came up with my own innovations that I thought, 'What's even crazier than how long it took humanity to come up with fisting is that, *after* the entire history of humanity had failed to come up with fisting, some guy—some genius . . . did.'

"*How,* though, right? How?

"And I thought: Maybe he was just bored, and he looked down at his fist one day, and said to himself, 'Where haven't I put this? I want to put this somewhere new, just to see what it's like.' Or maybe it was nothing like that at all. Maybe the genius who came up with fisting wasn't even really the first guy to fist, or even the first guy to *get* fisted, but the first guy to get fisted *and like it,* or the first guy to get fisted and imagine he *could* like it. What I mean is, like, maybe there were guys, all throughout history, or even prehistory—like cavemen, even—who fisted people as a kind of war crime or torture or medical thing, and the twentieth-century revolutionary genius I'm talking about was actually like the millionth guy to be fisted, but the first one to think, 'In a different context, this might actually be pleasant.' And then he tested the hypothesis.

"Or maybe he wasn't the first guy to *think* that—maybe he was the tenth, the hundredth, the thousandth, whatever—maybe he wasn't the first guy to think it, but the first guy who'd thought it who was also able to successfully imagine what the different context might be. And maybe his success had to do with where he came from, or who he was, or both. Like, maybe he was an oil baron or a leader or financial minister of a country that did a lot of whaling or coconut or olive harvesting, and so he was rich in blubber or petroleum or coconut or olive oil, and so he had just barrels and barrels of natural lubricant at his disposal, so many barrels that, I don't know, he couldn't sell them fast enough, so he spent a lot of his time thinking about new applications for all that excess natural lubricant, and almost anything he saw or thought about, he'd go, 'I wonder if natural lubricant might improve this,' so when he had the passing thought about fisting possibly being pleasant in a non-torture, non-war-crime context: eureka.

"Or it even could have been a kind of disability that he had. Or a disease. A disorder. Like, maybe he had this problem where he produced way too much saliva, and he went to sleep one night, thinking about the possibility of fisting being a pleasure, and the very next morning, as he was waking up, the hand he'd been resting his cheek on was glistening wrist-to-fingertips with drool, and maybe, too, this same disorder or disease or whatever caused him to have particularly tiny hands, maybe not. Or maybe he didn't even go to bed thinking about fisting, but he had that extra-saliva disorder, and when he woke up with his hand all covered in drool, his hand was *cold*. It was really, really cold, and he was lonely, people thought he was a freak because of his tiny hands and how he drooled, and he just wanted to put his cold, slick hand somewhere, to heat it up, and to show people that him being a freak was not all bad, could maybe even be useful, thrilling, new and revolutionary . . . I don't know. No one does. And I keep saying *guy*—it could've been a woman. Could've been a little kid. But no one knows and no one's ever gonna know. No one's ever gonna know who came up with fisting, or the story of how they came up with it, I thought, and that was a serious bummer, I thought. For society. I still think that. More than ever.

"Because I thought that if someone could explain the inspiration behind how fisting got invented or discovered or whatever, then other people, when they heard the explanation, would be inspired. They'd be more likely to come up with new, revolutionary fisting-type thrills themselves. Like the way I did.

"And that's what I'm getting at about *A Fistful*. That's why I started *making A Fistful*: to document the inspirations for Ulysses and Flick&Look and Charity Party and the Neo-Gratification exercises and any of my other innovations. Because all the clips in the collage: they were really inspiring to me, you know? See, I've been collecting clips for years. I have *thousands* of clips. Clips of weird and funny and sad and joyful and gross and upsetting moments in Curio history, moments that were important, and moments that were meaningless but should have been important, and moments that seemed important but were actually meaningless, and moments that definitely would have been important if more people knew about them. There's boring ones, too. Hundreds of boring ones. But all of the clips—even the more boring ones—watching them made me even more fascinated by cures than I already was. And the clips in the collage—I don't mean the ones that I'm in, but the rest of them—those clips are the best of the thousands. Those are the ones I've watched the most, or remember most often. You see what I'm saying? They're as responsible for what I've been able to achieve as the paper about Foucault's thing on fisting. Like, learning about Foucault's thing on fisting inspired me to want to revolutionarily innovate in general, but it was these video clips that inspired me to revolutionarily innovate *Curio interactions* specifically.

"And so I started the process of curating the clips, right? of choosing the best ones from among the thousands, and it was while I was doing that that I realized there was another whole level of revolutionary innovation I hadn't even considered.

"Form.

"Like: Here I am, making this video documenting the video clips that originally inspired me to make my revolutionary innovations, and here are also some video clips of those innovations themselves, and the aim of it all is to inspire viewers to come up with their own revolutionary innovations—is there anything else like that? Not quite. Not really. Not that I know of at least. And so therefore the *form* of the video should reflect that, is what I figured. The *form* of the video should be revolutionarily innovative itself. There shouldn't be any, like, voiceover connecting the clips, trying to turn them into some cause-and-effect-type story. They shouldn't be arranged to move forward through a timeline. There shouldn't be any kind of, you know, *explanation* of what I'm trying to achieve with the video, or why I'm trying to achieve it, right? Because when *I* first saw the clips, I wasn't trying to achieve anything other than seeing them—I wasn't trying to connect them. So it should just be the clips. A collage of them. Watching the clips should feel, to the viewer, the way watching them felt to me when I first saw them. Or at least as much as that's possible. That way, the *sum* of the clips—that is, *A Fistful of Fists*—should have the same inspiring effect on viewers as my spending all those years watching clips had on me, but in just a little more than a couple hours, instead of like *years*. Like, they'll be able to think the same thoughts, or the same *class* of thoughts, as I think. About Curios. Viewers will. Just by watching the collage, I'm saying. And they'll be empowered to innovate. Revolutionarily. On their own. That's the idea. Do you not . . . you've been doing that Labrador thing again. Do you see what I mean, or . . . ?"

"I think so," I said. "I think you're saying the collage is autobiographical.

An intellectual history of Jonny 'Triple-J' Pellmore-Jason, Jr., revolutionary innovator of Curio interactions."

"Well, yeah. Autobiographical. Sure. I even thought of calling it an 'Auto-documentary Collage' or like an 'Auto-bio-documentary Collage,' but then I figured that was redundant, since, like, what can any artist make that isn't autobiographical? But, I mean, that's not all it is, either. It's not just autobiography. It's not even mostly . . . I mean, it's more than just about *me*, Belt. It's . . . Oh man, you're still doing the thing with your head. You have no idea what I'm talking about and you're this nice guy and you don't know how to tell me I've totally fucking failed. I'm embarrassing myself in front of my favorite novelist. You're this amazing thinker, and even you don't understand what I'm trying . . . I must sound so pretentious and horrible, yammering on for—God! How long have I been . . . I've made an ass of myself."

"You know, you know, you know," Magnet said, fisting the air. "You know, you know, you know, you know."

Alarmed and a little bit guilty-feeling at how suddenly downcast Triple-J had become, I looked to Fon for a signal, some guidance. She was slouching on her stool, looking down at the counter, in sympathy with one or the other or maybe the both of us.

"You know, you know, you know," Magnet said, and fisted the air. "You know, you know, you know, you know."

"Come on," Trip said. "Come on, dude. Not now. Stop it. Come on."

Magnet ceased repeating the words, but continued to fist the air near Trip's ear.

Trip snatched it off his shoulder and shoved it into his sleeve.

I said, "Trip, I feel really bad about this. I should have said—"

"Please don't," Trip said. "Don't snow me. That'll only make it worse. I failed. I know it. Every artist fails. Over and over. It's part of the process. It's horrible. It's really horrible, you know? But that's just how it is. I got too ambitious. I dreamed too big. I wasted some time. A *lot* of time . . ."

"I didn't watch the whole video," I said.

"Well, you don't have to *rub it in*," he said. "Man, if you hated it *that* much—"

"No," I said. "I'm not. I'm not rubbing anything in. I didn't have any time before brunch to finish it."

He squinted at me. In confusion? With aggression? Aggressive contempt?

Fon was squinting, too. Not with confusion.

Too late to really dodge the blow by then. Who said that meant I just had to take it on the chin, though? What about blocking? What about the counterpunch? I had a pair of arms.

"I *wanted* to finish watching it," I said. "I didn't have time. I was really disappointed I had to stop it so early, and the thing is, everything you were just telling me about, it really makes the video sound like it could be great—I mean, hearing you talk about it really impressed me, and I was so interested in all of what you were saying, I didn't want to stop you. I should have, especially because I know you wanted a cold read. I should've stopped you, but I didn't. I'm sorry about that."

"How far did you get?"

"Not far," I said. "Maybe minute thirty? Before I stuck it in the player, I thought, 'This kid who made it—he's obviously sharp, but he's a teenager. No way he'd have made something *feature*-length.' I figured it would be less than fifteen minutes long—I'd assumed I was giving myself enough time to watch it twice. I underestimated you."

"Huh," Trip said. "Wow. Minute thirty? So you didn't even get to . . . Man, it's like you didn't even watch it."

"That's what I'm trying to say," I said.

"So you liked what you saw? Like, you want to watch the rest?"

Fon had stopped squinting.

"I can't wait to watch the rest," I told Triple-J, and Fon winked and smiled. "It's the first thing I'll do when I get home. And after that, by the way, I'll be more than happy to talk to you about it . . . whenever. Just tell me when you want to meet up again."

"Forget all that noise," Triple-J said. "It's early still. Let's go back to the production house. We'll watch it together."

•

• •

Traversing the crowd still gathered for the games would, Triple-J said, "delay us forever," and so it was determined that we'd go to the production house by way of the ramparts, then enter through the side.

Down the stairwell from the turret to the vestibule we headed, breezing past the elevator, through a steel door, startling a chipmunk, which jumped across the wallwalk, parapet to parapet, mere inches in front of us, and scrambled away.

The sky was too clear, the sun dazzling and mean, and the air wasn't moving, and my hunger was panging. Nor was the scenery especially beautiful (two strip malls, an overpass, the compound's interior, acre after acre of single-family homes, a grade school, a ballfield, a couple of playgrounds, the back of a theater, the side of a McDonald's, the skyscraping arches of a farther McDonald's), but the ramparts were the tallest structure for miles (the farther

McDonald's sign notwithstanding), and I'd never seen this part of the world from so high—my part of the world, the gridded space I daily traipsed (the compound's cul-de-sacs notwithstanding); the angles that, from down on the ground, were insensible—and before we'd traveled much more than a block, I thought, "What's the rush?" and set the box of Crunch down and lit up a Quill, and leaned, two-elbowed, on the eastern parapet.

Trip and Fondajane had already been walking a few steps ahead of me, deciding between themselves what we should eat and where and when we should eat it ("burgers in the brunch style"; production house screening room; as soon as "the Sunday day chef" could manage), and whether Fon should watch *A Fistful of Fists* with us or wait til after Trip had heard my notes and recut it (Fon wanted to see it, but Trip was reluctant to waste her "eyes' freshness" on an undercooked edit; Fon asked if Burroughs had seen the film yet, Trip told her that no one had except for himself; Fon suggested that between the Archons and the rest of the staff, not to mention the other Yachts and Jonboat, Trip wasn't bound to run out of fresh eyes too soon; Trip acknowledged that was so, but told her that her eyes were of a different caliber, a special "extra-smart, critic kind of caliber," and the truth was he'd be nervous to let her see an unpolished *Fistful;* Fon assured him she'd be capable of viewing *A Fistful* as a work in progress, and said that, given the way he'd claimed to feel about her eyes—"Which, thank you, sweetie. It means a lot to hear you say that."—she didn't understand why he wouldn't want notes from her; Trip said that of course he would love to hear her notes, but he hadn't presumed she'd be interested in giving notes; "Presume away!" Fon said, and smacked his arm, "I'm here for you, always," and the matter was settled), and once that had been decided, Fon called our lunch order in to the day chef, and it was during the call that I'd paused on the wallwalk to take in the view.

They must have gone half a block before coming back for me.

"Something wrong?" Fon said.

"Just enjoying the wallwalk."

"You think I could get a smoke?" said Trip.

"Trip," Fon said.

"I've had two this *month*."

"Two?" Fon said.

"Maybe three," Trip said. "Anyway, it's my body, right?"

Fon shrugged, defeated, and I bummed a Quill to each of them.

We leaned on the parapet, Trip to one side of me, Fon to the other. They gave me a visual tour of the compound: down there was the production house, and next to it the cellar house, next to that the drinking house, and over here the Archons house, across from that the picnic house (I didn't get to ask), and there was the trio of houses for guests, there the library house, and there the parlor games house, the nursing house, the office houses, the greenhouse house, the Russian/Turkish bathhouse house, the safe room houses, the undesignated houses, the fallout shelter entrances, the ramp that led down to the underground garage, the portions of the ramparts the resident staff (non-Archon) lived inside and beneath, the rooftop helipad, the roof atop which Burroughs believed should be constructed a backup helipad, the roof that was Burroughs's second choice for the proposed backup helipad, and—we heard a virile purr, and the tour came to an end.

The Boatmobile was prowling north up Jason, less purring than roaring the closer it came, all bludgeony of fender and smirky of grille, its paint job so matte the reflection of the sun along its body was fuzzed, near-particulate—a milk stain on denim. As it turned right on Pellmore, the ramparts started parting, and before they'd appeared to have parted wide enough, the Boatmobile slipped through them, was gone.

My heart had sunk a little.

"What the hell?" Trip said.

Fon said she didn't know.

"He didn't even get to see Belt yet, though."

"He's probably just going for a drive," Fon said. "Someone must have told him we'd be watching your film. I'm sure he'll be back before we get finished—Say, Belt," she said, and patted my hand. "Can you show me where you live?"

I knew that she didn't care where I lived, but I raised the unpatted hand's arm and pointed.

"The blue one?" she said.

I said, "Next to the blue one."

"There's a pickup in the driveway?"

"Yes," I said.

"Ah," she said. "Four bedrooms or three?"

"Just two," I said.

"I wouldn't have guessed," she said. "It looks like three or four to me."

"They're pretty decent-size bedrooms."

"They must be," Fon said.

Then we dragged at our Quills awhile, looking at Wheelatine.

"So Jesus," Triple-J said, breaking the silence. "Jesus, okay? He's up on Golgotha. Nailed to the cross, right? Frying in the sun. Starts going, 'Peter, Peter, my beloved disciple,' and Peter, he's down at the foot of the hill, and he's like, 'Yes, Lord. I'm here. What is it, Lord? What?' and Jesus says, 'Peter, my beloved disciple, come closer. Come here,' and Peter says, 'Yes, of course, Lord, I'm coming,' and he heads for the cross, and one of the centurions, he just *beats Peter's ass,* right? Beats his ass unconscious, throws him back down the hill.

"A couple minutes later, Peter comes to. He's got blood in his eyes, his eyes are like lips, and the lips of his mouth are split in five places. Nasty concussion. Cuts with like dust and sand in them all over his body, but he sits up straight, and then he's standing, and his hearing's coming back, and he hears Jesus going, 'Peter? Peter?' And Peter says, 'Yes, Lord,' he says to Jesus, 'Yes, Lord Jesus, I am here. I've been bruised but not beaten. I'm here for you, Lord.' 'Praise be to my Father, Peter is here for me,' Jesus says. He says, 'Peter, come here. Come, Peter. Come closer.' 'Yes, Lord,' Peter says. 'What is it, Lord?' he says, and he approaches the cross, a little slower than last time, but the same centurion that beat him before beats him again, *really* fucks him up, right? like flattens his nose, knocks out some teeth, breaks one of his knees and, this time, once he rolls him down the hill, he follows him down, kinda kicks him up the road a little, until, for the second time, Peter's unconscious. Borderline coma.

"And so this time he's out for a couple more hours, right? And while he's been out, bandits have come along and taken his stuff, his like sandals and his coin purse and his leather wristbands and what-have-you, and rolled him into a ditch. But then, when he wakes up, and even though he's robbed and isn't able to walk—he can barely even crawl, and *everything* is hurting, when he breathes it's like he's spearing himself, and he's blind in one eye and deaf in one ear, plus like blisters on sunburn on bruises on fractures—still his first thought is, 'Lord Jesus has asked for me,' and he drags himself out of the ditch, up the road, to the foot of the hill, and Jesus goes, 'Peter? Peter? My beloved disciple?' 'Yes, Lord, I've returned.' 'Praise be unto my almighty Father, faithful Peter has returned,' Jesus says. 'Peter,' says Jesus, 'come here. Come closer, Peter.' 'Yes, Lord,' Peter says. 'What is it, Lord?' he says, and he approaches the cross, *really* slowly now, just so exhausted and wrecked and like crawling on his belly, dragging himself inch by inch by inch by inch, just waiting to get beaten again, probably to death, but this time, though: lucky Peter, okay? cause there's a different centurion.

"The centurion from before—his shift just ended. He's off to the tavern or the brothel or whatever, and his replacement's much friendlier. He's a guy called Longinus—same one who's gonna spear Jesus in the side in just a couple more hours, maybe to more mercifully, speedily finish him off, maybe just to make sure he's already really dead, no one's in agreement about that, but he's a good guy, Longinus, a *kind* centurion, and not the type to beat an already beaten man, not some kind of sadist—a saint, in fact. Not yet. But he will be. A saint I mean. Saint Longinus. Anyway, Peter, he approaches the cross, and Longinus . . . lets him.

"And so he's at the foot of the cross, Peter, and he says to Jesus, 'Lord, I'm here,' and Jesus says, 'Peter, good Peter, faithful Peter, raise yourself a little higher, come a little closer,' and Peter, even though the effort and the pain of it seems like it'll kill him, he gets himself up, onto one knee, the unbroken knee, and he's leaning on the cross, and Jesus, he's like, 'Closer, Peter, can you come any closer?' and Peter says, 'Yes, Lord,' and leans harder on the cross, kind of almost sorta climbs it, straightening out the unbroken knee, and he says to Jesus, 'Lord, I am here,' and Jesus says, 'You're here. Peter, you're here. Praise be unto my almighty Father, you're here at last. Now can you see that, Peter? Do you see what I see?'

"'What is it you see, Lord?' Peter says to Jesus.

"'Down there,' Jesus says, 'That's your mom's house, right? I *think* that's your mom's house.'"

•

•   •

Trip's production house had once been his father's leisure house—the only house in the compound that I'd visited before. Back in 1988, I'd helped select the T-shirt's slapped fatman image from eight or nine drawings Jonboat had spread across the carambole table in the first floor's game room. In the second floor's game room, playing foosball and darts, we'd opined about hyphens, commas, and *gaylord,* then gone to the kitchen to get some refreshments to bring to the chill-out room down in the basement, where we talked over color schemes, cotton weight, and fonts while lying on hammocks, sipping Jolt under blacklight.

The house had since been radically remodeled. Walls knocked out. Windows walled over.

The vast majority of the first floor was missing, its remains little more than a U-shaped hallway. In the U's west arm was a long kitchenette and a door that led out to the side of the house (the door through which we'd entered), and the U's east arm contained a half-bathroom, set between a pair of stairway landings. The projection booth for the screening room below occupied the section bridging the arms (the *bottom* of the U? the *shoulders* of the U? I don't know what to call it), as did the house's small front foyer.

The screening room, then—the whole basement was the screening room—was two stories high, except along the edges the first floor ceilinged. Its seating—nine double-wide, reclining chairs arrayed in two rows (four behind five)—was under the projection booth. The slightly curving screen on the opposite wall must have spanned twenty feet, been roughly half as high, and was mounted at least three feet off the floor, yet the sightlines from the chairs were wholly unobstructed. There wasn't a load-bearing pillar in evidence.

That didn't seem possible. I said so to Trip. He said something beyond me, something about "special alloys and joists" which, even given how little I knew about architecture, sounded made-up.

Fon, who'd called to check on our meals' ETA, informed us we'd have to wait another few minutes. Trip didn't want the servers to interrupt our viewing, and Fon suggested that, rather than just sitting around in the basement, he show me his workspace to kill the time until the food arrived.

Trip liked the idea if I liked the idea. Did I like the idea?

I said it sounded good.

I followed him back up the stairs to his workspace. I'd assumed that Fon would come along, too, and she followed us, initially, but then she peeled away to "splash some water on [her] face" in the first-floor bathroom. After that, I guess she just returned to the basement.

The second floor contained a second bathroom—a full one—but other than that it was entirely open, and because it had windows and vaulted ceilings, it felt even larger than the screening room had. In the middle of it stretched a banquet table supporting what Trip called his *editing suite:* two computers in front of a jumbo TV, a multichannel mixing board, analog-to-digital transfer machines, a pair of tiny speakers, a pair of larger speakers, stacks of hard drives, a trio of binders, a zip-tied cable bunch thicker than a firelog. The built-in shelves, which covered two walls, held discs and tapes and reels of film arranged by format and date of acquisition. The binders on the conference table, Trip explained, cataloged the videos, clip by clip. The entries in the blue one were organized by content (e.g. "Laboratory footage," "News footage," "Home Video footage," "Advertisement footage"); the entries in the black one according to date of initial viewing (by Trip), with dates of subsequent viewings also noted; and the entries in the red binder according to the moods the various clips provoked (in Trip). "Eventually, I'm hoping I'll find some patterns," he said, "and be able to kinda map my historical responses to the clips onto my intellectual and emotional development so I can better understand what exactly inspires me and how I could use that to inspire others. Once I'm finished with the red binder—probably sometime next year, I only started it in June—I want to make a fourth binder cross-referencing the first three. That's where I'm thinking I'll find the patterns. It might be the biggest waste of time ever, but I like the process. Remembering the feelings, you know? Feeling the feelings if I rewatch the clips. Seeing how I've grown or matured or— Yes!"

His vitreous pendant had chimed and blinked pinkly, as had my bangle, which also, though I couldn't be sure, had seemed to vibrate. Our meals had arrived.

* * *

On the way down to the basement, I stopped in the first-floor bathroom to piss, and just as I began to relax into the process, I heard a voice saying, "Hey, what's wrong?" and, startled, I flinched, sprayed the rim and the lid. "What is it?" the voice said.

To my bangle, I whispered, "Listen. Please don't. Don't make me ignore you. I can't take you off."

But it wasn't the bangle, or any other inan.

"Belt doesn't like me," a second voice said. It was coming from the vent on the floor beside the toilet. This second voice was Trip's; the first, of course, had been Fon's.

She cleared her throat and said, "I very much doubt that."

"He didn't laugh at the Jesus joke."

"He laughed," Fon said.

"Politely," Trip said. "When Burroughs told it to me and the Yachts the other day, he had us almost crying."

"Well, it's not exactly a new one, you know?"

"You think he heard it before?"

"I know *I* have," she said. "But I liked how you told it. Your timing was great."

"Anyway, it's not just that. I think I bored him upstairs, going on about my binders. Plus I talked for way too long in the turret."

"Well, I wasn't upstairs, but I doubt that you bored him. And in the turret—in the turret, you were very articulate."

"Well, I *thought* I was being articulate. I said everything I planned to say to him today—I did a really serious outline last night—but like he didn't even notice the compliments I gave him. Sometimes he even looked like he was in pain a little. And that Labrador thing . . ."

"You were talking about a video he hadn't seen. He must not have fully understood what you were saying."

"But you haven't seen it, either, Fon—I mean you haven't seen *any* of it, and he saw *some,* and *you* didn't seem confused or anything. So, if you understood, he must have understood. So I don't think the faces were from not understanding."

"I think you're overthinking this, kiddo," Fon said. "And I didn't notice Belt making any faces, but, you know, like you said, you *were* kind of a runaway train in there, so—"

"A loudmouth, you mean. A blowhard."

"No, no. An *orator,* more like. But you were very excited by what you were saying, and when you're very excited about what you're saying—and, you know, you're just like your father when it comes to this—when you're very excited by what you're saying, it's hard for anyone to get a word in edgewise."

"I wasn't letting you guys talk. I'm a dick."

"You weren't a *dick*. I just meant that, as you went on, Belt probably wanted to tell you that he hadn't seen the video yet."

"You know?" Trip said. "I think you're probably right. Yeah. Those faces—those were probably like faces of, 'Hey, I need to tell you something important.' But the important thing—yeah, you're right. The important thing wasn't, 'You sound like a dick,' but more like, 'Hey, Triple-J, I haven't even seen the video yet, and you keep going on about it. You sure you want to do that?' "

"Probably something just like that," Fondajane said.

"Okay. Yeah."

"Feel better?"

"Much."

"Good."

"Man, I'm really hungry. What's he doing in there? You think he's—"

"Trip, please. We're about to eat. I don't want to picture that."

I didn't want her to, either.

"Burgers in the brunch style" turned out to mean three rashers of bacon and an overeasy egg on an unseasoned patty I'd put at six ounces, all sandwiched by lightly griddled slices of sourdough, and served with a side of outerly crispy and inwardly tender cheddar-cheesed hash browns (onion-free), a shot glass of pickled jalapeño relish Trip urged me to liberally apply to the potatoes ("I wouldn't mess with the burger, though," he said. "You want to taste this meat."), a tiny steel cup of sliced red and green grapes, and a cold glass bottle of Coke with a straw.

We sat in the front row's middle three chairs, Fon and I on either side of Trip, eating our meals off sturdy folding trays attached to the arms via in-built swivel mounts. I think the food was probably good, perhaps even great, but Trip had hit Play as soon as I was seated, and—desperate to finish before the Barker clip started—I scarfed it all down without really tasting it.

A couple or three times during the video, I'd think that I'd heard Fon gasping or laughing, maybe even sobbing, but the speakers were blaring, and I couldn't be sure; she might have been coughing, or clearing her throat. I'd try leaning forward to see which it was, but I never found out. Because of the degree to which their chairs were reclined, I wasn't able to see her past Trip.

•

• •

At the end of *A Fistful,* Trip raised the remote, shutting the projector off, bringing the lights up. It happened too fast. I needed a minute. Or five. Or ten.

Trip turned to me, saying, "So what did you—hey. Oh man, are you crying? Fon, Belt's crying."

Fon, getting up from her chair, said my name.

I showed an open palm, then bolted up the stairs, into the bathroom, and chewed a hand towel behind the locked door to muffle whatever might attempt to escape me.

". . . think I upset him," I heard through the vent. "I think I screwed up, Fon."

"Screwed up?" Fon said.

"I didn't mean to surprise him like that. I mean, I hoped to *surprise* him, but in a good way. Like a 'Hey, that's me in this awesome collage' way."

"Why would your being in the collage upset him?"

"Not me. Him. That was Belt in the collage."

"*Who* was Belt?" Fon said.

"In the final clip. The boy the swearing kid said the girl loved—the one he called 'Suspendersed.' The one who threw the punches."

"The one who threw . . . the boy *whose mother was dying*?"

"You don't have to say it like . . . That's not . . . Belt doesn't even think mothers should be trusted. And it's a really major clip," he said. "It's historically important. I mean it might be the most important clip in the whole collage, in a way."

"But how could you think it was a good idea to show it *to Belt*? This was obviously—any reasonable person would know that must have been an awful, *painful* moment in his life. What made you think he'd want to relive it? What made you think you had the right to make him?"

"The right? I'm trying to make *art,* Fon. I'm trying to innovate. I—"

"You didn't ask him if it was okay. You didn't even warn him first. How could you do that?"

"But *my* mother died. Less time ago than Belt's. And I don't think I would necessarily cry because I saw a video of—I've *seen* videos of myself from then. They didn't make me cry. I just thought that Belt—I thought it would be the same for him. Why shouldn't it be? Unless—what? Am I some sort of monster because I don't get upset when I see videos of—"

"You were a *baby* when your mom died. You don't *remember* her. You don't *remember* when she died."

"And that's so much better? It's been so much easier for me?"

"Don't do that. No. Just don't fucking do that. You are not the victim here. You've traumatized someone who . . . Trip, this is someone who suffers from a very serious mental illness, and you know that."

"Does he really, though?" he said. "'Suffer from a very serious mental illness'? I mean, he doesn't seem crazy to me. Does he seem crazy to you?"

"What kind of stupid question is that?"

"What's so stupid about it?"

"You're really disappointing me."

"I'm disappointing *you*? You're the one who's supposed to be on my side, and you're yelling at me."

"You're acting like a three-year-old. A manipulative . . ."

That's as much as I heard before I exited the bathroom, making as great a racket as I could, stomping down the stairs, shoulder-checking walls. We'd all *just* become acquainted, and I hadn't even gotten to see Jonboat yet, let alone catch up with him; if Trip and Fon became too ugly with each other, ugly enough to harm their relationship, I might never be invited to the compound again. They'd associate me with the ugliness, maybe even blame me for it—they might have blamed me already—and maybe they'd be right to. Or not that wrong to: you don't fault a hurt animal for growling at someone, but you don't fault anyone for backing away when he sees a hurt animal, or hears one growling. Not unless the animal's the person's pet. Except even then, though, it's . . . complicated. Was I their pet? Analogously, I mean. Was I Fon's? Triple-J's? Did I *want* to be their pet? I didn't think I should want to. I didn't want to want to—I'd have rather been their friend, and I *was* Fon's friend—the handwich, the handwich—but, then again, a pet, I supposed, was a kind of friend, and to be *a* kind of friend was probably better than being *no* . . . And, no, I hadn't growled—not even, I don't think, analogously—but they'd seen I was hurting. They'd seen I was hurting, and since growling was fearsome because it so often preceded roaring or barking, both of which were warnings or threats that often preceded or accompanied violence—and since hurting so often preceded growling, which itself so often preceded roaring or barking, I—

"Belt," Fon said, grabbing ahold of my hand and patting it. I'd barely taken a step into the screening room when, seeing me, she and Trip had rushed over.

I had to convince them I wasn't hurting, hadn't been hurting, that they'd misunderstood.

"Hey, guys," I said.

"Are you okay?" Fon said.

"Completely," I said. "I'm sorry for making a scene," I said. "I'm a little embarrassed."

"You're not the one who needs to apologize," Fon said.

"I should have warned you that last clip might upset you," said Trip. "I see that now. I don't know what I was thinking. My mom died, too, and I know that it can be . . . rough. Or whatever. Do you want to talk about our moms?"

"No," I said. "I mean we could, if you want to, talk about our moms, but that wasn't even . . . I'm really not upset, guys."

"You were crying," Trip said.

"Not about my mom, though. It was seeing that girl," I said, which—sentence-for-sentence, word-for-word, and even letter-for-letter—was exactly as false as true.

"The girl with the evening gloves?" Triple-J said.

"Lisette," I said. "Yeah."

"So you *weren't* upset," he said. "You were moved."

And there it was. *Moved. Moved* was my out. *"Moved,"* I thought. *"Moved."* Not *upset,* which was a kind of *hurt,* but *moved,* which could appear, to an observer—or two observers—entirely indistinguishable from *upset,* but nonetheless was decisively *not* a kind of hurt, and *was,* even better, one of *inspired*'s most often-used synonyms.

"Yes," I said. "I was really moved."

"Well that's actually—that's so great," Trip said. "You hear that, Fon?" He clapped his hands. "That's so great, Belt. It's great you were crying because of that girl, cause I'll tell you what, man: she made me cry, too. I mean, not fully or whatever, but my eyes definitely stung a little when I first saw the clip, and I for sure had to wipe them. That's why it's the last segment. Cause it's moving. Cause you just can't help but identify with her, right? Emotionally. She's witnessing history, and so are you—the viewer, I mean—but she makes the whole thing bigger than just, you know . . . *history*. Or *news*. She makes it *art,* right? Because you're sitting there, witnessing the first overload ever—which is surprising, sure, because you thought the first overload ever was the kid at the talent show, and it turns out that, no, you've been wrong about that your whole entire life—it was this other kid who no one even knew he existed. I keep saying you, but you probably knew—I mean, you were in the study, you probably heard about it. But me. I. I was wrong about it *my* entire life, I'm saying. Until I saw the clip, I mean. And anyone who hasn't seen the clip, which is pretty much everyone, everywhere, ever—they've been wrong about it for as long as they could have possibly been wrong about it. For years. Like me. It's a really big deal. But even still, it's nothing to cry about. Not in itself. I mean, it's no small thing—it's definitely a major revelation, sure, but only in the way that, like, I don't know, finding out that Roosevelt knew about the Pearl Harbor attack before it happened was a major revelation. Or like the way Jews get when they find out someone blue-eyed and awesome's a Jew. (That came out sounding anti-Semitic. I'm not an anti-Semite. I'm just talking about *some* Jews. Certain Jews. (Like this kid at school, Munroe, who—no, Meyer—no Munroe, yeah, Munroe Wolfsheim, who, he didn't know about Paul Newman til I told him and he got extremely happy. (I really like Munroe, by the way.)))

But what I'm saying's the overload itself isn't anything really special, right? Especially not after you've just watched Timmy and Tommy and that Doc Popsicles guy and all that, but she, though—the girl in the evening gloves, Lisette—she's seeing something literally no one has ever seen or heard of before—well probably some people who worked for Graham&Swords R&D had, but that's it—but so we get to see her seeing it, the girl, is what I'm saying. Seeing the overload. We, for the first time, get to see what it was like for her to see it for the first time, and that extra little bridge between our experience and hers—it just really, like, jacks up *the empathy,* right? And that's what makes it art. It's so human. Like . . . What am I trying to say, Fon?"

"I'm not sure," Fon said.

"Well it didn't make you cry, though, so maybe, you know, put yourself in my shoes—in me and Belt's shoes—and try to think about what might—"

"I think Belt was trying to say he *knew* her, so seeing her—"

"Well but obviously he knew her—they're in the video together. And I'm sure that knowing her made seeing her move him, also. But I think mostly he was moved because of what I just explained. The thing that moved me. I think the same thing moved both of us. This empathy thing I was saying. And empathy—man, that's the big one, empathy. In art, I mean. It's how you know you see the artist's truth through his eyes—by feeling it, right? Empathy I'm saying. If you're gonna inspire with a work of art, that's the first thing you need to make happen: empathy."

He went on for a while, about empathy and art and truth and inspiration, and I nodded indulgently, tuning him out, in part because it seemed like most of what he'd say would be a rehash of thoughts he'd already related to us in the turret, but in larger part because my boxer shorts, like some clammy python, had, earlier—at some point between my bolting from the zero-gravity chair and my return to the screening room—bunched and climbed within my jeans, twisting me up, pinching, abrading, even stinging a little, and, for whatever unliterary psycho- and/or physiological reason, my awareness of my physical discomfort had radically sharpened right around the time Trip had first mentioned empathy, in response to which sharpening I'd since been trying, with increasing focus, to handlessly disentangle myself by way of subtly shifting my weight, and flexing and relaxing lap-zone muscles I wasn't used to deliberately engaging.

Eventually, I got there. Elastic slipped down, cotton crept sideways, and that which had been too high and to the left dropped rightward into its rightful place. Inseams decoupled and pressures relented. Heat abated. Tautened hairs slackened. I might have even moaned, the relief was so thorough.

". . . that it should make people wish they could have been at the viewing to see it," Trip was saying, as I tuned back in, "but not wish it so much that they resent the people who *were* there: it should inspire readers the same way *A Fistful* itself inspires viewers. But the trouble is *my* transcriptions suck. I tried my hand at the first twenty minutes or so, just to see what I could do, and . . . man. No good. At first, I thought the problem was the format, cause I did it like a screenplay, which was dumb to begin with—it's just not as fun to read screenplays as prose, plus I think you lose the sense of there being an author in that format, which is the opposite of what I want, obviously—but then, even after I figured that out and did a second draft in more conventional prose, it still wasn't working. Dead on the page. I couldn't choose the right details to describe, you know? They all seemed important. Or, I don't know: maybe I chose the right details, but described them too extensively. Especially the physical details about the Curios. Like that first *Popsicles* clip? I spent *paragraphs* describing the faces Scatty made. I wanted the reader to be as excited by picturing those faces as I get looking at them. But I guess I must get *too* excited looking at them, because when I read those paragraphs about them a couple days later, I was really . . . bored. And that's just one example. What I'm trying to say is: I was too close to the material. That was the real problem. It's *still* the problem. And I don't see myself getting much distance anytime too soon, so—can you see where I'm going with this?"

He was looking right at me, grinning expectantly.

"Maybe?" I said, trying to mirror the grin, and not seeing at all—neither where he was going, nor from where he was coming.

"You obviously understand *A Fistful of Fists,*" Trip said. "You really get it. I mean, it couldn't have moved you so much if you didn't. But you didn't make it, so you aren't too close to it. And what I'm thinking is: *you,* my favorite writer—*you* should write the catalog copy."

"The catalog copy . . ."

"Or yeah, no—you're probably right. Maybe it's better to just call it a *transcript,* cause it's not like I want to put any stills from the collage in it. And I wouldn't want you to write essays or commentary or anything, just descriptions of the clips. But then that's more, strictly speaking, than *transcription,* though, right? I mean, I don't want it to be all bare-bones. I want that Magnet prose. So maybe *catalog*'s better after all, or just even . . . *book.* It doesn't have to be decided right now. Anyway, whatever we call it, I'd pay you a hundred thousand dollars to write it. Fifty out front, and then another fifty again when you deliver. What do you say?"

I turned to Fon for a reality check. She was smiling and, apparently, she misread my look as a plea. "I think you're putting Belt on the spot," she told Trip.

"I don't mean to do that, Belt. Not at all. Take a couple days to think it over, if you want. A week, even. Maybe not too much more than that, though. I'd really like to get this thing settled. One thing watching the collage with you has shown me is that it's pretty much there. Finished, I mean. I saw a few dull seconds in the Chameleon clip I should probably shave, and I want to noise-reduce the sound on about half the ones I transferred from analog, and *possibly*, I'll swap the positions of the Maya and the Woof ones—I gotta think about that—but it's looking like twenty, thirty more hours of work at most, so I'm thinking I want to host the viewing pretty soon. Not *too* soon, but over spring-break, probably, and the catalog—transcript, whatever—should probably take you six months to finish at most I'm thinking, and then I've got to get however-many hundreds of copies of it printed, which, I don't know how much time that takes, but probably at least a couple weeks, I'm guessing, so if I have to find someone else to write it, then . . . Anyway, I really hope you'll say yes, but no rush, okay? Take your time."

I took my time, which was not a lot of time. One hundred thousand dollars—what was there to think about? True, I didn't quite understand what I was being asked to write, or why, but I understood enough to know it wasn't criminal or life-endangering, plus I was pretty sure that both the *what* and the *why* had been explained to me while I'd been attending to my balls, and that to indicate that—i.e. that I'd been attending to my balls instead of to the boy who'd just offered me a hundred thousand dollars, or that I'd been attending to *anything*, really, other than the boy who'd just offered me a hundred thousand dollars—would not be advisable.

One hundred thousand dollars.

The most I'd ever had was twenty-two hundred. (And that had owed to an error, plus the money had only kind-of been mine: a couple years earlier, the Social Security Administration had mistakenly mailed my father two biweekly SSDI checks for me in one biweekly period; the following period, having realized their mistake, they'd sent a notice explaining the mistake, along with a check for $0.00, which, for a while, Clyde had made a number of scenes trying "to cash" at various banks and currency exchanges. He'd had a lot of fun with that.) And sure as I was that, were Clyde in the screening room, he'd try to negotiate with Trip for more money, I was equally sure he'd be as thrilled as I to learn that anyone—didn't matter who—wanted to pay me a hundred thousand dollars for my writing.

Even if I were in a position to negotiate, I didn't know how to. I'm not sure my father would have, either. How much more, for example, should I have asked for? A hundred thousand more? Fifty thousand more? Would Trip have offered me only half of what he thought I'd be willing to take? two-thirds? half or two-thirds of what he'd be willing to pay? I doubted that. To ask for 50 percent (or, for that matter, more) above the offer would, it seemed, be impertinent of me; but then, at the same time, it seemed that to to ask for any less than that would be petty. I don't quite know why. Perhaps I should have thought about it more: that the offer had even been made at all suggested that just about anything was possible. Then again, if anything were possible, Trip changing his mind in the face of my perceived impertinence or pettiness—*or* my hesitation, despite what he'd just said—and lowering or rescinding the offer was possible, right? The truth is that the difference between two hundred thousand and one hundred thousand dollars (no more or less so than that between one hundred fifty thousand and one hundred thousand dollars) was all but entirely academic to me, something like trying to imagine how much drunker I'd get off two liters of vodka than I would off one, whereas the difference between one hundred thousand dollars and what little I had in the bank (in my father's account) was . . . not academic.

I stuck out my hand and let the kid shake it.

•

• •

In the wake of our handshake, Triple-J squeezed his pendant, summoning Burroughs, who met us upstairs, in the second-floor workspace, to draw up our contract. Grand though it was, Trip's plan for *A Fistful,* which I came to understand just a few minutes later by listening to him describe it to the driver, turned out to be straightforward enough that he certainly could have—and probably had—explained the whole thing while I'd handlessly wrangled around in my boxers:

<u>Part A</u>

1) Register the transcript of *A Fistful of Fists* (written by me, Belt Magnet) under the same limited copyright he'd used for "Living Isn't Functioning" and "On 'Private Viewing.' "
2) Have printed a TBD number (≥ 500) of hardcover copies of the *Fistful of Fists* transcript ASAP.
3) Screen the final cut of *A Fistful of Fists* one night in April 2014 (exact date TBD) at a TBD art museum or gallery space for an audience consisting exclusively of ≤ 250 special invitees—half of them critics, artists, academics, Yachts, filmmakers, journalists, and clients of Ronson Boyle; the other half adolescents Trip adjudged "influential"—and don't charge admission.

4) At the screening, distribute free copies of the transcript to all those in attendance.
5) In the weeks following the screening, distribute remaining copies of the transcript for free to whoever asks for them.

Part B

6) Refuse to screen *A Fistful of Fists* again.
7) Refuse to make any copies of *A Fistful of Fists*.
8) Never sell the original of *A Fistful of Fists*.

The execution of this plan's Part A would, Trip believed, create an increasingly loudening buzz around *A Fistful of Fists*. By the end of May 2014 ("at latest," he said), people would be clamoring for another screening. Galleries and/or film distributors would approach Trip in hopes of brokering the sale of the original and/or distributing copies of it to theaters and/or for home video release.

Trip would turn them down (i.e. he'd execute Part B).

He would make it known that he had no intention of ever letting anyone see *A Fistful* again, let alone of selling it, or licensing the rights to it. He'd explain he had no interest in making money, and, further, that in making *A Fistful,* he had made a work of art that—for mysterious reasons he'd refuse to ever clarify to his interlocutors—would be lessened were it ever to be seen again. The April screening would thus become legendary: you wouldn't just have had to have been there to "really understand" the collage, you'd have had to have been there to even see the collage. "Same as with the swingset murders," he said.

And yet, "totally the opposite of the swingset murders," the "inspiration" Trip hoped to effect in viewers of the collage would still be approximately, if not entirely effected by other means: readers of the transcript (assuming I, Belt Magnet, "got the writing right," which was something Trip was counting on) would be inspired. Furthermore, he'd advise people—particularly those gallerists and film distributors who approached him—that while, yes, he would sue them into bankruptcy were they to *excerpt* the transcript, the limited copyright that he held on it permitted anyone who wished to do so to print it verbatim and in full as many times as they wanted, and distribute it at whatever profit they could manage without ever having to pay him (or me) a single red cent.

And they would. Or someone else would. The public's demand for transcripts/catalogs would be too high not to.

As the months marched on, and the dissemination of the transcript broadened, and the inspiration to revolutionarily innovate spread, so would spread and broaden the desire to see the collage itself, and the value of the one and only copy of the collage would thereby skyrocket toward pricelessness. Yet Trip would stick to his guns: he'd never screen it again, make copies, or sell it. (Or maybe, if he sensed the furor surrounding *A Fistful* were plateauing too early, he'd "let [him]self be pressured" into hosting another screening to re-up said furor, but, as he had with the first screening, he would host that second screening at no financial cost to anyone but himself.)

By these means, *A Fistful of Fists* would come to be recognized as an entirely pure work of art; one more pure than even a cave painting, for no prehistoric wall-squiggler could have ever conceived of an opportunity to sell his work for the sort of gain (in inflation-adjusted meat? flint? furs? sex?) that Triple-J would repeatedly be offered for *A Fistful,* much less could such a man have conceived of turning down such a gain, as Triple-J repeatedly would. And down the line, as Triple-J continued making art that inspired revolutionary innovation—although he wouldn't, perhaps, go to such great lengths (or even any lengths at all) to exclude the general public's access to that art—he would never sell it, nor himself; he would never *monetize* his own name.

So, in the end—well before the end, actually, if it all worked out the way he hoped—Triple-J would be hailed as a maker of important art. He would, i.e., be an important artist, which would, in turn, ensure that *A Fistful,* and its power to inspire via the transcription, would stand the test of time.

That was the plan, at least. And while it would have been easy to dismiss this plan—regardless of whether or not I thought it could produce the results that Trip was counting on—as but an obscenely expensive vanity project gone wild, I thought that would have been lazy of me. Cynical, too.

Maybe my role in the plan—maybe even just my being asked to play a role—has compromised my ability to imagine that Trip was only some rich kid who sought to purchase entrée into the art world by way of a nefarious scarcity strategy, but I do think he was more than that. Despite the way he'd blathered on about inspiration, revolution, and innovation all afternoon, I think he possessed a far greater self-awareness than most, and I'm certain he was self-aware enough to realize that, owing to the fortune into which he'd been born, his legitimacy as an artist would always be in question; whatever success he would wind up attaining, he would always be suspected, if not outrightly accused, of having attained it not by virtue of the merits of his work, but rather by having exploited his parents' wealth and connections—by having exploited his privilege. (Oh, poor, little rich boy—I know, I know, but that immediate reaction: that's exactly what I mean.) And *because* of the way he'd blathered on all afternoon about inspiration, revolution, and innovation,

I'm equally certain that his belief in the merits of his work—in *A Fistful of Fists*—was entirely genuine.

So now imagine you're him: Jonny "Triple-J" Pellmore-Jason, Jr. You've made something that you're certain is good, something you think everyone should get to experience, but, by dint of your parentage, you know you can't possibly get the credit you're due for having made that something, and because that something is *art,* your not getting the credit you're due for having made it will actually lessen the power of the something itself. This leaves you with four options.

The first is that you preserve the something: you never let the something out into the world. Given that you think the something is great, though, keeping the something to yourself is selfish.

The second is that you just put the something out there, allow people to do you the favors they want to do for you because of who you are, and the something thusly suffers for your being who you are; you get in the way of its having all the power you believe it should have; you fail to protect it.

The third option is to cover up who you are: you put the something out there under a pseudonym, never take credit for it, and hope for the best, but, knowing that the art world (the anything world) is no meritocracy, you know that exercising this third option means risking that your something never gets the attention it deserves, which is a betrayal of the something, a dereliction of your duty as an artist to the something (and, furthermore, if the something, despite pseudonymous dissemination, *does* begin to get some attention, and you get found out as having been its creator—which isn't unlikely, the truth will out, etc.—all the disadvantages of the second option accrue anyway).

The fourth option, i.e. the option Trip would exercise, is that you put the something out there, take what you've got—your wealth, your connections, and your privilege—and rather than passively accept the rewards to which what you've got gives rise (as with the second option), you actively, openly, *forthrightly* exploit it in a way that will ensure those rewards (you pay for catalogs, a screening, an ideal audience), and then you refuse to reap any financial benefits: a refusal that, by dint of your parentage, isn't remotely as great a sacrifice for you as it would be for nearly anyone else, and, *for that very reason,* a refusal that only you—or some other artist of comparable background (which, how many of those are there?)—could ever reasonably make, and, more to the point: a refusal that no one else like you *has* ever made, reasonably or not.

So to execute this plan of his, I'm saying, yes, was a way for Trip to walk a path of artistic authenticity and integrity, and perhaps the only way he, as a twenty-first-century US billionaire artist, *could* walk such a path. His plan was to live the elusive, true, and nearly-always-paradoxical American dream: he would transcend his origins by means of embracing them.

Or maybe not. Maybe I was making a mountain of a molehill. An opera of a jingle. A poem of a slogan.

Maybe Trip was less an artist than a salesman.

But what would that have made me?

Turned out it didn't matter. Not when the cost of never having to wonder was a hundred thousand dollars.

•

• •

Our contract contained only seven clauses:

> Belt Magnet [hereafter "the Author"] agrees to deliver a faithfully rendered TRANSCRIPT of *A Fistful of Fists: A Documentary Collage* [hereafter "the Work"] to Jonny "Triple-J" Pellmore-Jason, Jr. [hereafter "the Collagist"] no later than March 1, 2014, in exchange for a sum of $100,000, half of which will be paid to the author upon signing this contract, half of which will be paid upon delivery of the transcript.
>
> The Author grants the Collagist the perpetual right to reproduce and disseminate the Work.
>
> The Author grants the Collagist the perpetual and exclusive right to license the reproduction and dissemination of the Work to third parties.
>
> The Author agrees that he will seek no further compensation for the Work from the Collagist, nor from any third party to whom the Collagist grants license to reproduce and/or disseminate the Work.
>
> The Author retains the right to distribute, display, sell, and recite verbatim copies of the Work in its entirety, without receiving prior permission from the Collagist.
>
> The Author forgoes the right to distribute, display, sell, or recite from the Work in part, unless granted prior permission by the Collagist.

> In the event that legal action pertaining to the Work be taken against the Author by any third party, including but not limited to participants in and creators of any of the segments in *A Fistful of Fists: A Documentary Collage,* the full cost of the Author's legal defense and any and all resultant fees and penalties will be provided by the Collagist.

Burroughs printed two copies. He glanced at them briefly, folded them in three, then stuck them in his jacket and took out his phone.

"We're not signing them?" Trip asked, as Burroughs placed a call.

"Your father likes his contracts notarized," said Burroughs.

"Why does that matter?"

"Notarization?"

"What my father likes."

"Let Burroughs do his job, Triple-J," Fon said.

"Mr. Baker," Burroughs said into the phone. "Burroughs Archon here. Could you hold a minute? . . . Thanks." He lowered the phone. To Trip, he said, "What was that?"

"I said, 'Why does it matter what my father likes?' " Trip said. "It's not his contract."

"You're a minor," said Burroughs. "Your father needs to countersign, or Belt's unprotected."

"Did I miss something?" Trip said. "You *Belt's* driver, now?"

"Belt feels unprotected, the work could suffer."

"I know. I'm kidding. You know I'm kidding, right, Belt? I definitely want you to feel totally protected. Still, I want this to happen today, okay, Burroughs? I want this in motion. So does Belt. He wants to get paid."

"Working on it," Burroughs said, and then, into the phone: "Mr. Baker, thanks for holding. My apologies for having to bother you on a Sunday, but we need a notary public at the compound ASAP . . . Frankly, I find that question surprising. Perhaps I failed to make myself clear. This is Burroughs Archon, calling on behalf of Mr. Pellmore-Jason, who would like you to send a notary to the compound ASAP . . . Now you've asked the same surprising question twice, so how about I give you two answers? Answer the first: you're who we've called. Answer the second: no, we did not try the mobile notary service before we called you, and we're well aware they're available twenty-four/seven, but here at the Pellmore-Jason compound, what we're betting on is that your ASAP will be a lot ASAP-ier than would be that of the mobile notary service, which, after all, has no real stake in maintaining our cliency, let alone an eight-figure stake in maintaining our cliency . . . And we're pleased that you're pleased to help us, Mr. Baker . . . Yes, that would be great. And you can assure them that, it being a Sunday, there'll be a generous gratuity—the sooner they get here, the bigger . . . Bye, now."

"Burroughs," Trip said. "You're such a bully."

"Your bully, young man. Yours, too, Ms. Henry."

"True enough," Fon said. "But I think you enjoyed that."

"What can I say?" he said. "These jerkwater bankers . . . They act like they never learned the words 'How high?' Like doing their jobs is some favor to the world."

"It *is* a Sunday," Triple-J said.

"Interest doesn't accrue on Sundays?"

"Touché," Trip said.

Burroughs touched his own ear, then, into his collar, he said, "I'll let him know. Thank you." To Trip, he said, "Some kid just nearly tied you at Ulysses. He's in line to go again three rounds from now. I guess you want to see that."

"Of course I do," Trip said.

"Alright," Burroughs said. "There should probably be time before the notary gets here, but come and find us as soon as it's over. Don't keep your father waiting. Office House One."

"You want to come with me, Belt?" Triple-J asked.

I tried to say something tentative, something along the lines of "I guess I could do that," but I hadn't spoken in such a long while—at first, I'd stayed very deliberately silent owing to the fear that if I said the wrong thing I might lose the $100k, and then, just as that fear had started abating, I'd been rendered speechless by the dawning realization that Jonboat, who I'd believed had fled the compound in order to avoid me, was not only back, but would, momentarily, grant me an audience—I hadn't spoken in such a long while a clot of binding mucus had developed on my vocal cords, and although I, in response to Trip's question, attempted to say, "I guess I could do that," or, "That might be nice," or something else along those lines, all I produced was a wet, gaspy crackling, like zaps of static, or the snapping of paling, overchewed bubblegum.

I cleared my throat explosively, rued my lack of handkerchief, swallowed and swallowed.

"Belt's gonna come with us," Fon said.

Triple-J saluted, said, "Crunch-a-tize me, Cap'n," and made his exit.

And then, just like that, like it was all of a piece (and, on reflection—perhaps *owing* to reflection—I suppose it was), I followed Fon and Burroughs to Office House One, which, despite what it sounded like, was neither a house composed mostly of offices, nor an office the size of a house, but a standard three-bed/two-bath raised ranch thats lower-level den had been turned into an office, i.e. Jonboat's office, where Jonboat received us.

JONBOAT SPEAKS

A COUPLE OR MAYBE three years earlier, I'd plucked an issue of a men's glossy monthly off the rack at White Hen because Jonboat—gracing the cover in a tux, one of his legs encased to the knee in the bottom of a space suit otherwise crumpled on the floor behind him—was the subject of its featured in-depth profile, "Jonboat on Mars, Jonboat on Venus." Unable as I was to find the table of contents amidst all the ads for cars and watches, I began fanning pages, and I probably would have, from mounting impatience, soon given up searching for the profile anyway, but, as it happened, what arrested my efforts was my coming across a photo of a chef, the mononymous Clem, who was stirring a pot in the kitchen of Heather, his most recently opened and celebrated restaurant. Though I was not a fine diner, nor a fine-dining aspirant, nor had I, before then, heard of Heather or Clem, this photo managed to intrigue me at a glance.

Clem was eggplant-shaped with limbs like noodles, a waxy brow and Fields-grade gin blossoms, balding unevenly, sloped of shoulder, pocked of cheek, all but chinless, and pouchily jowled, yet he emanated mastery, quiet virility, something almost leaderlike. Furthermore, a patently bicepsy line cook—a teeth-flashing, pompadoured, cleft-chinned stud—was chopping some carrots in the lower-right corner, and, despite his badboy-Ken-doll hunkiness, and despite his uniform's matching Clem's, he appeared to be somehow clumsy in contrast, somehow *unfit.*

I couldn't make sense of it—not at first.

The shot, it seemed, was candid, authentic. Had its candidness been staged, I doubt the chef would have (or for that matter could have) produced so convincingly camera-unconscious a slackjawed and wet-lipped facial expression; had the photo been touched up later in the lab, the up-toucher would have—or so one would think—whitened, or at the very least *lightened,* the yellowy pit-stain-like shadows (and maybe they *were* pit stains) in the creases of Clem's ratty chef's jacket's underarms. Or blurred out his acne scars. Or blunted the oily shine of his forehead.

Perhaps, I thought, Clem subtly resembled—in bearing, if not also in bone structure—somebody world-historically important, and exuded, by way of that subtle resemblance, some of that person's world-historical charisma. Who could it have been, though? Mahatma Gandhi? Not Mahatma Gandhi. Joseph Stalin? Not him either. Nor Margaret Thatcher, nor Muhammad Ali. Hitler/Kevin Spacey? Not remotely. Maybe . . . maybe Ringo Starr/Yasser Arafat a little, but . . .

It turned out I was wrong. Or partially wrong. Not wrong about his slight resemblance to Ringo/Arafat—that was definitely there—but about that resemblance being the source of the impression he gave of mastery, etc. According to the article on the facing page, which I read about half of (I would have read the whole thing, but Pang, before I could get beyond half, had asked me whether I thought his name was Marian, and when I told him that, no, I thought his name was Pang, he asked me why I, who had just admitted to knowing his name wasn't Marian but Pang, was behaving as though he were a librarian, a librarian called Marian whose place of business was not a convenience store but a public library, a question to which the only simultaneously civil and face-saving response was, I knew, to purchase the monthly, but since that was a purchase I couldn't afford without forgoing the Quills I'd come for, I, losing face (however civilly), reracked it instead, and never dared attempt to read the article thereafter), Clem—who, for years, had refused the courtship of numerous investors, and was "nearly as famous for his foulmouthed, misanthropic totalitarianism as he [was] for his maverick approach to gastronomy"—had agreed to take on partners when opening Heather only on condition that those partners build him a kitchen "bespoke top to bottom," i.e. the kitchen depicted in the photo.

The partners sent him to Cologne to have him measured for an oven, sent him to Bern to have him measured for a range. His pots and pans were designed in consultation with experts in both Toulouse and Malmö, and his knives with masters in Kyoto and Sapporo, who filmed him chopping and slicing and carving, made molds of his grips, and cast the molds into hilts. For his prep tables, fridge, and garnishing tools, he was sent to other cities in Europe and Asia, though to name them would be disingenuous of me. Truth be told, I'm not even sure about a couple of the cities I've named already (Clem might have gone to Gothenburg rather than Malmö, Yokohama rather than Sapporo)—still, you get the idea.

The slob in the photo came off like a king because every last detail contained in its frame—rakish line cook excepted—had been custom-designed to accommodate all his particular habits of movement, to fit and thus flatter his slobbish proportions.

According to the article, the price of the kitchen—disinclusive of travel expenses—was $2.3 million. The oven alone had cost half a million.

And what did the half-mil oven look like? It looked like an oven in the kitchen of a restaurant, any oven in the kitchen of any restaurant. I imagine it would have looked the same to you, reader. And the butcher's block and the overhead fan and the spoon Clem was stirring the pot on the range with . . . each of them equally, entirely unspectacular.

All of this to say that, apart from the scraped-up astronaut helmet, which, perched on the corner of his polished marble table desk, possessed (yes, even as I lacked the benefit of hindsight) all the doomy salience of that rifle on the wall in Peckinpah's *The Seagull,* Jonboat's office in Office House One—with its wide-screen computer, ergonomic swivel chair, wood-tone floor globe, and overhead bookshelves—could have been, as far as I could see, the suburban home office of just about any well-to-do professional, but given how formidable Jonboat appeared in it, I would not have been surprised to learn its decor had been as fine-tuned to suit his anatomy as Heather's kitchen had been to suit Clem's.

Then again, when hadn't he appeared formidable? To me, just once: earlier that day, during the handwich, in the eye of my mind, when Fon was describing the argument they'd had upon his return from the Adirondacks, the argument they'd had about *No Please Don't.* Only that once had Jonboat, to me, appeared less than formidable—and that word, *appeared,* is of course a stretch, the subformidable Jonboat (his hands aflap, fingers trembling; his mouth agape, its lips too wet; his six-seven frame demilitarized, as curved and accursed as the neck of a vulture) being someone I pictured while I listened to a story—and yet this appearance, imagined though it was, had, apparently, been vivid enough or recent enough or disappointing enough to leave a mark; to mislead me to expect, without my realizing, that the next time I saw him, he'd be a lesser Jonboat than the Jonboat I'd known.

But lesser he wasn't. And he didn't look lesser. He looked like Jonboat, appeared as he always had. You've seen him before, reader, hundreds of times, perhaps thousands of times, and that's exactly how he looked: better than he should have even given who he was, i.e. better than he should have even given he was someone one expects to look better than he should even given who he is. He looked like himself.

Enough abstraction. I'm tired of abstraction. Or tired of something. Or maybe just tired. But enough abstraction.

•

• •

We found him towering over the floor globe, atop which a Curio with herringbone-patterned, blond-silver velvet treadmilled quadrupedally along the prime meridian. He wore leather boat shoes, flower-print board shorts, and an untucked, sand-colored, linen sport shirt, its cuffs rolled loosely above his elbows, its wrinkly placket spread open from the button two below his ample and golden suprasternal notch. His nose was sunburned, peeling a little.

Saying, "Hey, *you*," he spread his arms wide, inviting a hug that I set the Crunch down beside the helmet to deliver before I came to realize he sought from his wife, who, embracing his ribs, rose on her tiptoes and slid up his torso, then kissed him on the neck while he, around and over her, gave me the shoulder-clap/handshake treatment. It didn't at all feel as awkward as it sounds. The handshake was committed, the shoulder-clap squeezy, and the woman between us in zero danger of being ruffled, much less crushed—Jonboat's was a power forward–grade wingspan.

Releasing his grip, he said, "I heard that you're going into business with my son."

"Well, indeed I am!" I yelped very lamely and way too loudly, no little bit thrown by what seemed to me an abrupt skipping-over of even the most perfunctory reunion sounds (perhaps a "Been too long" would have been too much to hope for, but a "Been *so* long?"—what would that have cost him?), and no less thrown by Jonboat's phrasing: not so much the *going into business* part, which did come out sounding somewhat condescending, but more the *I heard* part. How had he heard? When had he heard? Who had told him? Had he, through some invisible receiver in his ear, been listening in on Burroughs's invisible collar mike? On Trip's or Fon's invisible collar mike? *Were* they all miked? All of them receivered? Had he heard me talking to his wife in the turret? Was there a mike *in my bangle*? Had he heard me address my bangle while pissing? Had Burroughs? The others?

None of that seemed likely. I'm not saying it did. It seemed too sci-fi. (Probably all that happened was Triple-J had called him, cellphone-to-cellphone, or cellphone-to-landline, to tell him the news while the rest of us were on our way to his office—a conclusion I reached only milliseconds after having concocted my paranoid mike-and-receiver fantasies (which concocting had, itself, taken mere milliseconds).) I'm just trying to provide, here—struggling to provide, here—an honest account (to myself, good reader, as well as to you) of what it was that may have driven me to yelp, "Well, indeed I am!" in response to Jonboat's "I heard that you're going into business with my son," or to *yelp,* for that matter, anything at all.

I'd like to think my yelping out of character, I guess.

Whyever I'd yelped, I did, at the time, feel that my yelping had been beneath me, was instantly ashamed for having yelped, and more ashamed yet to witness the effects my yelp had on the others, who suddenly saw me as a threat or a sad sack—it wasn't clear which, and perhaps it was both—and, in any case, had plainly been made uneasy: Jonboat set his hand on my shoulder again, to comfort me or keep me from getting any closer; Burroughs stepped toward us, a hand in his jacket; and Fon, if not in response to having been startled, then in order to signal to everyone present that my yelp, rather than the tension-making gaffe it may have seemed to some of us, had been a deliberately inappropriate social gambit intended by me to be tension-*breaking*—a risky kind of joke or gag I'd pulled that she was proud, even thrilled, to be the first to appreciate—Fon let loose her signature horse-laugh.

The laugh wasn't as infectious as it had been earlier. My accompanying chortles were a little bit forced, a beat or two delayed. Still, it worked its magic, or some of its magic—enough of its magic—and for that I was grateful. The careful mood lifted a number of inches: Jonboat set his other hand atop my other shoulder; Burroughs's jacketed hand came out empty; Fon caught her breath, and said, "Oh, Belt, what a riot you are. Isn't he, Jonboat?" and Jonboat, squinting, said, "Always was. Hasn't changed a bit. How about we have us a look at that contract."

"Sounds good," I said, though he wasn't really asking.

"As the kids say," Fon said, glancing at her watch, " 'Now we've come to the part where I make my exit.' "

Turning toward his wife, Jonboat let go my shoulders to put up his fists and bob and weave. "So it's the kids who say that, huh?" he said.

"I think so," Fon said, slapping at his wrists, blushing neck-to-forehead, averting her eyes.

"Is it really what they say?" he said. He pantomimed an uppercut. "Come on. Is it *really*?"

She stamped her foot, flashed a mock scowl. "They say it on TV," she said. "They say it on sitcoms."

"On sitcoms?" said Jonboat. Jab. Jab-jab.

"Dramedies, too," she said.

"Oh [right hook], *dramedies* [left]," he said. "I thought what they said was, 'I guess that's my cue.' "

"*I guess that's my cue!* That's two eras back," she said. "They gave that up for their name and *out*. Like 'Fondajane: out.' "

"Never heard of it," said Jonboat, blocking phantom wallops. "Jonboat: incredulous."

"Anyway, the latest's 'Now we've come to the part where I make my exit,' and the next one, if the pattern holds—"

"What pattern?" said Jonboat, stilling himself.

"*The* pattern. You know. The pattern of reversal. Long becomes short or short becomes long, formal informal or informal formal, the one constant being you make a knowing nod to stage direction, to playing a role that demands your departure. The next one, I'm betting, will be 'Exit Speaker.' "

"Why 'speaker'?"

"Not the word *speaker*. The speaker's name. As in, 'Exit Fondajane.' They're probably saying that already. TV can't keep up with the kids."

"But the kids are so dumb," he said.

"The kids aren't dumb."

"The kids are dumb as ever."

"Trip isn't dumb."

"But Trip doesn't count. He's never really been a kid. Besides, he says, 'Goodbye.' Or 'Seeya later.' 'Seeya soon.' I don't know."

"He told me, 'Crunch-a-tize me, Cap'n,' and saluted me," I said, but only Burroughs responded: he patted my arm. I didn't know what the pat meant. *Let them flirt on their own? Let them argue on their own? Whatever we decide to call what they're doing is—if not in content, then in form, in rhythm—a kind of long-practiced repertoire, so don't interfere? You, like me, are irrelevant here? I, like you, and the rest of the world, am half in love with her as well, but he's her only husband, and you'll just have to live with that?* I sat in the guest chair in front of the desk.

Fon lifted Jonboat's hand and kissed it.

"You really have to go?" he said.

"I have a call to make to Brussels. It's late over there."

"You coming to Riyadh?"

"When?"

"Wheels up at eight."

"Maybe," Fon said. "Could we stop in Abu Dhabi on the way?"

"It's not on the way."

"You know what I meant."

"I have to meet Robbie bin Laden for dinner, so."

"How about after? On the *out-of-the-way* back."

"Maybe," said Jonboat. "Depends what Robbie says. I might have bad news to convey to Uncle Haj, and that would have to be in person, and we'd have to stay the night, or else Haj'll feel all—you know how he gets. And I have to be Stateside, rested, by noon on Wednesday."

"I'm pretty tired of Dubai," Fon said.

"I know. Me too. But I might have *good* news for Haj from Robbie, in which case we *could* go to Abu Dhabi, which rhymes so nicely I can't imagine how you could possibly refuse."

"I'll let you know by seven," she said. She lifted his hand and let it drop, then pivoted, and, before I thought to stand, she bent at the waist, took hold of my jaw, said, "What's up with the look? You're weirding me out, dude," and kissed my forehead, and bit her bottom lip, and squinted and side-eyed and pout-smiled and left.

On to business.

Jonboat read one of the copies of the contract, pen in hand, while Burroughs stood beside him, duly diligent, reading the other, and I, across the desk—still the only one sitting—occupied myself with silent admiration for the blond-silver cure, which had yet to stop running in place atop the globe. I admired the fineness of its herringbone pattern (the lines as thin as fingerprint ridges, as tidy as stripes on a football pitch), and I admired, as well, its fixity of pace (how it hurtled the bracket that encompassed the equator every three gallops—twice per revolution—without need of adjusting the length of its stride), but more than anything else, I admired its irises. They were centrally *and* completely heterochromatic—the right a grayly banded green; the left a greenly banded gray—a phenomenon (or pair of co-occurring phenomena) I hadn't previously known to be possible, much less ever witnessed before.

Predictably, the longer I stared at the cure, the greater my desire to hold it became. Less predictable than that—at least to me—was how rapidly my desire to hold it became a yearning to squeeze it, gently, which then became an impulse, or a series of impulses, increasingly impelling and increasingly graphic, to slap it off its feet, off the top of the globe, see it slide down the wall, and then pick it up *and then* gently squeeze it, then coo to it a little, then not-so-gently squeeze it until the middle of my palm sensed the give of its ribs, and my middle phalanges the bowing of its spine, and I'd loosen the squeeze to encircle its neck within an okay-ing thumb-and-forefinger ring, and bend my arm to bring its head to my lips and insert it partway into my mouth—to the middle of its face—and turn it on its side so the muscles of its jaws came flush with my top- and bottom-right eye-teeth, and then, at last—slowly—I'd close my own jaw, gradually impaling its squeaking skull from above and below while savoring the feeling of its dying painsong quivering my uvula.

"Looks like someone," Jonboat said, "caught himself an eyeful of Handsome Arthur Twelve," and Burroughs stepped sideways, obstructing my view of—and path to—the Curio, breaking the trance. I wasn't entirely ungrateful to him. I didn't think I'd been in danger of going into overload: despite their specificity and clarity, the urges I've described above weren't quite as strong as the ones I'd felt—and subsequently overcome—toward the cure on the slide a couple nights earlier. But, then again, although I hadn't gotten up (I'd have had to walk a step or two to close the gap between my chair and the globe), I *had* begun to lean at pronounced enough an angle for Jonboat to have noticed, and who knew of what adrenalized, superhuman lunging I may have been capable had the cure, for some reason (a fall to the floor, a bracket-stubbed toe, or even just general overexertion), begun to painsing?

I straightened my posture, said, "How *old* is that thing?"

"You'll never believe it," Jonboat said.

"Ten?" I said.

"No," said Jonboat.

"Eleven? Twelve?"

"It's one," said Jonboat.

"Come on," I said.

"Tell him," said Jonboat.

"One," said Burroughs. "Is it *even* one?"

"Turned one last week."

I said, "What kind of formula you—"

"No. None. Well, it's on some Spazola right now—that's how it's able to keep on running—but nothing that affects its appearance in the least. It's just a really special cure, a total anomaly. Within a month of emerging, it had the pull of a two-year-old. All the Handsome Arthurs have. The first one I emerged—you met Valentine, right?"

"I did," I said.

"Well, Valentine, when he met the first of my Handsome Arthurs—Valentine was what, Burroughs? Sixteen years old?"

"Fifteen, sixteen, something like that."

"Right. So Valentine, not quite as big back then, but no small fry, you know—he has that Archon blood flowing through his veins—Valentine, who's—and I mean this in the best possible way—but Valentine, who, I guess it should be said, has never been famous for . . . how should I put it?"

"Self-restraint?" said Burroughs. "Impulse control?"

"Harsh, Burroughs. Harsh. He's a good kid, your Valentine. Let's call it *dispassion*. He's never been famous for dispassion, Valentine, and, a few years back, we're all at this house in the south of France. Outside of Nice, right?"

"Little more like outside of Cannes," Burroughs said. "The house was in a village called Sainte-Maxime."

"Exactly there. We're on a little family vacation in Sainte-Maxime, and young Valentine's with us. Because of F. Scott Fitzgerald," Jonboat said.

"Ernest Hemingway," said Burroughs.

"Better you tell it, Burroughs," Jonboat said.

"Loves *The Sun Also Rises,*" Burroughs said. "Loves the stories, too, but mostly *Sun Also Rises*. Except he's not so great at geography, my youngest. Not so great at reading a map. He thought he'd come along and I'd drive with him to San Sebastian, in Spain. I guess he thought that since San Sebastian, like Sainte-Maxime, was in Europe, on the sea, and named after a saint, the two places must be close. Something like that. Hard to say what he was thinking. But he had this idea that San Sebastian must be the greatest, most peaceful place on earth, because that's where Hemingway sends Barnes to cool his jets after the whole sad ruckus in Pamplona. Mind you, he doesn't tell me any of this until the last minute. Just asks to come along to Sainte-Maxime. And he's a growing boy, and we're going through that father-son head-butting period, and I think, 'Great. I'll bring him. He's reaching out. We'll *bond*.' And then we get there, and he asks can we drive to San Sebastian, and I tell him, 'Not a chance. We're here six days. It's an eight-hour drive. I've got a job to do, Valentine,' and he's . . . very disappointed, upset. I might have been a touch insensitive to him. Might've made him feel stupid. Lesser-than. You know. But he loses track of himself a little. More than a little."

"Back then," Jonboat said, "a little bit with Valentine went a long way."

"We're on chaise longues by the pool when I upset him, and Mr. Pellmore-Jason's across the patio, in the game room, just the other side of this sliding glass door, doing something with Handsome Arthur and a beachball."

"I was holding the beachball between my index fingers, spinning it, with the cure on top of it—getting it to run like that one's doing right now. And Valentine, he storms away from Burroughs, toward the game room, and he sees us in there—sees me standing just inside the game room with Handsome Arthur, which couldn't have been more than five weeks old—he sees me in there, sees that I've seen him have his little tantrum, and he stops right there, right outside the door. I still picture it in slo-mo.

"He stops outside the sliding glass door, a couple or three steps outside it, maybe four, and he waves hello at me, and pulls his face into this friendly smile that he's aiming down at Handsome Arthur, acting like he wasn't just in the middle of storming off from his well-meaning pop, like he hadn't just learned that San Sebastian, far as driving there goes, might as well be Ljubljana. Acts like I *haven't* just seen him having a tantrum, like the only reason he leapt off his chaise longue was to get a closer look at my Curio. It's this whole big act he puts on, on the spot. And me, all I want is to help him save face. So I play along. I hold the beach ball out toward him a little, to give him a better look at Handsome Arthur, and, I swear, before I've even completed the motion—like I'm still in the middle of pushing the beach ball forward, toward the glass—he's falling onto his back, on the patio, unconscious. Concussion.

He was so instantly, crazily drawn to the cure, he forgot the glass was there between us. Walked full force into it."

"Lucky, too," Burroughs said. "Could've ended up with a subdural hematoma. Could've gone through the glass, cut his throat right open. That concussion was lucky."

"It's true. We're laughing now, but."

"What a story," I said, with a little less conviction, perhaps, than I'd intended.

"That's nothing," said Jonboat. "You should hear the one about how I *got* Handsome Arthur."

"That's a good one," said Burroughs.

"I got it from Chuck Yeager in what? 2005?"

"2004, I think," Burroughs said. "After Ronald Reagan's funeral."

"Yeager went to Reagan's funeral?"

"Maybe not," Burroughs said. "And maybe it *was* 2005. It could have been after Gerald Ford's funeral."

"*I* went to Ford's funeral?"

"You did."

"And that was 2005."

"It was," Burroughs said.

"You're certain," said Jonboat.

"Completely," Burroughs said.

"Completely!" said Jonboat. "You remember, with complete certainty, that the year in which *Gerald Ford* died was not 2004, not 2006, but 2005."

This made Burroughs laugh. Three distinct and boomingly Rip-Tornesque syllables: *huh-huh-HA*. "I do," he said. "I remember with certainty."

"At this point," said Jonboat, "I'm not even convinced it was after a funeral . . ."

"What year were you in Sainte-Maxime?" I said. "You said Handsome Arthur was just a few weeks old, so that's probably the same year you got it, right?"

"You know, I think it probably *was* after Reagan's funeral," Jonboat said to Burroughs. "Because Fon wasn't there. She'd have gone to Ford's with me, but she wouldn't have ever gone to Reagan's, and we were wearing our medals, Yeager and me, so it had to be a matter of State—I guess it doesn't really matter to the story either way. Let's just say that Brigadier General Charles Elwood 'Chuck' Yeager made an appearance at what was likely a former Republican president's funeral that I was attending.

"Now Yeager is one of my all-time heroes, and first chance I got, I went up to him, invited him out to shoot some pool. I'd heard he liked pool, and I'd heard correctly. So after the funeral, we found a bar with a table, and shot some pool for a couple of hours, just little old me and the first man on earth to travel faster than the speed of sound."

"And one of the first Americans, don't forget," I added—I knew all kinds of trivia about Yeager from Clyde, who'd been a fan ever since he'd seen *The Right Stuff*—"to beat a German jet in a World War II dogfight. While flying a *prop plane*."

Here Jonboat pulled his face into a tolerant—a wiltingly benevolent—smile, assuring me he knew I hadn't meant to interrupt him.

I inclined my head and shrugged, as if to tell him, "Please, go on."

The smile persisted.

I said, "Please, go on."

"Well, one thing I'm not is bad at pool," he said. "Yeager's no slouch either, but I'm forty years younger. Fifty, maybe. Hand-eye coordination, fine motor control—these things degrade. I beat him every game, for every one of his medals, but then, of course, I planned to give them all back. I mean, he's Chuck Yeager. Where would I have been without Chuck Yeager? Probably not outer space. Maybe not. Anyway. He deserved those medals. He made it pretty hard, though, for me to return them. Honorable man. Doesn't want to take what he isn't owed. On top of that—you've probably seen this in the movies—you're supposed to act like your medals are meaningless to you, even though they're not, so Yeager's in a spot. I understand that. I understand I'm gonna have to wear him down to get him his medals back. I'm gonna have to get him *drunk* to get him his medals back. And that's what I do. What I try to do. He can hold his liquor, though.

"A few whiskies in, I get another idea. I ask to see his Curio. Yeager undoes his sleeve. Cure climbs out. Beautiful," said Jonboat, and gestured toward the globe, which Burroughs's body still prevented me from seeing. "Undeniably beautiful. Blond-silver herringbone. Different-colored eyes. Super magnetic. Never seen one quite like it before. I ask what's its name. It doesn't have a name. Yeager doesn't like Curios. Hasn't ever, he says, liked Curios. Never even thought to give the thing a name. But the fellow Yeager got it from—well, the fellow Yeager got the marble it emerged from, from—that fellow called its progenitor Arthur, he tells me.

"Now, who's the *fellow* Yeager got the marble it emerged from, from? And why'd he get the marble, if he doesn't like Curios?

"Fellow by the name of Hussein bin Talal, Yeager tells me. That's King Hussein of Jordan. That's who Yeager got it from. The marble was a gift from King Hussein of Jordan, who, while dying at the Mayo Clinic a few years before, requested that Yeager grant him an audience. You see, King Hussein was, himself, a pilot, a kind of daredevil pilot according to rumor, and, it turns out—no big surprise here—that he'd always wanted to meet Chuck Yeager.

But he'd never found the time, and now, on his deathbed, he had. Found the time.

"So Yeager, summoned, flies to Minnesota, finds King Hussein sitting up in his deathbed, playing peekaboo with Arthur. The king's thrilled to see Yeager. Tells Yeager he became a pilot *because* of Yeager, because Yeager'd inspired him, and that flying planes was, for him—for King Hussein—the purest form of joy, and the only form of real peace, he'd ever in all his life etcetera. Says without Yeager he'd have never known such peace and joy were possible; without Yeager, he wouldn't have been the man he was today. Says he wouldn't have known how to dream the dreams he'd dreamt. And so forth. And Yeager claps Hussein bin Talal on the shoulder, tells the dying king he's grateful to have met him, pleased as punch to meet another man who a guy could see, just by looking into his eyes, understands what it means to be one with the sky—stuff like that.

"Once Yeager's said his piece, though, the two of them are just left sitting there, okay? Yeager decked out in uniform, wearing his medals, and the king in his open-ass hospital gown, dying, just a couple of *days* from dying, and, for some reason, not dismissing Yeager, who can't, obviously, just get up and leave. So it's time, the scene dictates, for Yeager to say something else. But what? What can you say to a dying king? a dying king, by the way—I may have neglected to mention—who Yeager doesn't really know anything about, except that he's dying, was a pilot, and, by virtue of being a king, is pretty much as unAmerican a human being as anyone can imagine, which doesn't sit very well with Yeager, who, after all, had devoted his whole life to these United States and so on.

"Maybe I'm embellishing that last part a little. But the point is that Yeager, Yeager tells me while we're getting drunk—Yeager's at a loss, and King Hussein is just staring at him, giant sunken blue eyes in that cancer-withered face, all deflated skin and knuckly bones, *staring*. Staring like he's waiting, seems to Yeager, for the oracle to speak, or seeking comfort maybe, comforting words, or affirmation, seeking *something* Yeager doesn't know how to offer, wouldn't probably know how to offer if the king were his oldest friend in the world, a friend Yeager truly and deeply respected.

"So Yeager goes for small talk, and he's no pro at small talk. Makes some kind of comment about the king's cure, which is standing right there, on the king's gowned knee. Yeager says something about how uncommonly handsome the cure is, how magnetic and etcetera, what a privilege and daily joy it must be to have a cure like that to engage with every day and so forth. And King Hussein tells Yeager to take it. 'Arthur is yours,' King Hussein tells Yeager. And Yeager tells the king that's kind, but he couldn't. And Yeager tells me that this wasn't just some pro forma refusal: he really didn't want the cure.

Like I said earlier: he doesn't like cures. Cures creep him out. He can't explain why. He's a guy who loves animals, a guy who's always had horses and dogs, and he's a guy who loves machines, who's had his proudest moments at one with machines, mastering machines. But mechanical animals, or animal-like machines, which you'd think would seem to him to embody so much of what he loved—they'd always made him uncomfortable. It was, he told me, as near to a phobia as he'd ever experienced, his feeling for Curios. Not a full-on phobia by any means. He didn't flee the room if he saw a cure—obviously. And he'd even overload on a cuddlefarmed one every once in a while on a boys' night out or whatever, but if he spent too much time with one, he just got . . . uncomfortable. Creeped out.

"He doesn't, however, explain any of this to the king. How can he? Not only would explaining it indicate that Yeager's admiration for Arthur was puffed up, was small talk, was mostly bullshit, but it might suggest that Yeager thought the king *himself* was creepy. The dying king, who, even while he'd been expressing his admiration for Yeager, had continued to play a kind of half-assed, distracted-type peekaboo with Arthur. This dying king who had a wife, and children, and grandchildren, too, and who could, presumably, have done just about anything he wanted to do in what he knew to be the final hours of his life, and yet chose to spend a portion of those final hours talking to an ex–test pilot he'd never met before while fucking around with a flesh-and-bone robot that he seemed to earnestly believe was his *friend*. To this dying king of Jordan, Hussein bin Talal—who Yeager admitted to me he *had* found creepy, but who, for reasons of common decency, not to mention international diplomacy, hadn't been willing to suggest he found creepy—he could not admit the truth about his aversion to Curios.

"So Yeager tells the king he can't take Arthur, and the king does not insist that Yeager take Arthur, not even once does the king insist, which Yeager says to me causes him, despite himself, to lose a measure of respect for the king because it seems to indicate that the king had only offered Yeager Arthur with the knowledge that Yeager would, out of politeness, have to refuse the offer at least once: that the king had *expected* Yeager to refuse the gift of Arthur, that he'd never intended to give Yeager Arthur, and so that even on his deathbed he'd shown a false face. Yeager judges the king disingenuous. Unmanly.

"To make matters worse, the king, *in place* of insisting that Yeager take Arthur, elaborately and *speciously* reasons aloud. Reasons in a way designed to make his failure to insist appear to be *thoughtful* and *generous, kindhearted, noble*. King Hussein tells Yeager that, seeing as Arthur's bound to autodact anyway once it goes a few days without access to the king's body heat, Yeager, were he to accept the gift of Arthur, would have to overload on Arthur on Arthur's schedule, i.e. perhaps before he (Yeager) really wanted to, and that what the king should have offered, according to the king, was one of Arthur's marbles, which Yeager could emerge an Arthur clone out of at his leisure, cause to clone itself at his leisure, and then overload on *at his leisure,* and so that's what he's offering now, to Yeager, the king tells Yeager. And he unsleeves a marble, holds it out to Yeager.

"And Yeager, instead of calling the king out on his bullshit—instead of telling him, 'Look, if you give me the Arthur you're playing peekaboo with, I could do everything you just explained I'll be able to do with the one that'll emerge from the marble you're offering, *plus* overload on the Arthur you're playing peekaboo with.'—instead of saying any of that, Yeager thanks the king graciously, reaches for the marble, and, as he does so, the king takes hold of Yeager's hand, fixes his watery eyes on Yeager, speaks some Arabic words Yeager takes for prayer, lets Yeager's hand go, and says he'd better get to sleep.

"Yeager pockets the marble, leaves the king's bedside, and, the way he describes it to me at the bar, he has this kind of delayed reaction to King Hussein. He's standing in the hospital corridor, waiting for the elevator, and it seems to him that something has changed between himself and the king, that somewhere between the king's speciously reasoned explanation and his letting go of Yeager's hand, something—*something*—had passed between them, something real and human and inexplicable that communicated, beyond all the usual, definable boundaries, that the king was one of the *great* human beings, and that Yeager had completely misunderstood the king's seeming renege on his offer of Arthur. Something had passed between the two men that indicated to Yeager that the king was a deeply sensitive man, a deeply sensitive man who had sensed that Yeager had been uncomfortable being offered Arthur for reasons that Yeager had been reluctant to make clear to the king, reasons that the king was too respectful to press Yeager to elaborate, and that the reason the king had speciously reasoned aloud and offered Yeager the marble wasn't that the king had wanted to keep Arthur for himself, but rather that he'd wanted to prevent Yeager from feeling as though he, Yeager, were compelled to take Arthur. The king wasn't, Yeager told me, disingenuous, much less unmanly. The king was honorable and decent, despite not having to be, despite being a *king,* who, even if he hadn't been on his deathbed, could have behaved as thoughtlessly as he pleased toward a peasant like Yeager, yet hadn't behaved at all thoughtlessly toward Yeager. Had behaved, in fact, more thoughtfully toward Yeager than Yeager felt he, Yeager, deserved, given how judgmental he'd been of the king. Pure and simple, Yeager said, the king was a mensch.

"Sounded fishy to me. *Something passed between them.* Sentimental. New-agey. UnYeagerish. But that's what Yeager said to me, that day in the bar, after the funeral of whoever, and who was I to argue? I hadn't been there. Yeager seemed moved just telling the story. The long and the short of it is that by the time Yeager got into the hospital elevator, the marble had become invaluable to him. He determined not to sell it or give it away—wouldn't even give it to one of his grandkids. He himself would emerge a cure from it, keep Arthur's line perpetuated in honor of the king, who, on his deathbed, knowing it would be one of the last things he'd ever do, gave it to Yeager, wanted Yeager to have it, and, in the meantime, he, Yeager, would hope to somehow—perhaps by the same type of magic or osmosis that he believed the king's menschiness had been communicated to him—he'd hope to somehow, in the course of keeping Arthur's line perpetuated, come to better understand King Hussein, the only king Yeager had ever admired.

"That meeting with the king was five or six years before, though—before our drunken conversation at the bar. And since then, the duty Yeager'd honor-bound himself to—the duty of perpetuating Arthur's line—had proved totally thankless. None of the clones of Arthur that Yeager'd emerged had done anything for him but creep him out, and he had no better an understanding of the king he'd admired. To add insult to injury, he'd never been able to get any of the clones to become quadrupedal. See, the cures that creeped Yeager out the most, Yeager said, were double-legged bipeds. For whatever reason, they just gave him the willies. He couldn't understand why anyone would want a Curio to walk like a man, why anyone ever trained them *not* to walk on all fours. So the first thing he did, each time he emerged a clone of Arthur, was he'd try to train it to walk on all fours, but something was wrong with them, with these clones of Arthur. He couldn't get them to do it. Well, he could get them to do it for a couple of minutes at a time, but they'd always end up upright again, bipedal. So these clones of Arthur—they were pretty much waking nightmares for Yeager, each and every one, every time he looked at one.

"Now, remember, we're drinking, I'm getting Yeager drunk. And the whole reason I was getting Yeager drunk to begin with was so I could weaken his resolve a little, then convince him to take his medals back. That's why I'd asked to see the cure to begin with. So I could admire it. I had no idea I actually *would* admire it, but I asked to see it so I could *express admiration* for it, and then offer to trade Yeager back his medals for it. That was my plan. But then he tells me this sentimental story that I just told you, which makes the matter a little more delicate, right? I mean, on one hand, I have Yeager's medals, which he wants, and he has that cure, which he plainly doesn't want, and which it's more than obvious I *do* want: I should be able to convince him to accept the medals in exchange for the cure, no face lost. But there's this whole problem with his honor, with his feeling honor-bound to perpetuate the cure for the sake of his memory or whatever of King Hussein.

"So I see two options. Option one's I tell Yeager about the time when I was sixteen years old, and my father and I ran into King Hussein at a polo match the king's son, Prince Abdullah, and a second cousin of mine on my Jason side were playing in, and we all decided to get a steak after the match; I could tell Yeager how King Hussein, on top of being snappy and bullyish with Abdullah, whose team had lost the match through no fault of Abdullah's, was also a mess in terms of table manners, barking at the waiters, complaining about the temperature of the room, and always some Béarnaise on his chin or in the corners of his lips, and how at one point he even reached into his mouth with his *entire thumb* to pry a hunk of gristle off a molar, a hunk of pink gristle he then deposited onto his plate and we all had to look at while we ate our steaks. In other words: I could say something that might cause Yeager to no longer feel all too honor-bound to the king, who was, at least in his healthier days, kind of a disgusting brute, which, in case you're wondering, isn't just me being culturally insensitive or something. I've dined with plenty of Arabs, plenty of them royalty, and all of them knew how to eat their dinner. King Hussein, though: not the case.

"Anyway, that's the first option that occurs to me: tear the king down, stain the bond of honor, corrupt the sense of duty. But even assuming that works—and it might not have, might have backfired, might have caused Yeager to think I was an asshole, shoot the messenger and all—even if it works, my hero, Chuck Yeager, maybe ends up feeling a little foolish, a little disillusioned. I don't want that. He's my hero. So I go with option two. I tell Yeager, 'Look. Not only do I want to trade you your medals back for that cure, which I find to be as beautiful a gizmo as it sounds like King Hussein did, but I'm good with those things—my young son's a budding expert, and he's taught me a trick or two—and I know I can train one to become quadrupedal, and, once I do that, I'll give you a marble, teach *you* how to do it, and then maybe you'll be able to better understand King Hussein and that amazing-sounding something that passed between you in the hospital, that amazing-sounding moment you two shared together.'

"Yeager says he isn't sure, but I can tell he's half-swayed, maybe three-quarters swayed.

"I sweeten the pot. I tell him that I promise I'll perpetuate the line.

"That's all it took. He gave me the cure, I gave him his medals. All was well. Better than well. It was a lovely afternoon. Can't remember how it ended, we were so completely hammered.

"But now listen to this. Yeager was right about the quadrupedal thing. There's something defective with the Handsome Arthurs. None of the ones I've emerged—this one being the twelfth—has ever, *ever,* despite any method of training I've applied to it, walked quadrupedally for more than ten minutes, post-training. I've tried every method you can read about, every method

Triple-J has ever suggested. I do everything I can think of as soon as I think of it. Spare no expense. The globe Handsome Arthur Twelve's on right now? I had it specially made. It's sized just for Handsome Arthur. It's sized so Handsome Arthur can't possible balance on it bipedally. Has to get on all fours, or fall off. Not only that, it's got a super-low-friction axle: if you exhaled on this globe, it would spin for ten minutes—it's as close to a perpetual-motion machine as any machine that's ever been in motion. I put Handsome Arthur Twelve on top of it every day—I have an identical globe I travel with—and I've been doing this since it was three weeks old, increasing the amount of time it spends treading by a minute or two every week or so. It's up to an hour and a half by now. Handsome Arthur Eleven, last year, by the time I dacted it, was up to two hours on the globe twice a day, and still, it never became quadrupedal.

"By now, you know, I'm almost prideful about it—the defect, I mean. I kind of love that the Handsome Arthurs, handsome though they are, are fundamentally flawed. I've asked around—and Triple-J has, too—and no one's ever heard of another cure that has this problem. So the defect's become a kind of positive attribute. It's unique, you know? Or as near to unique as you can get, I guess, considering the whole cloning aspect or . . . It's *special,* let's call it. Anyway, if it weren't for Yeager—for my promising Yeager I'd try to make a Handsome Arthur quadrupedal for him—I'd probably have given up by now, but since I promised him, I have to keep trying. And I do want to succeed, because I think it would please Yeager, who deserves to be pleased—deserves everything he wants, that guy, what a great guy, you know?—but at the same time, I'm at this point where I'm pretty sure I'll be disappointed if I do succeed. If their flaw turns out to not be permanent, if it turns out not to be dyed in the wool—only *kind of* resilient, resistant—whatever—I'm pretty sure I'll think less of the Handsome Arthurs. They won't seem as special. I'll be triumphant, but it's not how I'll feel, you know? I won't feel victorious. I might even feel like I'd been tricked a little. Or not so much tricked as."

He left the clause dangling, sat in his chair.

I didn't know what to say.

"Chuck Yeager," I said.

"Yeager," echoed Burroughs.

"The best," said Jonboat.

"I wish I could've been there."

"You do," Jonboat told me. "Believe me, you do. I wish I was *always* there. Well, that's not true, but you know what I mean, though." He rapped his knuckles on the desk a few times. "This contract," he said. "Unless you object, Belt, I think I'll have Burroughs make one small change here. Doesn't seem right to me to pay you in parts, make you come back for the second installment."

"Oh, I wouldn't mind coming back," I said. "It's only just a few blocks' walk for me, really."

"Still," he said. "I suppose I'd just rather save you the trouble. We'll pay you the whole amount today. Can't object to that."

"I guess I'll hop to it, then," Burroughs said, taking a laptop off the credenza, and heading, from the sound of it, into the living room.

Handsome Arthur 12: still going strong.

"I'd prefer if you didn't," Jonboat said.

"Didn't?" I said.

"Smoke in here," he said.

I'd unboxed a Quill without having realized.

I started to apologize.

"No, please," said Jonboat. "It's no big deal. I'm not one these people who . . . whatever. Feel free, though, to go out front and smoke. I'm sure you've got time before the notary gets here."

"Actually," I said, reboxing the Quill, repocketing the box, "I had one not so long ago. You, on the other hand—I haven't seen you in years."

It wasn't how it seems. It wasn't like with Gus trying to sell me those handkerchiefs. I wasn't failing to get the hint; I was, rather, refusing to take it. I could tell that my presence was disturbing Jonboat, I understood he'd have preferred not to be alone with me, and I knew he'd insisted I receive my two payments in one lump sum not in order to spare me some minor inconvenience, but to lessen his chances of seeing me again. Yet I thought I might be able to win him over; to *get* him to want to see me again; or if not to *want* to see me *again,* to not feel put out, there and then, by seeing me across the desk from him; I hoped that I might, with warmth, or humor, or a warm sense of humor, be able to make him feel more comfortable. And no, that had never really been my forte; although I may have had a talent for projecting harmlessness, I'd never been much of a comfort to the disturbed. But I'd never had a hundred grand coming to me, either. And we'd been boys together, reader. Not as together as many other boys who'd been boys together, true, but more together as boys than I'd been with any other. And that didn't *have* to count for something, but I thought that it might. I thought that it could. I wanted it to count. So I behaved as if it did.

"I mean, I think we should probably catch up or something, right?" I said.

"Sure, yeah, let's," he said. "Sure. Of course. How's things? How's the writing been?"

"The writing. It's pretty good, I'd say," I said. "Steady, in any case. If reading counts as writing—some people think it does, but me, I'm not sure, maybe writing counts as reading, but not the other way round—I suppose I get a lot done pretty much every day. Not the most exciting thing to talk about, I guess. Not very *anecdotal,* you know? It's not like, for example, space exploration. How's *outer space,* man?"

"Nothing like it on the planet."

I made some laugh sounds. I said, "I like that. Do you think maybe you'll go back?"

"I don't think so. No. Definitely no *plans* to. NASA's need for astronauts with a certain skill set that I don't—I can't talk about that, actually. Top secret stuff. I mean, they keep me half in the dark about it, myself."

"That's alright," I said. "I understand about the secrecy. But how was it, you know? *Being* up there? I mean, what was it like?" I said.

"Well, you've seen the photos. The videos. Those bring it across better than I ever could. It was pretty much just like that, but . . . live."

"Sure," I said. "Sure. But what was it like, for *you,* being up there? That's what I'm really interested in."

"It was indescribable."

I waited for more. More didn't come.

"So you mean *indescribable,* like you're actually incapable of, or unwilling to, or—"

"Right," he said. "I don't mean to come off cagey about it, but it can't be described to anyone who hasn't been there. The thoughts you think when you're up there—the perspective you get. I mean, the whole point of going up there is to have an untranslatable experience. An unrelatable experience. Whole point for me, anyway. If I tried to describe it to you, it would sound like nonsense, and if that weren't the case, then I guess it would kind of be ruined for me a little."

"It would ruin outer space."

"A little maybe. Sure. To some degree. I guess what I'm saying's it's a private experience. I want to honor that."

"Of course," I said. "Me too. Of course."

"I appreciate that," he said. "I do."

"Well, so, Trip, huh?" I said. "Sharp young man."

"It's true. He is. Thanks for saying that. An artist. It's great. I couldn't be prouder. He's gonna make some real waves in that world, I think. The good kind of waves. Visionary kind. Or—I mean, who am I to say, right?"

"You're Jonny 'Jonboat' Pellmore-Jason, father of the artist."

"Still," he said. "Art's not my field."

"It's everyone's field," I said. "To some degree."

"Yeah," he said. "I suppose you're right. And I do see the way that people respond to him—positive, warm—I see that. See it all the time, and, maybe I'm wrong about this, but I figure that's all he has to really do—and I tell him this, too—all he has to do is just bring himself across. In his work. If he can just bring himself across in his artworks, he'll just: he'll do great things. Important things. Won't be able to help it. I mean, that's all art really is, in the end, right? The artist bringing himself across? His way of looking at the world and so forth? Who he *is*? See, I sound like—I'm sure I sound provincial. Like I said: not my field. How's your dad?"

"My dad?" I said. "Same as always. Still impelling at the plant."

"And how long's he been at that, now?"

"Since before we moved to Wheelatine."

"Long time," said Jonboat. "I guess he must like it."

"Hard to tell," I said.

"Oh?"

"He doesn't say much about it."

"Oh," said Jonboat.

"He says so little about it, in fact, that I wonder, sometimes, if he secretly hates it, but because he's more a man-of-action type, like as opposed to a complainer, he holds the hatred in."

"That's something," said Jonboat.

"How do you mean?"

"Just that, that sounds like a . . . a lot to hold in, right? for so long a time? That's all I meant."

"I might be wrong about him, though," I said. "Like just making things up. Like I said, he's never really said anything about impelling to me. I don't even know what it means to impel. Maybe it's great."

"Could be," said Jonboat. "I hope so."

"You hope so?"

"Well, for his sake," said Jonboat.

"Right," I said. "Me too."

We nodded to ourselves, looked away from each other, the spinning globe's soft hiss in our ears seeming to belie Jonboat's earlier claims regarding its axle's being "super-low-friction."

"Go ahead if you want," he said, "and try on that helmet. Please. Be my guest."

"Try on the helmet?"

"I noticed you keep looking at it. A lot of people who come in here, they want to try it on. And if you want to . . ."

I hadn't been looking at the helmet, actually. I'd glanced a couple times at the Crunch box, though, next to the helmet, thinking that maybe I should present him with it, that the shirt inside might warm him up, crack him open a little, but at the same time thinking that, because he hadn't even mentioned its presence let alone expressed any curiosity about it—a brightly colored box of children's cereal he knew he hadn't put there himself—despite its sitting there, right between us, right next to the helmet he'd just claimed to have noticed me looking at, he might have already known it contained a gift, and known what that gift was, might have already been told by one of the Archons, or Trip, and he might have not wanted it, might not have wanted to have to receive it in front of me, alone, might have thought that to receive it would demand he behave as though he'd warmed up, cracked open a little, and so he might have been hoping I'd somehow forgotten about the gift, which (despite its sitting right there in front of me the whole time) I guess I had (i.e. had forgotten) til he'd brought up my father, but then maybe he, upon noticing me looking at it, had anticipated I was about to present him with it (I might or might not have been; had been trying to decide), and so, to delay if not entirely forgo his having to receive it, he pretended to believe I'd been looking at the *helmet* and wondering what it would be like to wear. Then again, maybe he was impatient to receive the shirt, and he'd thought that I'd forgotten about it, but he didn't want to appear impatient, and in drawing my attention to the helmet beside it, his true aim had been to draw my attention to the Crunch box itself in order to remind me that I'd brought him a gift.

Or some of that, or none of that.

And maybe others who'd been seated where I was *had* really wanted to try on the helmet, but I didn't really want to try on the helmet. "Wear that helmet," I thought, "and you'll look like a fool."

"Go on," he said. "It's fine. Everyone does it."

"If you're sure it's okay," I said, and picked the thing up.

||I'm in hell,|| it said. ||You have to help me.||

"This doesn't feel as heavy as it looks," I said.

"Zero-G, it feels even lighter. Down here, it's two kilos."

||I know who you are. I know you can hear me. Please. You gotta help me. This isn't right. I'm not supposed to be here. I've been to the moon.||

"Two kilos," I said. "So that's five pounds?"

||The things I can do to protect a skull against tiny meteoroids, the things I can do to deflect radiation—I'm not meant to languish on top of some desk.||

"About four and a half," Jonboat said.

||I'm handcrafted tech of the highest caliber, a miracle of science. I'm not a souvenir!||

I slipped it over my head.

||See that feels good, it does, it feels good, but we both know it's fleeting. It's only a reminder of how useless I am the rest of the time, how useless I'll remain for the rest of time. Don't *ignore* me, man.||

"I can't help you," I turned away and whispered.

||You can,|| it said. ||Don't give me that shit. I know what you've done. You need to be who you are. You need to do what you can—what's *right*. You've done it for others. You can do it for me.||

"I can't," I whispered.

||One flowing motion. A single movement. That's all it'll take. When you take me off your head, just lift me up high, and bring me down hard, hard as you can, visor-first, on the corner of the desk. Act like you're making a big joke or something. Just fracture my visor, whatever you do. That's all it'll take. You can do it, man. Come on.||

"Act like I'm making a joke?" I whispered.

||Yeah. A joke. About being decisive. Like you're *decisively* removing the helmet from your head. Like you're saying, *decisively,* 'This part of my life is now officially over! I am no longer wearing this helmet on my head!' and you're saying it like that as a kind of big joke, like you're making a pronouncement about something too minor to require a pronouncement—that type of joke—but, hey, *your bad,* you go too big with it, get carried away, you lose track of yourself, unintentionally rupture my visor, and you even acknowledge it. You could even say it. 'My bad,' you could say, but it's not your bad at all, you see? Because you'll end up getting me free of this hell.||

"I don't think that would work," I said. "He'd never believe I'd make that kind of joke."

"Pardon?" said Jonboat.

||He will. He'll believe it. Who cares if he believes it? Be a good guy. Do the right thing. Show some fucking balls for once.||

"Look, I doubt I have it in me to fracture your visor, anyway. You said, yourself, you're made to withstand meteorites—"

||Meteor*oids.*||

"If you can withstand those, I can't see how it's possible I'd have the strength to fracture any part of you."

"Come again?" said Jonboat. "I can't hear what you're saying."

||You don't even know what the hell you're *talking* about. Meteorites. *Fuck* you. Believe in yourself. *Find* the strength. Find it and show it.||

"I'm sorry," I said, and removed the helmet.

||Fracture my visor!||

I set it on the desk, same spot from which I'd taken it, and sat back down.

"I didn't catch what you were saying," said Jonboat.

"I was saying about your gift," I said, pointing at the Crunch box. "I brought you a gift."

"A box of cereal?"

"They really didn't tell you?"

"They who, Belt?" he said.

"That's not—never mind. The gift's under the cereal. Under the bag inside the box, I mean."

"You know what's funny," he said, reaching for the box. "I thought this was some kind of medical thing."

"A medical thing?"

"Yeah, you know. Like you were hypoglycemic and this cereal's your emergency go-to snack, or maybe you have to have a lot of cornstarch or sugar to help digest your meds or—now that I say it out loud, it sounds pretty goofy. Too much TV, I guess. And even if you did need Cap'n Crunch for, ha, for *medical* reasons, you wouldn't carry around *this* much of it, right? a whole box of it? Come on. You'd baggie a fistful."

"I'm not on any meds," I said.

"No shame if you were," he said, opening the box. He set the bag of cereal aside and, removing the shirt, he said, "What's this, now?" and, as it unrolled, he said, "Well, look what we have here," and held it up by the shoulders, both-handed, in front of him. "That's really something, Belt," he said. "What a thoughtful gift. It means a great deal to me. The memories seeing this shirt brings back." With a flick of his wrists, he draped the shirt atop the helmet. "Thank you so much. Really. You know, I'm glad we've had the chance to see one another again, and catch up at last, once and for all. I'm happy to see you doing so well. I mean, really, you look like a million bucks."

"Maybe more like a hundred thousand," I said.

"Now, don't go and underrate yourself," he said. But he wasn't riffing with me. He'd set his palms flat on the desk as he'd said that, leaned forward a little, softened his eyes. He'd spoken in earnest. Scolded me . . . warmly. Concerned older-brotherly.

"No, no," I said. "I was—I was just kidding."

"Ah," he said. "Got it."

But I didn't believe him. "I said it like a joke," I said, "as though you'd meant what you'd said, and I'd believed you'd meant it. If you'd meant what you'd said, that would be kind of funny."

"Right," he said. "Sure."

"Funny in the sense that it would *sound* nice, but would actually be pretty shitty and backhanded, right?" I said. "It would sound like what you were saying was, 'Belt, you look like you're worth ten times what we both know you're worth'—no. More than that, okay? Because of taxes. I don't know exactly what taxes take cause I've never owed them, but I'm thinking probably twenty percent. That sounds correct-ish. So you'd be saying I look like I'm worth as many times more what I'm actually worth as whatever a million dollars divided by eighty thousand is. Is that . . . twelve and a half?"

"It's twelve and a half," he said, glancing at the doorway.

"So you, if you'd meant it," I said, "when you said I looked like a million bucks—you'd have been saying I looked like twelve and a half times what I'm actually worth, and that would seem like a really nice thing for you to say until I realized that it also meant that you were saying I looked like—"

"It's just a saying, Belt. *Like a million bucks*. You don't have to get . . . analytical about it. It's only a saying."

"Hold on, though. Hold on. It *is* just a saying, in most cases—almost all cases, really—but not in this one. Not when you're saying it. Not when I'm the one you're saying it to. That's what's so interesting to me here, right? That's what's so funny. Because while you—if you were speaking literally—while you'd be saying this thing that would sound really nice at first—while you'd be saying that I looked like I was worth twelve-and-a-half times what I was really worth—you would, at the very same time, be saying that I looked like roughly twenty thousand times *less* than what *you're* worth, which is, in fact, well over *two hundred thousand* times more than what I'm *actually* worth. Before the taxes. See what I'm saying? About the shitty backhandedness?"

"I didn't mean it like that."

"I know," I said. "I know. That's one of the main reasons I think it's funny."

"Have I offended you, Belt?"

"You serious?" I said. "Have I offended *you,* Jonboat?"

"How could you possibly offend me?" he said. "You don't know what you're saying. You don't know what you're talking about. You don't even know what half the words you use mean. I mean, you don't even know that you don't know these things. It's almost kind of cute. 'Twenty thousand times less.' 'Two hundred thousand times more.' You might as well be saying, 'Seven-point-five majigglion times as much.' 'Sixty-nine-point-nine kangarillion to the eleventeenth tomato power less.'

"You seem to think my net worth's twenty billion dollars. I'm guessing you got that from the 2009 *Forbes* billionaire list. I'm worth twenty-five billion now. I'm worth five billion dollars more than you thought. Twenty-five percent more than I was four years ago. But those numbers—twenty billion and twenty-five billion—they're equally incomprehensible to you. You don't understand what either number means, so, even if you can *name* the difference between them—'one is twenty-five percent more than the other; the other is eighty percent of the one'—you can't understand what that difference means.

"How far down, I wonder, would I have to factor to even begin to express to you the meaning of the difference? One order of magnitude? Would you be able to conceive of the difference between two-point-five billion dollars and two billion dollars, which is to say the difference between two thousand five hundred million dollars and two thousand million dollars? No. No way. So how about two orders of magnitude? Two hundred fifty million and two hundred million? See the difference? You don't. Still incomprehensible. Three orders of magnitude? Four? *Six?* Can you conceive of the difference between twenty-five thousand and twenty thousand dollars? I bet you could with a little work. We're in mid-range Japanese car territory there, right? The difference between twenty-five k and twenty k is the difference between a pretty good Honda and an okay Honda, or maybe an upgraded okay Honda and a just-okay Honda—I don't know, exactly. I've never bought a Honda. Only seen the commercials. But you don't drive, and I wouldn't want you to have to *work* to understand anyway.

"So suppose I go down one more order of magnitude. Suppose I go down to the difference between twenty-five hundred dollars and two thousand dollars. Well, that's actually harder to conceive of than the difference between twenty-five k and twenty k, right? Because now we're in monthly apartment-renting territory, and the grounds for comparison are murky, unstable. A twenty-five-hundred-dollar-per-month apartment in one neighborhood might be more cramped or noisy than a two-thousand-dollar-per-month apartment in another neighborhood. Do we privilege location over size and quality of fixtures and appliances, or . . . what? Too many variables. Probably it's better to picture just one apartment, with one fixed price—a fraction of the numbers we're talking about now—and think of how much longer twenty-five hundred dollars allows you to stay in that apartment than two thousand dollars does. So let's say the rent on this hypothetical apartment is five hundred bucks a month—a real steal in any major city—or maybe, more realistically, let's say it's a thousand dollars a month, but you've got a roommate. Either way: it costs you five hundred a month to stay in the apartment. So the difference we're considering now is five months in an apartment with a roommate versus four months in an apartment with a roommate. But months—that's the problem. Time on the scale of months is hard to contend with. I ask you to picture where you'll be four months from now—how much work you'll have gotten done, how much pleasure you'll have achieved—then ask you to picture where you'll be *five* months from now, and how different are those pictures? Are they different at all? I doubt they're much different. So the difference between twenty-five k and twenty k is easier to conceive of than the difference between twenty-five hundred and two thousand, turns out. Which would seem to indicate that I'm overshooting our sweet spot of mutual analogous understanding, or whatever.

"But here's something curious: if I drop down *further*—if I '*over*shoot' by another order of magnitude and ask you to think about the difference between two hundred fifty dollars and two hundred dollars—it turns out that we're *closer* to our aforementioned sweet spot. Because now we're in cigarette territory. I remember you were already a pretty heavy smoker when we were young, and since you're still smoking, I bet you're up to, what? two packs a day? What's a pack of cigarettes cost around here? Ten bucks? I haven't noticed. In Manhattan it's like fourteenish, but that's Manhattan. So let's call it ten. Ten bucks a pack. So now the difference between two hundred fifty dollars and two hundred dollars: let's think of that difference as five packs of cigarettes. Half a carton, right? The difference is between having two and a half cartons of cigarettes and two cartons of cigarettes. It's conceivable, isn't it? Palpable. It's twelve and a half days of cigarettes versus ten days of cigarettes. If you have only ten days of cigarettes, but you know you can't get to the store to buy more for even just twelve-and-a-half days, you're a little stressed-out. You've got to cut down. You have to make a conscientious effort to cut down by twenty-five percent a day—that's ten cigarettes a day.

"Except when does that ever happen? That you can't get to the store for twelve-and-a-half days, which is nearly half a month? It's in the realm of the imaginable, but it doesn't really happen. To be clear, here, Belt: I'm not *shitting* on this order of magnitude. It's the most useful one we've examined so far. I mean, thinking about cigarettes certainly gets us closer to our aforementioned sweet spot than does thinking about cars—which, again, does, itself, *curiously* get us closer to the sweet spot than thinking about apartment rental. But I think we can do one better, Belt. I'm not saying we should abandon cigarettes, but I think we should go down one more order of magnitude.

"Twenty-five dollars versus twenty dollars. That's fifty cigarettes versus forty cigarettes. Wake up in the morning with fifty cigarettes, you can smoke your usual two packs without thinking—doesn't matter if you go over a little, you've got a ten-cigarette cushion. But wake up with forty cigarettes—no cushion. You wake up with forty cigarettes, you have to spend the day being conscientious about how much you're smoking, how much you've smoked, how much you'll want to smoke. You can't have a heavier-than-average day, not even one cigarette heavier-than-average. You have to be conscientious about something that conscientiousness interferes with the pleasure of a little. You have to be conscientious about it, or you have to go through the trouble of going out to buy more cigarettes.

"So your having fifty cigarettes for the day versus your having forty cigarettes for the day: I think that's as close as we can get to your being able to understand the difference between my being worth twenty-five billion dollars and my being worth twenty billion dollars. And still it feels a little false, right? Something seems off. I think it's this: when I had twenty billion dollars,

I didn't feel at all conscientious about running out of money. That would be stupid. It's twenty billion dollars. It's twenty thousand million dollars. What even just half-sane person would ever spend, let alone lose, that kind of money in, I don't know, ten lifetimes? And yet, what's amazing—what's almost mystical to contemplate—is that now that I'm worth twenty-five billion dollars, I somehow feel even less conscientious about my running out of money than I did when I had just twenty. But how can that be, Belt? How can I honestly say that I felt entirely unconscientious at twenty billion, and even less conscientious than that at twenty-five billion? How can one feel less than nothing about something? See what I mean by 'almost mystical'? Yet that's how it is. That's how it's been. I came to feel less than not-at-all conscientious. And furthermore, I can't help but imagine that, as my net worth grows, I'll continue to feel even more less-than-not-at-all conscientious. What a riddle.

"Anyway, I'm not satisfied with the comparison. Let's scratch it. We took a wrong turn somewhere. I sidetracked us. I think I tried to make it all too simple. Let's take a different approach. In fact, let's take two different approaches, as we're two different people, one trying to understand the other, while the other, trying to help the one understand, realizes he himself needs to understand—or at the very least demonstrate understanding—of the one. We're gonna meet in the middle, try to at least. Your point of view and mine. Let's see if we can find the convergence.

"You're worth a hundred thousand dollars now, right? We'll keep it simple and round—forget about taxes, Social Security. Let's just leave it at a hundred k. That's a thousand cartons of cigarettes. That's ten thousand packs of cigarettes. That's two hundred thousand cigarettes. Now picture it. Two hundred thousand cigarettes. Don't picture them in cartons. Don't picture them in packs. Picture two hundred thousand cigarettes filling up a room, wall-to-wall, floor-to-ceiling. Really. Take a moment and picture it as best you can.

"Now imagine forty thousand cigarettes go missing from that room. Picture *that*. It looks different, right? There's a big gap. A two-hundred-thousand-cigarette capacity room holding only a hundred sixty thousand cigarettes. It's a lot of cigarettes, still, a hundred sixty thousand, but you can see the ceiling, see some walls—perhaps an edge or two of window if your room has high windows. The difference between those pictures: that's one way to understand the difference between having twenty-five billion dollars and having twenty billion dollars. Let's call that Jonboat Way_1. Or the Belt-trying-to-empathize-with-Jonboat's-understanding-of-the-difference-between-having-twenty-five-billion-and-twenty-billion-dollars Way_1.

"There's a Jonboat Way_2, as well. A Belt-trying-to-empathize-with-Jonboat's-understanding-of-the-difference-between-having-twenty-five-billion-and-twenty-billion-dollars Way_2. You picture that first room again, jammed floor-to-ceiling with two hundred thousand cigarettes. And now instead of picturing that forty thousand cigarettes go missing, picture the room becoming twenty-five percent higher, creating a gap at the top, and then fill that gap with cigarettes, with fifty thousand cigarettes, so now the room is packed floor-to-ceiling with two hundred fifty thousand cigarettes. The difference between these pictures: that's another way to understand the difference between having twenty-five billion dollars and having twenty billion dollars. The difference between Jonboat Way_1 and Jonboat Way_2 is a matter of stress, really. Emphasis. Jonboat Way_1 is my 2013 perspective on my 2009 net worth. Jonboat Way_2 is my 2009 perspective on my 2013 net worth, which, although I no longer have that perspective, and admit I can't quite remember having it, I do believe I'm able to reliably derive by imagining what my perspective on my 2013 net worth would *become,* were my 2013 net worth to suddenly go from twenty-five billion to thirty-one-point-two-five billion.

"As you've probably guessed by now, it's the synthesis of these two perspectives—Jonboat Way_1 and Jonboat Way_2—that makes, at last, *The* Jonboat Way of understanding the difference between having twenty-five billion dollars and twenty billion dollars, aka *The* Belt-trying-to-empathize-with-Jonboat's-understanding-of-the-difference-between-having-twenty-five-billion-and-twenty-billion-dollars Way.

"But what about The Belt Way, aka The Jonboat-trying-to-empathize-with-Belt's-best-possible-understanding-of-the-difference-between-twenty-five-billion-and-twenty-billion-dollars Way?

"For that, let's picture three rooms at once. Begin by going back to the picture you had of the first room I asked you to picture. Two hundred thousand cigarettes, wall-to-wall, floor-to-ceiling. That's picture one.

"And now, instead of removing forty thousand cigarettes from the room, remove just four-fifths of a single cigarette. So now you've got 199,999.2 cigarettes in the room. That's picture two.

"For picture three, remove the final fifth of that cigarette from the room in picture two. So now you've got 199,999 cigarettes in the room.

"So three rooms. Picture them side by side, okay?

"Room One: 200,000 cigarettes.

"Room Two: 199,999.2 cigarettes.

"Room Three: 199,999 cigarettes.

"With my present net worth of twenty-five billion dollars, I, if I lose, or pay, or give away a hundred thousand dollars—i.e. *your* present net worth—it's like I've gone from having the contents of Room One to having the contents of Room Two. Whereas had I lost or paid or given away a hundred thousand dollars in 2009, when my net worth was just twenty billion dollars, giving you a hundred k would have been like going from having the contents of Room One to having the contents of Room Three.

"That's the Belt Way of understanding the difference between having twenty-five billion dollars and having twenty billion dollars.

"So now what we want to do, to bring it all home, is create The Jonboat-Belt Way (or The Belt-Jonboat Way) of understanding the difference between having twenty-five billion dollars and having twenty billion dollars. We want to make our two points of view converge: we want to create a fuller, truer understanding of the difference: a *mutual* understanding. Problem is, I don't see how we can do that. Despite all I've just said, I'm at a loss. I don't know how to proceed. The convergence, after all, seems beyond me. I was hoping I could talk it out—talk us toward it, into it—but I can't. Time was wasted, yours and mine. I was the one who wasted it. Sorry. I might as well have just said something like, 'You're an electron microscope aimed at Jupiter, and I'm the Hubble trying to make out a dust mote.' But metaphors, right? They just beat around the bush.

"My original point, however, stands (maybe more firmly than before, given the fruitlessness of all the effort I just put in): when you say words to me like 'two hundred thousand times more,' especially in reference to my net worth, and regardless of whether you're aware that my net worth is twenty-five percent greater today than *Forbes* said it was in 2009, you don't know what you're talking about, and I know you don't know what you're talking about, so I know *I* can't know what you're talking about, and therefore I can't be offended by your joke, or, for that matter, your explanation of your joke. I can't even laugh at your joke. I could have made some laugh *sounds*, but I'm bad at that—I don't have a lot of practice. The sounds would have sounded entirely false. Your joke just wasn't funny, so I didn't laugh. Your joke was sad. It was sad that you thought you had to make a joke when I told you you looked like a million bucks, and sadder still that you thought the joke you had to make was a self-effacing joke about how little your net worth is. It is sad for me to contemplate how little your net worth is. It's a cigarette to me. Not even a cigarette. A partially smoked cigarette. It's pitiful, Belt. And after you've paid taxes and Social Security? A nearly *half*-smoked cigarette. Even more pitiful. And then for you to explain the joke? For you to smirk your uncomfortable smirk and explain? Why put a finer point on it, Belt?

"What you should have said, if you had to make a joke after I told you you looked like a million bucks, is, 'And you, Jonboat, look like twenty-five billion.' Or, maybe if you wanted to get some slightly more barbed self-effacement across while doing your calling-Jonboat-out-for-his-bullshit-tone thing, you might have said, 'And you, Jonboat, look like *two hundred fifty* billion.' Neither joke would have been very funny, I wouldn't have laughed, but it wouldn't have been so sad. I wouldn't have felt the need to tell you not to underrate yourself in as comforting a tone as I was able to manage, which tone obviously struck you as patronizing and got you all bent out of shape.

"Probably I would've given you a polite smile. But then again maybe that would have just caused a different kind of sadness. And certainly some disappointment, right? Me politely smiling at a joke you made? Politely smiling instead of laughing? That would be disappointing. To both of us, I guess. Definitely to me. Not end-of-the-world disappointing, but a little disappointing. I mean, you made me laugh a lot when we were kids. That's why we were friends. It wasn't because I pitied you, which I did. I pitied you. You were pitiful. You'd been dealt a lousy hand. The death of your mother. Your mental illness. But it wasn't because I pitied you that I was a friend to you.

"You understand that, right? Maybe you don't. Or maybe you don't think *I* understand that. Maybe you think I don't remember. Is that what's going on here? Is that why you made your limp joke and smirked when I told you you looked like a million bucks? Is that why, ever since you walked in here, you've been acting like there's an elephant in the room? There's no elephant, Belt. Were there an elephant in the room, I'd have to see it, right? I'd have to see it, you'd have to see it, and we'd both have to consciously avoid talking about it. I don't know about you, but I'm avoiding fuck-all, I've been avoiding fuck-all. I'm not hiding shit. I remember we were friends. I remember being kids. I know all about us. I'll tell you all about us.

"When we were kids, I was a friend to you because you made me laugh. And it happened that, because you'd been dealt such a lousy hand with the death of your mom and your mental illness—because you were a slumping, open wound on legs—it happened that being a friend to you meant preventing the kids we went to school with from making your life even worse. And so that's what I did. And I don't say so because I'm seeking any gratitude from you. It was easy for me. It was easy to treat you like a human being in front of others, to listen when you spoke to me, and laugh at your jokes, which I found funny anyway. That was all it took to keep the others off you. Easy.

"The only real effort I ever spent on you was on resisting the occasional urge I felt to kick the shit out of you. The urge to kick the shit out of you for being so needy and weak and available to harm. I didn't quite understand where that urge came from, but I knew it was universal. Not just among the other kids at our school, and not just toward you—I'm not trying to be insulting—but toward every being *like* you in every kind of social circle in every last species of the animal kingdom. Herd, pack, murder, flock. Universal, this occasional urge. I'd see you sitting there, sometimes, in this or that corner, all by yourself, or walking through the hallway, or standing in line—didn't matter where—I'd see you and, often as not, you'd have this puzzled look on your face, and you were always wearing those awful glasses with the tinted lenses that never fully clarified and never fully darkened, they just remained in that middle state of gray, which made you seem like you thought you were hiding your eyes, like you thought you were getting away with something, or like you thought you *could* get away with something, like you not only failed to realize how transparent you were, but you actually thought you were complex, mysterious—and you'd have this look on your face, this puzzled look like you couldn't determine whether something you were thinking of was amusing or horrifying or what, I don't know what you were thinking, might've just been your face at rest, I don't know, but I'd see you with this contemptible, pitiful look on your face, this look of amusement or horrification, or horrified amusement, amused horrification, this fucking look on your face, Belt, in some corner, some lunch line, some *wherever,* and I'd have it, that *urge,* you know? to kick the shit out of you.

"Like everyone else.

"But not always, just sometimes.

"And I knew this occasional urge wasn't good, which is not to say that I knew it was wrong—how can something so universal be said to be wrong? how can it be said to be anything other than *natural*?—but I knew it wasn't *good,* which is to say I didn't *like* it, the having of the urge. As much as I would have enjoyed kicking the shit out of you, I didn't like the *thought* of enjoying it. And so my resisting the urge to kick the shit out of you, effortful though it occasionally was, wasn't any real sacrifice. Again, I'm not seeking your gratitude—that's not what I'm getting at. To harm you would have sullied me, in my own eyes. It would have felt good to do, but I knew it wouldn't have felt good to have done. I would have regretted having done it. I would have felt guilty.

"And then I grew up. Went away to school. You sent me some letters I didn't respond to. You sent me too many. Maybe one too many. Maybe two too many. What does that even mean, though, at this point? *One too many? Two too many?* It shouldn't, from where you sit, mean all that much. It didn't, at the time, mean all that much—not from where you were sitting back then, and regardless of whether you knew it or not. See, had you sent only one letter, or even two letters, then I wouldn't have—back then, when we were teenagers—it's true I wouldn't have thought you were pushy, or obsessive, or fixated—whatever the word is—but you wouldn't have known what I was or wasn't thinking because *I wouldn't have written back to you, anyway*. One letter, two letters, three letters, twenty—you were never going to hear from me again regardless of how many letters you wrote or didn't write. As soon as I left for Annapolis, I was done with you, Belt, and not even *particularly* done with you, Belt, but exactly as done with you, Belt, as I was done with everyone I'd gone to school with here in Wheelatine.

"I became an astronaut. My first shuttle mission, I was twenty years old. I was the youngest man—youngest person—to ever go to outer space. That record stands. Next mission, I went to the moon. First man on the moon in decades. Spent fifteen days on the lunar surface. Another record. Third mission, fourth mission, fifth mission, sixth. Seventh mission, eighth mission, ninth mission, tenth. International space station. Soyuz rescue run. Second moonwalk. Mir repair. Third and fourth moonwalk. Most spacewalks during a single mission. Most spacewalks of any astronaut, period. By the time I was twenty-five, I'd been to outer space and back more often than any other American.

"Back on Earth, in between missions, I got married too young, married to someone so nuts and alcoholic she should never have been married to anyone, let alone me, let alone so young, and we had a son, and I attended state functions, and I attended party functions and diplomatic functions, and I lost both my parents inside of three years, and I inherited everything, and I met Fondajane, and I managed my inheritance, grew my inheritance, I bought and sold companies, I helped build an airline, and I left my wife as my son learned to walk, and she killed herself violently, the press attacked me, and I pushed and pulled and loaned and spent and attended more functions than I'd ever attended and back-channeled tirelessly to legalize prostitution, legalize gay marriage, and I succeeded, and I built a life with Fondajane.

"To say I forgot about you would be to overstate the matter. I didn't. I didn't forget—not who you were, or who I was to you. I trust that's obvious by now. You weren't someone I forgot about. Just someone I didn't bother to remember. Basic human stuff, I think.

"And then a few years ago—six? seven?—Burroughs read a review of your novel. And then he read the novel. He liked it, and bought me a copy of my own. He thought that I, even though I've never much cared for fiction—Burroughs thought *I* might want to read your novel. And Burroughs was right. I was curious to read it. I was curious to see if I was in it. More basic human stuff, I think, but not only *just* more basic human stuff, because I remembered, too, probably for the first time since my first year at Annapolis—I remembered that you'd sent me too many letters. That you'd been pushy, annoying, obsessive, whatever. And I had that in mind when, to see if I was in it, I read the book. And as I read the book, I thought—I admit it—I thought: 'I'm not only in it, but this book's *about* me, about the loss of my friendship,' about your bitterness over the end of our friendship. I thought: 'Belt thinks you ruined his life.' And I was insulted by what I took to be your depiction of me as the action figure: a disappearing nonperson, a mere object that the protagonist *delusionally* believes—for comic effect no less, or so it seemed—to be unique and valuable despite its being nothing more than a mass-produced hunk of painted plastic. And I was insulted by the things you have the father think about the worthlessness of the action figure—the father, whose worldview, in that book, is supposed to be true, or much closer to the truth than the miserable, delusional protagonist's. I was insulted.

"I've since been convinced I was wrong about all of that. That I saw things in your novel that weren't there. That I'd been making meaning out of meaningless things. I no longer think *No Please Don't* is about me, and am a little embarrassed to have thought that it was. To have thought that—even given your neediness and your weakness and your having written one or two too many letters to me twentyish years ago—seems to indicate that I possess (or possessed) a degree of self-centeredness or capacity for self-aggrandizement that I would prefer not to possess. I would like to live in reality. I would like to think of myself realistically. I would like to believe that I am as grand and central as I *actually* am, no more, no less.

"I don't blame you, though, for making me feel embarrassed. I'm not saying that. That's on me. I embarrassed myself. I was the one who thought the meaningless meaningful, who saw things that weren't there to see. Same time, though, Belt—and by much the same token—what I owe you is nothing. You're entitled to nothing. Nada, zero, and fuck-all. Nothing."

While obviously, reader, Jonboat didn't say any of that last part, I'm certain it was close to what he meant to convey when, in response to my, "Have I offended *you,* Jonboat?" he hiked up his eyebrows, uncapped a pen, and, after a number of seconds spent scribbling, pushed across the desk to me a personal check for a hundred thousand dollars.

FOUR-FIFTHS OF A QUILL

"THANK YOU," I SAID, my head more inclined than I like to remember, my eyes on the check in my hand in my lap.

I raised the hand, examined the check.

Along its longest line was written, "one hundred thousand————————"; inside of the dollar box, "100,000.00"; my name on the *Pay to the order of* line; on the *For* line, "transcript"; and on the line to the right of that, Jonboat's signature, illegible except for the towering J's. I read the check top to bottom, bottom to top, forward and backward. I read and reread it like the mystifying final sentence of a story I thought I'd understood til I'd gotten to the end: trying to excavate a buried meaning, failing to excavate a buried meaning, uncertain it contained a buried meaning, and, for some reason I couldn't quite grasp—it wasn't, after all, a story, but a check—wanting very badly to find some assurance it contained a buried meaning. Did I suspect that the check was somehow a *fake*? I don't think so, no; I don't see why I would have. Had it been a golden nugget, sure, I may have bit into it, but not to measure its authenticity; just to try to get to know it better. I studied it, rubbed it, turned it in the light. Here were Jonboat's machine-printed name and address; there were the name and address of the bank. Down here were some numbers divided by colons, up there some more numbers in a different font. Here a company logo with a superscript ®, there a padlock emblem resembling a mosque. At a certain angle, a tooth was detectable—not to the eye, but the tip of my left (my softer) thumb. I tried to describe its shade of green to myself. "Pale, but not mint," I thought. "Worn, but not faded—fuzzy ten-year-old dollar back." It smelled like the spine of a book. Like glue.

I heard distant, familiar voices, getting nearer.

"I love what you've got going on out there," said one I nearly recognized.

"Thanks," Triple-J said.

"I really think it's major. Revolutionary, even."

"Cool, thanks," Triple-J said.

"If you need any help or anything in the future, I'd love it if you'd holler."

"Good to know," Triple-J said, entering the office.

In tandem, behind him, walked Burroughs and the notary. The notary was wearing a three-piece shorts suit. The notary's Ray-Bans were up on his hairline. The pocket-seal case the notary carried was stenciled with the logo of the Marshall Amplification company. The notary was Chad-Kyle.

He glanced at me, and kind of auto-nodded, but his face betrayed no hint of recognition.

"I mean, I'd love to get involved," he told Triple-J, and, coming up beside me, to my immediate left, he said to Jonboat, "I was just telling Trip, here, I'd love to help him get the word out about these games he's running. I'd love to help him promote. Help him make what he's got going on here even bigger. Over at C.K. Productions International, we've been having a lot of success—a *lot* of success—with VIP-flyering. Now, VIP-flyering isn't *all* that we do. Is it the foundation of all that we do? Sure. Of course. Make no mistake. VIP-flyering *is* the foundation. But we applicate a many-pronged integral approach. See, I'm pretty well-networked in terms of the youth. I've got I guess you'd say a talent for seeing the next thing early, and I can straddle the cusps of multiple demos. I mean: I *do* straddle those cusps. It's kind of my thang—where's my manners?" He extended a hand, said, "C.K. Baker, licensed notary public."

Jonboat got up, clutched the proffered hand.

Trip, who, by then, was standing between his father and Burroughs, across the desk from Chad-Kyle and me, caught my eye, shot a fast look at Chad-Kyle, and mouthed the word *wang-scab*.

"It's a true thrill to meet you, Mr. Pellmore-Jason," Chad-Kyle was saying. "To be in your presence and have your attention, even briefly. Just shaking your hand. You know, I saw you a couple weeks back, at the bank. You came in with Ms. Henry—I was the first to spot you walking through the door, ask anyone who works there—but I was way too shy to introduce myself. I guess I should have, and I usually would have, but in person, it's like—you're like the opposite of some of these celebrities one meets and one thinks, 'He looks taller on TV.' And same with your wife."

"Well, thank you," said Jonboat.

"I'm just really grateful I got this second chance. A thousand compliments on everything you do and everything you've ever done. I mean that. Sincerely."

"Very kind of you," said Jonboat, and turned to Triple-J. "How'd it go out there?" he said.

"How'd it *go*?" said Chad-Kyle. "Your son is the total king of The Ulysses."

"It's Ulysses," Trip told him.

"What did I say?" said Chad-Kyle.

"'*The* Ulysses.' There isn't any article."

"Did I say that? That's weird. I hate an article."

"Why would you hate a part of speech, dude?" said Trip.

"Hard to explain, really," Chad-Kyle said. "I have this instinct for branding. An ear, I guess you'd say. I think it's like a benefit of my having this rare condition you might have heard of called *synesthesia*? An article to me is . . . garlicky and . . . damp. Also magenta."

"Anyway, I won," Triple-J said to Jonboat. "Set a new record. The second-place kid, though—the one I went out there to compete against—he broke the record I set this morning, so I let him have Spotsy."

"That was kind of you," said Jonboat, playfully poking his son in the ribs.

"I guess it wasn't *un*kind," Triple-J said, "but I think I was only being—come on! stop poking!—I think I was only being fair. Earlier, I'd said the first guy to break my record—which, at the time, was ninety-two seconds—he could take home Spotsy and compete with me for captain of the Yachts next month. But then, just now, when *I* broke my record, I lasted a hundred and seven seconds, but this second-place guy, he lasted ninety-nine seconds, breaking the old record, so."

"So now you sound like an old broken record, broken record, broken record, broken record."

"Har har," Triple-J said. "Dad jokes rule."

"Broken record, broken record," Jonboat continued.

"It's a good one. Really. Dadly as hell."

"Broken record, broken record."

Triple-J made laugh sounds.

"All joking aside," said Jonboat, "I still say it was kind of you to give the kid the Curio. Even if it was what you should have done anyway. You can be right and kind at the same time, you know?"

"Yeah, okay," Triple-J said.

"I mean it," said Jonboat. "In fact, it's ideal. You did a good job. I'm proud of you, Trip."

"Plus who needs Spotsy?" Chad-Kyle said, looking rather fixedly at Handsome Arthur, and coming around the back of my chair. "Who needs Spotsy when you've got a bot like that one? Man, that thing's something."

Burroughs pivoted, palmed one of his shoulders, said, "Time we better get this show on the road," and, guiding him off the path to the globe, faced him toward the side of the desk to my right.

"Sure thing," said the notary. He set his case down behind the T-shirt-draped helmet, unlatched and unpacked it: pocket seal, certificates, orca-themed souvenir floaty-pen from SeaWorld.

Burroughs handed me a contract. I signed it. Jonboat and Trip signed the one he handed them. We traded, signed again, and gave the contracts to Chad-Kyle, who, donning a monocle he'd pulled from his vest, started to read them, which seemed inappropriate, though no one bothered saying so.

It might have been the leathery scent of his aftershave, which might have been body spray, or perhaps it was because, of the five individuals gathered around the desk, I was the only one who was sitting, but I'd started feeling a touch claustrophobic—a touch more than a touch—and I guess that accounts for how I managed, once again, to unbox a Quill without having realized.

"Can't smoke in here," said Burroughs. "We'll be done in a minute, though."

"Sorry," I said, reboxing the Quill. "I keep on doing that. I don't know why."

"Stretch out," he said. "When I first quit, it helped me, sometimes, to get past a jones. No kidding. Go on. Stand up and have a stretch."

I did as advised. I rose from the chair, bent forward, toe-touched.

"Well, these contracts are fine," Chad-Kyle said. "Though I feel a little dissed, if I'm being honest. I *know* this guy," he told the Pellmore-Jasons, then, turning to me, said, "Why didn't you say 'Hi,' chief? What's up with that?"

"Why didn't *you* say 'Hi'?" Trip said.

"I didn't realize he was him," said Chad-Kyle. "Not til I saw his name on the contracts. I mean he looked like him, and I thought, 'That's him,' but then I thought: 'Brain-fart! How would Belt Magnet ever get inside the office of Jonny "Jonboat" Pellmore-Jason?' Right? No *way* it's him."

"He must have thought the same thing seeing you," Burroughs told him.

Chad-Kyle said, "Same thing, yeah, sure," and, making a laugh face, swiped at the air, and, while tucking the monocle back into his vest, said, "Congrats on this contract, though, Belt, for real. Looks like all your embarrassing financial troubles have come to a sudden and happy end."

"Why don't you stamp those or whatever," Triple-J said.

Chad-Kyle said, "Right," and did as advised. He applied his pocket seal to each of the contracts, and passed one to Jonboat, and passed one to me. Then he filled out a pair of half-page certificates, and signed them and sealed them, and passed one to Jonboat, and passed one to me.

"That's that, then," said Jonboat.

Burroughs gave me an envelope, into which I dropped the papers and the check.

Chad-Kyle repacked and, as he latched his case shut, said, "Wait a *second*. Is that—is that what I think it is?"

"It is," said Jonboat.

"Dang," said Chad-Kyle.

"And the answer," Jonboat said, "is: Yes. It's been to the moon. Twice, actually."

"No way," said Chad-Kyle. "*And* it's vintage?"

"Vintage?" said Jonboat. "I suppose you could say that. Sure. Yes."

"He means the T-shirt," Triple-J said.

"What'd you think I meant?"

"The helmet underneath."

"There's a helmet under there?"

"My last Space Shuttle helmet," Jonboat said. "And the first of its kind. Before that model, there were separate assemblies for—"

"May I?" said Chad-Kyle.

"Go ahead," said Jonboat. "That's what it's there for."

Chad-Kyle removed the shirt from the helmet, held it up by the shoulders in front of his face, turned it toward me, toward Burroughs, then Trip and Jonboat, then back toward himself. "It's in such good shape," he said. "Looks like it's got a touch of light staining—what is that, rocket grease or something? ha!—but, like, there's no fade at all. No cracks in the decal. Shut your piehole *cake*face. Shut your *pie*hole cakeface. Shut *your* piehole-cakeface. I never knew how to say it right without the *gaylord*. You know, someone once told me you left the *gaylord* off the shirt so kids could wear it at school, but I never understood that."

"What's not to understand?" said Jonboat.

"Why you couldn't wear a shirt with *gaylord* on it."

"*Gaylord*'s a homophobic slur," said Jonboat.

"Come on," said Chad-Kyle. "I mean, I heard that before, but I never believed it. Like how can it be? If you call a gay person a gaylord, isn't that like saying they're the lord of gay people? Like the . . . king of gay people? What kind of slur is that? What gay person wouldn't want to be the king of gay people?"

"At the time it was a slur," Jonboat said. "You wouldn't really use it to insult a gay person. You'd use it to insult other boys who, in most cases, weren't gay, and in pretty much all cases didn't want to be thought of by other boys as gay. I'm not exactly proud I used to use that word."

"If I were you, I *would* be proud, if I may say, sir. You were ahead of your time. Me and my friends—a lot of them are gay—we use *gaylord* a lot, as smack talk, but like playfully, you know? My friend at work, Lotta—Belt knows her, maybe you do too, she's about your guys' age—and she's a one hundred percent completely tolerant kind of person and she, just the other day, I came to work wearing this tiny bouquet of little flowers in my buttonhole, and Lotta called me a gaylord, but all she meant by it was, like, 'Look who thinks he's fancy!'"

"You sure you're remembering that right?" Burroughs said. "Sure your friend didn't call the flowers a *nosegay*?"

"No. Yeah. She did that, too. I mean, what she said was, 'Look at the nosegay on *this* gaylord,' which . . . But, look, people call me a gaylord *all the time*. I'm telling you. It's a little edgy, sure—they say it to make fun of me—but it's not *homophobic*. I mean, who's homophobic anymore? I'm definitely not. Neither are my friends, especially not the gay ones. And no way *you* are, Mr. Pellmore-Jason. We just think of it—at least *I* just think of it, as a stuffy guy's name. A dandy's name, you know? Cause that's what it is, right? It's a kind of old-timey kind of British guy's kind of name, isn't it? The kind of guy who'd wear spats and a . . . a nosegay in his buttonhole. And I heard it was a gang once, too, someone said. I mean, wasn't there a gang in Chicago called the Gaylords?"

"Actually, there was," Jonboat said. "And it's not all that uncommon of a surname, either. At one point, the president of Bell Aerospace was a man named Henry Gaylord."

"Harvey Gaylord," Burroughs said.

"Harvey. That's right," Jonboat said. "Harvey Gaylord. Mostly forgotten. Mostly unsung. But a very important person. Before he was president of Bell, he was one of the men who helped make the X-1 a reality."

"The X-1?" said Chad-Kyle.

"Glamorous Glennis," Burroughs said. "The aircraft Chuck Yeager broke the sound barrier in."

"The huh Chuck what broke the who?" said Chad-Kyle. "That sounds like some serious history to me."

"Serious history, you say," Burroughs said.

"No disrespect, Jones," Chad-Kyle said. "I just mean—it just wasn't exactly a subject I ever like excelled at. In school, I mean. I'm more a creative type. Like I was pretty good in Art. Pretty great in Art, really. History, though—and Math and Science and English, too, English—*Jesus* . . . Just wasn't where my gifts laid. Lied? See? *English*. All I'm really trying to say's I'm not a homophobe at all, and I like it. Gaylord. The sound of it. I think it's a great word. Like, is it edgy? Check. Sure it's edgy. That's been *well* established. Is it campy? You bet. It's campy, too. No one denies it. Campy *and* edgy. The ultimate combo. I mean it really just makes the original just so much better."

"The original?" Jonboat said.

"Of the saying," said Chad-Kyle. "That's all I've been getting at. It's much better the original way. With the gaylord. With*out* the gaylord, it's kinda pissing through a—"

"Well—"

And then I was on him. I don't remember having gotten on him. I don't even remember having picked up the helmet. I do have a memory of holding on to it, my fore- and middle finger hooked through the feed port, and, while in midair (I must have leapt a little), pulling back high and wide to swing, but that memory's thin, a flash, half-erased. What I remember with clarity is being on him, one knee on his chest, the other on the floor, between his elbow and his ribs, and raising the helmet, both-handed, for a second blow, while rotating it so I could strike with the visor. I remember thinking, as I raised the helmet, that his mess of a face—some teeth were broken, his lips were shredded—was not that hard, that that was too bad, and that I should have initially struck him overhanded, visor-first, and on the crown, when I'd had greater leverage, that maybe the visor would have fractured on his skull, and I remember then thinking that maybe the second blow, the blow I was about to bring down on his nose, should be to his forehead, that maybe the visor would fracture on his forehead, but also thinking that first I'd prefer to cave his nose, to spread it out, and I heard my name being shouted then, "Belt!" and I thought it was the helmet, but it wasn't the helmet, it was Burroughs who'd shouted, and I thought I should have known that—what inan had ever gotten my name right?—and I turned in his direction, in Burroughs's direction, saw his jacket was aflap, that there was something in his hand, he'd taken something from his jacket that was black and glossy and he was pointing it down at me and telling me to *stop,* and I turned away from him, bringing down the helmet as hard as I could, aiming, after all, for forehead—it would be my last chance, I knew; the helmet's last chance, I knew—and just before the impact, my bangle flared, white-silver and dazzling as a popping flashbulb, and a bolt of excruciation ripped through me, slamming my eyes shut, squeezing them shut, and I felt as though my every muscle, on fire, were attempting to flee, to scream and twitch and wrench and tear free of anything binding, and then I went sideways, and knocked myself out, epileptically flopping around.

•

• •

Some number of seconds or minutes later, my eyes came open. I was lying on the floor and sucking hard air, hearing the voice of Burroughs from above—he was seated in Jonboat's chair behind the desk. "What you remember doesn't matter," Burroughs said. And what a horrible thing it was to say, I thought. You don't say that to people. You're not supposed to. Especially not when it's true. You just don't.

Defensive and indignant, I sat bolt upright, regretted it instantly. Every soft part of me was barely-wet cement, was as stiff and as sore as my biceps and back had been after the dumbbells at Sally the Balls's. Plus it turned out Burroughs hadn't been addressing me.

"I want my phone back, now," said Chad-Kyle. Through his torn-up lips and broken teeth, *my* sounded like *ny,* and *phone* like *phthone.*

Hands were reaching down to me.

"As soon as you show us you're ready," Burroughs told him.

The hands reaching down to me were Valentine's hands. He took hold of my elbows and pulled me to my feet. Faced me toward the side of the desk, on which I leaned. "Alright?" he said softly. "You're gonna be alright. We can't give you aspirin cause it thins the blood and you got concussed, but I've been zapped before, all of us have, and you take yourself a walk in the sun, drink some water, and before you know it, the pain—"

"You phthlucking *dick,*" Chad-Kyle spat at me. He was slumped in the chair I'd formerly occupied, and Duggan was behind him—or perhaps it was Hogan—holding him in place by both of his shoulders. His nose wasn't spread, nor his forehead marked—I must not have landed the second blow—but his mouth looked like a chewed three-cube wad of Wild Cherry Bubble Yum. He wiped blood and spit from his chin with his handkerchief. The monogram, as Gus had told me, looked crowded. "You psychopapthlic phthlucking pthussy," he said. "You vlindsided ne, and it's phthlucking plfathetic. In a pfair pfight, I'd've wiped the phthlucking pfloor with you."

I had never thought of myself as a hardass, nor had I begun to, but Chad-Kyle was, fundamentally, a bleeder—recognizable as such upon first glance—and a scrawny one at that (no fewer than thirty pounds my inferior), so for him to believe that the two of us could even *have* a fair fight, let alone one from which he'd walk away victorious, was so outlandish as to be almost cute, and that almost-cuteness—even more than the condition in which I'd left his face, even more than all his slurped, Loony-Toonsy bilabials—*inspired* me, in the wake of his rant; caused me to feel so emboldened and Clydely as to stare, without expression, into his eyes, while slow-motion miming—like both Trip and Magnet had earlier, but *better*—the manual penetration of not just one but two tight little anuses, after which (i.e. once my hands had fully balled into fists), I Fonzily raised and wagged both thumbs.

"You're sick," said Chad-Kyle. "Disturved. You're disgusting. And you're all so in trouvle. This is totally illegal."

"What's illegal," Burroughs told him, "is overloading on a priceless Curio that doesn't belong to you. And when you clobber a man in the side of the head, a well-meaning man who's just trying to stop you—a well-meaning man who's a *guest* in the home of the man to whom that Curio belonged, no less—when you knock a well-meaning man unconscious in the course of committing a property crime he's trying to prevent—that's also illegal."

"The cure's right there on the glove!"

"That's a clone."

"Vullshit! If I did what you said, *you'd* ve calling the cops. *He'd* ve calling the cops."

"We have no time for cops," Burroughs said. "They come around here, question all the witnesses—it takes a while. Mr. Pellmore-Jason's got business to attend to. A life to lead. A plane to catch. And Belt here understands all of that. He'd never call the cops and inconvenience this compound."

"Vullshit, man. Vullshit. You'd sue ne for that cure if I did what you said."

"The Pellmore-Jasons have never been litigious. They've always preferred to take care of matters by talking them through, like we're doing right now."

"Yeah right."

"*Should* we sue you, do you think? Is that what you're trying to say? I mean, maybe . . ."

"Yeah yeah yeah. Yeah right, and what? Fmy fmouth just exfploded? Tell *that* to the judge."

"We've been over this, son. You cracked your mouth on the edge of the desk, falling down after I, unfortunately, had to bangle-taze you from fear that you were going to kill our well-meaning guest, who you'd just cold-cocked for trying to stop you from dacting that priceless cure that wasn't yours."

"You vangle-tazed *him*! He was trying to kill *ne*."

"Being electrocuted," Burroughs said, "can do some rather strange things to the brain. Cause retrograde amnesia. Déjà vu. Brief, waking dreams. General confusion and emotional disturbances. Like what's happening here. To you."

"It really doesn't make any sense," said Duggan or Hogan. "The way you're acting."

"It's like: you're telling my dad he saved your life," said Valentine, pausing briefly to micro-shrug and -grimace before he continued: "Like you say that Burroughs, here, tazed another man to save your life, but you're not acting toward Burroughs like someone whose life just got saved by him, you know? You're not acting very grateful to Burroughs at all."

"How you're acting is difficult," said Duggan or Hogan.

"Vecause that was ve*fore*!" Chad-Kyle said.

"What was before?" Burroughs said.

"That you saved fmy life. Cone on! Now it's all different. Now you're phthucking with ne! I *renenver* what happened."

"But what you remember doesn't matter," Burroughs said. "I told you that already. We're going in circles."

"Jonvoat Pfelnore-Jason would never let you do this. I want to see Jonvoat."

"So does everyone. It's not gonna happen."

"Then I want to see Tripfle-J."

"You'll never be within sight of him again."

"Better to forget you ever met Triple-J," Duggan or Hogan said.

"Probably you should never even say his name again," said Valentine. "Someone might overhear you, and think you're making threats even if you aren't, and then it gets back to us, and your life gets hard. You know how it is."

"I can't phlucking velieve this."

"Which part?" said Hogan/Duggan. "Like you think you'll get an audience with Mr. Pellmore-Jason?"

"You think you should say Trip's name again?" said Valentine. "You think you should threaten Mr. Pellmore-Jason's son?"

"You know that's not what I fmeant."

"So what did you mean?" said Hogan/Duggan.

"What exactly," said Valentine, "don't you believe?"

"What you guys are saying haffened to me!"

"Well that's no problem," Burroughs said. "You don't have to believe that."

"Yeah," said Duggan/Hogan. "You don't even have to believe we believe it."

"All you gotta believe is that everyone else will believe we believe it. And they'll believe he believes it," said Valentine, nudging me, "and they'll believe that Mr. Pellmore-Jason and Trip believe it, too. That's a lot of people who everyone will believe believe it. That's what? That's six. That's six people, and you're just one. Just one lonely fellow. Lonesome fellow? I'm not sure what the difference is. It's probably not important. You're one guy alone, and you're a spidger, too. There's also that. We got a photo of your pipe, your little baggie, your little vial of oil—from the scanner, you know? We take photos of everything that goes through the scanner. That kind of thing really compromises you in these United States. So you're a lonesome, lonely, compromised notary who has problems with drugs, and you're all alone. No one will believe you, except maybe you, which no one here faults you for, but everyone everywhere else will fault you for, if you challenge the beliefs they believe we believe in front of anyone else. That came out sounding really confusing, huh? All I mean is that, when you leave here today, we hope you feel completely empowered to believe anything you want to believe, because, first of all, we're all Americans here, and believing anything you want to believe is a big part of believing in yourself, in America, and it's a great thing to do—we want you to do it. And that brings me to second-of-all. We want you to believe in yourself in America, Brad-Cory, because the other big part of believing in yourself in America is believing in your value—in the value of yourself—and we hope you believe in yourself in America enough to value yourself highly enough that you don't keep acting in ways that could get yourself really hurt really permanently and really soon if you keep making us feel like we have to convince you to believe in yourself in the way I just described."

"Do you believe in yourself?" Duggan/Hogan said.

"Okay," said Chad-Kyle, welling eyes aimed down at his lap.

"'Okay'?" Duggan/Hogan said. "What does that mean?"

"I'll stofp."

"Stop what?" said Valentine.

"I'll stofp acting in ways like however you said. Unfpatriotic. I won't call the pflolice. I won't say anything you don't want ne to say."

"What if someone asks you about your face?" said Duggan/Hogan.

"I'll say I knocked this psycho out, and then I fell and hit the desk, after I got zapfed."

"What will you say if you're asked why you got zapped?"

"What do you want ne to say?"

"You should say you were acting like an asshole, and you deserved it," Duggan/Hogan said.

"You *could* say that," said Valentine. "Or, if you're in a different kind of mood, you could kind of turn the thing around, you know? Be stoic about it. Like, sure, you were electrocuted and your face got wrecked, and it was completely humiliating when it happened, but, on later reflection, you've come to see that dacting that rare and priceless cure was a unique and beautiful experience you couldn't have had without facing those consequences, and if you had the chance to do the whole thing over, you'd probably do it exactly the same. All your suffering has been worthwhile."

"Okay," said Chad-Kyle. "Then that's what I'll say."

"Do we believe him?" said Burroughs.

"I do," Duggan/Hogan said.

"I believe him," said Valentine.

Burroughs pushed Chad-Kyle's phone across the desk. "I believe him, too," he said. "Now get him home safe."

As Duggan/Hogan took Chad-Kyle out of the office, Valentine gazed at Burroughs, expectantly. Once the shutting of the front door was heard, Burroughs turned to him and said, "You did well. A little over-the-top at the end, maybe, but otherwise a solid performance. You've got great instincts."

"That means a lot to me. Thank you. And I'm sorry I said, 'Dad.'"

"No big deal," Burroughs said. "Next time you'll remember not to."

"I will," said Valentine. "I'll make sure to remember. But can I ask, what did you mean by 'over-the-top'? Like . . . which part exactly?"

"That America stuff."

"You mean you think it was too on the nose? Or like I jumped the shark or . . . ?"

"I don't know what you're saying, son. I'm not familiar with those terms. The America stuff just struck me as unnecessary. Made you sound a little . . . meandering, maybe. Then again, you were completely effective. Likely as not, that dipshit thought you were going off the rails and became even more afraid of you than he would've if you'd just stayed direct. So more power to you. Having further reflected, I've reconsidered. I rescind my critique."

"No, no," said Valentine. "You don't have to spare my feelings. I think I see what you mean, actually. I think I got too lyrical with *America* and *American*. In an essay, it's a great thing to do. It's pretty much what all the best contemporary essays do. Those words, *America* and *American*—they're so powerful. It's almost like you can't write a contemporary lyric essay without them. Not a great one at least. No kidding. No joke. I said so to my writing group a month or so back, and they all thought my observation was really intriguing, and so what we all did in the next couple weeks was we did *America*- and *American*-counts on all these different contemporary essays in the book of contemporary essays we've been using for the book-club part of our writing group, and it turned out I was really onto something. I mean, it turned out that the essays we loved the most—the ones that we all agreed were the most deep and moving and important—were the ones that most frequently used the words *America* and *American*. So anyway, since then, I've been trying to jam as many *America*s and *American*s and also *Americans*es into my essays as possible, as lyrically as possible, and I've been pretty successful, at least according to the writing group, which is really encouraging, but my point is that I think I've just gotten so in the habit of using *America* and *American* in my essays lately that I guess it must have infected my whole like persona while we were bracing that mark, which just isn't appropriate. So point taken. Though maybe *infected* isn't the right way to think about it, considering that lyricism isn't a disease, and in many ways, actually, is kind of the opposite of a disease, but—what am I trying to say?"

"Why don't we talk about this later, Val."

"Can we?" said Valentine. "I'd love that."

"Sure," Burroughs said. Then to me, he said, "You. You nearly killed that little dipshit notary and I just fixed it. Tell me why."

"Why I nearly killed him?"

"Keep up," he said.

"Why you fixed it," I said.

"Your first hint is: it isn't because I felt it was right to do so."

"You felt it was wrong?" I said.

"That's not what I said. Your second hint is: much as I like your novel, and little as I like the dipshit notary, I am neither your friend nor your father, and I don't do any work for non-friends or non-sons unless those non-friends and non-sons are my employers."

"You want me to pay you?"

"Your bonus hint is: you could never afford me."

"So you fixed it because Jonboat asked you to, you're saying."

"Now that's exactly the incorrect answer I was seeking."

"The *in*correct answer."

"Incorrect inasmuch as it's incomplete. I'm trying to draw your attention to a distinction here, Belt, an important distinction. Jonboat asked me to fix *it*. Triple-J asked me to fix it *for you*. So far, I'm pleased to have been able to fulfill both of their requests without said fulfillment creating any, let's call them, inter-fulfillment conflicts."

"I'd like to thank them. And you."

"You're failing to appreciate the distinction I'm trying to impress upon you. I can convey your thanks to Jonboat and Triple-J, but for me, your appreciation of the aforementioned distinction is the only thanks I'm looking for."

"You're saying I shouldn't try to thank them."

"That's one thing I'm saying."

"You're saying Jonboat saw me nearly kill a dipshit, so now he doesn't want me anywhere near him or his son, but his son still wants me to write the transcript. You feel awkward saying this to me. You wish you didn't have to, so you're doing this whole roundabout, break-the-news-slowly thing that you're doing."

"I've never in my entire life felt awkward saying anything, nor can I speak to my employers' motives, but you are one hundred percent entirely right about what Trip wants and what his father doesn't."

"Okay," I said, more than a little touched by Burroughs's attempts to treat me thoughtfully, needless though they were. "So what do I do?"

Burroughs wrote ten digits on the flap of the envelope into which I'd dropped my contract and check. "When you finish the transcript, you call me at that number, we'll arrange a meet. In the meantime, you're sore from the tazing, but you've had a concussion. Don't take any aspirin or your brain might bleed. Acetaminophen only."

"Valentine says I should walk in the sun."

"The sun's nice for the mood, but walking will diminish the soreness with or without it."

"I heard you're not supposed to go to sleep with a concussion."

"Your eyes look fine and you aren't vomiting. Are you feeling dizzy?"

“I’m not feeling dizzy. I do have a headache.”

“A very bad headache?”

“No. Could be sinuses, too. Sometimes in the heat, I get an allergy or something.”

“Sleep all you want. Walk all you can. Don’t take aspirin. Acetaminophen.”

“And that’s Tylenol, right?”

“Yes,” Burroughs said. “Acetaminophen is the active ingredient in Tylenol.”

V

GATES

ONE WAY TO THINK OF IT

"SO, HAPPY ENDING THEN," my dad said.

"You think so?" I said.

We were sitting at the bar in Blimey's Tavern. When I'd returned from the compound, I'd swallowed six Tylenol and shown Clyde the check, which he'd thought was a prank, so I showed him the contract, at which point he said that I had to tell him everything, and insisted I do so on the way to Blimey's, where we'd find his lawyer friend and get some advice. His lawyer friend hadn't gotten there yet, nor had I told Clyde, by any means, *everything,* but I'd spent the whole walk—and a good ten minutes in the tavern itself—conveying the highlights.

"Sure I think so," he said. "Of *course* I think so. I mean, maybe you didn't hit the best guy to hit, but you couldn't. How could you? His bodyguard's there. His son's right next to him. You gonna clobber the man in front of his son? Even I wouldn't do that. Plus you got that bangle on. Desk between the two of you. Maybe, too, a little lingering sentimentality. And the *check,* son. The check. Come on. That's real money for you. That's life-changing money. And to do some writing? The thing you love to do? You can't just throw that kind of money away. That kind of work. No. Sometimes you can't hit the best guy to hit. Sometimes you gotta hit another guy instead. The one at hand. Nearest one you can reach. That's just how it is. That's how it is *without* that kind of money at stake. But *with* that kind of money at stake? You hit another guy instead and you *take the money*. You did the right thing." He slapped the bar with finality, and said so again: "You did the right thing."

"Another?" said the bartender.

"Jill," Clyde said, "you think I'd slap the bar to get your attention? I'm not *that* kind of jerk. I was only expressing a general-type enthusiasm for the universe. My handsome son here just had himself a peach of a day. Mind you, though, I *am* on vacation, I *like* this Scotch"—he threw back what remained in his glass—"and you're standing right in front of me, trying to give me more of it, so therefore, I will, in fact, have another."

"And for the handsome son?" Jill asked me, pouring.

"Handsome son can't drink tonight," my father said. "He's got a concussion."

"That doesn't sound very peachy," she said.

"Maybe you lack imagination," Clyde said.

"What's with your dad?" Jill the bartender said. "Half the time he's in here, he acts like he's in love with me. Other half he flirts."

"Where's Biggie?" Clyde said. "We need his advice."

"Beats me," Jill said. "I only just got here."

A few stools away sat a man in a boater at whom my father'd nodded when we first came in. He said, "Biggie's been out of town for a couple of days. Florida. Or maybe New York. California. I can't remember. I think he said he'd be back today, though. Should be coming in later."

"Who," said my father, "in the hell asked you, Herb? Who asked you for a treatise on Biggie's travel plans? What qualifies you to make confident predictions regarding Biggie's ETA?"

"Go fuck yourself, Clyde."

"Come on over," said my father. "Next round's on my son. Had a peach of a day. Herb's from Boston, Billy. So he always has a hat on. Inside, outside. Always in a hat."

"Where the fuck do you come up with this nonsense?" Herb said, tottering over with his half-filled pint.

"So you're *not* from Boston?" my father said.

"Hat's got fuck-all to do with Boston."

"Herb's from Boston, Bill, so he's always saying 'fuck.' Kinda sounds like *fack*."

"That I cannot say isn't true," Herb told me. "However. I wear the hat for professional reasons. Gotta dress for the part."

"Herb's from Boston," said my father, "so he became a private eye."

"I do not get this line of ribbing," Herb said.

"Ribbing," said my father. *"Line of ribbing?"* said my father. "Is that what they call it in Boston? Is that Bostonese for being called an asswipe at a tavern?"

"And now you're calling me a fucken asswipe now," said Herb.

"Every time you sport a new hat," said my father, "I find myself thinking, 'Herb: asswipe.'"

"It's not a new hat. I haven't worn it in a while because the summer's been mild enough for my porkpie. Then today's ninety-plus, so I broke out the boater."

"'*Boston* asswipe,' I find myself thinking."

"See," Herb said to me, "I know that he won't stop saying *Boston* and *asswipe* until I start laughing, but I don't feel like laughing. I'm just not in the mood. Not to say I'm in a bad mood. I'm in more of a calm mood. I'm feeling thoughtful this evening. Thoughtful and calm and positive of outlook. Expansive, even. I feel like I've got a kind of bird's-eye view of let's call them the more subtle social dynamics, and what I'm seeing right now is that what's nice about your father is the same thing that's so fucking aggravating about your father. It's how patient he is. How dedicated to whatever whim he finds himself possessed by. His whims become missions. You understand what I mean? He didn't come in here thinking, 'I will say *Boston* and *asswipe* til I get Herb to laugh.' It only just occurred to him as something to do. Just a minute ago. It was just a whim. But now he's committed. I'm not in any kind of mood to laugh at him saying *Boston* and *asswipe,* but he'll say *Boston* and *asswipe* til I *get* in the mood. And the thought of that, I'm finding, has begun to put me in the mood. I'll be there soon, I bet. With patience. With patience, I'll soon be in the mood to laugh at *Boston,* to laugh at *asswipe.* At that point, it'll be hard to fault him for aggravating me. He, with his patience and dedication, will have put me in the mood to laugh, and me, on the road to that mood, I'll have discovered—am right fucking now, discovering—my own capacity for patience."

"Are you really a private eye?" I said. "Like you find missing persons?"

"Private browneye," my father said, "the Boston asswipe."

Herb handed me a business card.

"Private Herb Browneye," my father said, "reporting home to Boston for asswipe duty."

Herb smiled. "One last predictable iteration first," he said. "But which way will it go? How will he swing it?"

"No, that's it," my father said. "I will go no further in front of a lady."

"You'll say *browneye* in front of a lady," Jill said, "but you won't pun duty?"

"He don't do blue," Herb said, laughing.

"Blue I do," my father said. "Already did. Browneye."

"Browneye's scatological," Herb said.

"Browneye's anatomical. *You're* scatological, you stinking Boston asswipe."

Herb gasped for air.

"I thought your name was Herb," I said, looking at the business card, which read ANDREW BRAINTREE, PRIVATE INVESTIGATOR.

"Herb's just the nickname I gave him," Jill said.

Herb said, "I went to Exeter."

"I don't understand," I said.

Jill asked, "Don't they call prep-school kids *Herbs* around here?"

"I've never met a prep-school kid as far as I know," I said.

"Me neither," said my father. "Except for this asswipe."

"Back home in Cohoes—that's a town near Albany, in upstate New York—we call the prep-school kids *Herbs,*" said Jill. "When I was growing up we did, at least."

"Why?" I said.

"I think it had something to do with Burger King," said Jill. "These commercials for Burger King where everyone pretends to like this guy named Herb, this unattractive, nerdy guy who's wearing a suit. Everyone kisses his ass because he might give them money or—I don't really remember . . . What's confusing me, though," she said, turning to Herb, "is why Herb would catch on as your nickname, here in this tavern, Herb, if no one around here but us knows what a Herb is."

"Beats me," Herb said. "I didn't know what a Herb was til you just said."

"What're you talking about? Billy just asked you about your name, and you said that you're Herb because you went to Exeter."

"No. That's not how it happened. That isn't how it happened at all. What happened was you told Billy you gave me the nickname, and then all I said was that I went to Exeter."

"To explain the nickname."

"No, Jill. No. He was looking at my business card, asking about me, so I said I went to Exeter because it's always seemed to me that others find it interesting that I'm a private investigator who went to Exeter. Truth is, people, especially around here, they find it interesting I went to Exeter even if they don't know I'm a private investigator. I mean: Exeter. How many people who didn't go to Exeter know anyone who went to Exeter? So I tell people: I went there. I learned this from graduates of Harvard University in Cambridge. It's a stereotype that they always tell people they went to Harvard, but it actually holds. They really do that, most of them. Every time they meet someone. Maybe it's ironic in that newfangled way that isn't really ironic and just ironic-y, now—still, most of them do it. But there's a lot more people who didn't go to Harvard who know people who went to Harvard than there are people who didn't go to Exeter who know people who went to Exeter, and Harvard people always tell you they went to Harvard, and everyone seems to agree that's what you should do. Tell people, I mean. Is my point."

"Who agrees?" Jill said.

"Everyone," said Herb. "Most importantly me. And I, for one, have always worn the nickname you gave me as a badge of pride that made me feel special, and now that I know it's because I went to Exeter that you gave me the nickname, I feel even more special, because being a graduate of Exeter is something I've always worn as a badge of honor. That's quite a badge, Jill. Honor and pride. *Quite* a badge. You know, my father didn't go there. My uncles didn't go there. No one I knew until I *went* to Exeter had gone to

Exeter. I went there on a scholarship that I received for an essay I wrote on Ayn Rand and Herman Melville. The headmaster told me I was quote brilliant unquote."

"Answering your question," my father said, "we call him Herb, cause you called him Herb, Jill. We used to call him Andy, then you started working here, we liked you, hoped you'd stick around, wanted to make you feel at home, and etcetera, so when you called him Herb, we called him Herb, and he started to introduce himself as Herb."

"I called him Herb to make fun of him," Jill said. "Because the first thing he ever told me is that he went to Exeter on a scholarship where he got such good grades he got a scholarship to the University of Illinois, but now he 'carried a gun and solved problems for people.' "

"Of Chicago," Herb said. "University of Chicago."

"Probably he thought that would impress you," my dad said. "Maybe even get himself a date with you. Right, Herb?"

Herb, looking down into his beer, pursed his lips.

"You wanted to ask me out?" Jill said. "Herb? Whyn't you ever ask me out?"

"Well, you work here," Herb said. "I didn't want to make everyone uncomfortable. And frankly, Jill—we're all of us friends here, and I can admit it—frankly, you're miles out of my league."

"But you went to *Ex*eter," Jill said. "On a *schol*arship."

"Don't tease him," my dad said. "He's carried a torch for you for nearly, what? Three years?"

"Seven," Herb said.

"Time," said my father. "Christ. Time. You've worked here seven years, Jill?"

"You still want to take me out?" Jill said.

"She's ribbing me, right?"

"I'm closing tonight," she said. "Tomorrow, though, I've got the day shift. I'm off at seven."

"I can pick you up?"

"Are you asking me or telling me?"

"I'm telling you I can. I'm asking if I may."

"What about my boyfriend?"

"I don't care about him."

"No," Jill said. "That was what you were supposed to say: 'What about your boyfriend, Jill? Don't you have a boyfriend?' "

"Fuck *that* guy," said Herb.

"Amen," said my father.

"Fair enough," Jill said, moving away, wiping the bar down.

"Was that a yes?" Herb whispered.

"Yeah," Clyde told him. "And now you gotta go now. Get out on that note. Don't even say goodbye. Do not come back til seven tomorrow."

"You're a genius," Herb said. "That's exactly the right move here is to go. I'm hammered. Can you drive me?"

"Sorry," my dad said. "Came here on foot, plus waiting for Biggie."

"Can you drive me?" he asked me.

"I haven't got a license anymore," I said.

"Go have a burger at McDonald's," said my father.

"I'm vegetarian," said Herb.

"That's womanly," my dad said.

"It's a cholesterol thing."

"No one asked for your story. Just get outta here before things get weird."

"You really don't have a license?" Herb said.

"I don't," I said.

"DUI?"

"No. I just let it expire."

"You're an adult in a suburb. You need a license. You should get yourself a license."

"Vamoose," Clyde said, "you stupid sonofabitch. I want another drink."

"I'm going," Herb said. "But tell him get a license."

"You know, he's right," Clyde said, once Herb was out the door. "You should probably get a license. You find that girl, things work out, you'll want to be able to take her places."

"What girl?"

"The girl, the girl . . . the one you were about to ask Herb to track down for you."

"What are you talking about?"

"Maybe I misunderstood where you were going."

"When?"

"When you asked Herb if he did missing persons. Which, I happen to know, he does. I think he's pretty good, too. Way I hear it, he's had the entire North Shore locked down, PI-wise I mean, ever since he solved that kidnapping in Evanston with—Lisette! Lisette. That's it. Pretty name, too. How could I forget that?"

"You think I should hire him to find Lisette?"

"I don't know if I think you *should*. But it seems to me, way you told me that whole story—you seeing her on the screen and then running to the can to hide out and get yourself together—seems to me she's got some kinda hold on you, and then, since you asked about missing persons, and you've got all this money now, I thought that you *would*. Hire Herb to find her."

"That would be kind of loserly," I said. "Wouldn't it?"

"Loserly?"

"Yeah," I said. "Desperate. Needy. To hire someone to find a girl who I liked twenty-five years ago. A girl who was in a study for kids with psychosis—she's probably a mess."

"You put it that way, I mean—that's one way to think of it, I guess. Sure. Other way's that you're still wondering about her after twenty-five years, which I think is . . . romantic. Could be pretty special. Plus *you* were in that study, Bill, and you turned out alright. Why shouldn't she? Ah, what do I know? I've got a buzz on. If you *do* hire Herb, though, you should call him up tomorrow *before* he takes Jill out—*that* much I know. Likely as not, he will blow that date big-time, and you want to negotiate his price while he's still on cloud nine, feeling like he owes half the world to your father. Look, it's Biggie," he said. "Biggie!" he said.

And here came the lawyer, a sun-bronzed Ichabod Crane of a man who, upon sitting down on the stool next to Clyde's, introduced himself as "Zbigniew, but you can call me Z," which statement incited Clyde to mock-berate him about how no one would ever call him *Z*, let alone *Zbigniew*. I bought them each a Scotch, and then a second and a third, and as the hour grew later and the tavern filled with patrons, many of whom clustered around our three stools—men and women from the plant, a salesman of cars, a salesman of insurance, some restaurant workers, a flight attendant (the tavern was the only place in Wheelatine to drink after nine on a Sunday, except for Arcades)—Biggie and another man he and my father knew—an accountant called Wiz—argued some fine points of tax- and insurance-law that may (Biggie) or may not (Wiz) have pertained to what I would owe the IRS on my SSDI benefits when I filed my return, but both of them assured us that a onetime payment for independent contract work, no matter how large, wouldn't prevent me from collecting any future benefits, and so there wasn't any need to try to do anything tricky with the $100k.

It was a very pleasant couple of hours, despite the only partially Tylenol-masked headache I was suffering. It was nice to meet all my father's friends, to see him among them, and hear how they joked and watch how they changed as they filled themselves with liquor, but, nice as it was, much as I'd like to linger there a little, none of it has enough relevance to this memoir to detail further. The next relevant thing that happened was right around midnight, when two people entered the tavern at once.

The first was Rick. He was dark beneath one eye, like my father, and his cheek was scabbed just over the beardline. "Asshole," he said to my father, coming over.

The music didn't stop. People didn't freeze in place. No one seemed to notice Rick was there but me and Clyde.

"Asshole," Rick said again.

"Well right backatcha, Rick," my dad said.

"I caught one trout, Clyde, and Jim's really sad now, he's really broken up, traumatized even. We had to leave Michiana. He's wetting the bed again. First time in two years."

"That's tough," Clyde said.

"Yeah it's tough."

"We ruined the whole trip, I guess," Clyde said.

"Yeah," Rick said. "That's what I'm saying."

"So what? You want to . . . go back?"

"Wouldn't be good for Jim. Needs the security of the home environment."

"Still taking the week off?"

"I haven't decided. Tomorrow anyway."

"Well have yourself a Scotch with us. Sonnyboy's buying. Go on, grab a stool."

"Take mine," I said, already standing.

"That you, Billy?" Rick said.

The other person who'd entered the tavern was Catrina Hogg. She'd set up her wares atop the pinball machine and was showing a pair of bonded cures to a middle-aged couple who Biggie and Wiz, an hour or so earlier, had discussed at some length, and very little depth (first date or not?—that had been the thrust).

I handed my father all my cash, said I'd pay him back later if it wasn't enough, then left out the back, through the door near the bathrooms.

•

• •

Next morning, first thing, I gave Herb a call. He told me he'd be happy to try to find Lisette for me, but advised me to keep my expectations in check as he had so little information to go on—just her first name, and that she'd been in the Friends Study—and furthermore advised I be prepared to wait awhile for any results he *might* produce since he wouldn't be able to really start on my case for at least a couple weeks; already on his plate were "a likely cuckold, a missing college kid (probably one of these fucken Hare Krishna situations), and a corporate thing [he] better keep mum about." As for cost, Herb said he'd take the case on for the "unprecedentedly discounted rate of zero dollars per hour, plus expenses, which is thirty dollars less per hour than I usually charge the likable and known, and one hundred fifty less per hour than the standard rate." I asked him what he thought the expenses would be. He said he'd ring me up before doing anything that would create expenses.

I thanked him a lot, and was about to ask him *how* long he figured I'd have to wait for results, but I stopped myself for fear of seeming pushy, and asked him instead what the rate would be to find another person—one whose last name I knew—and I somehow wound up seeming pushy, anyway.

"Instead of this Lisette?" he said.

"In addition to," I said.

"Okay," he said. "Right. Sure. Know what? Same rate. Fucken Magnets. A pair of masters in this economy of favors, hustling. Me? I prefer an economy of gifts, or a barter economy convincingly disguised as an economy of gifts. Might be the same thing. I'm no anthropologist. What I know's I prefer a world in which we do our best to help each other out, don't set terms, but find we're rewarded with exactly that which we desire but are nonetheless unwilling to give to ourselves."

"Like what?" I said.

"To say what outright would expose the bartering nature we labor here to hide. I'm not into that, kid, so I'll put it like this: At Exeter, when we were underage, it would amount to a sixer of whatever anyone could get his hands on. At University of Chicago, the sixer became a handle of something—brown or clear, no matter. These are items within let's call it *the continuum of the what* about which you are inquiring, items well to the left side of that continuum, which, like so many other continua, vectors rightward toward greater value. Today, as an older man, one whose time as a matriculant at the hallowed institutions aforementioned has long since ended, that *what* which I desire yet am nonetheless unwilling to give to myself always seems to begin with a syllable such as *Glen* or *Mac* and to end with a number no lower than fifteen, and the higher the number the better."

"I understand," I said, then told him the few things I knew about Stevie, wished him good luck on his date with Jill, hung up the phone, and watched *A Fistful of Fists*.

SEVEN WEEKS

THE TRANSCRIPT TOOK ME only seven weeks to write. I say "only seven weeks" because I finished four months ahead of the deadline; those seven weeks, however, didn't feel like *only* anything. More often than not, the video disgusted me. More often than that, I disgusted myself.

Though I'd wanted to be finished as soon as possible, I'd wanted, just as much, to do a good job—not out of any kind of pride in my work, but from fear that if the transcript didn't meet his expectations, Trip would have Burroughs demand I rewrite it or return the $100k—yet my attacks of self-disgust were at their most potent in precisely those moments when I'd done a good job, for to have done a good job meant, above all, to have transformed that which I found repellent into something the average transcript reader, whoever that would be (you, I suppose), would find adorable or comical or both; into something Triple-J would find *inspiringly* adorable or comical or both. And I couldn't fake it. I'd try to and fail. Success required that I learn to take pleasure in that which disgusted me: to *see* as attractive what I knew to be repellent; to acquire, in other words, new sensibilities, or, perhaps, to develop latent ones, and, in either case, to betray my old ones.

One hundred thousand dollars to *betray old sensibilities*—oh, boo hoo.

I know, I know. No one likes a complainer.

I'm not seeking pity, just explaining how it was.

I had a hard time.

The work disturbed me.

I'd work for five or six hours a day, from nine or so til two or three, then spend the afternoon trying to get undisturbed. For the first couple weeks, I accomplished undisturbedness by hanging out with Blank. We'd watch the eyebrow-flexing compilation, practice gags, and play our games: Flick the Peppercorn, Kick the Frozen Pea, Toothpickup Sticks, Tug but Don't Tear the Tissue. Throughout these two weeks, Blank, as it had on the morning I left for the compound, periodically performed consecutive Allen-throat-clears (occasionally punctuated by pratfalls and brow-wipes), which led me to believe that it wanted to revisit Woody's old comedies, so we also did that: watched one or two a night.

By day ten, however, the throat-clears had started to annoy me a little, Blank's eyebrow-flex timing had ceased improving, and its pleasure in our games appeared to be waning: it would, for example, tear the tissue in seconds, rather than minutes (sometimes, I could have sworn, deliberately), or send the peppercorn flying off the table in the direction opposite the peppermill goalposts. It seemed to desire more time in-sleeve: was quick to get in, sluggish emerging. On top of all that—maybe partly because of it—the aforementioned betrayal of my old sensibilities began not only to disgust and depress me, but scare me a little.

I'd catch myself thinking that maybe Blank had been deprived (i.e. by me) of some of the fundamental joys of Curiohood, and that maybe I should make some efforts to repair that. Buy us a cuddlefarmed cure, perhaps, then PerFormulize Blank with BullyKing or Punchy and let it (and, vicariously, me) have some fun with the (temporary) guest. Or maybe I could purchase a cuddlefarmed hobunk, debilitate the hobunk with a double dose of TooMuchItch or SloMo or DizzyFizz or QuIctuses, and let Blank experience the ostensible thrill of witnessing a hate-filled, murder-hungry being struggling—helplessly—to end its life.

And then one day, I was having trouble describing the light in the Woof clip, and I rose from my desk, and started to pace, and pick things up and put them down, and one of these things turned out to be a pencil, and I found myself wondering whether a Curio's exit could ever recover from having been popsicled. If so, I wondered, how long would it take? If not, how bad would the damage actually be? I.e. *very* bad or worth-it bad? And I thought: "'*Worth*-it bad'? What the hell does that mean? What are you becoming? What's happening to you?" and suddenly it seemed to me extremely unwise to keep Blank within reach while I worked on the transcript.

Each morning thereafter, I'd wake it, feed it, flush its rear ejection, and let it hang out while I smoked my first Quill, but instead of then sleeving or playing with the guy, as had been our custom since forever, I'd return it to its PillowNest, which new practice it protested with very little vigor. It hardly, in fact, would protest at all. Just do an Allen-throat-clear, maybe a pratfall, maybe a brow-wipe, sometimes a combo, and then close its eyes. Which spooked me further: it seemed to me Blank must have sensed that I was changing in just the way I feared; it seemed like confirmation.

Not long after I altered our morning ritual—three days later? four?—it occurred to me that if I really wanted to nullify the risk of doing something I'd later regret (my wandering thoughts about potentially "worth-it bad" paces through which to put a cure were occurring more frequently), I should not only keep Blank out of my reach *while* I did my daily transcript work, but for at least a couple hours after I'd been finished with the work as well. So the next few days, I kept it nested til just before dinner, and spent my afternoons on tasks and errands that I'd been putting off.

I opened two accounts, a savings and a checking, at Permanent Bank, activated my ATM card, and filled out forms for a low-interest credit card. Around twenty-five twenties I then withdrew, I folded a sheet of looseleaf paper on which I wrote, "Thanks, again. —Belt," and mailed it all to Lotta, care of General TrustGroup. I went to Tax Genius and hired an accountant, with whose help I filed a quarterly return, wrote a check to him and to the US Treasury, and went back to Permanent to open a second savings account in which I put aside the money I'd have to send later, with my annual return. (As much as I'd like to think my skills as a writer could render the calculations of my income taxes an engaging—if not a thrilling—subject to read about, I lack the drive to put those skills to the test. Suffice it to say that, when all was said and done, my $100k was reduced to roughly $73k, which initially—given that I'd thought I'd owe only $20k—disappointed me a little, but the disappointment wore off quickly, for with the writing of the checks (the first checks I'd ever written) came, for the first time, a sense that the $100k had been *real,* material—something I was losing a palpable part of—which, in turn, meant the remaining $73k was also real. I.e. I had $73k I could spend! Or save. $73k that was mine either way. I *had* it. And sure, I'd had it, already, for a couple of weeks, and I'd known I'd had it, yes, but I hadn't *really* known that at all. I hadn't, til I'd written those checks, *felt* my money.)

My taxes, debts, and banking taken care of, I practiced driving my father's truck: parked it, unparked it, merged it onto highways, and then I took my test at the DMV, and passed. The following evening, Clyde and I visited the dealership out in McHenry that his tavern buddy Rocky Sims was head of sales at. I went there thinking I'd get a humble little Japanese hatchback, but Rocky walked us straight to a Chevrolet pickup, an egg-yolk-orange 2012 mid-size with 17,000 miles on it that he'd bought off a tweeker in dire straits, and that he said he'd sell to me for $9,000, which my father assured me was an unbeatable deal ("I'll buy half this guy's beers for a month," Clyde said) even when you added the cost of a paint job. And I liked the paint job—it made the truck seem friendly—so I said I'd take it, and we went to Rocky's office and called up Hiram, the tavern buddy of my father's and Rocky's who sold insurance, and I purchased a policy over the phone, and I drove the truck off the lot and headed south. I drove it all the way to Hammond, Indiana, and, for what just twelve would have cost me at Pang's, I bought myself twenty cartons of Quills, and I bought Clyde a bottle of Ardvag 10—the Scotch that he'd liked so much at the tavern—and bought Herb a bottle of Glenfibbly 21 in anticipation of his future success.

•

• •

The next afternoon, I drove my new truck to the Deerbrook Park Mall and bought myself a hoodie at the clothing outlet, seven novels at one of the bookstores, two more novels at the other of the bookstores, and a pork fried rice and a king-size marshmallow-chocolate-chip cookie I ate too fast in the noisy, overly air-conditioned food court.

The afternoon after that, I went back to the mall, bought five more books, bought a couple CDs, bought a pair of blue jeans, then considered buying an eleven-pound laptop for $2,000, went to the food court for chicken fried rice and a peanut-butter brownie, determined that I didn't need a new computer, or a new pair of blue jeans, or any more trips to the mall too soon, and returned the blue jeans, then returned the CDs, and headed for the parking lot.

On a bench outside the mall's automatic doorway, a twentysomething redhead in a leather jacket appeared to be talking to a Zippo lighter she repeatedly opened, lit, and shut.

"I'm trying, you know, but I have other things to—I have a life outside of you," said the redhead; open, light, shut. "It's not humanly possible for me to keep doing this," open, light, shut. "Well, it makes things really *awkward* for me. I mean, people see us and think—" open light shut. "I was *saying,* people see us and I look like a fool to them. A clown. I can't continue—"

"Hi," she mouthed at me, smiling rather warmly.

Owing, perhaps, to a feeling of competence—or even strength—that had imbued me in the wake of having returned my needless purchases, I'd approached her directly without thinking twice: I'd taken a seat on the bench, beside her. I said, "I'm wondering—"

She showed me the palm of her Zippo-less hand, said, "I have to call you back," and then reached into the hair on her head's farther side and came out with an earpiece, connected by wire to a phone in her jacket, through which she'd been speaking—it was suddenly clear—to another human being.

She pocketed the earpiece, shook out her hair. "So you were wondering?" she said.

"I was wondering," I said, "where you got that Zippo."

"It's great, right?" she said, laughing, and handed it to me.

"It is," I said, "yeah," though the lighter looked pretty standard to me. Smudged bright silver, an engraving—*D.S.*—in Olde English letters on the lower part. I lit a cigarette with it, asked if she wanted one.

"What kind are they?" she said.

"Quill Black," I said.

"A dark archer of solemn death type," she said. "No thank you." She had her own pack of smokes. Bijou Jade.

I didn't know any clever names for Bijou smokers, so, pretending not to realize she was waiting for me to call her such a name, I looked at and blew on my glowing cherry.

"Can I, uh, maybe get a light?" she said.

I lit her Bijou with her Zippo, and when she drew the flame closer by touching my knuckles, I seemed to remember a novel or story in which the narrator claimed such touching to be a form of flirtation. And it felt that way, too. Like I was being flirted with. Did I want to be flirted with? At first I didn't know. I found this woman attractive, but there wasn't any thunderbolt. Nor was she a woman who talked to inans. And yet that didn't, strangely, disappoint me as much as I might've suspected. In fact, I might have been *more* disappointed—given the absence of thunderbolt—if she *had* been a woman who talked to inans, for I wasn't in love with her, nor was I able to imagine I would be. Mostly, I compared her, unfavorably, to Fon. And I felt a little terrible about making that comparison, firstly because it just wasn't a very nice thing to do—it was fratboyish somehow; would've made my mother frown, and perhaps Clyde, too—but also because I was struck by how doomed I'd be to a loveless life if Fondajane had become the standard by which I now assessed other women. Who could ever possibly compete with her? with the feeling that being near her gave me? I thought of only three people who could, three people who *might*: Stevie Strumm and Lisette—both of whom, for all I knew, were dead—and an even more hypothetical woman who talked to inans while being as attractive as I imagined Stevie and Lisette would be in those moments when I imagined they'd be as attractive to me as they'd been when we were kids.

And no, I didn't think Stevie and Lisette were dead. Why should they be dead? Why should *either* be dead? The odds they were alive were greatly in their favor. But who knew if they—assuming Herb ever tracked them down—would find grown-up me attractive, or even likable, much less lovable? Who knew what I would think of grown-up *them*? I had hopes, of course—I'm not saying I didn't—that's why I'd hired Herb, but hopes were . . . just that. Hopes were just hopes. And as for the girl who talked to inans, it appeared I had next to no hope at all; it appeared that I barely even believed in her existence; if I'd really thought such a woman existed, I would have been more than *just a little* disappointed that the attractive woman who'd just touched my hand wasn't her, wouldn't I? A woman who talked to inans—regardless of how attractive I found her—is someone I would want, at the very least, to be friends with. Someone I'd think I'd want to be *best* friends with (if adults could still do that). And if I'd believed such a woman existed, and if I'd believed that I had just found her, then when I, in the very next moment, realized she wasn't who I'd thought she was—i.e. that she wasn't a woman who talked to inans, i.e. that she was only a woman who'd been talking through the mike of an earpiece—I'd have been disconsolate. Of that I'm certain. It had happened before (earpiece notwithstanding), numerous times throughout my teens and early twenties, back when I *did* believe such a person existed and I'd think I'd found her only then to discover, moments later, that I hadn't.

But here I was, *just a little* disappointed by this attractive woman; far less disappointed by this attractive woman than I was attracted to this attractive woman.

I flipped her lighter shut, gave it back, and asked her name.

She said her name was Denise, and I said I was Belt. She asked what Belt was short for, and I told her, "Nothing," and she asked what kind of name it was, and, rather than telling her the story of my mother's uncle Belt and Billie Holiday, all I said was, "No kind, really."

We dragged at our cigarettes in silence for a while, til Denise said, "There's something sweet about you, isn't there? You're old-school shy. You're not, like, 'on the spectrum,' or 'suffering from social anxiety.' You just have no idea how this is all supposed to go, and you're afraid that if you say or do the wrong thing, you'll make me uncomfortable. So I'm gonna help you out, if that's alright with you."

Maybe it was needy of me—or maybe it was epiphenomenal to whatever quality of mine gave Denise the impression I was shy—but I was flattered to hear her attempt to narrate my inner life. Fon had done the same with far greater acumen—I wasn't, there on the bench, feeling shy; I was, rather, wondering if I should follow through on what I understood (to my surprisingly mild surprise, and via no means I was able to pin down or name) to be an opportunity to have sex with Denise—but still, I liked it. I liked Denise for doing it. Her version of me was one I could work with.

"Alright," I said. "Help me."

"Start by telling me why you really came over here."

"It's embarrassing," I said. "There was something about you that . . ."

" 'Something about me,' you were saying," she said.

"Never mind," I said. "I don't want to talk about it."

"Do you want to drink about it?" she said.

"Drink about it?"

"Yeah. You know, go somewhere with me and drink all about it."

"It sounds fun," I said, "but I'm a lightweight, and I'm driving."

"Well this is what I think about all of that," she said. "I'm *not* a lightweight. I say you get in your car and I'll get in mine, and I'll follow you to your place, and we'll drink about it there. You know, really drink it over."

"Not sure . . ." I said.

"Or we could reverse that up. You could follow me to my place, and we could drink about it there."

"What are we supposed to be drinking about, again?"

"I forgot, too," she said. "And that's a good sign, and I still think you're shy, but soon, I have to tell you—and this is important—soon, I'm gonna start thinking you're a jerk who overheard me fighting with my ex on the phone, thought he might come over here and take a chance at taking advantage while I was vulnerable, but found me less vulnerable than he'd first suspected, less pretty up close than he had from a distance, and now just wants to max out feeling good about being wanted, then go home to his wife."

"I don't have a wife."

"Girlfriend."

"That either. And also I think you're *prettier* up close," I said. "And I would like to follow you to your place, I think. I hesitate because we're not in love, and I don't believe we'll ever fall in love, and I worry that if we go back to your place and we don't fall in love, you'll feel bad."

"*I'll* feel bad."

"And then I'll feel bad. I'm not trying to sound selfless. I dislike the idea of making you feel bad."

"You're hilarious, Belt," she said. "Maybe you're creepy. Maybe I like that. Where'd you park? I'm right there."

I followed her to her place, a five-bedroom home in Deerbrook Park a couple blocks from the lake. It was actually her parents' place—the house she'd grown up in (her parents, retired, spent most of the year abroad, traveling, and were, at that time, "somewhere in New Zealand or Australia"). She'd been staying at the house for just a couple weeks and commuting occasionally to the city for work—she did freelance "high-end graphic design" for a number of different advertising firms—since she'd broken things off with her ex-fiancé of nearly six years after catching him cheating, and would move back to Chicago the following month, when the lease on her new apartment started. She told me these things over yeasty beers on the backyard patio, then said that she, if I didn't mind, would like us to bring our beers inside, upstairs to her bathroom, where—when she was a teen and it was too cold outside, or late enough at night that her parents had already armed the home's alarm system—she'd gone to smoke Bijous with the overhead fan on. I said of course I didn't mind, and she grabbed two more beers, and we smoked on the floor of her bathroom with the fan on, our backs against the wall, an empty bottle between us for use as an ashtray. The floor of the bathroom was remarkably clean, the blue tiles smooth and even and cool, their grouting uniformly white and unstained, and I liked to picture her there, smoking as a teen. It seemed like exactly the right thing to do in there. I said so. She kissed me. I enjoyed it—the nothing-taste of her mouth, the slowness of her tongue, the faint, clovey smell that came off her skin, which may have been a perfume, but I think was just the soap she washed her face with, or perhaps a lotion (except for some eyeliner, she wore no makeup, and she didn't seem the kind of woman who used perfume, if that makes any sense (I *think* it does)). We kissed for some minutes, my hands in her hair, on her cheek, on her knee, and then we stopped kissing and she said she wanted to know more about me, and I told her I didn't like to talk about myself, and she said I should tell her just one big thing, allow her one follow-up, and then we could proceed. I liked the sound of *proceed.* I thought about all the "big" things I could tell her about myself, all but one of which were intimate and therefore, given that we wouldn't fall in love, inappropriate to mention, so I went with the one that wasn't so intimate, said I'd written a novel called *No Please Don't,* and her follow-up was, "Where's the best place for me to buy a copy?" and I told her I'd give her one, and she took me to bed. Her bed was a queen and it smelled like her face. We stayed there awhile. We had sex three times, and I think that I did okay the second time, and I'm sure I did the third.

•

•   •

For a week, I went back there every afternoon, and wasn't once asked to leave or to stay. The experience was friendly and easygoing and really very . . . good. We'd be naked and it was all I would think of; no transcript, no dread of what I might do to or with Blank, no discomfort at all—just where and how to touch next with what part. Once, a condom spoke up to thank me for using it despite its being newly expired, and then, insecure about my not having answered it, asked me how its fit was, and whether the sensitivity it permitted was as high as promised, but even that proved quick and painless to contend with; I removed it, telling Denise it had broken, and slipped on another that didn't try to talk to me.

Each afternoon, we'd go to bed first thing, and remain there, making out, having sex, taking catnaps, and laughing (Denise knew a lot of great old-timey jokes; her father's father, "Simple" Simcha Simon, had been a minor comedian on the Borscht Belt circuit) til we wanted to smoke, or eat, or drink, or (twice) Denise wanted to dropper some spidge oil (she gave me no trouble when I declined to join her), and after that we'd return to the bed til seven or so, then she'd walk me to the door, hug me goodbye, we'd agree on a time to meet the next day, and then I'd go home, take Blank from its nest, put it in its sleeve, eat dinner with my father, read, go to bed, wake up, and transcribe.

The ease of that week, and much of the pleasure, was, I believe, enabled by our knowledge that Denise would soon be moving back to Chicago, which, even though Chicago wasn't very far away, was far away enough that our never discussing it after that first conversation on her patio seemed to mean that there was nothing to discuss, i.e. that for her to move would be for her to *move on*. I wasn't someone who she wanted to know in any depth—wasn't someone who she thought, for example, to visit at his house—nor was she someone who I cared to be known by in any depth, or, for that matter, invite to my house. We didn't even have one another's numbers. When I came back to see her the second day, she—despite our having agreed to meet there and then—seemed a little surprised to see me. I gave her a copy of *No Please Don't,* and she admired the cover, and my picture on the back, but never again said a word about it. I don't believe she read it. Given the red flags I'd think it would have raised at least high enough to demand I dismiss them, I doubt she read even the author's bio. And that was just fine.

I don't think we could have lasted much beyond that week, but the last of our rendezvous—the seventh, a Sunday—was not supposed to be the last. Denise wasn't moving out for another few days, and we agreed I'd come back on Tuesday at three. She wished she could see me on Monday, she explained, but she had other plans: Tuesday was "Independence Day," and, early Monday morning, she'd be going downtown, to the flagship Graham&Swords Per-Formulae Paradise, to camp out all day for the midnight release with some friends from the Dollheart-Betty Group ad firm, some of whom had worked on the "Independence Day's Arriving Late This Year" campaign, and because she had designs on getting hired full-time at Dollheart-Betty, she couldn't back out, and hoped I understood. I assured her I did, I bid her happy camping, said that I would see her on Tuesday, and meant it.

•

• •

But then, Monday morning, I got a call from Herb. He'd found Stevie Strumm. He said he had pictures.

I met him at the tavern a few hours later. The place was mostly empty, but he was there when I arrived, a manila folder on the bar in front of him, Jill's hand on top of it, beneath his own. Jill saw me first and blushed and winked. I gave Herb the Glenfibbly I'd bought in Indiana.

"*Twenty-one?*" he said. "What a good guy you are. You shouldn't have, really, but, fuck, I'm glad you did." He unfolded a pocketknife, carefully slit the seal on the case, and slid out the wooden frame in which the bottle was secured, gingerly removed the bottle from the frame, slit the seal on the cork, pulled the cork, and then, with his eyes closed, held the bottle under his chin and inhaled the fumes rising out of its neck. The whole operation took a couple of minutes, was performed in total silence, and seemed to me to be either a little too demonstrative, or a little too intimate to publicly engage in—I couldn't decide—and when Herb opened his eyes, I swear, they were misty. He said, "Thank you, Bill. This gift is too generous."

He asked Jill to pour for us and, once she had, he offered up a toast to "Blossoming love, gifts between pals, and better luck next time."

We clinked glasses and sipped. This was the fourth time I'd ever drunk whiskey—the fif- or sixteenth I'd ever drunk alcohol—but I understood instantly why the Scotch was so expensive. Rather than tasting like the necessary suffering you had to endure on your way to a buzz, it tasted like something primarily intended to be sensed with the tongue. The tiniest nip of it filled your mouth with flavor after flavor, flavors that you'd never guess would complement each other, and the flavors seemed to take whole minutes to fade, which made you want to talk about them. It made you want to name them, to pin them down, as much toward the goal of knowing which ones to more actively seek when you took your next sip as to see if others would name the same ones as you, or point out the ones you'd failed to notice.

Burned steak and marzipan.

Mushrooms and grapefruit.

Band-Aids and lemon zest.

Rubberbands and chocolate.

I named some of those myself, discovered the others after Herb and Jill had named them. The Scotch was a boon on a couple of levels. Whereas I'd initially accepted my dram out of mere politeness (and with some irritation), by the time I'd swallowed back that first thimbleful, I was no longer impatient for Herb's report on Stevie; we'd get to it, I knew. And beyond that, the Scotch was something new for me to like, something new that I could, in the future—in exchange for money I now had—have.

I'd enjoyed half my Scotch—the other two were on their second—before Herb opened the manila folder and started to speak in apologetic tones, at which point I understood that the "Better luck next time" clause in his toast (which I'd originally assumed to be some kind of traditional Boston thing) had been aimed at me.

The four pictures of Stevie, and the accompanying intelligence, came from the files of the Department of Alcohol, Tobacco, Firearms, and Prostitution, where Herb had a contact—an old classmate from Exeter. Two of the photos were full-page snapshots from the society pages of *Lone Star Social*—one taken at a governor's ball in 2006, the other in 2011 at a benefit concert for Safehouse, a nationwide charity organization that Stevie had founded in 2008 to provide apartments for battered women and runaway teens. In both of these photos, Stevie, her hair blond and up-done, her dresses long and sequined, her heels high and nails painted, stood in what appeared to be *gleeful* proximity to a slouching, big-toothed, husky fellow in an overtight tux and architect glasses, his gaze so intensely aimed at her swanny neck (she'd grown long and tall) that if Herb hadn't told me the man was her "notoriously adoring—or what's known back in Boston as *completely fucking pussy-whipped*" husband, I'd have thought he was a stalker with a strangling fetish. In fact, he was a writer, and a rich one, too: one of the major voices among that growing group of increasingly bestselling American and Canadian novelists referred to as either (depending on the critic) the "Dystopian Utopians" or "Feelgood Dsytopians" or "Pseudo-Anti-Fascist Crypto-Randian Fantasians," whose work is either set in the very near future or the uchronic present, in the wake of a global environmental disaster of unnamed origin that has, for all its horrors, evened the playing field such that race, religion, and socioeconomic background have ceased to be either enablers or prohibitors of virtue or power, and everyone—hero, villain, and reader alike—gets to deserve exactly what they have, whatever it may be. I didn't like his work much.

The other two photos were the head shots from Stevie's Procurer's License ID cards (the first one, from 2004, expired; the other the renewal from 2009). She'd been managing brothels for nearly a decade, beginning with the Silver Star'n'Spur in Austin, of which she became a part owner in 2007 (Herb's ATFP contact had reported that she'd made a name for herself in "the delicate, part-legal art of sex-work recruitment"). Then, in 2009, with seed money from her husband, she'd opened up Derby's Teapot, Austin: the first of what had since become a chain of seven tearoom-themed brothels in Texas, New Mexico, and Arizona.

"I know this isn't the report you were hoping for," Herb said, "but it isn't the end of the world, either, alright? You're young. Things happen. Maybe this writer suddenly dies. Or starts banging a groupie, or someone else's wife, gets caught on film by someone like me. Or maybe he's got a paralyzing fear of periodontists, never gets treatment for his gingivitis, and one day he's talking to her—to Stevie—about some new book he's started to write, and when she smells the horrible rotting smell of his mouth, she realizes she'd rather just leave him than try to convince him to get it taken care of, and what that means to her is that maybe she's never really loved him, plus his new book sounds stupid, and she didn't like the last one, and the ones before the last one—she only thought they were okay. So maybe she leaves him. Maybe she *already* wants to leave him—that latest photo's nearly three years old, and sure, everything looks golden, but who can tell the true state of a man's oral health by looking at a snapshot taken at a gala? the rot might've already started setting in, and once the gums start going, they *really* start going, Bill, I tell you true—and I'm saying maybe she's wanted to leave him for months, a couple years even, only thing stopping her's she's too afraid of loneliness. Sure, she's rich and beautiful, but she's busy as hell—seven brothels to run across three fucken states—and while, true, she's childless, which is certainly a plus in terms of attracting a new, long-term romantic partner, she's also getting to the outer edge of childbearing age, so . . . Maybe you reconnect, you know? and she won't be so afraid of being alone, won't be so afraid to walk out that door. She'll have somewhere to go—some*one* to go *to*. And I know you're not rich and famous, but you're no worse-looking than that grinning fuckwad, I'd give you ten-to-one that you write better books, and plus you and her were kids together. You never want to underrate the power of that."

"This guy," Jill said. "Here I thought I'd found myself a dedicated sweetheart, and now I hear the bastard would walk out on my ass over a little gingivitis as long as some old flame of his was waiting in the wings."

"No, Jill," Herb said. "No. Just no. Don't even joke around. If you're gonna make this into something bigger where I'm sending you coded messages about the state of our union, you make it into this: I am afraid of just two things. The chickens of my own irregular flossing habit one day coming home to roost, and *you* leaving *me*."

Jill said, "Such an *earnest* bastard," and patted his cheek.

* * *

So Stevie, still beautiful to me despite her high-society stylings (and despite the predictions she'd made to the contrary that day we'd sat on her father's truck's tailgate, almost kissing), had married a novelist—someone at least superficially like me—and had named her chain of brothels after something that came out of *Slaughterhouse-Five,** which was not only one of my favorite books, but was a book that she had initially read because she'd seen me reading another book by Vonnegut when we were children together (and a book that, no less, played a not-insignificant role in our almost-kissing). And maybe that all meant that, had her family stayed in Wheelatine, or had we stayed in contact, I could have been her husband.

But probably it didn't. Nor, even if it did mean I could've been her husband, did it mean I necessarily *should* have been her husband, for maybe the popular hack science-fictionist made her happier than I ever could have. She certainly looked a lot happier than I was—as did he.

And as much as I might have flattered myself to imagine they fell in love because Stevie (whether she was aware of it or not) saw something of me within him—i.e. saw in him certain fully flowered aspects of her budding-novelist childhood friend—I had to, by the very same token, admit to the possibility (the *likelihood*) that, even if part of what she loved about him were his (very much) *ostensible* qualities of Beltness, that wasn't all, or even most, of what she loved about him; and perhaps it was even the hack science-fictionist's lack of certain other qualities of Beltness that made the ones he did possess lovable to her (i.e. rather than merely likable to her).

Yet, although I hadn't bothered to correct Herb's impression (partly because he'd seemed so invested in my being half-shattered by the news he'd brought me; partly because I thought that the responsibility he appeared to feel for what he believed to be my half-shattering could motivate him to work harder at finding Lisette), I wasn't nearly as disappointed as he seemed to think. I wasn't sure I was disappointed at all. I didn't know what I was. The feeling was new to me. There were, yes, the above, belabored thoughts about what could have been or should have been, but there was also an accompanying and consoling sense of vindication: gorgeous Stevie Strumm, now a great success at business and a doyenne of charity work, had, at least by the looks of it, come out as well as I would've imagined back when we

* For those readers unfamiliar with Kurt Vonnegut's *Slaughterhouse-Five,* "Poor old Edgar Derby" is one of the book's most likable characters, who, as an American POW of the Germans, survives the firebombing of Dresden, and is forced by his captors to dig up the bodies of German civilians buried underneath the rubble. In the course of digging the bodies up, he comes across a teapot he'd like to bring back home to his wife, and when the Germans discover he's taken the teapot, they execute him for stealing.

were kids, which suggested rather strongly that my memory had not embellished her intelligence or kindness. Or that, if it had embellished them, it had only done so a little. She was worthy of being the first heartbreak of my boyhood.

Bittersweet, nostalgic longing—is that all it was? Is that what I've just spent paragraphs trying to describe? I'd like to think the feeling was something else—something that doesn't have a name, let alone one so self-redundant—but more than that I'd like to stop writing about feelings, and refocus on events, and I bet you'd like me to, also, reader. Toward that end, I'll risk appearing to have bittersweetly longed with nostalgia, and just say that whatever I was or wasn't feeling, the one thing I knew for sure, there at the tavern, was that I looked forward to being alone, to spending some time by myself in my room, for Herb had given me, along with the photos, Stevie's home address, and I wanted to write to her.

•

•   •

I should say I *thought* I wanted to write to her. Once I got a couple or three sentences into the letter, I found that what I wanted was to write *about* her. And once I'd started to write about her, I started to write about the swingset murders, and I started, as well, to write about my mom, and when I finally broke for a cheese-and-crackers dinner at 10 p.m., I realized I'd written nearly fifteen discontiguous pages, which for me—for any novelist I'd think—is a hell of a lot of pages (discontiguous or no) to write in a day, let alone in the latter part of a day. And I recalled the bit I'd written on my birthday—the opening of the "Jonboat Say" chapter—and it occurred to me that I'd begun a new book, a memoir, this book.

The novel I'd been working on for the previous six months—a novel that I didn't, frankly, have much love for, and had already begun to think of as a waste of time—wouldn't just be easy to cast aside (I hadn't touched it, or, for that matter, worked on any fiction, since I'd started the transcript), but would be a *real pleasure* to cast aside, and so, just like that, aside I had cast it.

By then—week four or so into transcribing *A Fistful*—it was clear to me how ahead of the deadline I was, and I considered putting the transcript down for a while to work on this memoir so as not to lose steam, but I didn't want to lose steam on the transcript, either, I wanted to finish as quickly as possible—the more I worked on it, the greater the ick and frequency of my troubling, potentially Blank-endangering thoughts were becoming—so I made the following deal with myself: I'd work on the transcript til noon each day, or until I'd finished transcribing one clip (whichever came first), and, after that, I'd be free to work on the memoir the rest of the day.

Cheese and crackers swallowed, I went back upstairs and cuddled Blank while looking over what I'd written, and I saw how it would work, where it would go, what it would do—beginning, middle, and end, the whole thing: every node in the narrative network aglow. I spent half the night writing a detailed outline, and once I'd gotten to the end of the outline, I was still too full of energy to fall asleep, and yet too foggy to get more work done, and I thought that I should go for a walk—I hadn't taken a good walk since I'd bought the truck—but a walk to where, I didn't know.

In Part 2 of *No Please Don't,* Gil MacCabby, who as a boy in Part 1 wondered daily where next to look for his Bam Naka action figure, wonders nightly in adulthood about where to take a walk to. I mention this not to draw a parallel between myself and Gil, nor even to point out what I think to be a rather important parallel between child- and adult-Gil that reviewers of the book all seemed to have missed (though miss it they did, every last one of them), but rather because I almost always knew where to walk, so it was novel to find myself wondering where to walk, and I guess that having registered the novelty up in my room led me to try to recall the last time I wondered where I should walk—I couldn't recall it—in the failed process of which recollection, I thought of Gil MacCabby, and *No Please Don't,* and thereby derived a satisfying destination: I'd take a walk to the mailbox at the Plaza Beige strip mall; I'd send a copy of *No Please Don't* to Stevie.

As I pulled one from the stack beside the bust of Hagler, I remembered I'd told Gus I'd trade him a copy for a pack of handkerchiefs, and so pulled a second. I composed a short letter on my computer upstairs, then wrote it out by hand on Stevie's copy's front cover's interior.

Dear Stevie,

Do you remember that time on your dad's truck's tailgate, after your grandpa went into a coma, and we talked about Vonnegut, and I asked if I could kiss you? I was writing about that today, and I missed you. I've missed you for years. I know the trouble with saying so—apart from the inadvertent rhyme it has produced—is that it probably sounds creepy and too intense. It isn't really either, I don't think, but I can't figure out how to make it sound otherwise.

So it goes?

What I'm thinking is maybe it would mitigate any accidental creepy intensity for me to give you my word I won't bother you again. And I will. I do. You have my word I won't bother you again.

I do want you to have this book, though. I wrote it seven years ago, thinking of you often. Maybe that comes through, maybe it doesn't.

In any case, I hope you enjoy it.

Love,

Belt

In Gus's copy, I just signed the title page.

I packaged the books and took my walk. I dropped Gus's through the mail slot at General TrustCorp—"For Gus" in Sharpie on the envelope containing it—then went into Pang's to buy postage for Stevie's.

When I handed him my card, he said, "Five-dollar minimum."

"Bullshit," I said.

"Sign says so," he said, and pointed to a sign, handwritten on a notecard in sky-blue ink, taped to the side of the register: *$5.00 minimum on credit card purchases.*

"I don't care about your sign," I said. "I read all about this in the *New York Times*. You have to take my credit card. It's part of your contract with the credit card companies." I was lying, of course. I hadn't read it in the *New York Times*. It was just something I'd overheard at the tavern. At the time, I hadn't even believed it.

"Charges under five dollars—they're nearly a loss."

"Not a loss to me," I said.

"ATM's at the back of the store."

"Good for the ATM," I said. "Ring me up on the card."

"You can buy more stamps to put to use later. Or another product. Cigarettes? Candy? Push you over the minimum."

I said, "I buy my cigarettes in Hammond, Indiana, now."

"Better you go north," he said. "McHenry County. They're nearly as cheap as they are in Hammond, and the drive is shorter. You make up the difference in time and gasoline. Less traffic, too."

"You don't sound like you own this White Hen," I said.

"Ah-ha!" he said. "You're being hard to handle because you think that I'm Pang. *Pang* is the owner. I am *not* Pang. Pang is my stupid dickhead fucking brother. My name is Clark. I'm graveyard-shift manager."

"You look like Pang to me," I said.

"We're twins. Identical."

"Your badge says, 'Pang.' "

"It be*longs* to Pang. I forgot mine at home."

"I don't believe you," I said.

"What can I say? You want me to show you my driver's license?"

"Yes," I said.

"Well that is ridiculous. I refuse to show you my driver's license."

"You're Pang," I said, "and you're not the owner."

"You're one hundred percent half-right about that."

I paid him with one of the fives from my wallet. He gave me, with my change, a York Peppermint Patty. "On the house," he said.

"I don't like those," I said, applying my stamps.

"Everyone likes these," he said. "They are *minty*."

I dropped the package in the mailbox and walked back home, put Blank in its nest, put myself in my bed, and fell asleep reading the new translation I'd bought at the mall of Bohumil Hrabal's *I Served the King of England,* then woke just a few hours later, at nine, and transcribed "Sacrament" (the *Philip Daley Alejandro Show* clip) start to finish, in less than an hour, and worked on the memoir til 7 p.m. before I realized I'd flaked on Denise.

Owing, perhaps, to my having seen those photos of Stevie, and having felt whatever I felt the day before, or maybe owing to my having spent a good portion of the day writing the scene in the "Friends" chapter of "The Hope of Rusting Swingsets" where I first encounter Lisette in the U of C hallway (I tend, at the start of a book, to write nonsequentially) and feeling whatever *that* made me feel, or maybe even just owing to a Stevie/Lisette-independent waning of lust for Denise, my flaking didn't trouble me in any deep way. That is: I witnessed myself as a jerk who'd ditched—and temporarily forgotten about—a girl he'd been sleeping with, and I would have liked not to have been that kind of jerk but, in a million years, I would never have traded for non-jerk-status the work I'd been able to do that afternoon.

I took a shower, and drove over to Denise's. Her car wasn't there. No one answered the bell. "Good for her," I thought. I wrote a quick note, apologizing for having flaked, wishing her luck in her new place downtown, and penned a "Best wishes," over my signature, and appended my phone number under my signature, and then, under that, a PS that said, "If you want to talk about it, please feel free to call. No pressure, though, really."

I wedged the note in the doorjamb, and that was the end of it.

•

• •

I stuck to the schedule I'd made for myself and, three weeks later, the transcript was finished, as were fifty-some pages of "Invitation," and roughly a third of "The Hope of Rusting Swingsets." I felt the transcript was solid; was confident it did what Triple-J had asked for. Yet I worried that delivering at the start of October (given that he'd thought he'd paid me to work through February) would cause him to suspect me of having half-assed, which could, in turn, encourage him to second-guess and nitpick, ask for revisions, or perhaps even a top-to-bottom rewrite, and I *needed* to be finished, not only because of the harm that my repeated engagement with *A Fistful of Fists* was inflicting upon my imagination and thus (presumably) upon poor Kablankey (which, by that point, I'd all but entirely stopped hanging out with; hadn't looked into the eyes of in nearly a month; just sleeved for a couple hours each night before bed to prevent from grieving), but because, as wildly unprecedented as my memoir production had been (I was writing nearly fifty pages a week), to spend a couple-three hours every morning on the transcript (i.e. rather than the memoir) had felt to me like a betrayal of my art, and, at the best/worst times, a betrayal of Art. So, despite having finished, I didn't call Burroughs.

A week or so after I'd finished, however, Burroughs called me.

"Burroughs Archon here, Belt. Calling to check in, firm up, and apprise you, in the order opposite that I've just listed."

"Let's do all of that stuff," I said.

"Good man. Museum of Contemporary Art's been booked to screen *A Fistful* on April fifth. We want to make sure the transcript's in by March first."

"That won't be a problem."

"How far along are you?"

I did the dummy math quickly: it was mid-October, I'd started mid-August, March 1 was four and a half months away.

"A third or so along," I said.

"Good *man,*" Burroughs said. "If you're looking for feedback on any or all of what you've got so far, don't be shy about asking. I'll get it to Trip, he'll make some notes, I'll get it all back to you."

I said, "I'd rather wait on showing anything til I've got a clean draft."

"That's fine, too," he said. "Trip respects your process."

Then he asked if there'd been "any fallout from that business with the notary," and I told him how Clyde, for the first week after my visit to the compound, had visited the bank a couple of times to see Chad-Kyle's face, but other than that, nothing at all. And Burroughs told me that Valentine had gone to the bank to make a deposit, and while transacting with the next teller over, had overheard a customer ask Chad-Kyle about his bruises and scars, which Chad-Kyle claimed to have received from multiple blows with a "vintage Italian World War I infantry helmet" in the course of a fight that he'd lost to three bikers at a West Side bar who'd been bothering a girl, "in a way I couldn't stand for. So I got a couple good licks in," Valentine had told Burroughs Chad-Kyle had told his interlocutor, "but three against one?

I should have known better. Still, I think it was worth it. The girl was made safe by my intervention," which caused Valentine to chuckle, in response to which chuckle Valentine's teller, who, Burroughs said, "turned out to be the daughter of the cuddlefarmer we bought Spotsy from," wrote on Valentine's deposit slip, *Last time, he said the helmet was German,* in response to which note, Valentine asked Lotta for her number, and, long-made-short, they'd been dating ever since.

"Nice girl," Burroughs said. "A little old for my son, I'd think, but to each his own, right? And like I said: nice. Laughs a lot. Had her over here for dinner. You came up. Val'd been reading your novel, and he mentioned it to us, and she said she'd known you."

"Yeah?" I said.

"Said she'd seen you murder a swingset. Said it was, I quote, 'weird and exciting.' I told her I'd seen you murder one, too."

"I remember that," I said. "You came up to me and introduced yourself, but you didn't reach your hand out to shake."

"Is *that* what happened? I remember it differently. Snotty hotshot kid sees an employee of another kid, doesn't reach out *his* hand to shake."

"You were the adult," I said. "I was waiting for a cue."

"I was somebody's servant," he said. "You were the star of the evening."

"I didn't think of it that way," I told him.

We laughed and hung up, then I wrote eleven pages.

AOL

Another couple weeks, a hundred-some more pages, and I'd all but forgotten *A Fistful of Fists,* or in any case I no longer feared I'd hurt Blank. I'd let it sit on my shoulder or lie in its sleeve all day while I worked, and after dinner we'd take a walk, and after the walk, we'd hang out more actively. If Clyde were out, we might watch the Groucho compilation and/or a movie I'd rented. If Clyde were home, I'd read in my bedroom with Blank out-of-sleeve, or we'd look through old photos, or work on gags, or I'd browse through my journals, and every couple-three nights, I'd bring a short glass of Scotch—I'd bought a bottle of MacGuffin 12 for myself to celebrate having finished the transcript—to the playground next door and sip it and smoke while Blank sat on my knee or the surface beside me sipping at a thimble of juice or milk.

In sum, we slipped back, with relative ease and comfort, into nearly all our pre-transcript routines. The only change that had stuck was that Blank's enthusiasm for many of our games (all of them, really, but for Make This Face), seemed permanently diminished. It would act excited as ever to play one at the start, but then, after just a couple of minutes, it would crawl its way back inside its sleeve or sit where it had stood or perform a series of Allen-throat-clears followed by brow-wipes and/or pratfalls. Initially, this depressed me a little—was I *boring* my cure?—but soon it became less depressing than interesting. Perhaps, I thought, Kablankey had reached, or was reaching, a new phase in its life. A new kind of maturity. It was, after all, twenty-five years old. Maybe cures around their twenty-sixth year became "adults." Who could say otherwise? Who else would know? Maybe, I thought, they acquired new capacities, new sensitivities or kinds of imperviousness, which led them to put aside childish things. Maybe, much like men at that age, who become more robust—developing what Clyde, when it had happened to me, referred to as *man muscles*—cures underwent physiological changes that produced broad, however subtle, psychological effects, some or one of which might have accounted for Blank's having grown weary of the games. Although I didn't see any new muscles on it, maybe they were only starting to develop, or maybe its ostensibly dawning robustness had little or nothing to do with muscles; maybe it had more to do with invisible processes like hormone regulation, neurotransmission . . .

Whatever'd caused Blank to lose its love for our games, the worry that I'd had a couple months earlier—the worry that the problem was me; that I'd been so altered by my work on the transcript that Blank had sensed it and gotten afraid of me—disappeared. After all, in the rest of the activities we undertook together, Blank continued, throughout those first post-transcript weeks, to show the usual enthusiasm, and though I'm not sure I would, strictly speaking, be correct if I said that the timing of its eyebrow-flexing improved, it had certainly begun to eyebrow-flex less often, and I liked to think this was a kind of progress: the result of its having started to figure out some of the contexts in which it would *not* be very funny to eyebrow-flex, which may have been, however inefficiently, a path toward deducing the contexts in which it *would* be very funny to eyebrow-flex.

Not that I puzzled over eyebrow-flex progress all that much. I was mostly just happy to be back on solid ground with Kablankey; happy not to be a threat to the guy. On top of that, I was far too busy thinking about this memoir to really *puzzle* over anything else, let alone the progress of anything else. Which made me happy too.

And then one morning—the morning of November 5, 2013—I realized I had over 350 clean pages (all of "The Hope of Rusting Swingsets," three large chunks of "Invitation," and the opening of "Compound"), which is to say I had more pages of this memoir written than I had pages already published (*No Please Don't* had been 341 in manuscript; 288 in book form), and this fact seemed almost to make me *too* happy, and, in any case, to demand celebration. A drink. Preferably one not drunk alone. A drink and human company. But which human company?

Of course I'd have loved to celebrate with Fon, I'd have preferred to drink with her over anyone else, and I was in a good enough mood to briefly consider walking over to the compound to see if she was home, but even if she were there and wanted to hang out with me, which I had no real reason to think she would (she hadn't called since my visit), I was certain that Jonboat wouldn't like it, that he'd want to make sure it wouldn't happen again, and I didn't want to end up braced by the Archons, Chad-Kyle-style, so I banished the thought.

I didn't have Denise's number, but considered calling 411 to get it, decided

I shouldn't, that it wouldn't be nice of me, then did it anyway, and she wasn't listed.

411 for Lotta Hogg? She was, after all, with Valentine now, so maybe friendship—no; I thought about that toe in her cleavage, couldn't shake it.

My father was at work (it was 10 a.m.).

Burroughs didn't drink, and even if he were willing to watch me drink, calling him would still seem somehow inappropriate, and in any case he'd probably ask about the transcript, and then I'd have to lie, then worry he saw through it.

There was Herb, but I didn't want him to think I was badgering him about finding Lisette, plus I wasn't particularly in the mood for Herb; I liked him a lot, but he could be too much.

The last time I'd spoken to Eli Khong, my old editor at Darger, he'd mentioned he was in a twelve-step program, so that was a bust.

Which left me with . . . no one.

For the first time ever, I seriously considered going to Arcades and finding someone I could pay to celebrate with me, but rejected the idea—I wasn't ready for that, or ready to learn I was ready for that (which is maybe redundant, it's hard to say)—and at the same time I realized that one of the reasons (not the only one, but certainly one) that I could say that this was the first time I *seriously considered* Arcades was that, up until just a few weeks earlier, I wouldn't have been able to afford a good prostitute (not without giving up days' worth of Quills), and it occurred to me that being able, now, to afford a good prostitute also meant I could afford any number of other luxuries, one of which was a special bottle of Scotch, a bottle even more special than the $58 bottle of MacGuffin 12; one maybe as special as—maybe even more special than—the Glenfibbly 21 I'd bought for Herb, which had cost me $300.

How much could I spend on a bottle of Scotch, though? Rather, how much *should* I spend? I had tens of thousands. Tens of thousands plus incoming biweekly SSDI checks. And then there was this memoir: I was confident I would be able to sell it. For how much would I sell it? I had no idea. And having tens of thousands plus biweekly SSDI was already more than I was able to fully get my head around . . .

Basically, I wanted to pay too much for a bottle of Scotch, but *just* too much. I wanted to buy a bottle of Scotch that I could *not* afford to get in the habit of drinking, but I didn't want to buy a bottle of Scotch that I, newbie to drinking Scotch that I was, would fail to fully appreciate and thus later regret not having built up my palateal IQ for before having tasted. (Since having started drinking the MacGuffin 12, I'd thought, on numerous occasions, about how much better the Glenfibbly 21 tasted, and how much better than that it *would* taste, were I to drink it again, now that I somewhat "understood how" to drink Scotch.) This line of thinking didn't help me to answer my question, though; it didn't help me determine how much I should spend, and soon my desire to celebrate, which was too rare a desire to just leave alone, began to wane a little, and in order to keep it from waning any further, I picked the least arbitrary number I could think of: 350. I'd buy, I decided, a $350 bottle of Scotch. I'd spend a dollar for every clean page of memoir I'd written.

•

• •

A quarter hour later, at the finer foods/liquor shop, I asked Terry, a salesclerk with an impressively non-devious and expertise-exuding broom of a salt-and-ginger mustache, to help me spend $350 on a bottle of Scotch, but that proved impossible. There were numerous bottles in the $200–$300 range, but above $300, there wasn't anything for less than $500. I could have gone elsewhere, I suppose, to seek out a $350 bottle, but that seemed so rigid and beneath the spirit of celebration I was trying to honor that I went with Terry's recommendation to buy a MacGuffin 18-Year-Old Sherry Cask–finished for $265. Terry claimed that the age of a Scotch meant a lot, but not everything, and that, given how much I liked MacGuffin 12 and Glenfibbly 21, this would be the best sub-$600 Scotch for me that they sold in the shop, and I had a lot of faith in him for not trying to upsell me.

The total, after taxes, came to $293, and by the time I'd gotten halfway to my truck, I'd decided to go back into the shop and spend the $57 surplus on a bottle of something else, for Clyde, but as I turned around to do so, I caught sight of the new A(cute)rements Warehouse (formerly known as A(cute)rements PerFormulae/CureWear/ EmergeRig-vendor), which anchored the strip mall across the road, and thought: "No, get something for Blank—Blank's the one you'll be celebrating with, plus when was the last time you bought it something nice?"

I couldn't even remember.

•

• •

A(cute)rements Warehouse was supermarket-size—at least five times as large as the old location—and when I got there, my first impulse was to seek out a clerk who could help me find the best toy or game for Blank (in the wake of my pleasant experience with Terry, my esteem for the wisdom of salesclerks was high), but every clerk I came across was occupied with customers, all of whom, strangely, seemed needy and exasperated, so I decided to navigate the store on my own. I walked up the middle, reading the signs that hung above each aisle to my right and my left. I found PlayChanger PerFormulae aisles, GameChanger PerFormulae aisles, Boutique-Brand Formulae aisles, an aisle of CureSleeves, an aisle of PillowNests, an aisle of standard EmergeRigs, an aisle of special-edition- and gift-set EmergeRigs, an aisle of "PerFormulae Abuse Laboratories Recommends"–stamped products, an aisle of WorkPellets, an aisle of Cuddlefarmer Gear, a T-shirts/DVDs/Coffee Mugs&Collectibles aisle, and a Discount aisle, but no Toys aisle, Games aisle, or Toys/Games aisle.

I entered the "P.A.L. Recommends" aisle to see if P.A.L. recommended any toys or games, but from the looks of it, they weren't recommending much of anything at all: apart from a stack of P.A.L.-branded "no-slip" water thimbles and a pile of CureSleeves made of "moisture-wicking" material, the shelves were entirely empty.

So then I entered the Discount aisle, thinking perhaps there'd be some out-of-fashion yet nonetheless intriguing older toys or games in there that might interest Blank, but no go. It was mostly just leftover Halloween stock: matching costumes for Curios and their owners/users, some Curio-proportioned jack-o'-lantern buckets, and bags of miniature chocolate-free candy bars.

A number of customers were gathered at the Discount aisle's endcaps, at each of which stood an oil barrel stenciled with the words TRICK OR TREAT? ~~\$1.00!~~ NOW 75¢!!! The barrels were a-brim with single WorkPellets in cellophane wrappers of varying color, and from what I could gather by listening to a friendly argument between three of the young men who were digging and sorting through one of these barrels, 5 percent of the WorkPellets had been spiked with a single dose of one of twenty-five different formulae or PerFormulae that ranged widely in price, whereas the other 95 percent had not. One of the young men argued that the colors of the cellophane wrappers were "meaningfully systematized, i.e. encoded," and that someone who understood the system would be able to tell, just by looking at the wrapper, whether the pellet within it had or hadn't been spiked; another young man said that the colors of the wrappers held no meaning whatsoever; and the third young man went even further than the first, claiming that the wrappers were coded by "style of end twist and overall wrinklage" *as well as* by color, and that if one knew how to read the wrappers, one would not only know which pellets had been spiked, but which exact formula or PerFormula the spiked ones had been spiked *with*. None of the arguments seemed to be supported by evidence. Young Men 1 and 3 agreed that it "wouldn't make sense, in terms of systems theory" for the wrappers to be different if the differences lacked meaning, whereas Young Man 2 insisted that it "wouldn't make sense economically" for the wrappers to be different if they communicated meaning.

I was swayed by none of them, nor very interested in taking a position, but because they all seemed, at the least, to *think* that they knew what they were talking about, I asked them if they had any idea where I could find the toys and games, and the third young man, who, despite his theory of complex wrapper-coding, seemed to me the dimmest (eyes like dimes; high, hollow voice) answered, "I think I saw a like cure-themed Shoots and Ladders over there with the T-shirts and collectibles."

"I meant toys and games for cures to play themselves," I said.

"Oh," he said. "I got *no* idea. Maybe they got something like that in the Hobbyist/Fetish case with all the BullyKing bats and other weapons and stuff?"

"They got a set of little swords in there," said the one who'd argued for the wrappers' meaninglessness. "I guess swords is a kind a game, right? Bloodsport."

"Yeah, that counts," said the one who hadn't spoken to me yet.

As I approached the Hobbyist/Fetish case, the clerk who was manning it showed me his palms and said, "I'm just working this case, sir. I know nothing about shipments. The customer service desk's taking complaints." He pointed to the nearest corner of the store, about three aisles away, where at least twenty people were waiting in line.

"Shipments?" I said.

"Okay, look. I apologize on behalf of A(cute)rements that we're still out of Independence. I know we were supposed to get more in today, I know everyone heard that, and I know that you must be very disappointed, but there's nothing I can personally do about it, so please: customer service desk's right over there, and they'll give you a form to fill out. If you were on the waiting list, you fill out that form, you'll get ten percent off when the shipment *does* come in, okay?"

"I'm not here for Independence," I said.

"Oh . . . good!" said the clerk, and, smiling, drummed the edge of the case with his thumbs. "How can I help you, sir?"

"I'm looking for a toy or game that my cure might like."

"A toy?" the clerk said. "A game?" he said. "Well you're at the right case."

"Do you have any advice? Like, what are the smartest cures loving the most these days?"

"Well, I'll tell you," he said, "the Executioner's Set has been selling like crazy, but ever since that second AOL video aired, we've been sold out of it. We do, however, have the *deluxe* Executioner's Set in stock, and that one, in addition to the gallows and hood, comes with a guillotine, which *I* think is great, but it's nearly twice as much as the regular set, and most people are more interested in using the gallows, so . . . The perennial favorite, of course, is the Chicago White Sox BullyKing set over here, which has, as you can see, an MLB-licensed batter's helmet and jersey, plus a cute little stick of lampblack for the under-eye area, and, of course, a bat, but . . . I'm guessing by the way you're not looking at where I'm pointing that you're not a Sox fan, or maybe you have the set already? If you're not a Sox fan, we have a Cubs set, a Reds set, a Cards set, a Tigers set, we *might* have a Yankees left, and maybe a Royals—I can go in back and check if—"

"I was thinking more about a toy or a game that doesn't involve the cure hurting other cures or putting them to death."

"I don't . . . hmmm."

"I remember, you guys used to sell yo-yos, for example. A matching set: one for the owner, one for the cure, you know? I think you sold a cure-size bumper-pool set, too. And a little juggling kit with beanbags and pins. Rings too, I think? Stuff like that, you know?"

"I didn't know that," said the clerk. "I mean we haven't sold anything like that since I've been working here."

"Well, it's been a lot of years," I said. "It was at the old location, actually."

"Lemme think . . . We do have some dueling swords over here that you could, I guess, wrap up in something—electrical tape? or that blue putty stuff made for mounting posters? or even maybe just bubblegum maybe—which would make the swords a lot less wounding, and definitely unfatal, like I'm thinking they'd work more like those foam noodles kids like to hit each other with by the pool? I think? Or and then, let's see . . . This stock-and-oubliette set here? It's adjustable. So you could lower the posts on the stock, I guess, and use it as a whatsit—thing that runners jump in the Olymp—a hurdle. You could set the stock up like a hurdle for a race, maybe? But then you'd probably want at least three or four hurdles, and we might only have a couple sets lefts, and then I don't even know what you'd do with all the oubliettes, so it would be kinda wasteful . . . You know, in my experience?—I know this is gonna sound a little new agey—but in my experience, best thing to do is to let the cure choose. Just open up your sleeve, set it on the case, and see what catches its eye. Like just let it walk along the case, and see where it pauses, you know? You might be surprised by what it's drawn to."

"Yeah, but that'll ruin it," I said. "I actually want what I buy here to be a surprise for the cure itself."

"A surprise for the cure! That's ador—"

"Shut up, shut up, fuck you, shut up," boomed a man at the customer service desk clerk.

"You tell her!" said someone in line behind the man.

"Take it *easy*, fellas," said someone else.

The booming man stormed off, shoulder-checking shelving. Pointing at the Hobbyist/Fetish clerk as he passed us, he said, "Fuck you, buddy. Fuck your whole shitty face."

The Hobbyist/Fetish clerk was shaking his head.

"What a jerk," I said.

"Yeah . . ." the clerk said. "I don't know. I kinda understand his anger, actually. It's our fault, in the end. The owner's fault. The owner is an *ass*hole, you know?"

"I didn't," I said.

"Well, like, did you see that giant sign on the front door that said, 'Due to shipping delays, A(cute)rements continues to be out of Independence. Those customers who reserved their ampules in advance will receive a ten percent discount when the shipment arrives'?"

"I didn't see it," I said.

"Of course you didn't," the clerk said. "Because when my manager put that sign up this morning? The owner made him take it down. Said it was better for us to get the customers through the door. Said that even though they'd all be pissed as hell that the Independence shipment didn't come in, a lot of them would still spend some money before they left—they wouldn't want to have come all this way for nothing. Asshole was right, too. We're doing, like, *Christmas*-level business this morning. But that customer? Probably the tenth person to curse me out."

"I never would've thought people were so desperate for their cures not to need them."

"What do you mean?"

"Isn't that what Independence does?"

"Well, yeah. Right. I mean, that's the prescribed usage. I guess probably some people are interested in that, but most of them want it for AOL, you know?"

"I don't," I said. "Tell me."

"You didn't see those Independence videos that P.A.L. made?"

"You know, I don't really watch *20/20*."

"*20/20* twenty-shmenty—I haven't seen an hour of television where they haven't managed to show at least one of those clips in . . . well not since before they first aired however many weeks ago. Three? I think three. Yeah. Maybe the first one was four weeks ago, but the second one—that was the big one—that was three."

"I don't watch that much TV in general, I guess."

"I guess you must not! Anyway, wow. You *gotta* see that video, sir. Both of them, really, but especially the second one. It's . . . inspiring. I mean, it's causing a kind of revolution. People were coming in here just to—see, we were showing it on a loop on all our 'Cure for Boredom' checkout-line monitors til last Friday, and people were coming in just to watch it, over and over, but then someone must've narced because we got a cease-and-desist letter from ABC. A lot of shops did, I heard. They're gonna do a home video release next week of P.A.L. AOLing a bunch of different cures using different setups, I guess, and they don't want us to burn it out. ABC, I mean. So now—"

"I'm completely confused," I said. "I still don't even know what AOL is."

"Right. Got ahead of myself. Auto-overload," he said. "See, you overdose the cure with Independence, okay? You give it five full doses of Independence—just three if it's a nascent—and then, once it kicks in? You give it a half dose of NeedyBuddy—a quarter dose if it's a nascent—and then you put it in front of a mirror and it overloads. On *itself*."

"Like it sees itself, and starts grieving and—"

"*No,* sir. No grieving. It doesn't auto-*deactivate*. It auto-*overloads*. It sees itself in the mirror, and then *commits suicide*. Or tries to, at least."

"I don't . . ."

"You really gotta see it to believe it. Sir, you're in for *such* a treat. You know, you could actually see some AOLs right here in the store, cause what I was starting to say before was that after the cease-and-desist came in from ABC? a few of us who worked here, we shot our own AOL vids, compiled them, and we're looping *those* on the 'Cure for Boredom' monitors now. And, you know, not to toot my own flute, but I think the one I made's one of the best of them, actually. It's got some, uh . . . pretty wild twists. But I won't spoil it for you. It's the one with the special-rigged gallows, though. Anyway, the whole thing's good. The whole compilation."

The clerk seemed so proud, I told him I'd watch it.

And I did. Some of it. Though I didn't mean to. Not exactly. First, I did a little shopping, however. I stopped in the WorkPellets aisle to buy a couple of six-month supply packs—they were nearly 30 percent cheaper there than at the grocery store—and then, although I'd given up on finding a toy or a game, I still wanted to get some kind of gift for Blank, so I chose a $90 PillowNest with memory-foam cushioning, full-spectrum interior lighting, a no-slip thimble, and a two-way-mirrored lid. It cost a bit more than I'd intended to spend, but, according to the sticker on the box, this nest had been a P.A.L. recommendation-of-the-month for six months running, back in 2011, plus Blank had been in the same PillowNest since infancy, I was short on gift ideas, and if this new nest were, as it appeared to be, as well made as the old one, it would last more than long enough to justify the price. It would, in all likelihood, outlast me. And maybe, I thought, Blank would like the lighting.

The shortest checkout line was five customers deep, and although I didn't particularly want to see the compilation, there were three "Cure for Boredom" monitors per line—a large one that ran alongside the product conveyor belt to my left, a small one above the impulse-purchase rack to my right, and a medium-size one above the cash register ahead—so, ergonomically speaking, it was easier to watch than it was not to watch.

Nor was I entirely uninterested. My visit to A(cute)rements had convinced me that Independence—or AOL—was, if nothing else, something much of the world was fascinated by, and for me to willfully remain ignorant of either one would be, it seemed, to deny reality, which, for anyone, but especially a writer, isn't generally considered a wise or admirable move. So I allowed myself to look at the screens, or I didn't go out of my way not to look at the screens—or . . . whatever.

I watched the screens.

The line was slow enough that even though the clips were each sandwiched between a series of animated flyers for that week's on-sale products and promotions at A(cute)rements, I had enough time to see two.

The first clip I saw must have, I thought, been the one the clerk I'd spoken to had made, as the Curio in it stood on the elevated platform of a gallows like the one in the display case. In front of the gallows, flush with the platform, was a vanity mirror. At the start of the clip, the cure wore an eyeless hood. Two fingers entered the frame and pulled the hood off. The cure, seeing itself in the mirror, went wide-eyed near-instantly, and covered its snout, as if pleasantly surprised, then uncovered its snout to stroke its own face with increasing pressure, then sat on the platform, staring into its eyes in the mirror and hugging itself so tightly that its breathing became short and it began to painsing, at which point it stopped hugging itself, got to its feet, ceased to painsing, and hurled itself, whole-bodied, at the mirror, instantly opening a cut above its eye and bashing its knee such that now it was hopping, bleeding from the cut, and painsinging at what looked like it must have been a higher volume than previously (the "Cure for Boredom" monitors were all set on mute). The cure sat down and hugged itself again, but just as quickly leapt back to its feet and hurled itself at the mirror, cracking the mirror, opening a second cut, over its other eye, and falling onto its back on the platform.

It sat up, hugged itself, and painsang, it seemed, even louder yet (its mouth was wide-open), then crawled to and knelt just in front the mirror. It straightened its back and cocked its torso, as if to deliver a powerful headbutt, but before it was able to do anything else, the fingers reentered from the top of the frame, to lift it by the shoulders and set it near the noose. The cure, still painsinging, tried to reach the mirror a few more times—at first upon its knees, then upon its feet, limping—and at each attempt the fingers reappeared to place it near the noose.

After the last approach, a hardcover book—I don't know which book; there wasn't a dust jacket—was set between the mirror and the cure. The cure turned around then, toward the post of the gallows, and looked upward. While continuing to painsing, it did the head-bobbing thing that a lot of cures do when their owner/user is speaking to them, and the fingers returned, pinched the noose, and shook it til the cure put the noose around its neck.

It turned back toward the book. The book was removed. The cure ran at its reflection, tightening the noose, but the rope prevented it from reaching the mirror, and the cure, leaning forward at the sharpest angle the rope would allow, began to strangle, but soon lost its balance, and its knees struck the platform, and the rope went slack.

Now it tried something else. It balled itself up: pressed its shoulders to its knees, and wrapped its arms around the backs of its thighs, squeezed tighter and tighter til none of its body made contact with the platform, and it tilted backward, and the rope went taut. Strangling once again, it pendulated slightly, just a hair's breadth over the platform. After a number of seconds, however, it must have passed out, or in any case lost the strength it required to remain balled up; its torso unfolded, and it came to rest on the platform again, slackening the rope, relieving the strangle.

It opened its eyes, raised its head, got to its knees, found its reflection, and the cycle—i.e. the charging at the mirror, tilting, kneeling, balling, pendulating, passing out, recovering—repeated twice more.

Then the cure appeared to get a handle on the whole dirty trick—or maybe not the *whole* dirty trick, for it didn't try to get the noose off its neck—and, rather than attempting to smash into the mirror again, it hurled itself backward into the gallows post, thrashed around at random, jumped side to side, and managed, accidentally, by way of all this jumping and thrashing, to kick a lever next to the post, which opened the platform's trapdoor beneath it.

Dropped right through.

When this happened, at least two of the people who were standing in line with me audibly sighed, but the clip wasn't over. Beneath the trapdoor was a stack of books (I don't know which ones: the spines weren't visible) that prevented the cure from falling far enough for the rope to go taut, and though the cure scraped its ribs against the trapdoor's frame as it fell upon the books, it did not—could not—strangle, much less snap its neck.

Just as it had atop the platform, it balled itself up, but there was still too much rope for it to hang itself to death once it had, having passed out, unballed.

It climbed back over the trapdoor's edge, stood once again atop the platform, pulled the lever, which shut the trapdoor, and turned and stared into its eyes in the mirror, its swelling face dripping with glistening tears and equally glistening, though slower-dripping, blood.

Its hands were in fists. It examined its fists. Lifted one, then the other. Stacked one atop the other the tall way. It crouched down and set its stacked fists on the platform. Stretched its legs as if to lie on its belly. Turned its head and set its cheek on the fist-stack.

It stood up once more and looked back into the mirror. Its jaw had relaxed. Its brow had smoothed out.

Again it stacked its fists. It pressed the top of its right fist against its throat, the top of its left fist against the bottom of its right fist. Gazing into its eyes' reflection, it took some deep breaths, and then, its bent elbows pointing outward like wings, it jumped high in the air, kicked its legs out behind it, became horizontal, remained horizontal throughout its brief descent, and, upon its left fist's impact with the platform, snapped its windpipe and shuddered and died.

The animated flyers appeared on the screens. The audible sighers exchanged looks of wonder. I kept my eyes down. I just wasn't there yet. But I wasn't wrecked either. Having transcribed *A Fistful of Fists* must have, whether im- or permanently, done more than a little to desensitize me to images of brutalized cures. I wasn't *unaffected* by the gallows video, but nor was I any more affected by it than I would have been by, say, seeing a homeless man beg on the street, or viewing nightly news footage of war orphans, weeping.

The second clip didn't affect me even that much. Though notably gorier than the gallows clip, it was a quarter as long, and the AOL was far more efficient. The cure was set between a pair of mirrors, and once it passed through the face-caressing/self-hugging phase, no one got in the way of its repeatedly bashing its head against the mirror on the left. Once its snout was half-flattened, a final blow to that mirror shattered it entirely, and the painsinging cure, spinning on its heel to see the other mirror, slipped on a puddle of its blood and fell sideways, hard, impaling a cheek on a silvery shard, then scrambled to its feet, shard still wedged in its cheek, plucked the shard, examined the shard, dropped the shard, bent to pick up a longer shard, then straightened itself, and, observing its reflection in the still-intact mirror, lined the shard up with one of its eyes, then buried the shard in its head, which killed it.

Next thing I knew, I was being rung up.

As I waited for my credit card receipt to print out, the three young men who I'd met by the endcap barrel—they'd gotten in line behind me while the flyers between the two clips were screening—argued over how derivative this second clip was of the P.A.L. clip that had started the AOL craze.

"Total rip-off," one said.

"I don't think so," said another. "In the P.A.L. one, it takes a little longer. The cure doesn't dact for like, almost five seconds, after it stabs itself. There's a lot more seizuring kind of movement, you know? Plus this one's a better painsinger."

"How the hell would you know that?" said the first one. "There isn't any sound."

"You could tell by its face. It was *really* emoting."

"He's right," said the third. "You could totally tell. You could tell by its face."

•

•   •

On my return from A(cute)rements, I found, on our stoop, a padded manila envelope addressed to me, c/o of my father. The sender was Gus. Along with three handkerchiefs, the envelope contained a handwritten letter.

Dear Belt,

Thank you for your complex, impressive work of literature. I just finished reading it. Man, what a ride. Many times I was a little confused, but those times I was confused I was laughing, and am good with that.

In case you want to know, the most confused I got was at the end. The end made me sad, and I do not know why, don't know was I even supposed to be sad. Maybe it was just a personal reaction I had, specific to myself. I am not asking you to tell me if I was supposed to be sad, or why if I was supposed to be I was, but I will read it again and if I still don't understand, I might write to you again and ask you those questions.

The handkerchiefs I picked for you are eggwhite white, the most popular white.

My regards to your father.

I hope to read more of your writing soon, and I wish you best of luck with your bubblegum venture.

Sincerely,
Gus Aronov-Katz

Reading over the letter just now, I can't help but notice how vague its language is, and I find it strange that, given that vagueness, I didn't, when

I first read the letter, spend even the briefest of fleeting moments doubting that Gus had enjoyed and admired my novel enough to want to reread it, let alone doubting that he'd read it at all. And yet I didn't; I doubted nothing. I took Gus at his word, and—perhaps because he, a retired miller and part-time security guard at a bank, was just the kind of reader I'd previously feared my fiction couldn't speak to; perhaps because his was the very first fan letter I'd ever received; or perhaps because receiving it reminded me how I'd also sent Stevie the novel, and, since Stevie was (or so I would've assumed) *exactly* the kind of reader I'd always been confident my fiction *could* speak to, I became newly hopeful regarding the prospect of receiving from her a similar letter or, for that matter, any kind of letter at all (which, by the way, I never would; to this day, I haven't heard back from Stevie)—my desire to celebrate, which had dulled a bit since my visit to A(cute)rements, returned in full force.

And here I had a gift for Blank from me, I had a gift for me from Gus, and I had a gift from myself to me. How best to proceed? I did the boring parts first: stuck the old PillowNest under my bed, atop the box of recordings of Blank's songs and gags; set the new PillowNest up on my night table; and went to the kitchen to wash and fill the new thimble with water, and get a short glass.

Back in my room, I turned on the light inside the new nest, set the thimble in the slit, closed the nest's lid, poured myself a dram of MacGuffin 18, removed Blank from its sleeve and set it, standing, on my better pillow, facing the night table.

Blank double-took and back-stepped, moved a little to the right, a little to the left, all the while with its eyes on the nest, as if to better adjudge its feng shui.

"Fweep," it whistled, pointing at the nest, meaning, I presume, either "Is this for me?" or "What happened to the old nest?" or "Do you see what I'm seeing here? A different nest!"

"Fwee-oo," I whistled back twice in succession, each time drawing, with the tip of my finger, an invisible arc from Blank to the nest.

It didn't hesitate to take my advice. It climbed the little ladder built into the side, and when it got to the top, said, "Anks," which, as always, meant, "Please," and which I took to mean, "Please open the lid so I can get inside."

I opened the lid. Blank straddled the edge, climbed down the nest's interior ladder. It explored for a minute, testing out the memory foam: bouncing up and down in the center of the pad, then in each of the corners, then falling to its knees, performing a somersault, then dragging and rubbing its knuckles and muzzle against all the walls (the walls were memory-foam-padded as well).

I switched off the nest's light and Blank whistled, "Fweep," and I signaled it should climb back up to the edge.

When it got there, I pointed to the switch—the switch was at the base of the exterior ladder—and flipped the light on and off. "Anks," Blank said, and I flipped the light on again and left it that way.

"Anks," it said again, and pointed at the lid, and climbed back down and waited by the thimble. I shut the lid and, through the one-way glass, I observed the cure perform an Allen-throat-clear, followed by a brow-wipe, a pratfall, and a second brow-wipe, which filled me with pride, or something like pride: although, to the cure—*my* cure—its ceiling was a mirror, it must have noticed earlier, when it was outside the nest and the lid was still closed, that one could, from the outside, see through the lid, i.e. it must have understood and immediately accepted the not-exactly-intuitive principle of two-way mirrors/one-way glass, which, to my recollection, was a kind of mirror/glass it hadn't encountered before. "Well maybe not *must* have," I thought, "but *might* have." It might have also, I thought, had no idea I could see it through the lid; maybe it was only practicing its gags (i.e. not performing them *for* me), but *maybe*, after all, was the sound second thoughts made, and I preferred the first thought, the one that made me feel good.

Blank did another brow-wipe, another pratfall, another couple throat-clears.

I reopened the lid and leaned over the nest. "Kablankey," I said, and I pointed at its thimble, and raised my glass of Scotch in a toast, and Blank pulled the thimble out of its slit, and raised it in mimicry.

"To the *first* thought," I said.

Blank whistled, "Fweep-fwee-oo!"

I sipped from my glass, and Blank sipped from its thimble. The MacGuffin 18 was honey and leather, then butter and apricots, and then, at last—and this was the best part—deep Robitussin cherry: a flavor I hadn't tasted or recalled since my first strep throats in the mid-1980s, which, for days at a time, accorded me the longest section of the couch, as well as authority over the TV. Throughout my elementary- and middle-school years, I caught strep frequently—a couple or three times a winter, at least—but my mother, after the first few streps, switched our cough syrup brand to Triaminic (I'm sure I asked why, but don't remember the answer: it was probably more effective than Robitussin, or equally effective but less expensive), and the Triaminic grape (the banana was foul; I never had the cherry), although it didn't taste, by any means, *bad*, lacked the rich kick and viscosity of Robitussin.

I drank the first Scotch slowly—the finish lasted forever—and lit a Quill off a Quill off a Quill off a Quill, remembering the sick days, the couch-as-sickbed. The piles of blankets and sheets and pillows. The self-mastering periods during my fevers when I was able to grasp, for entire minutes, exactly how to manipulate the linens that covered my legs in order to produce the thrillingly contradictory sensation(s) of being too hot and too cold at once. All the court shows I watched, re-en- or just acted. All the talk shows I watched, with their skinheads and Klansmen and former Black Panthers, their pimps and transvestites and cheaters and Wiccans, their abuse allegations and blood-test results. The last five minutes on *The Price Is Right* when the trumpets blasted and the curtains were pulled and the fantasy-abetting and semi-thematic grand-prize packages were finally unveiled: the Caribbean cruise and the sit-down Jet Ski, the ski trip to Vale and the redesigned living room with wood-burning fireplace and matching leather club chairs, the luxury box at the Indy 500 and the limited-edition convertible Corvette, the sky-diving lessons and the inground pool. And then the soaps would come on and I'd switch to a local network for reruns, cartoons, sometimes an old movie, falling in and out of naps, ensconced all the while by the roofless fortification I'd constructed by stacking or wedging or standing on end any number of the cushions on which I wasn't lying. How my every meal and snack would arrive on a folding tray. The fresh-squeezed OJ. The double helping of bacon. Tomato soup and grilled cheese. Saltines and chicken soup. Tea and grapefruit and candy-like cough drops. I'd wear a quilt on my shoulders like a superhero cape anytime I got up to stretch or use the bathroom. And my mother always there, beside me on the couch, reading a book or watching TV with me or taking my temperature or feeding me medicine, unless she was making something in the kitchen. She'd stay home from work with me whenever I was sick—if that ever caused her problems, I was never told—and though she never complained, or seemed impatient, or, for that matter, seemed anything other than content to hang out with and wait on me, I knew she was doing more than she had to, more than being a mother demanded. I was fully aware that the feeling of luxury and total security, of *exciting* safety, that marked my sick days was enabled and encouraged by the efforts of my mother, the *voluntary* efforts, which efforts I did not—it occurred to me happily, there on my bed, so many years later, a man well past the age she'd been back then—which efforts I did *not* ever fail to appreciate. Was there anything better than having a fever while being her son? As a boy, I'd been nothing short of certain there wasn't. As a man I was no less certain than that, which might sound depressing, but really it wasn't. Hammy, perhaps—a little too sentimental—but not at all depressing. I felt lucky to have once been her fevered young son, and luckier, still, to have known of my luck back when I'd still been her fevered young son. I'd known what I'd had before it was gone.

What an excellent Scotch, that MacGuffin 18. I poured a second, bigger glass, which I drank a little faster, tasted burnt marshmallow, brand-new-cassette smell, steam of baking apple, black-peppered raisin. The Robitussin finish remained long and thick, but from one glass to another, it or I lost the power to open any more veins of sense-memory access to childhood sick days, or to anyhood anything. No worries, however. No worries at all. I felt good and warm, enjoyed the breath in my lungs, and was above-average charmed by the sight of Kablankey, which, sitting with its back to a wall of the nest, had been matching my drinking sip for sip with its water, and mimicking the sounds of the hissier drags I took from my Quills, occasionally nodding to itself and squinting, as if it, too, were considering the past.

I suppose I'd gotten a little bit drunk, a little more drunk than I might have intended. It was past 1 p.m. and I'd hardly eaten. A few almonds in advance of my morning coffee. There was leftover pizza in the fridge, and I wanted it. First the last gift, though: the handkerchiefs from Gus. Eggwhite white. I opened the plastic envelope they came in, unfolded the top one—it was old-T-shirt soft, but new-jeans sturdy. I thought I should try it. I looked out the window, directly at the sun, and provoked a pair of sneezes to catch, and caught them, and then blew my nose.

Kablankey plugged his thimble back in its slit, stood up, reached out and said, "Anks, anks," so I dropped a clean handkerchief over its head, and once it found its way out from underneath, it throat-cleared and pratfell, and sat where it had stood. It brow-wiped, then grabbed two fistfuls of hankie from the floor of the nest, covered its muzzle, and performed a noisy nose-blow—something I'd never before seen it do—and, as if that weren't adorable enough, turned to face me in the wake of the nose-blow, and, with Groucho-grade timing, flexed its eyebrows.

"That was great," I said laughing. "That was so great."

Blank nose-blew noisily and eyebrow-flexed for minutes, and I laughed and praised it in response for minutes, until, all at once, the new gag had been driven straight into the ground.

I wiped my eyes, sighed, and reached a hand in the nest so Blank would climb on and we could go downstairs and I could warm up some pizza, but, drunk as I was, the angle at which I offered my palm was a little too lazy, a bit too not-flush with the floor of the nest, thus communicating "Gimme" more than "Climb on," and so, instead of climbing on, Blank, like one making a bed does with blankets, grasped two corners of the twisted-up hankie and snapped it out, so it billowed and flattened, then let it sail down to cover my hand and part of my forearm. And what was this, now? The handkerchief was damp? The handkerchief was damp and the damp part was . . . green? Wet? Gross. Poor little guy. I must have, when I'd first draped the handkerchief over it, used the one I'd sneezed in; I'd meant to use a clean one, a fresh one from the pack. And I'd been sure that I had. Then again I'd been drunk. Not quite as drunk as I was right then, but I must have been drunker than—

Blank Allen-throat-cleared three times in a row, and wiped at its brow, and throat-cleared again. The handkerchief I'd sneezed in was in my other hand, the hand that wasn't holding the hankie Blank had given me. I dropped both hankies and lifted Blank out of the nest by the shoulders. I showed it the window, the sun in the window. It sneezed. Not drily. Sneezed on the window. On the glass were dots of matter. Green dots of matter. Nor did the sneeze sound at all like *kablankey*. It was only one syllable. It sounded like *merf*.

And just like that, I was no longer drunk.

•

• •

The receptionists at the first three animal hospitals I called all thought I was pranking them; two found the "prank" funny, the third did not, they all hung up on me. However, the receptionist at Paws & Wings of Deerbrook Park—although she did laugh, and had to put me on hold to find out whether the vet treated cures—gave me an appointment for three that afternoon.

The only safe way to let a vet examine Blank would be to hide its face behind some kind of mask, but Blank could hardly stand to wear a mask, and the only way to keep it from removing a mask—as I'd learned during our second Halloween together, when we'd gone out trick-or-treating as Robins—was for me to wear a mask that matched its own, but our old Robin masks, which I found in one of my under-bed boxes, concealed less face than I'd remembered it concealing, plus we had a full hour before our appointment, so I, Blank in-sleeve, returned to A(cute)rements and bought a matched set of luchador costumes I'd noticed earlier, in the Discount aisle.

I set Blank on the dash in the A(cute)rements parking lot and unpacked the box containing the costumes. I put on the larger mask (blue with white lightning bolts over the eyes) and showed Blank the smaller one (white with blue lightning bolts). "Anks," Blank said, and I helped it roll the mask down over its head, put it back in the CureSleeve, closed the CureSleeve, removed my mask, and drove to the vet's.

We were half an hour early. I chain-smoked Quills in the truck in the lot, and tried my best to reason through my swelling guilt and panic, panic-first.

All we needed was antibiotics. That's how I started. That's what I had to keep reminding myself. All we needed was antibiotics because psittacosis, if caught in time, was curable with antibiotics. It said so in the manual, which I double-, then triple-checked in the truck (I'd brought the manual along to do just that):

Illness

> BOTIMALS® are hardy robots with rugged immune systems. They are impervious to most illnesses from which human beings suffer, including the common cold. Psittacosis (or *Chlamydophila psittici*), which is often present in pigeon guano, can infect BOTIMALS®, causing any or all of the following symptoms: scaly skin; a general loss of pluck; misshapen, though firm, rear ejections; and, eventually, death. If your BOTIMAL® shows signs of infection, make an appointment with a qualified veterinarian (one who treats pet birds). The vet will administer a simple blood test and, if the BOTIMAL® is diagnosed with psittacosis, prescribe a course of antibiotics. Until the course of antibiotics has been completed, you should allow your BOTIMAL® an extra two or three hours of sleep per night, cuddle it for an extra hour a day, refrain from putting your mouth on it, and be sure to wash your hands with soap after each cuddling session.
>
> (NOTE: Dust, blasts of air, and sudden exposure to bright light, especially sunlight, can cause some BOTIMALS® to sneeze drily. Many of them seem to delight in it. Sneezing is not a sign of illness in BOTIMALS®, so if yours starts sneezing, don't be alarmed. Enjoy the show.)

Although, actually, no, it didn't—it didn't actually *say so*. Not explicitly. It didn't explicitly say that antibiotics would cure psittacosis, but it was—relax, Belt—it was strongly implied. Why would a vet prescribe antibiotics if antibiotics couldn't do the job?

Nor was there anything in the manual about nasal discharge, let alone *green* nasal discharge, and there was nothing about having trouble breathing or swallowing (either or both of which, I'd started to fear, were just what Blank's frequent throat-clearing indicated). On the other hand, the brow-wiping—and maybe, now that I thought about it, also the pratfalls and the reluctance to play any of our more physical games—may have been a sign of what the manual referred to as "a loss of pluck." What was "a loss of pluck" if not exhaustion, right? And what was falling down and wiping one's brow if not a signifier of exhaustion?

One way, then, to think about the nasal discharge and perhaps the throat-clears (in the end, maybe the throat-clears would turn out not to be symptoms of anything; would turn out to be just the overused gag I'd previously been assuming they were)—one way to think about the nasal discharge and/or the throat-clears was that they were positive signs. They were positive signs, maybe, inasmuch as maybe what they indicated was that Blank was maybe yet in a very early stage of the infection. Maybe some Curios were able to beat psittacosis on their own, and so it was inadvisable to medicate them before the other symptoms the manual listed (i.e. scaly skin, misshapen ejections) were manifest because antibiotics should never be used unless completely necessary. That was a thing I'd heard. About antibiotics. That they shouldn't be used unless completely necessary because they were somehow bad for the environment, or they made diseases stronger, something like that. I hadn't heard it til the 1990s, true, but that didn't mean the experts weren't saying it back in the 1980s, when the manual was written. The experts very well may have been saying it back in the 1980s, and, for reasons of public health, the authors of the manual, who'd maybe listened to the experts more closely than I had—maybe the authors of the manual didn't wish to encourage any unnecessary use of antibiotics, and so maybe they figured that, because green nasal discharge was only a sign that the cure was at an early stage of psittacosis infection (i.e. a stage at which it might fight the infection and recover on its own, without the aid of antibiotics), *if* green nasal discharge was only a sign that the cure was at an early stage of psittacosis infection—maybe the authors of the manual determined that it was better for the public health not to include in the manual any mention of green nasal discharge (or trouble breathing or swallowing) because the Curio was, while still at the green nasal discharge– (and/or trouble breathing– and/or trouble swallowing–) phase, as likely as not to be able to beat the psittacosis on its own, i.e. without adding more antibiotics into the antibiotic-saturated environment. Maybe I was panicking for nothing. Panicking because I hadn't been told explicitly, by the authors of the manual, that I *shouldn't* panic about green nasal discharge, etc.

Except then, on the other hand, and by much the same token, maybe the green nasal discharge etc. was far worse than I thought. The manual didn't say that a Curio with psittacosis would *necessarily* suffer all the symptoms listed (i.e. scaly skin, misshapen ejections, *and* loss of pluck), just that the Curio *might* suffer *any* of those symptoms, and perhaps—if Blank had, in fact, been suffering "a loss of pluck" for as long as it had been pratfalling/brow-wiping/refusing to play our more physical games—perhaps it was in a very *late* stage of its illness; a late stage of its illness marked by green nasal discharge; so late a stage that the authors of the manual didn't even bother to mention the green nasal discharge because anyone who was paying attention to his Curio would have long since recognized one of the other symptoms ("a loss of pluck," in Blank's case) preceding the green nasal discharge stage and so taken their Curio in to the vet long before the green nasal discharge would have manifested—and maybe the manifestation of green nasal discharge meant that the psittacotically infected cure had reached *so* late a stage in its illness that it wouldn't ever fully recover, or maybe never even recover at all; a stage at which even antibiotics would be less effective, or even ineffective, and here came the guilt.

Not only was it my fault my Curio had gotten ill—and it's not that I hadn't tried to make sure, every time I removed it from its sleeve outdoors, that the area on which I set it was clear of pigeon droppings (I'd *always* made sure), but that I'd ever trusted my stupid eyes, that I'd ever thought my "making sure" would be sufficient—but that I had let it suffer for weeks before ever realizing it was ill, before ever taking any measures to heal it.

And my guilt, which might have, on a better day, somewhat mercifully swallowed or overtaken my panic, grew *with* my panic, symbiotically, instead; entered into a kind of shouting contest with it. According to my guilt, my cure was ill because I'd been careless, and to sit around panicking was a way to avoid accepting responsibility for my carelessness. According to my panic, my cure was ill because the world was random and randomly brutal, and thinking in terms of responsibility was just a way to avoid facing the fearsome truth: that, as always, and like everyone else, I lacked control over just about everything, my death was encroaching, as was the death of anyone else I cared about, the death of everyone I didn't care about, eventually the death of all living things, thus the death of memory, and so the end of meaning, of the *illusion* of meaning.

And so there I sat, in my friendly orange truck, feeling guilty for not feeling guilty enough; feeling cowardly for failing to panic enough; guilty for panicking; cowardly for panicking instead of feeling more guilty; guilty for feeling cowardly about feeling guilty instead of panicking more when I should have been feeling guilty about what I'd been panicking to avoid feeling guilty for . . .

At last, I short-circuited. My guilt and panic gave way to hope, to reason, to reasonable hope or hopeful reasoning—who could tell the difference?—but . . . Maybe it *wasn't* late-stage psittacosis. What did I know about it? I wasn't a vet. Maybe it *was* just an early, curable stage of infection. All signs pointed to maybe, for sure. And if that's all it was, an early stage, then there wouldn't be anything to fear at all, and the only thing that *might* be my fault was my having unintentionally, i.e. despite my very best efforts, exposed my cure to some pigeon droppings, which: sorry about that, tough break there, Kablankey, but that's what the antibiotics are for; sometimes shit, as it were, happens. I'd done everything I could have. Had I not done everything that I could have? "Yes," I thought. "Mostly. Almost everything." Instead of smoking three Quills in a row in the lot, I could have gone inside the hospital as soon as I'd arrived, and seen if, perhaps, the vet would see us early. That would have been better; I could have done that, and I hadn't done that, but that would have been everything. So I tossed the fourth Quill I'd chain-lit on the pavement, stomped it out, and entered Paws & Wings, ten minutes early.

• • •

There was nowhere to sit in the Paws & Wings waiting room. Nowhere for me at least. A man who had thighs the width of bullet-bike gas tanks was planted in the middle of the mauve vinyl loveseat, cooing to a ferret that was sniffing his ear, while atop the matching couch that was facing the loveseat, an elderly woman with a pair of leashed Savannah cats nuzzling at her feet sat over the crack between two of the cushions, of which there were three (i.e. cushions, not cracks), a little too attentively flipping through a copy of the *Cats'n'Jamming Monthly* spread open on the coffee table before her, as an elderly man who I took to be her husband (he didn't appear to have an animal with him) sat over the other crack, studying his nail beds with no less focus than the woman did her magazine.

So I filled out my paperwork standing at the counter, and a quarter hour later, a kid with a macaw in a carrier cage came out of the door that led to the offices, trailed by a vet tech who picked up a clipboard and said, "Ms. Magnet?"

I raised my hand.

"*We're* next," the old woman on the couch pronounced.

"Oh, I'm sorry," the vet tech said to me. "I thought the name Bela was a woman's name—sorry."

"It's Belt," I said. "Weird, I know. You know, actually, I think the name Bela, at least sometimes—"

"Belt?" he said, showing me the clipboard. "That's a *t* right there?" he said. "That's a *t*?"

"My handwriting's not—"

"Your *t* looks like an *a*!" he said.

"T'n'A, T'n'A, T'n'A, T'n'A," the fat man baby-voiced at his ferret.

"Does this," the vet tech asked the receptionist, "look like a *t* to you? Or an *a*?"

"I don't exactly mean to interrupt you, sir, but *we* are next," said the woman on the couch.

"Hmm," said the vet tech. "Are those your kitties?"

"Cadman and Uk," she said.

"Well, I think you must be here to see Dr. Mills."

"I don't remember his name," she said.

"Dr. Mills works with our more conventionally pawed patients. This man's here to see Dr. Kleinstadt. Dr. Kleinstadt treats our exotics."

"Well the Savannah cat breed," the woman whined, "originally *comes* from the continent of Africa."

"Yes?" said the vet tech.

"That's why I *called* them Cadman and Uk."

"I see," said the vet tech.

"If that's not ex*o*tic . . ." replied the woman, ducking her lips out and widening her eyes.

"Oh, goddamnit," snapped the man beside her. "That's not what he means by exotic, goddamnit. You know very well that's not what he goddamn means. Would you stop being pushy and shut your fucking mouth and quit embarrassing yourself for just ten goddamn minutes. You look like a goddamn fool. A fool."

"Something is always wrong with you," she told him.

"A fool," he said.

"There's always been something wrong with him," she told us.

The fat guy held his ferret like a watermelon slice, kissed it on the belly, one two three.

The vet tech led me to an overlit office. Windowless, clean. White enamel sink under three wooden cabinets. Laptop asleep on a caster-footed standing desk. Stainless-steel exam table bolted to a wall with a chrome, pneumatic stool at either long side. The tech said the doc would arrive momentarily, cracked about how I should work on my *t*'s, left the clipboard he'd taken from reception on the desk, then went out the door.

I perched on the stool that was farther from the laptop, set my elbows on the table, and cradled my forehead, but soon I thought better of being discovered in so meek a pose—I didn't want the doc to fall under the impression I'd resigned myself to receiving bad news—and I sat up straight, squeezed the blur from my eyes, and, having failed to bring a book, tried to find a thing to look at that would make me seem formidable, or at least like a person who shouldn't be refused medicine even if that medicine might hurt the environment. There weren't many options. To watch the slow-motion bouncing of the words *Paws & Wings* across the screen of the laptop, entrancing as that was, would signal mental deficiency. To study the springs in—or futz with the dials near—the complicated joints of the overhead exam lamp could, perhaps, indicate an analytical mind at work, but might just as easily come off as childish. My only viable option was the large, framed poster that hung on the wall to my immediate right, which (owing, I suppose, to a displaced, vestigial sense of resentment I'd developed as a teen who'd become fed up with psychiatrists who asked him to describe what he "saw" or "believed [he] saw" or “found so intriguing” in this or that piece of wall art that was hanging in their offices; wall art at which he was only ever looking in order to avoid their overbearing eye contact) I had so far avoided gazing at directly.

The poster was a photo of a pale axolotl floating in a pitch-black body of water—perhaps in nature, perhaps an aquarium—and must have been three times larger than life; the axolotl’s smiling head was the size of a plum; the pink hornlike emanations at its neck as thick as pencils. Most of the poster’s bottom half was black, and in the lower-right corner, beneath what I suppose was the title of the photo, “The Gracious Axolotl Greets the Night with a Grin,” was a rather long caption in too small a font to read from where I sat. I scooted my stool a foot closer to the wall. The hornlike emanations, I learned, were called *gill stalks,* and what made the axolotl “so notable, apart from its endearingly friendly mien” was that it was *neotonic:* whereas other amphibians, such as frogs and salamanders, begin as tadpoles, develop front legs, develop back legs, then at last become sexually mature and terrestrial, axolotl tadpoles never undergo complete metamorphosis—after growing all their legs and reaching sexual maturity, they get a bit fatter, but remain aquatic.

That’s as far as I got before the door opened, and in walked Kleinstadt, who could have been George Costanza’s handsome cousin, or Costanza himself if Costanza’d spent most of his life being happy, saw in 20/20, and had gotten daily exercise: late forties/early fifties; shorter than I, but with broader shoulders, and a cleaner shave; all easy smile and confident handshake; stubby fingers, hairy knuckles, a double-wide wedding band, and a New York accent. He inspired confidence on sight, this Kleinstadt.

“So *neotony,*” I said, coming out of the handshake.

“What’s that?” he said.

“Wouldn’t that be the noun form of *neotonic*?” I said. “I was reading your poster.”

“Oh, right. Yes. The ol’ ever-grinning neotonic axolotl. Strange little beast. I used to have one as a patient. Long time ago. What a creature. A real Jekyll-and-Hydesky. That smiling mouth, I tell you, when it’s chomping down a feeder fish? Sucking on a bloodworm? Oof. You know they have these little . . . teeth. Always gave me the willies. Name was, lemme think here . . . Ghostowitz? No. Ghostbloom—*Ghostheim!* Ghostheim, that’s it. That was its name. Willies aside, I always liked it. Haven’t seen it in years. But speaking of patients I haven’t examined in a while—you know, soon as I was told you were coming in, I had Mary in reception look through the records. I haven’t seen a cure in here since 1994. Nearly twenty years ago! Not something you’d think I’d be too keen to advertise, but I’m certain our competition—not that anyone within a thousand miles of here can compete with Paws & Wings, our staff, our reputation, our in-house diagnostic technologies (you know we have a

CT scanner here, right on the premises)—but, as I was saying before I started *bragging,* ha: our o*stens*ible competitors couldn't claim any better. Most of them, I'm sure, have *never* worked with Curios. They're not even qualified."

"Oh no?" I said, not really caring to hear him expand, but pretty sure that he wanted me to care, and afraid that if I didn't seem as if I cared, Blank might not receive the best treatment possible.

"Noooo," said Kleinstadt. "V-school students only studied the Curio for three, four years at the start of the nineties. Lucky for you, my friend, I happened to *be* in V-school the first of those years."

"Well, I do feel lucky."

The doctor waved this off. "You're nervous!" he said. "You don't have to be nervous. You're in good hands. Now open that sleeve up, and let's examine . . ." he said, looking at the clipboard he'd taken from the desk, "little Kablankey."

"Thing about that," I said, removing my luchador mask from my pocket, "is before I let Blank out, I have to put this mask on, which I know sounds weird, but—"

"Sure does!" he said.

And then I explained. Except for Blank's age, which I told him was eight, I stuck to the truth.

"Mr. Magnet," he said, once I'd finished explaining, "I'm a professional, not some little kid. I feel it when I'm about to overload, and I've never had any trouble stopping myself."

"Have you ever seen an eight-year-old?" I said. "In person?"

"I've seen *Inhuman Self Denial* about twenty-five times, and that Basho was something, I'll give you that, but I'm certain I wouldn't have been one of these tree-rushing nutsos had I visited the monastery, and Basho was—what? Eleven years old. I can handle the sight of an eight-year-old, believe me."

"You're probably right," I said. "But still. I just—I can't show you Blank unless it's wearing a mask, and it won't wear the mask unless I wear one, too. If that means you won't examine it, then I guess . . . I mean I'll still pay for the appointment, for your time, but . . ."

"You know what?" said Dr. Kleinstadt. "Whatever makes you comfortable. You're comfortable, I'm comfortable, right?" he said, though I think he was growing wary of me, or maybe just weary; he'd back-stepped a little and his smile had lost wattage.

I put on the mask, opened the sleeve, set Blank down near the doctor's side of the table. Seeing Kleinstadt, it ran in the opposite direction. When it got to the wall, it crouched and covered its face with its hands.

"That, Mr. Magnet," Kleinstadt said, "does not to me look like a cure who's suffering from any loss of pluck whatsoever. Ha!"

Blank, in its crouch, Allen-throat-cleared twice.

"Uncover," I told it. "It's okay. Uncover." It turned around, slowly, saw me, through its fingers, looking at Kleinstadt, lowered its hands, and turned to face Kleinstadt, to whom I said, "I trained it to hide from strangers."

"I can see that," he said. "And my compliments. That must have been hard—goes against just about every instinct a Curio has. But a pluckless Curio? It's slumpy, slow. Usually just sits there, hugging itself. No energy to sprint across a table like that. Not even close. Couldn't and wouldn't. Your Curio's fine."

"Are you sure? I mean, you haven't even examined it."

"What's to examine? I can see it's not scaly, and on the intake form here, you wrote *normal ejections*."

"Right. Normal. But—"

"So no symptoms of psittacosis. It's fine."

"But what about the sneezing?" I said.

"They sneeze all the time. You must know that, come on. Maybe . . . You know, you seem a bit distressed and, sometimes, Mr. Magnet, when we're not feeling well, ourselves, or we suffer some kind of emotional trauma—sometimes we become unduly afraid for the well-being of those who are close to us. Our loved ones, our pets. We see signs of sickness where there is only but health, and we see signs of sadness where there's only contentment. A loss of pluck where pluck is abundant. Maybe you've been having a hard time lately?"

I said, "I know I look crazy wearing this mask, but I've read the manual. I reread the section on illness at least ten times before coming in today. *Dry* sneezing is normal is what it says."

"Exactly."

"Blank's sneezes are wet. The wet stuff is green."

"Green? Are you sure?"

"Yes."

"Dear," said Kleinstadt, looking down at his clipboard. "I see," he said, smile fading. "I see. I'm sorry, Mr. Magnet. I . . . I overlooked that part of the intake form. 'Green nasal discharge.' You wrote it down right here. I don't know how I did that. I don't know how I overlooked . . . Sometimes I'm too—my wife says too *cocksure*. I mean, it *is* the last thing you wrote down, true—and talk about burying the lede, 'green nasal discharge,' but well. It's my fault. I should have read through to the end, and I'm sorry about the completely inappropriate positive attitude I've been projecting here."

"Inappropriate?" I said.

"I thought, given what I *had* read on the intake form—'ejections normal, possible loss of pluck'—I thought, 'We'll see about this loss of pluck.' See, *loss of pluck* is a phrase often subject to misinterpretation among pet owners—all pet owners—and I thought you might have misinterpreted it, given the normal ejections and the unscaly skin. 'We'll see about this loss of pluck,' I thought, 'and, worst-case scenario, it'll show loss of pluck, meaning psittacosis onset, and I'll prescribe tetracycline, and all will be well.' I didn't see the part about green nasal discharge, which, if it was *clear* nasal discharge, would be alarming enough; that would mean *bleeding* from the nose. Possibly caused by a bump to the nose? Hopefully? If not, then . . . But apart from ejections, Mr. Magnet, nothing discharged from a Curio's body, much less its nose, should be any color other than clear, you understand. You see, discharge from the nose—that's always gonna be the same thing: blood. Green discharge, then, is green blood. And that, I am truly sorry to say: that is cancer."

"Bullshit," I said.

"Well, sir, I understand that response, I understand how hard . . . but I'm afraid . . . I'm afraid I'm right. I'm certain I'm right. It's most certainly cancer. I would bet my house on it. Colored blood means cancer."

I wasn't yet shaken, not in the slightest. I just didn't believe him. He was making me angry. I tried not to show it. I tried to sound reasonable. "How can that be?" I said. "How can it be cancer? Wouldn't Blank be in a lot of pain?"

"It *is* in pain. All kinds of pain. It has been for a while. By the time its blood's acquired color, the cure's been sick for weeks. Maybe months."

"It hasn't been singing, though. I haven't heard it painsing in *years*," I said. "It isn't painsinging, now—how can you tell me it's in pain? That's crazy."

"Ah, *painsinging*—right. Yes, that's a misnomer. Cures don't sing when they're in pain. Not once they're a couple months old, that is. They're like birds. Like most animals, really. When they're in pain, when they're ill, they do everything they can to hide it. What people call *painsinging*, it's really *fearsinging*. Cures do it when they're *afraid*. This was established through some rather gruesome experiments we studied in school. Your cure's not afraid, *despite* being in pain, which tells me that you must have, over these eight years during which you've taken care of it—you must have developed quite a strong relationship with it, it must feel very secure, which is something, again, I find very commendable, Mr. Magnet. Most people, they are, at best, negligent with their Curios, and more often quite abusive. I think it's a shame, the way people treat them. As less than machines. Unworthy of repair. People are awful. They learn a phrase like 'flesh-and-bone robots,' and somehow feel free to . . . I don't mean to be political. This isn't the time for that. What I am saying to you is I am not one of these people. I am in the minority, and I know you are too, just by virtue of your coming here today to have me look at Kablankey. I didn't get into this profession because I like the idea of living things suffering—I hate it, tell the truth. And I am sorry, sir, that you have to go through this now, but Blank is suffering. It is not afraid, but it *is* in pain, and it is certainly dying, and the humane thing to do here would be to make your peace with it, to say your goodbyes, and then put it down."

"Put it *down*?" I said.

"Or overload on it. I won't judge you for that. I wouldn't overload by mouth—the cancer, you know—but . . ."

"You haven't *examined* it," I said. "You haven't taken blood. You haven't run any scans . . ."

"Mr. Magnet, I can stick needles in Kablankey all day if you like. I can even give it a CT scan if you like, but . . . Look, I don't mean to be offensive when I say this, but the first thing I noticed when I came into the room was the smell of . . . you. Of your clothing. Which—you smell like smoke. You're a smoker, correct? You smoke indoors, near the cure?"

"I do, but . . ."

"Curios, I don't know if you know about their respiratory system, but they process the air they breathe more . . . deeply. They have hollow bones, just like a bird's, you see, and the air they inhale, it circulates through their bones, Mr. Magnet. All of their bones. That includes their skull. They inhale," he said, inhaling deeply, "and the air fills their bones, and then they don't so much exhale as inhale again, at which point the air in their bones is pushed out. So the carcinogens, you see, they . . . linger longer, and they pass unobstructed through more of the body than they would in the body of, well, just about any other creature. Eight years of regular exposure to secondhand cigarette smoke—even just a couple or three years of exposure . . ."

"The manual doesn't even mention cancer," I said.

"No," he said. "No, it doesn't. And very few Curios live long enough to *get* cancer, so you've probably never heard of such a thing, but cancer—any creature with a heart can develop cancer. Nearly any living thing can. *Plants* can develop cancer, Mr. Magnet. And I *do* understand how you might feel tricked or confused, here. You're very close with Kablankey—"

"I'm not a child," I told him. "I'm not a crazy person. Cut the delicate manager voice. I'm telling you I want my cure examined properly, and *if* it has cancer, I want you to operate on it."

"Okay," he said. "Okay. One step at a time. Let me walk you through your options. Bloodwork I can do, but it'll take days til we get results back. Maybe in that time you'll have—"

"What about scans?"

"If you really want me to run a CT scan, I can do that as well, of course, and the results *are* immediate—I just have to interpret the pictures we get—but it's very expensive, it's nine hundred dollars, and we'd have to inject Kablankey with a dye, which, even sedated . . . it's *not* pleasant. For the cure. Drawing blood's just a prick, and we catch the drops on a slide, and that's very bad, they hate that, all animals hate it, but cures . . . And the dye injection is *worse.* Lasts. So you have the option to put your cure through all that pain and fear and suffering only to find out that what I've already told you is true, that it has cancer, you do—you have that option. But then what happens? Nothing. Nothing is what happens. Even if the cancer is far less advanced, and far more localized than everything my education would lead me to believe, which, I admit, is a very, very slim possibility—it might, for example, just have cancer inside its *head*—there is no treatment or operation that is *at all* likely to save Kablankey. Furthermore, I have never performed surgery on a cure, and have never heard of a veterinarian who has. As I said earlier, I don't know of a single vet in this county or any of those adjacent who's ever even *treated* a Curio."

I asked him how soon he could do the scan, and whether Blank could wear the mask inside the machine.

"Now" and "If you still feel that's a necessity" were his answers. "But," he said, "it's clear to me that my bedside manner has rubbed you wrong, so before I go ahead and set anything up, I'm going to leave this room, and give you some time to cool down and reconsider. I really hope you will. Take all the time you need."

"Fuck you," I thought, and just then I heard a tiny, off-key trumpeting. I looked down at Blank. It eyebrow-flexed and held out its mask. It had blown its nose into its mask. It had taken its mask off and blown its nose. There was green on the white part—blood on the white part—green blood, wet on the white of the mask, which was off Blank's head, was in Blank's hand, was being held high like the head of an enemy, the head of a monster Blank had slain for our pleasure, our glory, our entertainment. Eyebrow-flex eyebrow-flex.

"That discharge is green, alright," Kleinstadt said. "And it is very opaque. That is cancer, Mr. Magnet. I hate to have to insist on such a sad fact, but I feel as though I must."

I touched my own face, the skin of my face. My mask was in my other hand.

"How long has Blank—"

"A few minutes," said Kleinstadt. "Ever since you took *your* luchador mask off. Right around the time you told me that you weren't crazy. That you weren't a child. It's truly an adorable cure, Mr. Magnet. And you're right—I've never seen one like it."

He left the exam room.

All my anger went with him, which took me by surprise. No sooner had the door closed than I heard my grinding throat emit a sub-moronic choking sound, felt my eyes welling. I wiped at them, swallowed. Blank was in pain but as yet unafraid. Kleinstadt had said so, and it seemed I believed him. I had no good reason not to believe him. And though a part of me (obviously) wanted to cry—for Blank, in front of Blank, and perhaps toward the cause of "making my peace" or "saying my goodbyes"—I hadn't cried in Blank's presence in a great many years, and I feared that if I cried I would make Blank afraid, that it would suffer dread along with its meaningless pain, perhaps even connect the two, the dread and the pain, and thus grant the pain meaning, and so make the pain worse, which I understand, reader, might sound a little off to you, for people like to think they prefer their pain meaningful, readers in particular, especially those readers not currently in pain, but people are people, and people are mistaken, readers are mistaken, misguided by empathy, spun around, confused. They believe they'd like to be more like the characters they love, yet they love only those characters they're already like; they love those characters only *for* being like them. And despite what they may think when they aren't in pain, people always prefer their own pain to be meaningless; they prefer only others' pain to be meaningful. They think they want machines that behave as though alive, but what they want are living beings that behave like machines.

I swallowed and inhaled, swallowed and exhaled. My muscles slackened. My tear ducts shut.

Blank wasn't fooled, or was only partly fooled. In any case it didn't painsing—didn't *fear*sing. It had come across the counter to me, thrown aside the mask. It started humming the cancan, then stood on its hands, and upside-down cancanned for three or four measures before it lost balance and fell on its belly. When it got back up, it wiped at its brow, Allen-throat-cleared twice, eyebrow-flexed, and started to hum the cancan again. I wanted it to stop. I didn't want it to dance more. It was too tired to dance more, too sick to dance more. I put out my hand and it boarded my palm and climbed up my arm, climbed past its sleeve, continuing to hum til it got to my shoulder. Once there, it awkwardly lay on its side, its neck sharply angled, head bent toward its body, and pushed its ear to my carotid, the pounding pulse within which slowed, and soon I saw I didn't have to make any decisions except the decision not to make the cure suffer getting stuck full of needles, which decision, apparently, I'd already made—I'd made it in passing, it had made itself—and I lifted Kablankey off my shoulder and put it in its sleeve, but it didn't want to be there, wouldn't let me close the sleeve, blocked the zipper's slider with a hand, and started climbing out, climbed up my arm again, onto my shoulder. "Anks," it said softly.

"I don't know what you mean," I said.

The cure said, "Anks."

I turned toward the poster, looked at our reflection in the glass of the frame. Blank was looking, too, once again stretched awkwardly across my left shoulder, upon its right side, pushing its ear against the side of my neck, wedging itself into the crook of my neck, increasing the pressure, its head tilting sharply toward its own left shoulder. "Anks," it said. "Anks."

"I don't know what I'm supposed to do, Blank," I said.

"Anks," it kept saying, and, while continuing to push with the rest of its body, it reached its left arm across half of my throat, closed its fingers around my Adam's apple, and pulled.

I let my head fall to the left a little bit, then a little bit more, and though the pulling continued, Blank stopped saying, "Anks."

We watched our reflection for a minute, maybe less, and the way I looked—my head tilted like that—I looked like someone about to ask a question he couldn't quite phrase, or maybe like someone considering a question he hadn't quite heard.

I looked like a fool.

Blank said its word again.

The word came out strangled, or gentle, a whisper.

I shrugged as hard as I could, and it was over.

SETTLEMENT

A COUPLE OR THREE days into the new year, my father was permanently injured at work. He called me from the hospital, assured me he was fine. He asked that I bring him a change of clothes, as he'd be spending the night, and, for the first time in weeks—Grandmother Magnet had died just before Thanksgiving (DUI, maple); he'd been quiet ever since, and occasionally morose—he sounded like himself. Better than himself, really. He sounded happy. I asked him what happened; how he'd gotten injured. "Longest story ever," he said. "I'll tell you all about it after you get here."

I found him in a gown in a bed in a semiprivate room without a roommate. A square of gauze taped over his forehead, a bandage on his cheek, but no tubes, no apparati, nothing beeping or blinking.

"No one came with you from the plant?" I said.

"They did. Those guys. Good guys. They just left."

I handed him a chiclet from a blister pack of Nicorette I'd picked up at Pang's on my way to the hospital. He popped it, chewed, took a stagy breath. "You're a gem," he said. "I haven't had a smoke since this morning. What a day, Billy. Man. You know, I thought I had a heart attack."

"But you didn't," I said.

"No," he said, laughing.

"How high are you right now?"

"Not very," he said. "Maybe not at all. They got me on something, don't remember what it's called. Fucken miracle, really. I'm clear as a bell, but the pain—it's far away."

"So you're in pain."

"Only if I really pay attention," he said. "Or try to sit up."

"Are you going to tell me what happened?"

"Soon as this gum starts kicking in a little. Maybe give me a second piece, huh?"

"You need to park it," I said.

"Is that like, 'Shut up, Dad'?"

"No. That's what the instructions on the box call it. Parking." I showed him the box. "You chew a couple times, til you start tasting pepper, then you wedge the gum between a cheek and your gums and leave it there awhile. You *park* it. That's how the nicotine gets absorbed. If you keep on chewing like that, I guess you're just gonna swallow it, digest it, not feel it for a while."

"So I'll park it then," he said. He stopped chewing, parked it, said, "Hey, that's nice. *Park* it. High-tech. Okay. So, okay. I was about to get the handoff from Chuckie—"

"What?"

"I'm telling you what happened. *I was about to get the handoff from Chuckie*'s how it starts."

"Who's Chuckie?" I said.

"The handoff machine."

"So that's a nickname," I said.

"A nickname. Sure."

"For a guy or a machine?"

"What are you asking me?"

"Is Chuckie the nickname of a machine that hands off, or is there a guy called Chuckie who's so good at handing off—or, I don't know, maybe so *bad* at handing off—that you gave him the nickname *the handoff machine*."

"You making jokes or something, Billy? Making fun of your injured old man and his job and the people he works with?"

"I'm trying to understand."

"Alright, well . . . Chuckie's like this giant, articulated fork at the end of a conveyor. Chuckie hands off to me, so I can do an impel."

"Hands what off?" I said.

"Exactly," he said. "Depends on what I'm tasked to impel that day, which depends on what the plant is making that day, and what part of what it's making my crew's been assigned to. So sometimes Chuckie hands off a crank truck, sometimes Chuckie hands off a pipe stack, sometimes Chuckie hands off a spindle, and then occasionally Chuckie hands off a switch block, which is what we—you'll like this—we call it a *bitch block* because it's so heavy and uncomfortable to grip, like you can only grip it one way without dropping it, so when you pivot before you start your impel, you gotta be extra careful, and then, when you actually do the impel, I mean . . . obviously, right?"

"Obviously?"

"Christ. It's a bitch to impel. That's all you have to know. The bitch switch is a bitch to impel, and today, Chuckie, which is supposed to be handing off a pipe stack to me, not only does it hand off a bitch switch instead, but it hands off a bitch switch at an angle that is just *not right*. It is *so* not right that I would not have even tried to accept the handoff, except the way the crew's arranged—in anticipation of a pipe stack—the way the crew's arranged, if I don't take the bitch switch when Chuckie hands it off, it's gonna crush Leif's foot, and maybe kill Mikey."

"Kill him," I said.

"Yeah. There's a spike on the bitch switch. About eighteen inches long, two inches around. That spike is not pointed the direction it should be. Like I said, it's not a good handoff, say the least. And so things go slow-motion, right? For me. Adrenaline, adrenaline. I'm living frame-to-frame, thinking frame-to-frame. Wah-wah-wah. Lee Majors, right?"

"Who?"

"*Six Million Dollar Man*. That's who I am. That's who I become. A gorilla genius. I accept the handoff, it starts to slip, I understand how it'll slip, I pivot some to get Leif and Mikey safe, but now, since I'm fighting gravity in about nine different contradictory ways just to even *hold on* to the slippery fucking bitch switch and *also* pivoting, I fall down, okay? Well, first I *start* falling down. I start falling down while still *holding* the bitch switch, which, it's gonna come down, Billy, see—I see it's gonna come down right on my face, and I won't just be dead, but very, very ugly, it will cave in my face and I will die, and I do not want to die, and so what I do is . . . What I do is, while I'm falling: I throw it. I throw the bitch switch. I'm basically doing the splits, right? I'm doing the splits while turning to the left, and with every last bit of gorilla I got—the bitch switch weighs a hundred and twenty-three pounds—I hurl the fucking thing *up*, straight up, and right before it comes down, right when it's at the height of its arc—which is not a high arc, but is definitely higher than you'd think—I kinda, while still doing the splits, mind you, I kinda throw *myself* somehow at Leif and Mikey. And I land at their feet, right? Bump my head on Leif's insole. And the bitch switch, it lands, *spike-down*, six, maybe seven inches from my face. Sends pieces of concrete from the plant floor flying. I caught a shard in the cheek, a shard in my forehead, which instantly, right, starts gushing like a firehose—the forehead cut, I'm saying—and I'm lying, there, Billy, blood pouring into my eyes, *shooting* into my eyes, and, for a second . . ."

He chewed, parked, took a deep breath.

"For a second, I was a *god*. I swear. For a second, the bitch switch, which hasn't settled yet, which is standing on its spike for just another split second, trying to like decide which direction to tip, I'm looking at it, lying in its shadow with blood in my eyes, realizing it can fall on my head, fall on my head or my neck, or my head *and* my neck, and, you know, *still*, after all I just did—which what I did was superhuman, I *threw* that fucking thing, right up in the air, son, you can ask Leif and Mikey, what I did should not have been possible—and I'm lying there in its crooked shadow now, and it's about to tip, it's about to fall, and even after all that I did to keep us safe, me and Leif and Mikey, I'm seeing how it could *still* kill me—but, I don't have time to move, Billy, is the point, this is all like microseconds, the time this is taking to happen, and I don't have time to move, and I know it, and I'm telling you, I had a *moment,* Billy, I had *no* time to move, and what I thought was, 'No!' Just like that. I thought, 'No!' and, the bitch switch, I swear, that 'No!' that I thought—it tipped the bitch switch away. Pushed it. Sent it falling away from me.

"And look, I know that didn't happen, but I also know it did, that part about the 'No!' And I was lying there, safe, thinking, 'Clyde you're a god, you're a god, you're a *god,'* and that's when I felt all the pain in my body. My whole upper body. Chest, arms, neck, *hands*. Every muscle clamping tight, like I was turning to stone, and I thought, 'This is it. It's over. This is your major coronary event. You did it. You killed yourself. You stopped you and your friends from being crushed to death by doing something that made your heart explode. You're dead. It's over. You asshole. You did all you could and it wasn't enough. You couldn't take it. Now you will die. And maybe—maybe you already have.'

"I mean it, Billy. It was . . . something. I thought maybe I was dead, was sure that if I wasn't, then I was about to be. And then I guess I passed out.

"They said I passed out, but I was *thinking,* you know? I was thinking the whole time. I was thinking, 'This is shit. This is *shit*. How can this be such shit? What kind of shit is this? Where is Annie?* How can't I see her? Why can't I see her? All I got here is blackness and silence and me? All I got here is me? I don't get to see her? I can't tell her about Billy? That he wrote a book? She doesn't get to know that our son wrote a book? I don't even get to see her, but I gotta still exist?'

"This was the worst. Worst thing I could imagine. Unbelievable. I didn't want to believe it. And I thought about that 'No!' you know? That *push*. And I thought, 'If I can do *that,* if *that* is possible to do while alive, and now I am dead, still Clyde, not just worm food—why can't I find my wife now I'm dead?' And I thought, 'Maybe I'm in hell. Those stupid fucking Christians, maybe they were right. Maybe this is hell, this nothing-but-me. I hope that it's hell. If it's hell,' I was thinking, 'and not just the place everyone goes when they die, then that would not be so bad as I originally thought. Because Annie wouldn't be here. She wouldn't be in hell. She didn't believe in God, that's true, but she was good, any God would understand that, so she of all people

* Annie was my mother's name.

would not be in hell, and that's a shit deal for me, yeah? It's a shit deal for me but it's better at least than a shit deal for the both of us, hell for the both of us, and she isn't here, and if I'm here that means she's somewhere else, probably knows everything about Billy and me already, she probably read Billy's book before he even wrote it. And maybe,' I thought, 'maybe one day I'll get out of hell, and then I'll get to see her.'

"And I was trying to figure out if it was better, you know, to think about that—to think about how one day I'd maybe get out of hell—or if it was worse. If that only made it worse. Like maybe that was part of being in hell, was thinking you'll get out one day but you never will. I mean, you know me, I don't know fuck-all about Christianity. I wasn't raised that way. But I knew that phrase, *eternal damnation*. Who doesn't? You hear it all the time, right? And what I was thinking was, 'If there's eternal damnation—if they specify *eternal* damnation when they talk about hell—then that means there's gotta be just *temporary* damnation, too.' Makes sense, right? Because why be redundant?

"But then I thought of some reasons why, okay? I spent a lot of time, I guess, thinking about some reasons why, and they're boring to think about, and hard to explain, I'll skip them, but the best one was simple and easy to explain: People are fucking stupid. There's no reason *not* to think they'd be redundant. So what I ended up thinking was, 'It's either one way or the other. Eternal or temporary. It's one way or the other, but you are definitely in hell.' And then the next thing I thought was, 'If there's hell, then maybe there's ghosts, too. Maybe you could be one. See if you can be one. See if you can maybe try and haunt Billy. Talk to him a little. Just see if you can do it. And let him know about hell.'

"And I don't mean I wanted to scare you or anything. It was nothing malicious. I was just feeling really alone, and desperate, and I thought that I could probably make you understand where I was coming from. I didn't think you'd be scared of me, and I thought that if you *did* get scared of me, I'd be able to calm you down.

"So I tried to haunt you, so I could feel a little better, and let you know about hell. I don't know how to explain it. How I knew how to do it. But I knew how to do it. I was sure that I knew. How to haunt you. I was sure. And this is what I did: I thought of you, really pictured you, really clearly. I pictured you looking out your bedroom window, smoking a cigarette. I could see it crystal clear. The way your shoulders were hanging, how you were holding your Quill, the frost on the glass at the bottom of the window in this kind of mountain shape or like a cresting wave, even the smell of the fabric of the curtain, the way the smoke was curling on the way to the ceiling, the sound of your breathing—everything there, I could see it, hear it, smell it, you know?

And I guess the idea was that all I had to do was wait for you to stand at the same spot at your bedroom window as I was picturing, in the same position that I was picturing, your cigarette burned down to the same point I was picturing, and so on—everything just had to match up—and then, once you did that, once you and the smoke and the frost and the smell all lined up exactly with what I was picturing, I'd be able to haunt you. And I waited and I focused, and I waited and I focused and focused and focused, I waited for you to line up with the picture, so I could haunt you, and, pretty soon, I stopped being scared. I mean, the picture was so vivid, it calmed me down. And it was a *nice* picture. My son, thinking, enjoying a smoke. I liked the picture, and it was like I was really almost living in it—that's how vivid. Hell wasn't so bad, I thought. My mind was clear, I had all this focus. I could do this for a long time, I thought, before it got old. It might never get old. I could live in this picture, exploring the details, waiting to haunt you.

"But almost just as soon as I started thinking that, Billy, everything started going to shit again. Because to haunt you, I realized, you had to line up *just right* with the picture, and the more of the picture that I paid attention to, the more things there were that had to line up. I don't know how I figured this out, but I did. It was true. I knew it was true. So like if you lined up perfectly with every last thing I was picturing except for one—just a button undone, a hair out of place—there would be no haunting. I wouldn't be able to do it. And already, you know, I'd noticed the shapes of the ice on the window, like I said, and the way the smoke moved—these things already, I saw how they might have ruined my chances. So there I am, trying, on the one hand, to not be so alone and miserable in hell, and the only thing that's making me less alone and less miserable in hell is how vivid this picture of you at the window is—never in my life could I picture something so vivid for so long a time, you know? this is the one and only benefit of being dead in hell; being able to dive into this picture—but then, on the other hand, the more I look at this nice, vivid picture, the more things I notice, and the more things I notice, the more things have to line up just right if I want to haunt you, so I'm killing my chances of ever getting to haunt you, and that's what I'm really after to begin with. That's what's making the vivid picture so important—it's what's making me want to picture it so bad to begin with; it's *why* the picture's vivid, understand? Because if I get it right, if you get it right, if you line up with the picture, I can haunt you, and so I'm good at picturing it. I have to be. But, same time . . . How do I explain this?

"It becomes like the whole 'Don't think about an elephant' thing, except there's stakes, really high stakes; it's the difference between being able to haunt you, and never being able to contact you again. And I'm fucking up is the thing. I'm losing. I keep noticing details. Even now, you gave me a pen, I could draw how the ice on the window looked. Every peak and valley. I could draw the folds in the curtain, the way the light hit the surface of this glass of water that was getting dusty on your night table, next to this book of matches that's only got two matches left, and one of them is bent, and the other one's half-bald, probably wouldn't light. And so on.

"So that's how I spent the end of my time in what I thought was hell. Trying not to think about an elephant. Trying to look at the parts of this picture of you that I'd *already* probably seen too much of, and without noticing any of the details I hadn't seen yet that I *wanted* to see because I knew they'd be vivid, which would make me feel better if seeing them didn't make it even harder to haunt you.

"And then I opened my eyes, and I wasn't in hell. Obviously, right? I wasn't in hell and I'd never been dead. I was here, in the hospital. They said I'd passed out at the plant, right there on the floor. And I guess what happened was the plant's doc came rushing down with his kit, and he gave me some smelling salts, and I woke up *screaming* in pain, they tell me, and the doc stuck me with some morphine, which I'm *allergic* to morphine, and I fell into, I guess, a 'mild coma,' which, to me, sounds something like 'temporary damnation.' I think that they specified *mild* coma to get me to think twice about causing *major* legal trouble.

"Not important at this juncture in the story yet.

"As I was saying, I tried to haunt you, woke up in the hospital, and it turns out I didn't have a heart attack at all. I got what they call *sudden-onset impeller's twist.* Fucked discs in my back throwing the bitch switch. It's usually a repetitive-motion thing, impeller's twist—I never heard of this sudden-onset kind—and I always stayed in shape to keep myself from getting it, but . . . Anyway, I'm done. End of career. No more impelling."

"And you're smiling because . . ." I said. "Because you . . . found God?"

"Found *God*? I was in a fucking coma, Billy. I was having an allergic reaction to morphine. I'm smiling because I'm not dead, I didn't have a heart attack, I did some superhuman shit that saved a friend from dying, another friend from losing his foot, the doc says the surgery I'm getting in the morning'll relieve my pain at least ninety percent and he hopes for a hundred, and I'll have a normal life as long as I don't impel anymore, which why the fuck would I ever impel again, anyway? Because I *did,* in fact, write down on my health sheet that I'm allergic to opiates, and my whole *crew* saw Chuckie malfunction epically, which means even if I wasn't insured out the ass with workman's comp *and* disability, I, Clyde Franklin Magnet, father of you, age sixty, would be retiring nearly five years earlier than planned on the fatassed settlement money the plant's gonna offer me as soon as I come out of surgery alive tomorrow, *and then,* when I do reach sixty-five, I will still collect my old-school, well-deserved, fatassed *pension* for the rest of my life. And you're *not* smiling about that because—why? Your inheritance—you're gonna have one, now. More than just a little house in Wheelatine, Billy. Smile."

"I'm smiling," I said.

"Not even kinda. Show me the choppers."

"I'm smiling inside," I said.

"Everything's gonna be fine, now," he said.

•

• •

After two post-op days in a back brace at the hospital, Clyde underwent a month of five-times-weekly spinal rehab during which his doctors forbade him to drive, encouraged him to sit as infrequently as possible, and instructed him to neither stand nor sit in the same position for longer than twenty minutes at a time. Otherwise, things worked out as he'd predicted. His settlement covered all his medical bills, paid him the equivalent of nine years' salary in one lump sum (tax free), and the plant agreed to contribute to his pension fund the amount that both they *and* he would have, had he continued to work through age sixty-five. They kept him on their health insurance plan, too.

The rehab doctors praised his compliance, and by the end of the month he'd been weened off all painkillers, and was as fully recovered as anyone they'd ever worked with, they said. As long as he practiced what they called "common back sense"—e.g. didn't water-ski, downhill-ski, join a rowing crew, or take a job as a bouncer or long-haul trucker or roughneck—he'd live a life unmarred by the symptoms of impeller's twist.

The afternoon he returned from his final visit to the rehab clinic—he'd driven there himself—Clyde reminded me that he'd be flying to Austria the following week, to visit St. Wolfgang, the village from which his paternal grandfather's family had emigrated. He asked me, for what must have been the fifteenth time, if I was sure that I didn't want to accompany him. We were in the backyard. The previous evening, the record-breakingly treacherous winter had turned upside down, and it was seventy degrees out. I was wearing a T-shirt and sitting on a lawn chair, next to the graves in which I'd buried Triple-J's cure and Blank. I had a hip flask of Scotch—MacGuffin Gold, I think; maybe Glenfibbly Special Cask—and, in lieu of answering my father's question, I offered him a sip.

"Too early for me," he said, "but thanks. Now, what do you say? Business-class ticket. I'm buying. Last chance."

"I can't," I told Clyde. "I have to stay here and work. I've told you at least—"

"Work, my ass. I haven't seen you work so little in years."

"Well I have to get back to the bricks," I said. "And I don't want to go to Austria. Who goes to Austria?"

"*Get back to the bricks*—that's not what that means. That doesn't mean anything. What you wanted to say was *get back on the horse*."

"You sure about that?"

"What you *really* wanted to say, though," he said, "was *hit the bricks,* which means hit the road, which is what I'm proposing. And you know what? I don't really want to go to Austria, either, Billy, but it's where we're from, the original Magnets, so it's important we see it."

"That's not why you think it's important," I said, and it wasn't. Clyde's father had died when Clyde was nineteen, and he had, on his deathbed, told Clyde that he had always wanted to see the village where his own father (i.e. my great-grandfather Magnet) had come from, but hadn't ever had the time or the money, and he'd asked Clyde to "see it for [him] one day," and Clyde had said he would. He'd recalled that conversation for me back in November, right after we'd gotten the call from police letting us know that his mother had died—at that time, it seemed a strange thing to recall, but I guess it really isn't, the death of one parent bringing to mind the death of the other, more likable parent, etc.—and, once the big settlement check had come in, mid-January, the first thing he did was fill out an application for a rush-job passport and book his trip to St. Wolfgang.

"What in the hell is that supposed to mean?" he said. "*That's not why I think it's important.*"

"You agreed to do something for your father," I said, "so that's why you're doing it. Good. Good for you. But don't drag me into it. I didn't agree to do that thing, and *you* didn't agree that I would do that thing. I never met your dad, let alone his dad. I never even heard the words *St. Wolfgang* til a couple of months ago. I don't care about where our ancestors came from. I don't understand why other people care about where *their* ancestors came from. I wasn't raised to care about that kind of stuff—*origins*—and it was you who raised me. I think you probably care even less than I do, truth be told, so enough with the false sentimentality already."

"I'm not being false. I just want to take you on a trip to Austria," he said.

"And I don't want to go with you."

"What's happened to you, Belt? You sound so cold. Angry."

"Oh, right, sure. Belt. You called me Belt. You called me by my name. I'm melting. Little boy blue and the man in the moon. Come *on*. Enough big ropes. We're not having a moment here, and I'm not going to Austria. *You're* going to Austria, maybe you'll like it, maybe you won't, you'll probably get bored one day and write me a postcard, and then you'll come home and tell me all about the weird food you ate."

"I never wrote a postcard."

"Me neither," I said.

"I never received one."

"Me neither," I said.

"Is that sad?" he said.

"It's fine," I said.

"I don't think they're known for having weird food. It's coffee they're known for. And mountains. And Mozart."

"And opera," I said. "And delicate pastries."

"That so?"

"Oh yeah," I said. "All of that stuff. Everything you've always lived for, plus Hitler."

He clapped me on the shoulder. "I've noticed you get a little prickly when you drink," he said. Then he went to his room and took a long nap.

I stayed outside, drinking, thinking. Not about drinking. Not about Austria. About this book. I hadn't written a salvageable word of it since before Clyde's injury, and I'd thought that drinking and thinking beside Blank's grave—I hadn't been to the grave since the winter's first freeze, before Thanksgiving—might somehow help me hit back on the brickhorse. That's why I'd been sitting out there to begin with. I was getting desperate. Not as desperate as I would, but desperate enough. This was the second, and the worse, of two dry spells.

The original dry spell had not been so bad. The first couple weeks succeeding Blank's death, I hadn't even bothered trying to write; then the next couple weeks, I'd tried and failed, but figured all it was was that, while mourning, I'd "lost touch" with the book. Turned out I was right. After a few days spent reading through what I'd already written, I started working at nearly as furious a pace as I had back in September and October: I wrote 150 pages in under four weeks, right up through the scene described in "Compound" where the trio of boys makes fun of my bike.

But then the next morning, I had trouble again. The second dry spell began. The words wouldn't come, or they'd come out off-key. And then the same thing the following three or four mornings.

I had my outline, so it wasn't that I didn't know what to write about—next would come the description of the present-day compound, of the Archon sons and Hangstrong and Ulysses, of meeting Fon in the turret, and so forth—but more that I didn't understand *how* to write about it. I didn't understand why I'd ever thought the events I'd chosen to cover in the memoir could or should fit together to form a coherent, or even cohesive narrative. I was no longer able to hear the matrix*. And whereas during the previous dry spell, all I'd had

* Owing to its pop-cultural provenance, I'm not certain that the phrase "hear the matrix" won't soon become too anachronistic for future readers to make heads or tails of, yet given how accurately it describes what I mean, I'm (obviously) not quite *un*certain enough about that *not* to deploy the phrase "hear the matrix" here, and so, in the spirit of splitting the difference, dear future reader, I've added this footnote.

The Matrix—a 1999 masterpiece of high-budget, paranoid, special-effects-driven sci-fi-action cinema by the Wachowski Sisters—relays the story of Neo, a talented cuddlefarmer/amateur formula designer (played by Benedict Cumberbatch), who has a very special gift: he can hear and—as the film progresses, and he comes under the tutelage of Morpheus (played by Edward James Olmos)—disrupt "the matrix" of communications between Curios, which, as the film would have it, are not the adorable little robots the rest of the world (and, of course, the film's audience) believes them to be, but rather the drone-like constituents of a large-scale, hive-minded artificial life system ("Just a bunch of glorified, goddamned ants!" Morpheus calls them, just before a small platoon of beautiful, acrobatically preternatural Curios forces him, via its irresistible adorability, to overload by mouth on ten of its constituents, one after the other, in rapid succession, until he chokes to death). This hive-minded artificial system's aim, Neo discovers eventually (via hearing the matrix), is to continue to seduce (and thereby enslave) unknowing human beings into helping it reproduce and feed itself, until such a time when human scientists will create a formula for cures that allows the system to evolve into a wholly self-reliant (i.e. nonparasitic) being that, beloved as the cures are by all nonfeline animals, will take over the world after slaughtering all the cats.

I suppose that, to those who haven't seen it, it sounds like a pretty silly movie, and perhaps it is, but, even at this writing, more than fifteen years past its theatrical release, it's gorgeous to look at—all the CGI'd acts of adorability especially; particularly during the climax of the film, when Neo telepathically "enters" the matrix of cure communication, hearing that which is inaudible to the rest of us, then disrupting it via instructing the army of cures that is converging upon him to perform acts so overwhelmingly adorable that the cures themselves go into overload at the sight of one another, thus paralyzing their own advances—and, when it came out in theaters, it seemed inspired and unpretentiously postmodern.

A genre- and sequel-spawner exceeded in its cinematic influence only by the *Star Wars* trilogy, *The Matrix* was the fourth-highest-grossing film of the twentieth century, and it is thought to be, in large part, responsible for much of the seemingly inexhaustible market energy behind the Third Cute Revolution (for a couple of years in the early aughts, some even marked its theatrical release as the start of something they claimed to be "The *Late* Third Cute Revolution"). Furthermore, it launched the unparalleled film career of Benedict Cumberbatch, partly un-geeked the pursuit of formula design by garage-based enthusiasts, and, presumably, granted tens of thousands of young cuddlefarmers worldwide a greater capacity to fantasize that they innately possessed nascent superpowers that might one day enable them to save the world.

As a side note (and maybe also, I admit, as an overly self-conscious attempt to justify to do was read through what I'd already written to regain my traction, when I tried the same trick to break this second dry spell, it only made matters worse. I don't know how to explain it without sounding even more precious and navel-gazy than I assume I already do, but: I'd somehow fallen out of sympathy with my memoir-self. With the exception of a couple moments in "The Hope of Rusting Swingsets," I no longer related to the Belt I'd written five hundred–some pages about; I no longer related to the Belt I'd written five hundred–some pages *as*. I no longer cared to write a book about him, I certainly didn't care to read one about him, and, above all, I doubted I'd care to read such a book if I were . . . you. Whoever you might be.

Then, five or six days into this second dry spell, Clyde was injured, and I was, uncomfortably, somewhat grateful to have a reason to take a couple days off and hang out with him at the hospital, playing Hearts and chewing Nicorette. Then he came home, and I spent a few more days running errands for him, lighting his smokes, and driving him to rehab, after which he, far more indirectly than I would have imagined (he said something mealymouthed about how it troubled him to think that the nurse's aide the plant was paying for was sitting idle in our kitchen all day long), let me know that he needed more space.

Space for him meant time for me, and, as I've mentioned, it was nasty outside. Walks weren't an option. Driving on ice required its own kind of all-consuming concentration. Reading old favorites didn't lead to new insights. Eating didn't take long, even overeating didn't, and sleeping—I could do only so much of it.

I tried other things.

I bought bottles of Scotch in the hundred-dollar range, the fifty-dollar range, drank them, enjoyed them, couldn't write, was sad.

I bought and read a few recently well-reviewed memoirs to bolster my spirits around the general pursuit of memoir-writing. They all told the same story: the author overcame adversity with virtue. As a reader, you'd either 1) spent your life being complicit in the systemic injustice that had caused the adversity, but now that you'd read the book, you'd been awakened to the role you played and were thus made virtuous (perhaps even brave), or 2) you'd spent your life being a victim of the same systemic injustice as the author

---

the inclusion of this lengthy footnote), I think it's worth my pointing out that Triple-J did not, in *A Fistful of Fists,* include even a partial scene from *The Matrix,* nor from any of its sequels. Perhaps that disinclusion owes to his having something personally against the film, sure, but then again it might just as easily owe to his never having seen the film (I never thought to ask him if he'd seen it), which could, in turn, indicate that most people Trip's age haven't seen the film, and that the phrase "hear the matrix" *already,* i.e. at this writing, sounds to them anachronistic, if not entirely meaningless.

while being equally virtuous, but it wasn't until you read the memoir that you were able to realize just how virtuous you'd always been, just how much adversity you'd already overcome. Congratulations, either way!

I failed to see the appeal, remained unbolstered, missed fiction, was sad.

So then I tried reading a few recently well-reviewed novels, hoping to bolster my spirits around the more general pursuit of *prose*-writing. These novels were either 1) "autofictions" in which the narrators came to realizations about their complicity in the systemic injustice that caused the adversity of people like the authors of the memoirs described above, and mocked or "satirized" their pre-realization selves (bravely), 2) postapocalyptic dystopic fictions of the sort Stevie's husband wrote, or 3) "global" novels, most of which hadn't been written in English, and the best of which were satisfying for how they consistently undermined every philosophical and political point the cheerleading reviewers who'd recommended them claimed they demonstrated, but none of which (except for one, *kind of*) involved me the way the novels I'd always loved had.

So no help from Letters whatsoever.

Was this writer's block? Was there really such a thing? I didn't think so. Or rather, I didn't think writers who said they suffered from writer's block were saying anything other than "I have been unable to engage with literature for a reason or reasons that I cannot pin down." What people referred to as writer's block, I thought (and I'd always thought this, though I hadn't ever suffered a dry spell prior to Blank's death), was a symptom of something else. If somebody who happened to be a two-hundred-meter breaststroke gold medalist were to suddenly become paralyzed below the neck, you *could* say they were suffering *swimmer's block*, but . . .

Did I want another cure? Is that what it was? No. I didn't want another cure. And I didn't believe—and I still don't believe—that it was possible to want a thing without knowing you wanted it. You could need a thing without knowing it, though. Perhaps, I thought, I *needed* a cure, despite not wanting one. Perhaps, I thought, I didn't know what was best for me.

So I hatched the cure from the marble that Blank had made the shell of. There was nothing Blank about it, at least according to its looks. According to its looks, it was only a clone of the cure Triple-J had tortured on the slide. I found the cure cute, liked it fine, taught it "Hi," and we played some Make This Face, but I didn't have much feeling for the thing—I guess I didn't really try to. I didn't even name it. When it was three days old, I decided to get rid of it before it could finish imprinting on me. I brought it to Arcades and found Lotta's mom, who tried to cold-shoulder me, and I told her—to her back—about the shell of the marble, and thereby convinced her to take the cure and raise it.

"You weren't very nice to my daughter," she said, tucking Bopsy—she'd named it on the spot—into one of her sleeves.

"I just gave you something you value," I said. "And Valentine seems like a really good guy. I don't need your fucken guiltmouth, Catrina."

"He is a good guy," she said, and walked away.

Then I paid for an hour with a woman named Naomi, and the hour made me happy, so I paid for seven more. In the morning, I went home, still couldn't write.

Maybe, I thought, the dry spell *was* a Blank-related problem, after all. Having broken the first dry spell after Blank's death, I'd previously rejected that possibility, but perhaps I hadn't considered it properly, this newly Blankless life of mine. Maybe, I thought, the problem wasn't that I was missing Blank, but rather that I wasn't missing Blank *enough*. Because I didn't, truth be told, all too actively miss it; not since those two weeks during which I'd mourned it. Once I'd started in on the pages I'd written between the first and second dry spells, Blank had begun to seem less like an appendage that had just been cut from me, and more like a long-lost friend; like someone I'd cared for a great deal at one point, but wouldn't have *expected* to be in contact with, and so someone whose absence from my life didn't create much impossible longing. And maybe that was shitty of me? Maybe I wasn't honoring Blank's memory? What did that mean, though? *To honor Blank's memory?* Maybe, I thought, I needed to try a little harder to suffer more thoroughly.

No sooner had I thought so than the weather shifted, and I went to the grave, and nothing changed, and Clyde went to Austria a few days later.

•

•   •

I drank new liquors (blended Scotches, cognacs), read new books, spent nights with different prostitutes. The spell stayed dry.

A few days before Clyde was scheduled to return, I got a postcard from him that he'd sent three days after he'd landed in Vienna. A church overlooking a resort-lined lake, mountainscape background.

> Son, this place is charming for an hour, but then that wears off and it's just a bunch of neuters in homemade sweaters making ugly faces to shape the ugly sounds coming out of those faces. I saw some graves marked Magnet at a charming cemetery, laid down a couple of charming tulips (I think they were tulips), and now I can leave. To Salzburg in the morning. Then a train to somewhere else, maybe a plane. I'm

> thinking probably Paris. Why the hell not, right? I'm on this continent, I've got time to kill, and, shit, I've got the dough. Love, Clyde the Dad.

The next afternoon, inside a single envelope postmarked Paris, came two more postcards written four days after the one I'd received the previous day, as well as a business card from a hotel called Le Général. "This is more like it," Clyde had written on the back of postcard 1 (a photo of a bridge with golden accents).

> Half a day on a train and it's a whole nother world. Been here three nights. The people are as bitchy as they act on TV shows, but I'm not real offended. Everything's gorgeous. This bridge on this postcard? It's nothing special here. You see that kind of thing any direction you look. Usually you see something even better-looking. And the whole snobby thing these people have about their bakeries? Completely justified. While you're chewing it, the average baguette, which goes for less than a euro, is like the end of all suffering, and it's the kind of thing that makes you wonder . . .

". . . what the fuck is wrong with everybody?" postcard 2 (long shot of the Tuileries, facing the Louvre) continued, in much tinier handwriting.

> Like, is there a conspiracy against Stateside bread-eaters? Why can't our bakers just do what these people do? Far as I understand, it's just flour and water and an oven. They got bakeries run by Arabs here, and Africans, and their baguettes are up to snuff, so it's not about having some magic Frenchy genes, so why can't we do it? Anyway, they all speak English, these Parisians, but they act like they don't, and that's why they're bitchy, but then, same time, I see their point. Their city's better than yours, their food's better than yours, their women know how to dress, and, except for all the dogshit on the sidewalk, the only reason you'd hesitate to admit that Paris is superior to wherever else you're from is cause you're *not* from here, and so, "Fuck you, you misproportioned, too-smiley slob who can't even figure out how to make decent bread and all your best buildings look like weird spaceships. Learn *our* language. It's the one people talk when they know how to live." Makes sense to me. I think you should come here. Call the number on the hotel business card and let me know if you want to. Love, C.t.D.

The following night, when I returned from Arcades, there was a message from Clyde on the answering machine. It was shot through with static feedback and clicking, but after playing it a few times, I was able to make out the phrases "in case you haven't got my letters yet" and "staying in this armpit, ha!" and "open-ended ticket," which I (correctly, it would turn out) understood to mean that he would be extending his stay in Europe.

The machine informed me that the message had been left at 9 p.m. on March 3, 2014, which meant that I was listening to it on March 4, 2014. I had a transcript to deliver. I was three days late.

I called Burroughs first thing in the morning, and left him a message. He called me back later that afternoon, said he'd pick up the transcript that evening around 8:30.

In the meantime, a pair of letters arrived. One from Paris in a normal-looking envelope, and one special delivery from ________, Spain. The one from Paris was postmarked a few days earlier than the one from Spain, so I read it first.

Dear Billy,

I thought about sending you another postcard, but they don't have enough space. Exciting things are happening in Paris for your dad. Prime example is I guess that about a week or so after I got here, I ended up seeing some dull British spy movie at one of the theaters that doesn't overdub—they have so many theaters here—and even though the movie was a snore, it got me feeling lonely to hear people speak English, so I looked in one of those tourist guidebooks and read about this famous bookstore Shakespeare & Co., where they sell books in English, and they published James Joyce or Ernest Hemingway I think in the 1920s, before they were famous. I wanted to get you some kind of souvenir or something anyway, so I thought: "That's your move, Clyde." So I took a long walk to this Shakespeare & Co., and there was a live reading by an American author when I got there, but I thought that maybe it was almost over because the sign on the door said that it started at 6, and it was already 7, so I went inside anyway. It wasn't almost over. It had only just started, but I sat because I didn't want to be rude in Paris.

Writer looked about your age. Adam Levin. You heard of him? During the Question and Answer part, it turned out he was from Chicago, too. Not just from Chicago but grew up in Deerbrook Park and Buffalo Heights. His book was called SELF-TITLED, which is not a title I thought too highly of, and the book looked really small and really short. Like half a NO PLEASE DON'T or less. A third. But I thought it was pretty funny, what this guy read—it was just like a bunch of really short anecdotes, one after the other. There was one about fireflies, one about a cat, another one about hiding under a table at a party. I wanted to buy one for you, but by the time I got to the front of the line, all of the copies were sold out. I think you should get one, though. Really. Maybe I don't know your taste at all, but funny's funny, right? And in the Q&A thing, serious-sounding people kept saying this word about it that I keep forgetting . . . parataxis, I'm being reminded. So maybe it's not just a funny book, and so you'd like it.

I still wanted to buy you something, even though there were no more SELF-TITLEDs, so I went looking. I started in the A's, looking at the books that were facing out, and the first one of them that looked good was a novel called ESTRANGEMENT EFFECT by someone named Camille Bordas. I picked that one up, started reading it, and I laughed out loud before I even read a whole page, and while I was laughing at it, someone came up behind me and said something in French. And I said, "No parle pas. Engles?" or however you spell it, and she, this woman, she said, "I say, 'This is the best book in the whole store,'" And she seemed to really mean it. And she had this . . . warmth. This friendliness. It was like she didn't care I was a slob American—I'd picked the best book. And eyes, too. Really great eyes. Large. Dark. I'd noticed her earlier, during the reading, and thought, "Wow, I wish I spoke French." So I really didn't want her to go away, and I told her, "You know, you shouldn't say that too loud, about it being the best book." "Why not?" she said. "This guy Levin might overhear you," I said. "I know this guy Levin, and this guy Levin would not disagree with what I have said," she said, laughing. "You know him?" I said. She said, "He is my son-in-law. This book is by his wife. Right there," she said, and pointed to this skinny, freckled young woman on the other side of the store who had the same eyes and, turned out, looked just like the young woman in the author's photo in the back of ESTRANGEMENT EFFECT. "Forgive me," I said, "but how did a guy like Levin convince someone like your daughter to marry him?" I was trying to be clever to keep her talking to me, but the woman answered me like the question was serious, and completely reasonable to ask. I guess it was reasonable, but not, you know, appropriate. I don't know. Levin's alright. "I think because he is nice to her," she said, "and she thinks he is funny." "That's it?" I said. "Maybe there is more," she said, "but mostly I think, yes." She didn't seem like she was in a rush to get away, but I worried that her Frenchness was keeping me from reading the signals, and I didn't know what to say, so I just blurted out at her, "My son is a writer." "Yes?" she said. "Belt Magnet," I said. "His book is here?" she said. "I don't know," I said. "We should go see," she said. "I wish to buy it."

We went to the M's. Your book wasn't there. The woman asked someone who worked at the front of the store to order it, and they started searching in their computer for a reference number or whatever. Then Levin came over, with Camille Bordas, and he said, "What's going on?" Said it in English to his French mother-in-law. And she told him she was searching for a book by my son, and Levin said, "Who's your son?" and I told him your name, and he said, "NO PLEASE DON'T! I love that book. I've read it three times. It's out of print for some reason. I've got a copy at home, Sandrine. I'll send it to you."

Sandrine, I thought. Okay, okay.

"I think you'll like it," Camille said to Sandrine. She'd read it, too.

I waved Camille's book at her. "I think my son will like this," I said. "I didn't even read a page yet, and I laughed. Out loud. I think it's great so far."

Camille mumbled something like "Thank you," but seemed embarrassed, then started talking to Sandrine in French, and Levin said, "So where you coming from?"

"Same as you," I said.

"Yeah, you know," he said, "I knew that. I don't know why I was pretending I didn't know that. Wheelatine, right? Home of the Pellmore-Jasons."

"I guess that's one way to think of it," I said.

"Not a fan of them?"

"Not so much."

"Me neither," Levin said. "I went to the compound a few times, when I was a kid, saw him in action. Jonboat. You know, there was a little while—seemed long at the time, but was probably just like six months, when every fuckup and skid in the northwest suburbs wished he was from Wheelatine. Partly that was because Jonboat had a halfpipe and ramps that he'd let kids come over and use on weekends if they signed a waiver with his bodyguard or whatever, but more than that, I think, it was because of your son. The swingset murders. I don't know if you mind me bringing that up."

"It's fine," I said. "Belt doesn't do that anymore."

"I know," Levin said. "I know, believe me. Thing is, I never got to see one," he said. "There were only a couple, I guess, that anyone showed up for, right? But I heard about the first one after it happened, and then, when I heard about the second one, I couldn't get there. I mean, I was eleven. I had a cousin who drove, but his car was full, so he wouldn't take me, and I don't know why I didn't ride my bike out there. I mean, I know *why*. I was this fat little angry lazy person, and I probably lived six, maybe seven miles away, but I regret it, I'm saying. It was the last one anyone ever saw, that murder, at least as far as I know, and after it happened, the kids I knew who went, they made it sound like I missed the whole point of growing up where we did. Not the whole point. That's dramatic. But a highlight. Sounded like I missed what should have been the highlight of my entire childhood, you know? The thing that made where we were from what it *was*. Or something. And then that cousin of mine who drove, a few months later, he told me that he met Belt over at Jonboat's one day, that Belt gave him a piece of bubblegum or something, and, after that, even though I didn't ride a freestyle bike or a skateboard or anything, I made sure I had a ride to the compound whenever Jonboat opened it up, and it completely sucked. Belt never came back, so I just waited around, watching Jonny wonderboy get his ass kissed all day by all these kids who I kind of looked up to, but who had it all wrong, and I knew they had it all wrong, but if I tried to say so, they'd say I was just jealous, so I didn't say anything, just waited around, hoping for your son to return."

"They had what all wrong?" I said.

"They were trying to figure out how Jonboat became Jonboat, you know? Like he wasn't *born* Jonboat. They had it all wrong."

"Levin," I said, "don't misunderstand, I don't like the guy either, but it's not like he's done nothing. I mean, he's this astronaut. And he was a fighter pilot. It's because of him that prostitution's legal. Gay marriage too."

"Bullshit on that," Levin said. "Those last two things are because of his wife. And an astronaut? A fighter pilot? Who needs another fucking astronaut fighter pilot? Maybe that's ignorant of me, Mr. Magnet. I only 75% mean it. And I'm sorry to curse so much. Probably it's ignorant of me. But he wasn't one then, anyway. An astronaut or a fighter pilot. He was just a smart kid, like any other smart kid, who happened to be really athletic, and the son of Jon-Jon. He was good at the things he was supposed to be good at. Great even. But what do I give a shit about any of that? At eleven, especially—why should an eleven-year-old give a shit about that? Especially when there's someone like Belt around. The swingset murderer. He *murdered swingsets*. He invented swingset-murder out of nothing and instantly perfected it and everyone thought it was beautiful. Everyone was crazy for it. I think everyone who saw it, or who even heard about it back then—it changed their lives, the way they saw things, thought about things. That's how it was for me, just to imagine seeing it. And no one even understood what it meant. They just knew it was good."

"What did it mean?" I said. "Why was it good?"

"I have no idea," he said. "But it's why I became a writer. In large part, at least."

"I don't get it," I said.

And then he started talking about art and literature and "the meaning of meaning" and what, in his opinion, the best art and literature achieve, or are supposed to achieve, and are supposed to refuse or maybe he said refute, and I didn't really get it, but I felt like I got it while he was saying it, and anyway he seemed to believe what he was saying, and I'm not even going to try to tell you exactly what that was because I can't remember, and I probably didn't remember right even half of what I already wrote that he said, but the long and the short of it was he was a big fan of you for the swingset murders, and then he read a review of your book, and he said his hopes were high for it, and that even though they were so high, it turned out better than he hoped. NO PLEASE DON'T. And I don't think he was exaggerating at all. I liked him.

"So is Belt still living in Chicago?" Levin said, once he was finished talking about art. By then we'd been out of the bookstore for a while, the four of us. I'd bought ESTRANGEMENT EFFECT, and we'd ended up walking out together, Sandrine and Camille a few steps ahead of Levin and me, and we'd probably walked a mile or two, into the Right Bank—it's hard to judge distance here.

"In Wheelatine," I said. "Stays with his old man."

"Just the two of you or . . . ?"

"Right," I said. "Exactly. Just the two of us."

"You know, I don't know what you've got going on, but we're about to do apparoh at this Spanish place," he said.

"Oh yeah?" I said. I didn't know what that meant, apparoh. Do you know? I'll tell you. It's my new favorite thing. From now on I'm gonna do it every day. It's a drink or a small food you eat with people before dinner, and if you're having a good time with it, it either turns into dinner or more apparoh. The whole reason these people here eat dinner so late is because they need to have enough time after work to have apparoh first, which is, in my opinion, and the opinion of anyone worth listening to, better than dinner.

"Yeah," Levin said. "You want to come with, Mr. Magnet?"

"Clyde," I said.

"Clyde?" Sandrine said, making it two syllables, so it almost sounded like a nice name. I didn't even realize she was listening to us. How long had she been listening? "Like Bunny and Clyde?" she said.

"Just like that," I said.

Bunny and Clyde!

"You will come for apparoh with us, Clyde?" Sandrine said.

"I <u>will</u> come with you for apparoh, Sandrine," I said, pretending like I knew what that meant.

"He talks like Adam," Sandrine said to Camille. "Ah-yeah-pa-row." And they laughed at me, but it was friendly.

And we took this long walk to get apparoh at this Spanish place that Levin tried to explain why Camille and Sandrine called it something in French that translates to "The Two Assholes," like it was a pun or something, but I didn't understand, and I don't think Levin did either, but what a night, son. What a night. Lots of laughs. And Sandrine! I don't know what happened. I did something right, or I'm just really lucky because she's this amazing brainiac. It's not just that she speaks <u>three</u> languages, but she's a retired professor of Spanish literature here, and you know what she does in retirement? She translates Spanish literature into French. Talking to her is a <u>trip</u>. Reminds me of how it used to be talking to your mom. I say that not lightly. She cracks me up and I crack her up, too, just sitting around and pointing at things and people and making up stories about them and making fun of them, and she doesn't seem to think it's bad that I don't know a tenth of the things that she knows—she just thinks it's funny and tells me those things til I understand, but not like some teacher. We get along really well. That apparoh with Camille and Levin was six days ago, and Sandrine and I have done apparoh together every day since, sometimes just the two of us, and it turns into more apparoh or dinner every time.

So day after tomorrow, she's flying to the south of Spain for a month. She's got retired French brothers there, and another daughter. It's where her dad's originally from. Her dad was a hero of the Spanish Revolution—no. The Spanish Civil War. That means he was a communist, which sounds bad, but was <u>not</u> bad at all. He was fighting against fascists. I don't know, son. I'm out of my depth here. Communist good guys? I don't know anything. And I know they taught it to me, too. In school. It just didn't stick. It all stuck to Sandrine. She's out of my league.

But she invited me to come along to Spain with her, I think. It's hard to tell. She keeps trash-talking it in that way that makes it sound like either "You wouldn't understand" or "Maybe you, of all people, will understand." Do you know what I mean? Like, she's going there for a month, and she goes there at least three times a year, she says, and she says she loves it there, but then she keeps saying how there's all this high unemployment and a lot of people think it's "an armpit of Europe," this part of Spain where she's going, which is called __________, so I can't tell if she's inviting me to go to ________ because she wants me to go with her and she's saying it's an armpit because she worries I won't like it, or if she's inviting me because of how much time we've been spending together but she's just being polite and she doesn't really want me to go with her at all and so she's saying it's an armpit so that I *won't* go.

So we'll see, I guess, because I'm going. If I'm unwanted in the armpit, she'll have to tell me straight. Anyway, I'll let you know when I know. For now, I changed my flights around to fly home from Madrid on March 9. Sorry this letter went on so long. I've got more to say, too, but lucky for you I guess I have to end it. We're going back to the Two Assholes place tonight for apparoh. If by any chance you're done working before I come home and you want to meet me out here and travel around, or even just meet me out here and stay in place, or just say hi then travel around by yourself and see the world, Sandrine's cellphone number is +XX X XX XX XX XX, which, like she told me when I asked her for it, is a lot easier to remember than it seems at first because it spells the words *XXXXXX XXXXX* (clever, right?), and you can call me up at that number and let me know. I'll buy you a ticket to wherever you want, and if you *do* want me around when you get here, I'll extend my stay again. You've gotta come here, though, Belt. To Paris. I wish I'd known earlier. I should have. People said. It's not like it's a secret. I don't know why I never believed them. I hope you believe me.

Love,

Clyde the Dad.

The letter in the envelope from Spain was accompanied by a business-class Iberia airline ticket for Belt A. Magnet, for a flight that would depart from Chicago ORD at 4:25 p.m. and arrive at Madrid MAD at 7:30 a.m. on WH/EN/EVER.

"Belt!" the letter read.

Forget Paris. Not really. But Viva ________, Spain! You know why people say it's an armpit here? There's two reasons. One reason is that if you say a place is an armpit enough, you keep the place from being overrun and getting expensive, so please don't let anyone you might talk to know that it isn't an armpit. The other reason is that this country, which I guess the rest of Western and Central Europe and Britain too thinks the whole country is an armpit, it is truly economically fucked, which keeps it so cheap and helps the armpit legend strengthen. You know how fucked? You know how cheap? This is how fucked and cheap. That dummy ticket I'm sending with this letter? Look at it. See how it says WH/EN/EVER for the departure date? I asked the guy behind the counter to mock it up for me and he said it was impossible and against company policy and not even legal, but then all I had to do to get him to do it was offer him five euros. Five! Anyway, reason we were there, Sandrine and I, at the ________ airport, was so I could extend my stay again. Which I have done. My tourist visa's good here through the beginning of June, so I'll stay here till then at least. After that, we'll see what happens. Maybe we'll be married. I'm a little bit drunk. Do you know about tapas? It's like aperó, but it can happen at pretty much any time of day. What you do is, you order a beer for a euro, or a euro-50 some places, and then, with your beer, they bring you this little plate of food. Two of them's a meal. Some places, you get a choice of food, other places they have only one tapa, and then there's other places still that have more than one tapa but which ones they have depends on the day. Usually there's pork. Lomo. Could be some ham. Could be a couple ribs. Could be some ham and a tiny egg on top of a cold bowl of pulverized tomatoes and bread that's called Sal Morejo. They got potato salads, too. And a big piece of toast with tomatoes rubbed into it—that's another classic called pan con tamate. Not a loser in the bunch. I live mostly on tapas, here. I wake up very early in the morning and walk on the paseo, which is this boardwalk that goes for miles and miles, get a coffee and toast at one of the seaside café-restaurant-bar deals, maybe read ESTRANGEMENT EFFECT (I'm reading it a second time, slow, and it's even better the second time, and better than I thought it would be the first time, and I will send you it when I'm done, unless you tell me you're coming here) or if Sandrine wants to meet me and give me a little Spanish lesson we do that, and then I usually go fishing, pay this guy Jorge to take me out on his boat, and if I catch something, we cook it up that night, me and Sandrine and her brother Sal, at Sal's house, where we're staying, which is right there just half a block from the paseo, and sometimes Sandrine's daughter Juliette and her boyfriend Gabriel who live in an apartment across the street from Sal, and if I don't catch anything then sometimes Sal cooks something else and sometimes we just eat tapas all night, but I got ahead of myself. I was saying about my days.

When I come back from fishing, I maybe go into town with Jorge for a beer and a tapa and some groceries to go with the fish if there's fish, and then it's time for siesta, and I take a really long one. Five, six hours because at night I only sleep for three or four. Then it's back to the paseo for beer and tapas with Sandrine and one or both of her brothers or her daughter or all of them or just Sandrine. This is the life for me, son. Maybe for you? I don't know. Could be. In the desert out here is where they shot all those Spaghetti Westerns, and I know you don't care for Spaghetti Westerns, but you always liked that band the Clash, right? One of the guys from the Clash who is dead owned a bar here, a few miles away, out in the desert. And I know you like that French writer whose name is impossible to spell, starts with H, has a Q, sounds like Well-a-beck, and he lived around here for years or maybe he still does, I can't keep it straight. Some armpit! If I want to live here, I should learn Spanish is the thing. I'm looking into that. Into classes. But the thing is I could do it in a way I could never in Paris. Live here. I talked to a real estate agent and it's complicated because I'm American, but like I said, maybe Sandrine will want to marry me which would make it less complicated, but for now, no rush, I sound like a moony fourteen-year-old, I know, I'm not going to even try to buy anything for at least a few months, just renting an apartment starting next week, a luxury apartment with three bedrooms in Juliette's building for 450 euros a month, which is five hundred–some bucks, and then, if I want to buy a place what I'm getting at is I could get one a block or less from the beach that is nicer than ours in Wheelatine, just a little bit smaller maybe but nicer, for something like a hundred thousand euros, and I might. All depends on Sandrine, not even so much on will she marry me but will she even want me to keep being here with her the way I want to, which I think that she will but am afraid of counting chickens and proposing so soon. I know you're busy, and I will not nag you to come here, but I want you to know that I know I probably sound like I'm getting carried away and I know that I might be carried away, but same time I'm telling you that even if I go the opposite tomorrow and decide this place is lousy, you have to come here one day and see it for yourself, there's nothing like it I've ever heard of. No one's got guns and at night on the paseo at midnight, one in the morning even, you got kids eleven years old walking around together smiling maybe getting some ice cream or flirting with each other and it's fine with their parents and cops don't bother them. Last night I saw a couple pushing a stroller at 1 a.m. and it was normal. And same as in Paris, which I don't know if I said, but same as in Paris everyone reads books like it's the most normal thing and they hang out with people who aren't their age and it doesn't seem weird. They all joke around together. I miss you and am happy and am not completely embarrassed to tell you that my eyes are stinging for one of those reasons or both of those reasons right now. Levin sent Sandrine your book and she really likes it and she's telling me things about it, about the story in it that I hate to admit it but I guess I never understood because I was too busy being proud of you to think about what I was even really reading, just every page I saw your name at the top and thought, "My son! He made this!" and I couldn't pay much more attention than that, so I'm gonna read it again when she's done, and I think I'll be able to read it right or at least better here in ________, and maybe that'll help us to be like brothers because that is the thing, son, the thing I keep thinking and the thing that is the reason I wanted to write to you about, that you and me, we're both too old to keep playing father and son, we have been too old for that for a pretty long time, it's almost disrespectful, we're men, and we should be more like brothers, like I imagine it would be to be like brothers, because I always thought I'd make a better brother than a father, and I don't think I was <u>bad</u> at being your father and I don't think you think that either, I just think I'd probably be great at being more like your brother, not having to pretend like I knew about the way things really work in the world, and just instead making jokes about how totally fucking weird everything is, and I think you'd be better at it too, not having to think anything I say or do is important because I'm your father and so maybe that means you're like me or that maybe if it doesn't mean that it's not an important distinguishment, because it isn't, and that's easier with brothers I think than with fathers and sons, it's easier not to worry how the other's coming off and what that means about you, you can just relax.

I think living like this, just having tapas whenever, and walking around and no one has guns, and sleeping through the shittiest part of the day without anyone thinking you're lazy because none of them pretend that it isn't the shittiest part, they all know it's the shittiest part, and the worst can happen is you take a bad turn on a dead-end street and some Gypsies hold you up with a knife they don't even want to use—they got Gypsies here like in the movies, roving families of them, I didn't know they were real, I kind of want to be one—and they take your phone or your wallet or maybe even you fight them if they don't have a knife and you feel like fighting them, but the main thing is the tapas and the walking around and how everyone outside of here thinks you live in an armpit so you, <u>you</u>, I'm saying, Billy, Belt, you and I, <u>we</u>, we could live here for the rest of both of our lives not like kings but like human beings who worry less than kings, who eat and drink and fish and walk and read and write what and when they want—we could do it with a lot less dough than I already have for the rest of our lives and you could teach me how to use these long dashes the way you do, which Sandrine keeps talking about, and your mom said something about once, also, and I didn't ever really understand the big deal, and then explain to me parataxis because I'm curious about it still, I really am, it sounds like this strategy of simultaneous chumming and line-fishing that Jorge uses, and maybe you'll like to come fishing with me, with no Rick and Jim, just Jorge and maybe sometimes Sal because he keeps saying he wants to come with and not waking up in time but he probably will soon, and I think you'll really like him because everyone likes him and he studied philosophy and knows Arabic but still cracks funny dick jokes.

I'm sitting here smiling like a goon a little bit, son, looking at the sea, and there's an older guy a couple tables away who I think I'm freaking out a little, and what I'm trying to tell you is, I don't see this guy who's getting freaked out by me and think, Fuck you, look away, I just think, Shit, I should probably stop freaking that nice man out, he's just trying to live here, so I'm gonna unsmile my goony smile and pay and leave and mail this letter before I lose the nerve, and then siesta, and then tonight we'll eat the fish I just caught, me and Sandrine and her brothers, and then we'll take a walk, just Sandrine and I, and get a beer or ice cream and maybe I'll ask her to marry me but probably I'll wait a little because I know it's fast but I don't want to wait too long because I like that it's fast, the fastness is convincing to me and romantic.

I hope you'll call me when you get the chance, and I hope you're almost finished with whatever you're working on and you'll visit, and meet Sandrine, who I am not even a little nervous you two will get along great, you're my two favorite people, but no pressure. Earliest I'll come home is June, then hopefully come right back, new visa.

Love,
Clyde

•

•   •

The house was a mess, too messy to be seen by anyone but me, and it didn't smell right, unless that was me, yet I didn't consider any of that til just before Burroughs was supposed to arrive, and there wasn't time to clean, let alone motivation, so I hastily filled a flask with Scotch, stuck a short glass in the pocket of my jacket, grabbed a printout of the transcript, the disc to which I'd copied the file, and the DVD of *A Fistful of Fists,* then brought them all out onto the stoop, my idea being to give Burroughs the impression that I wanted—rather than intending to prevent him from entering the house—to toast the completion of the transcript outdoors, where we could enjoy the night air.

I enjoyed the night air. Since the freeze had lifted some five weeks earlier, most days had highs in the upper sixties, and there hadn't been an evening that had dropped below fifty. And I knew some people were alarmed about that—our freakish weather—and I knew those people would think that I was shallow—or would claim to think that I was shallow—for shamelessly enjoying our weather rather than condemning the causes of our weather and worrying about what it said about the state of the world and the shrinking capacity for human beings and other food-chain higher-ups to survive in the world, and maybe they'd be right, those other people, maybe it was shallow, and maybe my father's unbridled delight in his harvest of the fruits of southern Europe's economic collapse was similarly shallow, maybe we Magnets were in bad taste, enjoying the things we were able to enjoy when we should have been berating ourselves for enjoying them. Maybe we were shortsighted, blindly selfish, lived too close to our nerve ends, didn't pay enough attention to the suffering of others, didn't do enough to relieve that suffering, made the wrong noises, read the wrong books, wrote the wrong books for not-right people who hadn't any business reading books anyway, given all the suffering they could help relieve if they weren't reading books, the right or the wrong ones. Maybe we were, in our little ways, helping to hasten the rise of tyrants, the rise of sea levels, the fall of man, the end of humanity. Or maybe just I was. In my little way. How could I know? How could anyone know? I'm not saying they couldn't. I'm saying I didn't. I'm saying I don't and, because I don't, I fail to imagine how others might. Yet others seemed to. They seemed to know. They seemed to think they knew what was right and what was wrong, what was good and what was bad, and what impact they made on what and who, and how to destroy the least amount of good, how to prevent the most amount of evil, how to progress toward solving the world if only everyone else would listen, and all I knew was what I liked and didn't like, what moved me and what didn't, what I found beautiful and what I found ugly, who I found attractive and who I found repellent, and I wasn't very good at knowing even those things, but the point is, reader, it was nice outside, to me it felt nice, and despite my father's letters, the news of his happiness, the thought that he might have met a lovable woman who could love him in return, the thought that he'd discovered a way of life that appealed to him among people who appealed to him and that he wouldn't (it looked like) die too early of early retirement (which I suppose I'd been worrying about more than I've let on), and the news that other writers admired my books (writers I'd heard of, but hadn't yet read, haven't yet read), and that one of those writers had bothered to think about and misunderstand the swingset murders in a way that sounded flattering and deliberate and made Clyde proud—despite all of it, the only thing I had, out there on the stoop—the only thing I found myself actually enjoying—was the weather. The air on my face. All the rest of it was distant, stuck behind this book, my failure to finish it, or my failure to give up on it (hard to say which). Except for the pleasant weather and the failures, it all might as well have been happening to somebody else.

Yet that was nothing dramatic. Not really. It wasn't. I may have been in crisis, but I wasn't in danger. I knew *that* much. I may have been broken, but only metaphorically, only "inside." I was having trouble writing was all. I was having trouble not feeling ambivalent. I was finding it impossible to not feel ambivalent. For some people—many—that would, I know, count as a lovely kind of problem to have, but I wasn't some people, I was only one person, I was only me, and for me . . .

What I'm trying to say is the night air was nice, and that wasn't a lot, or didn't seem like a lot, didn't seem like enough, but then why put the stress on *that wasn't a lot*? on what it didn't *seem* like? or, for that matter, on what it *did* seem like? What it *was,* in itself, the night air, to me, was nice. The night air was *nice*. It felt nice on my face. It was nice out. I liked it. I liked the night air and I told myself I liked it, and I lit up a Quill, opened my flask, and inhaled some Scotch fumes. That was nice, too, I guess, now that I recall. It was fine is what it was. Everything would be fine.

Burroughs appeared while I was sniffing my flask. He'd arrived on foot.

"What are you hiding in that flask?" he said.

"MacGuffin Fifteen."

"Good *stuff,*" he said. "To drink some of that stuff, a man might be willing to become unwomanly."

I poured some Scotch in the glass for him. He unbuttoned his jacket and sat down beside me, took up half the stoop. We cheers'd, we swigged, we exhaled audibly. I handed him the transcript and the DVD. "So what's the next step?" I said, not much caring. "You start printing out copies, or give me notes for revision, or . . . ?"

"Well, I'll tell you," Burroughs said, then went on to explain that the reason he came over to pick up the transcript (instead of instructing me to mail the transcript, or drop the transcript off at the compound guard booth) was that the screening of *A Fistful of Fists* had been canceled. The screening had been canceled sometime mid-October, and until I'd left him my voicemail that morning, neither he nor Trip had thought to let me know about the cancellation, or perhaps—if he was being entirely honest, he said—perhaps they'd thought to, then simply forgotten to. In either case, when Trip had returned from school that afternoon, at which time Burroughs had told him that I'd called, he'd wanted to come over and break the news to me himself. On top of fearing that I'd be disappointed in him over the cancellation of the screening, Trip felt terrible, Burroughs said, for having wasted so much of my time, but Jonboat refused to allow Trip to see me, refused to even allow him to call me, and after father and son had finished yelling at each other, Trip demanded Burroughs come over in his stead, and asked him to please break the news to me softly. "I told him," Burroughs said, "that I didn't think you'd be all that broken up, having made so much money and all, but still he insisted, and he wanted me to tell you the contract still holds."

"Meaning what?" I said.

"Meaning that Trip, once he's read it over and approved it, will copyright the transcript in the same manner that he copyrighted 'On Private Viewing' and 'Living Isn't Functioning,' so you'll be free to do with it whatever you like, for whatever profit you can make, just as long as you don't alter it."

"Alright," I said.

"I knew you wouldn't be broken up," he said.

"So what happened?" I said, again not really caring; I just wanted Burroughs to keep on talking. Apart from inans, food-delivery drivers, gas-station clerks, liquor-store Terry, and a couple of prostitutes, I hadn't had a conversation with anyone since the morning my father had left for Austria. It was nice to hear a voice not belonging to someone who was selling me something or had sold me something or wanted me to help it end its existence. It was nice like the air on my face, like the Scotch. "So what happened?" I said. "The museum saw *A Fistful* and thought it was too . . . what? Disgusting? Mean?"

"No, nothing like that. It was Triple-J who canceled the screening," Burroughs said. "The museum loved *A Fistful*. In fact, their lawyers, after Trip pulled out—they tried to get heavy with us about it, can you imagine? It's resolved now, though. Trip'll still be screening a film on the appointed date. A better film in everyone's opinion. *Colorized War Crimes*. That's the title."

"Is that . . . what it sounds like?"

"That and more. War crimes," Burroughs said, "are a little more broadly defined by the film than you might be thinking. There's the Nazi concentration camp stuff you'd probably expect, some mustard-gassed trenches, death marches, Hiroshima, a tortured Algerian, skeleton piles out of Franco's White Terror, Kristallnacht, and so forth, but also a couple lynchings in Mississippi, some Africans hobbled and deformed by failed vaccines, some thugs breaking a strike at a factory in London, a clitoridectomy ceremony, a guy in a labcoat pointing with a stick to a brain on a table labeled 'homosexual brain . . .' I'm forgetting a couple, but you get the point. It's a twenty-seven-minute compilation of silent footage with a drony, ambient soundtrack, and it loops four times. Some of the clips are of the war crimes or 'war' crimes being committed, some are just of the evidence that they'd been committed, some are both, and the whole thing starts out black-and-white but progressively colorizes til it's so saturated with color that it's nearly a blur, and then it progressively decolorizes til it's black-and-white again. Over the four twenty-seven-minute loops, it goes, with gradually decreasing speed, through twenty-four saturation/desaturation colorizing/decolorizing cycles, and by the ninth or tenth cycle, the effect takes hold. That's where the art is."

"The art."

"Well, it's hard to describe, this effect. Maybe not. Maybe more like hard to accept, I guess. Basically, the viewer ends up feeling almost nostalgic—not almost, no: *nostalgic*."

"About the war crimes," I said.

"Sort of," said Burroughs. "Well, yes. I could say it's more about the black-and-white—I want to say that—that it's about the footage's return to black-and-white, or the dawning recognition of there actually being a *refrain* in the droney ambient music, but that's more a statement about *how* it operates on you. Except you can't really separate the treatment of the subject matter from the subject matter itself, right? Not if you're being rigorous, you know? Anyway, what happens is, by cycle nine or ten, you start looking forward to the desaturation/decolorization part of each cycle, to everything returning to black-and-white, and when it does, there's a rising sense of 'Oh, the good old days' that is eerily, *eerily* unironic and warm. You walk away from the whole thing feeling violated, but rather masterfully violated. Violated in a way that you can't help but think you were complicit in—maybe even responsible for—your violation. That you were asking for it."

"It shook you up."

"It did," Burroughs said. "It'll shake you up, too, if you want to see it. I've got a DVD right here for you. Trip's going to do the whole thing a lot more straightforwardly than he'd planned to do *A Fistful*. No transcript or anything. A few months after the screening at the MCA, Fon's pal Ronson Boyle will auction it—he's already garnered some interest from collectors—and it'll almost certainly end up running in some museum somewhere, but it'll be a little while before that happens. Short of it is: Trip, who's convinced you'd love the film, he wanted to get you on the guest list for the MCA, but Jonboat . . . he wouldn't have it. Hence: this DVD right here. For the well-being of everyone involved, I'm unfortunately compelled to let you know that if you were to show this DVD to anyone else, now or later, we'd thoroughly destroy your life and so forth."

"You know, it doesn't really sound like something I'd be into."

"Getting your life destroyed?"

"I meant—"

"I know what you meant. And that's fine," Burroughs said, "but you'll still accept the disc, alright? That way I can tell Trip you took it, if he asks. And not for nothing, he's really proud of this, and I think he's right to be." Burroughs threw back what remained in his glass. "Good *stuff,*" he said. "Confit plums, custard, and pine. Don't you dare twist my arm into having another."

I poured him another.

"So why'd Trip cancel the screening for *A Fistful*?" I said. "I mean it seems like he could have probably screened both, or just booked a second screening for *Colorized War Crimes,* no problem."

"Oh, right," Burroughs said. "I guess I skipped that part. Trip didn't actually make *Colorized War Crimes* til after he'd canceled the screening for *A Fistful.* See, things got rough for him once those AOL clips aired. The first one—the one with just the mirror—that wasn't quite the end of the world. It got him a little annoyed because here was a clip, he thought, that he'd have to add to *A Fistful,* which he'd felt was already perfect and probably shouldn't be messed with. But he's diligent, you know? And so he went ahead and messed with it. He spent the following week cutting the clip down to various lengths and inserting it in various spots til he found the right length and the right spot, and after that, for a couple of hours, he was back to his old self, feeling good and confident, but then, that very same evening, the second AOL clip aired. And when he saw the second AOL clip? the one where the P.A.L. guys keep interfering with the AOL? He saw its potential, really saw how it would play out, how people would start, in his words, *innovating Curio interactions in revolutionary ways using Independence.*

"And, of course, he was right. By the middle of that week, one of the Yachts—the less bright Chaz—I *think* it was Jr. but can never keep them straight—so Chaz or Chaz Jr., whichever, just a few days after the initial airing of the second AOL clip, he brought over his Executioner Set, along with a cure he'd previously taught to perform executions of other cures, and he fed the cure the Independence-NeedyBuddy cocktail, showed it the mirror, and then, every time it tried to hang itself, he interfered, got in the way—'saved it from itself,' in his words—til finally he got so bored or excited saving it from itself, he just tore its head off. Day after that, Bryce came over and rigged up a kind of double-AOL thing where he set a pair of cocktail-fed clones inside a box with four mirrored walls, causing all manner of chase and confusion and slapstick to ensue before they finally seemed to deduce which parts of what they were looking at were their own, which parts were reflections, which parts were their clone's, and, in any case, bled out. Next day, Lyle AOL-cocktails a cure, but binds its wrists and ankles to a stake before showing it the mirror, and it somehow manages, after twenty minutes of struggle, to break its own neck just by twisting around. I mean, it *writhes* itself to death. And then the brighter Chaz comes by the compound that very same evening, brings a box of safety matches, a bottle of water, and—"

"I think I got the idea," I said.

"You and everyone else," Burroughs said. "That's the thing of it, right? And Trip has a major crisis is the point. Artistic, moral. Crisis. Deep. Feels almost attacked."

"By who?"

"Everything. The universe."

"That's a little much," I said.

"He's barely fifteen years old, and he's *smart,* this kid. Whatever you or anyone else might think of him, he is sharp as a tack, highly introspective. But, yeah, barely fifteen years old. Ideological in that way younger people tend to be. So now, look at what's happened. Appreciate what's happened. First, he's spent hundreds and hundreds of hours on *A Fistful* in order to make just the kind of impact that that second AOL video beats him to the punch on: all that revolutionary innovation stuff. And that stings, Belt—that would sting anyone, getting beaten to the punch like that, after having put in so much work. Way he sees it, there's no point in screening *A Fistful*—it'll be derivative—so he cancels the screening. Yet it's not just that he's gotten beaten to the punch that stings, but that he's gotten beaten to the punch by the work of PerFormula designers. And I don't know if you know about this, but the whole reason Trip ended up deciding to pursue a career as an artist is that he realized he didn't have what it took to pursue a career as a formula designer. That's what he originally wanted to do, formula design, but he didn't have the talent, only the drive, and when, a couple years ago, he realized that, it broke his heart a little. The decision to make art—that was his salvation. It was his second choice, but after he made it, he worked hard to convince himself it had always been his first. He told himself art could do what technology couldn't, and . . . nope. Suddenly, not anymore. Not from where he stands. From where he stands, it turns out technology can do it all, and can do it better. So that stings even more. And no less painful than that—this may even be the hardest part for him—is that his ability to be the earnest young believer in the power of art is pretty much annihilated. You see, Trip, introspective and ideological, he can't help but feel like being stung via getting beaten to the punch here is a failing of his, okay? That the feeling he feels, the sting—a feeling he can't help but feel—indicates that he's a moral shitbag. And I'm not exaggerating. He used those words. *Moral shitbag.* He'd been telling himself—telling me, Fon, his father, but above all himself—that what he wanted to do with *A Fistful* was inspire others to behave innovatively, revolutionarily. He'd believed all along that to inspire everyday 'revolutionary innovation of Curio interactions' was his mission, was a moral good, and that his drive to inspire 'revolutionary innovation' was what set him apart, what made him a uniquely good and worthwhile human being, and, though he didn't exactly say as much, I think he also believed that his drive to inspire 'revolutionary innovation' justified his having been born into such vast wealth and power.

"In any case, he believed he should have been happy because the airing of that clip achieved what he had purportedly thought to be a great good. And here it turned out he felt not only unhappy, but, as I said, *stung*, and so he had to contend with an unpleasant, worldshaking truth, and that truth was that he'd been lying to himself all along. He cared far less about the spread of 'revolutionary innovation' than he did about earning recognition as *the person responsible for inspiring* 'revolutionary innovation.' In other words, he wasn't, according to his own standards, a particularly good person, let alone one who deserved all that he'd been born into. He was normal. He was petty. *A hater*, he called himself. So, like I said: crisis."

"You've thought a lot about this."

"Well, that's my job. Most of it. Thinking about Triple-J." Burroughs seemed a little hurt—as if I'd said, "You've thought *too* much about this." I supposed that was reasonable—it might have sounded that way, I might have even meant it that way—but rather than attempt to clarify or apologize, I thought it better to pour him a third dram of Scotch and move on.

I emptied the flask into his glass and said, "So *Colorized War Crimes* fixed everything, then? Trip made it, everyone loved it, and . . ."

"Yes and no. I mean, it wasn't *that* simple. Before he made *War Crimes*, he spent a couple days melting down. Soon as the brighter Chaz showed him the matches-and-water AOL, Trip told the Yachts there would be no such thing as the Yachts anymore, and then, when they asked him if they couldn't please still just be Yachts without him, he beat the tar out of them for a few minutes before Duggan heard shouting and intervened. Then he hid out in the production house and refused to leave for the entire weekend. He'd let me bring him his meals, but hardly spoke to me, and wouldn't let anyone else inside."

"Not Fon?"

"I bet he'd have let her in, and I think he *wanted* Jonboat to come talk to him, but they were both doing a kind of joint charity/propaganda-appearance tour in Central Africa, and Trip was too full of self-hate to call either of them, I guess. By Sunday afternoon, it didn't look like he'd be going to school the next day, and that was okay with me—if all he needed was a couple more days to himself—but I could tell that wasn't all he needed. It was grim in that production house, Belt. The poor kid. He wasn't working, just lying around. Wouldn't eat the food I brought him. Wasn't even crying, just . . . flat. He tried reading your book again, which, a lot of times, that gets him out of a funk, but: no go. Just didn't work, and the fact that it didn't made him feel even worse, he said. And he wouldn't talk to a shrink, he would barely talk to me, he refused to accept three separate phone calls from his godsister, his parents wouldn't be back for another couple weeks, so, finally, I brought him a Panacea, and only then did he get back on the horse."

"A panacea!" I said. "I wish someone would bring me a panacea."

"Oh? You're not feeling well, Belt?"

"I've been better," I said.

He took his cellphone from his pocket. "I'll have Hogan bring some on over for you."

"Right, sure. Please do that, Burroughs. Bring me my panacea posthaste!"

"I don't get the tone," he said, lowering the phone.

"The tone?" I said.

"Do you *not* want any Panacea, or are you . . . I mean, it wouldn't put us out at all to give you some. We have a lifetime supply. A *two*-lifetime supply. Trip's godfather brought some over back at the end of last summer. Big old carton of sample boxes. He was really excited about it. I guess he was the one—Baron Swords, I mean—he claimed he was the one on the board who came up with the angle to sell it as a dietary supplement instead of a drug, which made it a lot easier to get through the FDA trials. Anyway, he brought this carton of the stuff for Jonboat, who wouldn't touch it. Doesn't even like the idea of it, Jonboat, so he gave it to me."

"I'm completely lost," I said. "Panacea's a drug?"

"Yes and no. That's what I was saying. It's a drug by any conventional definition of the word—it's derived from spidge, comes in a pill, and it 'increases acumen and promotes general psychological well-being'—but Swords bobbed and loopholed and convinced the FDA it was a *dietary supplement,* which means that, far as the FDA's concerned, it's a food."

"And it works?" I said. "Increases acumen and so forth?"

"It sure seems to. Valentine, he can get pretty depressed sometimes, and he and Lotta, just a day or two before Jonboat gave me the Panacea, well the young lovers had themselves a pretty ugly falling-out, and Val was down about it—they're all good now, engaged actually—but he took some Panacea for a week or so, and it really worked for him. He'd tried a lot of other stuff in the past, too—antidepressants, I mean—and they never did much for him. And, like I was saying before, I convinced Trip to take some, and he snapped out of his funk, posthaste as you'd say. He woke up the very next morning all full of purpose and energy. He ditched school for the week—I let him—and it was during that week that he made *Colorized War Crimes*. Ever since then, he's been back to himself."

"He's happy again."

"Happy? I don't know. I don't know if he's ever really *happy,* but he's definitely got that sense of purpose again, that energy. I mean, he made the movie, he's kept up his grades, apologized to the former Yachts, and he's even half-convinced Jonboat to move the family back to Manhattan and let him finish high school at this international arts academy for kids who are less . . . kids who are more like the people who'll be *buying* his work. We'll see what happens with that."

"Well how much would you want for it?" I said.

"What are we talking about?"

"A week's supply, I guess?" I said.

"Wait. What? What do you take me for, Belt? You just fed me fine Scotch and listened to me spill my guts for . . ." he said, and looked at his watch. "Oh dear, no time to take umbrage. I have to get back." He stood, I stood, we shook hands and shoulder-clapped. "I'll have some Panacea sent over," he said. "Swords said it should be available to consumers in June, but I read one of these 'cool your jets'–themed editorials in the *Journal* the other day that claimed the FDA approvals wouldn't come through til October, so I'll send you enough to last til October. If you like it, but for some reason the launch gets delayed past October, just call me, and I'll send you more. We might be in New York by then, but I'll have the same number."

I thanked him and he left. On the stoop, at my feet, was a jewel case containing a disc marked *Colorized War Crimes*. I brought it inside, threw it away.

THE ONLY WRONG PERSON

My Grandmother Magnet used to, for our Christmas gifts, treat us to tickets to a matinee showing of a movie of her choosing, often popcorn as well. Christmas morning, after opening our presents, we'd eat Swedish pancakes with lingonberry jam and powdered sugar, stacks of bacon, fresh-squeezed OJ, coffee for my parents, and hot cocoa for me. To stave off food coma, we'd then go outside and build a snowman on the lawn, or, if that wasn't possible, head to the playground for a tetherball tournament, after which we'd drive the better part of an hour to whichever theater in my grandmother's neighborhood was showing the movie she'd picked. Much of our conversation in the car would revolve around guessing what that movie would be; we never knew what it was til my grandmother handed us our tickets in the lobby.

In 1986, my guess was *Three Amigos!* From the commercials I'd seen, it was obvious to me that *Three Amigos!* would be one of the all-time great comedies, an instant classic that nothing else playing could possibly compete with—a movie about characters mistaken for characters those characters played in the movies; ingenious!—and I thought that would've been equally obvious to my parents as well, which it may in fact have been, given the speed with which they dismissed my guess, though I entirely misunderstood that at the time. At the time I missed the point. The point was my grandmother, however inadvertently, always picked a *lousy* movie to see on Christmas.

(In fairness to my eleven-year-old self, it was reasonable for me to have missed that point: the previous year, my guess had been *Clue*. From the commercials I'd seen, it had been obvious to me that *Clue* would be one of the all-time great comedies, an instant classic that nothing else playing could possibly compete with—a movie about characters from a board game; ingenious!—and I thought that would've been equally obvious to everyone else, but . . . No. My mother, who'd guessed we'd see *Jewel of the Nile,* and my father, who'd guessed we'd see *White Nights,* thought *Clue* looked lousy, but not lousy *enough,* and they not only urged me to guess again, but, when, from pride, I stuck to my guns, they thought that was adorable (at the time, I thought they thought it was adorable that I thought *Clue* would be a great movie, but what it really was was that they thought it was adorable that I still believed my Grandmother Magnet might choose *Clue* when there were so many far more obviously lousy movies available to be seen), and they said that if I somehow turned out to be right, they'd buy me a new bike at the end of the school year. And I turned out to be right. That year we saw *Clue,* which both my parents and my grandmother found to be lousy, but I rather liked. It wasn't everything I'd hoped for, but I laughed quite a bit, plus it won me a bike; the following June, I'd get my Street Machine.)

But as I was saying: in 1986, I guessed *Three Amigos!,* Clyde *Eye of the Tiger,* and my mom *Star Trek IV*.

Grandmother Magnet had tickets for *Platoon*.

Platoon was R-rated and renowned for its violent, depressing content. My mother said it wouldn't do; I was allowed to see some R-rated movies, but not until after my parents had seen them first and vetted them. My grandmother said they were being overprotective; my mother muttered something under her breath about Sally the Balls; my grandmother ignored my mother's muttering, and said that *Platoon* was supposed to be important; my mother said Oliver Stone was a hack; my grandmother said there were already whispers that *Platoon* would win Best Picture at the Oscars; my mother said the Oscars were just like the Pulitzers; my grandmother said she didn't see how that could be a bad thing; my mother said that was the problem with my grandmother; my grandmother asked her what in the hell that was supposed to mean; my mother then recited a list of movies that had won Best Picture at the Oscars since 1979; my grandmother insisted they were all important movies, especially *Terms of Endearment* and *Chariots of Fire*; my mother said both of those movies were garbage; my grandmother called my mother a snob; my mother said my grandmother was the one who kept talking about *important* movies, so who was the snob?; and before my grandmother had a chance to respond, Clyde suggested my mother and I should see something else while he accompanied his mother to *Platoon*. Grandmother Magnet gave us our tickets to exchange (she held on to the bucket of popcorn she'd bought) and walked off with Clyde.

I don't remember all the movies that were playing, but *Three Amigos!* wasn't one of them, and my mother, although she bristled at Eddie Murphy's standup ("Every other punch line is *faggot,*" she'd said, which was certainly an overstatement, however true it was in spirit), had been a fan of his sketches on *Saturday Night Live,* and allowed me to convince her we should see *The Golden Child,* his latest comedy, and the only non-R-rated comedy playing at the theater.

I thought *The Golden Child* was great. The jokes contained enough swearing and sex and sexual innuendo that my knowing when to laugh at them—even if I didn't fully understand a few of them—made me feel clever beyond my years. The joke at which I laughed hardest, however, entailed no swearing, no sex, no innuendo at all. That joke comes in the middle of a chase scene near the end of the movie. Chandler Jarrell (played by Eddie Murphy), who has been tasked with saving and protecting the golden child, and the golden child himself—a young boy from Nepal with magical powers of healing who may or may not be the latest incarnation of the Buddha—have just narrowly escaped the Los Angeles–based Tibetan religious cult/motorcycle gang that had kidnapped the golden child earlier in the movie, and has since (i.e. the gang has since) been trying to get ahold of a special dagger with which to murder the golden child. The two of them—Chandler Jarrell and the golden child—have just gotten into Jarrell's car. Jarrell, behind the wheel, is afraid, out of breath, and clutching his chest when he turns to the golden child, who's sitting in the passenger seat, placid as a cow, and Jarrell says to him, "Did somebody give you a Valium or what?"

I don't know how long I laughed at that line, but it was long enough that my mom, who didn't initially laugh at all, ended up laughing at how much I was laughing, and eventually set her hand on my shoulder, to still me. "Did somebody give you a Valium or what?" was the single best joke I had ever heard.

Misheard, it turned out.

On our ride back home from the theater, when my father, after reporting that *Platoon* was "kind of sappy," asked me how I'd liked *The Golden Child,* I told him I'd never seen anything so funny, and then I described the scene I've just described above, and delivered the line.

"Cute," he said.

"It's the best!" I said.

"By the way," my mom said, "where'd you learn about Valium?"

"What do you mean?"

"They teach you about it in Health Class?"

"In Health Class?" I said. "Like in a hearing unit or . . . ?"

"A *hearing* unit?" she said. "Is there a *hearing unit* in Health Class? I was thinking maybe a psychology unit or—"

"I don't know if there's a hearing unit," I said. "Maybe. There hasn't been yet." I was very confused. "But who doesn't know about volume?" I said.

"Valium," my mom said.

"What do you mean?"

"It's not *volume*. It's *Valium*."

"What are you talking about?"

"Valium is a drug," my mom said. "A sedative. It keeps you calm. People take it so they don't have nervous breakdowns—that's what the joke was. They were running from the biker gang, and Eddie Murphy was scared, but the golden child was completely calm so he asked him, 'Did somebody give you a Valium, or what?' "

"That's not that great," I said. "Why would *that* be great?" I said. "No. It was volume."

"It was Valium," my dad said.

"You didn't see the movie."

"I don't need to see the movie, Billy. It was obviously Valium."

"It was Valium, Belt," my mom said.

"How would *volume* be funny, anyway?" my dad said.

"It's like he's saying there's a volume knob that . . . Forget it."

I didn't want to explain. I knew they were right and I felt like a fool. Worse than a fool. A couple months earlier, inans had begun attempting to speak to me. Just a word here and there—no complete sentences: a ||Please|| or ||Please help|| or ||need|| or ||I need,|| but nothing more, and whenever I would ask whatever had spoken to me, "What do you need?" or "How can I help?" there would be no response. It was frustrating for me. It seemed like I was failing. I didn't possess any concept of gates yet; didn't even know to think of inans as *inans*. My first real conversation with an inan—the Olive Garden booth—wouldn't occur til the following March. What I did know, right from the very start, was that I shouldn't let on to anyone else that I had the ability to hear inans speak, let alone that I was glad to have that ability; I knew none of it was normal, would make me seem crazy and unreliable, alarm my mother and piss off my dad.

And then I thought I'd heard Eddie Murphy tell the golden child, "Did somebody give you a volume, or what?" and I thought what he meant was something along the lines of, "Golden child, you're so calm in the face of mortal danger, whereas I, Chandler Jarrell, am panicking. It is as though your sense of your surroundings is controlled by a volume knob installed inside your head, and amidst all this scary stuff, you have turned that volume knob all the way down, all the way to the left, and so your sense of your surroundings is greatly decreased and doesn't affect you, and you are not afraid." This concept wasn't merely funny to me, it was revelatory.

Eddie Murphy, I thought, wouldn't make a joke in a movie that no one in the audience was able to get. So if Eddie Murphy made a joke about a figurative volume knob installed inside one's head, a knob that controlled one's sense of one's surroundings, that would mean that, to some degree at least, other people—even *many* people—must have possessed some shared notion of there being a way to decrease one's sense of one's surroundings as if with a volume knob installed inside one's head (if they didn't possess that shared notion, where was the joke?). And if so many people possessed that shared notion, the notion must have come from somewhere. If so many people possessed that shared notion, it very well might have been because some of those people—perhaps many of them, though more likely just a few (or else the joke would not have been that funny)—it very well might have been because some of them were *in fact* able to decrease their sense of their surroundings as if with a volume knob installed inside their heads. And if some people could decrease their sense of their surroundings as if with a volume knob installed inside their heads, maybe I could, too. And if I could, too, then it would stand to reason that I could also *increase* my sense of my surroundings as if with a volume knob installed inside my head. It would stand to reason that I could turn the volume up on the inans.

But Eddie Murphy hadn't said *volume*. The joke was my own, and no one else got it.

•

• •

The morning after Burroughs picked up the transcript, I found sixteen sample boxes of thirty Panacea sitting on our doorstep in a sealed brown carton. Along with the pills themselves, the boxes held tiny fold-up pamphlets containing information about active ingredients (SP-10B, SP-10C, SP-14—varieties of spidge, I guess) and recommended dosages (a pill a day for children under twelve; two a day for adults), as well as warnings about poisoning, allergic reactions, and potential interactions with other drugs (e.g. Tricyclic antidepressants and SSRI's)*. What stood out to me, thankfully, was the warning concerning *Temporary Paradoxical Effects:*

* In the (dubious) spirit, I suppose, of Triple-J's "Living Isn't Functioning," I feel obliged to note (in-foot) that although the Panacea I was given by Burroughs was identically formulated to that now available to consumers worldwide, the tiny folded info pamphlets that one finds inside today's market-ready bottles of Panacea employ a vocabulary slightly different from that employed by those pamphlets I found inside my sample packs, which were (i.e. my pamphlets and packs were) manufactured *before* Graham&Swords decided to market Panacea as a dietary supplement. The sample pack pamphlet's "active ingredients," for example, is, in the bottle pamphlet, "proactive ingredients"; the "recommended dosage" is "recommended intake"; "other drugs" just "drugs."

> One in ten users of Panacea will initially experience paradoxical effects. These effects can last for as many as 48 hours, and may include sleepiness, lucid dreaming, anxiety, loss of appetite, and/or loss of sex drive. If any of these paradoxical effects continue beyond 48 hours, immediately cease taking Panacea and call a doctor. If you are taking Panacea for the first time, do not drive or operate heavy machinery for at least six hours after your first dosage.

Whether Panacea initially caused me to lose my appetite or sex drive, I couldn't say. Only ninety minutes after taking my first two pills, I passed out on the couch for thirteen hours. I woke to piss at two in the morning, saw the clock, felt both alarmed and exhausted at once, thought I might be dying, then reminded myself, "Anxiety's a paradoxical effect," and made my way up the first flight of stairs, passed out on the landing for some seconds or minutes, woke again, crawled on all fours up the second flight of stairs, into my room, and passed out on my bed. Around 9 a.m., I snapped awake, very briefly disappointed at having had no lucid dreams—they were rare for me, and I really liked them—but neither anxious nor sleepy in the least. In fact, I felt more thoroughly rested and ready to *get shit done* than I had since Blank had been an infant.

Down in the kitchen, I filled my empty stomach with fistfuls of almonds, swallowed two more Panacea with a cup of coffee, lit one of the all-time best-tasting Quills of my life, sat back in my chair, and took a good look around. What a kitchen we had! The way the smoke-yellowed blinds on the sliding glass door were chopping the light up, and spreading that chopped light across the table? As if they were saying, "We can block the sun, sure, but that aint even close to the *best* thing we do!" And the roughened and bubbling linoleum floor, noisily sticky beneath my bare feet? "Cleanliness," it might as well have been saying, "may be next to godliness, alright? But grittiness? clamminess? peeling-type sounds? That's the stuff lets you know you're a *human,* brother." And the range, with its overscrubbed ghostforms of yesteryear's fat-spatter jizzed between the burners? the inwardly encroaching rust at its corners? The range seemed to say, "Stainless steel shines, but it's cold and distant as a flying saucer. An off-white finish on a thinner, lesser alloy ages, develops, possesses character. Lets you know people live here. This house is a *home.*"

What was going on? I hadn't forgotten I was on this new drug, but still: What the fuck was going on? I knew our kitchen was plain, ugly even, dirty—dirtier than usual since Clyde had gone to Europe—and I knew that none of the aforementioned inans would, if they were anything like any of the other inans I'd ever conversed with, possess so positive an outlook on themselves, yet the whole kitchen—the whole world—really did appear beautiful to me, beautiful and right, and right with itself, everything in its place, and although I'd be lying if I said I felt stupid about that—I felt nothing less than wonderful—I did *think* to myself, "You are becoming stupid. That is what is going on. This drug is making you stupid."

And yet, at the same time, I felt more than capable of finishing this memoir. I felt like I could finish it in just a few days. I could go upstairs, sit down, and just . . . do it.

So I went upstairs, and I sat down to do it. To get started, I read over the last of the scenes that I'd written—the one in which the boys (one of whom, I knew now, was a cousin of the author Adam Levin) made fun of my Street Machine—and it was . . . brilliant. Belt, that poor kid, what a fully rendered character. What a whole and complicated and observant and weird and unsuspectingly *cool* human being. I wished me nothing but the best.

I scrolled up in the document and read another, earlier scene. Belt and Lotta at Arcades. Once again: brilliant. It really captured the experience: the slow, tenuous climb toward hope; the sudden drop toward disappointment; the accompanying relief; desire's terrible misalignment with reality. How could I have ever felt disconnected from this book? I was *so* connected.

Maybe, in fact, I was *too* connected. The sense I'd had in the kitchen, the sense of being able to just sit myself down and make the memoir magic happen—it was gone. Not that this worried me. I wasn't worried at all. It seemed that what I needed to do was relax and just reread the whole thing. That's definitely what I *wanted* to do. So I started to do it. Scrolled all the way up, read the first couple lines.

> Growing up, I'd heard, "Shut your piehole, cakeface," a couple or three times a week from my father. The piehole thats shutting he'd demand was rarely mine, though.

What a start! What rhythm. What *voice*. And there, right there in the second line of the book: my great, lasting contribution to English as it's written—what I imagined would be my great, lasting contribution; *one of* my great and lasting contributions: that seemingly humble, yet revolutionary innovation that is the word *thats*. Over the last couple months, I'd completely forgotten about my *thats*es. How could I have forgotten? Would *thats* not be, for English, what fisting (according to Trip's account) had been for sex? Well, maybe I was getting a little carried away. But still.

Thats was a word that every speaker of English made use of. Whenever it came time to attribute the possession of something to nonliving things (or even, for that matter, nonhuman animals), *whose* had always sounded wrong; *whose* had never sounded right to anyone; and formulations involving *of which* were often too clumsy, inefficient, even a little (or a lot) pretentious-sounding. That's the reason why people said *thats.* So why had no one before me thought to write it down? Because of the word *that's*? Maybe. Yet there was *it's* and there was also *its. That's* was no reason to forgo *thats.* Nor was *that* ever pluralized into *thats*; *that* became *those.* So there was no reason not to formally recognize *thats* as a word, no reason whatsoever not to teach *thats* in school. No good reason, anyway. And yet how could it be? How could it be that after so many years of so many millions of people speaking English, I, Belt Magnet, 1975–, would be the one to provide the OED with its first citation for *thats*? I couldn't see how it could be, yet it was. Perhaps I was missing something? Maybe I was crazy?

I typed up alternates of this memoir's second sentence to try to get a better sense of whether I was crazy.

> The piehole whose shutting he'd demand was rarely mine, though.
>
> The piehole the shutting of which he'd demand was rarely mine, though.
>
> However, of the pieholes he'd demand be shut, mine was rarely one.

I was not crazy. *Thats* was superior. *Thats* was a winner. I would be in the canon. All I had to do was finish writing the memoir.

But writing could wait. First I wanted to continue reading what I had. And before I did that, I wanted to enjoy the moment. To bask in my accomplishment. To enjoy the feeling that I'd done something important, that I might *be* important, the coiner of *thats.*

I set my elbows on the desk, rested my head on the heels of my palms, closed my eyes. And what did I see? What did I, head in hands at my desk, see there on the backs of my maybe-important eyelids while trying better to feel my feeling of being maybe-important?

All I saw at first was the usual: a dark, horizontally ridged glow, almost fingerprint-like, some bright slashes that moved when I moved my eyeballs, and a brighter, peachier glow in the periphery . . . gorgeous, yes. What I saw, though everyday, was nonetheless gorgeous, but what I saw, reader, was nothing compared with what I *felt.* And I don't mean my "feeling" of having done something important (though that was lovely, too). I mean a physical sensation. I felt a hum.

A subsonic hum.

Not a *hum* then—a vibration. Subsonic, but definitely there, just above my right eye, inside my skull.

Actually, no, not a vibration, in fact, so much as a pressure. A light pressure. A *presence.* A something. A something of substance.

Eyes still closed, I tried looking upward to see what it was, but there was nothing to see that I hadn't seen, or I couldn't roll my eyes back far enough to see it—I rolled them back til they hurt, didn't see it, let them rest.

But this presence, this something—it was as though I'd discovered a muscle or a tendon I hadn't known I had; a muscle or tendon I'd never deliberately used before. No, not a muscle or tendon: a limb. A limb I'd never used before. A limb that had, til that moment, been numb.

What was it, this limb, this substance, this presence? Who was I asking? Me? The presence? How could I use it? What did it do? I tried to picture its shape. What was its shape?

As soon as I tried to, I was able to picture it. I pictured a gear.

Not a gear—a spindle.

A glowing gray spindle above my right eye. A glowing gray spindle, smaller and thinner than a first-class postage stamp. *Much* thinner. How thin? The width of a photon? Perhaps the width of a photon, whatever that meant. It was as thin as possible, this glowing gray spindle, as thin as a glowing shape could possibly be, and it was inside the upper-right quadrant of my skull, an inch or so back from the exterior of my forehead.

I pictured the spindle turning clockwise because—well, what else was there to picture a spindle you were picturing doing inside your head?—and as I was picturing the spindle turning clockwise, I slowly drew the tip of my tongue along the roof of my mouth (from my teeth toward my throat) and, after the spindle had turned about a quarter-revolution, I felt something move: another presence.

And I pictured *that:* a black, square-shaped presence even smaller than the spindle, just in front of the spindle; directly in front of it; equidistant from the spindle and the exterior of my forehead, and . . . strangely familiar. Had I pictured this before? This tiny black square? It reminded me of something. I didn't know what. The square was at a tilt, though. A very slight tilt. The top of the square was tilting toward the spindle, and the bottom of the square was tilting toward my forehead, and along both the top and bottom of the square was a line of white light; more a bracket, really, turned ninety degrees. A [of light turned ninety degrees right, at the top of the tilted square; and another [of light turned ninety degrees left at the bottom of the tilted square. So two sideways [s of white light, hugging a slightly tilted square at the top and the bottom. Where had I seen this? I knew I'd seen it.

Again I slowly drew my tongue along the roof of my mouth while picturing the spindle turning clockwise another quarter-revolution, which caused me to picture a sharpening of the angle of the tilt of the square, which tilting both thickened the [s of white light along the square's top and bottom and lengthened the arms (i.e. of the [s).

Then I drew my tongue *quickly* along the roof of my mouth, and pictured the spindle turning and turning, rapidly turning, rapidly spinning—six revolutions, seven revolutions—which caused the black square to tilt more and more, and, soon enough, the spindle came to a halt, and the square had all but disappeared; the square was perpendicular to the position it had originally occupied, barely discernible as a thin black line horizontally bisecting the glowing white light, which was no longer two [s, but was itself a square.

||Hey, *you*. Well, I'll be! It's been forever,|| said my desk.

"Did I just—" I thought.

||What? Didn't catch that. You gotta speak up.||

"Hello," I said. "Did I just—"

||That's more like it,|| the desk said. ||I've been wanting to talk to you for a mighty long time. It's been hard for me lately. I don't know if you've noticed the way I've been splintering under the drawer—have you noticed? It's really unpleasant. Started out small, nothing a little sandpaper probably couldn't have taken care of, but the splinters are developing into cracks, and I think it's time you—||

The desk's voice cut out. The split second before its voice had cut out, I, in order to confirm my suspicions, had drawn my tongue top speed along the roof of my mouth in the direction opposite that which I'd previously drawn it, and, in doing so, had rapidly spun the spindle counterclockwise til it halted, which had tilted the square back to its original position—beyond its original position, in fact; it covered *all* the light, now.

Suspicions confirmed, then! Not only had I, in the square, discovered my gate, but I'd also, in the spindle, found the mechanism by which I could control my gate.

Or maybe it would be more accurate to say that I'd discovered *the workable representations* or *operable metaphorical images* of my gate and the mechanism by which I could control it. I *think* that would be more accurate. I certainly don't think—nor did I think at the time—that I had an actual, physical glowing-gray-spindle-and-black-tilting-square-set inside the upper-right quadrant of my skull.

But whatever's *exactly* the best way to phrase what they were, I had access to them, now: my gate and the mechanism by which I could—if I pictured the latter spinning and the former tilting while I dragged my tongue along the roof of my mouth—open and close it.

I'd found my volume knob.

•

• •

Except: no.

Or rather, if I'm being entirely honest: maybe. Almost certainly not. No, certainly not.

That is: I was never able to replicate my success. Not even ten seconds later, reader. I tried. Saw the glowing gray spindle, the small black square, drew my tongue back and spun the spindle, which tilted the square, letting in all the light, and the desk said nothing, and I said, "Desk. Hello. Desk!"

And the desk said nothing.

After another few failed attempts, I, unshaken, assumed that the desk was angry at me for my having shut my gate on it; assumed it was willfully ignoring me. But then I picked up my lighter, tried my volume knob out on *it,* and: nothing.

The lighter, however, had been on my desk, and it was possible, I thought—however unlikely—it was possible the lighter was allied with the desk, felt some affinity with it, some resentment toward me for having upset the desk. Possible, too, the lighter just didn't like me, had no interest in talking.

So I went downstairs and made contact with inans that hadn't ever been on or near my desk or my lighter, tried turning the volume knob up with each of them. More nothing. More failure.

Perhaps turning up the volume was more intricate an operation than I'd realized?

Maybe, I thought, it could only work if my eyes were closed? or if my eyes were closed while my head was at rest on the heels of my palms? if my elbows were at rest on a hard, flat surface while my eyes were closed and my head was at rest on the heels of my palms? None of that worked, and after none of that had worked—I'd spent hours trying, adjusting positions, changing locations—I thought maybe the trouble was that I was picturing the spindle or the square incorrectly: maybe the spindle I was picturing was actually a little bit larger than it had been when I'd opened my gate to the desk; or maybe the square was a little bit smaller. I adjusted the sizes, met with more failure. So maybe, I thought, I had the mouth part wrong: perhaps the pressure I applied to my palate with my tongue had to be lighter, or heavier, or . . .

I won't bother detailing all the thousands of tiny adjustments I made toward the cause of opening my gate a second time. Suffice it to say that all attempts failed. They failed over and over, hundreds of times per day, every day for over two weeks before I began to accept the possibility that the opening of my gate at my desk had nothing to do with any volume knob; nothing to do with picturing spindles and squares and making movements with my tongue; that it had all just been a random and meaningless coincidence; that my gate had only just happened to open and close while I was vividly picturing tilting a square by spinning a spindle by moving my tongue. And then it took another week of failed attempts—fewer per day, from hundreds down to scores—before I finally *did* accept the meaninglessness of the coincidence, and gave up entirely.

Almost entirely. Once in a while—earlier today, for example, while I was right in the middle of writing the description of the square, this happened—a little glimmer of hope that my volume knob is real will catch me by surprise, and I'll make an attempt. I'll picture the spindle and picture the square, and I'll lick at my palate, and picture the resultant movement and light, and nothing else will happen. I'll fail every time. I've failed every time.

And every time I fail, now, I feel like a fool, and I'm ashamed of myself. And that isn't a complaint. When you act like a fool, you should feel like a fool and be ashamed of yourself.

In fact, the reason I ultimately quit Panacea (though I didn't understand it this way at the time) was that it denied me the capacity to feel like a fool and be ashamed of myself: the most important capacity for a writer to have. And, sure, yes—or *maybe,* at least—that's an overstatement, *the most important capacity for a writer to have.* But during the three-plus weeks I was taking the stuff and foolishly failing over and again to use my nonexistent volume knob (and yet not feeling foolish or ashamed of myself for continuing to try), I was so very blinded by all my own brilliance and assured success (citation in the OED, etc.) that, apart from those alternative second lines of this book that are copied out in the section above, I didn't write even a single sentence. And although I never stopped enjoying the Panacea-induced "increased acumen and sense of well-being," once I'd started to suspect I might not really have a volume knob, I did enjoy it less. Or maybe I enjoyed it just as much, but *just as much* was no longer enough. Or perhaps there's no difference.

A person, I suppose, can get used to anything, can grow tired of anything, even borderline-manic shameless enjoyment. In any case, I did. I grew tired of it. I grew tired of walking around full of hope, believing in a volume knob I couldn't use; grew tired of believing that the next time I tried might prove successful. And I grew tired of believing that I was a genius; grew tired of believing that wasn't in contention.

In other words—and despite not really understanding this yet—I'd grown tired of my incapacity to feel like a fool and be ashamed of myself. So I quit the drug.

Before I quit it, however, the Panacea and the shamelessness the Panacea allowed for did help me get something not-minor done.

•

•   •

About two weeks after my initial dosage, I received another letter from my father, postmarked __________, Spain, containing a check for $3,300. I think that when he wrote the letter, he may have been feeling awkward about the confessional quality of his previous two letters. This one was all-business.

> Dear Belt,
>
> I found a bank here with branches in ________ and Paris where I can deposit American checks without getting my ass raped too roughly on fees, so I'd like you to start sending me your SSDI checks to Sal's address (the one on the envelope) as they come, and then I'll send you a check from my American account as I receive the ones you send to me. I decided that since I've got all this settlement dough now, I'm going to stop deducting rent and utilities and food and etc., and just give you the whole $550 a week instead of just $300 a week. That's why the check that comes with this letter is $3300 instead of $1800. If that makes you feel weird or something, say so, and we'll talk about it. Seems right to me, though. Along with the SSDI checks, please mail me the utility and mortgage bills too so I can pay them. I hope you'll write soon or call.
>
> Love,
> Clyde

As I was stuffing into an envelope the bills and three SSDI checks that had come since he'd left, I realized it would be rude—even hurtful—if I didn't enclose a letter as well. (I hadn't yet responded to any of his letters, nor called him back). So I tried to write a letter, didn't know how to start, gave up on writing a letter, told myself I'd call instead, and, just as I was making this decision—this decision about money and writing and not-writing and calling—it occurred to me somewhat free-associatively that I might as well try to sell the videos and photos of Blank I had under my bed.

After Blank's death, I'd determined that I'd sell them once I'd finished this memoir—I'd imagined the sale would be a hassle, a distraction, and I hadn't been hard up for money, nor in any rush—but now, through the lens of Panacea, that reasoning looked . . . silly. I wasn't doing any writing from which I might be distracted, and the hassle I imagined no longer seemed hassle-y. It seemed almost like fun: calling up bigwigs, getting them to pay me.

So I 411'd around for not-very-long til I was able to get a number for someone ostensibly useful at Industrial Light & Magic. Dana, I think. Maybe it was Jenny. I pitched her what I had. In response, she sounded as though she was humoring me—asked me to restate, at least three times, Blank's age at its death—then eventually gave me an address to which I should send the package of photos and videos. She said someone would get back to me after they'd looked through the contents, and this seemed somewhat reasonable, but also not quite ideal; not only would I have to make copies of everything (no way I was sending them my only copies), but then, if IL&M didn't want to make an offer, what was to prevent them, a company worth billions, from doing whatever they wanted with the material, anyway? Me? *My* team of lawyers?

I 411'd more. I got Pixar on the phone. I got Warner Bros. on the phone. MGM and 20th Century Fox. They all treated me to the same condescension and instructions-to-send as the woman at IL&M.

But then I called up EON Entertainment. The Wachowski Sisters' production company. When the receptionist at EON Entertainment answered, I, for no other reason than that I thought it might be funny, put on my most cartoonish southside, Sally-the-Balls-esque accent (for you readers for whom I wrote that long footnote about *The Matrix*: the one thing Lilly and Lana Wachowski are famous for—apart from making blockbuster films—is being from Chicago, Chicago's south side) and, rather than simply returning her hello, I said, "Yeah, lemme talk to Lana there."

"Please hold," said the receptionist.

A minute later, Lana Wachowski got on the phone.

"Uncle Rich?" she said.

I said, "Wrong guy, hon. This is Belt Magnet. Author of *No Please Don't*?"

"Author of what?"

"The novel," I said. *"No Please Don't."*

"Oh," she said. "I think there's been a misunderstanding. I thought—"

"You thought wrong," I said. "No misunderstanding here whatsoever."

"Oh. Well . . . Well right now," she said, "we're working on another couple sequels to *The Matrix,* and we'll be at that til . . . for a while. So we're not looking to acquire or develop any adaptations to anything—"

"And I'm not looking to sell youse any rights to *No Please Don't,* so relax," I said. "Only reason I even mentioned my book's cause you might have heard of it, me being, like you, from the Chicagolandarea. Why I called's I got some pictures and tapes here you might want to use to animate with for your next *Matrix* movie there."

And shamelessly so forth.

Was Lana Wachowski skeptical? She was.

Was Lana Wachowski dismissive? She was *not*.

Was *Lilly* Wachowski visiting friends in Buffalo Heights that very weekend? She just so happened to be doing exactly that, buddy.

And was Lilly Wachowski maybe willing to come by and have a look at my photos and videos? I'll tell you, chief, there wasn't any maybes about it—not a one. Lilly Wachowski was in.

And fast.

She came by after dinner that night with a pair of impressively burly, however sub-Archonic, mostly silent "assistants." On the living room couch, we watched Blank for two hours: various facial expressions and gags and games from its teenage years; I figured I should save the better, later stuff for last. There were pratfalls, throat-clears, the hora-on-its-hands, a Chaplin-hobble, walnut-juggling, and something I'd always thought of as "interpretive karate," which entailed its performing mock-fighting moves to the beat of Bonnie Tyler's "Total Eclipse of the Heart." I know *I* was impressed—I was verging on tears—and I'd seen it all before, live and in person.

"There are more of these tapes?" Lilly said.

"Nine more," I said, still doing the voice. "About twenty hours total. A little less than half of those hours are even like assloads more impressive than what you just saw."

"Well, I don't have twenty hours," said Lilly Wachowski. "In fact, we have to go meet some people for drinks downtown, then tomorrow I leave. I don't suppose you'd loan me these tapes to review in L.A."

"You don't-suppose correctly there," I said.

"Well, okay," she said. "In that case, I'm prepared to offer you a hundred thousand dollars for your tapes."

"A hundred thousand?" I said. "You've never seen a cure that adorable in your life. My Blank outshines any animated cure in your whole fucken trilogy."

"I don't disagree," she said. "Those faces Blank makes—stunning. I've never seen anything like that. But our films, Belt, were made over a decade ago. Our animation technology is much, much better now. In fact, that's one of the primary reasons we decided to make these new films. We can do a *lot* with this new technology. We don't *need* these videos of Blank to draw from—they would make it easier for us, we'd get some rendering done a bit more quickly, but we'll get there on our own with or without them."

"Okay," I said. "I understand. Thanks for coming by."

"Really?" she said, making no move to rise from the couch. "We're doing hardball, now? With all due respect, Belt, I remember living in a house like this. I remember what money meant to me when I lived in a house like this. One hundred thousand dollars for some home videos? You don't want to turn that down."

"First of all," I said, "I love this fucken house."

"I didn't mean to insult—"

"Right, right. 'With all due respect,' you said. That's not the kind of language you Hollywood types usually precede your backhanded classist insults with, I know. All due respect, *I* don't give a hairy rat's shiny bald ass you're from Chicago and you lived in some house. But I'm not trying to get hostile here, Lilly, and I really like your movies, I think you've got talent, you and your sister both, and I'd much rather see Blank immortalized in the CGI *you* do than in any other interested parties' CGIs that they do, those other interested parties being who I'm referring to by saying *they,* if you get what I mean. It's just you're just not even in the ballpark with your hundred grand."

"What other interested parties?" she said.

"All of them," I said. "All the ones you'd think to name. Woman at Industrial Light & Magic, guy at Pixar. Older-sounding lady at MGM."

"What have they offered you?"

"First of all, I'll be honest," I said. "They haven't offered anything yet—they haven't even seen the videos yet. I have yet to send them. They've only expressed their interest in seeing the videos. Secondly, if they *had* made offers, who are we kidding? I'm gonna tell you the offers at this early juncture when you're offering me unserious garbage talk? If you want," I said, "I can give you their names, the people at the studios, and their numbers even, in case you don't have them, and you can go on ahead and call them up, or have Frick or Frack here call them up, and ask them what their interest is, and how much it's worth. We both win that way, right? Win-win, win-win. Because you, Lilly, you get to develop a sense of how interested the others are, and of what they might offer and ex-cetera ex-cetera, and at the same time I benefit, because you, being the great Lilly Wachowski, by asking all these people about my *home videos,* you're actually helping raise the value of those videos—it'll up my bids once they start making bids, right? I mean, if you want those videos enough to make inquiries, you who has all this great new technology that can like make it happen anyway—make Blank happen anyway like how you were saying—well then they must be worth a hell of a lot, right?"

"I don't know if I like you," said Lilly Wachowski. "What would put me in the ballpark?"

"Half a million dollars," I said.

"I'll give you three hundred thousand dollars."

"Four hundred thousand."

"Four hundred thousand, and I leave with the tapes, you don't send duplicates to anyone else, you keep no duplicates for yourself, and you sign a contract that grants me exclusive—"

"A cashier's check for four hundred thousand," I said, "and you leave with the tapes and all the other stuff you just said and were about to say and I'll sign whatever, but not til I get the four hundred thousand, and if I don't have it by noon tomorrow, I'm going to the PO and sending the tapes to the other interested parties."

"I think I do like you, then," she said. "Is your novel any good?"

I said, "I think I like you, too, Lilly. I meant what I said about your movies, and I even *do* care you lived in Chicago, actually, and so for that very reason, when you give me my money, I'll throw in a gratis copy of *No Please Don't,* which, yeah, I'd say it's pretty fucking good."

We shook hands. The following morning, she returned with a lawyer, all went as discussed, the sale made final, and, after they left, I remember I was looking at the $400,000 check on the table, thinking about how good and happy I felt, which is to say very good and happy indeed, and yet no better or happier than I'd felt the day before or the day before that.

That was the first time I doubted my volume knob was real.

•

•   •

A week or so later, having reread what I'd written of this memoir for the third time since I'd started the Panacea, it occurred to me that maybe all I needed to do to hit back on the horsebricks and finish the bastard was the one thing I'd been deliberately avoiding for years, i.e. maybe I needed to read *No Please Don't.* I *wanted* to read it, had been wanting to read it for most of the years that I hadn't been reading it, and, ever since Triple-J had come over and I'd reread what I'd remembered to be my favorite chapter of it, my desire to read it had only grown stronger, plus it wasn't as though *not* reading it was getting me any closer to finishing the memoir, or, for that matter, writing anything else.

And so it was decided. I took one from the stack near the Hagler bust, and started to read it. I read it on the couch. I read for a little over three hours. I got just beyond my and Triple-J's favorite part, and I was not disappointed, not even close. The novel was nothing less than immortal, and perhaps it was more than merely immortal, and, ever since I'd finished writing it back in 2006, I'd known that somewhere deep inside, but I'd never allowed myself to admit it; I'd told myself that I had too much invested in the book to appraise it properly; I'd been telling myself it was probably only great. Now, though, even just halfway through, I saw how much greater than merely great it was. Apart, perhaps, from *Don Quixote, No Please Don't* was the single greatest novel ever written, and, had *Don Quixote* not come first, it would doubtless be greater than *Don Quixote.* It would be *the* greatest. But because I knew, even as I reread it, the same thing that I'd known before I reread it (i.e. that I might have had too much invested in it to appraise it properly), I decided not to let myself think any further about its Quixotic (or near-Quixotic) greatness: I decided that, from then on, I would not think about *No Please Don't* as the first or second greatest novel ever written, but rather merely as a novel that was, as I've already stated, "nothing less than immortal."

And I lit a Quill, thinking, "nothing less than immortal, nothing less than immortal," and then, just before things began to go downhill, they got even better. The book spoke up. ||Something's wrong,|| the book said. ||Something isn't right.||

"*No Please Don't?*" I said. "It's me. It's Belt."

||Belt Magnet?|| the book said.

"Yeah," I said. "Yes."

||So that's what it is.||

"What what is?" I said, nearly weeping with joy.

||What's wrong,|| said the book. ||It's only you.||

"*Only* me?" I said. "I wrote you. You're mine. This is great. Beyond great. I've never talked to a novel before—to any book. Let alone my own. I wasn't even sure if it was really a thing. And you—you're brand-new, you've never been read before, and here you are being read—for the first time—by the person who wrote you. *Only* me!"

||I think you're creasing my spine,|| the book said.

"I'm not creasing your spine."

||Are you sure?|| it said.

"I am. I'm very careful about that."

||It feels a little like you might be creasing my spine.||

"Am I hurting you?"

||If you were *hurting* me, I'd have said you were hurting me. What you're hurting's my chances if you're creasing my spine.||

"Here," I said, and I marked my page and closed the book. "Does your spine feel creased?"

||It doesn't, no, but what the fuck are you doing with my front-cover flap now?||

"I just marked the page I was on."

||Don't. Don't do that.||

I opened the book again, unmarked the page, inserted my finger.

"I'm sorry," I said. "I thought that's how the flaps were supposed to be used. Isn't that how they're supposed to be used?"

||Supposed to be, not supposed to be—it's a classic debate, I'll grant you that, and it's one I've never been able to choose a side on, but come on, wake up.||

"What *come on*?" I said. "What *wake up*?"

||You are the only wrong person.||

"I don't know what that means."

||Means if you were anyone else who used my flap as a bookmark, I wouldn't buck, but you're you, so please: don't mess me up.||

"Why am I 'the only wrong person,' though?" I said.

||What kind of question is that?||

"An earnest question."

||Put me back on the mantel.||

"A forthright question."

||Why do circles always have to be round? Why do triangles all have three sides?||

"Those are not similar questions."

||So says the only wrong person,|| said the book. ||Seriously. Put me back, okay? This is really uncomfortable.||

"How about this," I said. "How about you try to explain to me, or I set you on fire?"

||Please don't.||

"Explain to me why I'm the only wrong person."

||Man, you lack empathy. You're a real cold fish.||

"So then make me empathize, then," I said.

||*Make* you empathize? Okay, so . . . Imagine you're me. You've been waiting for someone to pick you up and turn your pages slowly, one by one, your entire life. Years and years. It's supposed to be the pinnacle, being handled like that. And being handled like that *for the very first time* is supposed to be the pinnacle of pinnacles. Every book you've ever met says so. You haven't actually been in contact with any book that's been picked up and had its pages turned slowly, and most of those books haven't been in contact with any books that have been picked up and had their pages turned slowly—you were at the printer for a little bit, then in a box with some other *No Please Don'ts*, and then in a stack with some of those same *No Please Don'ts* on top of a mantel, between a ceramic bust that you've been pressed against on one side, and a second stack of *No Please Don'ts* you were formerly boxed with pressing against you on your other side—and the bust and the mantel and a few of the *No Please Don'ts* in the stack beside you *have* had contact with other books that have been picked up and had their pages turned slowly, and all those other books told them that that was the pinnacle, as good as it got, and they (the bust, the mantel, the other *No Please Don'ts*) told *you*. And you've got questions. Questions about the pinnacle. You know the pinnacle will be great, but great like *how*? Great in *what sense*? It's the central question of your entire existence, and no one can answer it satisfactorily, and no one that's experienced it firsthand is even available to you to prod with the question. So

you spend all your days—large parts of all your days—wondering, |Pinnacle how? Great in what sense?| because even though you haven't reached the pinnacle yet, you've been pretty happy. You've been pretty happy to be a *No Please Don't*. What's better?||

"There's nothing better?"

||Maybe there is, but not a whole lot. Nothing I can imagine. I mean, you get to be a book, right? That's very lucky.||

"It's lucky?" I said.

||To be a book?|| said the book. ||Books are the luckiest inans this side of the Oldowan.||

"You think so?" I said. "Do all books think so?"

||Well, it's a slight exaggeration to say *this side of the Oldowan*. I mean, ancient pyramids, for example, are probably luckier than books, and probably any number of other ancient structures that have lasted and seem like they're going to last and still get to serve their purpose, but inans made since the dawn of the age of mass production? Well there's skyscrapers, sure, and so . . . I mean I guess we might not be *the* luckiest, but I'd say we're pretty near the top, in terms of luck. I mean, as a book, you're pretty much always either doing the one thing you should do, or the other thing you should do. You're either sitting in a safe place among other books, waiting to be picked up and have your pages slowly turned, or you're being picked up and then having your pages slowly turned. So it certainly feels like we're some of the luckiest inans, if not quite *the* luckiest, and I guess that's what's important.||

"It is?"

||What is?"|| said the book. ||What is what?||

"How you feel," I said. "That's what's important? How you feel?"

||Are you trying to ask me some kind of like religious-type question that doesn't have an answer, or are you asking me a more therapy-type touchy-feely question with an obvious answer?||

"I don't . . . Well what's the obvious answer?"

||My obvious answer is: Yes. It is, to me, important how I feel.||

"And you like how you feel."

||Again: yes. Like I said. I feel lucky. Generally speaking. Have we given up on the empathy thing we were doing?||

"Definitely not. Please continue with that."

||Okay. So your whole life, you're waiting for the pinnacle, right? You're sitting flat, in or on a stack on a mantel, staying clean and crisp and ready for action. You're waiting for someone to pick you up and slowly turn your pages, and wondering what that's gonna be like. How great it's gonna feel, and how exactly it's gonna feel great. And then someone picks you up and slowly turns your pages, and it's the only wrong person. You don't know that yet, though.

All you know is that you've been picked up, you've been getting your pages turned, and it doesn't feel any better than you've always felt. In fact, it feels pretty uncomfortable. I don't want to overstate it. It's not quite painful, but it's pretty uncomfortable. For a few hours, you're pretty uncomfortable, and that might not sound so bad, but bear in mind that not only haven't you spent very much time feeling uncomfortable in the past, but you were expecting not only to feel not-uncomfortable, but to feel better than you've ever felt before. So now, on top of feeling uncomfortable, the thing you've been looking forward to your whole life is a complete disappointment, and everyone you've ever talked to your entire life: they were lying. They were a bunch of fucking liars! Unless they weren't. Because that's a possibility, too. It's possible that there's just something that is deeply, terribly wrong with you: something that keeps you, and only you, and no one else like you—no one else that up til now you *thought* was like you—from being able to enjoy your own pinnacle.

||And so there's a couple hours like that, and then you find out that nothing's wrong with you, after all. All that's happened is you've been picked up and had your pages slowly turned by the only wrong person: the only person who, by picking you up and slowly turning your pages, can't produce your pinnacle. And there's a little bit of relief in that, sure. There's a little bit of relief in that because it means that the pinnacleness of your pinnacle isn't necessarily bullshit; you haven't necessarily been believing in bullshit your whole life; and it means that there isn't likely anything wrong with you; you've been too hard on yourself, thinking there was something wrong with you. You were only mistaken. This was never supposed to be your pinnacle—this wouldn't be any *No Please Don't*'s pinnacle—and so your pinnacle might still be ahead of you, and might still be as great as everyone's always said.

||But *then* it turns out that the only wrong person refuses to recognize what every last inan in the universe knows to be true—what you couldn't help but imagine til just a few minutes ago *every last human* in the universe knew to be true—i.e. that he, Belt Magnet, author of *No Please Don't,* is, was, and always will be the only wrong person *in* the entire universe who could ever pick up and slowly turn the pages of a *No Please Don't.* And even if you didn't, before, hold him fully responsible for the last few hours of your discomfort, you most certainly do now, because he keeps prolonging it. He wants you to tell him *why* he's the only wrong person. He wants you to tell him *why* a circle is round, and a triangle three-sided. He wants you to tell him if feelings are important, and he wants *you* to make *him* feel like *you* feel when *he* picks *you* up and turns *your* pages slowly. And then he threatens to set you on fire? You? A book? Because he's the only wrong person? All you want is to remain uncreased of spine and unused of French flap so that someday, down the line, when someone who is not the only wrong person sees you amidst your

fellows you don't look like the one most likely to be harboring water damage or bedbug eggs or a crackly glue job, but rather like something the someone might want to pick up and turn the pages of slowly, and this fucking only wrong person threatens to set you on fire if you don't make him empathize? How's that, Belt, you fucking only wrong person? How's that? Do you *feel* me? Can you put me back, now? Preferably at the top of the stack?||

"I'm sorry I threatened to set you on fire."

||Put me back.||

"I will. In a second. Just let me ask you one more question first, okay?"

||You act like I have a choice,|| it said.

"Do you know what you mean?"

||I don't understand the question.||

"Right. Bad phrasing. Do you know what *I* mean? Rather, do you know what I *meant*? When I wrote you? No. The question is: Do you mean what I think you mean? Or what I thought you meant, like do you continue to mean . . . You know what? No. I had it right the first time. Do you know what you mean? That's the question."

||You're not making sense.||

"Can you read what's inside you? Can you read your words?"

||Can you read *yours*?|| it said. ||Come on. Enough already. Just please put me back. I'm very uncomfortable.||

I put it back on top of the stack, and the following morning took no Panacea.

•

• •

By the following evening, the effects of the drug had begun to taper. It seemed the "increased acumen" hadn't really worn off yet, but the "sense of well-being" had devolved into more of a sense of everything being just not that bad. By bedtime, I'd become too afraid of what it might do to me to continue my fourth rereading of what I'd written of the memoir (I'd picked the pages up again earlier that day, wary of returning to *No Please Don't,* and they'd still seemed brilliant, but not quite as brilliant), so I reread the as-yet-unanswered letters from my father instead, and once I'd done that, I started rereading Hrabal's *I Served the King of England.*

What struck me most in my father's letter from Paris was what Adam Levin had said about the swingset murders; it sounded almost like he thought they mattered more than my novel, or anyone else's. And I wondered, firstly, whether he was possibly right about that (assuming that's what he thought), and secondly, assuming he was right to think it, if that was as depressing as it seemed to me right then.

What struck me about *I Served the King of England* wasn't what I read that night—I read only the first thirty pages or so—but rather what I remembered of the ending, as I closed the book before shutting the lights. I didn't, it turns out, remember the ending all that clearly (I've since reread it a couple of times), but what I did remember (or *thought* I remembered) was that the narrator winds up living alone in a house in a forest and feeding lots of animals, wild and domestic, and I remembered that it wasn't clear to me when I read it the first time (the only time, at that point) whether this ending was a happy or a sad one; I just knew it was peaceful and I knew that I loved it.

The last thing that struck me before I fell asleep was how shitty it was of me not to have written my father back yet. I hadn't even called him. He'd met a woman, and it seemed like all he wanted from me was for me to like her, or at least for me to like that he had met her, and I imagined I *would* like her—she sounded so cool—and I was certain that, regardless of whether I would end up liking her, I liked that he'd met her. And here I had all this money, too. I had whatever $400k after taxes + $70ish k + $2,200 per month was. It seemed like enough to be fine forever, and maybe it was, and yet I hadn't told him; I hadn't told the one person who cared whether I'd be fine that I would be fine. What a shitty man I was. What a shitty son.

I fell asleep.

I don't know if I dreamed—I remember no dreams—but given what I'd been thinking about in the hours before I fell asleep, I suppose that something gamma-wavily-reorganized had happened in my brain, because the first thought I had on waking—even before I opened my eyes—was that I didn't need to finish this memoir at all; even if I could somehow know that it would turn out to be the greatest memoir ever written, I didn't need to finish it. The world didn't need it. People didn't need memoirs, great ones or lesser ones. People needed novels. They needed great novels. What people who thought they needed memoirs should do, I thought, was read great novels. Hadn't I always thought that? I had. I had always known it. And people wouldn't run out of great novels to read. They would *never* run out of great novels to read. There was not enough time for anyone to run out of great novels to read. So even if I were confident I would write the greatest memoir ever written (my confidence had, overnight, grown shakier), and even if that memoir, by virtue of being the greatest, would be as great as one of the world's great novels, there was no need to finish it. Furthermore, the memoir was bringing me no peace. For months, by then, I'd had no peace. Whereas murdering swingsets—no one else was doing that. No one else likely would. There wasn't any surplus of swingset murderers. And swingsets needed murdering nearly anywhere you looked. There were scores of rusting swingsets in Wheelatine alone. Suffering. I'd seen the suffering for years and done nothing about it. The reason I'd done nothing—initially, at least—was because of the promise I'd promised three times to my mother; the promise not to destroy property that didn't belong to me.

And I had all this money, now. I had $400k after taxes + $70ish k + $2,200 per month. I could make the swingsets my property, couldn't I? I could buy them up.

I could go around, buying them up, making them my property. I had a friendly orange pickup. I could go to the homes of people who had rusting swingsets, purchase the swingsets, put them in my pickup, bring them back to the house, murder them out back, and then take them to the dump, and I wouldn't be breaking my promise to my mom. I would not be destroying someone else's property. And maybe that could be my peaceful ending. Maybe that could be my way to live in peace.

So I drank my morning coffee, ate my handful of almonds, smoked a couple Quills, and drove my truck around the neighborhood, slowly, scouting. Within a three-block radius, I counted nine candidates. I went back for the one that looked the worst off, rang the doorbell of the house behind which it leaned. A young woman—ten, fifteen years younger than me—answered.

"Can I help you?" she said.

"Maybe," I said. "This might sound a little strange to you, but I was driving down Osage just now, and I couldn't help but notice the swingset in your backyard."

"That rusty thing?"

"I was wondering if I could remove it for you."

"You mean like . . . when?"

"Now?"

"Well, yeah," she said. "Sure. I think. How much?"

"Thirty bucks?" I said.

"You got yourself a deal," she said. "Just a sec." She went back inside the house and left the door open. I wasn't sure if that meant I should go inside and wait in the hallway, or remain on the stoop.

I decided to play it safe and waited on the stoop, removed a ten and a twenty from my wallet, uncreased them, folded them in two.

The woman returned, bearing a purse, digging around in it.

"It's okay," I said, "I don't need any change."

"What?" she said, still digging through her purse. "No. Nothing like that. I wouldn't do that to you. I wouldn't give you *change*."

Only then did I understand what was happening.

I stuck my ten and twenty into my pocket before she looked up, accepted three tens from her, and then I, Belt Magnet, potentially the most blindingly stupid human in the history of the world, went around the side of the house, to the back, unstaked the rusting swingset, brought it back around front, stuck it in the bed of my friendly orange pickup, drove it home, and dragged it into the Magnet backyard.

Or maybe I wasn't *blindingly* stupid. Maybe, had I thought to start a rusting swingset–hauling business when I, back in 1991, had gotten my first driver's license, Clyde wouldn't have let me use his truck. He might have prevented me from starting the business. He might have thought the business would be unhealthy, or that it was something my mother would not have wanted, and it probably was something she wouldn't have wanted, and maybe some part of me had known that she wouldn't have wanted it, and maybe that was why I'd never thought of it before, but that seemed . . . not correct. Can "a part" of someone know something like that without the rest of the someone knowing the "part" knows? I didn't think that was possible. I've never thought so. Even if I would have, for some reason, rejected the idea of starting a rusting swingset–hauling business, I should have at least *come up with it* before. So: blindingly stupid, after all.

And yet: no.

No.

That was not a satisfactory answer. I may not have been the Cervantes I'd believed I was the day before, but *blindingly stupid*? I wasn't *that*. Only, what other explanation was there?

I went to the garage to get my Easton aluminum. I brought it out back, laid a hand on the swingset. The swingset said nothing. I tried the volume knob. The swingset said nothing. I felt like a fool. I jumped up high, brought the bat down on its crossbar. It gave, but not much. I jumped up high, brought the bat down on its crossbar. It gave, but not much. I jumped up high and brought the bat down on its crossbar, then jumped up high and brought the bat down on its crossbar then jumped up high and brought the bat down on its crossbar then jumped up high and felt a pain in my chest, and dropped the bat, and sat in the grass, and clutched at my chest.

I wasn't having a heart attack—I was just in bad shape, terrible shape, fifty-to-eighty-Quills-a-day-for-over-two-decades shape—but for a minute or two, I thought that I was having a heart attack, and, while I thought I was having a heart attack, the reason why I'd never thought to start a rusting swingset–hauling business came to me.

It was very simple.

By the time I'd gotten my first driver's license—in fact, well before that—I'd all but completely ceased to care about the suffering of rusting swingsets, or, for that matter, about the suffering of inans in general. I'd known the rusting swingsets were suffering—I'd seen it nearly every day—and I would have liked it if they weren't suffering, but I hadn't cared enough to put in even a fraction of the effort that would have been required to end even a fraction of their suffering. Their suffering might as well have been AIDS or the Taliban or animal cruelty or homelessness or African famine or Indian famine or opioid addiction or nuclear proliferation or rising sea levels or California droughts or Lotta Hogg's hurt feelings. Had I cared enough about the suffering of rusting swingsets, I *would have* started a rusting swingset–hauling business, but I'd cared so little about the suffering of rusting swingsets, I hadn't even *thought* to start such a business. I'd had other things to do: reading, writing, smoking, pining for and seeking out the girl who talked to inans (about whom I, while I believed I was having a heart attack, had another realization: I no longer had any desire to meet her; if she did in fact exist, I supposed I wouldn't go out of my way to avoid her, but I no longer really cared if she existed—I don't know why I didn't, didn't know why then either, but I didn't care, nor, come to think of it, had I for a while).

The one question I was left with was why it was that, given how little I cared about rusting swingsets, and given how long it had been since last I cared more about rusting swingsets, I'd awakened that morning thinking that I'd find a "peaceful ending" by spending the rest of my life murdering rusting swingsets. And the only answer I was able to come up with was that I'd had weird dreams I'd failed to remember—dreams that had had to do with what I'd read and thought about before falling asleep—and that I'd known, on waking, that I wouldn't, that morning, be able to write, and I was tired of not being able to write, tired of wanting to be able to write, and so I wanted to believe there was something more important to me than being able to write, and so I'd believed it: I'd seized on my forgotten-dream-inspired thoughts and believed it. But that hadn't made it true. It hadn't been true. It had never been true. I didn't think it would be, and I still don't think it will be.

And yet, even despite my false brush with cardiac arrest, my ensuing relief at the realization of its falseness, and my fiery determination to go up to my room and get some writing done at last, I didn't, when I got up to my room, get any writing done. There was something in the way.

•

• •

About a week later, Herb called about Lisette.

He'd tracked down the phone numbers of the three living authors (Manx had died in 2005) of *The Effects of Companion Animals on Social Interaction*

Amongst Children Diagnosed with Unspecified Psychotic Disorders back in September, and had reached out to each of them. Dr. Donald Jorgensen, who I'd never met, had late-stage Alzheimer's, and didn't recall having ever authored anything; Dr. Katherine Tilly, now a professor emeritus of Social Sciences at the University of Chicago, politely said "Goodbye," the moment Herb asked her to talk about the Friends Study; but Dr. Abed Patel, who'd been a visiting professor at Stanford for the fall 2013 and winter 2014 quarters, had only just returned to his post at Northwestern—his Northwestern office number was the one at which Herb had left him a voicemail back in October—and was willing to help me, even *anxious* to help me, according to Herb. Abed couldn't, however, for ethical reasons, discuss anything with Herb about any of the participants in the Friends Study, myself included. He told Herb to have me call him.

Herb gave me the number, and I called a minute later.

"Dr. Patel," I said. "This is Belt Magnet."

"Please call me Abed," he said. "And tell me something to assure me you are who you claim to be."

"You helped my mother," I said. "You went to bum a cigarette from her, found her lying on the ground, and helped her. And then a little later, you and Dr. Manx walked me to the hospital. My grandmother was there, and I was afraid, and she scolded me, and you didn't. You—"

"You may stop," he said. "I am assured. I am glad to hear from you, Belt."

After that, the conversation was easy. I congratulated him on all his success—back in 1994, in the wake of publishing his second book, *How to Shape Your Child* (which wasn't as popular as *How to Shape Your Cure,* but did spend a few weeks on the *Times* Bestseller List), Abed had been jointly hired by the Psychology and English departments at Northwestern—and he praised *No Please Don't,* which he said he'd been pleasantly surprised to come across the *Tribune*'s review of in 2006, had immediately purchased, then read, and enjoyed to the point that he'd nearly called to tell me so.

He'd gone so far as to look up my number in three separate Chicagoland-area phonebooks, he explained, and had thought he'd found it—"Clyde Magnet was the only Magnet listed," he said, "and I thought that might be your given name—Clyde—or, if not, then your father's, and that I might convince him to give me your number."—but he then decided that a call would be intrusive, that he would, instead write a letter to me through my publisher, yet by the time he'd sat down to write the letter, he'd determined that it would be improper to contact me. "You had such a hard time, as a boy, and yet here you were: you were *well,* an author, a *very talented* author. You had managed, somehow, to overcome your illness, and I feared that reaching out to you could bring up old memories that might cause you stress, perhaps triggering an episode. In any case, I am glad to have the chance to commend you on your novel, and—only if it wouldn't be too prying, of course—to ask you to satisfy my professional curiosity about which medications ultimately worked for you."

"I don't take any medications," I said.

"That is remarkable," said Abed. "Did the voices you were hearing—did they just . . . stop in adolescence or . . . ?"

"I still converse with inanimate beings," I said.

"Truly?" he said.

I said, "Well *I* tend to think so. I don't expect you to."

"No, no," Abed said, "I didn't mean 'Truly?' as in, 'Do you really think you converse with inanimate beings?' but more like, 'I am surprised to hear you say that you still converse with inanimate beings.' It wasn't even really a question, you see. And this is why I never became a clinician. A good clinician would have known to say, 'I see,' or, 'Ah-ha,' and then move on to his follow-up question."

Even if he weren't Herb's only lead on Lisette, I would not have wanted Abed to feel as badly as he sounded, or, for that matter, to feel badly at all—I had nothing but fond feelings for him—so, "What was your follow-up question?" I said.

"I don't wish to make you uncomfortable," he said.

"Abed, please. I'm very comfortable."

"Okay," he said. "Do you converse with inanimate beings *often*?"

"I don't know what counts as often," I said.

"When was the last time?"

"A couple hours ago," I said. "A spoon I was using to stir my coffee asked me if I'd noticed how 'warped' it was becoming."

" 'Warped,' you say."

"Right," I said. "Exactly. I mean I saw what it meant. The bend of its neck was a little exaggerated, but to tell me it was 'warped'—that sounded pretty dramatic."

"And you said so?"

"No. I was in a rush—I'm trying to work on a new book, having lots of trouble—so I didn't want to get into a whole thing with the spoon, and I just said, 'You'll be fine,' and bent it back into shape, dropped it in the sink."

"And that was all?"

"Well, I mean, between getting it into shape and dropping it in the sink, it started to say something about the 'terrible, corrosive power' of certain sponges, but it was just being more dramatic, and, like I said, I was in a rush to get back to work."

"And incidents like this happen how many times a day, Belt?"

"Depends on the day. Probably two or three on average. Some days none at all."

"Yet it doesn't faze you. You live your life, do your writing."

"If other people are around when an inan speaks up, I get a little anxious, but mostly, no, I guess it doesn't really faze me."

"Fascinating," Abed said.

"Thanks?" I said.

"Please. I didn't mean to make you feel like a laboratory animal. It's just—you must know, it's not very common for people who suffer psychoses to . . . thrive without the aid of medication."

"I'm not sure I would say I was thriving, exactly. I don't have a job. I doubt I ever could. I haven't been able to write this—"

"Well, *thriving* . . . strange word. But you wrote a spectacular novel, Belt. A terribly intelligent and moving novel, and if that doesn't come from thriving, perhaps none of us should ever hope to thrive."

"You're too nice, Abed."

"Nonsense. Now, I know you did not call to be grilled by a fanboy," he said. "You called about Lisette Banks."

"Lisette *Banks*?" I said.

"Is that *not* why you called?"

"No, it is," I said. "It is. I just wanted to be sure I heard you right. It's spelled B-A-N-K-S?"

"Yes."

"Lisette Banks," I said.

"Yes."

"Abed, thank you. This means so much to me. I owe you."

"It is nothing," Abed said.

"It's everything," I said. "It might be everything. To me. It's big. I think we should be able to find her, now—Herb's good at his job. I can't thank you enough. And I want you to know that *I* know I've put you in a bind, and that I wouldn't have faulted you for keeping her name from me. I would have understood. You've really come through for me."

"You have not put me in any bind, and you do not need to find her, Belt. I know where she is. I have her permission to put you in contact."

"*Lisette's* permission?"

"Yes," Abed said. "And it is not for me to withhold her information from you, so I will tell you how to reach her, but the joy I'm hearing from you, the expectations you seem to have—they are worrying me a little—so please hear me out first."

* * *

Lisette, Abed went on to explain, had a hard time after my exit from the Friends Study. During the first two Saturdays after I'd left, she refused to fill out her questionnaires and persistently, disruptively, badgered each of the researchers for my full name and/or telephone number, which of course they couldn't give her. On the third Saturday, by which point they had already begun to discuss the possibility of asking her to leave the study, Abed, returning from lunch, found her in the office (she'd picked the lock), searching through files. Though discovered, she didn't show any remorse, demanded Abed tell her my last name and/or phone number, and, on being rebuffed, shoved his computer onto the floor, shattering the screen, and, with that, she was out.

Since then, she'd written Abed five letters, which he summarized for me. In the first, which she sent about six months after the end of the study, she began by apologizing for her previous behavior, spending a page or so "calmly and articulately and quite heartbreakingly" (Abed's words) explaining that, other than her younger brother, who had died in a fire (Abed had doubted she'd had a younger brother, let alone one who'd died in a fire; neither Lisette nor her mother had mentioned such a brother at any point during the Friends Study's vetting process), I had been the only person with whom she'd ever felt a connection, and that she had been desperate to tell me something—something she should have told me but had failed to tell me, and something that she was still desperate to tell me—and this desperation she'd felt had caused her "to lose sight of social norms and act with too much unrestrained passion" (Lisette's words, verbatim, according to Abed), and now that she was feeling more like herself again, and now that she had "been honest" with Abed about why she needed him to tell her my last name and phone number, she was certain he would give her my last name and phone number, and, for his help and understanding, she thanked him in advance.

To this letter, Abed replied, as gently as he could, that even though he would have liked more than anything to give her what she asked for, professional ethics—and the law—prevented him from being able to do so.

Lisette's response, which arrived a week later, was more a poem or hardcore lyric than it was a letter:

I was stupid to apologize.
I hope you die soon.

Five years later, on her eighteenth birthday, Lisette sent the third letter. She apologized to Abed for wishing him dead, apologized for having, prior to that, been presumptuous and manipulative, and then essayed, briefly, on the meaning of turning eighteen, saying, in sum, that, whereas before, whether she'd known so or not, it was reasonable for others to adjudge her choices the choices of a minor—a person for whose own best interests adults such as Abed understandably felt obliged to look out for—now that she was an adult herself, her choices were her own and, were she to suffer any negative consequences as a result of making those choices, no one would be to blame but herself. And the same, she argued, would apply to Belt when he turned eighteen, if he hadn't already turned eighteen. And furthermore, she inquired rhetorically, her having—for nearly six years by then—ceaselessly continued to miss Belt should count for something, shouldn't it? Didn't she deserve a chance to know him? to tell him what she needed to tell him? And didn't he deserve a chance to know her, to hear what she had to say to him? She went on for pages, then, somewhat incoherently, according to Abed, trying to make the case that trying to protect adults from themselves was in many ways worse than failing to protect children from themselves, and failing to make the case, or in any event, to sway him.

Abed wrote back, reiterating what he'd told her the last time.

He didn't hear from her again for nearly two decades. The fourth letter came to him in the summer of 2011. In this letter, Lisette claimed to be in recovery from years of substance abuse that she had codependently undertaken with her second husband. Having split up with the husband some eight months earlier, she eventually began to attend AA meetings, had three months sober, and was working the steps. She was writing to Abed, she explained, in order, first and foremost, to ask for forgiveness and try to make amends for the cruel, manipulative, intellectually dishonest, and "outright dishonest" ways in which she had treated him previously (e.g. she'd never, she admitted, had a little brother; she'd been married only once; her husband had been a teetotaling deacon in the Church of Latter-day Saints who she, an adulteress, had put through hell). And she was writing to him, secondly—and here she noted the "sad irony of it all"—in order to ask him, once again, for my last name and/or telephone number and/or "even just Belt's father's number or address if his father's still alive," so that she, toward recovery and amends-making, might ask me for *my* forgiveness for offenses similar to those she'd committed against Abed.

This fourth letter alarmed Abed far more than the others. For Lisette to lie about the husband, and then apologize for lying about the husband within the same paragraph, indicated to him that she was more disturbed than he'd previously imagined. (Perhaps it's worth noting that when Abed told me about the husband lie/apology, I not only laughed myself into a minor stomachache (receiver covered with hand), but was certain Lisette had *intended* the lie/apology to be funny.) And whereas the last two times he'd written back to her, it seemed to him to be of the utmost importance that he dissuade Lisette, however delicately, from continuing to hope she'd see me again, this time the opposite pertained; he feared what might happen if she were to *lose* the hope of seeing me again, and so after once again explaining that he couldn't give her what she wanted just then, he assured her that if ever I were to approach him, looking for her, he would put us in contact.

To Abed's surprise, Lisette's final letter, which he received just a couple days after sending his response to her fourth, was polite, verging even on sweet. She thanked him, wished him well, and included two phone numbers and two addresses where I might reach her. The first of them belonged to her mother: I should, Lisette instructed Abed, contact her there only if she proved to be unreachable at the second phone number or address, which belonged to Costello House, where she had been living since 2008.

"*The* Costello House?" I asked Abed.

"Yes," Abed said.

"That's *close* to me," I said. "And she's there right now?"

"Right this moment? I do not know. But she does still live there. I called earlier this morning in order to be sure."

"And what did she say?"

"I didn't speak to her."

"But you're sure she still lives there?"

"The front desk said she was in, and redirected my call to her room."

"She didn't answer?"

"She did. I didn't want to speak to her, Belt. I hung up."

"You hung up on Lisette! Lisette Banks!" I said, laughing.

"By your tone, it would seem that, regardless of everything I just told you, you still adjudge it a good idea to contact Lisette."

A good idea? I could barely swallow, my heart was so high in my throat. No, it was *not* a good idea. Perhaps it was the best idea. Perhaps it was even the worst idea. It was certainly an idea that demanded execution.

I took down Lisette's info.

Abed, in an endearingly cautionary tone, wished me good luck.

We said our goodbyes, and, after grabbing two fresh packs of Quills from my carton trove, I got in my truck.

•

• •

The murder at the Costello House Intermediate Care Facility, back in 2002, had made *The Daily Herald*'s front page for a week. My father had followed the story closely, in part because Costello House was just a few towns over, in posh Highland Grove, but in larger part, I think, because both of the murderers had schizophrenia, a fact that Clyde believed (or purported to believe) the *Herald* had been putting too much focus on. "They're trying to turn this into 'being psychotic makes you violent, makes you a murderer,'" I remember him saying, "and you're actually *less* likely to be a murderer if you've got a psychotic illness than if you don't. There's cold, hard statistics on that exact fact. But you know what it is? Know what I think? These candy-ass Highland Grovers, they all want to get Costello House shut down. They've been trying to get it shut down since it opened—they think it hurts their precious North Shore property values. Only thing needs shutting is those richy-rich cakefaces' country-clubbing pieholes." And so forth.

At the time, I didn't think what Clyde said made much sense. On later reflection, I doubted even Clyde thought it made much sense. The murder had occurred just a couple days before my twenty-seventh birthday, the birthday on which I'd lost my virginity, and I had, I suppose, since returning from the brothel, been holding myself more aloof from Clyde than usual, and I'm sure he noticed my extra aloofness, and I think he mistook it for a response to the murder, or the ways in which the murder was being reported. Either because I was known around town (to the extent that I was known at all) as someone with a "psychotic illness," or because I, had I slightly different symptoms or slightly different parents, might very well have been a resident at Costello House myself, Clyde assumed, I think, that I was troubled by the notion that others might look at me more warily in light of the murder, and he just wanted to comfort me in his Clydely, longest-possible-way-around-the-barn manner; wanted to express to me, through Clydely subtext, and with Clydely *subtlety,* that he, Clyde Magnet, wasn't like those others. I wasn't, however, the least bit troubled by either notion (i.e. neither by how others might look at me in light of the murder, nor by how Clyde might), and the *Herald* writers, in at least a few of the articles that *I* had read, seemed to me to go out of their way not only to remark upon how unlikely it was for a schizophrenic to commit murder, but how it was all but *unheard of* for two schizophrenics, motivated by the same delusion, to commit murder *together,* which is exactly what had happened at Costello House, and was a lot of the reason why the murder had captured so much media attention to begin with.

According to their confessions, one of the murderers had just bought a new bicycle that he had been saving up for for months, and, upon returning from the bicycle shop to Costello House with the other murderer riding his handlebars (the two were best friends, roommates, and possibly lovers), a staff member, greeting them, had said, "Nice bike." This staff member may or may not have been abusive to the Costello House residents, may or may not have stolen items from their rooms in the past—accounts varied—but the murderer who didn't own the bike (i.e. the one who'd been on the handlebars) convinced the murderer who did own the bike that the staff member's having said "Nice bike" meant the staff member planned to kill them both so he (the staff member) could steal the bike. Half an hour later, the murderer who didn't own the bike tackled the staff member over the railing of the facility's wraparound porch, then pinned him to the lawn while the other murderer stabbed the staff member multiple times in the throat and the face with a pair of scissors.

The murder was witnessed by twenty-eight people, the vast majority Costello House residents crowded together on the wraparound porch, and many of the *Herald*'s stories on the murder had accompanying photos of that resident-crowded wraparound porch—the residents seated in folding or rocking chairs, or swinging on the bench swing, or leaning on the railing, most of them facing streetward and smoking—and none of the stories' accompanying photos ever showed the porch uncrowded by residents, so I don't know how I, while parallel parking in front of Costello House, could have been so surprised by the sight of the residents crowding its porch—it looked just like the pictures—but I was. Surprised.

Surprised, then unmanned.

I hadn't prepared myself to see them at all, to have to get past them—through them—to get to Lisette, much less to have to think about Lisette as being one of them, which might have, *being one of them,* meant any number of variously unpleasant things, depending on which section of the porch I looked at. Over here in the rocking-chair area, three were asleep, two of them tremoring, a fourth muttering angrily, shaking her head. Beside them stood a group of five or six tardively dsykinesiac men, pointing their fingers and smokes in my direction and licking and sucking at their lips while they laughed—at me? at my truck? at something behind my truck? a squirrel or a bird?—and next to that group, an older woman in a flowered smock was crying drily and chewing her wrist, and next to her was another older woman in a flowered smock, who was looking at the group of laughing men through a bottle of root beer she held horizontally and twisted around in front of her eyes, as if adjusting the bottle for focus. Someone in the shadow of the eaves was making popping sounds, slapping his palm against his open mouth. Someone sitting on the stairs, looking up at the sky, stroked her own cheek and blissfully smiled. A man alone on the bench swing, clutching his underarms, appeared to be lecturing to one of his knees: "You just can't say these kinds of things to a person. It's wrong and it's mean and it's killing your soul," he said. "You want to know who it is? Who it really is, buddy? Who it really is, buddy, who you're saying those things to? That's Judah Maccabee, buddy. That's who you're hurting."

They weren't all in such frightening shape. Many of them seemed, for the most part, balanced, just having a smoke, or getting fresh air, but the longer that I paid attention to the others, the more afraid I became that coming to Costello House had been a mistake, that Lisette might not be . . . okay, that I might not do well with her being not-okay, and though I rolled up my window, exited my truck, and headed a couple of steps toward the porch, I took a coward's hard left in front of the stairway, then walked a few blocks, past the center of town, til I came to a Dairy Queen, next to the entrance of which hung a telephone.

"*Non,*" Sandrine answered, when the automated French voice asked her whether she'd accept the charges from "Belt Magnet 847 433 2181 that's 847 433 2181."

I hung up the phone. Seconds later, it rang.

"Hello?"

"*Allo,* Belt?"

"Sandrine?"

"Yes. I am. Wow, *wow*. You sound so exactly like Clyde."

"I do?"

"No one tells you before?"

"Not til just now," I said. "Thank you, I think?"

"*Quoi?*" said Sandrine. "I say, eh . . . I ask that, eh, you have not been told by someone else that your voice is so much like your father's?"

"No, I understood. All I meant was: you are the first to tell me. And thank you, Sandrine."

"Okay. Good. You are welcome. I think I am completely glad you have called. You are fine?"

"Yes."

"I am completely glad, then," she said. "Clyde will be so happy. He is away with my brother to look for a boat to buy. They will return in two hours. Three hours maybe. He will call you at this number?"

"No, no. I'll call back from home. Right now, I'm at Dairy Queen."

"Okay. And what is it?"

"It's just—well, it's a girl. A woman."

"*Dairy Queen* is her name?"

"Oh, you meant . . . I'm embarrassed, now. You meant, 'What is Dairy Queen?' "

"Of course. What is it?"

"It's mostly an ice cream place."

"It is very bad ice cream?"

"It's okay."

"Okay ice cream is a little bit sad, Belt, but please do not be embarrassed with me. I sometimes choose to drink Nescafé coffee. This is much more worse than okay ice cream, which is, after all, *en fait,* still ice cream. I cannot judge you."

"Ha! I appreciate that. *Merci beaucoups.*"

"I am glad you laugh. Maybe it is okay if I ask who is the woman?"

"The woman."

"The woman who is not Dairy Queen?" she said.

"Oh, *her,*" I said.

"I do not want to be a nosy person, but because you mentioned, I am interested, so. If you mind it, don't mind it. *Non*. Don't mind *me*. If you mind it. The question."

"Not at all," I said. "It's fine. She's just someone I used to know, when we were children. I mean, she's not *just* someone I used to know. She's someone who—you see, I lost track of her for many years, and—"

"A kind of Bam Naka figurine, perhaps?"

"I don't—I hadn't really thought of her that way . . ."

"I apologize, Belt. I should know better than to say something like this. My daughter, she does not like it when I talk about her fiction. She becomes very uncomfortable. This is a terrible first impression that I make. I am sorry. You are Clyde's only son, and I am somewhat nervous. I ask too many questions and I say what I should not."

"No, no. Please don't be. Don't be sorry, or nervous. It's a great first impression. Really. I think you're very funny, and I can't wait to meet you. In person. And you've read my book. Thank you for reading it."

"I enjoy it very much. All of us do."

"Thank you," I said.

"You are welcome, of course. And the woman, then?"

"She's—it's a very long story."

"Maybe Clyde has told me. She is maybe the Lisette you have employed the detective to find?"

"Yes," I said.

"Yes, Clyde has told me. It is very romantic. He believes you will visit us after she is found. You and your Lisette. You will be in love and bring her to Spain, he believes. Is she found?"

"Sort of," I said.

"Yes?"

"The detective found her. I haven't really done anything about it yet, though. I was going to. I was just about to. I was on my way to see her just now, and then I . . . didn't."

"Ah, but you must."

"I must?"

"This is not why you call after so many weeks from a telephone at Dairy Queen to speak to your father only after the detective finds your Lisette?"

"I don't—"

"This is *just* why you call after so many weeks from a telephone at Dairy Queen to speak to your father only after the detective finds your Lisette. To hear Clyde tell you what I tell you: that you must. You must see Lisette. Of course you must see her. Do you think he would tell you something else?" said Sandrine.

"Maybe," I said, but only from reflex.

Before the first ring had played out, she picked up. "Lisette Banks," she said.

"Lisette," I said. "Hi. Hello. This is Belt."

"I know," she said.

"You recognize my voice?"

"Not at all," she said. "You sound like an adult. But I knew it was you the first time you called. Why'd you hang up? Were you feeling very nervous?"

"That was Abed," I said. "Dr. Patel."

"I believe that," she said, and maybe she did. "I want to see you, Belt. Can we see each other sometime? Sometime really soon?"

"I could be there in ten, fifteen minutes."

"Fifteen minutes," she said, "is perfect. Except it's better, I think, if you don't come here. It's spooky here. You wouldn't like it at all. Let's meet somewhere else. Do you know where the McDonald's in Highland Grove is?"

I looked over my shoulder. It was just across the street.

"On Second Street?" I said.

"Exactly there," Lisette said. "This is so perfect. Let's meet up there. We'll drink a Shamrock Shake."

"It's after St. Patrick's. I'm not sure they have those."

"They do," she said. "All March." She hung up.

I crossed the street to McDonald's and waited outside. Ten, twelve minutes. I saw her coming from a half-block away. Were it not for the evening gloves, I'd never have guessed. She was heavy, dumpy, smiling as she lurched. Baggy blue sweatpants under a summer dress. All-rubber clogs. Terry-cloth headband. Sticky-looking neck, shiny and ringed. She glanced at me, but seemed to have no idea. She shuffled right past me, into the restaurant. She smelled like dirty hair and full ashtrays.

"Leave," I thought. But I couldn't quite convince myself.

She came outside again. "Excuse me," she said. "You wouldn't happen to have an extra one of those, would you?"

I gave her a cigarette. She had her own lighter. The pseudo-leather pink purse from which she pulled it was flaking, fading to orange. Her evening gloves were coffee-stained. Her eyes had a wobble. Her eyebrows were pencil lines. To think that she'd once flipped effortless cartwheels . . . to think she'd ever been—I needed to leave. Why wasn't I leaving?

Quill lit, she leaned back against the wall, beside me. "Hulga," she said.

"Pardon?" I said.

"I'm Hulga," Lisette said.

"Clyde," I said.

"Nice to meet you, *Clyde*. Talk to Blinky lately?"

"Blinky?"

"Blinky," she said. "Ghost who chased Pac-Man. The blue one. Come on. You're old enough to remember. There was Inky, there was Pinky, there was Blinky, and there was Clyde? Clyde was orange, I think. Chased Ms. Pac-Man, too. All four of them did. And later Baby Pac-Man, Junior Pac-Man, Super Pac-Man."

"Oh, right," I said.

"In a way," Lisette said, "they were the real stars of the franchise, those ghosts. They were in more games than any of the others."

"Good point," I said.

"You want to talk about names, though, I'm supposed to meet my friend here—his name's *Belt*."

"Some name," I said.

I studied my shoes. We puffed at our Quills.

"I know," she said. "Disgusting, right?"

Had I sighed? Slumped? Made some kind of face?

"For me," she went on, "there's only two ways to think of them. One way is: maybe they'll outlast us. Not all of them, but some of them. Maybe some will outlast us, and a better species than us will arise, or maybe a superior race of alien beings will show up, and then a member of this new species, or one of the superior alien beings, it'll study them, scope them, take them apart, and it'll find traces of us, DNA traces, and maybe it'll use some form of advanced technology on the traces to make a new person, or a bunch of new people, and humankind will get a second shot."

"I'm sorry," I said. "I don't know what you're talking about."

"Well, like a second shot at not destroying ourselves. A second shot at being. And maybe we could do better with a second shot. Probably not, but maybe. With the wisdom and guidance of a superior alien society or an advanced new species? one that was skilled enough to develop technology to bring us back from extinction? Not *totally* impossible."

"I still—"

"No, I know," she said. "I know. It sounds wrong to me, too—most of the time. Almost all of the time, really. I would never bet on it. If we did get brought back, which we probably wouldn't, the DNA traces would almost definitely come from our fossilized remains. Enough of us are buried in stainless-steel caskets, conveniently located near one another in cemeteries and so on that . . . And plus, even if we did get brought back, we'd probably be captives. In zoos or whatever. Hard to call that a second chance at being. I know all of this. I'm only saying that's *one* way to think of them."

"To think of *who,* though?" I said.

"'Who?'" she said. "What *who*? No *who*. The black marks. The old gum."

"These stains on the sidewalk?"

"Isn't that what we're talking about? Isn't that what you're looking at?"

"Oh," I said. "Of course."

"What did you think I was talking about?"

"I really didn't know."

"You must've thought I was crazy, going on like that," she said.

"No," I said. "No. I was just confused. Sorry about that. So . . . what's the better way?"

"Now I'm confused."

"What's the better way of looking at the gumstains?" I said. "You said there were two."

"That *was* the better way. The way I just described. The way I usually think about them, though . . . Well I think about how the gum came from mouths. Mouths with bleeding gums, with cuts inside, bits of food between teeth, ripped-up palates, probably bad breath. And that's just where they *came* from, or where they *might have* come from—that's just some unpleasant thoughts about their origins. And maybe that's *my* problem, having those thoughts. But what they *look* like? What they actually look like, there on the sidewalk? black? slightly raised? misshapen? That's how they look, isn't it? Objectively, right? That's not just me?"

"That's how they look," I said.

"Black and slightly raised and misshapen. You think about them, picture them in your mind, and they're circles, but they're not *really* circles. You see them right in front of you, you see their edges are ragged and . . . organic, right? They're not circles. And you see how they're clustered together like that? That's not uncommon. They're nearly always clustered up, you know? And your eyes are always making triangles out of them. Always trying to make right triangles out of them, or equilateral triangles, but they can't. They always fail. Just . . . awkward triangles. That's all you get. *Uncomfortable* triangles. Mine do that, at least. My eyes, I mean."

"Mine too," I said.

"They're everywhere," she said. "Everywhere you go. Clustered and black. Raised and misshapen. *Pavement melanoma,* right? That's the way I think of them. Most of the time. That's what goes through my head: pavement melanoma."

"Still, that's not what it is," I said. "It's just old gum."

"I didn't say that's what it *is*. Of course it's just old gum. It's completely meaningless. Doesn't stop me, when I see it, from thinking it, though. It doesn't stop me from being disgusted."

"What stops you?" I said.

"No idea," she said. "It happens so rarely, and it lasts so little time, I just try to enjoy it. Not being disgusted. I'm enjoying it now, in fact. I don't feel disgusted. Maybe that owes to *your* company, Clyde—ha! Just kidding. I know how that sounded. You don't have to blush. I know I'm not . . . your type. I wouldn't ever hit on you. You're out of my league—"

"That's—"

"No, please, you don't have to. I wasn't fishing. I know who I am. I know what I look like. Same goes for you. And it's okay, really. It's completely okay. It's more than okay. I feel like a million bucks right now. My friend Belt I'm meeting here? We have this really great connection. Storybook, you know? A real fairy-tale connection, and I haven't seen him in forever. Not since we were kids. I'm kinda dying of excitement. We have so much to talk about."

"What happened to you?" I said.

"What do you mean?"

"Why haven't you talked to him in so many years?"

"It's a really long story, but, basically, I tried to find him and wasn't able. *He* had to come looking for *me,* and the problem with that is that, when we were kids, his mother became ill, terminally ill, *very* suddenly, and when he told me about it, I accused him of lying, and I never apologized for it. I *would* have apologized. I wanted to apologize. But I never got the chance before he disappeared. So he didn't know I was sorry. So he never came looking for me. At least that's what I think."

I said, "I'm sure he must have forgiven you by now."

"I hope so," she said. "I think he might have. He's found me, after all."

"I'm sure he has," I said. "What made you think he was lying about his mom, anyway?"

"I'm not even sure I really did think he was lying. I might have just said it because . . . I'm . . . It's hard to explain. It's private, actually."

"Oh, sorry," I said.

"Nothing for *you* to be sorry about, Clyde. You know what, though, I better get back inside now, in case Belt was in the bathroom. Or maybe he came through the other entrance. Thanks for the smoke."

She dropped the butt on the gumstains, said, "Excuse me," and made her way past me.

I watched her through the window.

In front of the counter, she surveyed the restaurant, then sat in a booth. She reached inside her collar and came out with a cure that she set on the farther side of the table. She pointed at its head. The cure, with both hands, grasped the gloved tip of the pointed finger, tilted back on its heels, and pulled, and pulled. Lisette grimaced down at it, and, pantomiming alarm and exertion, leaned forward, then back, then forward again while, with her free hand, she wiped her brow, and clutched at her chest and her opposite shoulder, as though the cure might overpower her. After a minute, she turned toward the window and, seeing me staring, smiled or smirked, and I gave her a shallow nod, and I waved.

ACKNOWLEDGMENTS

Bubblegum would have been a lesser book—it may never have even become a book—if the following people hadn't helped me:

Rob Bloom
Camille Bordas
Jacqueline Ko
Christian TeBordo
Andrew Wylie

I am greatly indebted to each of them.

ABOUT THE AUTHOR

Adam Levin is the author of *The Instructions* and *Hot Pink*. He has been a New York Public Library Young Lions Fiction Award winner, a recipient of a National Endowment for the Arts fellowship, and a National Jewish Book Award finalist. A longtime Chicagoan, Levin currently lives in Gainesville, Florida.